THE BOOKS OF THE GODS
PART TWO

Books by Fred Saberhagen

THE BOOKS OF
THE GODS
PART TWO

God of the Golden Fleece

Gods of Fire and Thunder

FRED SABERHAGEN

FANTASY

Published by arrangement with
Tor Books
Tom Doherty Associates, LLC
175 Fifth Avenue
New York, New York 10010

Tor® is a registered trademark of Tom Doherty Associates,
LLC.

First SFBC Fantasy printing: September 2002

Visit the SFBC online at *www.sfbc.com*
Visit Tor Books online at *www.tor.com*

ISBN 0-7394-2995-7

PRINTED IN THE UNITED STATES OF AMERICA

Contents

God
of the
Golden
Fleece

1

Proteus

THE WINNING END of a bitter and deadly struggle brought him up thrashing and splashing in salt water, stumbling waist-deep through the warm sea, emerging under a clear sky from which the light of sunset was fading fast. Leftover rage and fear poured fierce energy through his veins, but the memory of the disaster that he had just survived was fading faster than the sunset. Something had hit him in the head, and only fragments of what had just happened were still clear in his mind.

He had a vivid memory of a head as big as a farm wagon, two arms the size of massive trees, mounted on shoulders to match. One of the sea-going type of Giants, almost human above the waist in shape if not in size; but from the hips down, no real legs, only a pair of huge, twisting fish-tails, ending in something like whale-flukes instead of feet. The thing would never be able to walk properly, but it sure as all the hells could swim.

He had been on a ship, and the Giant had come swimming after it like a whale, bent on destruction. The deck and hull crushed in by blows from those tree-trunk arms, the vessel capsized, and everyone aboard had gone into the deep blue sea.

He couldn't remember how he had got away, but here he was. Now if only his head would cease to hurt . . .

When the Giant had reared up out of the sea, throwing everyone into a panic, the ship had been carrying its passengers to . . .

The survivor began to feel a new terror now, subtler than the fear of Giants, but equally unpleasant. It came with the realization that he could no longer remember why he had been aboard the ship, or where it had been taking him.

Or even who he was.

Start again. When the vessel broke up, when the monster sent it to the bottom . . .

No, start yet again. He was going to have to start much earlier than that. But he could not. Because he could not even remember *who he was*.

The man who waded might have broken out in a cold sweat, but it was hard to tell, when every inch of his skin was already soaked by the Great Sea. He could find not a single scrap of memory before his presence on that doomed ship. So, start with the ship, and try to work from that.

He could recall only a few more details, all trivial. Besides one or two clear images of the attacking Giant, there were only some additional colors, shapes, certain ugly noises . . .

The left side of the man's head, where his exploring fingers now discovered an aching lump, still throbbed from the savage impact of something hard. Turning to look backward as he moved, even as his feet kept taking him toward the land, he scanned the empty watery horizon in the direction opposite the sunset. Night was gathering out there, and stars were beginning to appear over the endless sea. Darkness was advancing from the east, but nothing else. There were no monsters in pursuit.

It was horrible that he could not remember where he had been going. Or why he had been on the ship. Or who he was . . .

A helpless groan came welling up, and the wader had to fight down panic. It seemed that virtually a whole lifetime had been swept away.

There was almost nothing left of himself at all, no solid identity anywhere. Who was he? What was he doing here, in what looked like and felt like, and so had to be, the middle of the Great Sea? There ought to be, there had to be, more to him than this, a naked wading body with an aching, almost empty head, laboring under a burden of fear and rage, a terror that wanted to hit back with murderous fury.

Damn the Giant! Could a man's whole self be erased by one medium-hard knock on the head?

Turning his back again on the empty, darkening east, he kept on trudging shoreward in the gentle surf. He was praying now, to every god and goddess he could think of, that his memories, his vanished life, would suddenly come back to him—and it had better happen soon. There were two small fires on the beach some sixty or seventy yards ahead, and a beached ship, with people milling around, and instinct warned him that before he met those folk, whoever they were, he had better have some idea of who he was and what he was doing in the world.

Looking down at himself, he realized that he was wearing nothing that might provide a clue to his identity, carrying nothing—not even a ring on a finger or in an ear. Not even an amulet hung around his muscular neck. The man paused in his wading, suddenly puzzled by his utter and complete nakedness. It was as if he had just left his clothing on a beach somewhere and gone in for a casual swim.

All this time he had been making steady progress toward the shore. Now the gentle waves surged up no higher than the wader's thighs, and every step forward raised him another inch on the sandy bottom's shallow slope. When his thick brown hair and beard had shed their weight of water they would be curly, but right now they were still almost straight, streaming and dribbling little threads of ocean. The unclad body gradually revealed as the water shallowed was no bigger than average, and looked to be in its youthful prime, no more than thirty years of age, strong and slightly rounded toward chubbiness.

Again he looked back into the darkening east, this time over one shoulder, as he kept wading forward. But still there was only watery emptiness to see, shrouded in advancing night.

What kind of reception he might get from the people on the beach ahead he could not guess. But he had nowhere else to go.

What *had* he been doing on that boat or ship, just before he was almost killed? It seemed unbearable that he did not know.

Going somewhere, trying to accomplish something terribly important, yes . . .

A certain great purpose, having some connection with a ship, yes, that was it! Not the vessel whose sinking had almost taken him down with it, but a totally different one. With a flash of disproportionate relief he realized that the ship he had been trying to find was doubtless the very one drawn up on the beach ahead.

Eagerly, now, the man emerging from the sea pressed on. The careened vessel was a new-looking bireme, lean and straight, and big enough to carry forty oars, two banks on each side. The new wood of her hull, except for the spots where it was brightly painted, glowed almost golden in fading sunset light.

One more slender shard of memory fell into place. It was a woman who had imbued him with the sense of purpose, maybe given him his orders—it might have been as simple and direct as that.

It was a blessed relief to feel that things were at least starting to come back. But what exactly the nameless woman had been trying to get him to do remained a mystery. Whoever she was, the man could *almost* see her face in memory, almost hear her exact words—almost, but not quite.

Still he kept wading forward almost automatically, toward the beached ship and the men around her, a sizable group on a long shoreline otherwise deserted.

It looked a pleasant enough place, and the wader somehow assumed it was an island, rather than a mainland shore. Bathed now in fading sunset light were green palm trees, pelicans, and other signs of peaceful nature . . . all reassuring. One last time he looked back over his left shoulder, seeing only the straight line of the horizon, and the gathering of night. The Giant that had almost killed him was evidently miles away by now.

His rage and fear were not gone, far from it, but now they had subsided, enough to be kept out of sight. Now he was close enough to see, in declining sunlight, the name on the ship's prow, above the painted, staring eye. And the word when he could see it—*Argo*—made a connection, established a faint link with all the memories that he had almost lost.

Overhead a gull was screaming, as if in derision, finding rich amusement in the way the world went on, how human beings and others managed their affairs. The *Argo* was long and narrow, the outer row of seats on each side slightly raised. The central deck, barely wide enough for two human bodies to edge past each other, was raised a little higher still, so the two inboard rows of oarsmen would actually sit beneath it, less exposed to sun and rain. In the middle of that raised deck would be a hole to hold a mast, whose foot would nestle snugly in a notch in the bottom planks below. And in fact a suitably long pole had been unstepped and laid aside, and a new-looking linen sail more or less neatly furled. No one was now aboard the ship, which rested tilted sharply sideways on the sand.

Every line of the long ship breathed adventure, and the man approaching could see a great, challenging, staring eye, blue with a white rim, and a thin black outline surrounding that, bigger than his whole head, painted on the near side of the prow, just forward of the name. The other side, of course, would bear another symmetrically positioned eye.

Right now the oars had all been shipped aboard. There was every indication that the rowers were all finished with their labors for the day. Half of them were swimming and plunging naked in the shallow water, mock-fighting with splashes like small boys, uttering rowdy yells, washing away the day's heat and the sweat of rowing. Their bodies were of all human colors, from tropical black to sunburnt blond, except that none of them were old. No gray hair was immediately visible.

The remaining half were up on shore, some clad and some not, mainly clustered around a couple of brisk small fires, from which a smell of roasting meat came wafting out to sea. A meal was in the middle stages of preparation. Someone had been butchering small animals on the beach, and had started the process of tidying up, bundling bones and offal and fat together, into packages that would soon be burned as offerings to certain gods. Meanwhile the humans as always were claiming the good meat as their share, a state of affairs to which no god ever seemed to raise objection.

It was hard to tell if any of the men up on the beach were servants; certainly none of them, at the moment, were wearing the fine robes of aristocrats. There were no women or children anywhere in sight, but plenty of weapons, a good variety of spears and bows and swords; it seemed a very military kind of expedition, or maybe a band of high-class pirates. The man just arriving felt a soothing, baseless certainty that he had come to the right place.

What now? It seemed to him that there was one man in particular he ought to find. The woman responsible for his being here had told him—had practically commanded him—something . . .

And as the newcomer drew ever closer to the gathering, he saw what he had somehow expected, that this was no crew of ordinary sailors. Youth and health and strength were everywhere, along with a kind of inborn arrogance. There was not a single metal slave-collar to be seen, though more than a few magic amulets hung on slender chains around muscled necks. Where scars showed on the hard bodies, they suggested the impact of weapons or claws rather than the lash.

A couple of men had turned now and were watching with interest the newcomer's arrival. But neither of them was the one man he had really come here to find.

Another of those ahead, standing waist-deep in the water at the center of a small circle of attention, had an air of leadership. For one thing he was very tall, and a kind of dominance showed in him, even in this superior company, even unclothed as he was. The newcomer changed the course of his steady, splashing advance to head directly toward this individual.

When the tall man turned his head to look in his direction, the man from the sea stopped a few feet away and said in a clear, determined voice: "Sir, if you are the famous Jason, captain of the *Argo,* I have been sent to join you." The name had popped into his head at the precise instant when he had to have it.

The leader's whole head seemed a dark, luxuriant mass of hair and beard. The closer the newcomer got to him, the stronger his arms and shoulders looked. He said: "My name is Jason." The dark eyes studied

the man before him with fatalistic calm. The voice was mild but au-
thoritative. "Where do you come from?"

The nameless stranger had lost his own identity, but he still knew
who Jason was. He thought that name would mean something to almost
everyone in the world. It was a relief to discover that certain parts of
his memory were still intact, things a man would have to know about
to function in the world. Jason's fame as a warrior, and particularly as
the heroic slayer of the Calydonian boar, had spread swiftly during the
last few years. It had been no trouble at all for Jason to recruit forty
volunteer adventurers to accompany him on a special quest, even if they
had no certainty of what its object was. As soon as the word spread that
he was undertaking a great adventure and wanted followers, hundreds
of men had come from everywhere, seemingly from every corner of the
earth, certainly from as far away as the news had had time to travel.
Very few were accepted, of those who applied without a special invitation.

"Out of the sea, Lord Jason."

The leader's voice was still mild. "No need to address me as if I
were royalty. I do not—yet—sit on a throne or wear a crown. And I
suppose, from the way you look and the manner of your arrival, that
you have some tale to tell of shipwreck?" Suddenly Jason's tone became
more casual, less interested, as a new thought struck him. "Were you
sent to us as a servant? Our original plan was to have several attendants
meet us on this island. But I sent word many days ago to cancel that
arrangement. What's your name?"

"Proteus." This answer, too, came automatically, for which the man
who gave it was deeply thankful; he took the timely access of memory
as a hopeful sign that other essential facts might come popping back as
soon as they were absolutely needed. Immediately his aching head began to feel better.

Jason was looking directly at him, but still Proteus had the feeling
that the leader was giving him only a fraction of his attention. The big
man said, as if he did not much care: "I don't remember anyone of that
name applying to join my company. Then you *are* one of the servants
who were originally to meet us here?"

Up on the beach, one of the young men had picked up a conch
shell and was trying to blow it, just for fun. But he had no idea of how
to do it properly, and was producing an ungodly noise, making Proteus
uncomfortable.

Before he was forced to find an answer for Jason's question, another
tall youth came splashing up to the leader and started talking to him
about someone called Hercules, who, it seemed, had been a member of

the company of Argonauts when they began their voyage a few days ago. Proteus, still distracted by his own secret problems, had some trouble making out just what the difficulty was now. As nearly as he could tell, this fellow Hercules and his nephew, named Enkidu, had been somehow stranded yesterday, left behind either by accident or design, when the *Argo* had put in along the shores of the river Chius, in the land of Mysia.

Other members of the crew of Heroes were now listening in, even as they boyishly traded splashes or just stood around nearby. Some of these made comments indicating they hadn't realized that two of their shipmates had been missing for a day. Evidently, out of this group of some forty young men, many were still largely unknown to one another, though they had been crammed together on a ship for several days.

Meanwhile, Proteus felt a growing certainty that the purpose, the compulsion, that had brought him here required, as a next step, that he find some way to join this noble crew. *She*, the nearly-forgotten but commanding woman, must have ordered him to join the Argonauts. More and more Proteus wanted to know just who that woman was, what had made her think she had a right to order him around. Also he wanted to find out why he felt it necessary to obey—he would be almost afraid to know the answer to that one.

Meanwhile, he was going to do his damnedest to keep secret his weakness, the fact of his ruined memory. Once he admitted that, why would they believe him about anything? And Jason and his crew must not know why he was here. Because it was a matter of life and death, that someone should not find that out . . . come to think of it, it was the nameless woman who had commanded secrecy. With an inward sigh Proteus acknowledged to himself that whatever secret she wanted kept was safe enough for the time being, since he himself could not remember what it was.

And then he was brought back, with a start, to his immediate situation. Jason had just said something that required a response, and was looking at him expectantly.

"I would like to know," repeated the leader, in a tone of patient tolerance, "just what happened to the boat? The one that must have brought you somewhere near this island?"

That question he could answer. "A Giant came up out of the sea, and broke it into bits. I fear that no one else survived."

Naturally enough, this produced immediate consternation among the men who heard him. Some of them went running for their weapons—as if such human toys would help them against that enemy—while others pressed closer to the source of news, urgently demanding more details.

Proteus needed only a couple dozen halting words to give them all the additional information he had available. Sudden, inexplicable disaster, splintered planks and terrified, howling faces, people drowning. Now surrounded by a ring of intent listeners, he explained that the boat had been sunk, he thought about a mile from the island—of that much at least he felt confident—and that unfortunately he seemed to be the only survivor. He'd had a good long swim to get here. It was faintly encouraging that as he spoke of the disaster, a few more of its details— screams for help, and thrashing human arms and legs—took shape in his mind. But nothing that answered any of his own urgent questions.

Several men, speaking at the same time, asked Proteus where he thought the Giant might have gone.

"I have no idea." Probably not to the nearest land; monsters like that one were as much at home in the sea as whales, but with their fish-legs had a hard time getting about on land. He shrugged. Trying to force his memory meant standing in front of a hideous, frightening void, big enough so that it seemed he might fall into it and be lost.

By now all of the men had heard his story, and none were more than moderately surprised. Giant attacks on ships were fairly rare, but certainly not unheard of. Vessels were lost at sea all the time, from a variety of causes, and people went down with them—servants were people, of course, even those who were slaves. But when you came right down to it, they were only servants. Too bad that useful workers had suffered and died tonight, but there were plenty of replacements to be had, and it was no great loss to the world, not to the important people in it. Jason, like his shipmates, frowned on hearing the unpleasant news, but it was not going to change his outlook or his plans. Whatever they might be.

One of the figures standing in the background observed: "Well, that settles one problem for us. There'll be no hangers-on or attendants on this voyage."

"That had already been decided," said another man, a trifle sharply.

"My name's Meleager." This change of subject came from yet another member of the crew, a big man, almost as large as Jason, who stepped toward Proteus with a hand stuck out in greeting. Plainly the kind who is anxious for you to know his name, and find out who you are, what kind of story you have to tell about yourself.

"Those who know me well call me Mel." His great hand swallowed the hand Proteus put out. "I've been keeping Jason out of trouble since we both were lads."

Mel turned to gesture to another. "And this is Haraldur." A grinning nod from a powerfully built, hairy man who was wearing a horned helmet, though at the moment nothing else.

How long the chain of introductions might have gone on there was no telling, for it was interrupted. Now one of the other men, somewhat older than most of the others, who had been standing by with folded arms and listening, spoke up and reminded Jason that some of the crew seemed to think the problem of whether or not there were going to be servants still had not been finally settled.

"I would remind you, sir, that as matters had stood when we left Iolcus, some of the Heroes enjoyed such a luxury and others did not."

"Yes, Idmon," said Jason patiently. "I understand that."

"Wouldn't have been much luxury for anyone, with half again as many people as we have now crammed aboard the ship," put in another who had been listening.

There arose a weary murmur, suggesting that this debate had been going on for a while and many were tired of it.

Jason looked vexed. "I think you are mistaken. I think all servants and companions have already left us." He looked around, as if his forty—if that was actually the right number—shipmates might be an unruly mob of strangers. "If there are any such still here, it is against my orders."

No one responded to that directly. But a voice from the background said: "If half of the intended servants were sent back days ago, and the other half have just been drowned, it seems to me there's not a whole lot left to discuss."

Someone poked the butt of a spear in Proteus's direction. "No survivors, this man was saying?"

But before Jason or anyone else could insist that Proteus provide more details of the disaster, another man, one of those who had been on shore, came wading briskly up to the leader, who still stood waist-deep in the lapping waves. Urgently this latest supplicant began haranguing Jason about the apparent absence of certain supplies. Someone should have thought to stow caulking materials aboard, and something to use for pitch! Sooner or later all ships leaked and required fixing.

Meanwhile, the news that a whole boatload of servants had been lost was spreading slowly through the ranks of Heroes as they splashed or lounged or worked at getting dinner. Proteus could see them frowning, shaking heads, murmuring. A bad omen, certainly. Probably those who had still been hoping for servants were upset because they would certainly have to do their own cleaning and cooking.

Jason's patience was unruffled. Maybe, thought Proteus, patience

was the virtue a leader needed, above all else. Now the leader was trying
to explain to his latest questioner about the caulking materials, and other
spare parts. The *Argo,* like most ships built for other purposes than
carrying freight, suffered from a lack of storage space in general, and
not much could be done about it. There were a couple of lockers, fore
and aft under the narrow fighting deck that ran down the center of the
vessel. Those important spaces had been packed full of necessary stores
of one kind or another.

There was talk of the spare sails. Proteus nodded to himself, un-
surprised. Some fund of practical experience, though he could recall
nothing of how he had obtained it, assured him that on a voyage of any
length at least one spare was practically essential, unless you would
really rather row. And if you got the finest, most expensive fabric and
workmanship—which Jason ought to have done to match the quality of
his ship—you could roll and fold the sail tightly enough to stow it away
in an amazingly small space.

Jason was going on with his inventory, and now it sounded as if
there were as many as two or three spare sails. There were also some
caulking materials, but you would have to dig them out.

All this was fine with Proteus. He and whatever other news he might
have been able to provide had to wait again. The expedition seemed
anything but well organized, and for the moment that was all to the
good, because it had spared him any probing, difficult questions.

Somewhere inland beyond the wavering spread of firelight, a male
voice suddenly began to moan in pain. Or more likely in passion, as
Proteus suddenly realized. None of the men around him were paying
any attention to the sound, so he decided to ignore it too. He supposed
it was possible that at least one woman had come along on this expedition—but on second thought, it was more likely that there were some
in this large crew of Heroes who found the absence of women no det-
riment to their love lives.

Now one of the figures in the loose gathering around Jason, the
slightly older man addressed as Idmon, had turned the conversation back
again to the absent Hercules. It sounded to Proteus like this Hercules
was a mere youth and a stranger who in a trial of strength had somehow
managed to make them all look like weaklings, which in this company
would be quite a feat. Inevitably more than a few of the chosen Heroes
would have considered him an offensive upstart, and probably out of
jealousy or resentment they had somehow arranged for him to be left
behind.

Proteus thought that a firm, decisive leader would not tolerate such
goings-on among his followers, and he was waiting for Jason to call

someone to account for this, try to determine the truth of what had happened.

Large Meleager and horn-helmed Haraldur were shaking their heads, looking vaguely embarrassed. But at the moment Jason seemed anything but firm or decisive. He seemed not the least bit eager to call anyone to account for anything. Watching him curiously, Proteus thought he gave the impression of wishing that all these splashing fools around him would simply go away, taking their worries about their spare parts and their servants with them, and let him get on with his private meditations.

Such an attitude made the newcomer uneasy. This was not the way a captain should behave at the beginning of a serious enterprise. Any voyage on the Great Sea was dangerous, and there was no doubt that Jason was intending a long voyage. Anyone who equipped himself with such a ship, such a crew, and such a plenitude of extra stores, certainly had in mind more than a brief and sunny cruise along the coast. If their leader showed no more enthusiasm for his task than this, Proteus foresaw a hard time ahead for the voyagers at best, and more likely real disaster.

The ongoing discussion soon degenerated into pointless wrangling. Standing by, now and then rubbing his aching head, occasionally looking back at the darkening sea from which he had mysteriously emerged, the new arrival was glad that the argument diverted attention away from him.

He had about decided that it was time for him to casually begin to move up on the beach, and get in line for some dinner, when suddenly there was splashing confusion around him, men crying out in alarm or excitement, everyone looking up. Jason, along with several others, was suddenly ducking and dodging, and Proteus raised his eyes.

A flying shape loomed close overhead, zooming over the waves at no more than treetop height. For a moment, fear of the monstrous in a new form gripped Proteus with paralysis. Screaming gulls darted out of the path of a figure that was much too big to be a bird. The sky was still bright enough to let him see that it was a man flying up there, or at least a figure that looked entirely human, except for the wings of magic sprouting from each ankle.

2

Joining

FOR A MOMENT everyone in the water and on the beach was startled by the rushing presence in the air above—then Jason and most of the others relaxed.

Once Jason had recovered from his initial start, the flying figure was no mystery to him. Turning to Proteus, who was still gaping, Jason assured the newcomer that it was no god or monster flying overhead, but only a man named Calais, one of the Argonauts. Calais and his brother, Zetes, had somehow come into possession of two pairs of some god's winged sandals. And now Proteus could see a second flying man in the middle distance, drawing near as if returning from a scouting flight.

"Come into possession?" Proteus marveled. "How?" Given the ruinous state of his own memory, he was not surprised to be unable to recall ever seeing anything of the kind before. But most of the men around him were as awestruck as he, to judge by the way they all gaped at the darting figures in the sky.

The answer to his question came from an Argonaut whose name he had not yet learned. "They're not saying. If some angry deity comes looking for them—well, that will be their problem."

For a moment Proteus stood gazing up at the two flying men, short cloaks streaming behind their backs, coming and going through the last rays of the setting sun, at the height of a good arrow shot above the beach. One flapped his arms in playful imitation of a bird, an action that made no difference in his flight. They waved to their friends below, and called down to them, words lost in the sound of surf.

"Don't tell me they've stolen them from some god, or pair of gods!" muttered one voice. "I've never even seen a god!"

Few people had. Another man put in: "But it looks that way, no? Where else would any human get such gear?"

"Wouldn't be any fun for us if the divine Hermes, say, got angry and came looking for his shoes."

The man standing next to Proteus nudged him with an elbow. "I admit, I've never seen anything of the kind before. Have you?"

"Not that I remember."

"If *I* could fly . . . well." The implication was that the speaker would be enjoying some glorious adventure of an entirely different kind than the one he had signed up for, a better prospect than pulling on a heavy oar for months at a time. Evidently a couple of days at sea, even in the company of world-famous Jason, had been enough to rob that prospect of some of its glamour.

Proteus was beginning to get some sense of the identities of several individuals in the little crowd around him. He suspected he was not particularly good at names, but now he knew Haraldur, Meleager, and Idmon.

A young man addressed as Telamon said to Jason: "Nothing suits you better than to abandon Hercules." A faint groan went up, in several voices; people were tired of that argument. But the reaction did not discourage Telamon: "I've heard it suggested that you planned the whole affair yourself so that his fame in our homeland should not eclipse your own, if we have the good fortune to return." The speaker paused. "Not that I really believe that," he added.

Jason showed no resentment at being challenged in this way. Calmly he denied having had anything to do with the abandonment of Hercules.

"Why should I be jealous?" he asked of everyone, looking around. "If one of my crew, Hercules or anyone else, should gain great glory, that's fine. It will only reflect well on me. All I want is to be peacefully at home, enjoying what is mine by right." After an inward-looking pause he added: "Release from toil is all I ask of the gods."

That struck Proteus as a poor attitude for a Hero setting out to seek adventure. It was as if Jason was tired before he started. But it seemed to have little effect on his forty followers, and Proteus wondered how many were really listening to anything the leader said. But then a few of the men did seem to be made vaguely uneasy by their leader's manner; they exchanged glances among themselves, and no one quite knew how to respond.

Jason seemed to suddenly become aware of this unfavorable reaction, for now he raised his voice decisively, saying he had decided it was time to make clear certain matters that seemed to be generally misunderstood.

Moving quickly, he waded out of the water onto the beach, put on some clothing to indicate the formality of the occasion, and called a meeting.

Proteus, who had slowly followed the others ashore, looked around at the members of the group he was trying to join and said: "I fear I will have to borrow clothing, if I am to have any at all." His hair and beard were still slowly dripping seawater.

"Come along, then." It was the large and hearty Meleager who volunteered to take him in charge.

His new guide led Proteus to the ship, which rested tilted sideways on its rounded hull. Avoiding the large steering oar that projected from the stern, the Argonaut climbed up into the portside outrigger. The bottoms of both outriggers had been solidly planked, to afford sitting and standing space for the outboard banks of rowers, creating what was in effect a triple hull. From there Meleager slid his large body in under the narrow fighting deck, where he pulled open the tight-fitting door of a locker—Proteus supposed there would be a number of other storage spaces distributed around the ship, given the necessity of carrying supplies. The opening revealed a small store of spare equipment, and the newcomer was soon provided with a loincloth and a plain tunic. Any question of his qualifications to join the company had been apparently set aside, at least for the moment.

———

Presently the Argonauts had all gathered round their leader, who had now put on tunic, loincloth, and sandals, and was standing in the full light of the twin fires.

"All of you must know," Jason began, "or ought to know, that I am the rightful occupant of the throne of the kingdom of Iolcus, where our voyage began a few days ago." He raised his chin as if in defiance, and as he gazed around at the assembled company he looked for the moment every inch a king.

Having achieved utter silence among his followers, Jason went on. "Some years ago my father, as you must know, ruled Iolcus from the high castle above the harbor, where now his brother the usurper sits." The captain paused to look around. "If there are any here with me now who do not already know the story of how my father lost his crown to the treacherous and false usurper Pelias, I will tell it to you."

He took the answering murmur as a signal to proceed, and plunged into the story.

Proteus soon gave up trying to follow the narrative through the technicalities of intrigue; who was descended from whom on which side of the family, and which claim took precedence over which other one. He gathered that Jason's parents were both dead. He couldn't tell if the captain had brothers and sisters or not. Various people were named as being in contention, but they might all be cousins and aunts and uncles. Alliances were made and broken, and hatred flourished everywhere.

Proteus decided that if the legends about Jason were true, he was probably a hell of a Hero when he had a weapon in his hands and an enemy in front of him; but no one was ever going to call him a spell-binding speaker. As for the transfer of power he was trying to explain, events seemed to have followed the path they often did in royal families, a dispute among close relatives. To those not directly concerned the outcome would probably make little difference.

But eventually Jason got around to his main point. Some months ago, when he had challenged the right of his uncle, Pelias, to rule, Pelias had spoken ringingly of oracles and of the will of the gods, and had sworn some high-sounding oath. The details of the arrangement worked out remained vague, but in one way or another the royal uncle had induced or compelled his nephew to set out on this voyage.

Jason sounded like a man fully convinced of the wisdom of his own actions, when he concluded: "The throne of Iolcus must be mine, and it will be, when I have brought back the Golden Fleece."

Brought back the *what*? Proteus wondered silently. Most of the men around him were nodding their approval of their leader's words, and giving the impression that they understood him; but if Proteus had ever heard before of anything called the Golden Fleece, the memory was part of the vast store that had been knocked out of his aching head.

When he tried to recall anything he might ever have known about King Pelias, he had but little better success. The name of Pelias seemed to be associated with a reputation for ruthlessness, but then the same could be said of most successful kings.

Jason's narrative had turned into an exhortation, and every time he paused for breath a polite murmur of agreement went up from his as-sembled crew, each response a little louder than the last. The second or third time this happened, Proteus joined in, though he had no more idea of whether Jason's cause was really just or not than he did of where the money might have come from to outfit this ship. From the reaction of the other Argonauts, he gathered that Pelias was generally considered mean and untrustworthy, even for a king.

Meanwhile, a couple of volunteers from among the Heroic company had managed to divert enough of their attention from the speech to tend the cookfires, and the smell of roasting meat promised a delicious dinner soon. Proteus's mouth was watering. He wondered how long it had been since he tasted food—then he thought it might be just as well that he could not remember that.

"The goal of our voyage is the Golden Fleece," repeated Jason, for the third or fourth time, making absolutely sure that no one had missed the point. This time fortunately he went on to provide a kind of definition: the Fleece was said to have come from a god-sent flying ram, the like of which had never been seen by anyone before or since.

"Flying ram?" Proteus asked the world aloud. A couple of his nearest neighbors looked at him, but nobody else paid any attention, which when he thought about it he supposed was his good luck.

Jason, having worked himself into a mood to talk, was recapitulating the story anyway. About a generation ago, this wonderful creature—or maybe it was some kind of a device, worked by odylic magic—had carried a man named Phrixus from the neighborhood of Iolcus halfway across the world to Colchis, where the fugitive had eventually married Chalciope, a daughter of the Colchian King Aeetes, and fathered several children by her.

"Two sons of Phrixus and the Princess Chalciope are with us now," added Jason, and motioned for the pair to somehow indicate themselves. "Phrontis and Argeus."

Two of the younger-looking Argonauts stepped forward into the full firelight, looking round awkwardly, as if they feared they might be called on to make speeches.

But Jason spared the brothers and his audience any such ordeal. He went on with his oration, driving home the essential point by repetition. "Pelias the false king has sworn, by all the gods and in front of witnesses, that if I can bring back the Fleece and give it to him, he will honor my just claim, and resign the throne to me."

Someone in the rear circle of listeners raised a hand. "Captain, this Phrixus is now dead?"

"Our father died several years ago," said Argeus, and went on to explain that he and his brother Phrontis had been mere boys when they left their grandfather's domain. But they could tell their shipmates of the old man's formidable reputation as a tyrant. Shaking his head, the speaker seemed to imply that they could provide plenty of evidence of that in the days ahead.

His brother, Phrontis, now took the floor and had more than a little to say about the journey that lay before them. He recited a list of the various kingdoms where they expected to touch land, on one side or another of the Great Sea. To begin with, there was the island of Lemnos, where women were now said to rule; and after Lemnos they would come to the mysterious domain of Samo-thraki, where travelers were strongly encouraged to take part in occult rituals. Then Bithnyia, where King Amycus brutally held power—and everyone who had ever heard of Amycus knew what a problem any visitor there was likely to encounter.

Proteus had not heard of Amycus, or could not remember if he had; and apparently he was not going to be enlightened for a while yet.

Young Phrontis, warming to his role of guide, was beginning to be breathless with excitement. After Bithnyia, he said, there were the filthy and odious Harpies that they would have to deal with, and after them the Clashing Rocks . . .

Around Proteus the listening men were nodding, grim-faced in the firelight but still enjoying themselves. Proteus's report of a Giant not far from where they were had not really alarmed this bunch, who were obviously not going to be discouraged by the possibilities of future danger; they had probably been hearing some of the same stories all their lives.

Someone standing back in darkness had a question in a different vein: "This Fleece must be a treasure of considerable value, then? I mean, whether it is really metallic gold or not." Proteus was glad to realize that others in the group were just about as ignorant as he.

Idmon answered: "That is a safe assumption. But the gold itself may be the least part of its value." In the firelight, it was easy to see that there was quite a lot of gray in Idmon's hair.

Proteus wondered suddenly if the crew, or any among them, had been promised shares in any profits of the voyage. That was a common enough arrangement on adventurous expeditions, most of which turned sooner or later into outright piracy. It was a prospect he was going to have to keep in mind, whatever the original impetus might have been that had landed him in this situation.

As for the pledge or promise that Jason seemed so certain of, from old King Pelias, well, it would be a bright sunny day in the Underworld before any king, let alone one with the reputation of Jason's uncle, would give up his throne simply because someone asked him for it.

One of the listening Argonauts now spoke up to raise this point quite openly, though he phrased it in somewhat more diplomatic language. When Jason retorted coldly that he had his uncle's promise, and was going to have the throne, the man who brought it up hastily added an assurance that whether Jason ever became a king or not, he was still eager to go on this expedition for the sheer adventure of it. He did not want anyone to think that he was trying to back out.

There was a chorus of agreement. It seemed that every other member of the crew had come along for the same reasons, and backing out would be the worst thing any of them could think of at this point.

"I plan to honor my side of the agreement scrupulously," Jason informed them all, driving the point home. "And I intend to see that my uncle honors his, one way or another." Another murmur from the men. Somehow the doubts raised about King Pelias and his pledge were set aside again without really being answered.

It was the youth called Telamon who wanted to know: "But tell us, Jason, what course are we are going to steer? I mean, we have heard of the various countries where we may land, but nothing yet of distances and bearings."

That question perked up the interest of the crew, who were already tired of dynastic squabbles and old horror stories. What really mattered was that they had been accepted into this company of famous Heroes, and that Jason himself, *the* Jason, Jason the Boar-Slayer, was leading them to new adventures.

"I will let another man answer that question," Jason said, and with a gesture of invitation stood aside.

A stocky, sturdy fellow, skin dark as ebony, got to his feet. "In case there is still someone on the crew who does not know me, I am Tiphys, your steersman and navigator."

Men looked at him respectfully; evidently he had a reputation. He was a very solid-looking man though not especially large, and Proteus saw that he had removed the compass-pyx from the beached ship, and was carrying it under his arm.

When it was time to shove off again in the morning, he would reinstall it, a job that any experienced navigator could easily accomplish with a few simple, routine rites of magic. Meanwhile, Tiphys acted as if the instrument were his personal property, treating it with the familiar care of a man who handles a treasure that has been passed down in his family for generations.

And he had a ready answer to the question that had already been asked about their course. Tiphys rapidly recited a firmly memorized list of seas and straits and coastlines; Proteus, yearning after his own lost memory, was impressed with the man's knowledge and his ability to recall. Proteus got the impression from listening that the land they were bound for, Colchis, must lie somewhere at the far end of the earth. The contemplated journey was going to last for months, perhaps for many months, even if all went smoothly. And they all knew better than to expect that.

When Tiphys had concluded, Jason asked: "Are there any other questions?"

Someone raised a hand. "Does Colchis lie at the edge of the world?"

"My compass-pyx has shown me that the world is really round. There is no danger of falling off an edge . . . well, argue about that if you like, but I know it goes on far beyond Colchis . . . anyone else?"

When no one else raised a hand, Jason's eye came steadily back to Proteus, who now realized that he had not been forgotten after all.

A silence had begun to grow, and others were also looking at the newcomer. The commander slightly raised his voice. "We must decide if this man Proteus, who comes to us from out of the sea, is Hero or servant. He might have died in a shipwreck with the other menials, but Fate decreed otherwise and he has come bravely through great dangers. If we judge him no more than a servant still, then we must leave him behind. The alternative is to make him one of our number, but before doing that we must see if he is worthy."

Listening to the talk around him, Proteus began to gain some understanding of the controversy over servants. Originally, each qualified and accepted Hero had been allowed to bring aboard one companion . . . friend, relative, servant, catamite, or some combination of those categories.

But Jason, in the aftermath of Hercules's abandonment, had decided that all such hangers-on or attendants had to go. Now that all the chosen Heroes were actually aboard, it was obvious that any such additional number would simply make the ship too crowded; and if not everyone could have an attendant, no one in this company of equals should.

Voices were raised in general agreement. If Proteus was to stay, it would have to be as a full-fledged Argonaut, a member of the company.

People looked at him uncertainly, and he looked back in the same mode. He found it gratifying that his unknown self at least did not feel terrified at the idea of being tested.

"Shall we have a trial of wrestling?" suggested Haraldur the northerner, in the tone of one who expects to get a laugh.

"That didn't work out too well when we tried it with Hercules," someone else recalled. And now there was a ripple of rueful laughter, mingled with resentment.

"Weapons, then." The man in the horned helmet looked at Proteus. "With what tools of death do you feel most at ease?"

"I choose the spear," he heard himself saying. Again, as when he was asked his name, he had no need to give the matter any thought.

Having said that, of course he had to borrow a spear, and several were immediately produced. He frowned at the selection, thinking there was something wrong about each of these weapons's heads, their points, though obviously all were well-made. But he could not have said exactly what the difficulty was, and at last he made a choice. The design of a dolphin had been worked into the spearhead with some skill, and it was good sharp bronze—which of course could never be as hard and enduring as the best steel, but some men still preferred it.

Now, if he could remember that with no trouble at all, along with so much else about the way the world worked, how in the Underworld could there be nothing left of himself except a name? But so it was, and he would have to deal with it.

Balancing the stout shaft in his right hand, Proteus looked about him, meeting expectant glances. "What must I do?"

"Fight three of us to the death. No, no, I'm joking!" And Haraldur bent over double, slapping his knobby knees in high amusement.

After grim news and edgy talk, everyone was ready to enjoy a joke. When the laughter subsided, it turned out that what the company were really proposing was that he should make a throw of a certain distance— someone paced off what was evidently considered a fair distance—and score a solid hit on a log of driftwood, on which some of the Heroes had already been practicing, leaving it chipped and scarred.

Someone jested that they could use as their target the very oaken keel of *Argo*. "She's not going to notice one little pin-prick there." Jason shot the man a look that said he was not amused.

Concentrating intently now upon his trial, Proteus nodded, stepped up to the mark, and with a casual motion of his left arm indicated that people should stand back. Then, without giving himself time to worry about it, he did precisely what he had been challenged to do. He did somewhat better, in fact—the spearhead went in deep, very close to the center of the indicated target. The long shaft stuck there quivering, as if it still had energy to spare.

He heard a muttering behind him: "Stronger than he looks."

The owner of the spear came to reclaim his weapon, and had to work at it to wrench it from the wood. Men thumped Proteus on the back, offering congratulations, bombarding him with their names, half of which he failed to remember the first time he heard them. He was invited to join the others in their dinner.

Jason, after being distracted several times by questions, finally said to Proteus: "Welcome aboard."

"Thank you, sir," the newcomer responded, gnawing fragments of roast meat from a bone. The meat was tasty, but suddenly he realized that what he was really hungry for was fish. Well, no doubt he would see plenty of that in days to come.

"And do you think yourself qualified in every way to join us in our quest?"

"I don't know the answer to that, sir. I've passed your test, I can handle a spear. I'm not sure just what other qualifications you expect." The mass of dark hair nodded judiciously. "A reasonable reply. Come to think of it, I believe Hercules had something of the same modest attitude."

When it came time to retire for the night, Proteus saw the steersman Tiphys carefully bring his compass-pyx with him to the place where he lay down to sleep.

The sight of the device stirred something deep in the newcomer's ravaged memory. Proteus asked permission to look at the fine instrument, hoping that something about it would jog his memory into further revelations. Tiphys rather grudgingly agreed.

Use of the compass-pyx was well-nigh universal. Navigation across the open sea, out of sight of land, was difficult enough even with the help of such devices, and would have been all but impossible without it. Probably Tiphys, like most other navigators of reputation, relied upon some special private magical addition to the instrument, an accessory he would try as best he could to keep secret.

The compass-pyx that Proteus was now privileged to look at basically resembled the similar instruments he could hazily remember seeing.

The pointer, or cusp of the device, balanced on a needle-sharp pivot, consisted of a narrow crescent of horn and ivory. A sliver of each of the disparate materials, identically curved and not quite as long as a man's hand, were bound together in a particular way. Some experts swore that silk was the only proper material to use for the binding, but Proteus saw now that Tiphys, like many other expert pilots, preferred the web-stuff of certain mutant spiders.

Once a pilot or steersman had attuned his mind to the device, it indicated with great accuracy the bearing that the ship should take to bring him to his goal. Few people placed any reliance on the compass-pyx on land; its effectiveness on the Great Sea was credited to Poseidon's having long ago given the device his blessing.

There were of course refinements in the construction and operation of the compass-pyx. Some extremely simple versions were good only for indicating true north; others, if the cap/cover was shifted to the first end, pointed to the nearest dry land.

Many swore that the compass-pyx worked best, indeed that it was only reliable at all, if hooked up with a strip of pure copper that ran deep into the central timbers of the ship. Whether Tiphys was going to reattach his instrument in that way Proteus could not tell.

The watches for the coming night had been assigned hours ago, long before Proteus had come wading out of the sea to join their company, and Jason had insisted on taking a turn himself, which was evidently his usual procedure with any kind of duty. So Proteus had no responsibilities as yet; anyway, he thought, his new shipmates were probably not ready to trust him with their lives. Belly satisfied with a good meal, he slept well through the night, stretched out on warm sand. The eternal sound of the surf was in his ears, and his dreams that night were of the sea. In them he was immersed in deep water, but somehow not in the least afraid of drowning.

In the morning, after breakfasting on the remnants of last night's feast, they all lined up along the ship's sides, and at a signal laid hold of her gunwales and pushed her back into the sea again. Proteus immediately scrambled into his newly assigned spot on one of the benches. Meleager was next to him, and he was beginning to recognize the names of others who were nearby.

The oar proved less familiar than the spear had been, but the business of its use was not that complicated, and he soon settled into the proper rhythm.

He felt a nervousness that he did not want to admit, even to himself. But there was no sign of any Giant.

As the new day wore on in rowing, Proteus found himself becoming more and more interested in the tale of the Golden Fleece, wanting to know more about it. He talked with those of the other Heroes who were the least standoffish.

That certainly included Meleager, whose garments, when he was wearing anything at all, looked rich and costly, a picture of size, confident attitude, and youthful vigor.

"Then this Golden Fleece is marvelous indeed," Proteus agreed. "But in what way?"

But Mel had to admit that he was the wrong one to be asking about that.

Every now and then, as the Argonauts talked among themselves, the name of Theseus came up, as it very often did when folks were telling tales of adventure. Everyone had heard the story of the Princess Ariadne of Corycus, her connection with Theseus, and the breathtaking reversals of fortune she had experienced on the Island of Dia.

Speaking of Theseus, almost everyone in the crew seemed to be surprised that that youthful adventurer, sometimes called King of the Pirates, had not shown up and demanded a place. But the time of departure had come and gone, and no one knew where he might be. Many assumed that his name had been on the list of those to whom Jason had sent personal invitations; if Theseus was not a Hero, who could claim that title? True, his remarkable career consisted of little but acts of piracy. But if a consistent concern for others' property was made a qualification, Jason might have a hard time filling his roster.

Jason had only one comment to make when the name of Theseus came up: "From what I hear, he is a thief and murderer, and to call him a king does dishonor to a royal title."

As they rowed, the conversation around Proteus touched on many things: to begin with, women, as might be expected. Then the sea and its wonders, and then something about women. The remote, ongoing conflict between Giants and gods, now supposed to be flaring into open warfare—but such mighty struggles were remote to most of the people of the world, and the conversation soon came back to women.

Proteus listened, mostly, now and then contributing a word or two; but to his surprise, what he had vaguely expected to be the chief subject of speculation, the Fleece itself, was scarcely mentioned.

Though he listened intently, he was still unable to discover just what kind of intrinsic value the Fleece might have, what were its magic powers—everyone assumed it must have some. How big it was, how many standard units of gold it weighed. Gradually it dawned on the listener that few if any of these men who were willing to risk their lives to find the exotic treasure, had any better idea of its nature than he did. They were here because Jason, a magnetic hero who would someday be king of an important country, was going to lead them on a glorious adventure, and so far that was enough for everyone.

———

Proteus found it oddly restful to spend another night at sea; he thought he could doze, slumped on his rower's bench, almost as comfortably as he would have slept in the safest, driest bed ashore. Most of the other men seemed to be having an easy time of it as well, napping at their oars, while clouds covered the stars. The sea was calm enough tonight, and Jason, who apparently did not completely trust Tiphys and his elaborate compass-pyx, decided to wait for dawn to push ahead.

Around noon on the second day since Proteus had joined the crew, Jason while taking a turn as lookout on the low raised deck—climbing the little mast would have been utterly impractical—caught sight of some green-clad hills. Within a couple of hours the *Argo* was coming ashore, her captain meaning to once more refill the collection of water jugs and jars and waterskins. Whatever part of the world this was, Proteus could not remember ever seeing it before.

When an opportunity offered, and when Tiphys had offered no objection, Proteus took a turn at crouching over the compass-pyx and with the aid of its powers called up a vision of the *Argo*'s destination. It was a mysterious vision indeed, and seemed to have little to do with geography.

Have I done this before? he wondered privately. He thought the answer must be yes. The ease with which he approached the instrument seemed good evidence that he had.

One routine means of operation, he knew, was to whisper aloud the name of the island, continent, or object that you were trying to reach by navigation, while resting your forehead against the ivory box. But in this case nothing of the kind was necessary.

If only he had known the name of his home, he would have tried to get a look at it. A vague attempt to think of home produced nothing. On impulse he tried imagining the Fleece instead.

On each trial the device showed Proteus, behind his closed eyelids, a new view of their mysterious objective, very slightly nearer than the time before but from the same angle. A shapeless mass that seemed to be hanging in the branches of a tree. And against that green it appeared to be golden indeed, but more like the shimmer of morning sun on the ocean, than any material object.

3

Lemnos

THE NEXT DAY seemed endlessly long to Proteus. Not that he was particularly wearied by the rowing, but the hours of labor were relieved only by intermittent talk with his new shipmates. The talk brought him no new knowledge on the subject in which he was most keenly interested—himself. And it taught him very little about the voyage to which he was now committed.

Throughout the long day he was engaged almost continuously in a silent struggle to regain his memory. But all the effort brought to the surface were scattered shards and images, almost nothing any earlier than the Giant's destruction of the ship. At one point the sight and sound of splintered planks came through clearly, then a more detailed look than he had had before at horrified human faces, none of which he recognized. And there was the sound of a man screaming, an ugly noise that ended in drowning bubbles . . . feeling his stomach growing queasy, Proteus gave up for the time being the effort of trying to force his memory.

But of course giving up wasn't as easy as all that. He could not escape his need to know the truth, whatever it might be. And so in a little while he tried again to find some remnant, some walking ghost of his old self. And got no farther than before.

All day the crew had been laboring almost continuously with the oars, which left them generally exhausted. It would have been only sensible if Proteus had found himself worn out too, but at the end of the day his muscles were not aching, and he still had energy. Nor were there any blisters on his palms and fingers, which, as he now thoughtfully noted, had been heavily callused all along. Whatever his true identity turned out to be, it would seem he was no aristocrat.

Maybe a common sailor, then, with an exceptionally well-conditioned body? Or possibly a professional athlete of some kind? Athletes often had to seek other kinds of employment. For all Proteus could tell, he might well have been one of the boatload of servants who had been scheduled to attend the Argonauts, before Jason and the others woke up to the fact that their narrow ship lacked room for so many non-Heroic bodies.

Athlete maybe, servant, maybe. But the more he thought about it, the more likely it seemed that he had been a sailor, one of the crew bringing a load of servants to their destination. In any case his earlier self, who he was beginning to think of as Old Proteus, had been nominally free; his neck was not encircled by any metal collar indicating slavery.

Servant, sailor, or whatever, the evidence said he'd certainly been accustomed to hard, physical work, and not unfamiliar with oars and spears. Now if only he could recall his orders from the mysterious woman—but they lay still tantalizingly out of reach.

It seemed ridiculous to feel uneasy about not getting tired, but the anomaly nagged him. Now stronger than before, the feeling grew in him that the Giant who had destroyed that ship and drowned those men would come and hunt him down if he knew that Proteus had survived. He, Proteus, had been personally stalked by some mighty power that was out to kill him. And if that power knew that he was still alive, it would come after him again.

━━━━━━━

The next day was also spent in rowing, and, for Proteus, in basically useless mental effort. And so it went on the day after that. On several occasions the *Argo* sailed entirely out of sight of land for hours at a time. Jason and his crew obviously were ready to trust their lives to Tiphys and his compass-pyx, and to the construction of their sturdy ship, and its outfitting with the finest silk and linen sails. From the superb quality of the gear, it seemed obvious that Jason had wealthy backers in his attempt to win a crown. Backers who were not only wealthy, but not much afraid of angering King Pelias. One alternative of course would be that Jason had been blessed with a family fortune, and had sunk that into this endeavor; but the captain made an occasional remark about his growing up in poverty, which seemed to dispose of that idea. Proteus asked a couple of his shipmates what they knew of the expedition's financing, but it seemed they had never thought about such mundane matters. A quest with Jason was sure to be a glorious adventure, and that was enough for them. The new recruit did not pursue the matter further; he had no wish to be suspected of being someone's spy or secret agent.

In the course of these same days Proteus began to notice how strangely often first one flying fish and then another, skimming the waves on a parallel course with the *Argo*, and at no great distance, just kept up with the ship. Maybe the actions of the fish were purely accidental, but now Proteus developed an eerie feeling that some unknown power, for some unknown reason, was keeping the vessel under surveillance. He kept this suspicion to himself.

Now and then during his long hours at the oar he raised his eyes, searching the clouds or the sunny blue, cursed by a vague fear that the *Argo* herself would suffer some direct attack, now that he had come aboard her. But so far there was no hint of anything of the kind.

Three days after leaving the beach where Proteus had joined them, Jason and Tiphys the steersman got together for a long, low-voiced talk. Afterward Jason stood up and raised his voice to inform the crew that their next port of call was going to be the island of Lemnos.

And at the same time, Proteus noticed Idmon opening a locker and taking out a waterproof sealskin pouch. From this in turn he carefully removed a book of modest size. The volume's pages were of parchment, and it was bound in what looked like sharkskin, which Proteus supposed would have some waterproofing effect.

When Proteus asked about the book, Idmon let him know that it was the ship's log, and entries were to be made in it daily, setting down events almost as they happened, so that when the voyage was over a detailed history of it would have been written.

Sitting cross-legged on one corner of the deck, the record-keeper dipped a stubby pen, made from a large feather, into one end of an inkhorn, and started putting words on parchment. When he paused for thought after a couple of lines, Proteus was still curious. "What language is that?"

The scribe looked at him in mild surprise. "An old one. Can you read it?"

It would not have surprised Proteus to learn that half the Heroes had trouble reading even the language they had been speaking all their lives. In this company, scholarship beyond that would be extraordinary. He said carefully: "I think I may have seen it somewhere before."

The scribe seemed about to put another question to him, when both were distracted by a debate that had begun on nearby benches, and had now grown vociferous. For several years now, word had been passed around the world (and in this matter the memory of Proteus seemed to be functioning normally) to the effect that Lemnos was inhabited solely by women. The most popular version of the story said that some years ago the Lemnian ladies, resentful of their husbands' having taken to importing mistresses on a large scale, had risen up in rebellion and slaughtered them to the last man.

Opinions on the truth of this story differed widely among the Argonauts, and a lively discussion went around the benches. Proteus listened, but knew nothing to contribute.

Nobody noticed his reluctance to speak, for plenty of others were eager to do so. Several of the Argonauts claimed to have actually visited Lemnos during the past few years, and these unanimously reported that the tales of mass murder were only rumors. All that had really happened on that island was that a kind of matriarchal government had been put in place.

Others, contradicting the men who claimed to be eyewitnesses, continued to swear that the stories of murder must be correct. When some of the men appealed to Jason, he had nothing directly to say on the question—again his mind seemed elsewhere, as it so often did.

But the dark rumor seemed refuted when, after a few days of moderately rough weather, and about a month after leaving Iolcus, the ship put somewhat warily into the small harbor of the city of Myrina, the only real port on Lemnos.

It was easy to see that the island was of substantial size though not as big as some—Tiphys said a little less than two hundred square miles. Here and there faint columns of smoke went up to enormous heights, over land much of which looked quite empty of human habitation; one of the older Argonauts said the smoke came from volcanic activity, that the ground here was always smoldering somewhere. Gentle hills in the western and southern parts of the island built up gradually to a single mountain, called Skopia, Tiphys said. The sharp-toothed crest stood about fifteen hundred feet above the level of the sea.

Once in the harbor, the visitors were relieved to see some of the wilder stories proven false. There were a fair number of men about— though it was true there seemed fewer males and more women than you would ordinarily expect to see on docks and quays. The waterfront was not particularly busy, but by no means deserted. Proteus observed one fellow standing at the end of a dock, who seemed to be posing with tensed muscles while he watched the *Argo* glide by, as if he wanted to impress the newcomers with his physique. If that was indeed his purpose, the effect was spoiled by his thin arms and pot belly.

Shortly after they had tied up, it was a woman who came to meet them as port official, with book and pen in hand, and escorted by a small armed guard who were also women. Briskly the official asked the newcomers their business. Jason met her courteously, and Proteus watching from a little distance thought they were having a reasonable conversation. In the end the visitors were granted full freedom to come ashore.

As the Argonauts gradually relaxed their vigilance, stepped off their ship, and began to see more of the town, it became obvious that for some reason the male population of Lemnos seemed content to leave both the business of government and the government of business to the women. It wasn't that the men were totally idle; but they seemed to be contenting themselves with an intricate system of activity involving both gambling and philosophical debates.

When Proteus, keeping a borrowed spear casually within reach, talked to a couple of the local men about the apparent lack of excitement on their island, the locals, turning calmly arrogant, informed him that they were expecting to depart within the hour. They said they were going to take part in a great adventure, whose nature they were not at liberty to discuss.

When the visitor looked around the harbor and asked which of the few visible ships they planned to take, they were unable to contain their great secret any longer. Each man swore soberly that they were waiting for Theseus to sail in and welcome them aboard his pirate ship for a cruise of pillaging and looting.

Their visitor thought the pair looked poorly equipped for any such adventure. When Proteus tried politely to convey that he still had doubts, he expected for a moment that the two were going to attack him, for they glared wildly and knotted their fists. But then they turned their backs on him and wandered off down the dock, arm in arm.

Another Argonaut, watching their slightly unsteady progress, snorted. "They're on drugs."

"That would explain much," put in a third.

The port official, a gray-haired woman with a look of harried pride, was looking after the pair also, with disdain. She explained that the fathers and sons and husbands of the island, or a great majority of them, were now spending most of their time and energy on taking some drug, or some combination of substances, that was supposed to make them clever, powerful, and handsome.

Then she added: "And what you are thinking about them is quite right. The drug does not work—not in the way they think it does. The only notable real effect, as you will observe when you meet more of them about the island, is to make them see themselves as Heroes."

"And to make the rest of us see them as idiots," Proteus muttered.

Somehow it made him feel a little better to see men who were worse off than he; there was no keeping their weakness secret from the world.

In passing he noted also that there were few small children to be seen around the island. Perhaps over the last few years the men of Lemnos had lost interest in other things besides work.

The idea of leaving all the practical affairs of life to women was one that a number of Argonauts found shocking. It led to a discussion of the half-legendary Amazons, another topic on which the men had strong opinions and very little knowledge.

None of Proteus's shipmates claimed to have ever actually visited Amazon country, though several said they were determined to get there before they died—rumor had it that impressive warriors were welcome there, and were royally entertained until they had impregnated large numbers of women.

Whatever the truth about the Amazons, Lemnos was real, and hard enough to understand. Those who said they had visited this port before observed that the situation seemed to have deteriorated since their last visit—by that they meant there were now even fewer men to be seen in public.

Leaving aside the organization of society, Lemnos did not seem to be a wealthy land. Every rooftop seemed to carry some kind of cistern, ready to catch rainfall; streams of fresh water were small and scarce. Sparse crops grew on hillsides visible from near the middle of town, and the workers in those tilted fields appeared to be almost entirely women.

But, soon after the port official had reported to the modest palace, messengers came from the queen, with word that the Argonauts were invited into their town and houses as friends.

And Jason was invited, alone, to visit the queen in her palace.

The Argonauts spent the interval when he was gone staying close together, trading stories and whetting blades, vaguely suspicious of some kind of treachery.

———

After about three hours, Jason returned to his men, looking quietly excited, more so than Proteus had ever seen him. When his crew had gathered around him, Jason reported that he had had a long conversation alone with the queen, and she had actually offered him the kingship of Lemnos.

A number of the Argonauts began to laugh at that, but Jason remained solemn. No, he was not joking. Then he raised a hand, quelling the beginnings of an excited celebration, and told his men that he had turned the offer down. At that a sudden silence fell.

Proteus felt inwardly relieved at the announcement, though he could not have said why Jason's political and dynastic plans should matter to him one way or the other. But then Proteus made the odd discovery that, for some reason that was still shadowy in his own mind, it was important to him that the Argosy go on.

Jason gave the impression that his decision had cost him a struggle, but once reached, it was firm.

Speaking into a continuing, wondering silence among his men, he said: "You will be asking yourselves why I have rejected a crown."

No one had any comment to make. Answering the question that had not been asked, their captain went on to offer several reasons for his refusal, chief among them the vow he had made and had to keep. "Not that I could have accepted in any case. I have made a solemn vow to return to Iolcus with the Golden Fleece, and that's what I will do."

There was also the fact that the current king of Lemnos would have had to be deposed. But rumor had it that that individual seldom took any interest in affairs of state, or in his queen for that matter, being totally absorbed in his life of drugs and games. His existence did not appear to be much of an obstacle.

Meanwhile, Proteus was thinking that Jason's true reason for turning down a throne might well be quite different: Lemnos was small and mean, almost a joke as an independent kingdom, and it would only retain its independence until some real monarch thought it worth his while to snap it up.

———————

Not much else of interest to Proteus happened during the adventurers' short stay on the island. There was a little excitement—vicarious for most of the crew—when three or four of the Argonauts sampled some of the drugs to which the men of the island were so ruinously addicted.

Proteus and a few others were standing at dockside, uneasy about getting far from their ship in this strange place, when the unmistakable sounds of a fight breaking out reverberated through the thin wooden walls of the tavern.

Haraldur brightened at the noise. "Sounds like fun. Let's go!" A couple of others shared his enthusiasm.

Proteus by contrast experienced only a vague sinking feeling at the prospect of a fight; but he went along, walking rather than running after his shipmates. His lack of eagerness did not matter, because the brawl, such as it was, was very nearly over by the time the first of his shipmates reached the tavern doorway, where Proteus looked in just in time to see Meleager felled by a thick glass bottle bouncing off the back of his head. The bottle did not break, and the thin Lemnian who had wielded it looked surprised at his own success.

Mel's shipmates lumbered forward, generally towering over the natives, exacting vengeance. Weapons hardly seemed required, in this tavern, in this town. And anyway, a spear was always awkward at close quarters. Proteus stood leaning on his, and watched.

The worst of the skirmish, from the Argonauts' point of view, was that Meleager had to be carried back to the ship, where several minutes passed before he fully came around.

———

Jason on hearing the story of the fight was plainly angry, the first time Proteus had seen him in that state. "Was it not possible to stay out of trouble for a few hours?"

A chastened Hero stammered out that drugs had been at the bottom of the dispute. The captain on hearing this blasphemed several gods and sent out a search party. A couple of Argonauts who had sampled the local pharmaceuticals had to be hauled back aboard by main force. Jason on hearing this went to look them over. Realizing their condition, he sternly warned them that any man who jumped ship from this voyage would open himself to lifelong embarrassment; then he ordered them tied up until the effects of the drug had passed.

One man had to be restrained from jumping into the harbor, saying he meant to swim to Colchis, pick up the Fleece, and be back to Lemnos in time for dinner.

The captain's indignation was quietly mounting. "If any of you have carried any of those drugs on board, I hope you'll pitch them overboard."

Haraldur, smiling slightly, had a comment: "It might be fun to watch a sunfish that thinks it's a shark."

Some men laughed, but Jason was not amused.

Fortunately there were no immediate repercussions from the brawl. In an effort to discover how much local resentment, if any, the fight had created, Proteus and several other Argonauts strolled to a different quayside tavern where they entered as casual customers. This like the other grog shop was one of the few places where local men were still working, tending bar.

Whining music came from a corner, where female musicians of

gnarled and charmless age sawed at their stringed instruments. The wine was not bad, and now he had consumed enough to make him feel well-satisfied with the world for the time being.

Looking round at his shipmates, Proteus decided that after all, getting truly smashed would be more trouble than it was worth—now that he had begun drinking, he had the feeling that serious competition in this field was not and had never been a regular part of his life.

The bartender who had been hovering nearby suddenly cleared his throat. "So, Jason is going all the way to Colchis."

Proteus raised an eyebrow. "That's the plan. Certainly no secret about it."

The man leaned toward him over the stained wood. "Take me with you." He looked a bit old to be starting out as an adventurer.

"You serious?"

"I am. Anything to get away from Lemnos." The tone was one of quiet desperation.

"Don't want to be ruled by women?"

The bartender shook his head, and looked at the musicians. "It's not the women who are driving me crazy. It's the men."

Proteus was shaking his head. "Sorry, but we're allowed no attendants aboard. It's been decided." Then he looked up at a familiar voice, and was surprised to see Mel back on his feet again so soon. Well, some skulls were thicker than others.

Another Argonaut joined in, making some drunken proposal to have the new applicant prove his worth by throwing spears. "Or maybe bottles? How 'bout that?" That was horrifying; glass bottles were rare enough to be considered of some value.

By now Proteus had had enough to drink so this even seemed a good idea to him. "Why not? It worked for me." But in the end the discussion came to nothing.

When the native men felt themselves insulted, which Proteus got the impression happened dangerously often, they were not shy of challenging some of the Heroes to fight. The resulting contests—if that was really the right word for them—tended to be very one-sided. Fortunately for the diplomatic atmosphere, no one was actually killed, and the native men bore no resentment. As long as they remained alive, they seemed able to convince themselves that their side had won, or at least that they had gone down gloriously, succumbing only in the face of overwhelming odds.

Meanwhile, some of the younger women had begun eyeing the visitors with frank interest. Three Heroes besides Jason received offers of marriage, none of which were accepted. Local prostitutes had seen their business fall off sharply, their bodies less attractive than the images produced by drugs in the minds of their former customers.

———————

They stayed in all three days on Lemnos.

"Three days." An oarsman grunted at his task. "Only three days? I thought it was longer."

Another shook his head. "Three days was plenty long enough. An unpleasant spot, for all that it was full of horny women."

4

Mysteries

MELEAGER'S HEAD WAS still sore from the knock sustained in the Lemnian tavern. But soreness was the least of his problems. He had not had much to drink, and had stayed away from the drugs, but his behavior had certainly turned odd.

Jason, as Mel's oldest friend aboard, was seriously concerned. "Let me take a look at him."

Proteus moved closer, watching over the shoulder of the would-be physician. External damage was slight. Mel's eyes were open most of the time, and he was capable of moving about, and sometimes responding to simple questions. He announced that he was ready to take his turn at rowing, but when he got to the bench he only sat there with the long oar idle in his hands.

When encouraged, and reminded of what he was supposed to be doing, he would pull steadily for a stroke or two, and then again forget where he was and what he was about. He just sat there looking round at his shipmates as if he wondered who they were. Proteus, on observing this behavior felt an inner chill, and rubbed his own head thoughtfully. The swelling had gone down and the spot no longer hurt, but a vast domain of vital memory remained totally out of his reach. Still, that crack might have left him much worse off than he was.

Another man, who claimed to have had some training as a physician, pronounced judgment on the case of Meleager. "I have seen this kind of thing before. He may come out of it, or he may not. Time will tell."

Everyone who thought he knew something about medicine took a turn asking Meleager questions, and peering into his eyes and ears and nostrils; none of these orifices were bleeding, which the self-appointed experts said was a hopeful sign. At last a consensus was reached that he should be watched, and allowed to rest as much as possible. His fate rested in the hands of the gods.

———

A few days later, the Argonauts were beaching their long ship at Samothraki. This was a rocky island, presenting barren cliffs to the sea around almost its whole circumference, but Proteus thought it beautiful in its own unwelcoming way. And it was certainly much different from their last port of call. Here there were springs and streams, obviously a good share of rainfall, and a single mountain four times as high as the single peak that Lemnos had. Samothraki was about ten miles long by seven wide, smoothly shaped with a regular coastline which offered few natural harbors. A shipmate with a mind for practical details told Proteus that exports included fruit and vegetables, especially onions.

More interesting to most of the crew than onions were the mystery rituals for which Samothraki was also well known. It was to discuss these, and the invitation issued to all the Argonauts, that Jason called a gathering of the entire crew beside the ship.

"There is a cave over there"—pointing to a spot on the cliffside that bulked up only a few yards from the harbor's mouth—"where certain rites, usually forbidden to visitors and strangers, are to be conducted; and we have been invited to take part."

Many were interested but everyone was wary. "We have? How did that happen? Who knew we were coming here?"

Jason would say only that the invitation had reached him through intermediaries. And Idmon casually let it be known that he himself had been an initiate for some time.

"What sort of rites are they?" someone asked. "What would be expected of us?"

"There are mysteries of which we must not sing," said Idmon, in a tone that suggested he was quoting someone or something. "I will say only this: that when you have passed through, you will sail on with greater confidence across the formidable sea."

Around Proteus several of the other men were making gestures and mumbling words that they doubtless thought had some magical efficacy. It came as no great surprise to him to discover that there were several would-be mystics and/or would-be sorcerers among the crew. But it turned out that no more than half a dozen men in all were eager to be introduced into the secret rites of the Cabiri.

That was a new name to Proteus. "Who or what in all the hells are the Cabiri?" he demanded of some of his shipmates. He didn't think they were divinities, for he had the feeling that among the vast store of largely useless rubbish his memory had somehow managed to retain, he could have found the names and folk histories of most of the gods— probably no human being knew them all. He could only hope that "Cabiri" wasn't familiar as mother's milk to everyone in the world with an intact memory. But it was still a new one to him, and there was nothing he could do about that.

The men to whom he put the question looked aghast at him, and one of them chided Proteus for a lack of reverence. But he got the impression that a majority of his shipmates probably did not know much about the Cabiri either. It was only that no entity of more than human power ought to be so casually treated.

For the rest of the day, and through the early hours of the night, when his shipmates whispered to one another about the Cabiri and their mysterious rituals, Proteus could only nod and smile, as if he really had some idea of what the others were talking about.

When the subject came up, Proteus felt a deep, instinctive reaction that he would be wise to avoid taking part in any secret rites himself. This feeling was only strengthened when he got his first close look at a dim hollow in the rock, fifteen feet or so above the high-tide level of the sea, and approachable only by a narrow ledge along the face of a low cliff. His first impression was of a shallow cave, no more than a grotto, but he supposed the appearance was deceptive. As he watched, a hummingbird came darting out. This, the Argonauts were told, was the entrance to the place where the mysteries were to be revealed—or rather, where glimpses of certain secrets were to be granted to a select few.

It all sounded somehow repellent and even unconvincing to Proteus. He asked: "What will these Cabiri look like when they appear?"

"Appear?" The informant, who obviously wanted to seem knowledgeable, shook his head. "They're not going to do that. They never do."

It turned out that the men who were to be initiated had been warned not to expect to actually see any of the Cabiri in the course of the rituals.

———

As the afternoon drew on toward dusk, Jason, dressed in a fancier tunic than usual, came looking for Proteus, and found him mending a small fishing net. "There you are. Do I understand that you mean to take no part in the ceremony?"

Proteus looked up from his work; the fact that his fingers knew how to tie a variety of useful knots seemed to bolster his theory that he had been a sailor. "That's right, Captain."

The big man shrugged. "I don't expect to gain much benefit of it myself, or to enjoy it either, but my position requires that I join in—those who made the offer may be offended if I decline. Half a dozen of our shipmates have decided to accompany me into the cave. I want to assign you, among others, a post to guard."

"The ship, you mean?"

Jason shook his head. "I have others assigned to stand regular watches, and most of the crew will be aboard anyway. You and one other—Telemon, I think—will be posted just outside the cave. Just in case there is anyone who means to do us harm, while some of us are busy and distracted in the ceremony. And while I think of it, it would be a good idea if you who are standing guard brought a few extra weapons to your posts. We will be allowed to carry no arms into the cave—but it would be good to have some available at no great distance."

Proteus stood up, trying to wipe the slime of fishy cordage from his hands. "Any reason to suspect any kind of treachery, Jason?"

The captain shook his head again. "No more than a feeling. Would you rather not be chosen as a guard?"

"No, I feel honored. I'll do my best."

———

Shortly before midnight, Jason and those of his shipmates who had chosen to take part in the ceremony entered the cave bearing torches, accompanied by several masked and robed figures who had come to escort them.

As soon as the chosen ones had passed inside, Proteus and Telamon, his fellow sentry, took up their positions, one on each side of the cave's mouth, below torches burning in sconces fixed to the rock. They had each, as inconspicuously as possible, brought along a few extra weapons, as the captain had requested. Proteus saw that swords and short spears, along with a couple of battle-hatchets, were stashed just inside the cave. No one could see the cache from outside, but men inside, expecting to find weapons there, could easily put their hands on them.

By the captain's orders, all of the remaining Argonauts were staying close to the ship. Tonight, Proteus thought that those orders would certainly be obeyed. Samothraki did not seem a promising theater for ordinary revelry.

Proteus knew, in the general way that he knew most things, that there was a simple art to standing sentry, as to most other military tasks. From somewhere in his demolished past the rules appeared when they were needed. Don't stand in one place, like a statue. Move often, but not predictably—if an enemy is watching, never allow him to be sure of where you will be a few heartbeats from now. Walk your post, whatever it is, with an irregular timing. Turn left this time, turn right the next time round. Of course there was very little room for any of these tactics on their small ledge.

Time passed quietly at first, and it began to seem the only danger might be utter boredom. Proteus and his fellow sentry exchanged a few words. Whatever the people in the cave might be up to, they weren't making much noise. Only a few strange sounds came drifting out from time to time, and the more Proteus tried to listen to them, the stranger they sounded. Some of them might have come from human throats, a kind of quiet chanting, and others from the squeaking strings of untuned musical instruments.

Apart from that, the night was peaceful, and exotic smoky smells came drifting from somewhere well inland. The moon lay sparkling on the sea.

Now Telamon whispered restlessly: "Why are these things always held in caves?"

Proteus shifted his grip on his borrowed spear, whose owner so far did not seem worried about getting it back. Fortunately spare weapons were in good supply on this voyage. " 'These things'? You've been to other parties like this one?"

His shipmate looked around uneasily. "One or two that were close to it. And I've heard stories about strange things happening here on Samothraki."

"I hope you told Jason. What are the strange things?"

The other man only looked wise, as if reluctant to speak.

Proteus asked him: "How long is it all going to take, do you suppose?" The question ended in a cough, for suddenly a cloud of strange smoke had come swirling out of the cave to embrace them in its crude pawlike eddies. If it smelled that strong out here, those inside would have to be careful not to choke themselves.

For Proteus, some odd flavor in the smoke rattled certain keys on the ring of memory. Suddenly, impulsively, he filled his lungs with one deep breath, trying to fit the key into the lock and turn it. The dark fumes made his head swim. He wheezed, and for a moment felt light-headed.

He had sniffed exactly the same pungent and intoxicating smoke before, but *when*, and *where* . . . ?

Proteus had the feeling that someone, somewhere, was urgently try-ing to tell him something.

A disembodied voice was saying to him: "You have managed to get yourself aboard the ship—excellent!"

"Yes, indeed I have," he said aloud.

And Telamon, at the other end of the short walkway, turned to him puzzled: "Are you talking to me?"

"No. No, I . . ."

"Proteus. Proteus!" His name was now sounded in quite a different voice, coming from a different place, some source firmly rooted in cold reality. A man's urgent whisper, repeated two or three times before Proteus focused on it. This voice was absolutely real, not coming out of any vision in his head, but from a place in the real world only a couple of feet behind him, on a rocky ledge outside a cave on the isle of Samothraki.

Telamon must have heard it too, for his young and almost beardless face had gone taut. "What was that? Did you hear—?"

"Good to see you on the job," said the whisper behind Proteus.

Something was also moving, silently, behind his fellow sentry; and in another instant Proteus was treated to the sight of his cheerful young companion being murdered before his eyes, his throat cut from behind with ruthless efficiency.

A single file of armed men, three or four of them at least, all utterly unfamiliar to Proteus, each of them as menacing as Death himself, had approached the sentries' position along an almost unnoticeable natural catwalk that ran just below the ledge of rock. These intruders all had dark paint of some kind smeared over their faces, and on every bit of exposed skin, trying to make themselves invisible in darkness.

The first two of them had climbed up, nimble and silent as a pair of cats, to the level where Proteus was standing, the nearest of them no more than a good spear-thrust distant from him. Meanwhile another, the whisperer, had somehow climbed into position directly behind him.

There passed a long and breathless moment, in which the intruders could easily have cut down Proteus in his half-befuddled state. But they only stood there gawking at him. This time it was the man first in line who spoke to him in a whisper, with fierce urgency.

"Proteus! You stoned, or what? Call Jason out of that hole." A jerk of the head toward the cave mouth. "We bring him greetings, from an admirer." And the fellow grinned, and shook his own spear in his brawny hand, leaving no doubt as to what kind of greeting he wished to give.

"I see," said Proteus. He leaned over the open side of the ledge, and for a timeless moment stared down at young Telamon, whose body had been pitched onto the rocks below, where it lay unmoving in what looked like a terribly uncomfortable position, trickling blood, that flowed dark in the moonlight, into the lapping waves.

Feeling his head clearer now, Proteus turned back. "Greetings to you," he added quietly, and with a flick of his wrist changed his grip on his own spearshaft. A moment later he had thrust the keen point hard and deep into the painted killer's throat.

Filling his lungs at the same instant, Proteus raised a cry. "Argonauts, to me! Assassins! Murder!"

From here it was impossible to see any portion of the *Argo*, but the ship lay at anchor only a few yards away. It was as if her entire crew had been sitting waiting for a signal, so quick was the reaction. Instantly Proteus was answered by friendly war-cries, and he could hear a tramp of feet and rush of bodies.

The men who had come here to kill Jason were offended, outraged, surprised beyond astonishment. "Proteus! Have y'gone mad?" barked out the second one in line.

And now a sudden rush of bodies stirred the atmosphere, drafting a wave of fresh air across the entrance to the cave. More of the anonymous attackers had been waiting in reserve, and here they came.

From the other direction rushed the Argonauts, meeting the painted enemy, head on. Forced to abandon all hope of stealth, the attackers were yelling like evil spirits now, a good way to throw victims into a panic.

But tonight the men they were attacking were hardly in the victim class. Proteus heard another voice, whether of friend or foe he could not tell, shouting out his name.

Two of the enemy were hacking at him, but neither was quite fast or strong enough to do him any harm. The spear in his hands felt as if it belonged there, though it was no perfect weapon, and in his hands it held like a defensive wall. Now he used the short blade like a sword, cutting with the iron edge against a bronze sword thrust at him, then thrusting back one-handed, to get a longer extension of his arm against a dodging foe. And as he fought, he let out rhythmic yells, a rallying cry for help.

The fight went on, in the timeless-seeming way of all fights. Some Argonauts advanced in single file, along the one narrow ledge readily available for passage. Others were managing to go round, scrambling and splashing along the rocky shingle below the ledge and cave, but that way took longer.

Still, thank all the gods, the crew of the *Argo* had the advantage of numbers. With no shortage of nerve and energy, brawny bodies moved with the spring of youth and the skill of veterans, pouring along the ledges and rocks and shingle into the shallow water before the cave. With heavy splashes, bodies of friend and foe were going off the rocks and into the deep water, one, two, three of them.

And at this point, better late than never, Jason and his few comrades in ritual came pouring out of the dark cave mouth with weapons in their hands, stumbling and retching in black smoke. It was easy to suppose that the attackers, suddenly outnumbered, had never expected anything of the kind.

And then abruptly, in the way of most fights, the bloody brawl was over. But in the mind of Proteus the eerie shock of it lingered on.

———

He stumbled, and someone took his arm and asked if he was wounded, and he shook his head. For a moment the world had turned gray before him, as if he might be about to faint, but then it cleared again.

It was not a reaction to the sudden treacherous attack, the blood and death, that set him reeling. Some part of his weakness came from the poisoned smoke and visions; but the true horror, what really made him gasp and stumble, was the fact that the attackers had known him on sight. Their leader had called him by name, and in the easy tones of comradeship. *Good to see you on the job. Call Jason out for us. So we can kill him.*

"Look out!"

And the fight that had seemed to be finished was not over after all. This time some of the enemy came from above, from the rocks over the cave mouth, as well as from below.

Proteus took a hard grip on his spear again, and used it to good effect. Those of the enemy who were not slain were driven howling in retreat.

He ran through one antagonist, saw and heard the man die with a gurgling cry, and clubbed another with the shaft of his handy weapon.

"Who are these bastards, anyway?" a slightly wounded Argonaut was gasping. "Are they Samothracians?"

"Damned onion farmers!" growled another shipmate.

Jason, once he had cleared his eyes and lungs of the befuddling smoke, used his steel sword with considerable skill and a kind of fatalistic calm.

When things got very hot for Proteus on the narrow ledge, swords coming at him from front and rear at the same time, he went off the ledge in a long dive that carried him past the shoreline rocks and into deep water.

Surfacing, he threw away his spear and reached ashore, grabbing two of the enemy, each by an ankle. In another moment he had pulled them off the rocks and into the rough waves.

Neither antagonist proved to be a swimmer, at least not in a league with Proteus. He shifted his handgrip on each man, getting them by their necks, and held them under water. As soon as they went limp, he let them go, and swam quickly to see what he could do for his beleaguered comrades.

To his surprise he discovered Jason in deep water too, grappling with a brawny foe who sought to stab him. Proteus reached the struggling pair in time to see that Jason stayed afloat while his enemy went under.

Now once again it began to seem that the struggle had been won. First Zetes and then Calais, on winged sandals, came overhead dropping rocks and then flying low to strike with sword and spear, striking terror into the enemy's heart. Whatever reserves they might still have had on hand turned away in screaming flight.

And then at last it was really, finally, truly over.

How many of the damned determined bandits there had been was hard to determine, because naturally some had run away. Estimates among the Argonauts ranged from a couple dozen to a hundred. Whatever their numbers, they had not been ready to take on forty well-armed men. Not forty who knew what they were doing when they had their favorite tools in hand.

Jason was looking around at everyone, not finding the face he sought. "Where's Mel?"

"He came running with us," a man told him, "when we left the ship. I saw him go into the water."

Roll call was taken hastily. Meleager had disappeared, and they had to assume he had gone into the water in the fight, and drowned. Jason dove in to look, going deep and coming up for air, bringing up only another dead enemy by mistake. There were currents here, and it was easy to suppose a missing body would never be found.

Meanwhile, men argued in the darkness on the shore. More torches were being brought, but one increment of light after another was added without doing any good. "But who in all the hells were they? Druggies who followed us here from Lemnos?"

"No, no. No men from that island would have wit or strength to get themselves this far, let alone fight like that."

"From King Pelias, then," murmured someone else. And no one spoke up to cast doubt on that suggestion.

Jason urged his men to try to find one of the attackers still alive, so they could hear his answers to some questions. But that was not to be. Many of the mysterious ones had run away, but everyone still within reach of the Argonauts was dead.

Proteus felt inwardly relieved; he wanted to hear the answers to those questions too, but not at the price of having one of the villains call him by name, and reproach him in front of his shipmates for being a traitor to the assassin's gang.

Jason, having given up the hopeless diving in search of Meleager, stood dripping over the first of the face-down corpses, thrust his foot under its shoulder, and turned the dead man over. There was a silence. "Anybody recognize him?"

There were blank stares, and shaking heads. Wiping the dark paint from the dead face did no good.

The captain went on to turn over the second in the same way, with no more helpful result. So it went with the remaining enemy dead.

When he had finished that fruitless task, Jason turned and vowed eternal loyalty to his friend Proteus, whom he credited with saving his life.

He laid a heavy hand on the shoulder of the shorter man. "I owe you my life, and I will not forget it."

"I would have done as much for any shipmate, Captain. Maybe you can do the same for me some day."

Still feeling lingering traces of the smoke, he went instinctively to plunge his head into the sea again. Under water, he groped around halfheartedly in darkness, but of course there was no trace of Mel. He came back to the surface, gulping a deep breath of air. The new attack he had been half-expecting had come, but it had not been directed at him. He supposed that fact ought to make him feel relieved, but it did not.

He was gnawed by the dark certainty that the attackers had only spared him at the start, because they thought that he was one of them.

Jason, and those who had been in the cave with him, had had enough of Samothraki rituals, and there was no thought of resuming any efforts along that line. Tersely the captain ordered his crew to reassemble at the ship. No attempt had been made to harm the *Argo*.

"They were no ordinary pirates," Jason mused. "I expect that what they chiefly wanted was to murder me." He looked at Proteus. "Did you hear them—say anything?"

"Nothing that I could understand, Captain." And that was certainly true enough.

Certain well-dressed Samothrakians, substantial citizens no doubt, came to express their horror, amazement, and regret. It seemed that none of them could recognize any of the dead.

That mattered not to Jason, who had already made up his mind. "I have no doubt that they were sent by my uncle. My arch-enemy. The usurper."

Idmon asked him: "Is it possible that those who invited you to take part in the ritual have some connection with—?"

"With the attack? I do not think so. No." The captain shook his head decisively. "But of course there were others here on the island who knew of the invitation."

But then, Proteus observed to himself, their leader was developing a strong tendency to feel doomed anyway. Now he had better cause for pessimism than before. Yet there was something about him that made his followers want to stand by and protect him, unite their fates with his.

———

Men kept searching for Meleager, alive or dead, until the hour before dawn. At that time Jason called off the search. Several Argonauts swore that they had seen Mel fall into the deep water, and he had never come out, and that was that. The voyage must go on, and the only reasonable assumption was that Jason's old comrade had died of wounds or drowned.

All the crew were able to agree on at least one thing, as they started to pull out of the harbor: They were eager to see the last of Samothraki.

Some of the men seemed chastened after the brawl, even though they had not been hurt. But others were in high spirits. "Nothing like a good fight, with blood spilled, to weld a crew together"—that was Haraldur's idea. And in an excess of good feeling he pounded one of his shipmates on the shoulder, fortunately choosing the man's unwounded side.

Some of the men began to sing, in raucous voices, an ancient-sounding chanty that Proteus naturally could not remember ever having heard before.

"So far, we have lost men, and blood, at every stop since leaving home," Jason groaned, sounding near despair. "How far can we go on like this?"

Proteus wanted to grab the leader, shake him, remind him to put a better face on things. But no one else seemed disposed to try to rally their commander, and they knew him better than Proteus did.

———

When it came Proteus's turn to catch some sleep, he curled up on the curving planks at the foot of his rower's bench. He had slept in this position before, but right now, despite having been awake all night, he could not have slept in a feather bed. He was haunted by the friendly words of the first man he had killed, just outside the cave, and the look of confident familiarity in his victim's face.

Good to see you on the job. Call Jason out of that hole. We bring him greetings.

He couldn't tell Jason that the sneaking murderers of Telamon and Meleager had expected him, Proteus, to help them butcher Jason too.

Proteus knew in his bones that he had not come aboard the *Argo* to do her captain any harm. The only purpose he now seemed to have in life was to help this captain and this crew complete their mission. Other men might have a vision of more glorious goals, but not the reborn Proteus. This ship had become his only home on earth, and Jason and the Argonauts his only friends.

With a faint shock he realized that one way or another, the voyage must someday be over. He wondered what he could possibly do then, and could come up with no ideas. But there was no point in worrying about that now. His chances of surviving that long were probably not great.

Seeing the glum look on his captain's face, he took it upon himself to make an effort to cheer Jason up.

5

Boxing

PROTEUS, SCANNING THE faces of the crew, decided that any of them whose secret goal had been gold and riches must be beginning to be disappointed. Of course those who had really joined the Argosy purely in search of adventure ought to be well satisfied.

"We have only been at this for a month and a half, but one cannot say that the voyage has been lacking in adventure." That was Haraldur's assessment of their situation now.

Idmon was shaking his head. "Adventure is always a story. It means something happening to someone else, hundreds of miles or years away from the people who enjoy it. Our story is too real to us to be adventure; but others will call it that."

"Call it excitement, then," said Proteus, and no one could dispute that. It would have been hard to make a reasonable argument that things had been too dull. In a sense the great gods were smiling on them, because good weather held, and the breeze was favorable, as it had been through most of their days at sea. But there were dead and wounded now, and the bloody proof that powerful enemies were determined that the Argosy should fail.

Jason had no comment to make about adventure. He was still beset with the gloomy feeling that a doom hung over him and his enterprise. He was making another day's entry on the parchment pages of the logbook, inside their rugged sharkskin cover.

The *Argo* pushed on, fast enough to put up a small white wave at her bow, with the great majority of her crew still alive and well.

One more Hero, a man of comparatively little fame, died aboard of wounds suffered at Samothraki. He was buried at sea, along with Telamon, whose mangled body had been conveyed on board. Various volunteers agreed that they would try to notify the dead men's next of kin when they got home.

It turned out that no one knew what their late shipmates' preferences might have been in funeral rites, and a majority thought it did not matter.

It was Idmon who said: "When you go down to the Underworld, you go down, that's all. Doesn't matter what happens to the clay you leave behind."

Others disputed that, though not with any real vehemence. Everyone on board had heard at least one ghost story—except, possibly, Proteus, who could not remember any—about a spirit rendered unhappy by some improper treatment of its no longer habitable corpse. It seemed that at least half the crew believed such things were possible.

When someone asked Proteus where he stood on the question, he replied that he only envied men who could be so sure of anything.

Several among the Argonauts who considered themselves most skilled in medicine took turns at looking out for the wounded, who were relieved of rowing duties for several days, and lay on the deck or sat and called encouragement to the rowers, or made light of each other's wounds. Each made it a matter of pride to resume his labors, at least part time, as soon as possible.

Casualties had made the crew a bit short-handed on the oars, but the weather continued favorably, there was no urgent need for speed, and they pushed on.

———

Proteus was still haunted by the memory of the assassin who had approached him with such cheerful confidence. The son of a carrion-eater had actually greeted him as a bosom comrade. *Good to see you on the job.*

He kept trying hard to find some alternate explanation, but kept coming back to only one. Old Proteus—that is, himself, back before he'd lost his memory—must have been involved up to his eyebrows in a plot to assassinate Jason. Might the plot have been led by the mysterious woman he could half remember? Maybe. But his memory could produce no indication that she had ever wanted anything of the kind.

So far none of the Argonauts had questioned Proteus regarding those bewildering first moments of the attack—exactly how Telamon had been taken by surprise, and how he, Proteus, had managed to survive. But his shipmates might grow curious, and one might bring the subject up at any time, either innocently or with suspicion. It would be a good idea to get some answers ready against that possibility.

. . . and still he kept coming back, in his mind, to that scene in front of the cave. The leader of the assassins had actually *expected* to find Old Proteus there, planted among the Argonauts so he could betray them. The carrion-eaters hadn't doubted for a moment that he was going to call Jason out to be killed. Surprise had come into their leader's face only at the last moment, when Proteus's spear point was already sunk a handsbreadth in his throat . . .

. . . and still he kept coming back to it, he couldn't leave it alone. Old Proteus must have been a secret agent, working for some deadly enemy of Jason.

The discovery raised several practical questions. To begin with, why—on staggering out of the sea and into his new life, with almost everything about the old forgotten—why had he felt from the very start an urge to *help* Jason and promote the Argosy's success? Why had he not stayed loyal to the assassins, instead of cutting them down without a moment's hesitation?

Proteus looked down at his own hands, tanned and strong and callused. What kind of man did they belong to? That still seemed to be a mystery, but he thought the evidence so far did not leave much room for optimism.

Dark thoughts were interrupted by Tiphys, who had been in his usual position kneeling before the binnacle, resting his forehead on his compass-pyx. Suddenly the navigator jumped to his feet and announced that he was ready to steer a course for Colchis.

"We are on our way to the land where the Golden Fleece lies ready for our taking," the sturdy man said in his precise voice.

Proteus thought that might be a slightly optimistic way to put it. At best there were still several intermediate stops to be made, and the next of these was Bebrycos.

Someone observed: "We probably ought to have dropped off our wounded before we got to Bebrycos."

This brought on a heated discussion, resulting in a general consensus that King Amycus of Bebrycos, who claimed to be a son of Poseidon, might have a reputation as the world's worst bully, but he could hardly enhance his reputation by stooping to pick on wounded men. "It's not the hurt ones who have anything to worry about. Amycus likes to pick out some big, strong lad, and beat him into a jelly."

"Son of Poseidon?" The speaker blasphemed several gods. "Son of a mad bitch is more like it."

"That may be. But he's a real man."

Haraldur the northman observed: "I'll go along with what the proverb says: There are no good kings, but there are certainly bad ones."

That comment brought a general murmur of agreement; Proteus noticed that Jason did not join in. If he was giving any thought to their next stop, beyond the plan of provisioning there, he did not show it.

Several of the Argonauts had visited Bebrycos in recent years. It was a pleasant enough place, according to their stories, or would have been, except for its monarch. It now had the reputation of being a good place for travelers to avoid, but at this point in the Argosy no one aboard—except possibly Jason himself—had any idea of avoiding an adventure.

Besides, some bad weather was finally blowing up, and the look of the sky combined with the chronic need for fresh water removed any doubts as to what the wisest course would be. Jason ordered the Argonauts to put in at the chief port of Bebrycos.

It was hard to credit the idea that the bully-king really insisted on boxing with every visitor—that would scarcely be practical, however great his appetite for combat. Some of the rowers could still not quite get it straight.

"You mean he challenges every ship? *Every* ship?"

"Well no, he doesn't fight every man aboard. But each crew must choose a champion."

"To go against the king's?"

"To go against the king himself."

"Amycus must be a tough one, doing his own fighting. To what does he challenge them, exactly?"

"Boxing."

"Hah, that's not so much."

"With gloves of hardened leather. They say Amycus has never lost a match, and more of his opponents have been killed than have been only stunned. Broken jaws and noses are routine. Many have had their teeth knocked out, and more than one has lost an eye."

"Huh. And what about him, in all these years of pummeling? Doesn't he get beat up? Has he never lost a bout?"

"Not that I've heard of."

———————

The island of Bebrycos was of moderate size, and its geography was unremarkable. Several merchant ships were currently in the harbor, taking on cargo in a routine fashion. The port was unremarkable, and there seemed no particular shortage of trading vessels. No doubt the king had learned to be selective in his challenges, not wanting to drive away useful shipping. Gradually a small crowd began to assemble at a distance of a few yards, first idlers, then more substantial-looking folk. They had the air of people assembling to watch a sporting event, leaving space for an arena.

"There are a fair number of ships," someone was saying two benches behind Proteus.

And the answer from still farther back: "Oh, I suppose he may let some get by, when he's feeling tired, or just on a whim. But if he knows that Jason is here, with a ship full of young men looking for adventure—" "It's not likely that we'll be given a free pass. No."

"Well." The speaker looked around at his shipmates, who were a tough and hardy-looking crew indeed. "I'd say it's not likely that we'd want one."

And indeed, they had not long to wait before word came from the king. They had been tied up at a dock for less than half an hour, and had not quite finished taking on fresh water. Boredom must have been rife at the palace; or maybe the news of Jason's Argosy had somehow got here ahead of him.

One of the minor officials of the court, a curly-bearded man who hardly troubled to hide his wicked amusement at what he considered to be their plight of having to sacrifice one of their number, let them know that the king was upset at not having been invited to take part in the Argosy. The suggestion was that long months ago Amycus had gone so far as to hint, through intermediaries, that he wanted to be asked. But Jason had chosen to ignore the suggestion, if in fact it had ever reached him.

Not that Amycus would condescend to join their expedition now, of course, the court official hastened to assure them. Not even if they begged him.

Only silence answered that remark. Moments later, Proteus heard Jason muttering that this monarch would serve as a model to him, of how not to behave when he came into his own kingdom.

"Here they come," someone said, and Proteus turned to look.

Amycus was having himself carried down to the docks in a litter, on the shoulders of eight brawny, gold-collared slaves; the king when he climbed out of the litter and stood beside it on his own two feet looked bigger than any of the bearers. He was a startlingly huge brute, looking every inch the champion boxer, a match for his reputation. Proteus thought that half of his opponents would probably be paralyzed with fright before a blow was struck.

Besides the slaves who bore the king's palanquin on their shoulders, he was accompanied by a numerous mean-looking escort, large well-dressed men the majority of whom were certainly not slaves. This crew settled in along dockside, where the construction went up in great stair-like steps of stone, as if they were looking forward to a show. Settled in, they began to pass around flagons of wine among themselves.

So far, no one had offered anything at all to the visitors.

"The hospitality here is not exactly lavish," one Argonaut commented.

Jason said in a taut voice: "Let's see if we can get some drinking water somewhere. But none of us should stray far from the ship. I suspect we may be leaving in a hurry."

"Best keep our weapons handy," Idmon advised. But no one needed to hear that.

Jason had hardly time to respectfully greet Amycus before the monarch threw down a black mantle with gold clasps he had been wearing, and a thick, crooked staff carved from mountain olive wood. Now the king stood forth in only a loincloth, obviously proud of his appearance and daring anyone to match it.

A few of the visitors might have done so, but none of them moved; this was not going to be a posing contest. Proteus, along with most of his shipmates, stood back with folded arms, watching with keen interest. The king looked to be in his middle thirties, in the prime of health and strength. His nose had been seriously flattened some time ago, testifying to the fact that at least one opponent had landed him a good blow. But the deformity only made him look all the more formidable.

In another moment, King Amycus repeated his challenge, in a loud and arrogant voice that suited his appearance.

"I feel like a little workout with the gloves today. If anyone among this crowd of weaklings thinks he can fight, let him step forward now! It will be better for the rest of you if one is willing to sacrifice himself." His substantial following of attendants and hangers-on made sure to applaud this speech swiftly and loudly.

If the king had hoped to overawe his visitors, or at least throw them into uncertainty and doubt, he had come to the wrong crew. Most of them only looked at him. Only one man responded to his challenge, and that very quickly, suggesting some kind of prearrangement.

The king looked somewhat puzzled at the figure who stepped forward. It was a man called Polydeuces, with whom Proteus had not yet exchanged more than a couple of words. Though Polydeuces was reasonably tall, he was far from the biggest in the company of Argonauts. Actually he was a slender youth, though strong and long-armed.

His eyelashes were long, his young face almost beardless, and gentle in appearance—or would have been gentle, were it not for the slight deformation caused by scar tissue on forehead and cheekbones. His eyes held sparks of youthful enthusiasm.

Though not minded to undergo a boxing trial himself, Proteus felt little personal fear of Amycus—nor indeed of any man, when he stopped to think about it. In the back of his mind there nestled a comfortable certainty that he himself had already survived at least one encounter with some mysterious opponent who must have been even more formidable. But he was somewhat surprised that none of the other Heroes stepped forward and tried to argue that they were better fitted for the contest than this slim youth. He had to conjecture that many of his shipmates knew something about Polydeuces that was not apparent to the latest man to join the crew.

Now one of the king's close associates, a court official of some kind who seemed to be acting as his second, walked out between the combatants and dropped a pair of rawhide gloves at each man's feet.

Amycus spoke up again, using the same tone of arrogance: "It may be the custom to cast lots for the gloves, but we're not going to do that."

Polydeuces nodded agreeably. He was being calmly polite as he took off his fine cloak (he had told his shipmates it was a present from his girl) and laid it carefully aside. "What does Your Majesty have in mind?"

"A decision that should make you happy—if your guts are not too upset just now to preclude any feeling of that kind. I don't want it said later that I played any tricks, so, therefore, I hereby make you a present of whichever pair of gloves you like."

Polydeuces murmured a quiet thanks. Without seeming to care one way or the other about the decision, he casually bent and picked up the pair that had been tossed in front of him.

Meanwhile the king's second, or steward, had been busy outlining the space on the dock in which the bout was supposed to take place. This was done quickly and efficiently, as if it had often been done before. Then the same official went through a swift recital of rules, in a high-pitched, sing-song voice, which Proteus had trouble understanding. Nobody seemed to be paying the slightest attention to the recital anyway.

When the formalities had been got out of the way, the two contestants lifted their large fists and went straight at each other.

The crowd roared, following the example set by their monarch's close associates, as if their champion had already disposed of his opponent.

Haraldur shrieked out something that sounded like: "Berserker!"

Some kind of strange northern battle cry, thought Proteus, shooting him a glance.

Subtle strategy played no part in the king's plan of battle. Steadily he advanced, firing one punch after another, giving Polydeuces no chance to pause. But that seemed fine with the younger man, who had the necessary skill to avoid these bull-charging tactics.

At one point the king, missing badly with a roundhouse swing, overbalanced and slipped to one knee. But Amycus was up again a moment later, red-faced and furious.

The crowd of onlookers was now growing rapidly, and on impulse Proteus scanned the faces nearest him. He was startled to encounter a pair of eyes looking back at him with what seemed to be recognition. They belonged to a youngish woman wrapped in a scarlet robe, a style of dress that in many places indicated the wearer was a prostitute.

"Got yourself a good thing going there, hey Proteus?" The woman, moving close beside him now, nudged him in the ribs. The gathering of people was now so dense that he thought the gesture might have gone unnoticed by anyone else.

The woman's face, not unattractive, was as unfamiliar to him as were all the other faces in the world, excepting only those of Jason and his crew. This one was leering and almost winking at him with an expression that claimed intimacy.

And she knew his name.

Her voice was so low that he felt sure no one else could hear it through the cheering. "Oh, you don't have to let on you know me. Glad to see you've come up in the world. I know you're the kind to remember your old friends." And she raised one hand a little, rubbing thumb and forefinger together in a gesture of universal significance.

At the moment Proteus had not a small coin to his name, and said so, a little roughly.

His rough words and a hard stare changed the woman's attitude completely. What came into her face was not greed or annoyance, but the look of deep and serious fear. She murmured something that sounded apologetic, in a whisper so low that Proteus could not really hear it, and backed away.

The roar of the crowd swelled up at just that moment, and he turned his head long enough to make sure both fighters were still on their feet. When he looked for the woman again he could not find her. Briefly he was tempted to go diving into the crowd in search of her, but this was not the moment to separate himself from his shipmates.

The circling figures in the ring had completed a preliminary period of sparring, feeling each other out, and now some hard blows were being exchanged. Actually Polydeuces, when you looked at the two men closely, seemed to have the slightly longer arms.

The young Argonaut kept circling, almost dancing, with the air of one who had played this game before; he was plainly faster on his feet than was the king, who simply kept plodding forward, going always toward his opponent.

There was now good evidence of something that Proteus had never doubted—the effect of hardened rawhide gloves was not to cushion blows, but only to armor the fists that struck. Soon both men were bleeding from the face, and from their arms, where the hardened rawhide tore loose patches of skin every time an arm caught a punch intended for head or body.

The Argonaut declined to stand toe-to-toe with Amycus, but kept stepping back and counterpunching.

"Stand still and fight, damn you!" Amycus roared, sounding a trifle short of breath.

"In good time, Majesty." Polydeuces spoke clearly; he still seemed to have plenty of wind left. His arms were bruised, covered with swellings and leaking red, but the muscles still had a good spring in them. His eyes were bright, and now he was the one who seemed to be enjoying the contest.

Polydeuces nodded to himself; it was as if he had so far mainly been taking the measure of his opponent, and now thought it time to get down to serious business.

Growing truly winded now, and obviously less confident than he had been at the beginning, the king lunged close to the Argonaut, and assayed a mighty swing that Polydeuces deftly turned aside, with just a touch of rawhide knuckles on the king's thick forearm at the precisely proper moment.

Now Proteus thought that the king, beginning to be winded, must have passed some secret signal to his official, probably in the form of smoothing his hair with one gloved hand. Because for no apparent reason the official immediately tapped a gong, signaling for a break between rounds.

Several Argonauts loudly raised objections about this procedure, but it did them no good. The steward explained coldly and clearly that no, the fight was *not* over. Having a pause every so often was simply the way they did things here.

A shipmate standing beside Proteus asked him: "I wonder what other new rule will be discovered?"

No one ever learned the answer to that question.

Evidently Polydeuces decided not to wait and see. Almost in the instant when fighting was resumed, the Argonaut struck overhand, a kind of punch he had not thrown before, catching Amycus on the right eyebrow and tearing loose a flap of skin that pulled the eyelid down and away with it, so that the right eye of the stunned king stared out, more wide-eyed than it had ever been before, through a gush of blood at his onrushing doom.

In the next moment Polydeuces threw a left hook, getting all his wiry weight behind the rigid curve of arm. It landed squarely just above the king's right ear. Proteus winced at the sound of impact, and thought he could pick out, in certain fine components of that noise, the crunch of breaking bones within the skull.

The sweeping right-hand punch that followed might have fractured a sturdy jawbone, but it missed its target, because the king was already falling, had already landed on his knees, eyes staring into eternity. A moment later, Amycus toppled forward on his face, never feeling what happened to his nose when it hit the dock. His fall had an utter finality to it, like that of a man with an arrow in his heart, or a slung stone embedded in his forehead.

There followed a long, breathless pause, before the winner stepped back, and several supporters of the king rushed to his side to learn if he still breathed.

Meanwhile, Jason had already stepped in front of his men and was issuing quick commands with silent gestures. The Argonauts closed ranks and kept their weapons ready.

"The king is dead!" The words were first spoken in hushed tones, then taken up by other voices, shouted across the docks and to the rooftops. There was strong emotion in the yells, but Proteus found it hard to tell as yet just what the emotion was.

Moments later, some of Amycus's shocked supporters had drawn swords and were doing their best to kill the Argonauts. Fortunately, the crew were at hair-trigger readiness to defend themselves.

Before anyone had had time to draw a good long breath, a major fight had broken out. The royal bodyguard, well-equipped with spears and hardened clubs, grabbed up their weapons and came charging at Polydeuces. But the fistfighter's shipmates were ready to defend him with their own spears, swords, and axes. In the first moments of armed combat, some of the high officials who had been closest to Amycus went down.

In retrospect the boxing match took on the aspect of a game, compared to what strong men could do to each other with edged weapons. For a long minute, there was bloody slaughter on the dock. None of those who took part were strangers to the art, and none of them turned and ran. Proteus, wishing for a shield, stood a little back from his comrades in their rank, hoping to be able to use the greater length of his weapon to the best advantage.

It was the royal party who broke off the conflict after the first clash. No doubt they were realizing that their king's death meant they were faced with other matters more important than seeking revenge for one whom they had never loved.

Jason backed away muttering: "Is there some curse on our voyage, that we must fight and die wherever we come to shore?"

Fortunately for Jason and his men, it was soon plain that most of the populace were more interested in hurrying home with the day's news, or in settling some old scores among themselves, than in punishing the visitors. And those leaders who had come to watch the fight, and who might have led a charge against the foreigners, were suddenly more occupied with seeing to their own futures now that everything had changed.

As they were accomplishing a slow retreat to the ship, weapons still ready, Proteus barked at Polydeuces: "Did you have to kill him? Wouldn't a simple knockout have done as well?"

The long-armed youth only grinned back, somewhat vacantly, as if the blows his own head had taken had left him a bit stunned.

Jason, for once seeming to exert some active leadership, gripped his own short sword and barked orders.

Once they were all aboard their ship, Jason had them row out a little way into the calm water of the harbor, where they prepared to defend against further attacks.

Jason was murmuring something, and Proteus looked around. "I couldn't hear you, Captain."

"I said, it is not good for any king to die in such a way."

The minutes dragged on and then an hour, and it was as if they had been forgotten. There were no more attacks aimed at the visitors, though they could see and hear that wild fighting had broken out in the streets of the city.

Idmon was talking in low tones, saying that certain factions must have been waiting in hopes of a chance like this. Two merchant ships had cast loose from their moorings, and were dipping oars at a good rate, and hoisting sail as well, but obviously their only intention was to make a prudent withdrawal, not to bother the *Argo*. Proteus could see two places, well inland, where buildings were burning. The columns of smoke gradually disappeared as darkness fell, but the glow of flames only became more lurid.

Zetes and Calais volunteered to fly ashore and reconnoiter, but Jason in his commander's voice told both of them to remain on the ship. The sight of flying men might bring on an attack, or at least draw the islanders' attention to the Argonauts again. "I think we can see all we need to see from here."

———

Toward morning, the situation quieted, as the various combatants on shore were becoming exhausted; there arose from somewhere inland sounds of cheering that could be interpreted to mean that one new leader had emerged victorious.

"What in the Underworld are they celebrating now?" someone wanted to know.

"Most likely that a new king has been chosen. Or one of the contenders has announced that all the people want him, which comes to the same thing."

"A likely interpretation." Idmon nodded. "Of course there may still be other contenders, as you call them, with different ideas. Whoever comes out on top will almost certainly want to consolidate his position in the palace and the capital before undertaking his next move."

"With any luck we will be gone by then. As soon as we have the tide, and the breeze—that now seems to be coming up. Hoist the anchor stone!"

———

The Argonauts pulled out of the harbor while the night was at its darkest, and at first light ran up their sail, catching a lucky wind that drove them on, in the direction the steersman had determined they should go.

Tiphys, who like most of his shipmates had come through the fight unscathed, now seemed a little more at ease than he had been. "Won't be any need to navigate for a couple of days, lads. There'll be plenty of land in sight. But the wind's not with us this time. Now you've had a little exercise, you'll be all loosened up for rowing."

A universal groan went up.

6

Harpies

THE KEEPER OF the logbook dipped his quill pen into the inkhorn, and recorded on tough parchment the fact that almost two months had passed since the voyagers departed from Iolcus.

Singing at their oars, inventing some ingenious new verses of an old song at the expense of the late, murderous Amycus, the crew of the *Argo* drove their sleek vessel on up the swift and swirling watery channel that the steersman and the Colchian brothers called the Bogazi.

And Idmon on that day copied into the log some of the impromptu verses, not bothering to cipher them into an antique translation.

Even Jason was more cheerful now than when they had left Samothraki. He told his crew that the name "Bogazi" meant "Ox Ford" in some ancient language. What an "ox" might be he did not know, but one of the more scholarly adventurers spoke up to say he thought it meant an animal, some type of mutated cameloid.

"Be ready for a long row and a hard one, lads," their navigator cautioned, leaning on the steering oar. The channel was almost twenty miles long, and varied in width from half a mile to more than two. At the start the scenery on both sides was of well-wooded shores, dotted with villages and what appeared to be the villas of the wealthy. But as they progressed slowly upstream, both banks became wilder, less populated.

Of the entire crew, only the two grandsons of Aeetes had ever traveled this route before, and their passage had been years ago, going in the other direction. Therefore their memories of the way were hazy. Few other members of the crew had ever seen any waterway similar to this one. Proteus, along with the great majority of his shipmates, could only shake his head in wonder. His damaged memory still offered him no clues as to whether he had ever beheld the like. But the steersman soon offered a simple explanation of the strange watercourse: this was in effect a great, salt-water river, a channel connecting two salt-water seas. Farther up the strait, he said, the land on both sides would be completely wild and uninhabited.

And Tiphys went on to explain, to the untraveled and geographically unsophisticated in the crew, that there were times when the Bogazi reversed its flow, certain seasons when it reacted strongly to the pull of the tides, as fresh-water tidal rivers were wont to do.

But now, approaching the peak of summer, the northern sea was receiving a great influx of fresh water from several large rivers, so the flow in the strait was consistently one way—the wrong way, from the Argonauts' point of view.

The vessel's painted prow encountered relatively few waves, but most of the time it was necessary to struggle against an increasingly swift and steadily rising current of cold water. Only when sail and oars could be made to work together was it possible to make satisfactory progress.

Two full days of hard labor at the oars, and the skill of Tiphys as steersman, were needed to win an upstream passage through the twenty miles or so of the strait.

Was it only his imagination, Proteus wondered, or did the *Argo* really make notably better speed when he was rowing, which was most of the time, than on the fairly rare occasions when it was his turn to rest?

Sitting at his oar, a position in which most of his waking hours were spent these days, he closed his eyes. Pull. Pull. Steadily, not too hard. Around him Heroes groaned and gasped, testing the limits of their endurance and the strength of their quivering arms, while what he chiefly felt was boredom. There, two benches away, was Polydeuces growing weary, who had outlasted Amycus.

Again it made Proteus uncomfortable to realize that he could have been pulling harder and faster than he was, without putting himself in any danger of exhaustion. In fact he thought he might even be capable of breaking the pine blade. As a practical matter there was of course nothing to be gained by his exerting an all-out effort; that would only have upset the rhythm of the bank, slewed the ship away from the exact course the steersman was trying to hold, as Tiphys sought to find a slower downstream current or an eddy.

A man would have to be crazy not to prefer strength in his own body over weakness. But the oddity still bothered him, because he could find no explanation for it. He couldn't remember being considered especially powerful, or notably capable with either oar or spear. Of course he could not remember ever being called a weakling, either. When he tried to compare the muscularity of his own body with those visible around him, he had to rate his frame as no better than average for this crew of adventurers.

It would be truly wonderful, Proteus thought, if he could remember being simply ordinary—but that comfort also was denied him. The woman standing on the Bebrycan dock had known him—probably had known nothing good about him, for one glance of annoyance from his eyes had been enough to send her in white-faced retreat.

The gaping void of ignorance about himself, the unavailability of information that had to exist somewhere, was like an infected wound, hurting more the longer he had to live with it. When the horror threatened to become too much for him, as it did now, he fought it in the only way he could, by turning his attention to other matters.

━━━━━━

Every now and then, at intervals during the day, the steersman put in to shore. Anchored by stones or tied to trees, *Argo* clung to the bank for a short time, giving the rowers a chance to rest. Those who wanted to switch places at the oars could do so; sometimes it eased the strain to shift from port to starboard, or from an inside bank to one of the shorter oars on an outer bench. As soon as the men had caught their breath they plunged back into the relentless struggle.

There were times when Proteus, rowing, fell into almost a hypnotic state. The briny water in its mad rush to the lower sea seemed like a living thing. From somewhere in the back of his mind came a suggestion that he speak to the flow as if it were a living being: *Why do you fight against us, Water? What god has you under his control, to force us so viciously downstream—and why? Or can this be simply nature?*

Just when it seemed they were about to be swept helplessly back where they had come from, a strangely powerful eddy current, coming into being as it were from nowhere, caught the *Argo* and whisked her lightly upstream, so close to the right bank that the raised mast brushed branches on the shore, and came away plastered with the leaves of an overhanging oak. Tiphys cried out in amazement, at the goal achieved so suddenly, when all his skill and the steady effort of the men for an hour had availed them almost nothing.

Panting, the rowers rested once more at their oars, this time for once losing no ground as they did. Some of the men were wondering aloud what god had been so kind as to help them. Proteus rested with them, and was silent. But in his heart he had begun to be afraid of what he did not know.

The next day they were out of the swift current of the strait, and into a much broader sea; and the day after that, they found the stretch of coastline and the harbor that they wanted, and brought their ship to rest. In fact they were still almost within sight of the coastline of Bithnyia, but it seemed to the weary men that they had rowed a thousand miles since leaving it behind.

During the last night before making port the men unwrapped such bundles of extra clothing as were still unopened, and huddled together for warmth. Though it lay at no great distance from Bebrycos, this was a harder, colder land, on the surface less hospitable than that ruled by the late Amycus. But here the welcome from the people was the very opposite of that. As if glad to see any visitors, they brought out food and flowers to the ship when it was tied up.

The next time Proteus slept, for once dry and snug ashore, his slumbers were uneasy, and he woke in terror from dreams of a murderous Giant.

They had now reached Salmydessus, the land ruled by blind King Phineas, who, as Idmon informed his shipmates, was tormented by Harpies—or at least that was what the stories said. No member of the crew had ever set foot on these shores before. And only a minority had ever seen a Harpy.

Following their experience in Bebrycos, the adventurers were nervous on first landing, but soon began to relax. The strangers of this land gave strangers a hospitable welcome.

The great wonder of this country was the peculiar curse that had afflicted its monarch for more than twenty years. According to a number of reliable reports, King Phineas hardly dared show his face outside the stone walls of his palace, for every time he did, a flight of ghastly Harpies appeared in the nearby sky and attacked him. For some reason that the newcomers had trouble understanding, it seemed impossible to fight them off, and the king's soldiers had even given up trying. The foul, unnatural creatures also devoured any food in sight, eating some of it, and scattering and befouling what they could not swallow or carry off.

Some of the Argonauts did not know what Harpies were, and the monstrous creatures had to be explained to them. Proteus could remember what they were supposed to be, though he doubted that his knowledge was based on any personal experience.

There were whispered rumors among some of the commoners that it was in fact the blind king's Scythian wife who caused him trouble. The queen's true feelings in the matter remained mysterious to the Argonauts, for she never appeared during the course of their visit, and her absence was never explained. Meanwhile, it was oddly true that none of the king's own soldiers or advisers had been able to help him overcome his strange curse.

Proteus had hardly been an hour in this land before he heard from a native one explanation of its royal curse that he found especially intriguing: that the king of Salmydessus had incurred divine wrath, more than twenty years in the past, by offering help to the refugee Phrixus, he who had come this way mounted on the famous and mysterious Flying Ram.

Both grandsons of King Aeetes were keenly interested in learning the truth of this story. If it proved accurate, they were determined to meet the man who had once helped their father in his time of need.

Argeus seemed the more scholarly of the two Colchian brothers, the more interested in finding things out just for the sake of knowing them. He thought the rumor very interesting, but doubted that it was true. "I don't know why the gods should have been angry at our father."

No one could offer him any enlightenment on that point; but of course gods were never obliged to explain anything they did to humans. Jason announced that one reason he wanted to stop here was a hope of hearing more details about the ancient flight of the Golden Ram, from Iolcus to Colchis.

Phineas proved to be quite the opposite of Amycus, glad to entertain interesting visitors, and quite willing to discuss the matter of Phrixus, especially with folk who brought him interesting stories in return. And he told the Argonauts matter-of-factly that he had seen the Ram, on that day more than twenty years in the past.

"What was it like?" asked Tiphys. "This Flying Ram, I mean?" In answer, the king only spread his hands, and shook his blind head slightly, as if to say that some things were beyond description.

"Yes," said Proteus slowly. "It would be good to glean any further word that we can about the Golden Fleece." Others nodded and murmured their agreement.

"Long years ago, when my eyes were young and keen—" he began his tale to the Argonauts.

Alas, the king's knowledge of the events proved very limited, and second-hand at that. He spoke of how a creature he described as a giant, flying ram had been stolen in Iolcus by a fugitive named Phrixus. Flying away on the strange beast had enabled Phrixus to escape from some unspecified trouble, but when the flight reached Colchis, it had come to a violent end.

Blind Phineas seemed glad to tell what little he could of the story again. Proteus, watching the people of the royal household, got the impression that they had grown so weary of the subject that they closed their ears to anything that the kind old man might have to say about it.

The hearing of King Phineas proved very keen, or at least, through long practice, it was finely attuned to certain peculiar noises. He suddenly broke off his tale of the old days, before any of the Argonauts' young ears had picked up the sound of what was coming.

The old king, showing an unsuspected agility, almost jumped to his feet. He raised one hand before him, its fingers spread and twitching; and the sentence he had begun to utter broke off in a wordless cry.

A moment later, Proteus could hear it, the leathery flap of distant wings, followed presently by the scream of high-pitched voices, taunting in an ancient language that he could only halfway understand.

The king was still standing in front of his chair, his whole body trembling. Now he pointed, quite accurately despite the quaking of his arm. "There! There! I hear them, and you can see! The curse is come upon me yet again!"

Following the direction of the old man's gesture, Proteus caught sight of what at first seemed to be a flight of odd-looking, thick-bodied birds, visible in the clear afternoon light. They were bearing in from the dim, gray north . . . from the direction of a line of ragged cliffs that he supposed might offer a good variety of nesting places.

Around him the Argonauts were murmuring in alarm, and snatching up their weapons, while the king's own guards, who ought to have defended him, were only tugging on his garments, intent on getting him safely indoors, and then seeking shelter for themselves.

"Will you not fight for your own king?" one Argonaut demanded of them.

The soldier looked startled, as if the idea had not occurred to him.

"Fight against the Harpies? We dare not. It is the will of the gods that our king is punished so."

Jason was outraged. "The will of the gods? To humiliate an honorable king in such a way? That cannot be!" Jason could not seem to bear the thought that any monarch should be subject to such abuse and humiliation, especially such a worthy monarch as Phineas.

Proteus was shading his eyes to study the approaching threat. The creatures now appearing in the sky were not much like birds at all, beyond the fact of having wings, and some of them with beaks. What he saw now were little more than large, inhuman heads with great pinions attached, and wiry legs ending in birdlike feet with savage claws. Of course the true scale of size was difficult to determine, but surely such shapes lay outside the ordinary forms of nature. Odylic magic had to be involved.

The creatures were closing in on the king's palace with remarkable speed. As soon as their captain sounded the alarm, the brothers Zetes and Calais went sprinting back to the ship to equip themselves with their borrowed sandals, while Jason stood shouting after them to hurry. The refitting took longer than some of their shipmates thought it should have. Earlier, someone had told Proteus that the magical footgear in the brothers' possession was really about the only reason Zetes and Calais had been accepted into the company of Heroes. But eventually Calais and Zetes were back, moving much faster than they had run away, flying now and brandishing swords.

Meanwhile the other Argonauts unanimously refused to be driven indoors, but stood their ground with spear and axe, sword and bow and sling.

When the foul Harpies swooped near the earth, they proved so hideous at close range that men found it was a joy to fight them.

Seemingly stunned by meeting such ferocious resistance on the ground, the enemy emitted astonished cries, were wounded by arrows and slung stones, and were soon in full retreat.

But their detractors had to admit that at the moment Zetes and Calais were acquitting themselves well, fighting back to back in a midair skirmish with half a dozen of the winged heads, all of the Harpies streaming long, tangled hair.

Flying near, the attackers opened beaked mouths that shrieked and honked with laughter, then swerved away as the fighting men once more responded fiercely. Some of the heads and faces were more birdlike than human in design, and others strongly resembled bats. It was hard to be sure of size at first, but when they came near, Proteus realized that they were built on a scale somewhat smaller than humanity.

———

By this time any lingering doubt about the Harpies' vulnerability had been dispelled. They were not ghosts, or visions, but as solid as so many crows or vultures, and with no sweeter voices. They could be hurt by sharp blades, carved up like so many crows if they persisted in attacking. The first wave of the monsters had drawn back, but the attack was not over. There were dozens of the Harpies now visible, and more were still approaching, as if attracted by the noisy uproar in the sky. The flying bodies too far away to be picked out individually made a small black cloud.

Jason took a hasty glance around and assured himself that so far none of his men had fallen, though the ground was littered with crumpled winged shapes. "Where are they all coming from?" Jason demanded.

Pointing into the distance, one of the natives shouted: "The creatures nest there in the high cliffs, where their caves are out of reach of climbing men."

"If this were my land," Jason vowed, "they would not roost there unmolested."

Among the attacking creatures Proteus saw one or two whose scalps were each thickly overgrown with a crop of hissing, writhing snakes. Another gripped in one set of talons what appeared to be a living snake, thick as a man's arm, and raised it like a weapon, ready to strike with the reptile's fanged and gaping mouth.

Moments later one of the larger creatures, its wings laboring frantically, drew close enough for him to see its bloodshot eyes, while squawking words at him. The language was one that Proteus had never heard before, but the content of menace, the intention to inspire terror, were unmistakable.

Suddenly it displayed a thin, bone-like arm, wielding a kind of twisted javelin. Evidently this version of the damned thing had six limbs in all, counting its wings. Proteus could also see the claws in which its thin legs terminated.

A moment later Proteus discovered, almost too late, that the flying horror, whatever it might be, also used its beak for a weapon. A savage thrust of head and neck just missed the Argonaut, and tore splinters from the shield of wood and leather that he raised in self-defense.

With his back against a stone wall now, there was no way to retreat, and no place to run. Instinctively Proteus thrust back with his spear, feeling the bronze point go into solid flesh. Another Argonaut dealt the thing a hacking blow, decapitating the snake, whose head stayed where it was, while the thick body writhed and fell away.

One of the flying creatures struck in midair by Calais dropped like a stone. Another, wounded, screamed and fell away, laboring to stay airborne with a damaged wing.

It was a battle against nightmare things. Those that entirely lacked legs looked grotesquely helpless when they fell to earth. One of these had been forced down in front of Proteus, and it could only lie there, like a winged egg, the ugly face tilted far to one side.

Proteus finished the beast off with his spear, then squinted upward, trying to shade his eyes from sunlight with one hand, and got a surprisingly clear view of some of the swordplay in the sky.

Even as he watched, another Harpy, stone-struck by a slinger on the ground, fell like a wounded bird, half-gliding, half-plunging toward the small river at the bottom of a nearby ravine.

He soon decided that after all, the beasts were probably not much more intelligent than birds, despite their ability to utter words, and the almost-human look their faces sometimes wore. Running in pursuit of the flailing, falling, flapping form, Proteus got a good look at one of the first Harpies that had been brought down. It lay on the ground surrounded by a growing litter of dead flies.

One of the other Argonauts called his attention to the fact that first one fly, and then another, had fallen buzzing to the earth and quickly died, evidently of poison, after being attracted to the fallen Harpy's wounds, or to small spots of its spattered blood.

Idmon, wiping dark foaming blood from the blade of his short sword, and giving counsel in his usual calm fashion, said it was obvious that they were flying more by power of magic than by strength of wing.

"These could not fly, nor could Giants walk, if they depended upon the powers of nature only." He was inspecting a slight scratch inflicted on his left shoulder by one monster's talons.

The struggle had taken longer than Proteus at first thought it would. But eventually the skies were clean again. Now word spread among the men on the ground that the Harpies, slow-witted monsters for all their physical agility, must have mistaken Zetes and Calais for flying gods, and fled away in terror.

One of the winged brothers landed, wiping his sword in triumph. "Ho ho! It's a glorious business, fighting in the air. I think the dull-brained beasts have taken us for gods, because we fly, and now they fall all over themselves getting out of our way."

Others looked at him in envy. "How about letting me try those sandals of yours sometime?"

"Not likely." The refusal was quick and definite. "Anyway, they're dangerous to wear. My brother and I were a long time practicing before we set out on this voyage."

A good argument was brewing, but Jason aborted it with practical questions. "Any casualties on our side? Apart from a few scratches?"

"Doesn't look like it, Captain."

That there might be none was really too much to hope for. Tiphys, like Idmon, suffered a scratch in this skirmish, from one of the monsters' claws, but brushed it off as only a slight wound.

———

When they told King Phineas that his enemies had been driven from the field with heavy losses, he seemed afraid, at first, to believe in his good fortune. For half an hour he kept wondering aloud whether his tormentors would return. But Idmon eventually persuaded him to come outdoors again, and told the king: "Now that they're convinced you have divine protection, I doubt very much that they'll be back."

7

Clashing Rocks

PHINEAS, IN GRATITUDE to Jason and his companions for ridding him of the monstrous pests that had tormented him for so many years, decreed a night and day of feasting and celebration. While preparations for this festival were under way, he engaged in conversation with Jason and a few of the other Argonauts. The blind old king had wrapped himself in a shawl, and emerged again from his castle to enjoy the relative warmth of the late afternoon sun, on a high terrace.

For the first time in many years, he told his guests, he felt certain that his fiendish tormentors were not going to hurl themselves at him out of the sky.

The king's hospitality went further than mere food and drink. Now, several dozen comely young women appeared as if from nowhere, the slave collars of some of them so thin as to be almost invisible, or to be mistaken for mere necklaces. These began to attach themselves to Argonauts in a most friendly manner.

Jason, as befitted his rank, was naturally the first to be offered his choice of partners. The captain still seemed to be debating which, or how many, to select when another girl approached Proteus, who was more than ready to enjoy such entertainment.

His smiling companion took him by the hand and led him a short distance apart, where she drew him down onto a natural couch of soft grass, warmed by sunlight and lightly screened by tall flowers. Yes, *this* he could remember doing, and he was certain that Old Proteus had enjoyed the experience many times. But there were no names or faces attached to the act.

A quarter of an hour later, when Proteus returned to the public area, he was somewhat startled to note that Jason was there, seated in a low chair almost at the feet of Phineas, and deep in intense discussion with the blind monarch.

It was hard to believe that the captain had declined the offer of intimate companionship, for he had appeared eager at the prospect. The alternate explanation was that Jason must have finished very quickly with his girl, or girls, and hastened back to sit beside his host. It was not hard to see that the captain's true interest lay here, in the chance to engage a friendly king in discussion of the questions and problems pertaining to royalty.

Proteus had not much curiosity on that subject, but had begun to have a fair amount regarding Jason. He sat down casually on a low wall nearby and listened with some interest to the talk between the king and the adventurer.

At the moment, Jason seemed to be answering some question about his own aspirations to become a king. The adventurer was speaking in hushed tones of the holiness, the blessed state of royalty.

And in return the king, gently shaking his sightless head, told Jason: "There is no need for you to envy any man who wears a crown. Even leaving aside the fact that your fame in the world is greater than my own, you now possess youth and strength, good eyes and freedom. You can enjoy a woman, run a race, watch a sunset, digest a feast—do you not think I would trade all of what you call my high estate, my royal glory, for the kind of wealth that you enjoy?"

Jason was respectful but stubborn. "Thousands of men are young and strong and free, my lord Phineas. But only a very few are granted the distinction and honor of being kings."

The blind man shook his head again. "Am I to suppose that you would change places with me this instant, if some god were willing to perform such a transformation?"

Jason's answer came without a moment's hesitation. "Most gladly, sir."

Proteus, silently watching and listening, shook his head on hearing this confirmation of his captain's madness. Apprehensively he looked to right and left, and even scanned the skies, wondering if some deity might have overheard. But the blue vault looked empty, and he chided himself for his own foolishness.

The king sighed. "No wise god would ever grant you such a wish. For good or ill, each man must live his own life, must read the knuck-lebones as they are cast for him by Fate."

Then Proteus must have made some movement, or uttered a sigh that attracted the blind man's attention, for the face of Phineas turned toward him where he sat five or six yards away. The king said: "There sits a man who has a certain smell about him—the smell of the sea." And his thin lips split in a faint smile.

"Or of fish, at least, my lord king," said Jason by way of explanation. "There sits Proteus, my good friend, my shipmate, and trusted adviser, besides being an excellent catcher of fish."

The blind eyes kept wavering in his direction. "What do you think, Fisherman Proteus? Would you rather be king, or god?"

Proteus did not answer immediately, but the king let him have time, seeming to divine that he was not left speechless by the question, but giving it serious thought. At last he responded: "Neither, Lord Phineas. It would be enough for me to know who I really am."

"There speaks the beginning of wisdom," said the old king softly.

───────

Presently the talk took a less philosophical turn. When Jason asked Phineas for advice on the next leg of their long journey, the king took the opportunity to warn his guests about the Clashing Rocks, which were said to represent a considerable danger at this season of the year. Not that he had ever seen them himself. Nor, he thought, had anyone who was currently available at his court. But he had heard terrible reports, of crushed and sunken ships.

"I have questioned Argeus and Phrontis," Jason assured the king, "who are King Aeetes's grandsons. They have heard the stories, like everyone else. But neither of them has any memory of any phenomenon called the Clashing Rocks. They passed this way but once, when they were only children, and probably at a different season."

Among other pieces of advice, the king cautioned his adventurous visitors to accept the gifts of warm clothing he intended to make them before they pressed on. The Argonauts were ready enough to believe what Phineas was telling them about the weather they should expect, as the air, even now in what ought to be the middle of summer, had already grown much cooler than most of them were accustomed to.

"What sort of reception will we be given when we reach the land of Colchis?" Jason wondered aloud.

Phineas asked Jason if he was acquainted with any of the Colchian royal family.

"Only with the king's two grandsons, who are valued members of my crew."

"Then they can tell you much more than I. Aeetes and I have never been friends, but certain things are more or less common knowledge. He has two grown children who still live at home. His son Apsyrtus must be thirty years of age by now—how time flies!—and his younger daughter, Medea, perhaps half as old. But wait, I am forgetting the older daughter, who you will doubtless encounter also. Chalciope, the widowed mother of your two shipmates."

Before the evening of celebration was over, blind King Phineas with the willing aid of members of his court pressed gifts on all the Argonauts. Warm clothes were abundant, as the king had promised. Proteus, allowed to choose from an assortment of fine weapons, got a good spear of his own. He thought it might have come from the same workshop as the borrowed weapon he had been using, for this spear, too, had the image of a dolphin worked into the metal head. He liked the balance, and the straight, keen point; yet still the vague impression persisted, that this weapon was lacking in something that would have made it the perfect spear.

Meanwhile Phineas, shaking his head, and briefly reverting to his look of depression, did not seem to think that family ties were going to mean much to his royal colleague, King Aeetes. He told Jason: "Beyond what I have already told you about the weather, there is little I can say that will be of help. You are obviously determined to go on with this."

For once, on leaving port, the Argo received an encouraging send-off. Proteus thought that Jason looked a little nervous until he had taken roll call again, and assured himself that no one had jumped ship in the welcoming land of kind King Phineas.

Swathed to a greater or lesser extent in garments of itching wool, Jason and his followers somehow maneuvered their long ship on upstream, watching vigilantly for the Clashing Rocks, which had been described to them as "perpetually shrouded in sea-mist."

"I see no magic rocks as yet," Haraldur cried. The northman happened to be taking his turn as lookout. "What I see are giant blocks of ice. Bergy bits, we call them at home."

"What in all the hells does that mean?"

"They are like crumbs from a true iceberg."

"From a true *what*?"

A majority of the Heroes had spent most of their lives in practically tropical climes, and from their complaints it seemed they would have much preferred another brisk swordfight to this kind of thing. "What sort of rock is it that floats with its head out of the water?" said one through chattering teeth.

"Only one kind that I know of—ice."

"*Ice?*" The cry had a sound of outraged disbelief. "Whoever heard of chunks of ice the size of houses?"

But someone chipped off a bit of one of the drifting things, and snatched it aboard—and as it melted in their hands, there was no doubt of what it was.

"Not all the oceans of the world are warm as a steam bath, like the one you mostly sail in." Now that the air had begun to turn frigid, Haraldur seemed to come alive, and was invigorated. He drew deep breaths, pounded his broad chest with energetic fists, and urged his shivering comrades to enjoy themselves.

What actually appeared now, in front of the ship and rushing downstream at it, was a series of ice floes, punctuated now and then by a fragmented berg—all ghostly silver and white, looming out of the white and silver mist. *Argo* absorbed a glancing blow from one of these that was fortunately very small, snapping off like toothpicks two oars whose rowers did not get them out of the way in time, and, as if in afterthought, hurling oarsmen this way and that.

"Man overboard!" One man who had gripped his oar too tightly had been sprung by it into the icy water.

Without pausing to think, Proteus sprang to his feet. In the next instant he had dived over the gunwale, launching his body high and wide off the stern to stay clear of the oars. The briny cold closed over him, but it seemed to him that he had no time to feel the shock.

A few quick strokes brought him to the side of the man who struggled convulsively, and at once Proteus had him in a grip that his frantic thrashing could not break.

Fortunately the current was bearing the ship straight down upon them, and very quickly Proteus had it within reach again. Someone threw a rope, and the victim still had the energy to seize it with ferocious strength—in another moment he had been hauled back on board. Then another rope, for Proteus, and he only had to catch hold to be pulled in and over the low gunwale.

Hands pounded him in triumph, deep voices roared congratulations. Now it was necessary to get the ship in to a bank, stop its rapid drifting, lest it be quickly carried all the way back to the mouth of the Bogazi.

But the next shock of glancing impact of a mass of ice, right against the starboard bow, was enough to stagger the few Heroes who were not on rowers' benches. They had all been served with a warning that they must avoid contact with any larger bergs.

That was advice easy enough to understand, but Phineas warned them it might be hard to put into practice.

In the legends that later generations were to build on *Argo*'s trip, the enormous power of passing time turned floating towers of ice into huge bulks of metal or stone, swung back and forth by currents, quite capable of crushing to splinters any ship that happened to be caught between them when they closed.

The northerner Haraldur said that he understood where the house-sized chunks must be coming from. They were nothing new to him, as they were to all the others.

"They are pieces of what we call a glacier, in my country, where such things are common enough."

More of what he called bergy bits, and even larger chunks that he named growlers, came riding the swift current down through the strait, in a flow made torrential by the late spring thaws.

Each mass of ice came trailing little wisps of cloud behind it, adding an air of magic to what Proteus now realized was a wonder purely natural. Gradually, as the day wore on, the whole scene became enveloped in mist, making it difficult to tell where either shore might be. Or how far away the next berg was, or the one after that, or to steer out of the way of any of them. Tiphys and Idmon had both grown feverish, and the skin around their respective Harpy-scratches looked puffy and inflamed. But so far, both men refused to admit that such small wounds might make them really sick. By now, all the wounded from the earlier fights seemed well on the way to full recovery.

The thoughts of the crew were on the ice, not on their injuries. Even a ship bigger than *Argo* could easily have been bashed to pieces, or crushed between huge chunks.

Visible bits of wreckage, maybe items of clothing, a broken oar, showed that this had happened to at least one vessel, somewhere upstream from where the Argonauts were laboring.

And now when the voyagers emerged again from the strait into an open sea, they saw that the cliffs on the land side were not of earth, or rock, but rather a towering wall like nothing most of them had ever seen before.

"By all the frozen hells!" Jaws dropped, and men forgot to row.

"What in the name of all the gods is that? Don't tell me that it's . . ."

"But it is."

The mass loomed bigger than any castle any of them had ever seen, yet it was no part of the natural rocky earth. It was gray-white, mottled here and there with suggestions of pastel color, smooth, sheer, and enormous. It was well over a thousand feet high, and still calving off huge bergy bits.

"I can't believe it—that's all ice?"

Only Haraldur had anything reassuring to tell his shipmates. He stood shading his eyes with one hand and squinting up. "I tell you, I have seen these things before—though none quite that high," he added under his breath.

And Proteus pointed. "There goes another. Look." Up at the top of the high wall, a slow crumbling, for some unseen reason. A majestic tumble and a huge, slow splash.

The weather was also turning much colder than most of the Heroes were accustomed to. Even bright sun did not bring what they considered real warming.

"If this is summer, what in the Underworld is winter going to be like here?"

"Just pray that we'll be long gone from here by then."

Somewhat cheered by surviving the perils of the ice, but gloomy with shivering and chilblains, and with their ship's sides scraped and dented, some of the joints of planking strained, the Argonauts landed in the home of King Amycus's arch-enemy, Lycus. They had heard something of this monarch before leaving home, and they expected him to be ready to offer a warm welcome to the conquerors of his old foe.

News of his hated rival's death had already reached Lycus by heliograph, and he was impatient to know details.

The latest monarch to offer the Argonauts his hospitality, a jovial rascal by the look and sound of him, made no effort to restrain his delight at the news, and ordered Polydeuces pointed out to him that he might pay the boxer special tribute.

He sat in his high chair, midway between two roaring fires, one at either end of his great hall, and waved enthusiastically for them to enter. "Cracked his head-bones, did you? With your fist? Ha haaa, I like it! No, I love it! Come in, gentlemen, come in! Sit down, let's bother with no ceremony! What can I do for you? Servants forward, ho, fill and refill their cups! You must all be my guests for many days."

———————

And so it turned out that the Argonauts enjoyed a whole barrage of feasts, and entertainment in every way equal to what they had enjoyed at their last stop. But with regard to their mission, Lycus could offer little in the way of practical help, and could do little more for the Argonauts than entertain them with a hunting party. Jason was reluctant to delay his sailing for another day, but realized that it would be rude to decline the offer. Meanwhile the great majority of the men were eager to remain a little longer in a place where many pleasures, not only those of the hunt, were readily available.

Several parties mounted cameloids and rode out into the royal hunting preserve, a few square miles of rugged land, where there were cliffs not unlike those in which the Harpies had been said to nest. Proteus scanned the skies at intervals, but there was no sign of any similar monsters here.

Unhappily, he had not much success in seeing signs of a boar, either.

But Idmon saw one, at extreme close range. The boar's tusk gashed his thigh, and he died, bleeding to death inside his suit of borrowed furs before any effective aid could reach him. By that time his mind was wandering, and none of the treatments attempted by King Lycus's physicians did him any good at all. Those who attended him at the end were certain that his weakness and inattention during the hunt were a result of his fever, caused by the single scratch on his arm inflicted by a Harpy's filthy claw, a small but ultimately fatal wound.

And an even harder blow now fell, in terms of the practical hopes for the success of the voyage. The fever of Tiphys, who had also been scratched by a Harpy's claw, grew worse and soon he too had breathed his last.

The navigator's chief concern in his last illness was how to dispose of his compass-pyx. He asked that it be brought to him, as he lay dying, and lay for an hour or more with the device clutched to his chest, as if trying to make up his mind how best to bequeath it.

In the end he chose Jason as his heir, though Jason was not the most skilled in the use of such an instrument.

———

Two weeks after their arrival in the domain of King Lycus, a double funeral was held. The company of Argonauts was again a little smaller than it had been. Idmon's counsel would be sorely missed, and in the loss of their navigator they had suffered what several of them feared might be a crippling blow.

Three months had now passed since the Argosy began. Four Argonauts had died on the journey, and the missing Meleager had to be presumed dead.

8

Medea

JASON STILL INTENDED that the log should be faithfully kept up—he had told his shipmates that he wanted as complete a record as possible of everything that happened on the voyage. Proteus supposed that the captain had some idea that written evidence might be useful to his cause, when he had brought home the Golden Fleece and stood confronting the current occupant of the throne of Iolcus.

"Captain, my thought is that nothing you bring before the king—excuse me, the usurper—is going to help you depose him. Nothing, that is, short of an army strong enough to do the job."

"We will see what we will see." And that was all that Jason had to say.

The business of log-keeping was under discussion now, because with Idmon dead, someone else had to take over the job. Anchaeus, who had assumed the duty of making entries, went on with the task, which was currently a joyless one.

In the process of selecting Idmon's replacement, the question had come up as to how many of the Heroes could read and write—when the captain called for a show of hands, it turned out that a substantial minority were practically illiterate, even in the common tongue that all of them could speak.

Proteus, glancing curiously through the log book, was struck by the fact that though Idmon at various times had used several little-known languages—maybe just to keep in practice with them—he, Proteus, could read all of them without any trouble. The only explanation that occurred to him was that sailors tended to get around the world a lot, and Old Proteus had evidently been no exception.

———

According to the new navigator's best projections and calculations, they had now covered well over half the distance between Iolcus and Colchis, where, as Argeus and Phrontis repeatedly confirmed, the Golden Fleece hung unsecured in its tree, just waiting for someone daring enough to lift it from the branches and carry it away. The distance had been halved between Jason and the treasure that he so keenly coveted, yet the captain of the *Argo* was moodier than ever, downcast over the two most recent deaths among his company.

This was a cause of gloom that Proteus could understand. The loss of Idmon and Tiphys at the same time was a hard double blow, and it was not surprising that the commander took it as an indication that there would be even greater tragedies to come.

Proteus also thought that he himself would probably have done well as the new navigator, particularly with the superb compass-pyx the successor of Tiphys had inherited. He would have liked to try, and had an instinctive feeling that he would have done well; it seemed to him very likely that he had some experience along that line which he could not remember in detail. But no one else had suggested that he take the job, and there seemed to be several other worthy candidates. And if he had said he wanted to replace Tiphys, naturally everyone would want to know, among other things, exactly what experience he had in using a compass-pyx. He was certain that he had some, but there was nothing specific he could have said.

When the captain kept on fretting about the losses his crew had suffered, Proteus wanted to tell him to quit bellyaching and get on with the job. But even when Jason was behaving stupidly, he retained his knack for making people want to like him and do things for him. Proteus was aware of being somehow subtly manipulated, but that did not dampen his enthusiasm for helping the captain to succeed.

He told Jason: "Captain, none of the bad things that have happened on this voyage were your fault. And everyone who volunteered to join your company knew the quest would be dangerous."

But it seemed he might have saved his breath, for the captain gave no indication that he heard. Instead Jason only voiced another complaint or two. "I do not want to think about how many men I have lost since leaving home. The whole enterprise seems to be under a cloud."

Proteus kept trying to give good counsel. "Some of your problems are certainly the work of enemies. Any man who wants to be a king is going to have enemies."

"That is true. Someone arranged that attack back on Samothraki. I wonder if I have other mortal foes besides Pelias?"

Proteus wanted to avoid speculating on that subject. "And some of them are just bad luck. You could hardly have ordered Polydeuces not to win his fight, but when he won that set off another battle."

Proteus found himself taking extra turns at an oar, making sure that the sail was well cared for, baiting extra hooks and casting lines whenever they stopped, to keep the crew supplied with fresh fish. King Phineas had seen that they were amply provisioned on leaving his domain, but storage space on the slender vessel was strictly limited, and more than thirty hard-working men consumed a large amount of food.

In the privacy of his own thoughts, Proteus often asked himself why the *Argo* and its crew should be so important to him. Until that sunset when he had come wading almost mindless out of the sea, he had never (as far as he knew) laid eyes on this ship or any of the people now aboard. The only answer he could find (and it was not very satisfactory) was the lack of any other purpose in his reborn life—except, of course, that of discovering who he was. Attaching himself to Jason and his cause had provided a kind of answer—at least he now had an identity as a member of a crew. By now, his own presence on the *Argo*, working hard for the success of the voyage, seemed to Proteus the most natural thing in the world.

But in connection with his own work, Proteus now faced another puzzle, one he could no longer dismiss as only a figment of his imagination. The ship really did make better progress when he was rowing than when it was his turn to rest, even though he never worked his oar harder or faster than anyone else. As far as Proteus could tell, none of his shipmates had yet become aware of this phenomenon. If any of them ever did, he meant to try to make a joke out of it somehow.

———

While Proteus uneasily enjoyed a feeling of accomplishment, things were obviously different with Jason. Sitting on a rower's bench—he continued scrupulously to take regular turns at the oars—the big man mumbled gloomy forebodings.

But the other Argonauts, to some extent following an example set by Proteus, persuaded the leader to brace up, and take some satisfaction in the fact that his marvelous goal was drawing nearer, hour by hour.

Proteus, in his ongoing concern for their success, was relieved to take note that no one but Jason was really grumbling. The others had all come for the sake of adventure, and so far no one could complain things were too dull.

Now at last they were drawing near their long-sought objective, or so the new steersman assured them, when he raised his head from the compass-pyx. And from here on it would seem that navigation should not be difficult.

After passing various sights, and avoiding a few more icebergs, the *Argo* came in sight of certain mountains, blue with distance, looming over the watery horizon. Phrontis and Argeus reacted with great excitement. Now, they said, they knew for certain that they were coming home.

Those high blue crags came nearer hour by hour, taking on the aspect of solid rock. It seemed now that they had come to the end of the open sea, and were entering the broad estuary of a sizable river. Jason gave orders to lower sail and yard and stow them in the mast-cage. Next they unstepped the mast and put it down to lie beside them, on one side of the long deck.

The current in this broad stream was comparatively gentle, nothing like the mighty flow they had had to contend with in the salt-water strait.

Men were calling back and forth across the benches, telling each other that they were in fresh water now. The smell of it was different, as always, and Proteus could feel the difference in the *Argo*'s lessened buoyancy. People were reaching over the side to scoop up handfuls of the stream that was trying to push them back to sea, and taste it. And it seemed to Proteus that whatever beneficial effect his rowing might have on the ship's progress had become decidedly weaker since entering the river. Still, pulling an oar as hard as everyone else did not tax him to anywhere near his full capacity.

Another day went by, and then another. The distant mountains came a little closer, then began to recede again, as the waterway the ship was following turned its course. The river was guiding them steadily inland, into what certainly must be the kingdom of Colchis, though so far they had had no contact, beyond a casual wave or two, with any of its inhabitants. They had to assume that word of their presence was being carried overland, much faster than they could row upstream, to the ears of the king in his capital city.

Now occasionally there were people along both shores, one or two or three at a time, laborers working in the fields, some riding cameloids. Faces kept turning in the Argonauts' direction, taking note of the foreign ship with the two broad staring eyes painted on her prow. Proteus supposed they might easily be taken for pirates, except that few people would believe that pirates could be so bold here near the center of Colchian power.

"We are almost home," Phrontis murmured, and it sounded as if he might be praying.

On the right bank as they proceeded upstream, Proteus saw, a short distance inland, the tops of a grove of tall trees, full green with the exuberance of what was undoubtedly a brief summer in these parts. Proteus supposed he might well be looking at the sacred grove supposed to hide the Fleece. What species of tree they might be he had no idea; if at any time in his life he had been a forester, that knowledge was all gone. But there was no spot of gold to be discerned among that forest of branches, and no sign of any dragon, or indeed of any living animal or bird.

And here Jason for the time being gave up taking his regular turn at rowing; it was as if he were expecting at any moment to be summoned to some great deed. With a sword now belted at his side, he stood or paced hour after hour on the slender foredeck, watching hungrily, having things pointed out to him by one or the other of King Aeetes's grandsons. Argeus and Phrontis were visibly excited at returning to the land of their birth, and kept pointing out remembered landmarks to anyone who would pay attention.

Argeus took one hand off his oar long enough to point into the midst of the grove of tall trees. "Up there. See? There is where they say the Fleece lies spread out on the leafy branches of an oak, while a great snake keeps watch and ward over it."

His benchmate did not seem at all impressed. "Yes, I see. What does the great snake eat all this time, do you suppose? Acorns and pine cones?"

"Maybe there are enough would-be thieves to keep him well-fed."

There was much speculation, some of it ribald.

"Aye, it's there among those trees somewhere," agreed Anchaeus, looking up from his rower's bench. "If all the stories we've been told are true."

"Are all the stories ever true?" demanded an Argonaut who liked to argue. "But if even half of them are based on some foundation, then the Fleece should be over there; somewhere in that very grove."

"See any glowing eyes, peeking out between branches? The treasure's supposed to be guarded by a dragon."

"I thought it was a snake. What happened to the snake? Ran out of thieves and acorns?"

"Dragon must have ate it," was another irreverent comment.

"Oh, it'll be guarded, certainly. By what, or who . . . I suppose we will find out when we talk to Grandfather. I'll be glad to be free of these damned oars for a few days."

One of the Argonauts, at least, was not notably quick-witted. "They say King Aeetes is brother to Circe the enchantress."

"Aye, so they do."

"Then let's see—if the king here is Circe's brother, or half-brother, then his daughters are Circe's nieces."

"They certainly are."

"And the king's son, Apsyrtus, who must be about thirty now, is Circe's nephew."

"Yes. Absolutely. I think you've got it now."

None of this was really news to Proteus, who was listening to it all with half an ear. Most of it fell into the vast category of impersonal things his memory had managed to retain, through the destruction of the old Proteus and the violent creation of the new—if creation was the right word. But it struck him now that there was probably a genuine relationship between Circe and King Aeetes—the enchantress was no goddess, by most accounts, and it would be unprecedented, Proteus thought, for any monarch to try to gain status by adopting her into the family. It was more or less expected that anyone asserting rights to a throne would work hard and imaginatively at manipulating his or her family tree, until some evidence could be discovered, or invented, for claiming at least one deity among the ancestors. Some families, by twisting their genealogies into complete fantasy, tried to establish half a dozen divine connections. Of course, folk tended to credit Circe with powers at least equal to those of many a minor goddess. And Proteus thought that the relative modesty of this claim tended to make it more credible.

Circe, he knew, was probably as famous as any other mortal woman who walked the earth. And besides that, she . . .

His hands stopped what they were doing, and for a moment he held his breath . . . in his chronic struggle to remember something of his own past, he had just brushed against something of great importance . . . but before he could seize it, it was gone again, hard to recover as a smooth rock at the bottom of a stream. Damn! He'd almost had it!

There was *something* else that he really ought to be able to remember about the enchantress, Circe . . . he supposed it was even possible that Old Proteus had met her. Why not? Even if the great ones of the world tried to keep themselves apart from common ordinary humans, they must sometimes encounter such folk, including sailors and fishermen.

And now he himself had met Jason, who was not a god, of course, but so famous that people would probably begin to think of him as one.

Abruptly it struck Proteus as odd that he had never heard Jason making out a claim for gods among *his* ancestors. But no doubt a deity or two would appear from nowhere, as a matter of common knowledge, as soon as Jason had managed to set a golden crown upon his head. Zeus would suddenly become his grandfather, or Hera his great-aunt.

"Not *the* Circe?" asked the slower-witted, marveling Argonaut, his thought lagging a speech or two behind the conversation, which had otherwise moved on.

"I don't know of any other." His bench-mate and sometime tutor looked at him impatiently. "People aren't likely to tag their daughters with that name, are they?"

That debate was drowned out by another one, more practical, between two other men: They were in disagreement about exactly how far upstream they had come, and which way they ought to be going.

"But which side of the river is the city on? Yes, as I thought. This one—that's the side where we want to land."

"Want us to take it right into the harbor, Captain, tie up to the central dock?"

"No, I think not," Jason said. And to Proteus the captain's increasing nervousness was evident.

But Jason's voice was calm enough as he gave directions to the steersman. They would land on the bank opposite to the supposed location of the Fleece—no use giving any of the local people grounds to suspect that the visitors had some particular interest in their famous treasure.

On the approaching shore, as the grandsons now pointed out, the wharves and piers of a real city were coming into view, though still a long way upstream. The number of people on shore actually watching the *Argo*'s arrival at this point in the river was quite small; Proteus was not sure that anyone would observe their landing.

They were within a mile of the real port when Jason chose their landing spot. A squall of rain had come to blur the river and the surrounding landscape, and it seemed entirely possible that they were unobserved when he gave quick orders to the steersman to turn them hard port into a marsh.

By the time the vessel came to a stop it was half-hidden by tall reeds from any curious watchers who might be passing on the water, or along the far shore. Here the *Argo* rested conveniently beside a narrow tongue of firm land, so the crew would be able to stand on something solid when they disembarked.

The men looked at one another when they shipped oars and dropped the anchor-stones, but no one made a comment on this odd choice of landing places. Proteus thought that anyone who saw them pulling in here was very likely to take them for pirates trying to hide.

Before anyone actually set foot on shore, Jason brought out from some hidden pocket a small flask of gold he had been saving, and poured into the river a libation of fine wine, saying as he poured that his offering was made to Earth, to the gods of the land.

Having done that, he sat for a while without speaking, as if reluctant at last to leave the ship, while his crew got up and stretched, and tried their feet ashore. Men got the impression that he did not know what to say; and if it had been anyone but Jason, they might have thought that he was frightened.

At last Anchaeus had to gently prod the captain. "We have come to our goal, Jason, the land of Colchis. Now we must consider how to go about getting what we came here for."

The captain nodded, but remained silent. His face wore an expression now all too familiar to his men, suggesting he did not know what to do next. It seemed marvelously strange to Proteus that Jason had led them this far without having made any firm plan for immediate action when they got here. At least their leader ought to have had one ready in his own mind. There had been no shortage of time to think and talk things over, and two members of the Colchian king's family had been on hand for consultation. But Jason seemed determined to rely mostly on his own stubbornness and intuition. Soon it was plain that nothing would be done until the morning, and Jason gave orders to make a kind of camp ashore. The men got busy, killing a few snakes who did not seem to mind the chill weather.

It was as if the mere thought of Aeetes, the stories of fits of rage, of cruelty beyond the ordinary, inspired dread. Though the Argonauts continued to talk bravely, in general it seemed to Proteus that they were more afraid of the king they were about to meet than they had been of any of the other difficulties they had encountered so far, including the boxing bully.

It had been easier to confront the brawler who only wanted to knock your teeth out. Polydeuces said to Phrontis: "From what I hear of your grandpa, I'd rather get into the ring with Amycus again." And the boxer rubbed his cheekbones, where the scars of that match were still not fully healed.

"So would I," offered Haraldur, overhearing. "He's dead!"

By now it was obvious, at least to Proteus, that the grandsons of
Aeetes were going to be of less help than their shipmates had been
fondly hoping. The two had only fairly remote memories of their grandfather, from a time when they had been really only children. But they
had a great fund of second-hand tales about the king, and could testify
to their shipmates of the old man's formidable reputation. As the time
for the expected confrontation drew near, the Argonauts were more and
more interested in hearing what Phrontis and Argeus had to say, but the
brothers seemed to look forward to the meeting less and less.

———

The night had been so cold under a clear sky that a thin film of ice
formed over the tall green grass of the marsh, to be dispersed like a bad
dream, or like the feeble ghost of an iceberg, in the light of the morning
sun. The men who had slept ashore blessed Phineas for having provided
them with blankets.

In a way, the lack of any Colchian reception at all was worse than
the hostility some of the Argonauts had more or less expected. No one
had approached them or their ship since they had landed, and it was
hard to say if any of the local inhabitants even knew they were lodged
in this trackless marsh, three-quarters hidden by tall reeds.

And now there was a decision to be made, that could not be put
off any longer. It was time for Jason, and whatever Argonauts he might
choose to come with him, to actually go to the palace and formally
announce first their presence, and then their mission, to the king.

The intruders' first good look at the distant palace, in clear morning
light, did nothing to ease their nervousness. The upper sections of several towers were just visible from where they were moored among the
reeds.

Jason issued orders in a quiet voice. "I ask those who are not coming with me to stay quietly on board, or very near the ship, with your
arms ready, while I go up to Aeetes's palace with the sons of Phrixus
and two other men."

Jason also chose Proteus and Anchaeus, as his new chief counselor,
to accompany him, so there would be five in the party in all.

"Do we go armed, Jason?" Proteus wanted to know.

"Of course." The answer came without hesitation. "Who knows
what we may meet along the way?"

Leaving the ship, the five men soon found a faint, irregular path that led them quickly to dry land beyond the reeds and water. From there, they passed on to higher ground.

Once they were sure that the way in front of them lay all on solid ground, they stamped and scraped the mud off their feet as best they could, and trudged on, still heading upstream though they were out of sight of the river now. The slate-colored tops of the palace's twin towers remained in sight, and what they saw as they drew closer confirmed it was a much more impressive building than any they had encountered since leaving Iolcus.

As the men walked on, the two grandsons of Aeetes entertained their shipmates with further descriptions of some of the people they might expect to encounter at the palace. Naturally Argeus and Phrontis were especially looking forward to a reunion with their mother, the king's older daughter, Chalciope.

"Mother must be about forty years of age by now. And I suppose our Aunt Medea must be fifteen or sixteen," said Argeus, who was scarcely any older than that himself. "I remember her as a mere toddler—now I have heard rumors that she, like our great-aunt Circe, likes to deal in witchcraft."

Proteus grunted something noncommittal in response. It seemed that everyone had heard those stories.

"And I," said Phrontis, "that Aunt Medea has something of a temper."

Once the delegation of Argonauts had got a hundred yards or so inland from the marshes, beyond the osiers and willows bowing over the wet ground, they entered a region where taller trees stood in rows, as if they had been deliberately planted years ago. It was not far from the city, in an area where one would think the need for lumber and firewood would be great; yet in these groves the absence of stumps showed that no trees had been cut down for a long time. The only likely explanation was that they had been set aside for some religious purpose.

The grandsons of the king confirmed the fact. "Look." Argeus was pointing upward.

There were corpses, swathed in wrappings and dangling on ropes from the tall trees' highest branches. Some were mere skeletons, with most of their wrappings fallen free, or undone by scavenger birds; others were comparatively recent, and rotting. Most of the stink of the freshly dead went upward, but now and then a thoroughly unpleasant whiff came drifting down.

Aeetes' grandsons explained to their shipmates that the Colchians would think it sacrilege to burn the bodies of their men. Here only women and children were cremated, a process which in many other lands was considered the only proper ending for dead warriors.

"How strange," mused Jason.

"The world is a strange place," said Proteus. No one was going to argue that point with him today.

Before they had emerged from the trees, they were met by a thick mist which spread gently from inland toward the river. It was so heavy that they almost had to grope their way.

Proteus was reminded of the thick smoke billowing out of the ritual cave on Samothraki, though here the smell was of nothing worse than earth and water. "Is this mist natural to this place?" he asked the brothers. "Or does some god wish us to pass through the city unseen?"

Phrontis and Argeus only shook their heads, as if to say they could remember nothing like this fog.

"Some power wants us to get lost and fall into the bog, more likely," grumbled the Counselor.

———————

The palace was perhaps a mile from where they had left the boat and most of the crew. As they drew nearer, now following a broad road, more people passed the Argonauts in the mist, some closely enough to take apparent alarm, despite Jason's cheerful greetings, at the sight of five armed strangers.

And at last there appeared in front of them a high stone wall that could belong to nothing but the royal palace. Phrontis and Argeus remembered the way to the front gate.

———————

On reaching the very entrance at last they paused. Two of the visitors at least were no strangers to palaces, yet even they found much to marvel at on surveying the king's courtyard with its wide gates, and the rows of towering stone columns, that seemed to have no purpose other than display.

Anchaeus remarked that the royal castle in Iolcus, perched on a crag as it was, was taller than this structure, and probably would be more easily defended. But in all other ways the home of King Aeetes seemed superior.

"Look at that, would you!" Yet another tower was looming out of the mist.

"It's impressive."

The guards who eventually appeared inside the closed gate showed no surprise when Jason told them his name, and told them that he had come, escorted by his trusted friends, to see the king. After only the briefest delays the visitors were ushered in, by sentries whose demeanor gave no clue as to whether such visitors might or might not have been expected.

There were gravel paths, curving artistically among neatly tended beds of flowers.

Another, lesser gate let them into an inner court, from which several sets of folding doors led out again, evidently to various rooms.

Here the visitors were kept waiting only briefly, before being welcomed by a well-dressed functionary, who without bothering to introduce himself said the king was busy with important business, but had sent word that his visitors should be entertained at dinner.

Given the early hour, it seemed likely that dinner would be hours away, but no one was going to quibble. "Then the king knows who we are?" asked Jason.

The man very slightly inclined his head. "Sir, your ship has been observed for several days by people along the river. Very little that happens here escapes His Majesty's attention."

But still the man made no move to escort them further. Now he was looking at their weapons with evident disapproval, and making small throat-clearing noises.

At last Jason asked him directly if he and his companions had unknowingly committed some offense.

"Sir, the king would be grievously offended if visitors should carry arms into his presence. We will not permit an armed invasion."

Jason turned his gaze on Argeus and Phrontis. Both native Colchians looked uncomfortable, as if realizing they ought to have known better, and to have warned their shipmates in advance.

"We thought we might encounter bandits on the way to the palace," the elder grandson offered lamely. The only response from the official was a look that made most of the delegation feel they owed him an apology.

But Jason, refusing to take offense, unbuckled his sword and tossed it on the ground, no better place of storage having been offered. His shipmates in turn all followed his example, Proteus being the last to give up his spear.

Then their guide at last led the way into the inner palace.

9

Challenge

AT EVERY MOMENT, with every new chamber that they entered, each new turning of a corridor inside the palace, the Argonauts were struck by some new detail, a fresh glimpse of size or elegance. To Proteus it seemed that everything here might very well have been calculated to stun the first-time visitor with an impression of overwhelming wealth and power. Well, this group was doubtless less susceptible than most. Neither Jason nor his Counselor were strangers to royal display. And this palatial exhibition half-awoke strange memories in Proteus, rather than striking him with awe. Why strange? he asked himself. Well for one thing, because the light in King Aeetes's halls, while bright enough, seemed somehow wrong. For any display as magnificent as this the dominant illumination ought to be greenish, or maybe blue . . .

He shook his head in wonder at his own thoughts. Maybe the effects of that knock on the head were even more long-lasting than he had suspected.

But this palace was indeed impressive. It was not only the height of the walls and hugeness of the rooms, but the marvelous tapestries, fountains, and statues to be seen everywhere. Any visitor who came from a truly rustic background would almost certainly be overawed and overwhelmed, but it seemed that none of the visitors fit that description. With the possible exception of Proteus himself, all backgrounds looked about equally familiar to Proteus. He could call up some general idea of what the inside of a palace ought to look like, as well as the inside of a fisherman's hut, and what he saw around him now matched with the former. Maybe, he thought, he had once been a member of some royal bodyguard. But where?

Where else, but at the court of the king—or usurper—who had chosen Old Proteus to be his secret agent? Jason's face as he looked around inside the palace wore an expression of faint sadness, as if he might be comparing the grandeur here with that of the castle that ought to have been his—and that someday would be his, as he had sworn.

To Aeetes's grandsons, of course, these marble halls were, if perhaps not exactly their childhood home, at least familiar to them from their early lives. Phrontis commented that everything looked smaller than he remembered it; but Proteus watching the two brothers got the impression that their life here had not been particularly happy or comfortable. They did not presume to behave in any way other than like visitors.

The visitors were conducted to a dining hall, where a large table was laid, as if in expectation of their coming, with utensils of gold, silver, and fine crystal. Attendants were already bringing in food and drink, as if a party of visitors had been expected. Jason and his companions were bidden to sit down and enjoy his majesty's hospitality; their guide said in his neutral voice that certain members of the royal family would greet them presently, and eventually they would be joined by the king himself.

Ordinarily it would have seemed somewhat early in the day for banqueting, but rations aboard ship had been lacking in variety for some time, and sometimes in quantity as well. The Argonauts were ready for a change, and fell to with a will. The wine and food were excellent, and seemed all the better after weeks of largely frugal fare.

Almost an hour had passed at the table, and they had practically finished a sumptuous meal, before the members of the king's family began to join them, one by one.

As soon as the entrance of the Princess Chalciope was announced, everyone at the table rose.

Proteus turning to the doorway saw a vaguely worried-looking woman of about forty years of age, wearing fine silks trimmed with fur. For the moment the princess ignored Jason's formal greeting, as she hastened to embrace her two sons. In a loud voice she reminded everyone that she had not seen Argeus and Phrontis since they were mere children. Now they were fully grown, but their mother swore that she would have known them anywhere.

Another figure was now pausing in a different doorway, about to enter the great hall, and inspecting the scene before him with what seemed sardonic interest. Proteus was certain of the young man's identity even before his name was mentioned. He wore gold and rich garments, worthy of a prince. Proteus thought that he did not seem especially formidable—until he recalled one of the king's grandsons earlier telling him: "I remember Uncle Apsyrtus—he seems very pleasant, most of the time." And then the youth had fallen silent, with an unhappy look.

Argeus looked that way now, as he caught sight of the waiting figure, and cleared his throat. "Good day to you, Uncle."

The older man nodded slightly. Obviously, if the decision depended on Uncle Apsyrtus, there was going to be no demonstrative family reunion. Phrontis in turn murmured something in the way of greeting, and bowed slightly.

Then, before any general conversation could begin, the king came in, not bothering to have himself announced. He was an old man of unhealthy but commanding appearance, dressed in silk and furs.

Proteus at his first sight of King Aeetes was struck with a maddening feeling that there was something familiar about the monarch's face—it seemed almost certain to him that this king had played some role in the life of Old Proteus, that he could not remember. But when the eyes of Aeetes rested on him, briefly, they betrayed no sign of recognition.

As soon as the king had taken his seat at the head of the table, his two grandsons stepped forward and bowed to him.

But before any conversation could begin, Chalciope, looking toward the doorway again, called out: "Come in, Medea dear. Come in and meet your grown-up nephews. And there are other travelers here, who have come all the way from your father's old home to visit us."

The king's youngest legitimate child now entered the banquet hall, a blond and elegantly dressed small figure. Old Aeetes greeted his daughter with a look of approval, and Proteus thought that the way he looked at her, and his murmured greeting, indicated some sincere affection.

Medea was dressed simply, more or less in the style of her older aunt. The girl's long blond hair was done in an intricate knot, and she was attended by a mousy-looking young maid. Suddenly Proteus was disinclined to believe the rumors that would have had this almost childlike person dabbling in witchcraft.

And Proteus noted that Apsyrtus appeared to be studying his sister carefully, as if he were trying to gauge her reaction to the visitors. And Medea seemed somewhat interested in the visitors, as was only natural when people were arriving from halfway around the world. He thought she paid particular attention to the two young men who were actually her nephews, though they surpassed her in age by a few years.

The glance that Medea returned to her older brother suggested that there was no love lost between the siblings. But that took only a moment; and now she gazed with frank curiosity at her two nephews.

So far there had been no sign of any queen or royal consort, and Proteus thought there probably would not be. According to the king's grandsons, Aeetes was now on his second (at least) wife (and queen), Eidyia, a woman of considerable beauty but who was seldom seen abroad. Rumor held that one of his intermediate consorts had not been entirely human, but rather an Oceanid or Nereid, called Idyia, Hecate, or Nearea, in various versions of the story.

There being no more interruptions, the king now methodically and formally greeted all his visitors, in a reserved voice, and heard their names from Argeus. Then in a grandfatherly way, he inquired of his newly-arrived grandsons how they had prospered on their long sojourn away from home.

Argeus began to tell their story, haltingly at first, then speaking more smoothly as the old man gave him an encouraging nod. Vaguely Argeus described how he and his brother had left home, filled with youthful determination somehow to recover certain unspecified possessions that their father had once owned in other lands. But they had to admit that effort hadn't worked out. And at this Phrontis nodded, smiling in rueful agreement.

Of course, Grandfather sir, they had really been on more than one long voyage. Speaking now in alternation, the two young men went on to inform the elder king of how they had come to hear of Jason's quest, bound for their homeland, and had made a great effort to meet the famed adventurer.

Here Aeetes raised one finger to interrupt their narrative. A certain rumor had reached the court, he said, to the effect that Jason had actually rescued them from shipwreck, in the middle of some earlier voyage. The king wondered aloud whether that might be true.

No, majesty, his grandsons explained, interrupting each other in their eagerness. At one point in their adventures they had indeed needed rescue, though not by Jason. It was simply that the ship they had been on at that time had failed. But the *Argo*, the ship that had now brought them back to Colchis, was quite a different matter.

Now they had come to a subject on which any sailor would be ready to enthusiastically hold forth. The young brothers explained eagerly what a superb ship *Argo* was.

Then the elder grandson, showing more enthusiasm than social awareness, started to introduce his shipmates all over again. "This is our captain, sir. Jason has led us here halfway around the world, by means of a long and difficult voyage, hoping you will make him a generous present of the Golden Fleece."

Two heartbeats after those last words were uttered, it struck Proteus that the banquet hall had suddenly grown very quiet. All eyes were on Aeetes, who, looking gently puzzled, raised a commanding hand. "Stop! Just stop a moment there. There must be some misunderstanding. *What* is it I am to let him have?"

The grandsons looked at each other helplessly. If there had ever been a plan of how to deal with this inevitable moment, that plan had been forgotten. What they remembered of their grandfather made them stutter and stumble as fear began to grow in them, neither of them wishing to speak the words that must now be said.

But at last one of them had to come out with it. "The Golden Fleece, sir. If, of course, you will do so freely and willingly. He has not come here to try to force you into doing anything . . ."

The young man's voice trailed off into a tense silence, for it was obvious to everyone that the king was no longer calm and welcoming, that in fact, though he had scarcely moved and was still silent, he was in a mounting rage.

Now the king, with a surge of energy surprising in an elderly man, jumped to his feet, with the result that everyone else scrambled to stand up also. A vein stood out on Aeetes's forehead as his words poured forth. "You villains!" At the moment he was glaring directly at his grandsons. "Get out of my sight at once. Get out of my country, before you meet a . . . Get out of here. Get out before I feed you a Fleece that you won't like."

Now the monarch was becoming almost incoherent in his rage. "Fleece, is it? I think I know better than that. You have in mind some plot to seize my throne. If you had not eaten at my table first, I would tear your tongues out and chop off your hands, both of them, and send you back with nothing but your feet . . ."

The floors and walls of solid stone seemed to be vibrating with the king's fury. But Jason, standing taller than the king, looked him squarely in the eye. And when the raging monarch had to pause for breath, began a soft and reasonable reply.

Proteus, wondering at his captain, thought: *So, this man can be very brave when ninety-nine out of a hundred would be speechless with fear. How strange, then, that I have seen him shudder and draw back at times when it would seem a Hero would find it easy to be brave.*

Meanwhile, Jason was still speaking. Proteus thought it was probably his fatalistic attitude that allowed him to infuse his voice with an hypnotic calm. "My lord, if you were offended by our show of arms at your front gate, I ask you to overlook that. We acted only in ignorance, no worse. We have not come to your city and palace with any such designs as you suspect.

"Destiny has brought me here, sir. Fate, and the would-be cleverness of a usurper. If you could find it in your heart to be generous, know that I will make your name and your virtue famous through all the halls of my homeland."

The king had now slumped back in his chair, his face a study in sullen deliberation. Meanwhile, everyone else remained standing.

The look on Aeetes's face told them all that his anger had not been dissipated. But now it had assumed a quieter and more thoughtful form. When he spoke again, his tone was calm and reasonable. To Jason he said: "Sir, there is no need for you to make me any more long speeches. If it is really the Golden Fleece you want, and nothing more—why, I will let you have it."

A breathless silence hung in the great hall. Obviously the king was not quite finished.

At last Aeetes went on. "That is, if you still want it when I have told you what you must do to get it." The old man looked up, almost smiling. "You should not confuse me with your ruler back in Iolcus, the man you hate so much, as you describe him; I am willing to be generous to honorable visitors."

Whatever Jason might be feeling, Proteus had to admire his ability to hold his voice level. "What test will you set us, sir?"

Now the smile had come fully back to the king's face. "It will be a test for *you*, sir. You alone."

Jason nodded his acceptance.

Aeetes said: "I propose to try your courage and abilities by setting you a task which, though formidable, is not beyond the strength of *my* two hands." And the king held them up, displaying many rings, and a set of arthritic knuckles. It was plain that his body had once been strong, but was now becoming gnarled with age.

He went on in the same tone: "Are you at all used to agricultural work? No? A pity." Again Aeetes paused for a time, looking from one to another of his audience, savoring the tension as it built. "There is a certain field of land in my domain, one that I want plowed, and sown with a certain, special seed, and harvested—all in the space of a single day."

There was a faint gasp of indrawn breath, almost inaudible, from the other side of the table. Proteus noted with a start that Medea had suddenly taken on a worried look, as if she had just realized what her father was driving at. And the inexpressive face of Apsyrtus had now developed a faint smile.

Meanwhile, the king, still steadily regarding Jason, went on. "Sounds impossible, hey? It's not, I assure you. I have performed the feat myself—do you think that you are up to it?"

"I will do my best, sir, if you will tell me or show me just what to do. What tools am I to use?"

"Aha! A good question. We come now to the most interesting part." The old man shifted in his chair. Obviously he was now truly beginning to enjoy himself. Proteus supposed there was nothing like a fit of rage to get the juices flowing. "What tools you are to use, and what crop you are to sow—and reap. Ha! Ha ha!"

Aeetes waved one gnarled hand, vaguely indicating a direction. "There's a place across the river—yes, over there. That's where you will yoke two very special cattle to your plow—they are Bulls with feet of bronze, and live flames in their very breath. And after plowing with these cattle, you will sow the field with nothing less than Dragon's Teeth. And—should you survive those early phases of your test—you will then be privileged to deal, to the best of your ability, with the resulting harvest." And the king's smile broadened once again.

The dining hall was very quiet as the king went on. His voice had fallen till now it was very low, but all in the large room could hear him clearly.

"I will tell you how I myself have managed the business in the past. After I have yoked the Bronze Bulls and plowed with them, I sow the furrows with the teeth of a monstrous serpent—never mind how I come to have such kernels—you will see.

"And then you will watch, and we will all watch with you, as those teeth grow up in the form of armed men—yes, that is what I said. But you see, I know how to deal with that crop of warriors, using my spear as they rise up against me on all sides.

"By the end of the day, I had done with my harvesting. Now if you, young man, can do as well as I did, you may carry off the Golden Fleece and take it home with you."

There was a heavy silence in the room. Proteus thought, with a sinking heart, that whatever power of will had kept the young man going seemed to be wilting away.

Jason stood before the king almost as if paralyzed, staring at the floor. *Say something, you fool!* Proteus wanted to shout at his captain. Had they not all been on their feet, he would have kicked him under the table. *Whatever you come up with will be better than just standing there like a lump of dirt, as if you were afraid to open your mouth . . .*

Into the silence the king said: "I am not unreasonable. You may have a certain minimal amount of help—someone to hand you the yoke for the Bulls, for example—but no more assistance than I myself enjoyed when I managed to achieve the feat. And that was very little, as anyone who watched me can attest."

"When is this test to take place, Majesty?" It was Proteus who had nerved himself to ask the question.

The old eyes flicked at him appraisingly. "Tomorrow, at dawn." The king returned his gaze to Jason. "And if you hesitate to yoke the bulls or shirk the deadly harvesting, I will take the matter up myself in a manner calculated to make others shrink from coming here and pestering their betters."

With dignity old Aeetes got to his feet again. Then he turned his back on his stunned visitors and marched out of the dining hall with a springy step, his head held high. Whatever might happen in the morning, he obviously expected to enjoy it.

Moments later the steward, looking no more and no less hostile than when he had ushered in the visitors, showed them out again. Their weapons had been moved from where they left them, thrown in a careless pile outside the outer gate, like so much garbage waiting for disposal.

"Not exactly a warm or joyous welcome," Proteus observed after a moment. No one else had anything at all to say.

———————

But when they had put the outer gate of the palace behind them, Argeus spoke up, saying that during the course of the meeting he had received several friendly glances from his young Aunt Medea. These he interpreted to mean that she would surely be willing to help, in one way or another.

"Yes," said Jason vaguely. "We must try to take advantage of that."

Phrontis quickly put in that he felt certain their mother would want to do everything for them that she possibly could.

And Argeus tearfully apologized for so clumsily blurting out the object of their visit.

Jason only shrugged, and clapped the young man on the shoulder, as if to say that the Fates must have wanted it that way. "It was necessary that we should tell the king sooner or later. I am not sure that any other way of telling him would have made the matter easier."

They all turned at the sound of softly running feet behind them, to behold a maidservant trying to catch up. Between gasps, the girl told them she had been sent by the Princess Chalciope, to invite the sons of the princess to come back through a side door of the palace for a private visit with their mother.

The young maidservant said: "If you are Argeus, and Phrontis, there is one in the palace who wishes to have a private talk with you. The king will not object."

This seemed to offer some hopeful prospects. After exchanging a few words with the captain, the two native Colchians went back with the messenger, while the three remaining Argonauts retreated gloomily to their ship.

After they had walked a few hundred yards in depressed silence, Proteus asked the captain: "What will you do, sir?"

Jason trudged on a few more paces before answering. "One thing is certain, Proteus. I will need help, if my mission is not to end in inglorious failure. Doubtless more help than Aeetes is willing to allow me."

"Of course." But Proteus fell silent, having said that much. At the moment he did not see how any help could be provided.

Possibly the captain had no ideas along that line either, for he made no immediate announcement of any plan. Instead he sighed, and asked: "Did you ever feel a great ambition, Proteus?"

"I don't think so, Jason. At least I can't remember having any."

"Then you are fortunate."

When they got back to the ship, Anchaeus discovered some favorable omens to tell Jason about, in an attempt to cheer him.

———

Meanwhile, back in the palace, Chalciope had eagerly welcomed her sons on their private visit, and hastily arranged for her sister to join them.

Medea had come with her maid, who stood by listening quietly. The younger princess said she was also eager to save her two nephews from the king's wrath, and had a question for her sister: "Are you implying, sister, that you would welcome my aid in the form of some kind of sorcery?"

Chalciope paled at the suggestion, but would not be discouraged. "I want to save my sons from our father's anger," she said simply.

The younger sister turned to the two young men.

"Tell me something, Argeus, Phrontis."

"Yes, Aunt Medea."

"When you are free again to go anywhere in the world you wish—where will you go?"

The youths looked at each other hopelessly. "That's hard to say," Phrontis replied at last. "There is much of the world that we have never seen as yet."

His brother nodded. "If Grandfather lets us go anywhere." He swallowed. "If he even lets us leave Colchis alive."

"My father is a grim old man," Medea agreed at once, surprising all her hearers. "I do love him, and I think he has some affection for me. But he can be impossible to live with. I really sympathize with anyone who tries to be his wife."

She paused there, and with a visible effort put some inner struggle behind her.

"But let us be practical. You are my nephews, and I mean to arrange matters so you will remain alive, and free to travel."

"Thank you, Aunt," said Phrontis.

"And what of our shipmates?" Argeus asked.

"Why, I will do all I can to save them, too, of course." And Medea smiled reassuringly.

Then she turned to her older sister. "To accomplish that, dear sister, I must talk with the captain of the Argonauts in secret."

Chalciope, with an arm round each of her sons, stared back at her half-sister. "That would be very dangerous!"

"It will be more dangerous, I think, if I do not."

———

The sons of Chalciope carried word to their captain of the time and place of the proposed meeting. Meanwhile, Medea equipped herself with whatever magic ointment she thought Jason would need to deal with the Bulls.

Of all the maids who served Medea, there was only one the princess truly trusted, the one who had come with her to meet the foreigners, and that young woman was called by her mistress "Mouse" because of her generally quiet and self-effacing ways.

The Mouse was, as usual, privy to all her mistress's secret preparations. The maid on learning of the contemplated project in odylic magic was not surprised. But she did appear concerned.

"Why do you hesitate, girl?" Actually the princess appeared to be a few years younger than her servant. "How long have you been with me now? Two years? You have helped me many times before in matters of this kind. Things that had to be kept secret."

Mouse nodded her dark head. "True, my lady, we have done a few such things together."

"Many times, I say."

The Mouse was obviously not going to argue.

———

As soon as the Mouse learned that Jason's voyage had originated in Iolcus, she was anxious to hear any news the Argonauts might have brought from there.

The princess was momentarily puzzled. "News? What on earth could it matter to you what news there is?"

The maid made a small dismissive gesture. "I—I once knew some people who lived there, my lady."

"Well, you'll be coming along with me when I go to talk to our visitors, so you can listen, I suppose." Medea's voice was preoccupied, she was intent on her own plans.

"What will you talk to them about, my lady?"

"Why, about the dangerous situation in which they find themselves. And how I can help them out of it."

"Is that all, my lady?"

"What else?"

"I'm sure I don't know, my lady."

"What else could there be? Here, these are the spells that I must work if we are to be successful." And Medea's arm shot out, thrusting toward the Mouse several pieces of parchment covered with close writing and intricately drawn diagrams.

———

Part of Medea's preparation for this effort was to clothe herself entirely in black.

She discussed her preparations with her maid, who catechized her on whether she had gone down the list correctly.

Carefully the maid unfolded the crumpled parchment. "It says, my lady, that you are to draw off the juice in a Caspian shell, after bathing your entire body in seven perennial streams—"

"Yes, yes. As for the 'Caspian shell,' we agreed last time on what that means; but what exactly is a 'perennial stream'? Have you any better idea than I do, Mouse?"

"I think, mistress, it means a spring or river that runs all year long. I fear we'll have to amend that part of the preparation. I doubt there are seven perennial streams within a hundred miles of here. Visiting them all in one night will not be possible."

Medea sighed. "Well then, we must do the best we can. We might leave that detail out. Then we have: 'and calling seven times on Brimo, nurse of youth . . . night-wanderer of the Underworld, Queen of the Dead.' And so on and so forth. That should be easy enough."

"Yes, my lady."

The list went on. There were certain dark roots that had been harvested, against some such eventuality as this. The princess began to recite, as if she were quoting from some old play or story: " 'The dark earth shook and rumbled under the Titan root when it was cut' . . . ah, what an adventure that was, Mouse, gathering those roots. Remember how the earth shook, when we tore out the plant? It really did, you know."

"How could anyone forget a thing like that, my lady?"

It was no more than an hour later when Proteus and Jason received through an intermediary a secret message from the princess, telling them that a meeting had been arranged in a Temple of Hecate. The messenger described this to the visitors as a half-ruined building that had been long unused, ever since the worshipers of that dark goddess were driven away.

The temple stood hard by the arboreal cemetery. They could probably find it without being specially guided. The one who had brought the message stood ready to guide them there.

"Do you suppose this is some kind of trick?" Jason pondered.

"Aeetes won't have to bother with trickery if he decides to butcher us. We can't afford not to take chances."

When the young couple met to speak for the first time, they knew that they were not entirely alone. Each was well aware that at least one companion, considered a loyal friend, was looking on from no great distance and overhearing at least part of their talk.

Proteus, who by now had earned his leader's trust several times over, had once more been chosen by Jason to accompany him as a bodyguard.

In asking him to come along, Jason gripped him hard by arm and shoulder. "I have lost Idmon and I have lost Tiphys. Let me not lose you."

"I am here, Jason. I am likely to stay here. I hope this is not another ambush, like the one on Samothraki."

"I do not think it can be. If it is . . ." And the captain gave a fatalistic shrug.

"If it is, we'll get through it somehow." *And if tonight another grinning assassin should call me by name, I will make him tell me who I am. Before I turn him inside out.*

Argeus and Anchaeus also went along as additional bodyguards, at least partway.

———

The temple, a middle-sized old building fallen greatly into disrepair, was dark, and an open doorway yawned on one side of the ground floor. Jason and Proteus as they approached could see a round room some thirty feet in diameter, illuminated by a single candle burning, unattended, on a stand in the center of the room. Entering the building cautiously, the Argonauts looked up stairways and into closets. All seemed innocently empty.

"I will wait in here alone," Jason decided, standing by the table where the one light burned. "Stand guard for me outside, at a little distance, if you will."

Proteus took up his position, and for a few minutes the night was still around him. Then, even as he thought he heard in the distance, approaching along an unseen path, what sounded like the soft footsteps of two women, he was suddenly distracted by the appearance of another figure, near at hand. This was no more than child-sized, and it approached from the direction of the palace in almost ghostly silence.

Seen at close range, this proved to be a mere lad, looking no more than nine or ten years old. Despite the chill night air, the boy's pale skin was totally unclad save for a kind of rich cloak or mantle that he wore oddly bunched up around his shoulders. In his left hand this strange attendant was carrying a small bow, no bigger than a child's toy, while in his right fist he clutched two little arrows.

The boy was walking straight toward Proteus and, just as the man was about to challenge him, came to a halt in front of him. Then he tipped him a conspirator's wink, and startled him by addressing him in a rasping, unchildlike voice, and with a strangely familiar manner. "Good to see you're on the job, my friend. The great ones are taking no chances."

"They seldom do," Proteus heard himself respond. He had no clue as to where that answer had come from, or just what it meant. Meanwhile he was thinking, in a kind of desperation: *Is this going to be the cave entrance on Samothraki over again? Another attempt on Jason's life?* But he dismissed that idea in a moment—no one who wanted to finish off the captain would dispatch a child armed with toy weapons to do the job.

Still, he could not keep from thinking: *Here we go again.* In his gut there was an ugly, sinking feeling that in recent days had become all too familiar—here was one more encounter with one more utter stranger who seemed more familiar with him than he was with himself.

He was about to demand some explanation from the boy, when along the same path came the princess herself, attended by the same mousy maid who had been with her in the banquet hall. Both women totally ignored the lad with his bow and arrows, as if he were some perfectly familiar attendant, and both smiled briefly at Proteus as they passed him. He caught a whiff of something strange, unpleasant, and thought it must be something that they were carrying—the maid held a little jar. He hoped that it was no one's idea of perfume. For a moment he was reminded of the smoke swirling out of the cave during the ritual of the Cabiri.

Meanwhile the boy had remained standing quietly at a little distance from Proteus, and now he spoke to Proteus again in his rasping voice. "Oh, and the great ones said to tell you: If you encounter an agent of King Pelias, kill him on sight."

Without waiting for an answer the youth walked on, following Medea and her attendant into the temple, leaving an open-mouthed Proteus to stare after him. Once the lad was inside the great room, he behaved as if he were indeed performing some kind of ritual, choosing a roughly circular path that took him clear around the waiting Jason, who totally ignored him. The boy came to a stop when he had reached a spot some fifteen feet behind Medea and her maid. The princess was facing away from him, alertly confronting the man she had come to see.

Proteus, puzzled, advanced a few steps toward the doorway and stood staring into the gently illuminated room. No figure however strange would have been very surprising back on Samothraki, as part of the Cabiri ritual. But what in the Underworld was an attendant like this boy doing *here*? He must have some connection with the magic that Medea was said to practice. Proteus decided he could only wait to see what would happen next.

What happened next came much too quickly for Proteus to do anything about it, and it completely froze the marrow in his bones. One moment the boy was simply standing there, his back against the gently curving temple wall. The next moment he had nocked one of his toy arrows to his little bow. Without a moment's pause he drew the small shaft to its full length and let it fly. Proteus, unable to lift a finger to prevent, stood watching the thin silvery streak go darting fast as thought toward the Princess Medea's unprotected back.

10

Bulls

PROTEUS STARED HELPLESSLY through the doorway into the interior of the temple, at a scene so close that he could see it almost perfectly, yet just out of reach. A moment ago, the small lamp near the center had shown him four faces in its circle of light—now there were only three. The boy had disappeared.

Reacting quickly to the bowshot, Proteus was on the point of leaping forward, but even before he moved he could see that there was nothing to be done. The archer had vanished simultaneously with his arrow, at the moment when it reached the body of the princess. And there stood Princess Medea, with her maid complacently beside her, not in the least troubled by young archers or little arrows, still facing Jason across the little table as their conversation got under way. To all appearances the princess was undamaged, and seemed completely unaware of any misfortune.

But an abrupt change *had* taken place. A new look had come into Medea's eyes, and the glow of some sudden emotion had inflamed her cheeks.

Proteus, on the very brink of dashing into the temple, held himself back. He would only make a fool of himself, by reacting to a mere vision, probably the lingering aftereffect of a dose of poison gas.

And during the long, frozen moment of his hesitation, he took note of the little attendant maid, still standing beside her mistress. The two were almost exactly of a height, and of similar slender build, the most notable difference being that the maid's hair was black instead of blond. What drew his attention to the maid right now was the fact that her big dark eyes were fixed on him. The girl looked nervous but was smiling at him slightly, as if she meant to be reassuring. Had she seen what he had just seen, the strange boy and the flying arrow? If not, then some high power had sent him, Proteus, a personal vision. The gods alone knew why they might do that. But if the young maid had seen the same thing . . . Proteus vowed to have a private talk with her, as soon as he could find a chance.

———————

Between the couple who had arranged to meet, it was Jason who spoke first: "Lady, I am alone. Why are you so fearful of me? I am not a lecher, as some men are, and never was, even when I am at home in my own country."

"My lord Jason, you mistake me utterly. I am not afraid of you." And as Medea spoke she took the small glass bottle her maid had been carrying, and handed it over to him. Proteus watching from outside the doorway could see that the contents were some dark and muddy stuff. Just before handing it over, the princess with a firm pull extracted the cork. Again the fuming smell of Samothraki stung the air, stronger this time.

Now, to the observer watching from just outside, it seemed as if she were in some way confidently taking charge of the tall man.

"Pay close attention," she was telling Jason. "Your life may depend on following my plan."

Jason started to interrupt, but then appeared to think better of it, and the princess went on. "When you have met my father and he has given you what he says are teeth from a Dragon's Jaws, anoint your body with what I have just given you, using it like oil."

The captain, listening respectfully, nodded. It was as if he could not find a word to say.

The girl's voice went on, charged with strong emotion. "If you do as I say, you will survive, and pass the test my father has set for you. Then you will be able to carry away the Golden Fleece. Take it home with you, or take it anywhere you like."

As she finished her speech, Medea's hands were clenched before her, and Proteus thought she was trying to keep from throwing herself into Jason's arms. She paused briefly, then in a voice charged with emotion added: "I ask only that if you ever manage to regain your home, you will remember my name, even as I will always remember you."

Her voice broke there. Proteus, staring incredulously in through the doorway at the princess, saw that she was weeping. She seemed like a woman saying farewell to her beloved husband or brother, rather than opening a conversation with a stranger she had seen for the first time only a few hours ago.

Jason too was obviously confused by the princess's display of emotion. But he seemed much in sympathy with it. Soberly he said to Medea: "Never will I forget the offering of help that you are making now. Of help and . . ." He had to pause there. The surge of love in the young face before him was obviously genuine.

At last the captain went on. "If you come to us in Iolcus . . ." He paused again, and took a deep breath, reading to the best of his ability the message in her eyes. Then he went firmly on, with the air of a man leaping over a precipice. "There will be a bridal bed for you, which you and I will share."

Medea's mouth opened in a soundless gasp. Jason seemed to have trouble getting control of his voice. The night around the abandoned temple was very quiet. At last he went on: "Nothing shall part us in our love till Death at his appointed hour removes us from the light of day."

What is going on here? thought Proteus to himself. *Have these two secretly known each other for years? Or have all three of us gone mad?*

Once the princess heard the Hero's pledge of marriage, her voice regained some measure of its normal tone. "So now, Jason—my friend—I will reveal to you the magic secret of the brazen Bulls.

"The secret has, strictly speaking, very little to do with magic. The truth is that the metallic things are no more dangerous than real oxen."

Jason was staring in fascination at the short girl before him. "Someone," he observed, "has told me they breathe fire." He sounded as if he dearly hoped that she was going to tell him otherwise.

Medea did not deny the point, but brushed it aside. While the glow of new love remained in her eyes, her speech was all practical business. "And so they do, in a way. So does a blacksmith's forge. But as the sparks from the forge are harmless, so are the apparent flames from the Bronze Bulls. Unless a man is foolish enough to hold his hand deliberately in them—I'm not sure what would happen then. So, too, the Bulls may knock down any human clumsy enough to stand right in their way.

"But they will *not* attack you. Because they care nothing about humans, one way or the other, nor do they care what humans may be doing near them, even right in front of them. They have no life in them, but are the lifeless engines of some ancient art."

Jason continued to watch the girl intently, as if he were still trying to guess what had made her do as she was doing.

There was a pause. Then Jason, as if waking suddenly from a kind of trance, asked: "How do you know so much about the Bulls?"

"Trust me, I do know." Medea nodded solemnly. "Perhaps as much as my father, and no one knows them better than he. Once, years ago, he put his knowledge to good use, plowing and sowing with the great bronze creatures, convincing all his subjects that he had the powers of a demigod."

"What are these Bulls?" The man put the question in a tense whisper.

And again Medea surprised her hearers: "I think the Bronze Bulls were once part of the Flying Ram, which twenty years ago brought Phrixus, who was to be the father of Phrontis and Argeus, here from over the sea. You know of the Flying Ram, of course?"

Jason was looking almost dazed. "I have seen its image in a statue."

Medea went on to explain that Phrixus had died before she was old enough to remember much about him. But in later years she had seen with her own eyes that the strange metallic things, by then called Bulls, could still be harnessed to a plow, and made to plow a field. Once when she was still a little girl, she had seen her father perform that feat, though how he had learned to do it was more than Medea could say.

"I might as well confess it to you, though the gods know what you will think of me when you hear it—some time after that, but when I was much younger than I am, I actually played with the Bulls myself! I did some of the very things the king now brags about."

Even the Mouse seemed astonished to hear that, and turned on her mistress a gaze of wonder.

Jason too was staring at the princess incredulously, and Proteus realized that he himself must be gaping in much the same way.

Medea, still focusing all her attention on Jason, went on with her explanations. She told him that it was in the nature of the Bronze Bulls that they would follow docilely enough the guidance of any human who walked between them with a hand on each.

And she had another revelation: though Aeetes had impressed his people by working parts of the trick, he himself had never sown more than one of the Dragon's Teeth at a time. Medea as a child had seen her father do so once.

"And did a warrior indeed grow from that strange seed?" Jason asked, in an almost childlike voice.

"Something grew." The memory made the young girl frown. "But it was more like a ghost than like a warrior."

That was a strange answer, and it took Jason a while to think of his next question. "And did your father duel with this apparition, and cut it down?"

The princess hesitated. "I did not see that part. I think he waited, a day or more, until the thing in the field had grown weak—but don't worry, the stuff I have given you will be a sure protection when you must fight!"

"Of course," said Jason, putting some conviction in his voice. And he looked down at the little bottle of dark stuff in his hand, now firmly recorked.

Proteus made himself look away from Medea, and shook his head to try to clear it. He was becoming more and more impressed by the Princess Medea's performance—he had the feeling of being slowly, delightfully, drawn in under a spell of true high magic. At a more practical level, he was beginning to be convinced that she might know what she was talking about regarding the handling of the Bulls.

But Jason, though he had already promised to marry the young woman in front of him, seemed not totally convinced that everything she told him was the truth. He said doubtfully: "A king may do many things that are prohibited to mere natural man, or woman."

Medea looked right back at him. "Only because he is a king? I do not think so. But a true Hero ought to be able to do more than a mere man."

Jason took thought. He said at last: "I hope you will believe, my lady, that it is not a mere lack of courage that makes me seem to hesitate. Any of my men will tell you that I have slain the Calydonian Boar— no, let me be precise, exactly truthful in my claim—I led a group of other men in killing that great beast, and so I gained whatever Heroic reputation may now be mine. But I am willing to confess to you that all the javelins I hurled at the beast may well have missed it. Still, I stood my ground when the Boar charged, and kept fighting till it was dead."

Proteus on hearing this remembered the late Meleager once telling him that when danger threatened, Jason's tendency was to stand still and endure it fatalistically—or, if it was something he could reach with a weapon in his hand, to hack away at it in the same spirit.

Mel had concluded: "In some situations such tactics are indistinguishable from great courage, and sometimes they bring victory."

You might also say, Mel had added, that Jason's real talent is in finding people who will somehow deal with difficult matters for him, or at least show him how to deal with them.

Proteus realized that he had somehow missed part of the conversation between Jason and the princess. "I believe you," Medea was saying now, her voice a lover's breath. "I believe whatever you say, and I do not care about your reputation. I know you are a Hero."

A soft footstep sounded behind Proteus, and he turned to see Haraldur, who in a whisper asked how the meeting was getting on. Proteus shrugged, and made a strong gesture enjoining silence.

Now Medea had returned to the subject of the Dragon's Teeth, and was apparently telling Jason all she could about them. Where her father the king had got them, she did not know.

Whatever Jason thought about this, he could hardly admit himself terrified to try a feat that this little girl assured him she had safely accomplished.

Of course she had stripped first, and anointed herself with the magic ointment. "That was in the days before I had my Mouse to help me," she explained, and turned her head briefly to the small maid at her side. "I'm sure my magic is much more effective now than it was then."

"I rejoice to hear it," said Jason solemnly.

When it had come time for the captain of the Argosy to bid the princess farewell—and after repeating to her his promise that included a bridal bed—the light in the temple was extinguished. Jason fell into step beside Proteus and Haraldur, and the three of them headed back toward their ship. Most of the walk passed in silence, as each man considered what had just taken place.

After returning to the *Argo*, Jason saw to it that everything was in readiness for a quick departure. He meant to do his utmost in the morning, but after their disastrous interview with the king, it seemed quite likely that desperate flight would soon become their only option. And then he urged his men to try to get some rest.

Assembling his entire crew, he told them all that he had been given hope by the princess, but he did not spell out the details of her pledge or his promise of marriage. He concluded his short speech with a warning that they must not interfere with the trial even if things should appear to be going against him.

There was much restlessness that night aboard the *Argo*, and in the small camp on the adjoining narrow ridge of dry land. All thoughts were on Jason, and the test that their captain must undergo, beginning early in the morning. Many people wanted to offer him advice on magic or on demons, and a few actually did so. Others kept urging him to get some sleep, and in the end he did manage a few hours.

The sentries posted near prow and stern of the moored ship were continually nervous, and there were several false alarms. Proteus was restless. Unable to sleep, he moved back and forth along the offshore outrigger for a while, stepping over the outflung limbs of sleeping shipmates, working his fishing lines, not quite as effectively as usual. But his thoughts were not on fish.

Wherever he looked, whatever he tried to do, a certain flash of memory kept getting in the way. Not the same old one. The face and words of the assassin on Samothraki had been supplanted by that terrible, heart-stopping moment when the peculiar boy had loosed his silver arrow at Medea's unprotected back. The dart could not possibly have missed her. There was nowhere else it could have gone but in between her silk-clad ribs. And the princess had totally ignored what ought to have been a mortal skewering. She had simply gone on talking to Jason; but from that moment, a great love for the man in front of her had shone as clear as lamplight in her face, and sounded in her voice.

And in the very instant when the small flying arrow disappeared, the figure of the archer had also vanished. There was no reason to think that any of the other people on the scene had ever been aware of the lad's presence.

Was it possible that he, Proteus, had only seen a vision, some aftereffect of the drugged smoke inhaled days ago? But he could not convince himself of that. So the little archer and his bow were more than natural, and more than merely a vision.

That drastically narrowed down the possibilities.

What ancient Boy was it who shot Arrows that did not kill, that wounded in only the strangest and most subtle way, inflicting only the most delightful pain? Proteus knew the inescapable answer—everyone did—but he did not want to think about it.

He had no choice, though. This time he had been recognized by a god, by the Lord Eros himself, known to some as Cupid, who had come on the scene to help Jason by causing the Princess Medea to fall in love with him. And in passing Cupid had recognized an old acquaintance, and stopped to chat with Proteus.

Good to see you're on the job, my friend. The great ones are taking no chances. Then, as if the god and the dingy assassin were working for the same cause, the Boy had made a point of passing on to him the latest command of the great ones—any secret agent of King Pelias should be killed on sight. But apparently, and luckily for Proteus, Eros had failed to understand that Proteus *was* the very secret agent whose death was to be accomplished.

Maybe, Proteus thought helplessly, he had lost more than his memory when the seagoing Giant wrecked and sank that ship. Maybe he was going crazy. Such an assumption would simplify matters enormously. But he had a feeling that the real explanation was going to turn out to be something even worse.

When at last he lay down and tried to rest, his sleep was fitful and troubled by strange dreams.

Most of the Argonauts were stirring before dawn on the morning of the trial, and soon every man was up. Each member of Jason's crew did his best to fortify himself for a hard day, some with rituals of prayer and token sacrifice, others simply with breakfast. The morning's fish catch, taken by Proteus whose luck at the game still held, was large enough to be considered a good omen, a pair of sturgeon or pike big enough to feed a crew of forty, along with a round of fried cakes left over from the night before.

Proteus beheaded and gutted his catch with swift, sure movements of his new steel knife—another gift from King Phineas. Yes, he was a good fisherman, skilled and lucky too, as old Phineas had thought. Careless of whether or not anyone was looking, he hungrily devoured a few bites of the raw, freshwater fish, earning himself some queasy looks from some of his more finicky shipmates.

The *Argo* and her crew had hardly begun their passage across the river, in misty morning light, when they caught sight of the king and his party, in several boats, performing the same crossing several hundred yards upstream. No salutations were exchanged.

Crouching beneath the raised deck to be out of sight of the Colchians while his shipmates rowed, Jason smeared himself all over with the ointment given him by Medea. Then he applied the same treatment to the head of the spear that he was carrying. The bad smell seemed to quickly evaporate once the stuff was put to use, and it became almost invisible as well.

As he did this he talked nervously to Proteus, telling him he had waited until now to use the stuff because he wanted it to be as fresh as possible when he put it to the test.

11

Plowing

PULLING STURDILY AT their oars, the *Argo*'s crew grounded their ship lightly not far from the royal vessel, on the riverbank near the broad meadow where the trial was to be. Visible a few hundred yards farther inland were the treetops of the towering grove where the Fleece was said to lie spread out on branches.

This time Jason carried a spear with him as he went ashore, because he had been told it would be needed in the trial. He had cautioned his men to bear their weapons with them as usual.

An officer of the king was waiting for him, and handed him a warrior's helmet, fashioned of bronze in an antique style. The helmet was inverted to make a bowl and Proteus, standing near, could see that the bowl was half full of what appeared to be sharp teeth.

The officer's tone was cool and punctiliously correct. "These are the Teeth of the Dragon, sir. The king has told you what you must do with them."

The captain nodded. "He has." Proteus was relieved to see that Jason looked calm and capable, ready to play the part of a captain of Heroes.

The Argonauts had all disembarked, following their leader. Two men had been assigned to keep a close guard on the ship. All the others arrayed themselves a few paces inland, with *Argo* riding at anchor close at their backs, and the field of the trial in front of them. This piece of land was lying fallow, and had the look of having done so for many years. But on close inspection it was possible to see the old, shallow ridges and furrows indicating that it had once been plowed.

Proteus had the feeling that this morning none of his shipmates really envied him the distinction of being chosen as the captain's close attendant. Now Jason passed on to him the helmet, doubly weighty with its cargo.

Proteus had heard no prohibition against touching the helmet's contents, so when Jason had turned away again he picked one of the supposed Dragon's Teeth out of its antique container and looked at it closely; and again he experienced a maddening moment of half-recognition. The object reminded him that there was *something* he ought to remember, in connection with things like this. Some association he ought to be able to make . . .

So strong was the feeling that he came near calling out to everyone that these teeth had nothing to do with dragons. In fact he was almost certain that they were really not teeth at all.

Proteus sifted a handful of the hard little objects through his fingers. They seemed about the right size to be useful in the mouth of a large animal, and almost the right shape, at least for a planteater. But he did not think that they had ever grown in any living jaws. Choosing one at random, he took a moment to study it intently. Mottled gray in color, beveled almost to a chisel edge on one end, and doubly pointed at the other, suggesting the roots of human teeth.

About fifty yards from where the *Argo* had nosed ashore, and the same distance inland, the king's attendants had been busy erecting a royal pavilion, a top and three walls of painted canvas, a sturdy tent that had doubtless seen its share of military campaigns. Aeetes, after keeping everyone waiting for another quarter of an hour, emerged from this shelter to make his official appearance on the scene. Several of his boats had carried across the river a full complement of attendants, and about a hundred heavily armed soldiers, a formidable bodyguard.

Meanwhile Proteus, scanning the field before him, its long grass silver-gray with morning dew, could see nothing of any cattle, either bronze or fleshly, and it crossed his mind to wonder if the whole challenge might be no more than some monstrous jest.

The Prince Apsyrtus was in attendance also, chatting with several military officers. And yes, there were the king's daughters, dressed in different finery than they had worn last night. Evidently Aeetes wanted everyone to witness the ignominious failure that the adventurer was going to meet, one way or another.

The king was gorgeously arrayed this morning, and looked confident, well satisfied with himself and with his plans. Aeetes called an expansive greeting to the assembled Argonauts, and then with fists on hips, planted himself in front of Jason. "And are you ready to meet the Bulls?"

"I am as ready, sir, as I will ever be."

"I take that to mean we should proceed. Sir, the field is ready, and so are your tools. Go to it."

Jason took a step or two into the field, and stood looking round him uncertainly. Still there were no Bulls in sight. The plow stood ready in the field, quite an ordinary-looking implement, fairly new and solidly constructed. A few yards from it lay the yoke, a heavy beam almost as long as a man's height, with curves carved smoothly into one side where it must be made to fit over the necks of the strange team.

Aeetes made a gesture to an aide, and that man did something that Proteus could not quite see.

Some fifty yards away, out near the center of the empty field, there came a stirring of the grass on the near flank of a low mound, over as wide an area as a man might span with his two arms. As the foreigners and most of the natives stared in wonder, a section of sod just that wide ripped open and peeled back, without apparent cause. Meanwhile, a door-sized aperture also yawned in some hard surface just beneath.

Proteus could hear the sound of the sod tearing, like the ripping of some heavy cloth, and then a muffled rattling noise, not quite like anything he had ever heard before.

"The Bulls," murmured one of the Argonauts standing a little behind Proteus, who had advanced a few steps in his capacity as authorized squire or attendant.

But of course, Proteus reminded himself, *they are not really bulls.* Medea in her secret instructions had insisted steadily on that point several times, but somehow he, and perhaps Jason, had not really grasped the fact until now. In the mind of Proteus matters became a little clearer than before.

At a glance he was certain that the two dark, bulking shapes were not even of flesh and blood. They were a couple of—of objects, things, that were alive only in the sense that a ship might be said to have life, or the wind. Now the pair of them, moving bull-like forelegs, had climbed clear of the opening in the mound and were standing, side by side, where everyone could see them. From time to time there was a small orange flare, as if the creatures were really breathing flames of fire. None of the Argonauts actually turned and ran, but Proteus could feel the impulse surge through the ranks. He was not totally immune to it himself.

At the first puff of visible flame, a little murmur of alarm went up among the onlookers. But the Argonauts retained their composure; Jason had told Proteus to once more pass the reassuring word that the captain had reason to believe he would be able to deal with whatever might happen today.

Now the two beasts that were not really beasts came moving forward side by side, leaving behind them the opening in the shallow hillside. Proteus was strongly reminded of something that he could not quite place, or fully visualize—it lay there in the ruins of memory, as did so many other things, just eluding his grasp every time he tried to pick it up.

The more he looked at the two creatures before him, the more certain he was that no blood flowed in their veins. To begin with, they were only calf-sized, not built on the scale of full-grown cattle. Their horns were stubby, little more than symbols, possibly projections designed for some other purpose entirely. (And it struck him also that the end of each horn had a broken look, suggesting that something had been attached above it. Here and there on the upper surface of each Bull were small, shiny, irregular spots, suggesting the stumps of broken metal branches.

And when these creatures moved, they did not change position casually or randomly, in the manner of normal animals or people. Instead, the Bulls either stood stock still or acted with seeming purpose, as they were doing now, when they moved a little apart from each other and turned their heads in the direction of the thin crowd who gaped at them from the field's edge. Proteus knew he had—somewhere, sometime— seen well-drilled soldiers act in such a way.

Somehow the idea that the two things that the king called Bulls might actually be demons had not occurred to Proteus as a serious possibility. And it had been obvious at a glance that they were not human beings, much less gods.

Coolly and thoughtfully Proteus surveyed them, wondering how he himself might try to do battle against such objects if he were forced to attempt it. They looked very strong, but still he thought there were some grounds for optimism.

Their unblinking eyes as blank as glass. They had no mouths that Proteus could see, and the weight of each rested upon two skillfully jointed, mechanical-looking legs in front, and two wheels in the rear, where a normal animal's hind legs would be. At first glance the creatures, or devices, gave an almost comical suggestion of beasts with their front legs on the ground, sitting in the very carts they were supposed to pull. And Medea had said at the secret meeting that they were components of the mysterious Flying Ram.

And now Jason, looking woodenly calm as he was wont to do in moments of desperation, had turned to him, was making a small gesture, wanting to make sure that when it came time to use the helmet half-full of the small, strange objects that were not teeth, Proteus would be ready to hand it over.

Now he muttered sharp oaths to himself. He had seen *something* of the kind before, but he was damned if he could say where, or when, or what . . . groaning with the futile effort of trying to reestablish some kind of connection with his unknown self, he dropped the pebble-like thing back into the helmet. There was someone who would be very glad to see a thing like this—someone, but who? Not the still-nameless woman whose orders had caused him to be here. But someone connected with her . . . He had now come that far, groping into the past.

The urge to know who he was, to try to establish what his life was supposed to be about, swept over him again. It was maddening, like an itch that could not be scratched or even precisely located. Like an itch, it was worse at some times than at others, but it never entirely went away. How could he accomplish anything else until he had freed himself of this nagging urge? And yes, what he really ought to do was bring this mysterious object, this fake tooth, to . . . to someone who would dearly want to see it . . . *someone*, but *who*—?

Jason was now as ready for his trial as he was ever going to be. In the next moment, before anyone could begin to question his courage, he sprang into action, charging directly toward the silent, waiting bulks of bronze. It was, thought Proteus, as if he were determined not to allow himself time to think.

Despite all orders to stay clear, Proteus took a tight grip on his borrowed spear and stood ready to jump forward and do what he could to rescue Jason if that proved necessary.

Fortunately the leader, once he had committed himself to action, lived up to his reputation as a Hero and stood in no need of help. He seemed to have decided he was going to treat his strange opponents as if they were the domestic animals they could not be.

Shooting out an arm, Jason grabbed the bull on his right side by the tip of its left horn, and gave a tremendous yank that got the creature moving toward him. A moment later, he brought it down on its knees with a sudden kick on one of its bronze feet. Meanwhile, the other Bull made a lurching, sideways movement toward the man, and was brought down in the same way with a single kick.

Now Jason took a solid stance, feet planted wide apart, and though the flame-like flaring of light at once enveloped him, he stood his ground unburned, and, still clutching one animal's horn in either hand, held them both down on their fore-knees where they fell.

Proteus had already handed the helmet on to Polydeuces, who was standing near. There was a long thong attached to the helmet, and by this Jason slung it around his neck. Now he picked up the heavy, massive wooden yoke and started to move it into position.

In tribute to this auspicious beginning, a murmur of relief and hope went up from the Argonauts. Proteus could see Medea, her whole life in her silent gaze as she watched the contest. At her side, the silent little servant called the Mouse again turned the gaze of her great, dark eyes to Proteus, as if for some reason she found him almost as interesting as the Hero in his struggle.

Meanwhile, Apsyrtus had his full attention fixed on Jason and the Bulls, as if the prince found this a more fascinating show than he had ever seen before.

Now Jason had gripped the wooden yoke, and was managing to fit it tightly over first one Bull's neck and then the other. In the next moment he had lifted the sturdy wooden pole between them and fastened it to the yoke by its pointed end. Now he grasped his spear and pricked both bulls on their flanks, in rapid succession. Then he slung the spear on his back again, and seized both handles of the plow in a firm grip.

When the spear-point stabbed against one of the creatures' sides, it made a sound as if Jason were tapping an iron shield. But it got his strange team moving. The iron plowshare began to cut the sod and turn the soil.

Scooping his hand into the helmet and bringing out clusters of pointed little objects, he cast them far from himself with many a backward glance lest a deadly crop of earthborn men should catch him unawares.

The bulls, thrusting their bronze hoofs into the earth, toiled on, and Jason kept pace with them.

———

Steadily the sun climbed in the sky. Hours passed while it turned through the zenith and began to sink. Hour after hour, Jason walked without pausing, plowing a long, straight furrow, guiding the Bulls through a sharp turn, and plowing back again across the field. Despite the duration of the struggle, few of the onlookers let their attention lapse for any reason. And those who did were soon drawn back irresistibly to watch.

The plowing was a lurching and uneven business, and Proteus suspected an experienced plowman driving a normal team could have finished the job sooner.

A murmur of amazement went up among the watching Argonauts, and every man among them gripped his weapons. Proteus saw to his amazement that the strange crop had indeed begun to grow.

It did not really consist of earthborn men, he could feel sure of that now. What was coming out of the earth and shooting up like corn were rows of objects that looked like miniature, dusty whirlwinds. The rows were as straight as those of planted corn, and they covered all parts of the field that Jason had already plowed.

Under his incredulous stare the things took shape and seemed to prosper, row after row of them emerging steadily from under the soil, growing as tall as men—but what were they?

Proteus had the sensation that the hair on the back of his neck was trying to stand up. For a moment he saw that first eruption from the ground as a tiny spout of clear water, the emergence of a spring. But there was no splash and flow of liquid. And as the odd little spout mounted swiftly to the size of a man, it lost its near resemblance to a fountain, taking on more the aspect of a cloud, or rather of some object spinning so fast that the details of its surface were no more than a gray blur. Now he understood a little better Medea's difficulty in describing her childhood view of a similar planting.

Some Argonauts were later to swear solemnly that in a matter of only a few minutes, the field in the wake of Jason's plow had bristled with stout shields, double-pointed spears, and glittering helmets—Proteus was willing to agree that there were shapes that might have been mistaken for such things.

The sight of the grotesque things suddenly triggered shadowy memories. Acting on impulse, Proteus snatched up a fist-sized rock that had been turned up by the plow, and handed it to Jason, meanwhile telling him in a fierce whisper: "Throw this among them! Hard as you can!"

Jason did not argue, but spun round and let fly with his strong arm, as hard as he could, so that the missile went bouncing far away along an irregular row of the earthborn things. An instant later, Proteus had crouched down behind the plow, pulling Jason down with him.

It was almost as if he had hurled a stone into a hornet's nest. Each impact along the row triggered a violent reaction. Each of the earthborn men, if that was what they were, struck out at his neighbors in some fashion. No actual weapons could be distinguished, not by mere human eyes at least, but the impression of combat was unmistakable. With explosive speed, the struggle spread from row to row, all across the field. First one by one, then in squads and detachments, the creatures fell back into their mother earth, as if a grove of small trees had been flattened by a gale. Jason had to do no more but crouch down with Proteus, while the creatures of the dark soil mowed each other down with amazing rapidity.

In less than a minute, the field was as barren as it had ever been.

When the time came, later, for creating legends, some Argonauts and some of the king's supporters too—none of them with quite as good a view of the field as Proteus enjoyed—were to swear that in the plowed field on that day they had seen armed men slaughtering each other; and there would also be testimony to rivulets of blood, running in the newly-plowed furrows. But Proteus, watching coolly and carefully on the day when it all happened, saw no bodies and no blood, but only a swirling and scattering of grayness, a vague, blurred wreckage that melted back into the earth even faster than it had sprouted out.

Proteus was not the only Argonaut whose eyes and mind saw clearly. One man behind him muttered: "Whatever those things were, they were not fighting men. And this king has built his warrior's reputation on knocking down such scarecrows?"

"Myself, I'd rather face some man with a sword," his fellow muttered.

Whatever the true nature of the peculiar crop, there was no doubt that the harvest was complete. The field was still again, and quiet, and whatever had been summoned up out of the earth had now gone back to it again. And it was time for the audience to leave.

Proteus's last sight of the two Bulls showed them standing motionless, a pair of bronze statues at one side of the broad field.

———

The king, without acknowledging in any way the upstart's victory, had turned his back on the scene even before the last of the strange creatures had been destroyed. His aides and his family hastened to follow Aeetes as he stalked away. Apsyrtus lingered a moment, surveying the scene thoughtfully, before he went.

Medea and her sister naturally followed their father and brother. Proteus thought that both women were looking deathly pale.

Proteus was just about to board the *Argo* again when the young maid who had been attending Princess Medea came hurrying up to him.

"My mistress wishes to see you."

This time, when she was near and looking directly at him, the maid gave Proteus an impression of wiry energy. He also immediately got the idea that for some reason she was seriously afraid of him, though she was trying to conceal the fact.

"You mean she wants to see Jason," Proteus told her. "Or is it that she wants me too?"

The young woman shook her head. "I mean what I said. Not Jason, not right now. You are the only one called Proteus, aren't you? It's you she wants."

"All right. Yes, I am the only Proteus among the Argonauts. What's your name, girl? Did I hear the princess call you 'Mouse'?"

"You did."

He was intrigued. "Is that your real name?"

"I answer to it quick enough."

"Have you a liking for it?"

"I like my mistress well enough, who gave it to me."

Proteus was on the brink of asking whether she had seen Cupid and his Arrow, but quickly decided he had better let that question wait. Hastily he told Jason what was going on, and said he would rejoin the captain and his crew as soon as possible.

When the messenger had conducted him to where the princess was waiting alone, Medea said: "We can speak freely in front of the Mouse, here. I would trust her with my life."

Looking into Medea's eyes, Proteus could not fail to see that the glow brought to her eyes by Cupid's Arrow still persisted.

Softly and eagerly she said: "Good Proteus, I am so glad you came to talk with me."

"It is my pleasure, princess."

"You are Jason's friend, are you not? His good, reliable friend?"

"I trust I am." And from the corner of his eye he noted that the Mouse was standing back a little, looking as if she seriously disapproved of this line of talk, perhaps of this whole meeting.

But to Medea it was obviously very important. "You are ready to stand by him, to risk your life to protect his?"

"Princess, I will take that risk for any of my shipmates." He could go as far as that and still tell the perfect truth.

But the princess was staring at him in such a way that he realized she had hardly heard his answer; she had already assigned him a role to play, and needed no confirmation. Now her tone was almost envious or jealous. "Have you known the Lord Jason for many years?"

"I'm afraid not, my lady. Only for a few months."

Still she was not really listening. She had her own idea of who he must be, and how he must serve Jason. "He seems to speak to you, to rely on you, more than on any of the others."

"I don't think any of us in the crew are really his old friends, my princess." Meleager would probably have been able to make some such claim, but none of the other Argonauts. Struck by an odd thought, Proteus added: "Somehow I doubt that our captain has any old friends."

That answer caught Medea's full attention, and she reacted with shocked surprise. "Oh, how can you say that? I'm sure you're wrong!"

"I have been many times wrong before, my lady." He did not want to waste this opportunity. "My lady, I have a question for you."

She was surprised again, but not unwilling to accommodate him. "Ask it."

"Now that Jason has done what the king demanded of him, what is going to happen?"

The princess had her answer ready at once.

"My father will be angry, of course—even angrier than he is already. But I think he will take no action immediately. He likes to think things all the way through before he moves, when that is at all possible. He will move cautiously when he moves."

"I understand you, Princess. So, we have a little time in which to get away, before your father takes action, as you put it. As soon as we can get the Fleece into our hands, we must leave directly. I fear that you will have put yourself into great danger by giving us your help."

"You are right about the danger, of course. So you must leave as soon as possible, even if you are unable to get the Fleece."

He was shaking his head. "No, my lady, we will not do that. Jason will insist on having the Fleece, because he still believes that if he brings it home, he can trade it for the throne of Iolcus. And even if Jason were willing to leave without his treasure, I think the crew might desert him if he did, having come this far and gone through all that we have endured."

"They wouldn't do that!"

"Forgive my directness, lady, but they would. They would consider him a false Hero, not worth following. And Jason absolutely needs the Fleece. Or he's convinced he does, which comes to the same thing. He believes it means a throne to him. Whether that is true or not—" Proteus shrugged. "But if he goes home without it, he will certainly have no kingdom. Whatever supporters he might have at home will desert him . . ."

"Not you, Proteus! Tell me you will never fail Prince Jason." And Medea reached out to grip his arm.

It was the first time Proteus had ever heard his leader awarded that title. It seemed to him misplaced, but he was not going to dispute with a princess over her choice of words. Now he admitted: "To serve him seems to be the only goal I have in life, my lady."

That answer pleased the princess very much indeed. "You do swear by all the gods you most hold sacred?"

"If it pleases you, I will."

"Thank you! Thank you, kind friend! I am so glad to hear that! Let it be always so."

And Proteus bowed silently.

12

Fleece

IN THE LIGHT of a glorious sunset the Argonauts recrossed the river in their ship, and put in very near their old landing place, about a mile downstream from the city and the palace. This time there was no question of trying to conceal their presence, and no one bothered to push *Argo*'s prow so deeply into the marsh.

The keeper of the ship's log, Anchaeus, careless now of whether Colchians might be watching him or not, lighted a lamp on deck, and tried to decide on the right words to set down a short description of the amazing events of the day just past.

He also noted that it was an apparent advantage of the cold weather that there were fewer mosquitoes in the swamp than might otherwise have been expected. But of Jason's triumphant success in his struggle with the Bronze Bulls Anchaeus wrote very little, and that in cautious words; and he set down nothing that he might have known of any secret understanding that might have come to exist between the captain and the princess. Jason had reminded him that it was not impossible that some enemy would soon be reading the log.

———

The last of the sunset had long faded from the sky, and the time was near midnight, when the Mouse came to where the princess waited in her room alone.

When the servant was slow to begin, Medea prodded her. "Have you seen the king?"

The maid looked over her shoulder before answering, and her voice trembled slightly. "Yes, mistress, and never in the years since I came into your service have I seen my lord the king so angry."

"Who are you to judge my father's angers?" But Medea herself realized that was a foolish question, and she did not pursue it. "What was he doing?"

"Only talking, my lady princess. To the prince, and to the other men who counsel him. But it was the look on his face . . ." Mouse shook her head.

Medea briefly closed her eyes. "I can well imagine. Go on."

The maid went on to describe how the king and Apsyrtus had summoned her for questioning in the royal council chamber. But when she was brought to them, they were not ready to hear her yet. She had been carelessly told to wait in an anteroom; and while waiting there she had been able to look out through a doorway and see the king and the prince, and overhear much of what they were saying to each other, and to the king's other advisers who were in attendance.

Not only had the maid overheard the talk, but she had made some shrewd judgments about the speakers. Aeetes was enraged by Jason's success, but at the same time impressed by the physical power and skill shown by the leader of the Argonauts. He had demonstrated more courage than Aeetes would have given him credit for, it seemed well within the realm of possibility that the foreigner might have had effective magical assistance. All these things made the king wary, but it was really the continued alertness displayed by the Argonauts that had kept him from impulsively taking any action against the visitors.

The maid also told how Apsyrtus had argued with his father that it was hard to see how the foreigner could have done what he had done without some kind of help from within the king's inner circle.

The prince had asked: "How many, Father, know the full secret of the Bulls? How many besides yourself?"

Apsyrtus as the heir had been fully informed of such matters. But Aeetes did not see how there could be anyone else. Certainly Phrontis and Argeus, who had left the realm as children, must be innocent of any such secret knowledge.

The Mouse hesitated before she added: "My lady, I think your father at first suspected your brother of some treachery."

Medea's red lips formed a round O. "Are you mad? That could never be. My father trusts Apsyrtus as he trusts no one else in the whole world."

"Then perhaps I am mad indeed, my lady. I can only tell you how it seemed to me."

"But what about my elder sister, whose sons are most in danger? And what about me? Did suspicion rest on either of us?"

"I would say, my lady, that neither the king nor Prince Apsyrtus seemed to consider either of you a real possibility."

Medea sighed with relief. Then she said, as if looking into some awful distance: "I think the king has a hard time imagining that any blood relative would really turn against him. Or that any might have reason to do so. That is why he is so angry with his grandsons." Her gaze came back to within the room. "Or that any woman might find it in her to be so bold and active. Truly he would deem it quite unnatural if she were."

Her servant thought about it. "My lady, the king mentioned the Princess Chalciope only once. That was when he said to his advisers that she would certainly be trying somehow to save her two sons from his wrath. I think he meant that your illustrious sister would come to plead with him, and of course she is going to do so."

"And he had nothing at all to say about little Medea?" And she touched her own breast with a forefinger.

"I heard nothing, beneficent lady."

Again the princess allowed herself a sigh. "Father has, I hope, no reason to suspect that I have ever bothered my head about such matters . . . I was only a little girl the last time he put his bronze toys through their paces."

Even as the maid reported to her mistress, the meeting in the council chamber was still going on, into the early morning hours.

The king and his advisers had to consider soberly that there were almost forty of the foreigners, a not inconsiderable number, all of them well armed, and good fighters if appearances and reputations meant anything in such matters.

Prince Apsyrtus said: "And also they are very much alert, tending to post guards, stay together, and keep their weapons handy. It would not be a simple matter to wipe them out. Hardly the kind of thing that could be accomplished quietly and unobtrusively."

One of the officers of the royal guard suggested: "Your Majesty might invite them all to a banquet, get them to lay aside their arms . . . but I doubt they would fall for any such trick now."

After the first three words, Apsyrtus had begun shaking his head. "I certainly wouldn't, in their place. Not after the way you have already spoken to them, Father. An invitation would only put them more on their guard, or send them fleeing—the usefulness of such treachery is overrated."

Aeetes shook his head. "They will be very reluctant to leave Colchis without the Fleece. And that, as we know, is too well guarded for them to simply snatch it up." He grumbled something more. Any way he tried to calculate it, trying to wipe out the Argonauts quickly, with only the relatively small number of troops he had handy in the palace, actually no more than a hundred, would most likely result in a prolonged pitched battle.

"And some inconvenient losses on our side," his son concluded. "Sir, to get the job done swiftly will mean using overwhelming force. I think you will have to summon reinforcements. Four hundred men would not be too many. Even so, we will have casualties. Of course that's not necessarily bad; I think our home guard could use a little real practice."

The king agreed with what Apsyrtus told him. Everyone knew that the king trusted his only son, at least more than he trusted anyone else.

Prudently the king and prince dispatched messengers, beginning the process of gathering the necessary force. To do so properly would require at least two days. It was Apsyrtus who suggested calling for warships; it was not impossible that the Argonauts would suddenly decide to run away, even without the Fleece they said they had come for.

"Should we set a close watch on their ship?" asked an officer.

"No, don't bother." The king smiled faintly. "It will be interesting to see just what they do, if they think they have their freedom. But send fast messengers, and while today's sun is bright, use the heliograph as far as possible. Order all my distant forces to be on the lookout for the *Argo*, and stop her if she should suddenly depart."

———

Meanwhile, Medea, still alone with her maid in the gray hour before cockcrow (she was much too excited to think of sleep), confided to the Mouse that her plans went far beyond simply aiding the foreigners. Whether her father suspected her yet or not was actually not of the first importance. "He will probably get around to doing so sooner or later."

"So what will you do, my lady?" As she spoke, the Mouse was busy about some trivial household chore.

Medea was standing looking out her bedroom window, which was half covered by a screen of stonework, at the dark void of the sky. "I will take control of my own life, so it no longer belongs to the king to do with as he wills. I mean to get away from here—clean away."

"In the ship of the foreigners?" The Mouse's voice was a frightened squeak.

The princess nodded. "And you are coming with me."

"My lady!"

"Of course you are. Don't be dull, Mouse. And don't be rebellious. If you don't come with me, and I am caught, I will see that you are implicated, and however bad the result may be for me, it will be worse for you."

"But *why*?"

"Why do I want to leave home, when I have such a delightful future before me if I stay?" The princess's tone grew mocking. "If I stay, I will probably soon be a queen somewhere—that is, I'll be the wife of one of two or three old men with whom my father would like to establish some alliance. Of course none of them are really *that* old, I might have thirty or forty years of humoring them into their senility." And her voice changed again, became fierce as she grabbed Mouse by her wrist. "This is the first real chance that I have ever had to get away, and it will probably be the last. I am not going to let it slip by."

Again she asked Mouse: "Are you sure that Father does not really suspect me?"

The maid gave her a helpless look. "I don't know what is in your father's heart, my lady. All I can tell you is what I heard him say. And he only asked me one or two questions, about what I might have heard the foreigners saying. Of course I had little enough to tell him about that. And he had no idea that you had met with the Lord Jason privately."

"That is good," said Medea, and for a moment she seemed lost in dreams.

Mouse cleared her throat. "It seems to me, my lady, that we now face serious practical problems. How will the Lord Jason, how will anyone, be able to get the Fleece, guarded as it is?"

That brought her mistress back to business. "I mean to see to that. And you of course are going to help me."

"I fear the Bronze Bulls were as nothing, my lady, compared to the one who guards the Fleece."

"I know that, Mouse. So Jason will now need a magic ointment that is much different, much stronger than the stuff I gave him to control the Bulls. So powerful that you will not dare to dip your finger in it— unless I show you how." And the lady demonstrated with her own small, white fingers the very action she had warned against.

"Of course, my lady."

"Do you know," the princess now remarked, seemingly diverted for a moment by a pleasant memory, "I think that ointment to protect against the Bronze Bulls really worked?"

"Of course, my lady. It seems obvious that your magic ointment was really very effective."

"Oh, Mouse! How wonderful!"

"Yes, my lady."

"And all my plans aside, I am truly in love with him—gloriously, marvelously in love! It happens in the stories, but I never thought that it would really . . ."

"I understand, my lady."

Medea talked about how suddenly her overwhelming love for Jason had come over her. Her heart was bursting with it, so she had to talk to someone, and she could trust no one but the Mouse—and, to a lesser extent, her sister Chalciope.

She could not begin to understand why, but she loved the strange dark foreign captain so terribly. She feared to do anything that would cause him to doubt her, or think less of her in any way.

Mouse was blinking at her. "So, my lady. So maybe this time you will also be successful in finding some effective protection against the one who guards the Fleece!"

That sobered Medea in an instant, and once more brought her back to business. For a little while she had actually forgotten about that guardian. "We must pray to all the gods that what I do will be effective. It must be!"

———————

If Mouse had understood and reported the council's deliberations accurately, and the princess had no reason to doubt she had, a day or two must pass before the king moved forcefully against the Argonauts. So at the first hint of daylight, beginning a day of expected peace and tranquility, princess and maid took to their beds to rest. Medea slept much of the time, or tried to sleep, and dreamt of her strong lover who was going to carry her away.

Around midafternoon, Medea took care to appear for an hour or two in the palace, and to act as if nothing very remarkable were on her mind. Then bringing the Mouse with her, Medea withdrew to the privacy of her own room, where the two young women began their most secret preparations.

What had worked against the Bulls was mere milk and honey compared to what was needed now.

"Once Jason has the Fleece in hand, he had better not delay his departure from Colchis by the space of a single heartbeat."

"That is very true, my lady."

"But the trouble is, if he departs from these shores without me, he is never coming back, and I will never see him again."

"That may well be so."

"You know that it is so. And I know that my heart will break, my life will be nothing without him; nothing! Have you ever loved anyone, Mouse?"

"My lady, I—"

But the lady had not really expected any answer, and pressed on without stopping to hear one. "I had thought that I knew what it meant to love, but now I realize that I had no conception of the thing at all. I will die, Mouse, if I am separated from Jason." And it seemed that the princess believed that it was so. "Therefore I must go with him."

The thought ran through Medea's mind that when a girl in one of the romantic stories ran away from home, she almost invariably left behind on her pillow a lock of her hair and a note, usually tear-stained, for her mother to find, saying only that she was going far away. But Medea's mother was long dead, and the king's current consort would not be much interested. If she left a note for anyone it would be Chalciope. Anyway, any such storybook gesture would be foolishness— some spy or snoop would be likely to discover the message before she could get to a safe distance.

Keeping all preparations to a very minimum, Medea went out to meet the Argonauts, taking with her as attendant only the faithful Mouse.

Neither of the young women carried with her anything but the clothes she was wearing—which in the case of the maid amounted to little more than a simple shift, and a woolen cape against the chill of the night air. Meanwhile the princess had on sandals and a couple of additional light garments, with a fine, soft, dark mantle over all.

Getting out of the palace unobserved was a trick that they had worked more than once before; they had learned it did not hurt to have the aid of a muttered spell or two, an invocation of Hecate.

They came to some doors that opened simply for them, in the ordinary way. One was held fast by a large, clumsy lock, that Mouse knew well how to pick, having picked it several times before, in the course of earlier adventures. Others, in apparent obedience to Medea's swiftly chanted incantations, swung open of their own accord. The princess ran in soft sandals down narrow alleys, holding her mantle over her forehead with one hand to hide her face, and with the other lifting up the hem of her skirt.

And the maid ran ahead, darting silently on small unshod feet, less worried about disclosing her own identity.

They passed under the trees where Medea had sometimes come to climb—or more often, to send her young maid climbing—in secret search of corpses, whose parts she needed for the most powerful spells and ointments. From there on they could only guess their way.

13

Guardian

PHRONTIS HAPPENED TO be the one standing guard, some yards inland from the ship, when he heard the two young voices softly calling. He called to his brother who was nearby, and the two young Colchians agreed that they were hearing the voices of their young Aunt Medea and her maid.

Jason, summoned at once, also recognized the voice of the princess. He sent Argeus hurrying to alert the other men, and soon all were awake and listening, practically speechless with astonishment.

The men marveled. "The *princess* has come to us? The young one? Are you crazy?"

"That may be," said Jason. "But I, too, know her voice." And he lit a torch at their small cooking fire and led the way toward the visitors.

When presently the two young women were guided in among the wondering men, Mouse gave Proteus a glance that he interpreted as asking for his approval. Not knowing what to make of this, he replied with a slight smile and nod. The maid seemed reassured.

Medea meanwhile went straight to stand in front of Jason, and raised her voice, as if to make sure that all the men could hear her.

"It seems that my father has discovered everything, and I am doomed if I stay here."

The Argonauts were all silent, wondering. And as soon as those words fell from Medea's lips, her maid looked at her for a long moment, in silent astonishment—that soon enough turned into genuine fear. *I think the princess is lying*, thought Proteus, and looked over Medea's shoulder, into the darkness she had come from.

"Were you followed, princess?" he asked abruptly.

She turned her gaze to him. "No, but all is discovered. We must sail away, and quickly, before the king can organize any pursuit."

Proteus immediately took note of that "we"—it suddenly made a kind of sense of her story. Meanwhile the princess was still speaking.

"Before we go, I will put the guardian of the Fleece to sleep," she was telling Jason, "and you yourself can lift the treasure from the tree." She paused, impressively, with the men all staring at her. "But one thing first. Jason, here in the presence of your men I want you to call on all the gods to witness the promises that you have made to me."

It still seemed to Proteus very doubtful that all had really been discovered; if so there would already be a hue and cry. He caught Jason's eye and slightly shook his head. But if the princess could really help them lay hands on the Fleece, then even if she was determined to come with them, accepting her offer might be their only real choice.

When there was really no time for hesitation, Jason could be decisive enough. "Then get aboard the *Argo* quickly," he commanded. "And your maid, too." Of course the servant must not be left behind, able to confirm that her mistress had really run off with the foreigners.

The maid began to move, but Medea reached out to grab her and hold her where she was. With neither woman stirring an inch, but only looking at Jason, he drew a breath and did as the princess had demanded.

"Dear lady, I swear—and may Olympian Zeus and his Consort Hera, goddess of wedlock, be my witnesses—that when we have returned safely to Iolcus I will take you into my home as my own wedded wife." And with that Jason took Medea's right hand in his own.

But marriage would have to wait. Flight came first, and for that very little preparation was required. Some Argonauts bent to their oars, while others began pushing and pulling on reeds and cattails to get the boat out of the marsh.

No one in the countryside around them raised an outcry at the sound, or tried to interfere with their departure. It seemed that no one had observed it. If Aeetes was setting a trap, thought Proteus, it must be an elaborate and subtle one; and the king did not seem the type for schemes like that. With Apsyrtus things might well be different.

But no trap had been set for the Argonauts or their ship in the river. There were only a couple of distant, moving lanterns to show how little traffic of any kind existed at this time of night.

They had left the fire burning at their campsite, but the *Argo* was showing no light at all as the men bent to their oars. Proteus was not trying to measure time, but the passage across the river seemed amazingly swift.

"Can we locate the place in darkness?" Jason fretted as they climbed ashore in darkness. In whispers he detailed several men to guard the ship, and hold her ready for a quick departure.

The young woman who was now clinging to his side gave him sturdy reassurance. "The Fleece itself will be our guide as we come near. It will show itself as bright as a golden cloud at sunrise."

"Are there no guards?"

The princess shook her head, whose long blond hair was now bound up closely under a scarf. "No need to worry about any human guards. No one but the king himself, and Apsyrtus, will go near the place."

"Then what about the famous dragon? Or snake, as the case may be?"

"Let me explain that later. With my magic to defend you, you need not worry about that—but just to be on the safe side, we will move as quickly as we can."

They made their way along a narrow path that wound between tall, dark trees.

Proteus found himself walking beside the Mouse, who boldly took him by the arm and pulled him a little nearer in the darkness.

When he bent down his head she whispered in his ear: "It sounds like the Lord Jason is expecting some kind of serpent guardian, and it really isn't that."

He kept his own voice very low. "What, then?"

"Maybe you should warn Jason, I don't know if he will listen to me, or if the princess is going to tell him the whole truth. The guardian of the Fleece is really a kind of Giant."

Those last two words echoed harshly in the mind of Proteus, awakening blurred nightmares—visions of a splintered and demolished ship, of human death on every side. "A Giant. Are you sure?"

"Oh, very sure. The kind that lives mostly in the water."

Proteus did not argue, but that seemed to him to make no sense. For longer than anyone could remember, Giants and gods had been engaged in a bitter war for supremacy over the whole world. That any one of those immense beings, traditionally antagonistic to all humans, would want to devote long years to guarding a treasure for King Aeetes was hard to believe.

Medea, walking with Jason at the head of the little column, led them along a path so faint that finding it at night, without a guide, would have been hopeless. Now Proteus, straining his vision, thought they might be entering the very grove of tall trees that housed the treasure. And now, still a little before dawn, before any of the foreigners had actually expected it, there was a light ahead, as faint and golden as the early dawn itself, but on a smaller scale. Only moments later they arrived at a small clearing in the trees, at one side of which the Golden Fleece hung waiting for them.

Their whole group, almost forty people, were standing in a kind of clearing in the grove, an open space twenty yards across, formed by the dead trunks of the other trees that must have been knocked down by the Ram in its violent descent from a long flight. The tree that actually held the Fleece was on one edge of this clearing, and at the crest of a low ridge; just beyond, the wooded land fell off sharply into an unseen valley.

Proteus as he stared, trying to make out some details of that dim fire in the darkness, recalled the fragments of the story he had been hearing from various people over the last few months. The tale had been passed down, from Medea's sister, of how the strange object had been flung into high branches by the force of the crash. Now, as the eyes of the Argonauts accommodated themselves to the deep darkness of the grove, they could see how beneath the broken tree trunks, and scattered for some distance all around, lay bits and pieces of strange material, the wreckage of something that once had been the Golden Ram, that had brought Chalciope's husband to this land.

Phrontis and Argeus were exchanging excited whispers; from what Proteus could overhear, he gathered that this was the first visit either brother had ever made to the sacred grove.

The light of the Fleece was not really strong enough to let them view each other's faces. Presently, at Jason's whispered order, one of the men uncovered a dark lantern he had been carrying, and they could all see a little more of their surroundings.

During the twenty years since the Ram's arrival, the grass and bushes had grown back thickly over what must once have been a deep hole in the soft ground . . . it seemed marvelous that the father of Phrontis and Argeus could have survived the impact.

The sons of Phrixus mourned and said hasty prayers over the spot, and Proteus could hear them mumbling promises to certain gods that later they would offer sacrifices.

Beside the hole there was a mound, overgrown with grass, and Argeus now whispered it must be the base of the altar that Phrixus had set up to Zeus. To Proteus, it looked more like a mound of dirt thrown up by some tremendous impact, as if a Giant's club the size and weight of a falling house had here struck at the earth.

Once he started to look around, it was easy to pick out other fragments, miscellaneous and unidentifiable, left over from the crash landing. Similarities in appearance strongly suggested to Proteus that the

Fleece and the Bulls had once been part of the same creature, or machine, the remaining parts of which lay smashed and scattered irretrievably.

Jason had now approached the hanging Fleece, and was reaching up with one hand to touch it tentatively. It would not be easy, Proteus thought, to reconstruct the details of that flight and its hard ending. Rooting with the toe of his sandal under some leaves, he uncovered a strange bit of metal, all twisted and black, as if it had been scorched. In the light of the single lantern, and the faint glow of the Fleece itself, he could see how other similar pieces were embedded in the ground, some in the trunks of trees. He bent quickly and picked up a bit of softer stuff, not glowing like the Fleece. It felt something like wool and something like grass, and it rang musically when it was touched. When he tried to squeeze it hard, his fist suddenly felt weak, and he hastily cast the object from him.

But all these things were only momentary distractions; they had come here for the Fleece, and there it was. To get directly beneath it, Proteus had to move around to the other side of the spreading tree that held the treasure up, some six or eight feet above the ground, within reach of a tall man.

In the moment when Proteus got his first full look at the object of their long voyage, the doubts he had begun to have of its divine origin were swept away, and he was struck with wonder. So were all his shipmates, Jason included. Only Medea and her servant, both of whom had seen the sight before, were less impressed. The princess kept glancing back nervously over her shoulder, in the direction where the unseen *Argo* waited, as if expecting her father's palace guard to appear at any moment.

In spite of all else, the Fleece drew Proteus's attention back to itself again. As if someone had frozen a sheet of golden flame, and somewhat dimmed its light . . .

The sight of it conveyed somehow the power of a huge waterfall, though it was not actually in motion. Still the tiny bits of substance that made it up seemed never still. It was quite big enough, as it sagged in heavy folds among the branches, to make a cover for a royal bed. Everyone present could feel the power of what hung there in the tree, or imagined that they could. The edges appear frayed, the strands composing them growing thinner and thinner as they stretched farther from the center, until they indeterminately raveled out into invisibility.

Proteus stared at the branches of the tree that held the Fleece, thinking to himself that they must have been transformed over the years, under the strange weight of such a golden burden. It was somehow disquieting that they seemed no different from any other branches on the trees around.

No two Argonauts were affected in exactly the same way. Some fell on their knees as if in worship, some hung back in fear, refusing to come near the tree. Meanwhile others' faces showed that greed had come alive in them. In the darkness before dawn the faint golden glow of the treasure before them transformed each man's countenance, so that he seemed something other than what he truly was.

The stuff where it was the thickest and most solid had the color of pure, raw, glowing gold, so intense that beside it Medea's hair, escaping from her scarf, had acquired a pale and lifeless look. Men stretched out their hands to touch it as it went by. Proteus impulsively reached with his fingers to brush the thing in passage. The feel of it was warm, with slow pulsations of even greater warmth perceptible.

"Take it, Jason, and let us go," Medea said.

Proteus could see how the muscles hardened in Jason's arms when he lifted down his trophy from the tree, but it was not too heavy for a man to handle. Folding it into a manageable bundle took a little time, and somehow the careful bundling was soon spontaneously undone.

But moments later, when Jason tried to run with his prize in the direction of the ship, he discovered that the Fleece somehow resisted any but the slowest acceleration.

———

The fabric hung as low as Jason's feet, as he held it in his arms, and the golden glow of it lit up his face. The very ground before him as he walked was dimly transformed to radiant gold. When Proteus touched him on the arm, he started nervously and looked up with a little cry. "What's that?"

"I said, Jason, we had better get into the ship and get moving as quickly as possible."

The leader seemed to emerge from a kind of trance. "Yes. Back to the ship. Shove off, and get everyone aboard as fast as possible. I'm coming as fast as I can, this thing is hard to carry." And he struggled with his burden, trying to form it into a more compact load.

"Shall I help you?"

"No, I'll manage."

For a moment Proteus dared to hope that they might manage to carry the treasure away without hindrance or delay, that the legends of one or another inhuman guardian were no more than legends. But that

moment ended when a strange sound turned all their heads. It had come
from somewhere behind the grove they had just left.

"You'd better hurry, Captain."

Jason was almost gasping. "I know that, Proteus—but by all the
gods, this is the strangest thing. Every time I try to run, it seems to
grow in weight and slow me down, as if I were pushing some enormous
rock."

But Proteus had turned his head away. "Damn all the gods, what's
that?"

There was a stirring, not loud, yet somehow vast, coming from the
little valley that lay just beyond the tree that had held the Fleece—a
sound like the crackle of trampled underbrush, but grown huge, made
up of the crushing and snapping of many branches of large trees—

In a moment Proteus's imagination created an awesome image—
despite the Mouse's warning, he wanted it to be a dragon or a snake—
but he knew, with the fearful certainty of nightmare, that it was really
a Giant coming toward them now, one of the transformed, mutant kind
whose legs and lower body had wholly metamorphosed into twin fishtail
coils.

Moments later the bad dream had come true. An enormous head,
surmounted by a whole thicket of hair, appeared just beyond the crest
of the low ridge passing through the grove. The skull was impossibly,
miraculously large, the span of an axe-handle's length between the eyes.
Proteus had seen people living in huts with smaller domes. The head
was very nearly human in its shape, but far too large to ever have fit
on any human body. It was easier to imagine a man or woman riding
inside it, peering out through one of the face-sized eyes.

Proteus sharply reminded himself to learn from the maid the source
of her knowledge—if they both survived the next minute or two, which
promised to be perilous.

The fragmented memories Proteus had begun to regain regarding
Giants informed him that most of that race were anything but comfortable when not in deep water. But there did exist a type, or subspecies,
whose lower limbs were practically reptilian—and that was what floun-
dered and rolled before him, almost like a great whale out of water.

It might be floundering now, confined as it was to land, but it was
nevertheless advancing with deadly speed, faster than a man could run.
Tree trunks bent and broke under the weight of the massive, practically
legless, amphibious body as it lurched and flopped and crawled toward
the Argonauts, most of whom were petrified. A thousand twigs and little
branches broke, making a ferocious crackling like that of a burning
forest. Proteus's stomach went queasy when he realized that the Giant

had freed one enormous hand from crawling duty and was actually swinging a thirty-foot tree trunk as a club. Birds and animals of every size uttered screaming cries and fled from the Titan's path.

Now that the Argonauts had been discovered, they had no choice— they were going to have to kill this hideous creature, or die trying, before they left this spot. At the moment, the men were falling back on every side, though to their credit most of them did not simply turn and run, but were backing away in good order, readying their spears and slings and arrows.

———

In a moment memory had transported Proteus back to a near-drowning in deep water, floundering in the middle of the Great Sea amid the wreckage of a demolished ship. The monster that had been trying to kill him then was very much like the one before him now. Both were Giants, and the identification brought with it something close to ultimate terror.

———

Medea met the challenge as bravely as any Argonaut. Displaying the courage of desperation, she attempted to take charge at once, while her maid could only fall down and hide her face. Proteus felt a surge of admiration. Standing as tall as she could with her arms raised, she did her best to stop the monstrous creature with her magic.

Meanwhile Proteus stood by with his spear ready, from the corner of his eye catching a glimpse of Jason who at the moment appeared to be paralyzed with terror.

As far as Proteus could tell, it was very likely that the girl's chants and her drugs were about equally ineffective. The intruders were going to need some other means of defense if they were going to survive.

And now Medea seemed to be coming to the same conclusion. "Run!" she cried to Jason. "Get to the ship!"

Jason had demonstrated his great strength in managing the Bulls, but something about this new task restrained him to a snail's pace, even when he tried to run.

Proteus raised his spear in the direction of their fallen foe, covering Jason's advance, and did not lower it again.

When the creature advanced, half-lurching, half-rolling forward with surprising speed, he hurled the spear as hard as he could, and with remote surprise saw the weapon bury itself up to the last hand's breadth of its shaft in the great monster's naked, hairy belly.

Jason, needing two hands to manage the Fleece, had dropped his spear, and Proteus now swiftly grabbed it up.

The surprising strength in his arm was matched by unsuspected skill. His second cast hit the Giant squarely in the middle of his chest, as easily as striking a wooden knot upon a log. At the same time, the other Argonauts around him were standing firm, shooting arrows or slinging stones. With a hail of missiles falling on the creature, it was all but impossible for anyone to see, in the poor light, whose stone or point was really doing the important damage.

The enormous monster was roaring like a thunderstorm. It had dropped its bludgeon, and was flailing with two arms themselves like mighty tree trunks.

Running forward, Proteus armed himself with a third spear, snatching up one that had landed short when cast by a shipmate. His next throw struck home in the Giant's left eye. The huge being let out an awful noise, and slapped his great hands protectively up over his face. Seizing yet another spear from the litter of fallen weapons, Proteus rushed forward and thrust it deep into his enemy's side. With a hoarse, terrible cry, the Giant fell. Moments later, writhing and crawling, he made a floundering retreat that carried him over the ridge again and down its far side.

Proteus ran after the thing just far enough to see what was happening to it. Downslope, the twitching arms were breaking off great branches. Sliding and slithering, the huge body dragged itself toward the lake and swamps below, visible as a sheen of water in the faint brightening of the morning sky.

Turning swiftly, Proteus ran back after his comrades, and had soon rejoined them. No one else was much concerned with the final fate of their fallen enemy, and it seemed that no one but Proteus quite understood what a key role he had played. They had won the fight somehow, with a hail of spears, stones, and arrows—a near thing there, for a while, but every man of them was used to winning fights. And now they had the glorious treasure to be marveled at.

Jason was on his feet again, apparently unhurt, stumbling on in the direction of the *Argo*, desperately clutching his treasure in his arms.

The young maid wept in fear as she crept aboard the ship, while the princess was fiercely jubilant. But Mouse was determined to serve her mistress, and even more determined that she herself would not be left behind. In only moments all the oars were working, and the ship was under way, headed downstream toward the open sea.

Their departure was just in time. Now there was plenty of daylight to see in the distance King Aeetes in his chariot, pulled by giant cameloids, at the head of a body of troops, chasing them along the riverbank. The king and his mounted troops gained ground but just missed catching up. There had been heavy rain upstream during the night, and the current was swift. Rowing downstream went much faster than the laborious coming up.

The captain stood looking back from his slight elevation on the deck. "He must have got together five hundred men, somehow. Row!"

Evidently the princess had keen eyes. "Yes, that is my father. And my brother too, I recognize their chariots, and the beasts that pull them. But they cannot catch us now!"

Even when they were almost a quarter of a mile downstream, Proteus thought he could still hear the great king's roaring in his rage. It might almost have been the bellowing of a wounded Giant, but Proteus knew that it was not.

They needed no further warning to know that a Colchian fleet would soon be in close pursuit.

The King of Colchis had been robbed of two great treasures, and what he would do to the robbers if he caught them was not something they wanted to think about.

14

Trapped

THE SCRIBE ANCHAEUS made mental notes of what the current log-book entry ought to be; he could hope that he was going to live long enough, and would soon be able to find the time, to actually scratch the words on parchment.

As the mouth of the river broadened and the banks fell away, delivering *Argo* to the sea again, all hands were fully occupied in propelling the ship or keeping lookout. And all rejoiced in glorious success!

One man shouted as he pulled his oar: "A hundred years from now, folks will still be making songs about Jason and his splendid voyage!" And for the moment at least that seemed believable.

"What top-notch pirates we'd have made!" cried out another.

The Argonauts, rowing in good rhythm now, were leaning hard into their work, but they all had enough breath left for a song, and the man who wanted to start a song got a good response on his first try. The Fleece was safely aboard, and so was the princess who had helped them and asked their protection in return.

When the Mouse's eye fell on the book, whose keeper had momentarily left it lying in the open, she whispered innocently that she liked books and would like to read this one. Then without waiting for an answer, she picked it up and looked at it. Most of those who saw her were surprised that she could read.

Meanwhile the princess was too busy staring back over the stern, and murmuring an occasional incantation, to pay any attention to a book.

Proteus at the moment was not listening to the songs, nor did he much care what was being entered in the log or who was reading or writing. Instead he was thinking furiously to himself, wrestling with private doubts as to whether any Giant ought to have been mortally wounded by a simple weapon in the hand of a mere human. True, the arrows, slings, and spears of some thirty strong young men could do a lot of damage. But Proteus had the feeling that most of those missiles had been no more than flea bites to the Giant. No, it was the spears that he, Proteus, had thrown, that brought the monster down. And the spear that he had thrust finished it off, sent it crawling in search of deep water in which to die. Even in the bad light before dawn, he had been able to read their huge enemy's reactions in sufficient detail to feel sure of that.

Others had probably seen the matter differently, as was usually the way in combat. Now some Argonaut was calling, with triumph in his voice: "Which way will you turn us, steersman? Find us another battle, or another monster?"

"And maybe another treasure, too!" chimed in another voice.

Judging from the comments, a good portion of Jason's crew had now had their fill of adventure for the time being, and would have voted to return home along the same course that they had followed outward bound. That route had certainly had its perils, but now it had the great advantage of being to some degree familiar. Meanwhile a minority of others, elated by their triumph, were in a mood for fresh adventures.

But there was no reason to expect Jason to call for a vote. Such decisions were better left in the hands of the steersman/navigator, assuming that he knew his business. The current occupant of the office could be heard muttering his hearty wishes that Tiphys had not died.

There was really no reason to doubt the new man's competence, and no one protested when he informed them they would have to begin their long journey home by a new route. He went on to explain that the decision was being forced on them, by the sheer need to get away from Colchis as fast as they could, and to avoid the forces that would soon be trying to hunt them down.

Once that was settled, Jason gave his men a little talk, toning down the mood of celebration. For the moment they were indeed free, but it would be foolish to think they had seen the last of that king's far-flung forces.

Proteus had to agree. They could all bear witness to the king's anger when Jason succeeded in the trial; and it was all too easy to imagine Aeetes's reaction when he could confirm that the Fleece was gone. Medea had reminded them that even before Jason's triumph, her father had sent word to his distant forces, by means of several fast, light ships, that the *Argo* was to be intercepted should she try to leave—and that order would remain in force until countermanded by the king himself.

―――――――

Some hours later, when the day was far advanced, the steersman appealed for help to the Colchians aboard; he was having some trouble understanding what his compass-pyx was showing him, and thought their knowledge of the surrounding geography might be of benefit. Princess Medea and her maid, proceeding in the easy fashion of people used to working together, began to draw with charcoal on an empty rower's bench a crude map of the maze of waterways ahead.

"Then it is likely we will be cut off," the navigator muttered, after a few minutes spent studying the sketch.

"We might try to slip through at night," one of Jason's advisers suggested.

The steersman raised his head and squinted at the sea and sky. Now he looked gloomier than ever. "That might work if we knew exactly which points were blocked against us. Also the skies are gray. Also traveling at night, in strange waters and under clouds, is a good recipe for getting lost, compass-pyx or not."

On returning to his post, the steersman spent the next few hours of the long day with his forehead almost continually pressed to his small ivory box, so that his face bore the marks of it when he straightened up. Only now and then he briefly raised his head, to inform Jason of some slight course correction that he thought they had better take.

As the day wore on, the princess spent most of her time standing alone (except for the almost constant presence of the faithful Mouse), holding on to a rail on the raised central deck. The two young women alternately looked back at the shores of their homeland, which were fast disappearing, and then cast their eyes ahead at the watery horizon, beyond which lay whatever new life they were to have.

Right now, Medea, the Mouse, and the man who clutched the steering oar were the only people on the ship not rowing. Medea, looking down at Jason laboring steadily on his bench, talked encouragingly to him as he pulled an oar. If the events of the last two days had exhausted him, he did not show it.

Proteus, pulling an oar steadily on a nearby bench, thought that the chief looked worried, even more than usual. Well, now Jason had good cause to fret, having made a deadly enemy of one of the world's most powerful monarchs. Not that it was easy to see how the captain could have avoided that outcome.

———

At last they were blessed by a favorable wind, so the sail could be hoisted and the oarsmen rest. Medea, thinking and planning aloud, considered it certain that there would be a determined pursuit, and likely that her brother Apsyrtus would be leading its main body.

"I'm sure that Father will send him, and not come himself. He'll not feel secure enough to leave his kingdom on any prolonged chase. And besides, he is an old man now."

———

When the wind began to fail again, and the men resumed their rowing, Proteus found himself taking the next shift right beside Jason—one of them sitting inboard and pulling on a long oar, the other outboard on a short one.

Now and then Medea glanced at Proteus and smiled, in the manner of a woman pleased by what a clever servant had done for her. He smiled back at the princess, and thought his own thoughts regarding her. A beautiful woman, but no more so than many others. Also, of course, as unreachable as a star for any common sailor, which made it possible to consider her objectively.

Meanwhile, Jason was speaking jerkily, getting out short sentences between pulls on his oar: "You need not worry, princess. No one's going to overtake us."

Medea looked at him thoughtfully. She said simply: "Perhaps not. But I know it is my brother coming after us." And she turned her head, looking back in the direction from which they had come. "He is more like our father than any man should be. But at the same time he is more cunning, so that I fear him even more."

Jason signaled to the man who had been resting to relieve him at his oar. Then the captain opened the door of a locker beneath the central deck, and set about trying to refit it as a kind of private nest for Medea, where she might be able to rest in a small sheltered space.

He said: "Come lady, I will prepare a place of greater comfort for you."

Her attitude seemed to say that it did not matter, that he should be devoting his time and effort to more important things. "I doubt that any such place can be prepared within a thousand miles of here."

But Jason only smiled at her, and set about doing what he had promised. The finished space was so small that Medea's attendant could not share it with her, but would have to sit just outside.

Proteus smiled at the maid, who was obviously frightened, and finally saw one corner of her mouth turn up in response. He sighed inwardly, foreseeing problems. All of the Heroes understood that the princess was firmly attached to Jason, and most of them would have thought her unattainable anyway, by reason of her royal blood. But here was another young woman, fairly good looking if no great beauty, and certainly of inferior social status. Several dozen young Argonauts would have her almost continually in sight for the duration of the voyage, with no reason to think that she was not fair game. However the girl chose to behave toward them, there were likely to be quarrels, which the crew could ill afford at any time, particularly now.

The presence of two passengers who never rowed really made the ship only a little more crowded, but the change seemed greater than it was.

"Good thing we are not trying to haul twenty or thirty servants," someone commented from a nearby bench.

"Aye, that would have been unmitigated disaster," said the speaker's mate. "Anyway, I think by now that most of them would be dead, or have deserted."

Princess Medea had already emerged from her nest, and was assuring Jason in a low voice that, yes, there were enough openings in her newly created private quarters to allow in sufficient air and light; she might have barely room to turn around inside, but for the moment nothing could be done about that.

Having thanked her rescuer for his trouble, the princess did not seem much interested in the little nest. Nor did she hear Jason when he muttered grimly to himself that the only reason that any spare space at all was now available was that the reserves of dried fish and hardtack, cheese and dried fruit, spare oars, and fishing gear that had formerly filled this space had by this time been put into action or consumed.

―――――

The wind no longer favored their passage, so the crew rowed all day, with only brief pauses for rest and natural needs, stretches and changes of position. Then they rowed on well into the night, favored by a clear sky with so many familiar stars that the compass-pyx became for a time unnecessary.

As the next few hours passed, Medea continued to spend most of her time out in the open, staying as close as was practical to the man who had pledged her his love.

━━━━━━━━

Tireless rowing afforded Proteus no escape from his own thoughts.

Again and again, behind the private screen of his closed eyelids, he could see that damned, deceptively tiny Arrow darting toward the princess's unprotected back. It had to have gone on to pierce her heart. Ever since then she had been crazily in love with Jason. So there was no doubt that the Boy who shot the Arrow had truly been Eros.

Then I have seen a god—that is the first marvel. I—alone of the ordinary mortals who were present—*could see him very clearly.*

Proteus had never seen a god before—or had he? The truth was, of course, that he could not remember. He knew that most people lived their lives and went to their graves without having any personal encounter with divinity. But on the other hand, many in the world's long history *had* met gods face to face, and no doubt some were still doing so.

One of the things that everyone knew about gods was that they could readily pass for ordinary humans, and might, just for their own amusement, choose to go about in the world as such. For every single one of them had been born a mortal human being, only to be transformed at some point in his or her life by somehow acquiring a god-Face.

But Cupid, on that memorable evening when he met Proteus, had not been interested in disguising himself. Instead he had made himself invisible—to everyone but Proteus. Because Cupid had a job to do, and also had something he wanted to say to Proteus. A few words that made less sense to the hearer the more he thought about them.

Like the whore on the dock in Bebrycos, little Eros knew me. Like that sneaky killer on Samothraki, he said he was glad to see me standing where I was. And then Cupid added, almost offhandedly, that I should kill a certain nameless man, an agent of King Pelias, as soon as I laid eyes on him.

Why would the divine Lord Cupid stop and talk with Proteus the common sailor as if they were old pals? Especially when Old Proteus was almost certainly the very agent, or one of them, that the great ones wanted dead.

It sounded like even the great gods must be monumentally confused. There had to be an explanation, somewhere, but Proteus was not at all sure he wanted to know what it was.

In the morning of the third day of their flight from Colchis, the fugitives tied up their ship on an unfamiliar coast, at the mouth of a river that the navigator said must be called Halys. Only he had any idea of where they were, and not even he could say which way they ought to go next.

Zetes and Calais were prevailed upon to fly, and soon took wing above the morning mist. Within the hour they were back with word that if the *Argo* held on anything like her present course, she was about to leave the open sea behind. They had now reached the fringe of what appeared to be a great continent, its coastline fragmented into a maze of islands and estuaries. Within the space of a hundred miles, the mouths of several sizable rivers emptied confusedly into the sea.

"We should be staying in the open ocean altogether," someone complained to the current steersman.

He snapped back at the questioner. "Don't talk nonsense!" And the flying scouts confirmed as much: "That way we're hopelessly blocked, by a score of ships almost as fast as we are. Maybe faster, if their crews aren't worn with rowing."

"Then how are we ever going to get home?"

"Look here." The steersman unrolled one of his several parchment charts, and thumped a knuckle on a spot. "We must be *here*—approximately. Of course we must eventually find our way back to the open sea. But to escape our pursuers, we must enter one of the mouths of this great river, then make our way upstream to a big freshwater lake . . . then out of that again by a different river, and so eventually back to the sea."

"Can we do that?"

"Easily enough—if there were no Colchian ships upstream from us. Which I fear is not the case. But we must do the best we can."

Making their way along the coast in a generally westerly direction, they were now passing through an area more heavily populated, and small boats frequently appeared at a distance, their occupants gawking at *Argo*, taking in the staring painted eyes that decorated her prow, and her many oars. No doubt a majority of these observers assumed that the Argonauts were pirates.

"Good thing we're not come here on that type of enterprise," Haraldur observed. "I don't see a lot of easy game." The small boats all seemed possessed of darting speed, as if the arms of their crews were energized by fear.

Above the *Argo*, as the steersman turned her into one of the great river's multiple mouths, and began to feel their way into the watery maze, towered rocky bluffs, crowned with an irregular line of trees.

The air was distinctly warmer now, and most of the cold weather had been left behind in Colchis. Mosquitoes began to be something of a problem.

After another mission, the flying scouts brought back a more detailed description of the pursuit. What they said left little room for optimism.

"Then it is as I feared, my brother leads them." And Medea's fingers almost convulsively knotted the fine scarf she had been wearing around her head when she fled the palace.

When Jason tried to be reassuring, it almost seemed that the princess could not hear him. "Some of my father's ships are very fast. And their captains are all terrified of him. They will not dare fail in their duty."

"Then the worst has happened," Jason groaned. With a sinking feeling, Proteus observed that the leader was slipping into one of his black, fatalistic moods. And it seemed true that the *Argo* had been cut off from escape.

———

Before long it was certain that the enemy knew where the Argonauts were. They had seen the *Argo* from a distance, and would be coming after her.

They passed channel after channel that the steersman refused to enter, because the compass-pyx gave him no hope that any of them could ever lead to freedom.

And there came a moment when he raised his head, and looked at his shipmates despairingly. "It is no use. There is no open way."

"Even if we go back the way we came?" asked Proteus.

"That would be the worst choice. That way leads only to an all-out battle against great odds."

The intrepid flying Argonauts took to the air again, but the only result was to confirm that the Colchians had the river blocked, both upstream and down, where it flowed amid a myriad of islands. The pursuers had now occupied most of these islands, with one notable exception.

"They have not occupied this island," observed Proteus, pointing to the nearest one.

"There's a big temple on it," the captain pointed out.

Not really very big, thought Proteus. But certainly a temple. Who but worshipers would build so elaborately on this scrap of land, where there were certain to be floods.

"But whose?" Anchaeus asked.

"Artemis, I'd say," said someone else. There was an image of the crescent moon atop its modest tower.

———

"Who among our crew is devoted to Diana?" Jason asked, evidently hoping to gain advantage from the goddess. It seemed to Proteus an unlikely source of aid, and that the captain was grasping at straws.

Men who heard his question looked around hopefully, but no hands went up. Adventurers as a rule had little connection with that great goddess, also known as Artemis. She was, among other things, the divine personification of the moon, eternally chaste and honorable, the patroness of childbirth and hunters, of fisherfolk and unmarried girls.

Jason looked out over the heads of his waiting crew, and raised his voice. "Who here can claim a friendship with any god? We stand in need of all the help that we can get."

Only silence answered him. That was the kind of claim that no one was eager to make—not when you came right down to it. The men were all weary, and they were all frightened, though their fear would have to grow a long way yet before it disabled these tough warriors.

Proteus suddenly recalled that Diana was also considered the twin sister of Apollo. And she had some close connection with Hecate, who in turn some said was Circe's mother. But the knowledge seemed of no current use at all.

"We are trapped, Jason. What are we to do?" asked another Argonaut, one who often gave advice, but now had none to give.

Now that the worst had happened, the captain seemed to be recovering his nerve. "If we cannot use the ship, we might as well get out of it and stretch our legs. I suppose we ought to go ashore."

———

Presently most of the crew had disembarked, stretching their legs and accomplishing what little exploring there was to do. Proteus was only slightly surprised when the Mouse seized the opportunity of being briefly alone with him; her meaningful glances had convinced him that she must have something to communicate in private, and a serious talk between the two of them was overdue.

They were walking for the moment in the shade, as much out of sight and hearing of all their shipmates as they would ever be able to get while on the island. Bushes more or less surrounded the couple, and someone might possibly be hiding in the bushes, but Proteus was certainly ready to take the risk.

After exchanging a few completely banal words with him, the young woman stopped in her tracks and said to him quietly: "Well, here I am."

Proteus stared at her. Somehow it had not sounded like a sexual invitation. The Mouse's hands were clasped in front of her, her shift still decently arranged if more than a little soiled by long days of being worn without a change. And there was nothing of the wanton in her pose.

When he remained silent, the young woman pursued him with a query: "I want you to tell me what our task is to be."

The request sounded simple enough. Except that he had no idea what the girl could be talking about. "Our task?"

She lifted her chin a little. "No need to dodge around with me. You are Proteus, and I was told to expect your coming on Jason's ship."

Another mysterious recognition—but this one was something more. He thought he could feel his jaw drop open. "Who could have told you I was on his ship?"

Restrained impatience showed in the girl's voice. "The same master we both serve in secret sent word to me. You pretend ignorance very well, but don't you see that now you are keeping up the pretense beyond all reason? That you are only making our job harder?"

He blinked at her. "And what is this job?"

She lifted her head with a look of brave defiance. Proteus realized with a slight shock that the Mouse was deeply afraid of him, just like the woman on the dock. No, not quite like that. Here he faced not only fear, but hatred.

But Medea's maid was not going to be conquered by her fear. "You are going to have to tell me. I will say it once more, I have been told to expect your arrival at the court of King Aeetes, as a member of Jason's company. A man of your name, your exact physical description." She paused. "So I would recognize you, even if I had not seen you before, in Iolcus." She paused, and now her loathing was more plain. "Even if I did not know *what* you are."

What am I? Who? He almost spoke the words aloud, but held back in fear of betraying his own ignorance.

Seeing his continued blank stare, the Mouse drew a breath and shook her head and tried again. "I am to obey your orders absolutely— whatever they may be." It had cost her a struggle to say that, but she had managed to put aside her dread, and smother her extreme revulsion.

"Ah." Proteus felt a sudden rush of anger. Not at the Mouse, but at the unfairness, the helplessness of his position. Half the people in the world seemed to know far more about him than he knew about himself.

Groping blindly for solid facts, and struck by what seemed a clever inspiration, he asked the girl: "I suppose this secret master is a god?"

"Don't be a fool." Now the maid was daring to be angry. "You'll have to talk sense to me sooner or later." But the Mouse did not turn and run away. She was not about to disappear, as had the others along the way who had dropped their enigmatic hints and vanished. His own anger was replaced by a tremendous inward excitement. Proteus found it almost difficult to breathe; he had the feeling that at last he stood on the brink of some huge revelation.

"How did this master, the one you say we serve, manage to send word to you?" That was the safest question he could think of at the moment.

The girl shrugged slightly. "Through one of a troupe of traveling players. They visit everywhere, talk with everyone."

"Ah, I see." That much at least was understandable.

The Mouse was silent while they walked on a few more paces. Then, with a sudden light breaking on her face, and in the tone of one who at last has caught a glimpse of sunlight through the clouds, she ventured: "Is it possible that he didn't tell *you* anything about *me*? Didn't even let you know that I'd be here, an agent in place to help you with your plan? By all the gods, that would have been a ghastly blunder on his part. But such things happen."

Craving solid information as he did, Proteus was ready to accept that "he" as certain proof that the secret master was not a woman. Which didn't help him much, because the only giver of orders to Old Proteus that he could remember had certainly been female. "You're right," he said. "He told me nothing about you."

"That explains your caution." His fellow agent—for so she seemed to be—was not going to let it go at that. "Then what *did* he tell you? Certainly he gave you some mission to accomplish when you reached Colchis? And I still think I must have been meant to play some part in it. Else why arrange to plant me here at all?"

The Mouse sighed, peering sideways at him in cautious puzzlement. "But I don't suppose he could have foreseen that Jason would manage to get the Fleece and the princess both on board, and would now be sailing free again."

"That would have been hard to predict," agreed Proteus. He strolled on in silence, furiously trying to think. Then he shook his head. "And I don't suppose we can count our current situation as sailing free."

"All right, all right." The maid's voice was vehement but she kept it quiet. Still afraid of him, yet still daring to be bold. "Don't tell me what the plan is yet. But I stand ready to follow your orders. I have no choice about that, as you well know." She paced for a few steps in silence, then added: "I only hope it doesn't involve anything that would hurt my lady. I've come to have a true regard for her."

"It doesn't involve anything like that," Proteus decided firmly.

"I'm glad of that at least. And glad to hear you admit that after all there is some plan, some thing we must accomplish."

Some of their shipmates were coming in sight, and their talk was broken off.

———

The temple island was roughly circular, not more than a hundred yards across. A hasty reconnaissance showed that they had the place entirely to themselves, except for a small handful of unarmed temple attendants.

A new arrival on the island needed only a minute or two to get a feel of its size. It was indeed so small that it was possible to stand near the middle of it and look out through trees and brush, to see the surrounding water on all sides.

The *Argo* was too big to hide, and within an hour of the Argonauts' going ashore, their Colchian pursuers had discovered where they were. Two warships took up symmetrical positions on opposite shores of the river, so they could keep every inch of the island's shoreline under observation. But so far Jason and his people were not molested.

One battle-scarred veteran said: "If I were the Colchian commander, I'd be setting fire to the good ship *Argo* right about now."

But another who looked equally experienced was shaking his head. "I wouldn't. Not if I thought I could sail her home as a prize. Ships as good as ours are rare."

Jason asked the princess whether Apsyrtus would be reluctant to attack them on an island dedicated to the goddess, and Medea brightened a little, agreeing that he probably would.

Now the captain and his royal passenger sat down together, borrowing an anteroom of the temple for the purpose, and tried to draw up a more complete map of their position, using charcoal on a plain board.

Proteus, invited by Jason to consult with them, watched the drawing grow. Here and here and here were the various islands, mostly overgrown with wild vegetation. Through all this twisted the courses of several rivers, or the branches of one river, if you preferred to think of them that way. Here, now firmly blocked by the enemy, was the way they had come into the maze. Way over *there*, seemingly out of reach, was the open sea they must eventually travel to get home.

Jason mused: "Your brother must feel very confident that we cannot get away—unless he lets us slip through his fingers. How long we will be safe on this island I do not know."

Medea answered: "Apsyrtus bears me no love—there will be no slipping through. But as there is a temple here, and he is a patient man, we probably will be safe from any violence—until we starve to death—or grow too weak to take up arms. Then he and his men will come and carry me away."

Proteus cleared his throat. "You say, my lady, that there will be no slipping through. But would it not be wise to establish some kind of contact with Apsyrtus? True, he may refuse to negotiate with us on any point at all. But we can't be sure of that until we try."

Medea looked sad, and quietly frightened. "I think there will be no trouble establishing contact. If I know my brother as well as I think I do, he won't simply order an attack. We will probably be getting a message from him, urging us to surrender, as soon as he knows exactly where we are. He is good at war, but he more enjoys diplomacy."

And sure enough within the hour, as if to confirm her prediction, a messenger from Apsyrtus came bravely alone in a small boat to ask for a parley.

Together Jason and Medea and Proteus went to talk to the man, who remained in his little rowboat some ten yards from the shore. He said: "My lady, your brother himself plans to come and speak with you."

Jason cleared his throat. "What escort does the prince plan to bring?"

The emissary shook his head. "No more than half a dozen men, sir, to row his boat. I will be one of them, and if you want us to stay in the boat, we will all—except the prince himself, of course."

What better meeting place than in the proposed sanctuary, one of the smaller chambers inside the temple of Artemis?

———

"Let us go," said the captain, "and make sure that those who are in charge of the temple have no objection."

When the door of the temple opened, Proteus saw the faces of a few young acolytes looking out, solemnly afraid. The priestess who came to meet the visitors was a quiet, frightened-looking woman who, when Jason courteously questioned her, quickly gave her permission for the meeting, and then withdrew to some inner, private room.

15

Murder

THE TEMPLE OF Diana, standing as near the exact center of the island as could be estimated, was an old structure, grown shabby through lack of maintenance. The lower walls were discolored on the outside, evidence of having been at least once inundated when the island flooded. Proteus thought that even when the structure was new, it could never have pleased the goddess much. It was plainly built of wood, and consisted of only a few rooms on the ground floor plus a kind of attic, with one main entrance and a couple of side doors. Here and there a panel, indoors or out, had been intricately carved in abstract designs, and stained in an attempt to add a touch of elegance. Proteus wondered if the building had originally been dedicated to some other deity altogether, or intended as something other than a temple.

No sooner had Jason agreed to a meeting, than Apsyrtus sent word to say he would be delayed—his sister interpreted this as an attempt to play on their nerves. A full day passed in this manner, with Argonaut sentries posted against surprise at several places around the shore. Meanwhile most of the men took the opportunity to catch up on their sleep, lying with weapons ready to their hands.

There was plenty of confirmation that the Argonauts were indeed effectively surrounded. A worn sandal and some fruit peelings drifting downstream testified to the careless presence of Colchians above. But sudden attack did not seem to be the real danger for the Argonauts, not when all Apsyrtus had to do was wait. It was easy to see that obtaining food for forty people was very rapidly going to become a problem.

Proteus was invited to listen in while Jason and Medea discussed the situation. By now, Jason had come to depend heavily on him for advice, and Medea was beginning to share the captain's view.

And the Mouse was present too—Medea maintained she had no secrets from her maid, and obviously relied on her as an adviser.

It was the Mouse who called their attention to the fact that a small boat was openly approaching, coming across the channel dividing the temple island from the next one over in the maze of waterways.

Taking a few steps to the shore, the princess looked out over the muddy current, shading her eyes with one hand. "Here comes my brother."

Silently a small group gathered to receive the visitor. Medea's brother seemed at ease, sitting in the stern of a small boat, and was dressed much as when Proteus first saw him in his palace. He was smiling faintly, and gave them a small wave as he approached. His curly hair and beard appeared to have been freshly trimmed and oiled, and his personal appearance revealed no traces of a hard voyage.

Even before disembarking, Apsyrtus complimented Jason on his seamanship, and the speed of his ship. "Your men are blessed with strong arms, and I envy you your swift vessel. Would it be impertinent to ask how you came by it?"

Jason was curt. "I have friends, and some of them are wealthy. There are many who see the justice of my cause."

"I see. Admirable. And what does your ship's name mean, by the way—*Argo*?"

"I have heard different answers to that question," said Jason distantly.

"Of course the superiority of your vessel and your crew will avail you very little, will it?—if your opponents are ahead of you as well as behind, and they have you outnumbered by about ten to one."

The captain said nothing. Apsyrtus looked directly at his sister and then away again. Evidently he had nothing in particular to say to her at all.

Jason was in no mood to prolong the verbal fencing. He asked: "On what terms will you allow us to go on?"

"May I not come ashore, where at least there is some shade?" Medea's brother showed his hands, open and well-manicured. "You can see that I'm unarmed."

"Yes, come." Jason gestured, and Proteus and the other Argonauts moved back.

The boat eased close to the riverbank, and Apsyrtus stepped to the muddy bank—the six men, apparently unarmed, who had rowed him remaining impassively in the boat—and when his sister offered him a formal greeting, responded coolly in a few essential words.

Proteus got the impression that the prince was ready to be tolerant of these amateurish adventurers who had foolishly tried to defy the power of Colchis. He was even faintly amused by their behavior.

Now with a word and a gesture he drew Jason aside, casually, deliberately leaving Medea out of their conversation. "I would have a word with this gentleman alone, dear sister." But the prince seemed willing to accept the presence of a bodyguard, and made no objection when Proteus silently walked along. Meanwhile Medea did not protest, or appear surprised. She waited, arms at her sides, chin lifted, a picture of royal poise despite the deterioration in her dress.

When the three men had gone a little way, Jason said: "If you come to parley, you must have some terms to offer us."

"Oh, I do." The Colchian prince had kept his gentle smile. "Nothing very harsh. To begin with, I am perfectly willing for you to keep the Golden Fleece. No, I mean it, really." With an amused attitude Apsyrtus raised a hand in a forestalling gesture. "The offer is genuine and I have no trickery up my sleeve. Believe me, I've no need for that."

Jason was silent, looking at him. Apsyrtus, taking note of the captain's expression, said in his aristocratic rasp: "Let me say again, Jason, that I plot no treachery. Really, keep the Fleece!" His long arm, pale and perfumed but still corded with wiry muscle, made an elegant gesture of pushing something from him. "If you want to know my true feelings on the subject, I consider the damned thing useless, nothing but a chronic cause of trouble. It's been hanging on a tree in that forest for as long as I can remember, and it seems impossible to realize any wealth from it, or derive any practical benefit. And once it's gone, we'll have no need of a fish-tailed Giant always lounging around, practically in our capital. The one that you disposed proved not much of a guardian in any case, and I suppose we should actually thank you for driving him away, however you accomplished it."

Jason, now looking downcast, murmured something.

"I understand your caution about taking me at my word," Apsyrtus went on, "but I've been considering the matter for years, and that is my conclusion. No, the Fleece is yours." Again he made an elegant small pushing motion, this time with both hands. "You honorably fulfilled the terms of your wager with the king."

"I did not consider it a wager."

"Whatever you want to call it, you succeeded, tamed the Bulls. I won't ask how, or who may have provided you with help."

Nor were Jason or Proteus about to volunteer any information on those subjects. The three men walked on.

"And Medea?" Jason asked after a few paces.

The elegant Colchian shook his head. "Oh, well, on that point I'm afraid we have nothing to negotiate. My father will settle for no less than having his daughter back. I assure you, my own head would not be safe if I went home without her.

"In the matter of his two grandsons, the king has announced formally that he wants to bring them to trial to answer for their crimes—he considers it a crime to have guided you to Colchis." Apsyrtus raised a hand, forestalling objection. "But between you and me, he doesn't really care about them. I say that Phrontis and Argeus can go on with you, and good riddance."

"She does not want to go home," Jason said, casting a glance back at the distant figure of Medea. Proteus looked too, and saw that her face was turned in their direction.

But the prince did not reply to that, or even look back at his sister. He seemed to be waiting for Jason to make a more meaningful response.

It took the captain of the Argonauts a while to find the exact words he wanted to use next. "I suppose King Aeetes intends to punish her."

"Well . . . my father *is* an angry man," Apsyrtus agreed, judiciously. "In fact, I don't believe I have ever seen him as angry as he is now. Probably you've heard the story that's recently been going around about that other king? The one who's said to have poked out the eyes of his sluttish daughter with long bronze pins? You mustn't think anything of the kind will happen to Medea. No, I very much doubt that any punishment my father has in mind would go as far as death or mutilation. If he did have some such idea, I'd certainly talk him out of it. My sister"—he nodded in her direction, without looking—"is after all a valuable asset to the crown. Eminently marriageable. Even after an—episode like this. Some new version of events will be developed. It will turn out that she's had a chaperone with her all the while she's been away from home."

"As a matter of fact she has. Her maid, the one called Mouse."

"Ah, there, you see? That will help."

With Proteus moving silently on their heels, the prince and the captain walked on, debating a little more around the fringes of the situation. Such matters as whether Aeetes had any additional complaints, what living conditions had been like for the princess aboard the *Argo*. But Apsyrtus was now taking it as settled that Medea would have to come home with him.

At length a silence fell. Proteus, nervously shifting his grip on his spear, had been waiting for some clever counterargument from Jason. Persuading people to do things for him was what Jason's life was all about. But now Proteus could tell by his leader's face that there was nothing of the kind in prospect. Proteus thought to himself: *I can't believe it. He's simply going to cave in. Unless he is planning some deception. Jason has the wit for that, if he would use it. He gave her all that talk of faithfulness and marriage. But the truth is he really cares for nothing and no one but his own ambition.*

Apsyrtus was evidently reaching the same conclusion. Confident now that he had won, Medea's brother remarked how unseemly it was for a young unmarried girl of royal blood to be living, day after day and night after night among a group of men, whether chaperoned or not.

Now the details of the surrender were being discussed, with some attempt at a face-saving arrangement for Jason. The Temple of Diana was conveniently at hand, and could be put to a good use.

The captain tentatively agreed that Medea and her maid would be put in charge of the temple priestess for a few days; and in that time the temple authorities would hear the case and judge whether she was to be sent back to her father or not.

Again an elegant gesture from Apsyrtus. "I am sure they will come to the right conclusion. Then, you see, there will be no point in our having a battle. You can take home the Fleece, as proof of having honorably succeeded in your mission. And I can go home too." By now the prince had evidently realized that Proteus was present as something more than a mere bodyguard, and was talking to him almost as much as to Jason.

Apsyrtus seemed to have no doubt at all as to how that judgment would come out. Proteus had to bite his tongue to keep from shouting protests and bitter accusations. It was only with a great effort that he kept quiet, and wooden-faced. He would only be placing himself and his shipmates in greater danger if he let an enemy see violent disagreement in the camp of the Argonauts.

When the meeting was over, Apsyrtus calmly climbed back into his small boat, which had been more or less keeping up with the men as they walked along the shore, and was briskly rowed away, in the direction of one of the large warships across the channel.

After waving a farewell, Proteus and his captain started back to rejoin the other Argonauts near the ship. Jason for once did not ask his opinion, and Proteus did not offer it. Instead, a taut silence grew between them.

But when they returned to camp, Medea was waiting for them and demanded to know what had been decided. Her voice was loud enough for most of the men to hear, and a small crowd of interested Argonauts began to form.

Jason would have been glad to avoid the confrontation, but he saw no possibility of doing so. "I will get to keep the Fleece," he began, and paused.

"I see. What else?"

The captain glanced momentarily at Proteus, but could see no help in that direction. He sighed. "You are to go back to your father."

For the first time since they had met, Medea was glaring angrily at the man to whom she had been fastened by Cupid's Arrow. It took her a while to get out any words at all. "I don't believe it. You must be lying."

Around them, the men had now formed a solid circle of still, listening faces. The maid seemed about to weep.

What had once been Medea's attitude of supplication was gone, had turned into something else entirely. Jason's soul was quailing before that gaze.

"My—my lady, I only wish it were not true." It was the first time that Proteus had heard him stammer.

The princess boiled with rage. She swore with fishwife oaths to set the ship on fire, to break it up and hurl herself into the flames. Clenching her fists, she screamed out her appeal to the sky. "Gods, give me power! Great Loki, give me fire to burn! Among all these spineless Heroes, is there not one with manhood enough to stand by me?"

Jason was obviously frightened, but he forced himself to regain some measure of calm. "Enough, my lady. I am no happier about this business than you are. But we are seeking to stave off a fight, encircled as we are by a vast horde of enemies, and all on your account."

"On my account? On *my* account?" Her beauty had been transformed, by an anger so great that it must push all else aside, so that Proteus marveled. Now she was her father's daughter. Now Proteus, glancing back over his shoulder at the poor little wooden temple, half-hidden among trees, thought he knew what the chaste and terrible Artemis must look like when she was calling some human to account for some offense.

At the moment, the Mouse was doing her best to make herself invisible.

But Jason, who had faced the angry king with patient argument, was not about to be unnerved by a mere princess. He was speaking with relentless calm. ". . . and if we faced them in the field, we should every one of us be slaughtered. Would it not mortify you even more if we were killed and left you to them as a prize?"

Proteus could see that prospect gave the lady pause, despite her rage.

Jason pressed on, looking at her hopefully. "I said that your brother and I came to an agreement, and we did. But what he and I have said to each other is not necessarily the final word in this matter. Any agreement can be repudiated, if there is good cause."

"This one *must* be."

Maybe, thought Proteus, *this man is somewhat deeper and trickier than I have thought.*

The captain was nodding. "As you say. But this truce of a day, before you are to be given into the charge of the temple priestess, will give us a little time to plan. My lady, you know your brother well. Can you think of any kind of stratagem . . . ?"

Medea stood looking at Jason for a time. She looked at Proteus. Eventually she said: "We have started down a road that will allow no turning back. Therefore we must go on. The decision to come with you was mine, to begin with—though I could have done nothing else. So now it must be up to me to find the remedy."

She raised the gaze of her blue eyes, until she was staring into the distance. "I will trick Apsyrtus into coming back to the island once more, to talk with me alone . . ." Now her gaze suddenly fastened on Jason. "Then, if you have the manhood to do it, kill him. That will throw their whole fleet into chaos."

Proteus felt a chill on hearing those words fall so calmly from such soft and pretty lips—but after observing the lady at close range for several days, he was not as utterly surprised as he would have been before the Fleece was taken.

But he thought that Jason was truly startled, and could almost read the captain's mind. The captain must have thought he was beginning to understand this woman, but saw now that she was still really almost a total stranger.

What a pair we have here, thought Proteus to himself, studying them; what a pair indeed. Either they will do great things together, or they will meet some truly spectacular end.

The Mouse was hovering at the side of her mistress. From time to time the maid cast a quick look at Proteus as if to see whether this plan met with his approval.

Ignoring everyone but Jason, who still had not responded, Medea repeated icily: "Kill him, I say. Do you fear I will blame you later for my brother's death? Never! As you have seen, he is ready to kill me."

Jason remained cautious. "He didn't say that. He said—"

"Bah, do you believe him? And as soon as the men aboard my

father's ships learn that he is dead, we must make our break for freedom, fighting our way through if necessary. I know the officers, and they will be uncertain then. At that moment they will break and yield, if you attack them fiercely enough."

A moment later, as if in silent agreement, Jason and Medea both turned toward him.

"Proteus, what do you think?" Jason asked him abruptly, while Medea slowly nodded. Meanwhile in the background the little maid seemed also waiting anxiously for his response.

Proteus cleared his throat. "I think, my lady, that, in the first place, if you are indeed turned over to the priestess in the temple of Artemis, we will not see you again, but your father will. Otherwise your brother would not have liked the arrangement so well."

The reluctant adviser paused before adding: "As to the plan you've just put forward, it is a treacherous business, and I can't say that I like it much. But at the same time I can think of nothing better. This has now become a war, and in war treachery has its place. We're less than forty men, one ship against a fleet. We'll not survive an open battle."

And even as he spoke, Proteus was wondering in the back of his mind how the goddess Artemis, the archetype of chastity and honor, would react to such murder and betrayal as the princess was proposing to perpetrate on her sacred island. But gods and goddesses tended to be remote and unpredictable—Proteus trusted his own instinctive judgment that it was so—and any deity was much less of an immediate threat than a determined prince who enjoyed a great military advantage.

Jason put the same conclusion in different words. "My princess, I would rather face an angry goddess than see you go to what may well await you at home."

Medea's look softened with relief when she heard this, and her color heightened. "Colchis is my home no longer." She seemed reassured by Jason's attitude, though Proteus, who had known him longer, thought the captain remained uncertain.

In a calmer voice Medea said to Jason: "I know something of my brother, and I know my father's officers, those who must be leading the forces that he commands here."

Jason was still uncertain. "I have seen unhappy omens."

"We cannot live by omens."

"And what good will it do us to kill one man, whoever he is? We'll still be bottled up by the king's fleet."

"I do not think so," said Medea in the new voice that had been hers since the great anger came upon her.

Now Jason looked at her with a new appreciation. It was not hard to imagine his thoughts: what a great queen the young woman before him would make, beautiful, intelligent, and ruthless.

But still he was seeking some way out of the Colchian trap, short of murdering her brother. The great persuader tried another tack. "What if we did not kill Apsyrtus, but took him alive and held him hostage?"

And the princess, though much shorter than the man who faced her, seemed again to be looking down at him. She said implacably: "And when and where would you set him free? Would King Pelias, in your homeland, thank you for bringing home the kidnapped son of King Aeetes? I think not. Taking him alive will only guarantee a relentless pursuit."

Jason tried another abortive argument or two, but in the end he had to agree that Medea must be right. "What do you think, Proteus?" he asked again, and got the nod of assent that he did not really want to see, or Proteus to give.

"Then the only remaining question," Proteus said, "is where and how are we to do it?"

Once the main decision had been reached, the details seemed to arrange themselves. An ambush was to be set inside the Temple of Artemis, at a time when all attendants would be out of the way.

Medea willingly undertook the task of explaining her plan to a larger group of Argonauts. She was certain that, once her brother was dead, the Colchian forces would retire in disorder. "Not a man of them will dare to bring that news back to the king. So it is when men are ruled by terror alone."

And the Argonauts marveled at her silently, but none objected.

"Who shall we send to Apsyrtus with the proposal?" And again their two heads turned together to look at Proteus.

Proteus was reluctant, but when Jason and Medea both pressed it on him, he at last agreed.

At first, he more than half expected the clever son of King Aeetes to see through such treachery, and refuse to come to any further meeting—but then he reflected that Medea must know her brother pretty well.

———

And the Mouse found another chance for a brief private talk. Giving Proteus a penetrating stare, she demanded: "It's Jason you are really after, isn't it?"

He shook his head. "Remember, if I wanted Jason dead, I've already had a hundred chances to do the job, before we ever got to Colchis. For that I'd have no need of fancy plans."

She seemed caught in an agony of wonder and indecision. "Then have you really turned your back on Pelias?"

"Judge me by what you see me do. Trust your own eyes and sense, if you won't trust what I say."

The Mouse chewed on her lower lip. "I can't stop you. I wouldn't want to, for I fear being dragged back with my mistress. But it must never be known in Iolcus that I have turned on Pelias. Such fearful things would happen—"

But at that moment they were interrupted, and he had only time to give the Mouse a nod and wink that he hoped were reassuring.

Later, in a more open talk, the Mouse told him she was ready to work hard for the success of any plan that kept her and her mistress from being dragged back to Colchis. "There'll be no brass pins there for my lady's eyeballs, and she knows it, whatever she might say. She just doesn't want to go back.

"But my own poor little body is another matter, and it might have to bear the burden of the king's anger. I'll be held to blame for not keeping my mistress at home in the first place."

The image of Aeetes taking out his wrath on the Mouse was entirely convincing, and it bothered Proteus more than he would have expected. "I wouldn't want to see anything like that happen to you."

She brightened slightly, but only for a moment.

And later, when they were alone again: "Do you know what, Proteus?"

"No, but I'm sure you're going to tell me."

"I have a strong suspicion that it's too late now."

"Too late for what?"

She made swift uncertain gestures. "I mean that something's happened to make it impossible for us to do whatever it was King Pelias sent you to do. Is that it? And you're afraid you'll have to tell Pelias of our failure? So is he going to take his anger out on both of us?" The Mouse was still quiet, living up to her nickname, but it was obvious that the prospect left her deeply terrified.

"No, that's not it," Proteus said on impulse. Suddenly he felt an urgent need to relieve her terror. "That's not it at all. We'll never have to see King Pelias again if we don't want to."

For a moment the Mouse stared at him helplessly. But once again other people were coming near, and once again she mastered her fright.

The story Medea conveyed to her brother, using her faithful maidservant as a messenger, was that Jason and his gang had kidnapped her, dragged her with them quite against her will. She was ready to return home with her brother, and even to help him steal the Fleece back from these marauders.

When the Mouse returned from delivering the message, she said she thought that Apsyrtus had no suspicion of what was being planned for him.

Proteus crouched waiting in the dark, amid trees and bushes near the temple entrance, watching the path which Apsyrtus would almost certainly travel when he came to the appointed meeting. Insects were loud in the nearby undergrowth, and now and then there sounded a whispered oath and slap. Half a dozen chosen Argonauts were waiting close beside Proteus. When Jason and Medea sprang their trap in the temple, these men outside would prevent interference by any escort that the prince might have brought with him. Meanwhile the rest of the Heroic crew were also alert and ready, keeping out of sight at a slightly greater distance.

The handful of men with Proteus had little to say, to him or to each other. He had the feeling that they were looking at him more than usual, in a way that made him feel uneasy.

At last he spoke up: "If any of you think this treachery dishonorable, well, I can only say that you must have little experience of war. Anyway, it is we ourselves, our whole crew, who are being unjustly held as hostages, surrounded as we are. We are free men, and I say we have a right to kill. To regain our freedom."

No one answered that. They were still looking at him grimly, their faces hardly changing; and he realized suddenly that he was probably arguing more with himself than with any of them.

Night fell, and the time set for the secret rendezvous drew near.

Medea's brother (who with an amused attitude had kept reassuring Jason that no treachery was planned) came just as arranged to meet with Medea. He had left his small escort outside the temple at a little distance, and he was personally unarmed as he entered the small room where she was waiting.

Now in Medea's eyes her brother looked different than he had when in council with their father, more as she remembered him from the good days of her childhood. He spoke to her warmly and kindly, recalling pleasant things that had happened when she was only a little girl.

His voice was mild. "You don't need to be terrified, little one, about going home. I promise that I will prevent our father's doing anything really horrible to you. You believe me when I say that, don't you? Don't you?"

The princess in turn looked at Apsyrtus wooden-faced, and told him that the simple fact of being forced to return home, of being separated forever from Jason, who now meant everything to her, would be quite horrible enough. As bad as having her eyes poked out with long bronze pins.

Apsyrtus seemed genuinely concerned. "Surely this ambitious stranger cannot mean that much to you."

"I tell you he means my life."

The prince was puzzled. "You first laid eyes on this Jason only a few days ago. And surely you can see he is too weak in some ways ever to be a worthy king—a man like him will come to no good end." Then the elder brother lowered his voice a little. "Tell me, Medea—are you still a virgin? Has he formally proposed marriage?"

"I love him—in a way that you are never going to understand!" And she gave the arranged signal. And saw in her brother's face that he had suddenly realized what was about to happen to him.

———

Jason leaped out of the closet, where he had been waiting in ambush, and ran at the Colchian prince with his sword raised.

Seeing his danger mirrored in his sister's face, Apsyrtus turned at the last moment, and his right hand went to his waist in search of the sword-hilt that was not there. But in any case the move would have been much too late. Jason's first thrust was true and deadly; Apsyrtus died with eyes and mouth agape in vast surprise, all elegance dissolved in blood. He fell clutching at old dusty draperies, a kind of tapestry depicting Diana on the hunt, and pulling the fabric down with him to the floor.

After striking the man down, Jason fell to his hands and knees, and went through a hasty ritual of thrice licking up blood, from the stones of the temple floor, and spitting it out.

It seemed that this particular superstition was a new one to Medea, and she recoiled from it. "Have you gone mad?" she demanded. Her voice was a mere rasp of breath. "What are you doing?" "Keeping a ghost at bay. I hope." And awkwardly he scrambled to his feet. "You who know so much of magic, have you never heard of that?"

Meanwhile, just outside the temple, the six men who had come as escort with the prince were alerted by a scream from within. They drew their weapons, but before they could move to interfere, Proteus and his chosen companions jumped out of concealment and blocked their way.

Proteus raised his voice in a commanding shout. "Your prince is dead, and there is nothing you can do about it."

And just as he finished speaking, Medea emerged from the temple bearing a lighted torch. Right behind her came Jason, carrying the head of Apsyrtus by its long, curly hair. He held up the gory weight so the Colchians could be sure that there was no mistake.

By now, the remaining Argonauts had come pouring out of their slightly more distant places of concealment, and the half dozen Colchians were fenced in on three sides by an overwhelming force of thirty men. Only the path leading back to their boat was open to them.

"Your boat is waiting," Haraldur told them harshly.

There was a stunned and angry silence. In accordance with Jason's orders, no blow had yet been struck outside the temple. The more of these Colchian fighting men who remained alive during the next few minutes the better, the more voices there would be to spread the word to their fleet that the prince was dead.

In another moment, the supporters of the murdered prince had turned and were jogging in retreat back along the path. The boat that had brought them to the island was anchored a little way off shore, with only one man in it; and while he waited with oars poised, wondering what had happened, the prince's surviving escort stood on shore screaming the terrible news out across the water to all the waiting Colchian ships. Their voices were hoarse and unsteady but very loud.

When the yelling had gone on for almost a full minute, Haraldur turned to Proteus. "Enough?" he asked.

"Enough." Proteus gestured, and the thirty Argonauts who had been waiting rushed on the six and slaughtered four of them—the other two quickly discarded their weapons, and managed to swim away in darkness. Meanwhile the one man in the boat had also opted for strategic retreat.

Having trotted back to the temple to report success, Proteus looked in to see the headless body of Apsyrtus on the floor, and Jason on his hands and knees beside it, licking up spots of the plentifully spilled blood, while Medea stood by icily controlled.

"By all the devils, man, what are you doing?" But even as Proteus voiced his shock, some dim recess of his memory produced a kind of explanation: a superstition claiming that by this means the ghost of a murderer's victim could be prevented from haunting him.

———

With Medea and the Mouse running as fast as any of the men, the entire body of Argonauts hastened to get aboard the *Argo*. In a few moments some thirty sturdy oarsmen were putting their whole backs into the oars, forcing them rapidly downstream.

Proteus had never seen Jason so shaken. It was almost as if the captain had never killed a man before; and Proteus knew that was not the case.

"I do not like the taste of blood," he muttered, wiping his smeared mouth on his sleeve, and hastily gulped down first a draught of water, then one of wine. Then he shuddered and looked around him, like a man in fear of immediate pursuit.

A few hours later, Jason also made such sacrifices as he could to Artemis, with the limited resources available on the ship. He said that such omens as he was able to detect were all unfavorable.

"One would think," Medea pondered, "that Diana might be angry with us too. Can anyone think of some way to placate her?"

"It is quite possible," offered Proteus, "that she didn't even notice." But those who heard him only looked at him strangely, and went on making their own suggestions. Each man and woman aboard had a firm personal conviction of what gods and goddesses must be like, though none of them had ever seen one.

———

Then they were all in the ship, and shoving off. Jason with vehement gestures silently urged the men to speed, and to quiet at the same time. The helmsman had turned *Argo*'s prow downstream, and they were making the greatest possible speed in that direction, in an effort to break through the ring of their pursuers while confusion reigned aboard the Colchian ships, and reach the open sea.

Never had the ship's more than thirty oars sounded so loud to Proteus as they did now. Once there drifted over the water, from somewhere in the darkness to their right, a sound of confused and muffled shouting, as if the crew of one or more Colchian ships might be reacting to the news of their leader's death. At any moment it seemed that one of the ships that had been standing watch might loom out of the darkness and cut off the fugitives' escape, but so far the darkness just ahead remained empty of their enemies.

Jason, seemingly well recovered from his horror, directed the steersman to hold in his mind the image of any peaceful, welcoming shore or island that might be available. Ideally this haven would be neither uncomfortably near, so pursuers would not stumble on it, nor more than a few days away. In earlier phases of their flight from Colchis they had often yearned for such a goal, but the compass-pyx had consistently refused to show them anything of the kind.

"But now I see it!" There was sudden elation in the navigator's voice, even while the man's face remained glued to his instrument. "Captain, a vision of the very place we want!"

The words sent a murmur of relief up and down the rowers' benches, creaking with the shifting weight of large, hard-working men.

"I will hold that thought too," Jason muttered. "How far have we to go?"

All the indications were that such an island was only about three days away, though no one could remember such a place being in this region, or what its name must be.

Proteus asked permission to take a look through the compass-pyx. When his forehead rested on the ivory box, there grew behind his closed eyelids a vision of an island, a beautiful place that seemed to him hauntingly familiar, though he could not recall its name. The vision was so clear, the island looked so large, that he thought it could be no more than a few days away.

———

When daylight came, there was no sign of any pursuit. It seemed that Medea's assessment had been correct, regarding what must follow on her brother's death.

The latest entry in the log said nothing of Prince Apsyrtus, certainly nothing of the manner of his death. It said little more than that the *Argo* had taken advantage of thick fog to slip past her blockaders.

And in fact as soon as the ship reached the open sea, a thick fog did indeed close in. Everyone aboard was willing to accept it as a sign that their luck had turned. The image of the welcoming island, only a few days distant, held firm in the mind of anyone who bent over the compass-pyx.

16

Isle of Dawn

THINKING BACK AS he rowed in darkness and silence, and observing the moon, which was just past full, Proteus reckoned that four full months had now elapsed since he had linked his fate to that of Jason and the Argonauts. A very short time, compared to the length of most human lives, but it was all he had in the way of remembered life. Before that stretched the void, shrouded in almost impenetrable fog, thirty years or so that were almost as much a mystery to him as if they still lay in his future.

When it came his turn to rest, and he fell asleep, there came to him strange dreams, in which he was aware of holding some kind of immensely powerful weapon, without being able to see it clearly, or knowing what it was.

Dawn found the *Argo* long since free of the maze of waterways. For hours they had been clean out of sight of land, headed for somewhere near the middle of the Great Sea. Patches of thick mist drifted over the ocean's surface, a most welcome sight to people who feared pursuit.

Through most of the morning, the hard-pressed crew kept up a weary struggle to make headway in a choppy sea. They were urged on by the steersman's latest report that now their goal, that still-nameless happy island where they would be able to rest in safety, could be no more than a day's effort distant.

Jason stared at him. "It was only a few hours ago when you said it would take us three days to reach the place."

The navigator was apologetic. "I cannot always read the instrument with perfect accuracy, captain. Now I am sure it will be much less."

"Let us hope that you are right this time." Then Jason wanted to know: "What is the name of this place we're headed for, and why did it not appear on any of our charts?" He sounded skeptical. "I still don't understand."

The navigator shook his head. "There is much in my craft that I have never understood. But there is no need, if we can obtain results. Just thank the gods, and the powers of the compass-pyx."

———

Dawn on that morning was no more than a troubled transition from dark to pearly gray, that brought little increase in visibility. Shortly afterward a low curtain of sea-mist parted, revealing near at hand their destination, an island of indeterminate size, lush with tropical growth.

Jason sounded numb. "First you said three days. Then an hour ago, you said one day. And now . . ."

"I am sorry, captain. I was wrong again. This is the place. I am absolutely certain."

The waning moon, no smaller now than when they had fled the temple island, was fading swiftly in new daylight, as it sank wearily toward a western horizon that was free of any trace of land.

Proteus was staring at the beach and ranks of vegetation now before them. "I have been here before," he murmured to himself.

Beside him, the Mouse shivered. "I do not think I like this place," the maid said suddenly, and wrapped her bare arms around herself, as if the warm air drifting over the warm sea had suddenly turned cold.

Medea, sounding as if she were suddenly in shock, murmured something about having visited this island once in a vision.

Haraldur had no time for visions now. "There's an easy beach, and a small stream to refill our casks. It seems to have everything we need. But . . ."

Proteus was suddenly, inwardly, completely certain of one thing. He got to his feet. In a clear voice he announced: "This is Circe's Island of Dawn."

Men around him groaned. "Then we are lost," one rower muttered, fatalistically.

But not everyone was ready to give in to imagined dangers, and others growled at the despairing one. Still, the men's reaction, as they leaned on their oars, coming into calmer water, was generally subdued. Frightening legends abounded about this place, the worst of them telling of men turned into animals, at the cruel whim of the enchantress. And many of the stories hinted that even greater horrors could happen here. "... things too terrible to talk about," someone was muttering.

Proteus almost laughed at that. He knew he had been here before and had survived. "Really? That's not the way people like to tell ghost stories, in my experience. Usually the most gruesome details are spelled out with loving care."

But the island waited invitingly before them, green and soft and welcoming. There was nothing in the least gruesome or alarming about the prospect.

How far was the Island of Dawn from Iolcus? Almost everyone aboard had a different opinion on that—Triton thought it was just about as far as Circe wanted it to be.

Something about the place—he couldn't tell if it was the sound of the gentle surf, or the aroma of spices on the offshore breeze—kept jogging Proteus's memory. Something very important to him had once happened here—but what? Vital clues to his real identity seemed to be bobbing like bubbles in the foam of the gentle surf, just out of his reach. Now he was absolutely certain that he had been to this place before.

The whole place looked entirely innocent, a spot of garden rimmed by surf and coral.

There were certain moments when he almost believed that the waves nibbling at the sand were speaking words, in a long-drawn-out splashy voice—words in a language he had once known, but had not yet remembered.

And more strongly than ever he felt a persistent sense of some stupendous revelation, hovering near—or was it only that he had had his head stuck into the compass-pyx too long? They said you put yourself in serious danger if you ever fell asleep with your forehead resting on the ivory box.

When he mentioned this to the Mouse, he got the answer: "If that's the worst danger we've got to worry about right now, we're in better shape than I think we are."

Another man complained: "What I don't understand is how the compass-pyx could be so easily deceived."

"There may be no deception," Proteus told him. "This may be a good place for our refitting."

In truth he suddenly had little interest in what his shipmates might be doing. The Island of Dawn was before him now, its sands beneath his feet as real and solid as any part of the earth that he had ever trodden. And the more he looked at it, the more he experienced maddening hints of familiarity.

Jason was urging Zetes and Calais to put on their flying sandals, and go scouting to see what might lie in the island's interior. The two brothers eagerly agreed. They promised to come back soon, and briskly took to the air.

Jason, shading his eyes, kept watch on them for a full minute, while they climbed on and on. "They look like sea birds," he finally remarked in a distant voice.

Those Heroes who were generally considered to have the keenest eyes kept up the watch when Jason and others had to abandon it.

"I've lost them." The Argonaut to give up the search seemed puzzled, shading his eyes and squinting. "There's only a couple of albatross."

———

While waiting for his scouts to return, Jason chose a spot to beach the ship. There was no problem finding an inviting place. They faced a long, broad, concave rim of white sand, curving along one side of a peaceful, half-wooded spot of land rising out of a warm sea. This was a much bigger island than the one they would all have been happy to forget, the little lump of dirt enclosed by a rough circle of freshwater shoreline, where the acolytes of outraged Artemis must still be hard at work trying to scrub away the bloodstains from the floor of the profaned temple. At least most of the Argonauts were assuming that Diana must be outraged—as far as Proteus knew, none of them had actually heard from her as yet. But the course their voyage had taken since the death of Apsyrtus seemed to show that some great power had taken an interest in them, bringing them here at an unnatural speed.

Circe's power was known to be formidable, Proteus thought to himself, but was it truly as wonderful as this? Had she some special hold upon the ship?

The condition of the *Argo* seemed to have deteriorated badly, over just the past few hours, and it needed work, on the central hull and both outriggers. Also they were running low on water, though naturally they had refilled all the jugs and skins before leaving the river.

And he had nowhere else to go. When he tried the compass-pyx again, it would show nothing but stark gloomy clouds, drifting over the open sea.

Proteus was driven by a mounting urge to explore the island on foot.

"Any chance we could just fill up our water jugs and skins and be on our way again?" one Argonaut was pleading.

"She is a goddess, no?" It was Haraldur who asked the question. His home was distant, and many of the gods and legends of this warm sea were still unfamiliar to him. "The one who turned men into beasts, in the stories. And this bit of land was hers?"

"It still is. And some of the stories do say that she's a goddess, but she's really not. Some call her a witch; I'd say enchantress." There were technical differences between those two.

"She hasn't come to welcome us," another man observed.

Proteus said nothing.

"You know her, then?"

Disbelieving looks were turned on Proteus, by men who had been forced to respect him by what they had seen him do. Yet the same feats made them jealous, and he knew they would be ready to mock at any false pretensions he might have, secretly rejoice at any failure.

He responded calmly. "She's only a woman, right? Is there any reason I couldn't have met her?"

His questioner considered. "One reason is, you've not been changed into an animal. I hear that one of her favorite tricks is to transform men into pigs."

The other was shocked. "Only a woman! Whoo! Might as well say that King Aeetes is only a man!"

He turned away from them, to scan the island again. "I do say that. As for Circe, she is . . . what she is."

Jason had made up his mind and uttered a terse order. They bent to their oars again, driving the ship firmly to the beach. And Proteus's shipmates, who had grown to know and trust him, were silent, looking at him strangely. But anything else any of them might have said was forgotten by the others in the subtle weirdness of the island as they drew nearer to it, and nearer still.

———

As soon as *Argo* ground her bottom on the beach, the men clambered out of the long ship, as usual groaning with relief to get their bottoms off the hard benches. Then, moving quickly in a practiced deployment, they ranged along both sides of their vessel to tug her up a little more securely on the land.

Even before the ship had been dragged entirely out of the sea, Medea was standing on the sand, her maid beside her. Both women were still wearing the same impractical garments, now torn and shabby, in which they had fled their homeland. Or some of them. Medea's soft mantle had long ago been lost, and the Mouse's felt slippers had dis-integrated.

The beach where the *Argo* now rested made part of the island's southern rim, bathed in life-sustaining sunlight. Here the surface rocks and white sand were pleasantly warmed. The sea shells on the strand were pretty . . . though Proteus had to admit to himself that there was something wrong with the shapes of some of them.

To the right of the new arrivals as they faced inland, there gurgled a pretty little creek, pouring fresh water into the sea. Ordinary seabirds flew up squawking, but as far as Proteus could see, the place was de-serted of intelligent life. Yet he had the sense that certain immaterial powers that served as guardians and keepers here were hovering close by.

Several members of the crew tasted the water of the small stream and one of them pronounced it clear and clean.

"But is it safe to drink?" another asked.

"If the lady of this island wants to poison you," Proteus assured them, "she can do it through the air you breathe, or the sunlight falling on your skin. So you may as well drink deep of her water, if you are thirsty."

A couple of men were already beginning to fill the casks and jugs, so they would be ready in case of a hasty departure.

Even before the *Argo* had been made secure—as secure as any ship could ever be made on this beach—Proteus, driven by a rapidly growing sense of familiarity with this island, turned his back on the others, and set his feet on a small path leading inland, through exotic vegetation. Before he had gone twenty yards, the growth around him was tall and dense enough to hide the sea behind him. It seemed to him that he almost knew—ought to know—where he was going. He felt a growing certainty that here he could find the answers he had been seeking for the past four months.

As he turned his back on the others, he could hear a querulous murmur of voices behind him, but no one asked him where he was headed. Just treading the white sand of this beach made people begin to behave strangely. For a start, it turned some of them uncertain in their thoughts and actions.

Not Proteus, though. He felt suddenly more certain of what he ought to be doing. Already he had become aware of whispering, giggling sprites and spirits, a small mob of half-material onlookers who remained somehow just out of sight. Or almost. He could get an occasional glimpse of one of them, from the corner of his left eye.

He had not gone far before he could hear the scuffling of several

pairs of feet following him swiftly on the narrow path, and he knew
without turning who was coming after him. If he listened he thought he
could pick out the faintly squeaking sandals of Medea and Jason, and
the patter of the maid's bare feet. Presently Jason and Medea were
practically at his elbows, the servant girl keeping close behind them.

"More and more," said Proteus, as if continuing a conversation already begun, "the conviction grows on me that I have been here before."

"When?" the princess demanded. And then, before he had a chance
to answer: "Have you met my aunt? This may indeed be her island, for
all I know, but I have never seen her."

Proteus ignored her questions. "It seems to me there is a . . . house.
Yes, a house built of cut stones, and it stands in toward the center of
the island, where the land is thickly wooded." At least he remembered
it that way. "There were palm trees . . ." And there had been other trees,
as well as certain growths that Proteus would not have known how to
attempt to describe.

Jason deftly caught a branch that Proteus had pushed aside, before
it could swing back and slap him in the face. The branch had leaves,
or buds, that when seen at close range bore a startling resemblance to
human hands and feet. The captain put in: "So, you've definitely been
here before? Can you be sure of that?"

"Almost sure. Could there be two islands like this in the whole
ocean? But still . . . no, I can't remember."

When Proteus tried to pin down in his mind the circumstances of
his previous visit, the only really clear image that came was that of a
young woman, sitting in the stone house. He tried to describe it to his
companions. "The woman was dark, and beautiful . . . and she sang as
she worked at her loom."

"A weaver?" Medea asked. "Some artisan or servant?"

"No. But working as great ladies sometimes do, for their own en-
joyment." He looked at Medea.

"They say my Aunt Circe is dark and beautiful. But I have never
seen her. What was she weaving?" Medea sounded truly interested.

"A thin—web of some kind." The material, as Proteus remembered
it, had looked incredibly soft and delicate. "Shot through with spectacular colors . . . you would think that no one but a goddess could have
created such a fabric."

Jason was looking at him strangely. "How did you come to be here,
Proteus? That other time?"

He was saved from trying to answer by the fact that the thin path
opened abruptly into a sizable clearing. They had come in sight of the
house, a low structure of irregular form; and it was truly strange enough

to be worthy of its mistress. The stones of which it was constructed might have climbed up out of the earth of their own accord, and formed themselves into a shape that was certainly not natural, but not like that of any other building that any of the visitors had ever seen. No sound came from the house, no smoke rose from its odd chimneys. Several low, broad, shutterless windows and doorless doorways stood open— there was no apparent way any of them could be closed. But as soon as Proteus approached the nearest entrance meaning to look in, all of the seemingly unguarded apertures quivered, like so many reflections in water, and disappeared, leaving only the inhospitable stone wall to foil his curiosity.

Involuntarily Proteus retreated a couple of steps.

"The place looks deserted," Jason commented.

"Almost," amended Proteus. And the visitors were treated to a peal of tinkling laughter, nearby but proceeding from some invisible source that none of the hearers could identify.

Putting one hand in a pocket of his tunic, he felt the "Tooth" he had stuffed in there before Jason underwent the trial of the Bulls. Proteus had believed when he pocketed the Tooth that he had known someone who would be very glad to have a thing like this—someone, but *who*?

Probably not Circe.

Something moved, gathered itself into an odd visual patterning at one corner of the house. Proteus supposed that there might well be some real creature in that position, just beyond the corner, gripping the stone corner of the building with some of its overgenerous complement of ill-assorted limbs. Could human fingers sprout from a bear's paw, or a crab's claw at the end of a pale and girlish wrist?

. . . or all these appearances could be nothing but strange illusion . . . and might not the whole island be little more than that?

Proteus had turned, skirting the edge of the clearing, and was soon heading briskly away from it along another path. Now he knew, he remembered before he saw, which way this particular path was going to curve next. His companions were keeping up with him.

"Where are we going now?" Jason for the time being had become very much a follower. Medea and the maid diligently kept pace, as if they might be afraid of being left behind.

But Proteus was gaining confidence. Instead of disturbing him, each new marvel presented by the island somehow made him feel more se-cure. "I think I know where we can find her. All this . . . is somehow very familiar to me."

On leaving the clearing that held the house, Proteus had thought that he was still headed toward the very center of the island, but once he got in among the trees things became momentarily confusing. Then all the elements of his mental map seemed to straighten out, fall into place again in a new configuration. His feet kept carrying him along the path, and before he knew it, another part of the beach was right ahead of him. And over there in the distance, though not in the direction where it ought to be, he could see the *Argo* run aground like a toy ship on those distant sands, and a clustering of Argonauts around her, some of them no doubt trying to get started with their repairs. Jason should have stayed back there with them, he thought.

But he spared no more than a brief glance for ship and Argonauts. Some ten or twelve paces directly ahead of him, a nude young woman stood waist deep in the warm water, bending gracefully to bathe her long, dark hair in the soft foam of the gentle waves. Unalarmed, she straightened at his approach, tossing her head to throw back her wet hair, and fixed him with a look that slowed his steps on the firm sand.

And a moment later, a look of blank astonishment had come over her face.

In a regal voice the lady in the water suddenly demanded: "Who in all the Tombs of Tartarus are you? And what are you doing here?"

17

Circe

SEEN AT ANOTHER time, and in another person, Circe's abrupt change from complete self-possession to amazement might have been comical. But Proteus felt no impulse to laugh. In Colchis, Bebrycos, and Samothraki, all lands entirely strange to him, he had been recognized—and here, where he had been certain he must be known, he was a complete stranger to the lady who knew so much.

He said to her: "My name is Proteus."

"Is it, indeed? Well, that means nothing to me." She tossed wet hair away from her face, and stared at him as if to see him better.

He said: "As to why I am here, I had hoped, my lady Circe, that you might be able to tell me that."

The enchantress was still puzzled. But not completely, not any longer. On some level understanding was beginning to creep in.

Now Circe was thinking hard, but had not yet quite found the explanation that she needed. "Proteus, is it? Am I supposed to know you, sailor? Your face is as unfamiliar as it is ugly. But you take a damned familiar attitude."

Proteus had no answer for that. While he waited for her to speak again, his gaze ran boldly over her unclad body—shapely, lovely almost beyond imagining. But some greater urgency hung in the air, formless but as effective as a threat of death, keeping his mind from dwelling on carnal matters.

Proteus did not turn to look behind him, but he knew his three companions must still be hovering there warily, in the shade at the edge of the forest. He had no doubt that Circe was fully aware of their presence, but she paid them no attention. For some reason she was still puzzling over her visitor, and at last she said to him: "I had better call you Bringer of Bad Dreams. That is who you are, today."

"Why 'bad dreams,' lady?"

Ignoring the question, she stepped up onto the dry beach, past a thin wrack of drying seaweed, and picked up a single garment that lay there, swirling it about her in a burst of fragile color. A moment later she stood garbed in something like a rainbow . . . a cloud of fine fabric, woven of all colors and of none.

Then suddenly she rounded on him again. "Now I begin to suspect what has happened. I see a possibility, at least . . . but if that is true, what else have I misjudged?"

Proteus waited silently.

In another moment Circe was nodding to herself. "It must be so. And if your friends hiding back there in the trees are the people I have been assuming they must be—the situation grows very interesting. Though not at all amusing."

"They are the Princess Medea of Colchis, and Jason the adventurer. And—"

"Yes, as I expected. You need not explain *them*. But you had better explain yourself, if you can."

"My self is one subject about which I know very little. I may as well admit to you, lady, that I have suffered a great loss of memory. But," he persisted, "why did you call me Bringer of Bad Dreams?"

"Loss of memory, is it? Yes, that fits." And again the lady studied him. The silence between them went on until he began to feel seriously frightened. When she proceeded it was with an air of caution, and on what seemed another subject. "Only a few hours ago I was terrified by a nightmare. I think it must have been sent me by the Prince Asterion of Corycus—have you ever met him? No? You will, one day—and he was trying to prepare me for your arrival here today." The lady paused. "I do mean to have some revenge on the prince, for sending me such a nightmare. I think I will dispatch him in return something that will not amuse him, to join him in his Labyrinth."

And there came another flash of returning memory. It was a startling image, come and gone like a reflection in the shattered surface of a pool. At some time in the past he, Proteus, must have been in the presence of Prince Asterion, and not in any dream, either. Clearly he could recall looking at what legend called the Minotaur, a seven-foot figure with the head of a bull on the body of a powerful man, dwelling in the Corycan Labyrinth.

Circe was speaking to him again. "Do you wish to know about my nightmare, you who now call yourself Proteus?"

"That is my name. Who were you expecting, if not me?"

The lady ignored the question. "It seemed to me as I slept that I saw all the rooms and walls of my house streaming with blood, and flames consuming all my implements of magic . . ." Circe's voice of silvery beauty faded, and for a moment she seemed lost in inward contemplation.

"And how did you deal with this nightmare, lady?"

"Successfully, as I deal with most things. The red flames I quenched with the blood of a murdered man."

"Of which you just happened to have a fresh supply on hand?"

"You are a bold little sailor, are you not?—and so in time the hideous vision passed. When morning came I arose from my bed, and as you see, I have been washing my hair and my body in the sea."

"If you are trying to terrify me, my lady Circe—"

She raised an imperious eyebrow. "Why on earth should I waste my time doing that?"

"—then I would say you are having—no more than a moderate success."

That drew a laugh from the enchantress. Standing in a bold pose, her hands on hips, she said: "Nor do I seem to be doing all that well in my actual endeavors. But enough of my difficulties." She was looking steadily at Proteus. "I suppose it is useless to ask what you have to report to me?"

"Report," he echoed stupidly. And suddenly, without warning, he almost knew, almost reached the beginning of understanding. It was like trying to recall an elusive dream, that kept slipping away even as you sought to grasp it. There was a frantic turmoil inside his head. Slowly he raised both hands, clasping his skull with the feeling it might be about to burst. Memories were clamoring more stridently than ever, trying to come through.

But the great explosion that must come sometime was not yet. He said: "There are matters I know I should report to someone. I feel certain that I have seen your face before, my lady Circe—"

"Oh, have you indeed? But the problem is that I have not seen yours. You are not the man I was expecting."

"—but what I see in you may be only a certain resemblance to the king of Colchis, who is said to be your brother. He of course looks very much older than you. But . . ."

Circe ignored the king of Colchis. "And do you know how and why this calamity befell you, this loss of memory? Were you attacked by a Giant, by any chance?"

"I was—but by what magic do you know that?"

"No magic is necessary, only a little thought. Tell me whatever details you can remember."

That did not take long. As Proteus finished the relation, he looked up, startled at the soft sound of approaching footsteps. For a moment he had forgotten that he had not come here alone.

Evidently Jason and Medea had gradually taken courage from the sight of what seemed a peaceful conversation, and had been emboldened to come forward out of the jungle, with the maid behind them timidly following her mistress.

But Proteus was not going to put up with an interruption, not just now. He faced back to Circe. "Who am I?" The question grated out in tones of desperation.

She squinted at him with what looked like sheer contempt, and the tone of her voice matched her expression. "You know full well who you are. Though it seems that for some reason you have been trying to deny it, even to yourself. Ah, what tricks the mind can play! Even a ruined one like yours."

As the three newcomers halted uncertainly a few steps away, Circe spoke decisively. "Come with me, all four of you. Come to my house." Then she threw a glance over her shoulder at the distant ship and the busy men around it. "Do you suppose your shipmates can manage to keep themselves out of trouble while we talk?—but never mind, I will send them something to keep them amused."

Then all four of Circe's visitors followed her as she walked briskly back to the center of the island. Once again the stone house displayed its full complement of windows and doors.

With a gesture she silently invited them to enter.

The interior was a cheerful place, with a small fire crackling brightly on a small hearth. A casual visitor might well have thought that some happy, industrious young woman, whose main concern in life was weaving, lived here alone. It took a closer inspection to discover the disturbing notes, like the peculiarities in the tiling of the floor.

But at the moment the sorceress looked anything but happy. Her great dark eyes were fixed upon Medea. When the enchantress spoke, there was true grief in her voice, and at one point it almost broke.

"You should realize that I had plans for my nephew Apsyrtus. He was to have done great things in the world, one day. But now you have murdered him—actually slaughtered your own brother—and I cannot forgive you for that. Now you are here, and I shall decide how you are to answer for your crime."

The girl gave a strangled little cry, covered her eyes, and collapsed in a heap upon the strangely patterned tiling of the floor, from which

Proteus had to tear his gaze away before it hypnotized him. If Medea's action was a ploy to gain sympathy, her aunt was no more affected by it than were the floor tiles. Jason moved to Medea's side and knelt by her, touching her hair awkwardly. Then he stood up again and confronted the enchantress.

"That will do no good, my girl." Circe, with a graceful swirl of her fine clothing, seated herself in an elaborately carved chair. "But, I must not forget my own responsibilities. While you are here, you are all my guests. Be seated."

Suddenly stools were conveniently on hand, for all but the maid, who sat on the floor, tucking her feet beneath her. In the background Proteus was able to detect a half-seen scurrying of inhuman servants, almost imperceptible to human senses. Covered dishes holding delicious food appeared suddenly on tables, as if from nowhere.

For no reason that Proteus could see, the maid had put her hands over her eyes, and groped her way to a corner of the room, where she cowered down in silent fear. Proteus suddenly felt sorry for the Mouse, and moved to her side and touched her gently. She seized his hand in both of hers and held on tight, meanwhile keeping her eyes tightly shut. Her mouth was twisted into an unhappy line. Proteus understood that Circe must have given her something to look at that no one else could see—that no one would want to see.

Again Proteus could feel flashes of memory coming and going. Someone, long ago in what seemed another lifetime, had once said to him: "Circe is not always kind . . ." Had the speaker actually been Prince Asterion?

Memory suddenly produced ghastly pictures, of fiendish tortures, men turned into animals, as in the stories. And the anonymous voice went on: "But she is Apollo's friend . . . also other gods have been here, upon this island, coming and going over a long, long time."

Meanwhile the enchantress had given herself over to a long contemplation of her trembling niece who was now seated on a stool, and looked, if anything, unhappier than her maid. Jason had seated himself beside her, and she clutched his hand.

When Circe spoke again her voice was chill.

"And so you, my brother's daughter, have not only murdered your own brother, but have been voyaging, practically unattended, halfway across the world with a boatload of strange foreign men." Somehow it did not seem incongruous that she made the two offenses sound approximately equal.

Now Medea raised her head and sat up straight. Her fear was momentarily overcome by anger, and hotly she proclaimed that she was still a virgin. And anyway, she had not been traveling unattended.

Her aunt acknowledged those points with a nod. "Then perhaps your crimes are not as bad as they might be," she admitted grudgingly. "But let me hear from your own lips the story of what happened to your brother in Diana's temple."

Sitting at ease in her own strange chair, the enchantress listened to Medea's version of her brother's death, interspersed with the girl's anguished pleas for forgiveness. The story was not too different from the way that Proteus remembered the events.

Then Circe abruptly interrupted. "And this one?" Her pointing finger indicated Proteus. "What part had he in this crime?"

"My part was one of loyalty," Proteus answered for himself. "To those I had engaged to serve."

The enchantress snorted her contempt.

He went on. "Call it a crime if you like, but it was no more criminal than any other stratagem of war. We were surrounded, unable to get away, defending ourselves against attack."

Circe looked at him as if she were disgusted beyond words. Proteus stared boldly back.

Jason spoke up at last. "What Proteus says is true. And had the princess gone back to her father the king, as he demanded, he would probably have killed her!"

"Would that not have been a just punishment for her crimes?" The enchantress shook her head. "But I really doubt that even Aeetes would have been so headstrong. Marriageable princesses are much too valuable in the games of empire."

"What else could we have done?" Jason argued weakly.

The enchantress stared at the captain of the Argonauts for a little, then looked away again, as if she considered him not worth even a comment. "I would see you all punished," she said at last. "But I begin to suspect that it is all out of my hands anyway. I see now that the great gods were foolish to depend on you to obtain the Golden Fleece for them."

Circe raised one slim hand toward Jason, and pointed two fingers at him, and his head nodded abruptly. In a moment he was fast asleep, though still sitting more or less upright on his stool. In the space of a few more heartbeats, Circe had done the same to Medea and the Mouse.

Now the enchantress and Proteus were effectively alone together. She arose from her chair and went to stand directly in front of him, while he let go of the Mouse's hand, and stood up straight, as if to be ready for anything. Circe looked directly into his eyes, for what seemed to him a long time. He was surprised at himself, at his own ability to stare back so boldly at this woman of whom most of the world would be utterly terrified. And indeed he was—no, not terrified, but wary, of what she might be planning to do next.

It was Circe who broke off the confrontation at last, took a few graceful steps around her room, and then turned to face her visitor again, this time from a slightly greater distance.

Her voice was regally amused. "I have said that *you* know who you are, and now I too have made sure of your identity. It was easy enough to discover, once I looked into your eyes. I saw more than a simple sailor looking back."

Now that the answer seemed almost in his grasp, he was afraid to reach for it. "How did you bring us here?" he asked. "You have some connection to the *Argo*, don't you? Some means of control, built into the very ship herself."

Her dark eyes smiled at him. "And where do you think the money came from, to build and outfit your Hero-captain's gallant ship?"

"Ah," said Proteus.

Circe smiled. "There were intermediaries, of course, who did their job quite cleverly. Jason has not the least suspicion, that I am—or was—his real sponsor against King Pelias."

"I see."

"Now let me ask you again, you who now wear the body of the common sailor and blackguard Proteus—which Giant was it you encountered, just before you found your way aboard the *Argo*?"

And with a little help from Circe, the scene of that disastrous shipwreck and his succeeding struggle in the water, came back to Proteus.

The memory, when it finally came, was vivid and luminous as a drug-vision, and left him sweating and swaying slightly on his feet.

Circe's voice broke through, recalling Proteus to the here and now. "I never learned that Giant's name," he said.

She seemed faintly disappointed. "Never mind, then, it matters little. But now do you begin to understand? About yourself?"

"I am a god." The words came out in a low voice, deep and confident. Even in his own ears it did not sound much like the voice of Proteus.

"Indeed you are! And which god are you? Such little details do make quite a difference, you know. Does your recovered memory extend that far?"

"I am Triton, one of the gods of the sea."

"Of course you are."

"And I killed that Giant, the one who wrecked the ship, after he came near to killing me." Now he could remember the frothing waves, all black with the monster's blood.

"And I am glad we have begun to clear that up."

And Triton, who for the last few months had been as one with the human Proteus, raised his head and looked at the woman before him with new authority. In his changed voice he said: "I begin to remember other things. A few more. You and I had an agreement."

"Better and better!" Circe clapped her hands, and in response shrilling little voices cried out in all the corners of the room. "Of course we did. That was when you were in your previous avatar—the human body in which you walked around before acquiring this one—you do still understand how the business works? Ah, good. Terrible things the Giants' weapon can do to a god's memory! But in your case it might have been worse, for certainly there is still a good deal of Triton left. Probably more of your memory will come back in time." She sounded as if that were a mere detail.

She was still looking at him, but her voice changed. "And Proteus, worthy sailor, how do you do? I suppose I must accept you as a colleague now." The enchantress paused, studying him again. "Hah, but perhaps even as a mere human you were more than a worthy sailor! Or should I say you were less?"

Now she raised a slender hand, bejeweled with several rings, and slapped him stingingly on both cheeks, back and forth. Again she looked into his eyes. Jason and Medea still slumbered on their chairs, and the Mouse lay curled up on the floor.

"Proteus the sailor, whoever you are, or were—probably some poor fool of a wandering tramp—do you understand now that you have the glorious good fortune to wear the Face of Triton inside your head? To enjoy his powers, to blend his memories—such of them as that befuddled divinity has left—with your own?"

Proteus/Triton was nodding slowly, in agreement. Circe nodded with him as she went on, as if musing to herself: "I can see now how it must have happened. Your avatar with whom I had made alliance was killed at sea, when a Giant attacked the boat that was carrying Jason's would-be servants. And you, lucky Proteus, whether sailor or servant, you were quick enough to save your life by grabbing up the Face of Triton when it came popping out of the dead man's head. That, you may recall, is what Faces always do when their wearers' lives are quenched.

"The Giant must have seen that the god he meant to destroy was about to take up his abode in a different body. For he blasted you again, blasted the new body, with that strange infernal weapon Giants have, against which not even the greatest deity can stand. That wiped away still more of Triton's memory, and most of the human memory that had just become attached to it.

"But, lucky for both of you, dear Triton and dear Proteus, the residue of powers remaining were great enough to somehow enable you to escape with your life."

"I tell you, I killed that Giant," said Triton's voice, coming again from the throat of Proteus. The man knew that the god dwelt in the god-Face now resting inside his head, and that for the rest of his life Triton must share his identity. Human and god, on terms of greater intimacy than could ever exist between two merely human beings.

Triton/Proteus looked down at his empty hands, and his voice grew puzzled. "Somehow at that point I still had my Trident with me, and I struck him down. Though where it could be now . . ."

He let that worry drop, for there were even more demanding problems to be faced. Now that he knew who he was, the answers to certain puzzles became terribly clear.

There was one important thing about him that Circe did not know. Old Proteus had been no mere wandering sailor, but the secret agent of King Pelias. Probably a trained and skilled assassin, under orders to kill Jason, or at least to prevent his taking the throne of Iolcus.

But at the same time, whether Old Proteus had ever suspected it or not, Triton in his previous avatar had been working on the other side, secretly allied with Circe and probably with the great gods too, somehow bound and sworn to help Jason get the Fleece—but then to take the treasure from him, and deliver it to the great gods to fit some purpose of their own.

Complications within complications. It was enough to make a man's head ache, or even a god's head, and it did. He was no longer a secret agent. No, nothing as simple as that. In fact he was now two of them, working for opposite sides, each of whom seemed to have good reason to kill the other.

It was even possible that Old Proteus had somehow signaled or guided the Giant who wrecked the ship to the spot in the ocean where he might ambush and kill the god. But that was not to be.

Instead, Fate had seen to it that what was left of the human assassin Proteus had been coupled for life with what was left of his divine intended victim. Then the sole survivor, the product of their union, a hybrid as innocent—well, almost—as a baby, had come wading out of the sea, his only surviving purpose to join the Argonauts.

It was all a monstrous jest, so magnificently horrible that Triton/Proteus began to chuckle to himself. Proteus/Triton thought that there was no way anyone else on earth could fully understand his situation. Not even the powerful enchantress, who saw only half of it.

"What are you laughing at?" Circe demanded.

"Nothing. Everything. The world." And his roaring laugh burst out again. The man who was now also a god, the god who could never be anything if he possessed no human body, clutched at his throbbing head and groaned amid his laughter, so did the laughter shake him.

Now he could understand about the Boy. The god Cupid, somehow recognizing his divine colleague Triton and indifferent to what avatar Triton might currently be wearing, had passed on the orders of the great gods, who wanted some man called Proteus dead.

Looking at the Mouse, who still lay on the floor, Proteus could now begin to understand her attitude toward him. Being originally from Iolcus, she must have seen him there, and now she saw in him nothing but the evil tool he had once been. What exactly might Old Proteus have done, to make her hate and fear him so?

The enchantress refused to be amused. "If it is nothing, I would advise you to stop this hysteria. We have practical matters to deal with."

Slowly he got his feelings under control. Even the wishes of the great gods would have to wait for a little while. The practical matter first in Circe's thoughts at the moment was her own anger with her niece, and with Jason as well, for somehow getting the girl involved in all this.

Of course Triton had been involved too. But being openly angry with a deity was a little different, even for Circe. Even though she snapped at Proteus: "Do not think you will be spared, just because you are a god!"

That brought his fading laughter to a conclusion. "Are those the friendliest words that you can find to say to me?"

Circe appeared to reconsider. "Let us not quarrel, Triton. The god of the Trident and the waves is welcome to my home, as always."

"My gratitude for your hospitality."

"Any favor I may do my Lord Triton will be reciprocated, I am sure." Certainly there was as much mockery in her tone as in his.

"I shall do what I can for you, in turn," Triton said, more seriously, and paused. After a moment he added: "I have wondered sometimes why you never seek divinity for yourself. You must know, sometime, when Faces become available. I have heard from other gods that Circe has turned down more than one opportunity along that line."

"I am content with what I have." Circe's smile was serene and private. "As I am sure the Lord of the Sea must know, the fire of divinity is a consuming one, when it catches in a merely human mind and body."

"I doubt that that is always so." Triton was not much interested, it seemed, in pursuing the subject further—and Proteus was afraid to do so.

"Perhaps, my Lord Triton, I remember some of your earlier avatars much more clearly than you do." And Circe smiled in a way that was as old as sensuality. And Proteus, old memories suddenly prodded into life, experienced a brief odd vision of seeing what seemed to be himself in a handsome but totally unfamiliar body.

"One additional word of warning, my friend," the dark-haired woman said, after the silence between them had stretched on for a little while.

"Yes?"

"It is for the man called Proteus, and not the Lord Triton, and it is only this: that the human body when serving as the avatar of any god will eventually wear through and collapse; there is a limit to how long the power of any god can sustain it . . . the immortality of the gods is only a cruel hoax where human beings are concerned."

"And I have a question for you, friend Circe. What of these people?" And he made a sweeping gesture that included Jason, Medea, and the Mouse.

Circe's anger now seemed mostly spent. "When they have given me the Fleece, they can go on with their voyage, and I will leave it up to the great gods to decide on what punishment they may deserve . . . do you go with the *Argo*, Triton?"

"I do. I find that I am still an Argonaut."

Now his hostess rose gracefully from her chair, in what seemed to be an indication that she was ready for her visitor to take his leave. The Mouse rose from the floor, and, moving with the air of a relaxed sleepwalker, found herself a chair.

One of Circe's thin dark eyebrows rose. "One final bit of advice."

"Yes?"

"I strongly recommend that on departing from the Isle of Dawn the Lord Triton should cease to tie his fate to that of Jason the adventurer."

"And why is that?"

"Because Jason will never be king anywhere." With her eyes closed, Circe added: "It is irritating to find a god in a new avatar every time I look around. I prefer some measure of stability. Not to mention intelligence. In the old stories the gods are forever disguising themselves as humans, ordinary mortals, and prowling around the earth in search of adventure. But in a sense such a disguise is no disguise at all."

The walls of the stone house were thick, but Proteus/Triton had a god's keen hearing. Outside the gulls had fallen silent, but in the pines some wild birds that few human eyes had ever seen were screaming frantically at one another, caught up in some conflict that had nothing to do with either gods or humans.

Something had distracted him, but Circe was still speaking. "It is not out of kindness that the mighty god who shares your body refrains from seizing total control of the flesh and bone. Kindness has nothing to do with it. The real reason you retain your freedom is that Triton, who is granted life and being by your body, has no real life at all without a human partner. And as long as you are his avatar, he can do nothing that the man Proteus does not want to do."

"If you know so much about it, woman, answer me this: Where did the *powers that are captured in the Faces* come from, in the first place? Who created them?"

"I think it is a pointless question. As well ask where we humans came from, and who created us." Then Circe looked at Medea, and added: "Bad things will happen to that girl, whether she is allowed to make good her escape from her father or not. I might forgive her— though I do not—but that would not be the end of the matter. I have said that her case must now be left in the hands of the great gods."

Triton suddenly put in: "Circe, more of my memory's coming back."

"Oh?"

"Yes. I now recall something of what our agreement, yours and mine, must actually have been about."

"So now you are going to tell me what you think it was."

"Yes I am. You told me that our side, the side of the great gods who fight the Giants, must have the Fleece, that it would somehow be of enormous value to them in the war. 'Our allies in their secret work- shops' is how you put it, now that I recall.

"You and I agreed that I should disguise my divinity and join the Argonauts. My avatar before this one was, like this one, a sailor— among other things. Our hope, yours and mine, was that the Giant who watched over the Fleece might not be on his guard if I approached him as only one of a group of common sailors. If he thought me no more than human, I could take him by surprise, get near enough to kill him before he realized the truth, then snatch away the prize."

"Very good, Master Triton." Now Circe's attitude seemed that of a schoolmistress grilling a difficult but promising student. "And what else do you remember?"

Slowly he shook his head. "Only that it seems to me I could have done as much without your help. What was I, Triton, supposed to get in return when I brought you back the Fleece?"

"That may come back to you someday. Let me know if it does." There seemed a hint of the demonic in her smile.

"There is one other point. If Zeus and Apollo want the Fleece, why should they not simply have gone to Colchis and taken it? Who could oppose them?" But even as he asked the question, the answer was there in his recovering memory.

"Oh. Giants, of course." Zeus and Apollo had feared to go to the grove in Colchis, because they knew it was guarded by a Giant who lay in ambush, ready to destroy their memories as soon as they came in sight.

Circe was saying: "Even the great gods have their weaknesses, and sometimes they even behave like idiots. But I am on their side in this; I have no wish to see the whole world ruled by Giants."

And she snapped her fingers sharply, once, and the walls of the stone house disappeared from around them, and the five people were all now sitting in chairs at the inner edge of a broad beach, with gentle surf a hundred feet away. In the distance Proteus could see the drawn-up *Argo*, and most of her crew busying themselves around her.

Once more Circe snapped her fingers, and the heads of three mortals rose from dreaming slumber, and their eyes came open. And Circe held out an imperious hand to Jason.

"Now bring me the Fleece!"

18

Waves

JASON STOOD UP from the chair in which he had been sleeping, drawing his clenched fists close in front of his body, as if the Fleece were in them. But he was wearing only a loincloth and sandals at the moment, and obviously the treasure was somewhere else. If he was astonished by the disappearance of the house, his face did not betray the fact.

When he spoke, his voice held raw defiance.

"That treasure is mine, my lady Circe. I will not surrender it, even to you. The crown that was stolen from my family must be restored—"

The lady put on the manner of a nursemaid, dealing with a noisy child. "Cease your babbling and bring me the Golden Fleece at once. Unless you want to lose much more than a mere chance at a crown." And she flicked the fingers of one hand in a gesture of dismissal.

Even as the enchantress spoke, Medea stood up from her chair too. Now the princess looked as if she might even be able to defy her aunt. She had heard the threat and was afraid for Jason, and seemed determined to drag him away from Circe before he met some truly terrible fate.

Meanwhile the princess was pleading for the man she loved. "Forgive him, Aunt Circe! He doesn't know what he's talking about. If you really must have the Fleece, I'm sure that something can be worked out . . ."

Circe only glared at her niece imperiously. Then, as if struck by a sudden suspicion, Circe lunged forward and seized her by her dress, the upper part of which she pulled violently aside. Circe stared intently at the skin between the firm young breasts, then spun the girl around, as if she were weightless, and inspected the corresponding location on her back.

Then she turned to once more confront Proteus/Triton. "Suppose you tell me, little sailor, did you see anything of Eros in the course of your journey? Perhaps when you were at Aeetes's court?"

Proteus/Triton saw no reason to aid the enchantress in her discoveries. He tried to sound obtuse. "The god Eros?"

The voice of Circe crackled. "Do you know of any mortal human going by that name? I certainly do not."

"No. But I don't see what connection you think Cupid might have . . . wait, though. There was a Boy. Somewhat odd-looking."

"Tell me about him."

"He was carrying a bow and arrow—so small that they looked like mere toys. I thought them ritual objects."

Meanwhile, Jason had seemed about to protest Circe's rough handling of Medea. But then he only bowed lightly to Circe and walked away in the direction of his ship, both fists still clenched. Medea walked by his side, tugging at him as if to get him away from Circe as rapidly as possible, and the maid, who had wakened with the others, went with her mistress. Circe paid them no attention.

No, thought Proteus, he's not going to give it up that easily. He'll try something desperate first. Proteus/Triton was uncertain exactly where the treasure was now stowed aboard the ship—he knew that Jason tended to move it nervously from one place of concealment to another. He supposed that Medea had done what she could to give its current hiding place some magical protection, but it was hardly possible that the princess would be able to hide anything from her aunt.

The enchantress still concentrated on the visiting god. "And where did you happen to observe this peculiar lad?"

"In Colchis, not far outside the walls of the capital. He walked past me while I was standing guard. Jason and Medea were having their first private meeting. The Boy was wearing an odd kind of cloak, or robe, bunched up around his shoulders—"

"Hiding his wings." Circe nodded briskly.

"By all the gods!" Triton/Proteus feigned surprise. Let the old witch go on thinking he was more befuddled than he really was.

"By some of the gods, at least," Circe corrected, carefully studying the deity before her. "I am sure that in this case Eros had his orders from above."

"But why would he want to hide his wings?"

"In case some human did catch sight of him, despite his wish to remain invisible."

Triton shook the head of his human avatar, as if in a futile attempt to call up ancient memories. "I took the Boy for one of Medea's attendants. I thought they were planning some ceremony, or religious rite, and that he must have some role to play. In passing he gave me a wink—as if he thought we shared some secret."

"Fool!"

The voice of Triton changed. "A dangerous name to call any god to his face, old woman. Are you applying it to Eros, or to me?"

"Both of you were idiots, and probably still are! But Cupid at least followed orders. He was told to hit Medea with an Arrow, and he evidently did."

"Are you in the habit of giving orders to gods?"

"Not to important ones. But I happen to know that they were given to the Boy, by Athena herself, or maybe Aphrodite."

There was a pause. Both natures of the dual being before her were impressed by those names. "But I ought to have recognized him," Proteus said at last. He gestured awkwardly at his own head. "The god Triton should have sensed the presence of another deity."

"Perhaps not, if the god Triton had been stunned by a Giant, and was only half awake, as even now he seems to be."

"I told you, enchantress. I have forgotten almost everything."

"So I see."

Triton looked down at the human body that had become his latest habitation. He flexed the capable fingers, appraising the play of muscles in the strong forearms. Of course what a god could do did not essentially depend upon the natural strength of his avatar, but youth and health and strength in the human body were all to the good. Triton thought he might have done much worse than this fellow Proteus—of course in the long run it would probably make little difference. The presence of a god-Face usually worked a considerable transformation in any human form it came to inhabit.

Triton was angry at Circe now, feeling, knowing instinctively that she was somehow responsible for the awkward and dangerous situation in which he found himself. His divine nature had been put at risk of complete destruction. It was common knowledge that no power in the world could destroy a god-Face; but totally wiping out a god's memory would be effectively to murder him.

And it undoubtedly was the god, not the sailor, who now spoke. "Woman, I can't imagine how you talked me into this, playing games with Giants. That's one of the very many things I find myself unable to remember. But there must have been some dirty trickery involved!"

Circe's haughty demeanor did not change. "If you cannot remember,

Triton dear, you do not know. And if you do not know what you are talking about, it would be wiser to keep your mouth shut."

"Tell me what kind of game you have been playing!"

"Would you believe me if I told you all the details? Why waste time?" And she turned to look at Medea's receding back, while the three ordinary humans continued their retreat. "Great Zeus, what complications! I never foresaw this. Now the girl is madly in love, of course, which I never expected to see in any niece of mine."

Triton/Proteus drew a deep breath. "But I think our effort to help Jason has been effective, so far. The great gods should be pleased with you and me."

"That may be."

"We helped him to survive the Bronze Bulls, and got the Fleece into his hands." Proteus paused, then added in the tones of argument: "If I am a god, I should be able to demonstrate some godlike powers."

"No doubt you can, at least when challenged by an emergency. Have you tried anything of the kind?"

"No, not really." But even as he spoke, Proteus recalled the improved progress of the ship when he was rowing, his tireless muscles, his easy swim through freezing water under icebergs, his consistent success at catching fish. There had been plenty of evidence, but something in him had refused to see it.

Circe ignored the comment. "When I have the Fleece in hand, I may be able to do something to help you regain your memory—but I would of course expect a consideration in return."

"I know who I am now, woman." He hesitated, but was reluctant to make any more bargains with this human trickster. "If I were to ask you for anything, it would be to let the Fleece go on with Jason. Our original idea was to help him, was it not?"

"The great ones' idea was to use him." Circe was brisk. "To get the Fleece away from the place where Giants guarded it. Now his usefulness is at an end. But Jason and his men can remain on my island for a time, if they choose, or they can leave. It will make little difference to me."

"What about Medea, and her maid? Perhaps you could free the princess from the spell of Cupid's Arrow."

"Oh?" The enchantress considered. "Does my Lord Triton also have a craving for her?"

"Medea is a beautiful woman." The god's tone implied that such were common enough. "But no. She and I are now bound together in quite a different way—by murder, and that is enough to have between us. Anyway, she is your relative, and I would think that you would want to show her mercy for that reason."

"My relative, as you call her, deserves no help from me. Rather would I see her punished for her crime. Besides, time and human nature usually provide sufficient antidote for Cupid's shafts."

"Human nature? I don't understand."

Circe evidently came to a decision that their talk had gone on long enough. "I have urgent business to take care of, and I will not stand here all day debating, not even with so eminent a deity as Triton." Her tone turned the compliment into a sarcastic taunt.

Now the woman, however great her powers, had gone too far. Triton said, in a quieter voice than before: "I think you had better stand where you are and answer my questions, until I tell you you may go."

Circe's fine, thin eyebrows rose in crooked arcs. "Bah! The little godling threatens, does he?" Her voice turned into a fishwife's shriek. "Remember who I am, little sailor! When you have put on the Face of Zeus, Athena, or Apollo, *then* you can come and give me warnings, and I will listen carefully, and bow my head and tremble. But the deity in charge of seaweed and seashells is not so terrible." The enchantress shook her head violently. "Not to me!"

Proteus stood taller, and met the gaze of the ancient, mortal woman with his own hard stare.

Circe was still not impressed. "If you think you can command the entire ocean, call its forces to your aid, you had better talk to Poseidon, and have your responsibilities and duties more clearly defined. I assure you that the Lord Neptune listens when I talk to him; he is master of all the water in the world, and he will be interested to discover that you are no longer his subordinate."

"Ah." The name of Poseidon, so confidently introduced, came as something of a shock. It tended to put things in perspective. Poseidon, better known to some as Neptune, was one of the triumvirate, with Zeus and Hades, who ages ago had divided up the universe among them— or so the tradition went. In that company, any powers Triton might be able to exert would dwindle to insignificance.

———

Circe put one hand out, in a reaching, grasping gesture that ended with the jab of an imperious finger. "Cease this stupid argument. Catch up with that fool Jason, and make sure that one of you brings me the Fleece!"

Now she had really gone too far. "Better think of who you are ordering about, woman. As for the Fleece, come and take it from us, if you can. Something tells me you may be lying when you say your only wish is to give it to the great gods." And having delivered himself of this speech, Proteus/Triton turned and walked away, heading at a deliberate pace down the long curve of beach toward the distant *Argo*.

Even as he walked, an awareness grew in him of ancient magic, tickling and probing at his mind. It was Circe, of course, doing her subtle best to confuse his sense of direction. But he could block that nonsense—Triton realized with satisfaction that he had not forgotten how to do everything. The woman was in for a surprise if she thought to treat him as an ordinary mortal.

Now he called upon the powers of the sea for help. And to his elation he saw the beginning of response come almost instantly, in the form of a rim of clouds beginning to grow along the horizon.

———

Striding on along the beach, Triton enjoyed the sensation of his returning powers rapidly replenishing themselves. A sense of unease began to grow in him, as he realized that he might have succeeded a bit too well. Help was certainly on the way, but possibly too much of it was coming, more help than he could readily control.

A few minutes later, with more elements of the god's memory still returning in a slow progression, he realized that he had actually summoned Scylla—the name meant She-Who-Rends—something he would probably not have attempted, had he been entirely in his right mind. Probably all he would really have needed would have been a couple of simple water-elementals. They could have provided all the help the *Argo* needed to get free of the Isle of Dawn.

And memory, still returning in small increments, increased the god's unease. He had called for help, for fighting power, for anger and destruction on a truly massive scale. And now he was going to get it. But it was too late now to revoke the summons, and he would have to deal as best he could with whatever it had brought him.

Suddenly a new worry occurred—if Scylla was near, then . . .

Yes. Having called the way he did, he was going to get Charybdis too. The Sucker-Down, as the name translated from some ancient language of which the god was only hazily aware, lying as it did on the clouded horizon of Triton's divine recollection.

But other elements of memory were firmer. Scylla and Charybdis were much alike, being huge, half-sentient knots of water-currents, ceaseless flows of liquid and energy all interwoven and entangled. If

Triton had ever known how such creatures came into existence, the details had been lost to him, along with so much else. But here they were, not half a mile offshore and bubbling closer—and had he been in full possession of all his wits, he would have tried to evoke such creatures only in a life-and-death emergency.

Well, perhaps that was really his situation now. With Circe it was always hard to be entirely sure. Anyway, the pair had now been summoned, and he would have to deal with them as best he could.

Was it only an accident that Charybdis and Scylla had been so conveniently nearby? He would come back to that question later, if and when he had the chance. Right now it was necessary to deal with the beings themselves.

Standing with arms folded, Triton watched the majestic progress of their approach. Thunderclouds that had just materialized from a clear sky now stooped to mingle with the sea, in a boiling turmoil that Proteus first caught sight of when it was still halfway to the horizon, but which closed with something like the speed of hurricane winds. Welling up a few hundred yards offshore, in forms that suggested to the water-god the waterspouts of tropical typhoons, they pleaded, in great howling, gurgling voices, to be released from their miserable existence. First one after the other, then both together, they moaned about certain uncanny adventures in the past, when they were called up by opposing magicians, to fight against each other. Humans could never have interpreted this bellowing as anything but the random raging of a stormy sea, but the ears of gods were far more capable. Stoically Proteus/Triton heard out the ghastly tale; he realized that unless he did, it would be hard to get the creatures to do anything.

Their voices came at him in a barrage of strange, echoing sounds, reverberating out of a dark green cave of curling wave that did not crest or break, but only stood its ground while the sea around it flowed up into it and through it, lending substance to its strange twisted shape.

The shrieking of Charybdis concluded with a question. "What do you say to that, Lord Triton?"

He tuned his voice to a volume higher than a mere human could have managed, not sure how well the raving, roaring things could hear over their own noise. "I quite agree, that you have both suffered great injustices. But such matters are all in the past, and not even Zeus himself can do anything about them. It is today that I would command your strength."

The response was another shriek and a whistle of wet wind. Now the monsters had concluded their ritual airing of complaints, they were ready to go to work. "What will you have us do?"

His right hand rose in a simple gesture of authority. "You will note a sturdy vessel on the beach, a little way ahead of me. The ship and its crew are to be set free from the island, provided with a lane of smooth water in which to ride, and given a swift current to carry them gently outward bound. Any powers on the island who might try to hinder this peaceful departure are to be pounded with your waves."

There was a slight pause. "Do you know who is on the island, Lord Triton? Who will be damaged and confounded by the work that you command?"

"I do know that, and that is my responsibility, not yours. Yours is only to obey."

"We hear and we obey!" The words of the answer dissolved in bellow and crash and howl.

And now, some truly tremendous water-walls began to stir and rise. Any mere human standing on the beach would have turned tail, if not suicidal, and run away. But the avatar stood firm, confident that the waves knew better than to strike at their lord directly.

At first, the powers Proteus/Triton had called into action were entirely obedient to the god's commands. Their hammering the coast with huge waves distracted Circe, and made her fear for certain works, some visible to human eyes and some not, she had established there.

Jason, marching stubbornly back to his ship with the two women, had looked up in amazement at the burgeoning storm and then had given the command for his men to gather close around the *Argo*, and shove her out to sea. Those Argonauts who were close enough to hear him, and able to move effectively, obeyed his orders with a rush. The Heroes were more than eager to leave the island, but at the same time understandably reluctant to put out into the teeth of a rising gale, what looked like the mother of all storms. But their terror of Circe, and Jason's orders, won out in the end. He was determined to save his treasure, or go down to the bottom of the sea still clutching it.

Suddenly a figure appeared ahead of him, running toward Proteus through the spume and sleeting rain. It was the Mouse, her single garment drenched and plastered wetly to her body.

"Jason sent me," she screamed at him when she drew near, her shouting barely audible over the mounting wind. "He wanted to be sure that you were coming. Didn't want to leave you on the island—" A brutal surge of wind and waves knocked her off her feet, left her floundering helplessly on the beach.

But even as her small figure was about to be engulfed by roaring tons of water, Proteus/Triton reached her side, and in a moment had scooped her into his arms. Briefly she tried to fight free of his grip, but the effort was completely useless. Two arms of divine strength held her in protective custody.

Instead of trying to dodge the next impending wave, he turned sideways to shield the burden he was carrying against his chest, and bore her right into the thunderous surf. When the Mouse, her eyes tight shut, drew in breath for a despairing scream, he clamped a broad hand over her nose and mouth, so that neither sound nor water might pass.

Then they were underwater, in Triton's natural domain. It came as no great surprise to Proteus to discover that he was able to breathe here (at least it felt almost like normal breathing) in perfect comfort. Of course he must have been breathing in the same way, without fully realizing it, when he rescued his shipmate in the ice-choked Bogazi, and on several other occasions after joining the Argonauts.

He looked down at the Mouse's face, still half covered by his hand. The girl was unconscious now, and of course she was going to have to breathe here too. But Triton could take care of that, and now he did.

Still looking at her, he thought: *It will be better if I can protect you here, in the sea, without showing you who I am.*

———————

The Mouse, on first recovering consciousness, thought at first that she had been dreaming. And then she became absolutely convinced that she still was.

With eyes closed, she heard and felt the thunder of the surf pass by. Moments later, still gripped and supported in the man's arms, she felt a very strange though rather comfortable stillness envelop her, and opened her eyes to the greenish light of several fathoms under water.

The figure of a strong man loomed before her. It was a figure she felt she ought to recognize, but still thought very strange. The man was bending over her, while at the same time supporting her with one arm. The curls of his hair and beard seemed all the same color as the water that was making each individual hair stand out, forming a great bushy mass.

In drowsy confusion the girl said to him: "I thought that you were Proteus. I thought—I thought that you were going to drown me."

"Why in the Underworld should I do that?"

When she only looked at him in dreamy silence, he went on, in his strange and watery-sounding voice: "Is this not a marvelous dream that we are sharing? I think we have Triton to thank for it. He is one of the sea gods, you know."

She drowsily nodded her agreement. At least she tried to nod.

Now the man who held her said: "You will be safe here." Then, as if he were trying to make sure of something, his fingers brushed her nose and mouth, and rested gently on her breast. "As long as you are with me."

In a burst of bubbles she released her pent-up breath. Her aching chest gulped in—

Great relief. After the tingling touch of her protector's hand, her lungs did not burn with the inrush of water, but accepted it as gratefully as air. In a moment Mouse seemed to be breathing normally.

Any lingering suspicion that she might not be dreaming vanished. "And who are you?" she asked. Her voice sounded strange, but it was a voice, not mere bubbling air. "You look like—like Proteus." She felt revulsion and fascination at the same time. This could not be the same man she had seen some three years earlier in Iolcus, doing frightful things—and yet it was so very like him.

"Why, so I am," the looming figure assured her in its godlike voice. "And Proteus and you are dreaming—a certain god who likes you both has sent the two of you a happy dream to share. When you awaken, it will seem to you no more than that."

"A happy dream . . . ?"

"Yes. Of course. Gods can do even greater things than conjure dreams. Did no one ever teach you anything about gods?"

Mouse shook her head. "Only that they never pay any attention to our prayers."

"That is not true, not quite true, although I know what you mean."

———

Here was a good place to bring a guest, with a clean sandy bottom, not too cold and dark and deep for a mortal to feel comfortable. And here, in the side of an underwater cliff, the dolphins and other natural creatures might with a little effort create a pleasant grotto for a god like Triton, and for any human he might choose to entertain in that environment.

Triton's guest today said, drowsily: "People tell many stories about meeting gods, and most of them are untrue, I suppose. I have never met a god, until now."

"Few people ever do. The man named Proteus had never met one either—until he picked up the Face of Triton, and let divinity flow into his head." He paused, and when he went on, it was Triton speaking, though there was very little difference in the voice. "There are not all that many of us—of gods, I mean. And most of us tend to stay clear of humanity most of the time."

The Mouse was staring up into the wavering faint light that filtered down from the surface of the sea. "Will the ship survive up there? The *Argo*?"

"I have given orders that it must." But having said that, he was not completely sure. Even if the local waves were gentle, the battered *Argo* might start to sink of her own accord. He would have to go up soon and look. But something caused him to delay.

In this environment it felt only natural to Triton/Proteus that he should grow a fishtail, and so he let the transformation happen. The Mouse stared, fascinated, as he demonstrated the extra speed of movement provided by the new appendage. His body reverted to full humanity as soon as he came to a stop again, right at her side.

"A moment ago you had a tail," said Mouse, with childlike directness. It was easy to talk that way when she knew that she was dreaming.

He nodded. "I did. A fishtail's a great help for serious swimming. Don't worry about it, it comes and goes as needed."

Her voice was suddenly so soft that he could hardly hear it. "I would rather not ever have one for myself, if you please."

That drew a chuckle from the god. "Don't worry, I have no plan of turning you into a mermaid. You shall remain as fully human below the waist as you are above. It would be truly a shame to change you in that way."

Triton knew that he himself would be able to see with great acuity, no matter to what depth he might descend. But any purely human guests that he escorted would need some form of light on going much deeper than they were now—in that event he could summon up some glowing creatures from the deep, who would accompany his party as guide and torch-bearer to the depths of the sea.

When Triton took thought, he remembered that there were certain ways in which he could entertain a human visitor to his domain with palatable food, not necessarily raw fish. Other varieties of entertainment could be provided too—he had done so often enough in the past, in other avatars. Now he could recall flashes, fragmentary hints, of a process for producing a good underwater wine . . .

Here in the depths the Mouse's sleepwalking eyes looked wider to Proteus even than they did in air. And the bottom of her shift, her only garment, kept rising up around her slender hips, making an image more seductive than ordinary swimmer's nudity. There were moments when Proteus thought she might be regaining consciousness, for her hands seemed to be trying to hold the hemline down.

"The next time you go bathing, you might take off your dress," he remarked, half in amusement, half in irritation.

"There wasn't time. Anyway, I wouldn't want to lose it. It is the only one I have." Her own voice sounded in her ears a little odd, but still she thought the words all came out clear and plain enough.

"Poor girl, you ought to have some better clothes . . . I'll see to that, when I have a chance." Then Triton suddenly lifted his head, listening. "In a little while we can talk. But first I must take care of some additional business. And you had better really go to sleep again; I will call a guardian to watch over you. Slumber deeply, and forget how we have talked. I tell you that you must forget."

———

What was Circe up to now?

Triton realized that she must know his abilities as well or better than he knew them himself. But it seemed the enchantress had convinced herself that she could defeat this minor sea-god, at least now while the god was dwelling in such an inexperienced avatar, and with his memory still lamed.

In this she was soon proven wrong. Circe's eyes went wide as she saw the chain of watery force, humpbacked as a whale but many times as large, rolling majestically up a slight ravine toward her house.

———

When Triton's head broke the surface of the churning sea, he saw with satisfaction that the two great monstrous beings had scrupulously obeyed his orders, inundating much of the island with enormous breakers. The waves did not behave in normal fashion, reaching a natural limit and then sliding back into the sea that owned them. Instead, each one seemed to gather itself for a second effort; a whole enormous mass of water, carrying a myriad of small common sea-creatures with it, went leaping, stretching, compacting and leaping again across the Isle of Dawn.

Meanwhile, according to his orders Charybdis and Scylla were leaving a narrow strip of relatively calm waters through which the ship could pass, with almost all its crew aboard. Proteus watching from a distance could see that Jason was pulling an oar as usual, presumably with the Golden Fleece stowed somewhere securely nearby or on his person. And he caught a reassuring glimpse of Medea's golden hair.

The waves and currents having been set in motion, they persisted for a time, simply in the way of nature. Now the bellowing, howling fountains that were Scylla and Charybdis came rolling up to Triton where he lay swimming in the deep, and reported to him that they had finished the job.

"Then you may go." Triton waved his free hand grandly. "You have my gratitude, for service well performed."

Yet still the howling vortexes lingered. One of the great elementals commented, in a voice of driving rain: "It is strange that Father Neptune has seen fit to punish Circe. They were on quite good terms not long ago."

Triton decided it would be best in the long run if he made certain matters clear. "What I have commanded you to do today is on my own authority, and Poseidon has nothing to do with it, one way or the other."

That news added volume to the watery uproar. "If Father Neptune calls us to account for this, we will of course say that it was done by your direct command."

"So be it."

———

The forces unleashed in the struggle had brought on something like a local hurricane, a natural turmoil that persisted after its instigators were departed. But the enchantress had managed to survive, though twice the wind had actually knocked her off her feet. From such sanctuary as she could find on shore, behind the rolling clouds of spume and spindrift, aided by such powers as she could hastily evoke, Circe shrieked curses at Triton and his latest human embodiment. She promised to call down on his head all the wrath of the great gods themselves. And in her fury she let slip, or gloated over, the fact that several of the Argonauts were still on shore and in her power. Some six or eight of them, who she was now holding penned up near her house, had started to turn into animals, displaying slender legs, with hooves on them, and fur.

When Triton through his divine powers saw at a distance what was happening to his shipmates, he was enraged in turn—Proteus could feel the divine fury as his own—and in some ancient-sounding tongue that Proteus had never heard before but now comprehended perfectly, began to work new spells upon the sea, threatening to drown the entire island, even submerging the enchantress's house, unless Circe let the whole company of Argonauts go, unharmed and fully restored to human shape.

Circe did not give up the unequal struggle against divinity until her island had been half-drowned in great waves, and herself with it. The stone stronghold at the center stood in danger of being buried in stinking mud, dredged up by her assailants from the bottom of the sea.

All that smothering mud was the last straw. When she saw that, she sued for peace.

The enchantress had no choice but to submit, and gave the necessary commands, freeing the men to run each on two human legs, through thick mud to the shore, where dolphins had been mobilized from somewhere to help them swim their terrified way out to the now-distant ship. Except that Jason's crew would now be two men short. The pair with winged sandals were gone for good, locked into the form of birds, beyond the range of her powers—or she said they were. It was beyond her powers now to change them back.

———

Circe expressed her surprise that Triton would be willing to stake so much on this contest, make an all-out effort on behalf of a handful of humans who were no close kin to him. But now the feelings of the wretched scoundrel Proteus were intimately involved. It was well known that when any deity passed into a new avatar, the quirks and emotions of the human became to a great extent those of the god or goddess.

———

Scylla and Charybdis in their departure from the vicinity passed so close to the ship that they endangered the vessel and crew again. But then Triton, working his way to full awareness of his rightful powers, contended with the vast whirlpool and saved *Argo* from being swallowed up and crushed in it.

Returning to the underwater grotto where he had left the sleeping Mouse, Triton dismissed her guardian, a killer whale, with a friendly pat on his blunt snout. Grampus gave Triton a glimpse of fifty enormous teeth, and with a swirl of rounded flippers turned away his thirty-foot black bulk, tagged with white on underparts, above each eye and on each flank.

"Come," the god said to the young woman. "Soon you will be awake again." Her eyelids quivered but did not open.

He had made certain pledges, and he meant to keep them. Triton was still a shadowy stranger, even to himself; and Proteus was still an Argonaut.

Today there was going to be no lengthy stay beneath the waves. He said to his guest: "We must return now to the ship." And he added in reiteration: "You must forget I am a god."

———

When the freakish storm and its aftereffects had completely died away, and it looked like there would be clear sailing for a time, the latest to play the scribe aboard the *Argo* took advantage of clear sunset light, and found time to make a long and very shaky entry in the log. It seemed to the writer that almost four months had passed since the ship's departure from Iolcus.

It was time for Jason to take roll call, and see just who was missing. Zetes and Calais were still nowhere to be seen.

19

Wedding

THE FORCES THAT had pried the *Argo* free of Circe's grasp had come near to destroying her in the process. The ship was no longer safe, even when the sea immediately around her had been calmed by the magic of a friendly god. After an hour or so of struggling at a distance to protect the *Argo*, Proteus, with the woman who had been called the Mouse still sheltering under his arm, caught up with the vessel and started looking for a way to get both of them back on board without being seen.

The need to return the Mouse was not his only reason for rejoining the *Argo* and her crew. He still felt himself drawn there, as naturally as a falling rock is drawn to earth; if he did not go back among his ship-mates, where else would he go? A god he might be, but in all the world he had no other home, no family or friends away from Jason's vessel and those aboard her.

Deep down, there was something in him now that feared the distant ocean and Poseidon's wrath. He feared he had usurped some of the greater sea-god's powers—Circe had probably been right about that. And he had not forgotten that the great gods had wanted Proteus dead.

Now the unconscious Mouse was quivering in his arms. Water temperature was something that Triton's avatar could ignore at his pleasure, but he could tell that it was currently in the range of comfort for most humans. Still, the long exposure was having its effect on the slender woman and he could feel her insensible body shivering.

The ship was only drifting at the moment, as the rowers changed positions. Clamping the limp fingers of the Mouse firmly over one gunwale, Proteus/Triton placed one of his hands on her head, and a moment later she had regained full awareness.

"There was a huge wave," Mouse told him, as if she were seeking confirmation for something she remembered. And Proteus could see in her face that she remembered very little more.

"There was indeed." He nodded vigorously. "In fact there were several enormous waves. But we have come through all right."

Then he gave the Mouse a boost, a good start at climbing aboard.

"There you are," he heard the princess say, her voice issuing from somewhere just out of his line of vision. "I had wondered whether you were permanently lost." Triton's head was under water again before the Mouse replied, and he could not quite hear her words.

Darting under the ship, Proteus/Triton grabbed the edge of the outrigger on the other side, and in a moment had hauled himself aboard.

One man who saw him come out of the sea declared that it was a strange time to be taking a dip, and he muttered some excuse about having to check the hull, but no one seemed to realize that he had not been on the ship when it left the island. Every man must have been concentrating on his own survival.

Looking back toward the domain of Circe, he saw that the huge waves his creatures had raised against the island were now rapidly subsiding, leaving behind them a surface of gray slimy mud, from which the trunks of coated trees, their foliage all sluiced and scraped away, protruded like the poison spines of some enormous monster.

An oarsman nearby groaned to his benchmate between pulls: "Some god is helping us make our escape!"

"Helping us? You'd describe the beating we've just taken as getting help? Another minute or two of help like that and we'll be drowned!"

Then a third Argonaut chimed in: "It may be that two gods are fighting, and we're caught in the middle."

The one who had spoken first now looked up. "Proteus, you're here, thank the gods—we could ill spare you. I thought you were lost overboard."

"No, I was up forward."

And a little later, when the men up forward questioned him, he was to say:

"I was back in the stern."

Listening to the men and watching them, he reassured himself that despite the events of the past few hours, none of Triton's shipmates were suspicious, at least not openly, that for the past few months a god had been helping them row their ship.

His next move was to ask Jason for a look at the Fleece, to make sure it had not been lost in the struggle.

The captain obliged, and dug out his treasure from the small locker where it had been bundled away. Both men were taken aback when they saw it. The bundle was notably smaller than it had been when he put it away. The Fleece was indeed diminished in size, and its brilliance noticeably dimmed.

"This is Circe's work!" Medea exclaimed. But Triton/Proteus doubted that. If the enchantress had had access to the prize, she'd have taken the whole thing away.

But what had happened to the Fleece was shocking.

"Where's the rest of it? Have you cut pieces off of it, or what?" Proteus demanded of Jason. But even as he spoke, he found it impossible to believe that Jason would do anything of the kind.

When the Mouse, looking over Triton's shoulder, saw the object of their concern, she was as puzzled as everyone else. There was a substantial deterioration. The golden glow had dimmed, and the fabric was more the size of a towel than a bedsheet.

Jason, dreadfully worried by the discovery, turned to Proteus/Triton for advice. But at the moment the trusted counselor had none to give.

Their scrambling escape from the island had pushed the men and their leader to the limits of their strength and endurance. And hope was fading that Zetes and Calais were ever going to reappear. Everyone had to acknowledge that the two winged Ar-gonauts seemed to be gone for good. One man who boasted of his keen eyesight now claimed to have actually witnessed the transformation of flying men into birds, and described it at length for his shipmates.

Jason sounded as numbly fatalistic as Proteus had ever heard him. "I fear there is no hope. Add them to the casualty list next time you make an entry in the log."

Medea was looking at him in dull wonder. Finally she asked: "How did we manage to get away?"

"The Fates were with us. And your magic . . ."

The princess shook her head. "People always say that, about the Fates, and it means nothing. I would like to believe that my magic was strong enough to get us free—but I cannot. There must be more to it than that. It may be that some god was indeed helping us."

Jason could come up with no better explanation.

When at last it was possible to cease an all-out effort to make speed, Jason took roll call of the exhausted Argonauts, most of them leaning on their oars while two men bailed; the strained seams of the hull were now taking water in several places. Only Zetes and Calais were missing.

The Argonauts were talking while they rested at their oars. Listening to them, Proteus realized that the men considered Circe and Medea to have been the chief antagonists in the duel of magic just concluded.

Since the getaway had succeeded, most of the men were now ready to offer the princess wide-eyed homage.

Jason seemed to agree with them. "It was the princess who somehow prevailed." There was wary calculation in the look he turned on Medea now. "It seems that you have saved us from your aunt."

The Mouse was still dazed, and only the princess herself seemed to have real doubts. She nodded in silence, then shook her head. First Medea's lips were trembling, then her whole body. Finally she murmured: "A storm like that . . . I tell you, I was not even trying to raise a storm. I cannot take full credit. Powerful help came to us from somewhere. But from where is a complete mystery."

———

No sooner did Triton feel confident that Scylla and Charybdis had really departed, than he realized, with a feeling of doom, that bad weather of purely natural origin was setting in, and there was almost nothing that he could do about it. Neptune might clear an entire sea of storms if he so chose, but feats like that were far beyond the lesser god's abilities.

Bowing his head while he once more labored at his oar, Proteus/Triton offered up a kind of quiet prayer: "I have this to say to the great gods: If any of them should feel inclined to step in and help us out of this ugly situation, they are quite welcome to do so. On the other hand, if they do not . . ."

He let it die away. He was filled with a sullen anger at the world, but there was no point in mumbling ridiculous threats against Poseidon and Zeus. If they took note of him at all, which he doubted, they would only laugh. And what would they say if he brought them that tattered remnant of the Golden Fleece?

None of their majestic forms appeared before his eyes. He realized that in the past he had probably not dealt often with such eminences, and he had no recollection of ever having met them face to face. Yet somehow he felt he knew them too well to feel surprised at their failure to respond to his prayer. Zeus or Apollo or Athena might have heard his outcry, had they been listening for it, but the chance of that was so small as not to be worth considering.

Several times in the past few days it had crossed his mind that the great gods might reward him when they saw what a good Argonaut he had been, helping Jason obtain the Fleece, and seeing to it that the treasure was brought back to where the great gods might get at it without fear of Giants. He, Proteus, might be able to claim some reward from Zeus and his confederates. Maybe after Jason had presented what was left of the trophy to Pelias, and derived whatever benefit he might from that act . . . which would probably be none at all.

He could remember vividly something that Circe had said: *"I see that the great gods were foolish to depend on you to obtain the Golden Fleece for them."*

But Proteus could not believe that the Fleece in its present wretched condition would be worth much to anyone.

If Circe had been right in her estimate of the current situation, all the Olympians would now be extremely busy, preparing for a major battle against the Giants. And even Zeus could only be in one place at a time.

Anyway, Triton feared that if Poseidon came to take a hand in this business, it might well be with a different goal in mind than either Proteus or Triton. So far Poseidon, like the other divine masters of the world, was inclined to be elsewhere. All of the gods feared the Giants' terrible weapon, and with good reason.

———

Not one of the voyagers was willing to put unquestioning faith in the compass-pyx any longer, not after it had guided them to Circe's island. But they were once again in the open sea, with no other means of navigation save the sun and stars. And they had an urgent need to locate friendly land.

Still there were some who wanted to throw Tiphys's heirloom overboard. One man snarled: "The last time we trusted it, it brought us to Circe. It's only by the help of some benevolent god that we're not all pigs, rooting with our noses in the dirt!"

After all the damage that had been done to Circe's island in the violent course of their escape, there was no doubt that the enchantress hated them, that she would gladly destroy the *Argo* and its whole crew if she had the chance.

———

Triton found he could be of no direct help in guiding the ship; whether because of his damaged memory or natural limitation, he had no better idea than anyone else of their exact location in the Great Sea. Proteus, after thinking things over, advised that before anyone relied on the compass-pyx again, they should rip out the copper strip that connected it with the ship's oaken keel. He suspected that that was the means by which Circe had been able to exert a degree of special control over the *Argo*. Jason at once gave the necessary orders, and the thing was done.

Then he turned to Triton/Proteus. "Some of the men are saying you have some special influence with certain gods."

Guardedly Proteus searched the captain's face. "I don't know why they say that, Jason."

"Well. Nevertheless, if there is any truth in what they are saying, Proteus, I pray you help me in this matter. If you can persuade some deity to help me, I promise him or her rich sacrifices—"

"I tell you, there is little I can do."

But Proteus was worried too. "Bah, what do any of the so-called great gods care for promises and sacrifice?" he barked out. Heads turned in his direction. Some would take that remark for fearful blasphemy, but Triton was in a foul mood inside the sailor's head.

Now everyone on board was aware of the change; Jason had left his failing treasure spread out on the deck, thinking perhaps confinement in the dark was the cause of its shrinkage and dimming. But sunlight and rain proved to be of no benefit.

Medea had no more idea than anyone else of what to do about the deteriorating Fleece. She continued to be despondent because her Aunt Circe was angry at her and would now certainly be more determined than ever to foil Medea's plans for Jason. Looking worn, her sunburn peeling quite unprettily, the young princess was obviously exhausted from her recent physical ordeals.

From time to time Medea looked at Proteus, but it was doubtful that she ever gave him any real thought, except as to how he might be even more useful. And obviously it had never entered her tired and sunburnt head that he might be a god. If anyone else aboard had that suspicion, they were keeping it to themselves.

Proteus had no intention of revealing his divinity to any of them as yet. He was certain that he had succeeded in making the Mouse forget the revelation.

Thinking of Mouse made him think of King Pelias, her secret employer. Proteus still had no idea of what the old bastard looked like, or any memory of ever meeting him. But it seemed almost certain that Old Proteus and the usurper had met, for Pelias would want to personally confirm the qualifications of any agent he entrusted with the task of disposing of his rival.

The more New Proteus heard about Pelias, the less he liked him.

Of course he had the same feeling about his earlier self, who had evidently been quite willing to work as a spy and assassin for such a human smudge.

But toward his earlier self he could feel no real enmity. He had realized some time ago that Old Proteus was dead.

———

Eventually the pictures in the compass-pyx came clearer. An attainable refuge was available, embodied in yet another island kingdom, this one named Drepane, only a few days' travel away.

Fortunately, the worst of the bad weather passed them by. But as the days dragged on the situation of the ship grew still more serious. Men were constantly bailing. Only one serviceable sail remained, and it had grown threadbare from constant exposure to wind and sun and salt, while the leaks grew worse day by day. He who ran out on his shipmates in this situation would be no Argonaut.

An ominous sight greeted the crew of the *Argo* as they rowed into the chief harbor of Drepane: a squadron of three large ships, marked with the insignia of Colchis. Weatherbeaten vessels, fresh from a hard journey, but still solid and capable. But at the moment there were no Colchians to be seen.

The first officials to greet the Argonauts on their landing were courteous but reserved. Thanks to Drepanian hospitality they were safely lodged on shore, well-fed, and their battered vessel temporarily secured against sinking. Some of the crew undertook such minor repairs as could be made without hauling *Argo* out of the water. Just now there was no drydock facility available, and there was no handy beach.

The ruler of this land, King Alcinous, had a widespread reputation for being just and fair. The Argonauts soon found, to their consternation, that the king was even now entertaining a strong delegation from King Aeetes, who was more determined than ever to get his daughter back at all costs.

Proteus heard with mixed feelings that the monarch of Drepane claimed to be a grandson of Poseidon; and for a time Triton thought of revealing his identity to this king. But that would not be a wise idea at all, if Neptune was truly against him.

Jason considered the idea of asking Alcinous for a meeting, at which he and Medea could confront their accusers; but none of his advisers thought that a good idea.

Ominously, only Medea was invited to see the king. But when she returned from the audience her news was not too bad. She described

Alcinous as kind and thoughtful, eager to listen to her side of the story; but all he would tell her was that he was still considering her case. Queen Arete had been present too, and the princess had appealed to her for help. Medea thought the queen was sympathetic to her cause. Making a formal appearance before King Alcinous, the officers of the Colchian delegation accused Jason and Medea of murder, in the slaying of Apsyrtus. They strongly implied that the mighty King Aeetes of Colchis would consider as enemies anyone who sheltered the fugitives.

Alcinous did not react favorably to threats, even when they were so indirect. But for the time he kept his own countenance impassive.

That night, Queen Arete, to whom Medea had appealed for protection, kept her royal husband awake by complaining, in a general way, of the ill-treatment to which fathers too often subjected their daughters, whether the daughters were guilty of anything or not.

The queen said: "Everything we hear about this old Aeetes suggests that he is capable of treating this charming Medea with extreme barbarity, if you give him the chance."

The king grunted something unintelligible. He was trying to get to sleep.

And, now that they were able to go ashore and find a little privacy, Triton/Proteus found himself walking gloomily with the Mouse, yearning to tell her of his troubles, and of the joys and privileges he had discovered in being a god. Not that his divinity had yet afforded him much in the way of joy.

At his suggestion, they sat down together in the soft seaside sand.

He pondered whether he ought to intervene on Medea's behalf, if the decision of King Alcinous went against her. He felt confident that Triton's power could somehow save the princess from being sent home. But what would he do with her then? The *Argo* was now chronically in need of fixing; he wondered if Circe had somehow managed to burden the vessel with a lasting curse. If she had, it was beyond his power to do anything about it. Vaguely he supposed that he might somehow seize control of a sound boat or ship, turn it over to Jason and his surviving crew, and wish them well.

The Mouse interrupted his gloomy train of thought, by saying to him: "Proteus, we are both of us still a long way from home."

"I don't know, Mouse—is that your real name, by the way?—I don't know where my home is."

Mouse was silent for a time, as if thinking something over. She picked up a handful of sand and let it trickle through her fingers. Then she said: "You claim not to remember my real name?"

"I don't believe you've ever told it to me."

"Then I suppose it possible that you don't remember my husband, either."

"I didn't know you had a husband. Certainly I've never met him."

For some reason that caused her to turn her face away. "He's dead now," she said. Then after a lengthy silence, she turned back to him, eyes searching his face intently. "Do you have a family?"

Proteus made a helpless gesture. "I don't know that either. I don't know if my parents are living or dead, or whether I have brothers or sisters. Given what I have begun to learn about my previous occupation, I think a wife and children are unlikely."

She looked at him for a long time in silence. "But now you are a different man," she said at last—but hesitantly, as if a shred of doubt still lingered.

"If you knew me, or thought you knew me, before I joined the Argonauts—then you must understand that I am now a very different man indeed. Something happened to me, I suffered a blow to the head, and almost all of my old self was wiped away."

"Really? Did any of the Argonauts know you—before?"

"No." Then following a sudden impulse, he told her: "My new self, I think, is—very small. Or would be, if—" *If half of me was not a god.* He couldn't go on like this! He wanted urgently to tell Mouse, to tell someone, but the words stuck in his throat.

"And a blow on the head accomplished this transformation?" Her disbelief was plain.

"No." Suddenly he could hold it back no longer. He was a god, wasn't he? To the Underworld with being cautious! He rushed on. "At the same time I saw the Face of Triton lying on a wooden deck before me; and I picked it up and put it into my head. It slid in smoothly, painlessly, just the way god-Faces do in all the stories. So now I am Triton, and I can do great wonders with the waves."

A silence began to stretch between them. She was staring at him in awe, in the way one might expect a mere human to stare at a god. At last she whispered: "With waves—and dolphins—and—"

"And breathing under water. Yes."

Mouse had a few more questions, and he did his best to answer them. At last she observed: "It sounds extremely complicated."

"Not really. It is easier to live with than to explain."

"Proteus—Lord Triton—hold me."

He held her. It was soon evident that certain elements of the sea-god's nature were emphatically human, with nothing of the fish about them. With a small part of the god's mind, he called up mist, and at a little distance sea-spray, to keep private, for a time, their little portion of the beach.

"Then I wasn't dreaming, that other time," she said after a while. "When we were coming away from Circe's island. Going under the waves with you."

"No, you weren't dreaming. I told you to forget, I wanted to keep my secret. But I was wrong. I need someone to talk to."

———

The Mouse was intensely curious about the details of his apotheosis, but actually he could tell her very little, though it was all he could remember, about the shipwreck, and his first fight with a Giant.

He concluded: "I suppose I had never seen a Face before, but I couldn't have had much doubt of what it was. I picked it up, and—here I am."

Mouse was silent for a time, her arms still around him. Then she said: "When I first saw you in Colchis, I hated you very much."

"But why?"

"Because I had seen you before, years ago, back in Iolcus, and there you were—a man who did horrible things. No, I don't want to say any more about it, please don't ask me to."

"I was a man who did horrible things, in the service of King Pelias."

"Yes."

"All right, I won't press you for details. I'm not that man any longer. And I'm glad that you don't hate me now." He stroked her tenderly.

"No, I don't. Now I will do whatever I am asked to do by the great Lord Triton, who has saved my life."

"When this voyage is over, Mouse, I will see what I can do, to arrange a better life for you. But don't expect too much. I have the powers of Triton, or some of them—I don't know how much I may have forgotten."

"How strange." She stroked his forehead tenderly.

"Yes, all new and strange to me. It may be that I can accomplish very little in the way of putting people on thrones, or knocking them off. I really don't care much about that. But I will at least keep you from being sent as a prisoner back to Colchis. I think I can promise you that much."

"I fear I can offer you no help in return, Lord Triton."

"You must remember not to call me that when others may be listening. I want to keep my secret for a while yet, if I can. And you have already given much help. The great Lord Triton, as you call him, finds himself in much need of such kind words and comfort."

———

Meanwhile there were two others, King Alcinous and his queen, Arete, who also lay wakeful in the night. The queen, considerably younger than her lord, was pleading with him: "My royal lord, save this unhappy girl from the Colchians."

"I have said that I will think about it." And Alcinous closed his eyes and tried, by regular breathing, to give the impression that he was already asleep.

The queen was not so easily deceived, but kept on talking in her normal voice. "Think all you want. Iolcus is not very many days of sailing from our island, and Jason may very well come to rule there. Whereas Aeetes lives far away and we hardly know anything about him but his name."

That stirred the king to a response. "We know he is a great and powerful monarch."

Ignoring what she did not want to hear, the queen took up another argument. "It broke my heart to hear all the troubles that poor girl has been through. She must have been out of her mind when she gave that man, Jason, the magic charm to help him deal with the Bulls." And she added: "He's the one who got her into this, you know. It's always the woman who pays."

The king grunted, in the way of listening husbands the world over, at moments when they would prefer to be asleep.

Queen Arete went on. "Then, as we sinners often do, she tried to cover one fault with another . . . why, only recently and not so far from us, the brutal Echetus drove brazen spikes into his daughter's eyes, and now the miserable girl is languishing in some dark dungeon."

Rolling over among a mass of pillows, Alcinous braced an elbow to raise his head. He asked: "Do you really believe that story about the spikes?"

Arete shuddered deliberately, making sure that the motion was strong enough to shake the bed a little, so that her husband would be sure to feel it. She said: "One hears the same version of the story from different people, which indicates there may well be some truth in it. And I know what terrible things I have seen men do."

The king shook his head: "I do have some sympathy for this little princess. As for the so-called murder she is said to have committed, doing away with her brother, it seems there was a kind of battle going on at the time. And in a battle, what do you expect but killing? But I should think twice before defying a just sentence from Zeus."

"We have no real evidence, my husband, that Zeus or any other god has any interest in the matter at all. That is only what the Colchian delegation tells us."

"True enough . . . nor would it be a good idea to hold King Aeetes and his power in contempt, even if he is far away. There is probably no greater king anywhere."

"So, what will you do?"

Alcinous sighed. "My duty, as best I can."

"And that is?"

"To give a decision that the whole world will acknowledge as the best."

The queen was nothing if not determined. "And what will that decision be?"

"If Medea is still a virgin, I shall direct them to take her back to her father. But if she is a married woman, I will not separate her from her husband. Nor, if she has conceived, will I hand over a child of hers to one who plans to punish her. Does that meet with your approval?"

The question was a serious one.

"My noble lord is wise as well as brave."

"I am glad I have finally convinced you of that elementary fact. Now let me get some sleep." Alcinous punched his pillows and lay down.

———

But before the queen joined her royal consort in his slumber, she arose quietly, without waking her snoring husband, and sent a trusted servant to inform the Argonauts of her lord's decision.

Jason and Medea rejoiced—she at the prospect of being married (belonging to a husband she could manage, rather than a father she could not), and the captain was happy to have found a sure way out of his present difficulties.

———

Medea and Jason were married within the hour. Someone took pity on the Mouse, and gave her a new dress, so she might make a decent figure in attendance. The couple entrusted the ceremony to a well-known local priest of Apollo, with the idea that it would be good to have an independent official, trusted by the king, who could if necessary give credible testimony that they were really married.

They went to bed together in a cave-room the queen had generously and secretly made available. The walls sparkled with a thousand mineral crystals, and in that setting the Golden Fleece that Jason spread out on their bed seemed to have regained something of its size and luster.

———

When Proteus had witnessed the ceremony, and had seen the couple retire to their wedding night, he looked around for the Mouse. But now he could not find her, and so went to his bed alone.

———

In the morning the young maid was still missing, and when Proteus finally inquired of the palace authorities, they had no word of her. When he went out on his own and questioned the local people, he learned that a fast Iolcan ship that had been in the harbor for several days had left, suddenly and unexpectedly, during the night.

Of course he had no proof that the Mouse had been aboard that vessel, but he had no real doubt of the fact either. She was speeding back to Iolcus to make her secret agent's report to Jason's rival.

Bitterly he thought that Pelias ought to richly reward one who brought him such important news: that his enemy Jason had now been fortunate enough to enlist a god in his cause.

———

Medea, fresh from her wedding night, and reveling in new-found freedom from her father's tyranny, found time to complain about the unfaithfulness of her missing maid, who had suddenly run off. Meanwhile Jason did not seem to care one way or the other.

Proteus felt a growing sense of betrayal, which soon turned to private anger at the Mouse. This he did his best to conceal from his shipmates.

Quite possibly the dead husband had been a lie. Certainly there would be an Iolcan lover of some kind, or lovers, who would welcome her back.

When in the morning the king's decision went against the Colchians, they trembled with fear, and readily admitted that they dreaded the wrath of their own king, should they return to him with such news. In the next breath they begged for sanctuary, which Alcinous immediately granted them.

"I will see that your decision is conveyed to your sovereign through some neutral source." The monarch went on to say that if the Colchian king wanted his ships back, he could send crews at any time to sail them away. "And in the meantime I will charge him no dockage fees. If Aeetes keeps sending his best agents far afield, he will soon discover that he has none of them left."

And Jason led a cheer: "Let it be so with every tyrant!"

After joining loudly in the cheers for the wisdom of good King Alcinous, the Argonauts soon completed their necessary repairs, and sailed on, rejoicing, with Jason and his bride aboard.

The Argonauts were more than ready to believe that their luck had at last taken a permanent turn for the better.

20

Triton

SO FAR, NO entry in the *Argo*'s log had mentioned the obvious deterioration of the Golden Fleece, and Anchaeus, still acting as logkeeper, did not propose to open that subject.

Several things of great importance had never been recorded. Evidently no one on the ship but Proteus had ever had the least suspicion that the Mouse had been a secret agent in their midst, working for Jason's archenemy. Proteus could not very well reveal the fact without disclosing the same thing about himself.

He was secretly relieved to find that the log book was still in its accustomed place—not that it would have done King Pelias much good if a thief had stolen it and brought it to him. Well, if the Mouse was on a fast ship bound directly for Iolcus, as no doubt she was, she would probably be carrying her exciting information to the king many days before the *Argo* came limping into home port—if it ever managed to do so. But the big news in her report would be something that had never been entered in the log.

Medea still grumbled now and then over what she perceived as the disloyalty of her missing attendant. But the attitude of the princess suddenly mellowed when it occurred to her that the Mouse might have met with foul play of some kind—it happened to young women sometimes, even in the most civilized of ports. Still, Medea spent little time fretting about her loss, for she was nagged by other worries. She told Jason and Proteus of a dream in which the ghost of her butchered brother had appeared, walking on water beside the ship, and seemed to beckon her to follow him.

But with grim determination Jason's bride managed to shake off the tentacles of guilt. Nothing would be allowed to distract her from her

purpose. "I will not put up with such things. I will not. I have done
what I have done, and that is that."

———

There came a time when Medea and Proteus were briefly alone, as much
as any two people could be aboard the ship. He saw her looking at him,
as if she had never quite focused on him before. And Medea said:
"Sometimes I wonder who you are."

Feeling a faint chill of alarm, he offered a slight bow, really only
a nodding of the head. "One who has served you and your husband
faithfully, lady."

"Granted. Though that is not quite what I meant. Oh, Proteus, good
Proteus! You are so devoted. If only life were that simple! But a woman
must look out for herself. You are a good sailor, and an excellent fisherman, but I would not be much of a success as a sailor's or fisherman's
wife." She gazed at him with the expression of a girl who had learned
early in life that nearly every man who looked at her could be enslaved.

Feeling somewhat relieved, Proteus/Triton replied: "There I must
agree with you, princess." Days ago he had begun to suspect that the
effect of Cupid's Arrow was wearing off; he seemed to remember Circe
saying that such was often the case, and the looks Medea gave her
husband were more thoughtful than adoring.

If there was a slight edge in his comment, the lady did not seem to
feel it. She only smiled, tolerating this very helpful man who was never
going to be a king.

———

No matter who now tried to read the compass-pyx, the result was cloudy
pictures and uncertainty—perhaps because no one on board still had
real faith in the instrument.

Day by day, and hour by hour, the situation of the Argonauts and
their hard-used vessel continued to deteriorate. Sails were useless, leaks
had become chronic, and there was not much that Triton could do about
it.

The driving wind and the smashing waves refused to bend to the
control of Triton's will. Instead, those great limbs of nature steadily
opposed him. His godhood had not been paralyzed, his powers were
still his to command. But they were completely overmatched by antagonistic forces.

The only explanation he could come up with, apart from the sheer

perversity of nature, was that Circe, or some other enemy, had successfully turned at least one of the greater gods against him. And of course
some powerful deities might be against him anyway, bitter enemies of
Zeus, taking the Giants' side in the ongoing war. Of course one excellent
candidate would be Hades. The Lord of the Underworld was said once
to have been a partner of Zeus, but for ages had been his chronic enemy;
not equal to the Thunderer in strength, but still a deity of enormous
power.

Doubtless more important, from Triton's point of view, there was
Poseidon, who, it was said, with Zeus and Hades had once divided the
whole universe among them. Triton had no idea of the great sea god's
position in the current struggle.

And Proteus had to believe that if the great gods were supporting
Jason, the Giants and any allies they might have must be his enemies.
Jason's destruction might even be the enemy's current chief objective.
If it came to another Giant attack, Proteus/Triton was the ship's only
capable defender.

Of course there was nothing compelling him to stay on board. It
would be perfectly easy for Triton to plunge into the sea, and have
himself borne by dolphins to some far corner of the world. No reason
he could not withdraw to some quiet place, where gods and Giants
seldom ventured, a part of the world where no one had ever heard of
the Golden Fleece.

If the ship does sink, he thought suddenly, *I will not be able to save
them all. But I will rescue Jason. Not that he is worthier than any of
the others, but saving him will deny the enemy, King Pelias and the
Giants, what they want most. I will save Jason, and as many of the
others as I can.*

It was damned strange to be aware of your own divinity, and at the
same time to feel trapped by circumstances, like some small, helpless
animal. Every scrap of knowledge that had stayed with him, the essence
of Triton's long, long lifetime, fed his certainty that he would be no
more than a worm in the hand of Neptune. It seemed only a matter of
time before the great gods would have time to spare to crush him, if
that was what they wanted.

———

The wind that drove the vessel seemed perfectly natural, yet it was so
strong that the only way to keep *Argo* from sinking or capsizing was to
turn and run before it. There was no thought of trying to raise a sail, it

would only be torn away. Scylla and Charybdis were somewhere far away, and out of touch with Triton, who felt very much alone.

Such overwhelming opposition as seemed to be arrayed against him could come, he supposed, only from the peerless Poseidon, who, like the other great gods Apollo and Zeus, and evidently Athena and Aphrodite too, wanted to see the Fleece go directly, and as soon as possible, into the workshop of Daedalus.

Triton had no doubt Hephaestus the Smith was a clever god— patchy memory gave some indication that it was so—and the human named Daedalus, also called the Artisan, might be something more than clever. Together those two could very well be able to wring some vital secrets from the unimpressive remnant of the golden wonder. Then gods might outlast Giants in their great struggle, and humanity would be better off.

They had reached the middle of another day of windy buffeting and helpless drift, when without warning a great calm seemed to come over their immediate surroundings. Then there was another upwelling of the sea, much more slow and solemn than that which had attended the appearance of Scylla and Charybdis, She-Who-Rends and Sucker-Down.

"What in all the chambers of the Underworld is that?" the captain gasped.

Triton was afraid he knew exactly what it was. "Prepare for some rough weather," he muttered, more to himself than to his shipmates.

An anonymous cry went up: "We're lost! Great gods, whatever that thing is, we're doomed!"

And some strange force, as far beyond Triton's ability to comprehend as it was beyond his skill to counteract, seemed to be holding the ship perfectly still in the water.

From the first moment of its appearance, he had no doubt of the identity of the mighty presence that had now taken control of the ship and everything around it. The Argonauts and their vessel were now in the presence of Poseidon, by some called Neptune. The great god was immediately recognizable on sight to many of Triton's shipmates, though almost certainly none had ever seen him before. Triton's own efforts to control the local water and wind were casually overruled, as was the natural gale that had begun to blow, so that for the moment the *Argo* was gently borne up in a sea of calm. Control of this portion of the Great Sea had been effortlessly assumed by its true master.

For a long moment, all of the other people on the ship were stricken dumb by their first sight of one of the triumvirate who had once claimed to rule the universe. In the eyes of mere humans, Neptune appeared a titanic figure, clad in gold, his golden chariot surrounded by leaping, bounding dolphins, and pulled by white horses which on closer inspection had something monstrously serpentine about some of their legs. He was not bothering today with a Trident—it would be foolish to think he really needed one.

The same Argonauts who had done their best to fight a Giant face to face were now cowering like children before this presence. One or two seemed to hope that they might be able to hide beneath their rowing benches. Even Jason's head was down, his face hidden in his hands. Medea was clinging to her husband's side, her own face buried in his chest.

Of all the people on the ship, only Triton/Proteus was on his feet, balancing himself with divine skill, keeping his body erect despite the swaying and dipping of the deck beneath his feet. Neptune was staring directly at him, with an unreadable expression, and Triton thought that in another moment or two, he would either be annihilated or his godhood would certainly be revealed to any of his shipmates who had not yet fainted.

Before Poseidon could say anything, there came a startling interruption. Half a mile from the ship, and with the ship between it and the god, there appeared a doubly fish-tailed Giant, bigger than a great whale, and breaching like a whale, dwarfing Neptune who like any other god must walk the world in human form, and be no more than man-sized after all.

The Giant's body broke the surface and fell back, with the roar and splash of some vast creature of the deep. In a flash, Triton understood that the Giant must have been tracking Poseidon and meant to destroy him with the special weapon.

In a moment, the monstrous panoply of waterspouts and clouds enshrouding Neptune had collapsed in a torrent of falling spray. The great god himself had disappeared. In his intense fear, Poseidon had quickly submerged to such a distance that the Giant, raising empty but powerful hands, could not take aim at him. Already even Triton, as he grabbed up a spear and dove over the ship's side, lost track of the greater god's exact location.

The mountainous disturbance resulting from Neptune's sudden plunge did not die away until it had engulfed the ship. Huge waves threatened to capsize the *Argo*, despite the stabilizing effect of the plank-bottomed outriggers on each side. Several men were swept overboard, and Proteus let himself go with the surge.

As soon as the waves had closed over Triton's head, he shifted into fishtail form, and launched a desperate counterattack, in defense of himself and his shipmates.

His previous encounter with a Giant in the water had taught him something about the tactics the enemy employed. What little Triton could recall of that now helped him form a plan of battle.

On seeing him submerge, the Giant too sank below the surface.

The only weapon Proteus had on jumping overboard was an ordinary spear, and he knew he would have to get very close to his huge antagonist indeed to use it effectively. Especially under water, where the throwing range would be enormously reduced.

His huge opponent, well aware that Triton would have to close with him to do him harm, kept turning so as not to be taken by surprise from behind.

At moments during the whirl and fury of combat, Triton caught momentary impressions of Neptune, now more than a mile deep in the Great Sea, and still retreating. Closer at hand he had a momentary look at Medea on the ship, still at Jason's side, her hands raised in a gesture that showed she had not abandoned all hope of being able to do something effective with her magic.

The struggle in the sea went on. Triton, his body fish-tailed and darting with a shark's speed through the water, called up a school of fish to screen him somewhat from his enemy. He had to keep the Giant from locating him and focusing the invisible weapon on him—one more blast from that might well leave him with no more memory than a clam.

Proteus/Triton had to assume that by this time any Giant he encountered was likely to know what had happened to one of their colleagues in the Grove of Ares—and also how Triton had killed another, months ago, in the midst of the Great Sea.

The Giant roared out a few words, from behind the murky screen of fish.

"Triton, is it you after all? I thought one of my comrades killed you months ago. Whose head are you hiding in this time? Come out, little godling, come out and fight, you wretched coward!"

That was the second time in a few days that Triton had been called a little godling, and he was tired of it. By a subtle power he had not known that he possessed, he caused his underwater speech to issue from the mouth of a great fish swimming on the other side of his opponent. "Matter of fact, he did kill me. But don't you know what happens when you kill a god?"

Evidently the Giant was not deceived as to his location. A wave of radiance from the magic weapon, stirring the water like waves of heat, passed very close on Triton's right side. He thought that if that had hit him, his mind would now be entirely gone; forgetfulness spreading like a dark cloud, until it engulfed even the ability to think. The propagation of the wave was very fast. Yet under water it was not so fast that an agile god had no chance to dodge.

———

He made some effort to draw his huge antagonist away from the *Argo*, so that the ship and the people on it might survive even if their god-protector died.

The inconclusive duel with the Giant dragged on, and seemed no nearer its conclusion when a beast of the sea that Triton had not summoned came darting near him, with a long burden in its mouth.

At first he spun away frantically from the approaching bulk, fearing that some creature allied to the Giant was about to attack him. But then he heard the shrill speech of a dolphin, garbled by the necessity of carrying a burden in its mouth. Instantly Triton doubled back in his headlong flight, to hear what the creature had to say. It seemed to be telling him that it came from Neptune.

Again the streamlined shape swam near. Reaching out his hand to seize the object carried in its mouth, Proteus/Triton blinked at suddenly finding himself superbly armed. His fingers had closed upon a spearshaft with a triune branching; the three separate, parallel spearheads looked like splinters of black obsidian.

Who might have fabricated this weapon, and when, he could not remember, but obviously something more than human skill and power had gone into it. This was his own Trident, his true Spear, of which all those he had been using over the last few months were only shoddy imitations. The whole unit had the look of a single piece of dark glass, rather than of metal, but the suggestion of fragility was utterly misleading, and he knew that all the parts of it were very strong. The triply-branching shaft was no more than about five feet long, and the three spearheads comparatively short, so any wounds they made must be less than a foot deep. Yet the triple impact of their keen points could strike with almost unimaginable force.

Neptune's messenger was a mere common dolphin, a being low enough on the ladder of importance to be impressed by the opportunity to talk with one as eminent as Triton.

Speaking in deferential tones and forms, the dolphin informed him that the Trident had been recovered from the bottom of the sea, about a month after the lesser god's last change of avatar.

The endlessly smiling dolphin mouth produced a form of speech that would have been opaque to merely human ears, but now that its mouth was free, Triton could readily understand. "The Lord Poseidon hopes that this gift will seal a reconciliation between himself and you."

Shifting easily into the rapid dolphin speech, Triton replied: "I have never considered myself our great lord's enemy."

The messenger looked at him closely with its very human eye. "Great Neptune now sees that the rumors of your enmity were false, and thanks you for your help against the Giant. He himself remains at a distance, because it may be that other Giants still infest this area. He advises you to seek your own safety."

"I thank Great Neptune for his concern. But tell the Lord of all the Oceans that I am much concerned with the survival of this ship, the *Argo*. If he wants to do me a good turn, he could help her on her way."

"I am to warn you, Lord Triton, that if you accompany the *Argo* farther in these waters, you must stay on the alert for more Giants. And for worse than Giants, too."

"*Worse?*"

"And I am to tell you, further, to expect no additional help from Lord Neptune just now. He urges you to put forth your best efforts to place the Fleece in the hands of the human Artisan, Daedalus. Lord Neptune cannot help you, because he must prepare for a great battle."

"Just what in all the watery hells of Ocean does he think we're having here?" the sea-god commented in a muttering gurgle.

"As to that I couldn't say, Lord Triton."

"All right. All right. Maybe Poseidon understands the situation better than I do. Bear him my thanks for this important gift."

The watery messenger signed assent, and a moment later had disappeared below the dark surface of the rolling sea.

Despite the Giant's continual wary turning in the water, Triton with his Trident in hand managed at last to get behind him, then dart in and strike before his enemy could bring the projected power of his hands to bear upon the god. In another moment the Giant was in floundering retreat, howling with the pain of deadly wounds.

Instead of beginning what might well have proved a long chase, trying to finish the Giant off, Triton/Proteus elected to stay with the ship. He had some hope that his restored weapon might be useful in a different way. But to his disappointment the Trident, shake and brandish it as he might, proved no help at all when he simply wished to counteract the prevailing winds and tides.

He even thought of trying to summon Scylla and Charybdis back, but he dimly sensed that they were far away; and earlier they had almost destroyed the ship, inadvertently, while under orders to protect it.

Once again he regretted, among other things, not being able to retain Circe as an ally. Well, maybe someday, a hundred years from now—with the enchantress doubtless looking not a day older—they would be on good terms again. Triton might very well have taken up residence in some new avatar by then, though that was not certain—a human frame infused with the powers of a god tended to last much longer than it would have done in the mere course of nature.

Certainly he must retain possession of the Trident, now that he had it back. But it might not be easy to do that, without alerting all his shipmates to his true identity. Casting about within himself for some power that might be of help, he came upon a means of magical concealment.

———

Currently Jason and his followers were having to contend with nothing worse than the natural aspects of the ocean, but those seemed quite sufficient to destroy them.

The most serious problem, and one beyond Triton's competence to do much about, was that the ship was damaged, her bottom leaking, and repairs were necessary. She was superbly constructed by any human standard—Triton thought that perhaps only the famed Daedalus could have done better—and any ordinary vessel would have broken entirely apart by now.

There was no choice but to find their way somehow to the nearest friendly beach, lying in the general direction they were being carried. They needed a place where a battered ship could come to land without having her bottom ripped out or being beaten to pieces on rocks. But for all any of them knew, including Proteus, the nearest beach of any kind in that direction might be hundreds of miles distant.

In his desperation, Jason continued to try to use the compass-pyx. Gladly he allowed Medea to take a turn, and anyone else who wished to try. Whoever was crouching over the instrument laid his or her forehead on the rest and held as clearly as possible the mental image of an anonymous, safe, and welcoming shoreline.

The ship's flying passage before the wind went on so long that those on board were in danger of running out of drinking water; but so far the driving rain fell thick enough, day and night, to keep them from total dehydration. The falling water was caught in pieces of a tattered sail, which were then wrung out.

———

The captain and his bride no longer seemed on the best of terms. Evidently, thought Proteus, Circe had been right about Cupid's Arrows. Their effects passed away in time, even as fire died out without new fuel. Love once planted could grow mightily, but then again it could be strangled. The couple still clung together, but there were hints of something wrong between them, deeper than a mere quarrel.

———

The driven ship was essentially lost. No way for it to reach any goal that the instrument might find. They were surrounded by a bleak seascape indeed:

Medea awakened abruptly from a deep sleep, announcing that she had just had a vision. "I saw a great gulf, or bay, from which no ship is ever able to escape, because of the fierce wind that drives all vessels on the shore. The water is shallow, and thick with tangled masses of seaweed. On the shore, there is nothing at all but sand, reaching out to the clouded horizon. No living creature stirs there, on the earth or above it."

———

And Proteus/Triton, when he fell asleep a little later, was drawn into the strangest dream that he could remember ever having.

It seemed to Proteus that he was wandering, afoot and alone, in some city where he had never been before, and with the secret knowledge that is given in dreams, he knew that everything around him was doomed to destruction. He stood on the portico of a great temple, surrounded by the statues of gods and goddesses, all of them sweating blood. A great inhuman bellowing sounded from somewhere inside the temple, so that even Triton grew terribly afraid.

Looking up into the noonday sky, he saw that the sun had somehow been eclipsed, and the stars shone out in the nighttime darkness that surrounded that terrible sight. Around the temple, men and women were wandering in the streets, dim ghostlike figures all wailing and crying out, some of them warning of war, others proclaiming that a plague was about to fall upon the land.

At last a figure approached Proteus directly, and it was physically monstrous, a great bull's head on a tall man's body, and he knew that he faced the Minotaur. But somehow the very strangeness of the shape was reassuring.

A quiet voice issued from the bull's mouth, saying: "I am Prince Asterion, of Corycus. It has been difficult to reach you, Lord Triton, god of the sea. I am glad to see that you have found the way into my house at last."

"I am only a godling," Triton heard himself reply.

"Welcome to my Labyrinth of dreams," the Minotaur said, and made a sweeping gesture with a very human hand. "It covers infinitely more space than my waking Maze on land."

Fear had receded from Proteus, and he asked: "Where does it lead, this Labyrinth of dreams?"

"Tonight it leads to sights that it would be well for you to see. Dreams can shadow forth reality. Have you met Hera yet? Or Aphrodite? They are divinities, of course, but like you they must dream, even as I do."

Out of the shadows beside the enormous temple loomed two shrouded female forms. Proteus knew, or thought he knew, that Hera, also known as Juno, was the wife of Zeus. And gray-eyed Athena, called by some Minerva, a traditional foe of Poseidon, but now here peacefully despite her helmet and her shield, seeming to demonstrate by her presence the unity of the great gods in this. From a few words that Proteus could hear them saying, he could tell that they were all here now as allies of Zeus, they all had a stake in helping Jason to succeed in his mission.

And somehow, with few words spoken, it was communicated to Proteus: The great gods were indeed on the side of Daedalus and Vulcan, and they had wanted Jason to get the Fleece away from its guarded place in Colchis. Their object was to take it away in turn from Jason, at the proper time, and hand it over to Daedalus, whose cunning wiz ardry would discover what secret strength it had to give its owner. For some reason, Zeus and his allies expected the Golden Fleece to be of great benefit in their ongoing war against the Giants.

"I know where the Golden Fleece is," Proteus heard himself saying in his dream. "It is in the hands of Jason."

"We all know that," Athena chided him in her deep voice, fixing him with ageless, depthless eyes.

"We all know that," said Hera, sweetly echoing. There was a peacock sitting in the graceful curve of her strong arm.

"What we must tell you," said the bull-man, "is that Daedalus may very well be here, on the island of Corycus, when the ship of the Argonauts arrives."

"You must seek out Daedalus," powerful Minerva commanded.

"You must give him the Fleece," Juno reiterated softly.

. . . and the goddesses and Minotaur all vanished, and Proteus dreamed that he was once more swimming with the Mouse. This time great metal fetters weighed her down, and he had to put forth all his strength to lift her from the very bottom of the sea.

Projecting upward from the muddy bottom was a strange object, like a huge tree-stump. Despite its being dead and underwater, it jabbered at Proteus/Triton in a strange language, saying words that he had never heard before, but yet conveyed a grotesque meaning:

> *"Full fathom five thy father lies;*
> *Those are pearls that were his eyes;*
> *Of his bones are coral made*
> *Nothing of him that doth fade*
> *But doth suffer a sea change*
> *into something rich and strange.*
> *Sea-nymphs hourly ring his bell . . ."*

Triton's dream showed him a last blurry vision of sea-nymphs, appearing as fish-tailed maidens, chanting that song of nonsense with the tree-stump. And even as the dream began to shatter and disperse, Proteus heard the voice of the Minotaur, sane and practical, telling him: "One thing that no sane mortal wants to do is to get caught up in a conflict between gods."

"I'll heartily concur with that," said Proteus. And thought he was starting to wake up.

He told no part of the dream to any of his shipmates. He saw no way that it could be of any help.

Help of some kind was definitely needed. From hour to hour in the waking world, the survival of the *Argo* and her crew hung in the balance. Another day and night passed, and no one knew whether their next hour might be their last, but finally there came the welcome noise and feel of sand grating beneath her bottom.

It was in fact a flood tide that had caught the vessel and swept her up to the inner shore, leaving her high and dry when the flood receded.

For a time the stranded crew were surrounded by an impenetrable fog. When that cleared, it revealed a landscape that was a close match to that Medea had reported seeing in her vision. Away from the sea, a wasteland stretched into the distance, unbroken and immense.

The worn-out crew dragged themselves off the grounded ship and staggered ashore. For their survival they poured out prayers of thanks, expressing their gratitude to a hundred gods, none of whom were likely to be paying the least attention. In the relief of the moment, several brave adventurers improvised vows that they would never trust their lives on any ship again.

Then, in that ghastly, fading light they made an exhausting effort to drag the beaten *Argo* even farther up on the beach, beyond all traces of the highest waves. When they had secured the ship as well as possible, they all crawled a little farther inland still, where they tried to take shelter from the wind behind a series of sand dunes.

One of the crew groaned: "The curses of Circe follow us even here."

Triton thought that all too likely. He was now carrying his Trident slung on his back with a frayed piece of rope, and thought he had succeeded in making the weapon invisible to all eyes on the ship but his own. But he still felt powerless, despite what ought to have been the reassuring nearness of the sea.

Nearby he could hear Medea weeping in exhaustion as she clung to her husband. She had no maid to attend her now.

The future seemed clearer than the past, and both were bleak and terrible. What good was divinity, if you were still effectively powerless?

The whole crew spent a bleak and miserable night. In the morning, the sun rose on a featureless sea and desert. Even the god who moved unrecognized among them had only a vague idea of where they were. For once no one had any plan to propose.

At least the sky had cleared somewhat, and the wind abated.

As soon as the rain stopped, the need of fresh water threatened to become critical. But they could hope the clearing of the clouds meant that the wind might soon reverse itself.

Then Medea, dowsing for water with a twig of driftwood in her hand, located a place some little distance inland, where pools of rainwater had gathered among the rocks. No one was going to die of thirst.

The ship was in need of serious repairs. Another acute problem was that so many oars had been lost or broken in the recent struggles with rough weather that half the remaining crew would ride in enforced idleness when the ship was launched again. On top of that, the last remaining sail was almost useless—a large tear had started. All the spare canvas had been used up long ago.

One of the ship's lockers still held some sailmaker's tools and materials, and at Jason's orders an effort was begun to mend the sail.

Careened on a beach, tilted sharply to one side—that was the only way *Argo* could rest on solid ground, given her cross-section. It was in this same position that Proteus/Triton had seen her first, but then she had looked eager and young and new, and though she was only a little older now, she certainly looked tired. Instead of a few months, years might have passed; and it occurred to him that the same thing might have been said about Medea.

Working in turn on different sections of the ship's bottom, the workers tilted *Argo*'s bulk from one side to the other, as it balanced on the central hull. The massive weight came down each time with a crushing thump.

"Here's where we really could use Hercules," one lifter grunted.

Some of the Argonauts had started a driftwood fire shortly after coming ashore, and kept it going. Now the fire was useful for heating tar, as men began to go over the ship, poking and pounding the fibers of shredded rope into the leaky seams, and pouring on hot tar as soon as it had been softened to the right consistency. The general opinion was that she could probably be made seaworthy again—or almost. If they encountered no more storms, she would probably get them home.

The ongoing search for firewood turned up a few surprises. There were many wrecks, some old, some new, up and down this coastline.

With here and there assortments of human bones, half buried in the sand, being unburied and reburied by the wind.

Haraldur was holding up a find. "Is this supposed to be a rib, or an arm bone? I'm not sure it's even human."

"What creature besides humans would haunt this empty land, without a plant or animal to eat?"

There were occasionally oars among the scattered wreckage, including a few of almost the right length.

"With work and perseverance we will win out," Jason assured his followers.

Still Triton had had no further word from Poseidon, and no more informative dreams. Triton supposed that the great sea-god, like Zeus himself and like Apollo, was simply too busy to pay much attention to this sideshow. The truly major deities must all be busy getting ready for the climactic battle with the Giants, and there was no reason to think that was going to take place anywhere around here.

At a time when no one was paying Triton/Proteus any particular attention, he walked along the beach until he was out of sight of all the others, then plunged in and swam out to sea, far enough to encounter several of its creatures, deep swimmers and a flying pelican, with whom he could converse. In a little while Triton had gained valuable information about the winds and currents up and down the coast.

On rejoining the others, he explained that a new vision had given him hope. In a few days, a seasonal change in the weather could be expected, and an offshore wind would set them free. They must be ready to take advantage of it when it came.

21

Corycus

JASON, WHO HAD now taken over the job of steersman for himself, lowered his head to gaze into the box of ivory and ebony. Presently he raised it again, and leaned upon the steering oar, turning the prow of *Argo* in what he now felt sure was the general direction of Iolcus. The Argonauts were setting out for home.

Something like five months had passed since the *Argo* had sailed bravely out of the harbor of Iolcus. "For all we know, Pelias may be dead by now," one member of the crew grunted as he pulled his oar.

Another shook his head. "I wouldn't bet on it. Old men like him will hang on to their power like grim death. You can tell by looking at him."

Proteus, who was listening nearby, nodded, not wanting to reveal that he had no idea what the old king looked like.

Another of his shipmates spoke up. "You saw the king in Iolcus? I never did. They say he keeps pretty much to himself in his high castle."

"Oh yes." His shipmate nodded. "He came down to the quay, to see us off he said, the morning before we left. I suppose to show that there were no hard feelings, between him and Jason."

"Not much there aren't."

"I didn't see old Pelias there."

"You only got aboard at the last moment, as I recall. He'd gone back into his fortress by then, a busy man with many things to do."

Someone turned his head to call out: "Captain, are we relying on the compass-pyx again?"

"What else?" Jason called back.

And indeed there seemed no other choice. But within a few hours, their journey began to be agonizingly protracted, as the precarious condition of their ship forced them to travel a zig-zag route, seeking out one mid-ocean island after another. Each time the weary crewmen came to land they had to labor on their leaky ship again.

At last the captain raised his head, his face indicating great relief. "I have a clear objective now," he informed his shipmates. "One you will be glad to hear. It is Corycus."

A cheer went up, and Medea clapped her hands. On Corycus, considered one of the most civilized of lands, a friendly welcome could be expected. Jason said that the island of the Minotaur lay almost in line with their course for home, and his own relief was evident when he announced that he was setting a course for the harbor of Kandak.

The man in the Labyrinth had been sending Proteus dream-messages whose full meaning was still far from clear to him—but they had strongly suggested that Daedalus was to be found on this island.

If that was true, then it should be possible to deliver the Fleece just as the great gods wanted it delivered. "Daedalus is on Corycus, is he not?" Proteus asked his shipmates.

But it seemed that none of them had any idea where the Artisan might be.

Meanwhile the princess, now that the pursuing forces of her father had been baffled, was looking forward to an interval ashore, hopefully in civilized conditions. She had her own idea of what would happen on Corycus.

"I will tell my troubles to Princess Phaedra, who has ruled the island since her father died, and the god Shiva was overthrown. Do you know Phaedra, Jason? I expect a woman will be more sympathetic to my case even than good King Alcinous. And Phaedra might even have some influence with my aunt. I hope she may at least allow me the luxury of a steaming bathtub in her palace. How fortunate she is to have her independence!"

Jason's mood had begun to darken again. He said he had never met Phaedra, daughter of the late Minos, nor her sister Ariadne, but had no reason to fear her enmity. "I can show her how it would be to her advantage to have me firmly established as king in Iolcus."

Proteus/Triton was as elated as anyone else aboard. He looked forward to this landing not only because Daedalus might be here, but because he had hopes of being able to visit in waking life with Prince Asterion.

Jason confided to Proteus his private worries that some of his men might be ready to jump ship when they came into this friendly port. So far only the maid seemed to have done that, but Corycus offered the most tempting refuge they had seen in a long time.

And in the discussion of recent amazing events on Corycus, the name of the Artisan came up. "I had heard that it was old King Minos who, before he died, brought Daedalus to this island."

Proteus simply nodded in agreement. If and when the moment came, he expected it would be easy enough for Triton to take the Fleece away from the captain. Of course Jason should also get some credit for the gift—Triton thought that would do the captain a lot more good than handing it over to Pelias.

Several days passed before they finally rowed and sailed their dangerously damaged vessel within sight of the harbor of Kandak. There were immediate indications that their stay might not be as peaceful as they had hoped.

The *Argo* was still more than a mile at sea when those aboard saw smoke rising from what appeared to be the center of the city, more smoke than could reasonably be expected from the cooking fires of even a large metropolis.

Whatever was burning on shore continued to burn, and the smoke kept ominously rising, but they really had no choice but to put in anyway. One more serious squall would almost certainly finish off the chronically weakened *Argo*. Unless an opportunity for major repairs could soon be found, her days were numbered, even if the Fates should grant them good luck and good weather.

When Proteus asked to see the Fleece again, Jason hesitated but then brought it forth, carefully wrapped in layers of cloth and fur. Exposing it on deck had only seemed to accelerate its deterioration.

It was now so shrunken that Jason could carry it inconspicuously in a pouch or pocket.

Looking at the poor thing in the bright light of day, Jason said thoughtfully: "If it should ever turn out that I cannot be king in Iolcus . . ."

"Yes?"

"Then I must manage to be king somewhere else."

Medea and Proteus exchanged glances. Jason was still contemplating the wasted Fleece. "I have been thinking," he went on. "In the last six months I have come to understand the ways of royalty somewhat better than I did when we began this voyage."

"I suppose we all have," Proteus agreed.

The captain did not seem to be listening. "It is all too possible that when I get home, Pelias will refuse to honor our agreement."

Again his hearers exchanged a glance between them. Proteus said: "I would say that's more than a possibility. In that case, there would be no use handing over the Fleece to the damned old tyrant."

Medea asked her husband: "What will you do then?"

"Other means must be considered. The right to the throne rests with me."

Triton/Proteus wished his ambitious shipmates well. But basically he did not give a damn which human rump might rest on which elevated chair.

What did concern him was the fact that, whatever happened when Jason brought his miserable treasure home, the Argosy would then be over. And Proteus/Triton would have to discover just what he was, what life might hold for him when he could no longer be an Argonaut.

The *Argo* was still separated by some hundreds of yards of blue water from the harbor's mouth, and the men aboard were still hoping that the smoke might have some innocent explanation, when Proteus suddenly had a sensation of familiarity. The port of Kandak was gradually coming into view before him, and there welled up in him vague memories of seeing this land and these buildings before, through mortal eyes. Suddenly he realized that for all he knew, his earlier, purely human self might even have lived here. That was an alarming thought, considering what he had begun to learn about Old Proteus—he could only hope that Princess Phaedra's men would not try to arrest the agent of King Pelias on sight.

It was soon evident that the authorities on Corycus had far more immediate things to worry about. The ship was now close enough to shore to convince its crew beyond all doubt that something was seriously wrong. At one edge of the city, not far inland, stood what had to be the royal Corycan palace, sometimes called the House of the Hammer. Right beside it stretched a vast, low-slung sprawl of walls within walls, walls upon walls, most of them roofless but mixed with low roofs and truncated towers. This could only be the fabled Labyrinth, the home of Prince Asterion and of a thousand legends. The great Maze was said to cover some four square miles, of which only a small part was visible from where the *Argo* lay offshore.

The smoke they had observed while still well out to sea could now be seen to rise from burning buildings, scattered about the city but all at some distance from either Maze or palace. It appeared to Proteus that some kind of war or insurrection must have broken out.

A weary groan went up and down the rowers' benches. "Not here, too!" a despairing voice cried out. "Is the whole world at war with itself?"

"Damn it all, but I was ready for a rest!"

"Not good." With a sigh Jason looked at the four men who were now bailing steadily. Yesterday two had been enough to keep the vessel afloat. "We have no choice but to put in. But let us not go into the harbor."

Jason and his crew had been out of touch with the world for several weeks. No ship outward bound from this port had encountered them at sea, to pass along the shouted news of any dreadful conflict.

The captain was pointing at a small boat that bobbed on the waves at no great distance. "Pull up to this fellow here, let's see what he can tell us."

Jason was looking at a single figure in a small fishing craft. The figure proved to be that of a gray-bearded man, tending a single fishing line. He was wearing nothing but a broad-brimmed hat, which offered some protection against the relentless sun. The fisherman looked up in fear at the *Argo*'s swift approach, and her practical appearance, but Jason soon put him at his ease. And if he was a man who kept up with the affairs of the world, it was even probable that he recognized Jason and his ship.

"What's happening ashore?" the captain called.

"Talus," was the laconic answer.

"Talus? But who's that? Or what? Some new kind of plague?"

The man seemed to be thinking it over. "Whether who or what is hard to say."

"Just what's that supposed to mean? Some invading king or pirate?"

"Worse than that."

"How could it be worse?" The Argonauts all turned blank looks on one another. Apparently the name meant nothing to any of them.

Surprisingly, the fisherman proved something of a linguist. "His name means 'sufferer'," he volunteered. "They call him that because of the awful noise he makes."

"But what is this Talus doing, apart from setting fires?" the captain asked.

"You'd not believe me if I told you, my lord Jason. But if you go into the harbor, you'll soon see for yourselves. You'd be better off to set your sail and head for some other island." Their informant shook his head sadly, and began to set his little oars into their locks. "I must go back into the port, but you don't need to."

Some Argonauts were ready to stop him, but the captain fatalistically shook his head. "Let him go."

"Then what are we to do, captain?"

"I think that under the circumstances it will be better not to enter the harbor. The surf's quite low. We'll pick out a spot on the outer shore, and run aground." Jason ran weary fingers through his hair. "And get out the repair materials again."

They had rowed only a little closer to the beach when one of the men pointed inland, and raised a cry of wonder. "A bronze man!"

Proteus turned his head, and saw the thing immediately. It was still almost three hundred yards away, but one look was enough to make him stare in wonderment. Nothing in his damaged memory was really any help with this—the nearest Triton's thought could come to it was a vague image of certain metallic entities that labored in the workshop of Hephaestus.

Some of the crew protested that the figure was not all that strange— it was only that the island had been invaded by some army wearing armor. But Proteus shook his head at that. There was only the single figure.

"It is a man in armor," said an Argonaut, squinting to see clearly.

His benchmate disputed this. "No, I don't think so. Whoever saw armor that covers a man's whole body?" Of course that sounded like a good idea, except that any mere human weighed down by so much thick metal would find it virtually impossible to move.

At first glance, the figure appeared unarmed and empty-handed, somewhere close to the size of an ordinary human. It seemed not nearly formidable enough to be responsible for a burning city. At the distance it was hard to be sure of details, but the person, or thing, looked nude and sexless. Very nearly its entire body was the color of bronze, with only a few spots of darker hue where there should have been a face.

"I know what it reminds me of," commented another Argonaut. "One of those misbegotten brass Bulls."

"Then maybe Jason can deal with it, as well as he did with them."

The face had two eyes, but they were as artificial-looking as the rest. There was almost no nose at all, and very little mouth, despite the loudness of the voice.

Jason sighed. "Well, we'd better find out who—or what—it is we have to deal with."

The Argonauts stared at Talus as they rowed, and Jason debated with himself, aloud, whether they ought to hail him. But before the captain could make up his mind, the figure startled him by calling out to him. In a loud penetrating voice, so harsh and metallic that it could come from no other source, Talus hailed the ship.

In his harsh, booming tones the Bronze Man announced that he had recognized the painted name upon the bow of *Argo*, and commanded those aboard to land immediately and surrender the Fleece to him. The tones of his voice made it indeed an awful noise, that turned the thoughts of Proteus to themes of suffering.

"Then someone does hold our find to be of value," Jason muttered. He filled his lungs and boldly roared back at the figure on the shore. "What master do you serve?"

"Hades!" The name came in a hideous shriek, so loud that Proteus felt the hair on the back of his neck trying to stand up.

And in the same instant, Talus bent to pick up something from the ground. Moments later a stone the size of a man's head came whizzing through the air, hurled by the bronze thing directly toward the ship, as if to prove that its demands should be taken seriously. The missile passed so closely above the deck that the men who were closest to its pathway dodged. It appeared the apparition did have fingers after all, at least enough of them to grasp a stone and hurl it with impressive accuracy and awesome strength.

At first some of the Argonauts, who had been looking elsewhere at the moment of the throw, insisted they were being bombarded with a catapult or trebuchet. But now all eyes were turned upon the uncanny thing as it stood on a seaside cliff. Again the bronze right arm flashed in the sun, quicker than a small bird's wing, and here came another flying rock, this one to send up a fountain of spray a few yards short of its target, then skip on to smash into an outrigger with wood-cracking force, so that the whole ship rocked.

"Armor or not," said a man on the right of Proteus, "that can be no man."

"No," responded another on his left. "But I don't believe it is a god."

"What else? What's left? It's not a Giant."

An Argonaut who had seen service in several navies exclaimed: "Truly it seems a kind of war machine, built in the shape of a man. But I have never seen the like of it before."

"Daedalus might make something of the kind."

"No mortal could!"

"We all saw those two other things, that had the shape of bulls. Who made them?"

Triton, knowing something of the habits of his fellow deities, suspected that Hades had found or created this creature somewhere in the

Underworld, and then sent it up in the hopes of gaining the Fleece for his own mad purposes.

For a time the men had ceased to work their oars. The ship was slowly drifting a little nearer to the shore, and when the Bronze Man came into view again, he had his back to them and was running inland. He had been only a few hundred yards away by line of sight, but that distance was rapidly growing greater. A long inlet lay between him and the spot where the *Argo* meant to land. If Talus wanted to get at them without swimming, he was going to have to go the long way round, perhaps a mile.

Now his almost featureless face turned back toward the *Argo*, even as he ran on in the other direction, and again the strange voice, inhumanly loud, came booming at them across the water.

"Jason of Iolcus! Surrender the Fleece to me!"

But why, Proteus wondered, would Hades want the Fleece? Possibly only to keep Zeus and his allies from getting any benefit out of it.

"The damned thing is trying to drive us away." For the first time, Proteus heard something like a note of hysteria in the voice of an Argonaut.

His benchmate answered: "Aye, away to the Underworld! One more hit from a rock like that last one will send us to the bottom."

And another man put in: "Maybe he wants to force us into shallow water, and sink us there. Probably thinks we're loaded down with plunder. Once he sees the Fleece, he may change his mind on wanting that."

Jason was calm as usual when things got nasty. "Bring her around, steersman! We might as well pull in to shore, and close our eyes to flying rocks. Even if he doesn't hit us, we're going to go down. We're taking water faster than before."

"What'll we do, Captain? Form a line with spears and shields?"

"No. Most of you will concentrate on fixing the ship, while I fight off this latest monster." Jason turned to Medea. "No more magic ointments on hand?"

Wordlessly she shook her head.

"So be it, then," he grunted. "I managed two metal monsters in Colchis. Perhaps I can handle one more."

Proteus refrained from pointing out that the Bulls were not known to have destroyed a good part of a large city, nor were they capable of hurling head-sized rocks like pebbles.

Medea was looking at her husband proudly. "To win this battle would certainly increase your fame, and also your chances of becoming king. Of course I will help you with my magic. Proteus and the others will do all they can. Proteus! Do I not speak the truth?"

"I am sure we'll all do our best, my lady. But I advise avoiding battle if that is possible. If not, Jason, you must certainly not face this thing alone. I will stand with you."

———

By this time Talus, who was evidently no swimmer, had vanished, running, somewhere inland. It seemed very likely that he meant to run around the inlet and close with the *Argo* when she came ashore.

Urging his men on, Jason got them to drive the *Argo* straight at the scrap of beach. While they were still in relatively deep water, Proteus dove in; a few moments' swimming and he was in the shallows, then running up the beach at his chosen landing place. He supposed he risked revealing his godhood by swimming at such a speed; but this was an emergency, and he expected the crew were too busy to concentrate on him.

Within a matter of a few more heartbeats he was standing, dripping, at the top of the beach, from which a hundred yards or so of open field extended inland, with a grove of olive trees beyond that, shutting out the view of the harbor and its immediate surroundings. Looking back into the gentle surf, he saw with mixed feelings that Jason too had leapt out of the vessel before it grounded, and was about to join him on shore.

Facing inland again, he observed that Talus had not yet reappeared. Well, if the damned thing was a mechanical device, like the Bronze Bulls, then Triton the god felt capable of handling it. He was unafraid of any war machine made by mortals. Even if it were a creation of the redoubtable Daedalus, he told himself, though he had to stop and ponder before he could feel sure of that.

Now, if only the Bronze Man did not change his tactics and retreat . . . but no, here he came, approaching the long way round the deep inlet, evidently still determined to get at the *Argo*. Sun glinted on a figure no longer sprinting as no mere human would ever have the strength and speed to run, especially in full armor, but moving more slowly, stalking like a predator with game in sight, his steady advance punctuated with small lateral movements.

Another pair of running feet, these merely human, sounded behind Proteus. Before he had thought it was really possible, here was Jason, sword in hand, standing right beside him.

"It is some god, I tell you," Jason whispered, staring at their strange opponent, who still charged forward. "Or else Hercules come back to be revenged on us."

Haraldur had joined them, and here came Polydeuces, all of them fully armed. They all looked as if they would welcome the chance to fight, for a change, some other opponent than the endless sea.

The boxer snorted. "Revenge for being left behind when we set out? Instead he should thank the men who played him that trick. And this figure's nothing like Hercules, except in strength. What god would it be? It looks like none I've ever heard of."

Proteus/Triton considered trying to persuade the warriors who had joined him to go back to the ship and let him handle Talus; but he could think of no way of phrasing the suggestion that they would not find offensive. Well, their lives were their own to dispose of as they chose; he would try to keep them breathing.

Triton for his part preferred to meet this strange and formidable opponent with his own back to the ocean, and as close to it as possible. With this in mind, he retreated a few paces closer to the sea, and there took his stance, on the highest ground in the immediate vicinity.

Meanwhile, a handful of local citizens had begun to gather at a little distance from the Argonauts, standing on some higher rocks that doubtless gave them the illusion of relative safety. Half of these Corycan natives were begging for help, while the others urgently warned the newcomers to shove off in their ship again, and flee while they still had the chance.

One man pleaded with Jason to give the Sufferer anything he demanded, so then the monster might depart from their island and leave them in peace. "If it wants something from you, please hand it over!"

Jason raised one hand in a wave, including all of these advisers. And then he ignored them all.

But Proteus raised his voice and called to them: "What more can you tell us about this awful enemy?"

The citizens looked uncertainly at one another, and voiced disjointed theories, none of them of any help. There was not even general agreement as to where Talus had come from. However he might have reached the island, or exactly when, since his arrival the Bronze Man seemed to have spent most of his time lying low, though emerging for bursts of terrible activity. Over the last three days, he had wiped out several squads of soldiers sent against him. Naturally by now everyone was too terrified to approach him. Princess Phaedra had summoned all her advisers, but among them only Daedalus had offered any hope.

"Then Daedalus is here?" Proteus asked sharply.

"Oh, yes sir, if the monster has not killed him yet."

"Let us devoutly hope not," Jason muttered.

One of the local men offered the opinion that the Sufferer must be a demigod, at least. He had heard that Zeus had given him to Queen Phaedra, to stand sentry duty over the island of Corycus by running clear around its perimeter three times every day.

With the air of one privy to great secrets, the man concluded: "And they say that he is also going to visit each village on the island, taking a regular census of the inhabitants."

The natives began to argue among themselves. Most of what they were saying now made very little sense to Proteus, or to Triton either.

22

Talus

THE BRONZE MAN had been advancing erratically, as if he might be focusing his attention on some prey closer to him than the Argonauts and their ship. And here, dodging between the trees of an olive grove that lay just inland, came confirmation of that idea, in the form of a lone human, running now at full speed toward the new arrivals.

Other people running had now and then come into view, in whatever part of the Corycan landscape Proteus happened to be looking at. But this man was the only one moving toward the Argonauts, and only he had Talus stalking after him.

The lone fugitive was lean and scantily clad, with gray showing in his hair. He was covering ground more speedily that most people of forty years or so could manage.

"It's Daedalus," Jason exclaimed suddenly. "I met the man in Iolcus, on the day of our departure."

Proteus stared when he heard that. Suddenly it seemed possible that the great gods had really begun to smile on him, after all.

As the Artisan drew closer, his appearance was somewhat disappointing. He was garbed in the clothing of a common workman, consisting of a mere loincloth and sandals, and a cheap vest whose small pockets jingled when he ran. Not with coin, Proteus saw now, but with delicate tools.

The name of Daedalus, if shouted in the marketplace, would not have created nearly as much excitement as that of Jason, but was perhaps just as widely known in the world. He was of no more than average height, with greenish eyes, a large nose, and brownish, gray-streaked hair tied behind him with utilitarian string. His fingers were ringless as a slave's, though there was no reason to believe his corded neck had ever worn a collar. Both hands were scarred, as if from the use of every kind of common tool.

He came pounding up to the Argonauts where they stood near the sea. He had lost one sandal somewhere, and his chest was heaving. "I am called Daedalus," he got out in a breathless voice. "And you are Jason."

The captain bowed. "Of course I recognize the famous Daedalus. You and one other, whose name and face have escaped my memory, were talking with Hercules, the day before we began our voyage."

When Daedalus turned to him, Proteus extended his right hand in greeting. It was enfolded by a callused paw that felt as hard as wood.

Then the Artisan, still breathing hard from what must have been a long run, turned back to the captain. "The machine means to kill me. Can you take me quickly out to sea?"

"Not as quickly as we would all like," Jason informed the fugitive. "Repairs are necessary." Then, seeing that the Bronze Man was not actually upon them yet, he turned away to help his crew in their rush to fix the ship.

Daedalus's face fell as soon as he was able to get a close look at the *Argo*, drawn up on the beach. Argonauts were laboring feverishly, with pieces of wood, canvas, and pitch, to patch two holes in her bottom planks. Medea was standing at a little distance, gesturing at the battered vessel, obviously trying to help in some way with her magic.

"I hope, by all the gods," panted Daedalus, "that Hercules is still with you. This island and its people have sore need of his strength today."

"He is not with us," Jason responded over his shoulder. He offered no explanation.

Puzzled, the Artisan looked to Proteus, who shook his head and said: "I have never met the man, he dropped out of our crew before I joined. What can you tell us about Talus? All we've been able to learn so far is that his name means 'sufferer.' "

Daedalus snorted. "Bah, the old word has nothing to do with suffering. It means an ash-tree. A smith told me that a race of bronze men once sprang from ash-trees. The charcoal from that wood burns with a tremendous heat, and so is good for smelting out the copper that must go into the alloy."

The Artisan sat down suddenly on the ground, as if his legs had grown too tired to hold him up. "Practical information about Talus is not easy to come by, but there is some evidence that he comes from the Underworld, and is in league with Hades."

Proteus said to him: "We have something we want to show you."

But Daedalus was wrapped up in some sudden new thought of his own. He called out to Jason: "You are on your way home, from your quest for the Golden Fleece?"

The captain turned his head again. "As you see."

"And was it a success?"

"It was," said Jason shortly, over his shoulder once again.

"Then may I see the Fleece at once? The matter is extremely urgent."

"That," said Proteus, "is exactly what I wanted you to see."

He looked hard at Jason, and after a moment's hesitation, the captain dug out the fragment from his belt pouch. It cost him another hesitant moment to actually hand it over to Daedalus.

The Artisan eagerly accepted the small wad, but then once again rising hope was dashed from his countenance. "Oh yes," he said in a lowered voice. "Marvelous stuff," he added glumly when he saw that some further reaction was expected. But his attitude belied the words.

A moment later he had handed the trophy back. "Marvelous," he repeated. "But useless to me. I already have a sample, very like this, in my workshop."

Proteus and the captain were both staring at him. "How can that be?" breathed Jason.

Daedalus threw a glance back over his shoulder, searching inland, but Talus still had not come into sight. He gave a slight shrug. "I managed to gain access to some of the materials left over when the Flying Ram was constructed, many years ago."

Proteus/Triton could feel himself growing irrationally angry. "Then you don't even want the damned thing after all?" he asked. "Are you sure? I heard—someone told me that the great gods were very eager to see this placed in your hands."

The Artisan did not seem at all surprised that the great gods took an interest in him. "One hears all kinds of things," he remarked, rubbing his forehead with a callused hand. He was still looking, wistfully, at the scrap of fabric as Jason stuffed it back into his pouch. "I was hoping that the Fleece would turn out to be something I had not seen before. Oh, this stuff is very interesting. At any other time I would be fascinated. But with Talus trying to kill me on the one hand, and the Giants to prepare against on the other, I have no time for merely interesting things. So keep your treasure, Jason, and derive from it whatever benefit you can. You have some kind of bet with Pelias, I understand?"

"But . . ." Proteus gestured his own disappointment.

Daedalus interpreted his puzzled look as a request for more information on the Fleece. "As a component of the Ram, it probably functioned to slow the vehicle down when a crash impended—then certainly it ought to have cushioned the final impact."

"Judging by the look of the Grove of Ares," said Proteus, "even twenty years after the final impact, as you call it, I would say it must have failed to do that. But are you sure that the great gods have no interest in this? I was certain they wanted it put into your hands."

Daedalus was getting his breath back, and now he regained his feet. He looked almost ready to run again—but only if he really had to. "Possibly they did, or do. But I fear Zeus and the others are somewhat out of touch with my work, having even more immediate threats to face." He turned to look inland again. "Where's Talus now? Do you see him anywhere?"

"No." Proteus was persistent. "I want to be able to tell the great gods that I have given you the Fleece!"

"I will tell them myself that you made the offer. I will also be happy to let them know that you have saved my life, if you have any way to manage that!"

Listening carefully, Triton could detect faint screams, coming from half a mile or so inland. The voices had a hoarse, male quality, that evoked an image of dying soldiers. "So, it's after you? You in particular, I mean?"

Daedalus nodded. "Unhappily, it is. Somehow it knows I am its only really dangerous opponent on the island. For days now I have been working, almost without sleep, to build a trap that will contain the Bronze Man if I can lure him into it."

Putting one hand in a pocket of his tunic, Proteus felt the "Tooth" he had stuffed in there before Jason underwent the trial of the Bulls. Proteus had known since he pocketed the Tooth that there existed someone who would be very glad to see a thing like this—and on an impulse he now held it out. "Here."

Daedalus took the gift, abstractedly, glanced at it and dropped it in a pocket of his vest. "Thank you."

What other comment he might have made was forestalled, by Medea who had now approached the men. She said to Daedalus: "There are still a number of ships and boats in the harbor. You might have got in one of those, days ago, and put out to sea."

Hasty introductions were performed, and the Artisan shook his head. "I might have. But I am pledged to defend the Princess Phaedra as best I can, and the princess refuses to leave her people in this crisis. But now it seems that I am cornered, and can run no more. Your ship may be my last chance to survive. I'll be no good to Princess Phaedra dead."

Jason was wrapping up the remnant of his treasure again. "What is this trap like, that you are building?"

"It is very complicated, sir. Not easy to explain." Daedalus swayed a little on his feet, as if his body dreaded having to run again. "Here comes Talus now. The gods be with us all."

———

Proteus turned to see that the bronze figure had reappeared, no more than a hundred yards away. The closer it came, the more human it appeared. It might indeed have been a man in armor, except that the waist and neck seemed too slender to have accommodated any normal human frame within them. If anything the figure now seemed a little smaller than Proteus had thought it when at a greater distance.

Jason was shouting at his men to heave on the *Argo*, get her back into the water at all costs, and they were scrambling to obey. Proteus glancing at the hull saw that some kind of patch, covering the worst leak, had been improvised with amazing speed.

When Proteus moved a few steps away from the Artisan, a little closer to the Bronze Man, the latter's attention stayed fixed on Daedalus. "I cannot run much longer," the great man admitted in small voice. His breathing had returned more or less to normal, but his face had a look of exhaustion. "You must let me board your ship. I must have rest."

"Of course," said Jason, and he was gone to join his men in getting the craft re-launched.

"I'm not sure the ship will be any safer," said Proteus. "Instead of that, stand close behind me, and I can probably protect you there."

Where were the great gods when they were truly needed? Proteus thought. He supposed, and Triton's experience held nothing to contradict the thought, that one thunderbolt from Zeus, or an Arrow from Apollo's Bow, could easily enough have reduced this Talus to a small heap of glowing slag. But according to all that he had heard, Zeus was elsewhere just now, very busy lying low and trying to decide on the best way to fight the Giants.

Meanwhile, a ragged formation of what must be Queen Phaedra's loyal troops had appeared in the middle distance, watching Talus from behind, and advancing on him slowly. Triton supposed the Corycan Army had been doing their best to defend their princess and their city, and probably Daedalus too. He could see that they had grown very wary of their terrible opponent.

To the Corycan soldiers' credit, they had approached to within about fifty yards of Talus, and were having another try from there. But slung stones, spears, and arrows only bounced loudly and harmlessly from Talus's metal body. The Bronze Man did not even turn his head to look at his assailants; and Proteus thought that as much as the fabric of his body might look like bronze, it had to be something even harder and stronger.

Triton was impressed as well as Proteus. "By all the gods, I think even Hercules could do nothing against this!"

Talus continued to ignore the barrage. He had concentrated his attention almost fully on Daedalus, and Jason. And now, having apparently satisfied himself that no trap or trickery awaited him where they were standing, he began a steady advance.

As the bronze thing moved forward, its color was changing, growing brighter . . . with a sinking feeling, Proteus realized that Talus had the hideous power of heating himself red-hot, through some internal source of energy.

"The day before yesterday," muttered Daedalus from close behind him, "some intrepid soldiers tried to catch him in a net. But he turned on the heat, like this, and it fell away at once in burning strands."

"The idea had possibilities," the Artisan admitted. "But a different implementation would be required . . ."

Seen at closer and closer range, the face of Talus seemed to be grinning fiercely—which might be, Proteus thought, some effect of the radiant heat. Slowly the Bronze Man approached, as if he respected Daedalus and was wary of some trap or trick. Or was it possible that he had somehow detected the presence of a god among these new adversaries?

Jason had rapidly retreated, trying to save his ship, and Medea had gone with him. Triton meanwhile had been calling his own powers into action.

———

Meanwhile, some thirty men, their muscles energized by fear, had shoved the ship back into the water, where it seemed in no immediate danger of going down, unless its planks should be punctured by another rock. Some of the crew, benefiting by their experience of recent days, were becoming wizards at the use of pitch and oakum and odd bits of wood and canvas.

Jason was standing on the deck, roaring out orders, trying to get his vessel out farther from the shore, to at least make greater demands on their foe's strength and accuracy. And beside her husband stood Medea, her lovely face a mask of rage, as she tried to use her magic to bring down Talus.

The *Argo* rode a smooth path out to sea, while her crew bent to the oars. Meanwhile, as in their escape from Circe's island, the swiftly swelling surf came crashing in to right and left.

Unslinging the Trident from his back, the sea-god held the weapon ready in his right hand.

Daedalus had not retreated to the ship, and it was plain that he preferred to seek protection by staying with Proteus. It crossed Triton's mind to wonder whether the Artisan had been consorting so much with gods that he was able to recognize one on sight.

Proteus danced nimbly back before the glowing horror, with Daedalus somehow keeping just behind him, then suddenly clinging fiercely to his back, like a small child seeking protection. The god's strength easily bore the burden. The surf had swelled abruptly, until the waves were house-sized, and then larger. The rushing billows split behind the sea-god's back, not touching him or the helpless human he was carrying. Then the great waves joined again in front of Triton, went pounding on to deliver their rock-crushing blows on the harbor breakwater and the small figure of glowing bronze that danced along it, now trailing a massive cloud of steam.

Triton was sure he could outrun any mere human, but his divine powers were much better suited to underwater work than to this earthly dancing; and he was slowed to some degree by carrying Daedalus with him. He understood very well that the protective powers of his godhood were definitely limited, and resistance to great heat might not be among them. He strongly suspected that if Talus was able to seize him, the body of Proteus might very well be crushed and burned to death, despite the fact that he was carrying a god-Face in his head.

Still, with his magic Trident ready in his grip, he felt confident of being able to deal Talus a devastating blow, as soon as the metal man came within reach. And now, as swift as thought, the Bronze Man was upon them, hands outstretched like the taloned paws of a springing beast. And just as speedily the Trident shocked the attacker into staggering back, producing as it struck his metal a pyrotechnic show, like the eruption of a miniature volcano.

Evidently Talus was made of tougher stuff than Giant-flesh, for the killing machine was not destroyed. Instead it backed away, just far enough to be well out of Proteus's thrusting range, and there it began to dance about, industriously picking up more rocks and throwing them again. Now and then, moving with lightning speed, it feinted a new dash to close quarters.

Proteus used his Trident to parry the flying rocks, and waited for his foe to come to him again. He himself was wary of advancing inland even a step more than was necessary. As long as Proteus stayed within the grasp of roaring waves, Triton could keep not only the three points of his Trident interposed between himself and his adversary, but a protective shield of water too. Each time the glowing, grinning thing of bronze advanced on him, masses of water battered it. Great waves were torn asunder by its heat, shredded into hissing, roaring steam, so that the figure of Talus beyond was visible only as an orange glow through a cloud.

So far Triton's tactics were succeeding, but he realized that the man he was trying hardest to protect now stood in some danger of drowning. Deftly the god maneuvered to get his back turned briefly inland. Then, with the monster for once between him and the sea, he gently set down Daedalus, and from the corner of his eye saw the man go scrambling away.

Talus made no attempt at pursuing the Artisan, evidently realizing it would be a grave mistake to turn his back on his new enemy.

Proteus/Triton had to lure his metallic antagonist out on a spit of land almost surrounded by the sea. Once there, he called on a flow of ocean, creating titanic waves that swept ashore and enveloped Talus in a cloud of steam.

The Bronze Man tried to advance across slippery rocks, but the huge masses of stone were not much impressed by his furious burning. His metal foot slipped on slick rock, and he began to fall. Moments later another big wave caught him squarely, and hurled him back shoreward in a fresh explosion of steam.

A moment later he was advancing again, as rapidly as before. But Triton had all the water of the Great Sea to call upon. He tried to speed the timing of the waves, but that was hard to do, once a natural rhythm had been established.

At last a cross-current of green liquid force swirled his bronze antagonist away. Mountains of cold water brought up from the depths exploded into steam, hammered Talus between them, and seemed about to beat him to pieces on the rocks. Now it seemed that process had begun, for one of the Bronze Man's hands was dangling uselessly.

A cheer went up from the Argonauts, whose ship was still riding close enough to shore to let them see something of what was happening; but not even Triton could hear the cheer, for the thundering of the surf.

Even after being wave-damaged, Talus managed to climb a cliff and was preparing to hurl another rock. But something inside him had been damaged, or exhausted, and he could no longer summon up the strength. He stood there for a short time, high on the jutting cliff. And then, abruptly, his legs could no longer hold him up. His strength failed, and he pitched forward headlong into the place where the surf beat on the rocks.

———————————

Later, of course, the legend-makers were to have their way with that day's astounding happenings. One story had it that an Argonaut wounded Talus in the ankle with a poisoned arrow. Others somehow gave credit to a passing shepherd for encompassing the Bronze Man's destruction; most awarded the chief honor to Medea, and her reputation as a magician was enormously enhanced.

———————————

As soon as Jason saw Talus fall, he urged his crew to turn their craft around and row straight for the harbor, in search of a place where again they would be able to resume their work of repair. *Argo* at the moment was not fit to begin the last leg of her voyage home.

Everywhere, along the seawall and the docks, crowds were gathering, cheering lustily for those who had somehow caused Talus to be destroyed. From a distance, Medea on her ship's deck had been far more visible than Proteus, where he stood almost buried in the surf that he had raised. So it was only natural that she should be given credit for the victory.

Gasping, his muscles quivering in the aftermath of exertion, but ready to fight again if necessary, Triton/Proteus held his position standing on a spray-drenched rock, waiting for the bronze head to appear once more above the waves. Minutes passed, and then an hour, and there was still no further sign of Talus.

———————————

It now seemed that, after all, nothing could stop Jason from bringing the Fleece home with him. Medea was obviously still determined to help him succeed in his mission.

And Proteus thought: *I have stood by him so far, and I will stand by him till he confronts his uncle and claims his crown. However that turns out. Jason will then be on his own. But before I leave Iolcus, I think I will have a word or two to say to Pelias on my own account.*

Triton had begun, with spells and unobtrusive gestures, to calm the waters still beating on the Corycan headland. He had also issued a silent summons, for dolphins to come and help in the search for metal parts. But it might well take hours for the nearest such creatures to reach the scene. Meanwhile, Proteus/Triton preferred to spend his own personal energy making sure that *Argo* was still safe, rather than seeking the remains of Talus underwater.

Within minutes after the fight ended, and long before the summoned dolphins could arrive, agile Corycan youths and girls were clambering on the wet rocks, braving the subsiding surf, plunging their shining bodies into the deep pools between rocks, from which a hundred rivulets were now carrying back the surplus to the sea.

There passed a quarter of an hour, then a half. So far, no more than a few brassy fragments had been recovered, from between the sharp points of the hard black rock, evidently part of one arm and hand. That was all.

And Daedalus, afforded the chance to make a leisurely inspection of a few little fragments of his deadly adversary, observed that he was strongly reminded of the Golden Maidens in the workshop of Hephaestus.

In these small bits of bronze-colored metal he found true excitement. The largest piece was a single finger, more or less intact. Daedalus vowed to pay a substantial price for any additional part of the wreckage that had been Talus, bronze in this case being deemed more valuable than gold. He asked that young people be ordered back into the surf to look for more parts, and he himself, weary as he was, dared to enter the subsiding waves to search.

———

Daedalus did succeed in carrying off whatever remnants of Talus could be found in the pounding surf. Still some thumbnail-sized pieces were being found, and not all of them were metal, a few being of stuff much harder to identify.

Medea was being acclaimed across the island, given credit for slaying the bronze terror with her magic. Daedalus, the only one who might have let people know the true state of affairs, said nothing, being utterly intent on his own ideas and work.

———

On the afternoon and evening following the defeat of Talus, Jason and Medea and all their shipmates were royally entertained on shore.

Triton/Proteus would take advantage of the delay of several days, while *Argo* was being solidly repaired with the help of a grateful Princess Phaedra, and would try to visit Prince Asterion in his Labyrinth.

Jason and Medea were mildly surprised to learn that it was their shipmate Proteus whom Prince Asterion wanted to see in private.

———

Escorted partway into the Labyrinth, Proteus/Triton found it vastly different in appearance from the site he had visited in dreams. His immediate surroundings were of reasonable dimensions. After only a short walk, through many turnings, he was shown into a comfortable roofed chamber and asked to wait. He was told that Prince Asterion would soon be with him.

While he waited, the man who had once come out of the sea to join the Argonauts found himself confronted by (for the first time in his life, as far as he could remember) a fine, clear mirror. And for just an instant it seemed to Proteus that he caught a momentary glimpse of the face of Mouse, as if she were right beside him, looking into the mirror too.

Surely he must have seen good mirrors at some point in his old life, and surely the god component of his compound being ought to be used to them. Still, this one was something of a shock, because of the image it presented. It was a fine sheet of glass or metal, beautifully silvered, and it gave him back an image that he thought must be very close to the reality. To what other humans saw when they looked at the man called Proteus.

It was not exactly what either Proteus or Triton thought he must look like, but he was ready to believe the glass could be right and his own ideas wrong.

Now it was not the Mouse, but the Bull-Man himself, the Minotaur in person, whose image joined his own.

Proteus turned and saw that this time the fantastic apparition was truly real, and Prince Asterion was standing just behind him.

"I have had it specially installed," the Minotaur told him, pointing at the glass with one huge but very human finger. "Because I want to know myself."

"I wish that I could know myself," said Proteus.

———

On that same evening, in the adjoining palace, Princess Phaedra offered Jason and his bride a new ship, in gratitude for the successful fight they and their people had made against the scourge that had almost destroyed her realm. He declined with thanks, preferring to complete his voyage in the same faithful vessel in which he had begun it.

When the princess expressed her curiosity about this decision, he told her that he had been granted a vision, to the effect that his fate and that of the *Argo* were inextricably linked.

Later Phaedra saw the visiting princess alone; what passed between the two of them was not immediately revealed.

———

The celebration of thanksgiving went on for several days. By that time Jason's ship had been made as seaworthy as the shipwrights of the port could make it, and he summoned all the Argonauts aboard. It was time that they pushed on for home.

23

Home

FOR SOME OF the Argonauts, returning to Iolcus meant truly coming home. But Proteus had no feeling of familiarity when the rocky landscape of the large island first came into sight, or when he first beheld the Iolcan ruler's castle perched atop one of the rugged arms of land enclosing the ample harbor. Somewhere up there in that pile of stones, Pelias would be jealously guarding the throne that Jason wished to occupy.

During the last hour of the homing voyage, Triton noted, with his divinely augmented vision for all pelagic things, how the seaward side of the castle overhung a wilderness of jagged rock, whose only visible inhabitants were a few hardy bushes, and some nesting seabirds. A little farther inland, pine-clad promontories reared up, surrounding the harbor on all sides, save for its narrow opening to the sea.

But it was the seaward surface of the rocks just below the castle that Triton found most interesting. Certain faint but broad traces of oceanic slime, too faint for merely human eyes to see but reasonably fresh, marked the oceanside cliffs just below the castle's frowning outward face. The sight of that trail strongly suggested the possibility that a fish-tailed Giant might have come visiting old Pelias. The marks were such as might have been left by a two-handed but almost legless creature of more than human size, and they broke off before reaching as high as the castle itself, just at the level of a particularly well-defined crevice in the rocks. Triton/Proteus supposed the deep crevice might possibly hide an opening, maybe even the entrance to a tunnel big enough to accommodate a slithering Giant who had some good reason to drag himself that high above the water.

The castle's lowest windows peered out some forty or fifty feet above the sea, clinging to the crest of a rocky peninsula. Looking up at the castle's inner face as the *Argo* pulled into the harbor's mouth, Proteus could see how in one place a merlon was missing from the battlement, like a broken tooth in a Giant's face.

Almost exactly one half year after her departure, the rundown *Argo*, her oars fanning the water jerkily like the limbs of a weary swimmer, bore her captain, his new wife, and his crew of tired Argonauts back into the seaport of Iolcus. The day of their return was chill and gray, the skies weeping gently at the beginning of what passed for winter in these parts.

Almost all of the tired men on board remembered that departure, and it seemed to them very little had changed in their absence; the harbor was still only moderately busy. The people on shore and on the piers who stood watching the long ship's arrival were wrapped in such clothing as they had available. Well, at least there were no mountainous walls of ice.

Princess Phaedra had given them a new sail, but there was simply not enough wind to make it useful, or Jason would have raised the mast and tried his best for a brave entrance. Anyway, it seemed somehow fitting that the last yards of the long voyage should recapitulate the difficulty of the rest. Everyone pulled smartly at the oars, and no one grumbled. They would make one last unstinting effort, and finish up the job in style.

Triton had been carrying his Trident ever since he struck down Talus. The three-pronged spear was slung quite openly on his back by a scrap of cordage, but it remained imperceptible to any ordinary humans. None of his shipmates could see the weapon, or hear the little sounds it made when it occasionally bumped or scraped on other objects. Nor could they even feel it, apparently, when one of them happened to brush past him. He had to be continually careful that no one was accidentally stabbed.

For the moment at least, there was nothing about either the port or the castle to jog his memory; they were as new and unfamiliar as any other place and any other royal dwelling he had seen on the long voyage.

His mind, compounded of human and divine abilities and memories, kept drifting back to Circe, trying to puzzle out what sort of agreement the previous avatar of Triton could have had with her. But the Triton of a year ago, a god with all his memories intact and dwelling in a different human body, was as remote and irreclaimable as Old Proteus. Whatever agreement that deity might have had with the enchantress had certainly been dissolved in those great waves pounding the Isle of Dawn, or buried in the mud that they had left behind.

Still, Triton toyed with the idea of someday paying another visit to Circe on her island, and trying to make peace with her. Well, after she had a good chance to cool down he might try it. There was no hurry. He felt reasonably sure that if he were to return to the Isle of Dawn in a hundred years, he would find her essentially unchanged. With a little effort on both sides, their relationship could be repaired. Vague memory assured him that the two of them had fallen out before, at various times over the centuries. Still their long-term interests coincided. Anyway, he seriously doubted the enchantress would be bothering him here in Iolcus.

In the meantime, the image of another woman kept intruding on Triton's thoughts. If the Mouse had come back here to report to Pelias, as it seemed certain she had done, then she was very probably still in the castle or the town. He told himself he wanted to see her just once more, just to make absolutely sure . . .

But absolutely sure of what?

———

Just as the *Argo* was poking her faded prow into the harbor, Jason suddenly brought up another gloomy detail: when preparing for this voyage, he had, as he thought, persuaded certain well-off foreign backers to invest in the construction and outfitting of his sturdy ship. Those backers would now surely be expecting some return on their investment—but any reward he might give them would have to wait until he sat on the throne. Meanwhile they must somehow have been putting up with the enmity of Pelias.

Proteus pondered whether he ought to tell the captain that his real sponsor had been Circe. Maybe someday, he decided. Now did not seem to be the proper time.

"Where we going to dock, Captain?" someone asked.

"We're not. We'd sink even while tied up at the dock. Unless people stayed on board to bail continuously, and I won't ask anyone to do that. I seem to remember that there's a little beach, over near the castle's foot. We'll run her aground there."

"Ship oars," was the last command ever given on the voyage.

After the bottom grated on gravelly sand, in a bleak and drizzling rain, there followed a long moment of silence, in which no one said anything, no one moved.

Finally the silence was broken when another Argonaut announced: "By all the gods, I'm glad I did it. But I wouldn't do it again, not for a dozen Fleeces and a crown." There was a murmur of agreement, stronger than Jason liked to hear, to judge by his expression.

Some of the folk on the docks had recognized the ship, and already a few onlookers had stopped and were staring from a little distance. One youth took a good look at the arrival, then turned and ran off with a purposeful stride. It would not be long before everyone in the city, and in the castle, knew who had come in.

One of the returning Heroes bent down and kissed the stones of the shingled beach, as soon as he had stepped ashore.

The two eyes painted on *Argo*'s prow, now staring into hopeless rain, were faded and worn almost to invisibility by sun and sea. Their blank stare encompassed the calm harbor, occupied by a fair number of craft of all descriptions. Here the *Argo* was not arriving in the midst of strife; but Triton/Proteus had a foreboding that she brought with her the potential for great violence.

Before anyone walked away from the ship, Jason insisted on conducting a brief memorial service on the gravelly beach where they had run aground, a pouring into harbor water of the last mouthful of poor wine, as a libation. The captain's muttered plea to the gods recalled to all their minds the names and faces of their shipmates who had died in the course of the voyage.

Five or six of the crew turned their backs on the *Argo* and her captain immediately after the service and walked away, having nothing more to say to their captain or any of their remaining shipmates.

The eyes of the remaining crew watched without emotion as the last of the wine was given to wet rocks and sand—all the rest was already gone, and there had been no thought of saving the good stuff for last. Much better drink was soon going to be readily available, a short walk away.

Someone brought up the subject of what was to be done with the logbook—as soon as the last entry had been written into it. The writer juggled it in his hands, once, twice, and for a long moment Proteus had the impression that he was about to hurl it away, into the deepest water his throwing arm could reach. Jason may have thought the same thing, for he hastened to take possession of the log. He tucked it into a small pack he had dug out from somewhere and was carrying on his back.

He was carrying the Fleece in there too, and after a moment of indecision he took out the remaining scrap of fabric and handed it to Proteus. "Will you keep this for me, shipmate?"

Triton hesitated only momentarily. "I will, Captain. But for how long? And why?"

"Only a little while. Because I think it will be safer with you, for the time being, than with me. It's possible that the usurper's men will be waiting in the harbor, to arrest me on sight."

You are not alone in that, my captain. But Proteus did not say those words aloud; he thought he certainly could defend the treasure if anyone should try to take it.

Meanwhile Medea was standing by, wrapped against the chill in a fine blanket given her by the sympathetic Princess Phaedra. She watched Jason hand over the Fleece as if it made very little difference to her what he might do with it.

When everyone walked away from the ship, for the first time in months leaving her unguarded, Jason and Medea followed slowly, lagging behind, deep in private talk or argument. For once they did not seem eager to have Proteus as a consultant, and this time he was well satisfied to let them settle their own affairs.

Others of the crew, now straggling forward in a loose gathering, had their own personal concerns. "I've not a coin left on me," someone was muttering behind Proteus. "Haven't had for months."

The line of Argonauts grew longer and more straggly, trudging around the edge of the water toward the buildings and the docks. One man raised an arm and pointed. "Look, lads. It's the very spot where Hercules threw us all in."

Haraldur chuckled. "I'll not forget that. Never felt so foolish in all my life."

"And the way the harbor water tasted."

"That's because you thought of all the sewage that runs into it."

"Never thought I could be glad to see the place again."

"Talk about not forgetting. There's many things been seen and done on this trip that we'll none of us forget."

For what felt like a long time, as their feet kept carrying them along the water's edge, it seemed possible that Circe had struck them with a curse of invisibility, so that now, when they had finally, actually, almost incredibly, regained their home port, very few people were going to take any notice of their arrival. But slowly there developed an additional movement of humanity along the docks, a slow gathering of onlookers.

Some of the voyagers, including Jason, Proteus, and Medea, had acquired new clothes on Corycus, but others had not bothered, and were still in rags, seeming to glory in their Heroic poverty.

"Use your imagination, man!" one of these was saying to another. "We won't need coins, not for a few days anyway. Anyone just back from a cruise with Jason, and bringing back the Fleece, will have the local barflies standing in line to buy him drinks and hear his stories."

"Wait'll they see the Fleece, they'll want their money back."

"But on the other hand," put in Proteus, "maybe some of us will be in no mood for telling stories." As the progress of the returning Heroes carried them closer to the quays and stores of the waterfront, he scanned the scattering of folk already there, trying to discover among them the men or women who might be already looking for him in the name of the king. The captain in all innocence thought that he, Jason, was the only one Pelias was going to be concerned about. Little did the captain know.

Proteus had no doubt there were anonymous agents of the king among the workmen and idlers who had witnessed the arrival of Jason and his ragged crew. It was very likely that he, Proteus, had already been recognized; and if he had not, he soon would be.

He had to fight down an irrational idea that the Mouse might somehow have learned that the *Argo* would be putting into port today, and that she would come down to the docks to greet her former shipmates. Perhaps to point him out to the king's officers.

One of his companions jarred him out of dark thoughts by bumping his elbow and demanding: "What's your plan, Proteus? Going to join us in the funhouse?"

"Not right away." He nodded more or less straight ahead. "I'll just wait yonder, in the big tavern, so I won't be hard to find. The king will want to see me."

Haraldur had fallen into step beside him. "So you wouldn't anticipate any trouble getting in to see the king?"

"Not in the least. I need only stand still, to be magically whisked into his presence. And if you're with me, Hal, you can expect the same kind of invitation."

Haraldur smiled at that, then, as the pair of them were entering the tavern door, frowned, as at some joke he had failed to understand.

"Sure, he'll ask you to drop in for a drink." Haraldur squinted at him, and his voice changed. "By the gods, I think you're serious." Then the northman seemed to experience a flash of understanding, followed by even greater mystification. "You mean you . . . have some connection with old Pelias?"

Proteus had finished the voyage without a coin of his own, but a day ago he had secretly arranged for a sea-creature to provide him with a few pearls, that he figured ought to serve at least as well as golden coins. He now handed one of these stones to a servitor, who looked at it with some suspicion and took it to the manager.

In moments the two shipmates were settling into tavern chairs, that felt so gratefully different from a rower's bench. Haraldur sipped from his mug—the server had swiftly returned—looked round him at the smoky room, which was sparsely populated at this time of day, and sighed with satisfaction.

"Used to have." Proteus turned his gaze toward the window, and the high castle beyond, looming over everything. "But it may be that he thinks I'm still working for him. If so, then as soon as he learns I'm back, and Jason's back in good health, he's going to want to ask me why a certain job never got done."

"What job?" The northman wiped mead from his mustache.

"He wanted Jason dead, and I was supposed to handle it." Proteus poured more golden liquid from the big jug left on their table by the server.

There was a pause, while the northman digested this revelation. At last he said again: "You're serious."

Triton/Proteus nodded.

"But you didn't."

"You wouldn't think a man could forget an assignment like that, would you?"

Haraldur leaned forward and lowered his voice. "Proteus, have y'gone raving mad? To betray the king and still come back here?"

"Raving maybe, but not crazy. Though my brains were scrambled; that's the point, you see. That's what caused most of the confusion. Remember the day I joined the company?"

The other leaned back. "Not likely to forget it. The way you buried that spearhead in the log. Then, I thought I was making a joke, when I said you had to fight three of us. But now I think you might have."

Proteus nodded. "Almost all my memory was gone. I didn't know who I was—anything beyond my name. When Jason asked me, I managed to come up with that. I didn't know who I had been the day before, whether I had family or not, or if I was coming or going. No idea what I had been trying to do before the Giant sank the other ship. I thought it was the knock on my head that had wiped me out, but I was wrong."

"What was it, then?"

"I know now I killed that Giant." Proteus drank.

"By all the gods!"

"But before I did, he swept me with his special weapon. Scrambled my brain for sure."

The northman was following him closely. "But their special weapon has no effect on us poor mortal humans. It works only against . . ."

Haraldur's speech trailed off gradually. He sat there while his face changed slowly, until he was staring at the man across the table from him in a way that Proteus had never seen him look at anyone or anything before.

Proteus nodded slowly. "That's almost right, shipmate. But it does work against human minds, sometimes. It works inside any human head where a god-Face has come to dwell."

"So you . . . are . . . oh, by all the gods, I should have seen it! What's your name?"

"I picked up the Face of Triton a couple of hours before I joined the Argosy. Right after the Giant killed the previous avatar."

"Oh, by all the gods!" The discovery called for a deep drink, from which Haraldur emerged once more wiping his mustache. "Triton! The fish, and everything. I should have seen it—I've met a god or two before. And the waves. It was you who pried us free from Circe's island." He made it sound like an accusation. "Or washed us free, was more like it. And then on Corycus. It was you finished the Bronze Man, it wasn't the princess and her jabbering."

Proteus nodded again. "I expect that Pelias already knows what's happened to his secret agent."

"How could he know?"

Proteus didn't answer that directly. "But just possibly he doesn't. In that case he'll be very interested in finding out why the man he sent to kill Jason has been so busy saving his life instead."

Haraldur wiped his forehead. "Not only saving Jason's life but getting him the Fleece—and what about that Giant in the Grove of Ares, I suppose you settled him too? Hah! And now you're just hanging around here so you can explain your conduct to King Pelias? You've got—" He stopped suddenly and lowered his voice, though no one else in the tavern seemed to be paying them any attention. "Were you a mere man, I'd say that you've got balls, standing up to a king!"

Triton nodded. "I do want to see old Pelias, face to face. There are some other things that have to be cleared up between us."

"Like what?"

"I don't know if I can explain it, even to myself. But I won't be sure of who I am now, until I know who I was before I became an Argonaut. Does that make sense?"

Haraldur snorted. "Shipmate, you're asking the wrong man about what in the world makes sense, what doesn't. Anyway, I'd give much to be there, when you confront the king and he tries to figure out if you're really a god or it's all some crazy story. Triton, by all the hells!"

"I was hoping you'd say that, Hal." Proteus sat up straight in his chair. "I have many of Triton's powers, but perhaps not all have come back to me. There are times when even a god can use another pair of hands, another pair of eyes to watch his back. I'd much like to have a reliable shipmate at my side when I go to talk to Pelias."

When Proteus had looked out the tavern window at the castle for a while, some ghosts of memory did indeed begin to stir. He remembered, or imagined he did, something of the vast structure's interior layout, as if he had indeed spent time inside it. Up there would be the private apartments of the monarch, and over there, somewhat lower, the long windows of the great hall. And lower still, of course, and almost windowless, would be the dungeons, which were still considerably above the level of the sea.

Half a dozen other Argonauts had come into the tavern, and settled at another table, where they began to drink and grumble. These were not men that Proteus would particularly have chosen as companions. Drifting over from their table came unhappy words concerning money. Well, considered as a pirate enterprise, the Argosy would have to be rated a financial disaster for those taking part, and for any backers they might have had; a lot of efforts at piracy ended that way, as did a lot of honest trading voyages.

Still, the casualties on such an expedition might easily have been much worse. And considered in terms of its real mission, the voyage could hardly be described as a failure. Jason had brought back the Fleece, exactly what he promised to do when he set out. Almost everyone else aboard had promised the captain they were seeking only adventure, and they could hardly allege they had been cheated out of that.

Those few among the Argonauts who had families or friends waiting in the city or nearby would no doubt be given a joyous welcome, as soon as their loved ones learned they had come home; but only a few of the adventurers were so lucky. In these men's young lives, there had yet been time for nothing but restless adventure. For them the voyage was not really over—for some among them, the Argosy had been only one leg of the long wandering voyage of their lives. Some of those men still had countless miles and many years to go. Others, Proteus thought a majority, were ready to return to their own homes and settle down—at least until the itch for change and danger grew in them again.

Wherever they meant to go, home, or to the nearest brothel, the great majority of the surviving crew had dispersed very quickly. It was as if they were tired of looking at one another, and listening to each other's voices.

The men at the other table all seemed to have come ashore with money. Still, they were voicing their general dissatisfaction with the world.

Now one optimist among them raised his voice. "Look at it this way—you can soon be getting laid."

"That might be easier if we would soon be getting paid. How's that for a rhyme?"

"You've missed your calling—should have been a minstrel."

Of course there was no prospect of anyone being paid off—not one of the crew had been a hireling.

Proteus produced another pearl, which he used to buy a round of drinks for the other table. The men there waved their thanks, and gave him a rousing cheer.

Proteus got the idea that not one member of the crew wanted to hang around with Jason any longer. Well, he could understand that.

"It was a wonderful voyage," said one of the men at the far table softly.

"More wonderful than you ever knew," Proteus called back.

They waved their respectful thanks to him for the drinks, and one called over asking him what he was going to do next. In response he only shook his head. As far as he could tell, not one of the crew, now excepting Haraldur, was yet aware that a god had been rowing and sweating among them as their shipmate.

Proteus thought whatever he did would have little to do with human politics. Kingmaking was not something that could be accomplished simply by stirring up a few big waves. And Triton certainly had no intention of trying to use his seagod's power to establish Jason on a throne—though maybe the man would be a good king. *There are no good kings*, said a proverb that might have been as old as the gods themselves, *but there are certainly bad ones*.

It was, or should be, up to those who were purely human to settle the matter of kingmaking among themselves. Gods really lived in another world; he knew that, though he could remember almost nothing of what that other world, the society of deities, was like.

It ought to be fun, trying to find out.

Meanwhile Haraldur had been pondering something, and at last he came out with it. "Will Pelias still be on his throne when you walk out of his castle?"

"I don't know. I suppose he can keep it, for all I care." Pelias was doubtless bad enough, but Proteus thought that he had encountered worse—Amycus, for example. Looking out the tavern window, he thought that most of the people in the harbor here seemed to be getting along fairly well. No doubt there were some in the castle dungeon who would disagree with that assessment, but the same thing would be true if and when Jason came to rule.

Hal was almost whispering. "Take a look behind you when you get the chance. What *have* we here?"

Proteus turned casually in his chair. Four tough-looking men, not uniformed but with a certain air of officialdom about them, had entered the tavern and taken a table. They looked toward Proteus and Haraldur from time to time. Proteus guessed they were prudently waiting until most of the Argonauts had dispersed before moving in on their prey. Hard-looking men, but probably not wanting to chance a fight with half a dozen of Jason's picked companions. Not when they had no need to hurry.

And now, here came Jason and Medea into the tavern—apparently some business outside had delayed them. Jason immediately went to talk with the other Argonauts at their table, where he was received respectfully but with no eagerness. Meanwhile the princess surprised Proteus by coming to where he and Haraldur were sitting. When they rose politely, creating room, she surprised him again by sitting down with them, though brushing aside the offer of a drink. When Haraldur made tentative motions as if to take himself away, Medea put a hand on his arm and asked him to stay.

Proteus asked: "Have you had any new word, Princess, about your missing maid?"

She gave him a puzzled look. "No. Why?"

Proteus said: "I suppose she may be here."

Medea blinked at him. "Here in Iolcus? Why? How?"

"It is only a feeling I have, my lady." He made a dismissive motion with his hand.

The princess gave him another strange look, then decided to get down to business. "The voyage is over, Proteus. What are you going to do?"

Everyone seemed to be asking him that. "I am not at all sure," he said, and it was sharply borne in on him that he really did not.

In a way he wished that the *Argo* had not yet reached this port, that the long struggle could still go on, giving some meaning to his life. The goal of the Argonauts, like the Fleece itself, had begun to vanish as soon as they achieved it—he was reminded sharply of something Asterion had said, about how goals were not meant to be achieved.

Thoughts of the Minotaur in his Maze suggested to Proteus that he might possibly return to Corycus—neither the god nor the man within him had any special attachment to that place, none he could remember anyway, but it would be good to talk to Asterion again. Princess Phaedra had been grateful to the woman she thought had disposed of Talus, and Phaedra would doubtless be just as grateful to the god when he told her the whole truth. It seemed strange to Triton/Proteus that a god might feel a need for human gratitude—maybe it was just human companionship he really craved.

There were other things he craved as well.

And now that the voyage was over, he noticed in himself also a yearning for the deep sea, the endless realms of ocean that existed far out of sight of land—and the pleasant knowledge, sure and secret, that the next time he went there, he would need no boat or oars.

Whether he went to Corycus, or sought the depths of the ocean, something would be missing. Suddenly he had a sharp, clear memory, carrying a pang of regret, of the curve and warmth of the Mouse's firm young body when his arm had cradled her, first beneath the sea and then above it. He had a good memory, too, of the satisfaction he had felt when his god-power forced deep water to treat her tenderly, induced the Great Sea to nourish her with dissolved air instead of drenching out her life.

. . . the warmth of the Mouse's body. The life and courage in her voice, even when she was afraid. Even the way the hem of her shift, underwater, had teasingly played around her hips . . .

But this was foolishness, because the woman he remembered fondly had gone to betray him to Pelias—he was almost completely certain she had done that. Well, there was certainly no shortage of other women. He half-remembered some old proverb, about there being as many as fish in the sea. As a god he knew he could enjoy almost any of them whenever he wanted.

Which made it all the more remarkable that there were moments—he expected there would be more in the future—when Proteus, and maybe even Triton, no longer wanted to be a god. Not that the avatar had any choice about it. Not as long as he wanted to go on breathing. Not even Daedalus, not even Hephaestus or divine Asclepius, could extract a god-Face from inside a human head without killing the avatar.

———

Meanwhile, the four hard-looking men were keeping a casually determined watch on Jason, and on Proteus. But the four were content to bide their time, remaining on their own side of the big room. If Jason was aware of their scrutiny, he gave no sign. He was still talking to the

Argonauts at the other table, where he had taken a chair and was sipping at a mug.

Medea was sitting with her back to her husband, paying him no attention.

She was purposeful and energetic. "You must remember, good Proteus, that I once made you a little speech about how unsuited I am for the life of a fisherman's wife."

"I do indeed remember it, my lady."

"I must have greater things. In fact I am determined to be a ruler somewhere, someday."

"I see."

She nodded. "That seems to be the only way I can be free. I thought my magic was powerful enough to bring me freedom, but it seems not."

Proteus wondered what spells she had most recently been trying out. Whatever they had been, evidently they had not worked. "I understand what you mean, Princess. So what is your plan?"

"Soon I will be leaving Iolcus, without Jason. He has his own plans."

"I see," said Proteus again, and Haraldur muttered something.

The young woman facing them went on: "Where I will go I am not entirely sure as yet, but it will be in the pursuit of power."

Triton/Proteus was curious. "I had thought, Princess, that there was a great love between the two of you."

"I had thought so too. No, it was more than thinking, there really was." She shook her head. "But that is all finished. What I am asking you, Proteus, is this: Will you come with me as my counselor?"

"As your servant, lady?"

She shook her head briskly. "Certainly not as a menial. The servant of a princess may enjoy high caste, even a status of nobility. Before you answer, I will tell you—and you, Haraldur—something even my husband does not know as yet: I now have wealth, in the form of jewels. Real wealth, enough to hire ships, and men, when I know whom to hire. Princess Phaedra was grateful for my help, and more sympathetic to my position than I dared to hope."

Proteus said: "I am glad of your good fortune, my lady. But no, I will not come with you."

Medea did not seem much surprised at this response, only a little disappointed that it came so quickly and was so curt.

With steely imperturbability she raised the offer. "Then will you come with me and be my friend? I do not mean my lover. But someday the commander of my navy, or even chief officer of state?"

"No, my lady, I will not do that either." And Proteus offered no explanation.

For a moment he thought that the princess was going to insist on one. But instead she only turned her gaze to Haraldur. "Then will you be my counselor, on the terms I have just stated?"

The northman needed no time to consider. "I will, Princess. Gladly. That is, provided you can first spare me a few hours, to keep a promise I have made to Proteus, here."

The princess looked at them both. "I see no difficulty in that." She rose to her feet. "Tonight we will talk again. I have been told I am expected at the castle." In another moment she was gone, walking gracefully.

Triton, looking up once more from the tavern window at the high castle, knew he would soon be going there. The god invisibly continued to push forward certain magical arrangements he had begun while the *Argo* was still miles at sea.

When Medea had gone outside, Jason, as if he had been waiting for his wife to leave, came over.

The captain approached without haste or excitement, and stood before their table. "I trust you have the Fleece still with you, Proteus? Let me see it."

Jason seemed not to care if the other people in the tavern got a look at his shabby treasure, so Proteus simply drew it from his pack and held it out. Jason only looked at it and nodded and asked Proteus if he would keep it for him a little longer.

Then Jason said: "I have one more thing to ask of you, Proteus, and you, Haraldur. You certainly have no duty to comply, for I am no longer your captain. Our voyage is over, and both of you have done very much for me already."

"Ask," said Proteus, and heard Haraldur utter the same word at the same time.

"Will both of you come to the castle with me, while I confront the man who now sits upon the throne? It may be dangerous," he added in frank warning.

Proteus pushed his tankard aside and got to his feet. "I was planning to see your uncle anyway." Haraldur stood up also, saying: "I wouldn't miss this for the world."

Jason blinked at him in surprise. He seemed grateful for what he took to be fervent loyalty.

"Jason, let me first have a private word with our shipmate here. Then we will join you outside," said Proteus/Triton.

When he was effectively alone with the northman again, Proteus said to him: "Since you are coming with me, there is something I want to do for you first."

The magical business took Triton only a few moments, touching Haraldur's axe and dagger with his hands, and muttering an old formula that came when it was needed. When it was done, he said: "I am not as clever at these things as Circe—maybe I never was. But there, that should do the job." And now he was satisfied that Haraldur's weapons would be concealed as well as his own.

The northman looked doubtful, inspecting the business end of the battle-hatchet that rode head-uppermost at his belt. "I see no difference."

"You and I will still be able to see the tools of our trade, both yours and mine. But I hope and expect that no other human eyes will be able to detect them."

Haraldur still looked doubtful. Then his eyes suddenly focused on Triton's Trident, riding over its owner's shoulder on a sling. "Where in all the hells did *that* come from?"

Proteus/Triton smiled. "A dolphin brought it to me from the bottom of the sea. Now do you believe me?"

They went out of the tavern and joined Jason. As Proteus passed through the door, he saw the four thugs getting to their feet, with a great show of casualness, and following.

24

Reckoning

ON EMERGING FROM the tavern under a gray sky, from which the drizzle had now ceased to fall, Proteus contemplated the slate-colored water at the harbor's mouth, and realized that he would probably never again travel any great distance from the sea. He might never again be entirely out of sight of deep water, or beyond reach of the smell of the sea-breeze, though he was sure Triton could survive a few such jaunts. Not even if his life extended vastly farther into the future than Old Proteus had ever dreamed of living. The god-component in his head was virtually immortal, and long after the body of the man Proteus had been destroyed, and his shade had descended to the Underworld, some trace of him would remain attached to Triton until the end of time. *Once a god, always a god.*

Assuming that Triton could keep from having his memory expunged entirely by another Giant. Remembering the faint trail of green slime on the outer cliff, he thought it quite possible that Pelias had arranged a special welcome for him in the castle.

Eyeing the strong-arm lads so patiently waiting to collect him for the king, Proteus wondered if any of them could recognize him from the old days. There had been a moment when one of them nodded in his direction, what could have been a kind of personal greeting. Another of their number kept looking back over his shoulder, as if he expected more Argonauts to come in at any moment—which was a real enough possibility to keep the king's men on their good behavior.

"Proteus." The leader of the king's irregulars nodded to him in a friendly way. "Ready for a little walk up the hill?"

"I've been looking forward to it."

"Really. That's good. The king says he wants to invite all the Argonauts to pay him a visit. Of course, it wouldn't be polite for you to carry any weapons in. If you've got any iron on you, might as well hand it over now." The fellow, despite his tattoos and suggestive scars, had a knack for sounding as innocent as a schoolgirl.

Proteus lifted his arms away from his sides. "Search, if you like." And he stood there smiling faintly, while another of the escorts briskly patted him down. The searcher was totally oblivious to the murderous Trident, although his probing fingers actually touched it more than once. Haraldur allowed himself to be searched also, and his eyes went wide and marveling when the procedure somehow failed to discover either battle-axe or dagger.

Jason had already disarmed himself, voluntarily, and so Proteus offered him no magical assistance.

Meanwhile, Pelias's respect for protocol had caused him to treat a genuine princess very differently. He had sent a carriage and a courtly official down to her with an invitation, which she accepted with the aplomb of one brought up as royalty. The carriage behind its two strong-pacing cameloids soon passed up the walking men, and was swallowed by the main gate of the castle.

_____

The three Argonauts and their four-man escort were steadily retracing the path taken by Jason and his men on leaving the *Argo*, trudging around the harbor toward the castle and the long ship beached at its foot. The closer they came to the great structure on the ridge, the older it looked to Proteus. Much older than the palace in which King Aeetes held forth, and its grandeur was of a different and more rugged kind. Torches and lamps were being lighted in its windows, against the cloudy dusk.

After their escort had conveyed them in through the first gate, there were many stairs to climb, first out-of-doors and then inside. Most of the climbing was done in silence.

Looking through a distant doorway from one of the last corridors they traversed, Proteus caught sight of the Princess Medea seated amid luxury, in what appeared to be a small anteroom. She was being entertained by the same courtly official who had come down to the town to fetch her.

———

Pelias was evidently as eager for the confrontation as Proteus. The Argonauts were kept waiting only briefly, just outside the brightly lighted chamber in which the usurper was sitting on a kind of low throne, attended by three men. Two of these were graybeard counselors, but one was young, and royally dressed.

Looking in from just outside, Haraldur nudged Proteus with an elbow, and whispered: "Looks like the king's son is here. Acastus. Must be wondering when he'll get to take over."

On entering the room, getting their first good look at the man on the small throne, the three Argonauts were all startled to see how ill and old he looked. Proteus had all along been picturing a more vigorous opponent. Directly behind the throne was a stonework screen, an intricate design of curving blocks and spaces. Some six or eight feet behind the screen were the massive stones of the castle's outer wall, here pierced by a couple of large windows, one on either side of the low throne. These apertures were generously wide and open, looking out as they did upon the seaward side, where it must have seemed to the builders that no attackers could ever climb. The space between the windowed wall and the interior screen was heavily in shadow.

Ignoring his other visitors for the moment, King Pelias glared at Jason for a time in silence, and then bluntly demanded of him: "What have you brought me?"

"What I promised I would bring, Uncle." And Jason held out his hand to Proteus, who in turn produced the ball of dull stuff, which Jason in turn held out to the old man. "It is the Golden Fleece."

The king stared at the shabby remnant for a long moment, then grabbed it roughly, so he could hold it closer to his old eyes. At last he growled: "Is this some joke? To me it looks more like a handful of asswipe. What could this do for me? Nothing but make me a laughingstock."

Proteus spoke up boldly. "Daedalus, on the island of Corycus, said he found it interesting."

The king and his attendants only looked at him. He half-expected to be ordered to keep silent, but no one bothered to do that.

Anyone who looked at Pelias with open eyes would have to judge him not to be many days away from death by natural causes. Acastus ought not to have long to wait. It seemed plain to Proteus that the old man was managing to deny within himself, clinging fanatically to power as a means of staving off fear of death and of the Underworld. *And why would a mortal man take the desperate step of attempting to ambush a god?* There was one likely reason. *Because whenever the avatar of a god died, a Face always became available. And to assimilate a Face into one's own body was the best way ever invented to stave off death.*

Jason now spoke up to say: "Had I not seen it gradually change, over the months, I would certainly have doubts too. But I remember how glorious was the Golden Fleece, what a miracle it seemed, when first we took it into our hands."

The king only made a strange sound, that seemed to be intended as a laugh.

Jason remained calm. "Whatever else it may be, Uncle, it is no joke. Men have died to bring it to Iolcus."

"Then it looks like they died for nothing." And Pelias barked out another laugh, that turned into a fit of coughing.

"Uncle, you and I had an agreement," Jason insisted. His voice was bitter, but not surprised.

"Did we?" The old gray eyebrows went up, an exaggerated miming of surprise. "You mean that nonsense about how I must abdicate in your favor, if you brought home this rag? There was some foolish rumor to that effect, or so they tell me, but why in the Underworld should I do that?"

Acastus, standing at the king's elbow, now spoke up, dryly, saying he wished to impart some information. A month before Jason returned home, his bargain with Pelias had been declared irrelevant, or moot, by the Iolcan Council, who referred to it only in a hypothetical way when they met to name Prince Acastus as his father's legitimate successor. Then just for good measure the council had passed a sentence of banishment on Jason. But the terms of the ban were mild, graciously allowing him to remain long enough to repair his ship.

Jason had no immediate response to make, and silence held in the great room for the space of several breaths. Then the old man on the throne said to his nephew: "Yours is a fantastic story, and no one will believe that I ever made any such agreement. Unless of course you have some proof to offer? Witnesses, perhaps? I thought not. My dear young fool, no one's going to believe you." There was a pause before he added softly: "I may as well let you go."

And the king scornfully crumpled what was left of the Fleece into a ball, and threw it back in the direction of Jason's face. "Get out of my sight. If you are wise, you will get your ship out of my harbor too. Unless you want to see it broken up for firewood, which is probably the best it's good for."

The soft little missile traveled more slowly than the king had intended—which might have roused his vanishing interest, had he been paying attention. Jason easily caught the balled Fleece in his hands at the level of his waist. "I will be moving my ship, Uncle, as soon as I can make it ready to sail again."

"See that you do." The king waved his hand dismissively, then shifted his gaze to Proteus and Haraldur. "You two men, remain here with me for a time. I would have some words with you."

Jason looked at his shipmates, evidently decided that this was not the time or place to tell them anything, turned his back on his uncle and went out.

———

The Princess Medea was still waiting, in the same neat, well-lighted anteroom, for her meeting with the king. And she was still burdened with the company of the same minor official who had been with her from the start, and she was beginning to be irritated with the length of the delay. To her surprise, another official, this one of higher rank, came to tell her that, regrettably, the king had been called away on vitally important affairs of state. His majesty sent his profound apologies, and he would see her on another day. Would tomorrow be quite suitable?

So, Medea thought, *he is going to talk to Jason*. She got gracefully to her feet. "I will consider tomorrow. Has His Majesty been taken ill?"

"I have heard no such rumor, Princess."

In a corridor immediately outside her anteroom she encountered Jason, looking no worse for his visit with his uncle. Medea was surprised and somewhat relieved to see that her husband was free to go; that his uncle had not handed over the kingdom to him came as no surprise at all. Beginning a quiet argument, much like other debates they had had in recent days, they started to look for the best way downstairs, while her previous escort diplomatically bowed himself away.

"Shall we take the private stair?" Medea suggested. That was how she had ascended, along the inner cliff and through the castle; the stair went all the way down through an enclosed tunnel, whose lower end debouched directly on the beach, near the place where the Argonauts had left their ship.

"No, the regular stairs are good enough for me." Jason started that way.

Medea sighed and followed him. There were a few more details she wanted to get straight with her husband, though it was already settled between them that they would separate.

As they began their descent, Jason told her of his short meeting with the man he called the usurper.

"There is no way I can force my uncle to my will."

"Obviously."

"I know that this is not what we had planned—"

"I know it too. Will it surprise you to hear that I am not surprised?"

"Medea, believe me, I—"

"Why bother asking for my belief? Jason, I am bitterly weary of this."

"Of what, my love?"

"I am your love no longer."

"I have been faithful to you."

"You mean that you have lain with no one else. If that is true, it is only because you care very little about women—or about men either, for that matter. All you really love is the idea, the image, of that golden circlet, that must someday rest in your black hair. But I think your hair will be quite gray before that happens. You are a cautious sort of Hero, after all. You may live for a long time."

It was as if he could not hear her words. "I think I have kept the essence of every promise I ever made to you. Here you are, in safety, a free woman, beyond your father's reach."

"You were ready to send me back to him. But you did marry me. That was one promise you kept—as soon as it became advantageous."

"And I have given you all I have to give."

"And in turn taken from me everything I had—which was much. Very much indeed. I gave you my innocence. I sweated and starved and almost died of thirst. And then for you I committed murder. I have lost my entire family, and made an enemy of my Aunt Circe, for you and your ugly Fleece. I suppose you still have it?"

Jason tapped the small pouch at his belt. "It was on our wedding bed. Remember?"

"How could I forget? It was a glorious sight then."

"Now much reduced."

"Still it is more than big enough," Medea said, "for all the lovemaking we are likely to do with each other from now on."

———

Proteus/Triton was morally certain that the king knew of his changed identity, and that he had been invited into the castle only so he could be ambushed by a fishtailed Giant. That dark space behind the throne, between the stone screen and the outer wall, was where he must watch.

At the invitation of King Pelias the monster would soon be climbing up the cliff on the seaward side of the palace, adding another layer of thin slime to the faint trail that Triton had earlier spotted on those steep rocks. It would have to be one of the smaller members of the Giant species. He doubted that any over fifteen or twenty feet in length would be able to actually enter the castle and move about effectively inside.

Pelias could not have known beforehand exactly when the *Argo* would come into port. Therefore there was probably no Giant hiding in the castle yet; but a summons would have been sent, somehow. And now that darkness had fallen, to conceal from the eyes of honest citizens the thing's climb out of the sea and across the lower cliff, Triton had to assume that a monster bent on killing him might make its appearance at any moment.

The king was letting his full anger show. Ignoring Haraldur, he said to Proteus: "Well, sirrah? Anything to say, before I order you skinned alive?"

"Only one question, Majesty: Did anyone warn you that a god was about to pay you a visit?" Even as Proteus spoke, he saw from the corner of his eye how Hal stood up straighter, and moved his right hand to what the guards must see as his empty belt.

The old man's eye stayed bright and steady, fixed warily on Proteus. He did what was apparently a kind of unconscious ritual, moving his eyebrows. "Oh, is that so? What can you tell me about this god?"

"One very important thing: He is already here."

And Triton/Proteus saw, with a pang of inner sickness, that Pelias was only smiling faintly at the revelation that should have stunned him. "Yes," the old king said, slowly nodding. "In fact they did warn me about that."

Triton saw that he had been right about the Giant, wrong about the timing. Now, minutes sooner than he had expected it, there came a slight stirring in the darkness behind the stony screen. Through its gaps there now protruded what could only be a Giant's enormous thumbs and fingers. One of the smaller specimens, indeed, though still enormous by any standard of humanity. From those digits the invisible, soundless beam that wiped out memory would, in the next moment, come lashing at the speed of thought.

But Triton was already rolling aside, getting himself out of the way of the weapon that would do Haraldur no harm at all.

The Usurper screamed out something, a warning or command, and

Acastus shouted also. The guards were not slow in getting their weapons into action, but they were still overmatched.

Two of the Usurper's men had fallen to Haraldur's invisible battle-axe before the others realized that the northman was indeed armed. The old king had tottered from his throne and was crouched down beside it, taking such shelter as he could.

In those first savage moments of the fight, several guards had lunged at Triton/Proteus, only to be scattered, flung away like mud from a spinning wheel, by the arc of the whirling Trident. Then the god hurled himself on the floor, rolling forward beneath the Giant's blast. One stroke of the Trident against the screen of stonework blasted a sizable hole.

In the next instant Triton had lunged forward, reaching through the gap, and stabbed the Giant on the side of his massive head. The triple impact of the Trident made an explosive noise in the confined space, and sent his huge opponent bellowing and tumbling down the secret chute leading to the open cliffside, and its sheer slope to the sea.

From the position in which he had finished his lunge, with his head and the upper part of his body inside the shattered stonework screen, Proteus could see the upper end of the tunnel whose existence he had already deduced.

The Giant had fallen that way, but was the Giant dead? Not wanting to take any chances, he plunged down after his defeated foe.

Meanwhile Hal had been using his axe to good effect, finishing off the guards. But now he looked around and discovered his partner gone.

"Damn it all, Proteus!" he complained to the empty air. He could easily enough kill the cowering king, or the paralyzed prince, or both of them, but that might create more problems for him than it solved. Triton had not been interested in killing them, and he, Haraldur, was here today as Triton's man.

He knew that reinforcements for the royal guard must be on the way, and he decided that a strategic retreat was definitely in order, a withdrawal at least until the god he served came back to look for him.

One glance down into the dark tunnel, with no handholds or foot-holds in sight, convinced him he was not going to take that route.

Choosing another way, Haraldur stepped through first one ornate door and then another, closing them quietly behind him, penetrating into luxurious lodgings, at the moment unoccupied. Here the quarters were a little close for convenient axe-work, and he drew his dagger and held it ready in his left hand. Feeling imprisoned by walls and doors and ceilings, he could feel himself growing confused and jumpy. There ought to be a stairway here somewhere, but perversely—might it have been done by magic?—the stairs seemed to have moved elsewhere.

Suddenly he froze, axe ready, listening to a single set of rapidly approaching footsteps now a room or two away. He could only hope they might be Triton's.

———

For a long moment after all the Argonauts had gone, there was near silence in the torchlit audience room. The only sounds were the ragged breathing of the two men who were still alive, and the muted roar of distant surf, drifting in through the big windows. Then slowly, shudderingly, the king got his old legs under him, and stood up from where he had been huddled beside the throne. Looking around, he saw that the only living presence in the room with him was that of his son, who, unarmed, had flattened himself against a wall where he clung, quivering. The bodies of several of the castle guards, all dead, lay scattered about the chamber, jumbled with their useless weapons.

Looking at the huge hole broken through the stone screen, Pelias assumed that the god had exited by that means, either in flight, or pursuing the wounded Giant into the sea. "Of course he may come back," Pelias muttered to himself. "That is quite possible."

He noted with satisfaction, by the look on his son's face, that the young man was utterly bewildered. Acastus still had no idea that his father had been trying to ambush a god, or why.

Now the prince had peeled himself away from the wall, and was standing near the center of the room, wringing his hands. "What in all the hell is going on, Father?" he demanded in a cracking voice. "What are you talking about?" And Acastus clutched at his father.

Pelias brushed him aside with a savage jerk of his arm. "I'll explain it to you later!" What if the god did not come back? Then all his planning and scheming would have gone for nothing. His chance for virtual immortality was slipping through his fingers.

Barking orders at his son, telling him in afterthought to summon the captain of the guard and search the whole castle for the man in the horned helmet, Pelias stalked angrily into the nearby room where, according to his orders, the Mouse had been brought for a confrontation. This room contained the upper end of a private stairway, and its outer wall was pierced by two windows similar to those in the audience chamber. Here there was no stone decorative screen.

Planting himself directly before the Mouse, Pelias told her: "I want to have another little talk."

Her response was to immediately collapse on the floor, either in sheer terror, or through weakness brought on by her days in a dungeon cell. Pelias noticed that the two guards who flanked the woman looked half stunned, like gods struck dumb by some Giant's weapon—of course they had heard the uproar in the adjoining room, and of course they did not dare ask the king just what had happened. They had continued to do their duty, guarding this important prisoner. Now they had simply let her fall.

Mouse's wrists were chained together in front of her, and from them more links ran down to a similar joining of her ankles. She was still wearing the same clothes that someone had given her, out of charity, at the court of King Alcinous.

Now Pelias ordered one of the guards to go and fetch the woman's two small children. Ever since sending her as an agent to Colchis, he had been careful to make sure that her offspring were still around, being cared for, more or less, by people on his household staff.

Taking a step forward, the king kicked the fallen woman where she lay—he could no longer kick with much force, but he tried—and said to the remaining guard: "Give this sow a taste of water, I must have some coherent speech from her." Then he shouted after the other man: "And hurry up with her two brats, I want them here!"

Someone splashed water over her, and rough hands hauled her to her feet. After the darkness of the dungeon in which she had spent the last few days, her eyes found even this torchlight almost painful in its brightness. A chair was pushed forward for her to sit in, and from it she stared in fear and amazement at the new presence that now stalked into the room. It was a smallish figure that seemed to be made entirely of metal, but shaped like a man, except that one hand was missing. It was utterly strange, almost incredible. The young woman listened with horror when an almost human voice came from the thing, a kind of screeching whisper. She heard with fear the words the incredible figure exchanged with Pelias, regarding the hunt that had now been launched for Triton, and for the god's companion, a burly man in a horned helmet.

The king addressed him, or it, as "Talus." The eyes of the Mouse's two guards bulged at the sight of Talus, but once more they continued to do their duty.

The Mouse's mind worried at the problem of the Bronze Man's nature, which offered at least a momentary escape from her own terrible situation. It might have been a man in a suit of metal armor, but the encasement fit too smoothly, tightly, and completely, and it was very hard to imagine that there could be a human being inside it. Besides, the right forearm ended in a jagged stump, as if wrist and hand had been torn violently away.

The king was allowing Talus to feel a taste of his royal anger. "Could Hades not have sent you to me more swiftly? You have given me very little time to prepare for Triton."

The screeching thing came boldly back, as if it were a god, and royal anger could safely be ignored. "Understand, Pelias, that I could not travel swiftly after the god did this to me." And the Bronze Man held up the stump of his forearm. The king seemed ill at ease in the thing's presence, and regarded it nervously. After a moment he turned his back on it, and once again gave the Mouse his full attention.

"Well, bitch? What have you to tell me now?"

He was not distracted by the quiet entry of Acastus into the room; presumably his son had followed orders, and reinforcements were on their way.

Mouse murmured something indistinguishable, about her children.

Pelias told her: "Your brats have not gone to join your husband yet, but I can assure you that they soon will. First, of course, they will get to watch what happens to their mother. What you knew would happen if you failed in your mission."

The woman whimpered. And the king allowed her a quick look at her twins, four years old, to show her they were still alive, and so far not much hurt. They had grown, had changed enormously in the more than two years since she had seen them, yet she had no doubt of who they were.

A chill of horror went through her when she saw that her babies were now wearing slaves' collars, their tender necks encircled by bands of some cheap silvery metal. The surpassing joy of seeing them alive was poisoned by the knowledge of what was going to happen to them soon.

"You have one more chance. Speak truly and I will let them live." The king leaned forward, cupping an ear with an old hand. "Speak clearly, so I can understand you."

She made an effort, gestured at her guards, and said: "I have been telling these men the truth ever since they kidnapped me. And the truth is that the man Proteus never gave me any orders."

"Then both of you were getting your instructions directly from certain of my enemies."

The woman let out a despairing cry. "Great king, take pity on me and mine! I have never been in anyone's pay but yours. As to who might be paying Proteus, I do not know."

"Is there perhaps something about him that you forgot to tell me? Some little detail, maybe—of how Proteus *became a god?*"

The Mouse started to shake her head, then slumped. It seemed that her determination to keep silent about Triton, to help him if she could, had gone for nothing.

"Let us see if I can induce you to remember it." The king drew a small knife, and gestured. The two men heaved the chained woman to her feet, and dragged her forward.

Pelias seized one of her manacled hands, and wheezing, began to dig the keen point of his knife under one of her fingernails.

The Mouse screamed, loud and hopelessly.

A wooden door that had been locked burst open, splinters flying. The Mouse looked up to see Triton/Proteus rush into the room, Hal brandishing his axe beside him.

25

End

ACASTUS TURNED AND ran from the room, with his aged father panting two steps behind him, falling a little farther back with every stride. The young man whimpered and ran faster as he felt a splash of warm blood on the back of his neck—the guards who had stayed to fight, whether out of bravery or necessity, were being cut down.

Triton for the moment was willing to let the Usurper and his princeling go.

He was amazed to find himself once more confronted by the Bronze Man, but he unlimbered his Trident, and used it again to good effect on Talus. The triple blast of the thrusting spear hurled the metal figure violently back, across the room.

Facing an opponent who had beaten him once before, Talus was evidently unburdened by any concern for honor, feeling no duty to die in his tracks. He turned his back on the angry god and sprang clear out the window. It was entirely possible that the long, skidding, and tumbling plunge toward the rocks and the sea that waited far below would do him less damage than the close-range anger of an armed god.

Gripping the Trident, Triton darted to the window and looked down, in time to see the metal body of his opponent vanish with a splash.

"See to the Mouse," he commanded sharply, and Hal bent over her. The children were clinging to their mother, who was unconscious. The northman tugged at the woman's fetters, then reached to take a key from the belt of one of the dead guards. In a moment the shackles and chains had been undone, and Hal tossed them rattling down the stair.

For the second time in as many fights, Triton/Proteus had seen the waves close over the head of Talus. This time he meant to finish off the Bronze Man, as he had just done for the Giant, but there were other matters to be taken care of first.

The deep water down there was reacting to his presence, to his staring eyes that conveyed his divine fear and rage. A whole arm of the Great Sea was stirring with an elemental kind of life.

"Mouse's fainted, but she'll come round," said Hal, panting and gloating at his side. "What next?"

"Now I think it is time for a thorough house-cleaning."

Reaching forth with all the power of magic that he still possessed, Triton evoked a great, gray-green foaming column, thick as a house and straining more than a hundred feet above the sea, brought it curling and foaming to such a height that its crowning spray blew in at the castle's upper windows. Triton could not maintain it at that altitude indefinitely, but he thought he could prolong the feat for long enough.

For the past two days, beginning while the *Argo* had been still many miles at sea, he had been silently calling for Scylla and Charybdis to approach the harbor of Iolcus, and to wait a few miles offshore for new tasks he would assign them. They had been far distant in the Great Sea when Triton's summons reached them, and only now had their amorphous shapes appeared on the horizon, moving under a strange sky, a sunset glowing through what looked like the natural cloud and lightning of an early winter storm.

Minutes ago he had urged them to come on at their greatest speed. And now they were on hand.

"Lord Neptune has urged us to follow you, and fight for you with all our strength!" came a great gurgling howl.

The god's voice roared in command. "Charybdis, Scylla, combine yourselves into one creature. Come to me now!"

"We hear, and obey!"

And by an act of concentrated will, Triton and his willing helpers set the roaring, rising column into full motion, even as the jet of a geyser explodes upward from the tormented earth, in some ill-fated land where the Underworld lies near the surface. The result was a great reaching fist of a wave, ready to strike with crushing force. More than a wave, but a great columnar upwelling that took within itself the power of many waves.

———

Looking out from one opening in the castle's wall, admiring his magical handiwork, Triton did not see the huge fingers of the second crawling, climbing Giant, as they reached inside the chamber through the room's other window.

One moment Triton was savoring the triumph of the powers he had set in motion; and in the next his conscious memory had been wiped away.

And in the moment after that, the head of the towering column of water he had raised came smashing into the high rooms of the castle and right through them, pulling the rest of the watery avalanche after it, like the body of some huge climbing serpent.

———

Haraldur saw the gigantic thumbs and fingers at the window, but his yell of warning came just too late. The hands were not quite as huge as he had once imagined those of all Giants had to be—only comparatively small members of their race could make the climb up through the hidden tunnel.

The Giant turned his massive head to see a single human rushing at him, apparently unarmed, empty hands raised as if they held a weapon. It was not a sight to make a fighting Giant try to dodge, or get away.

Hal took one sideways step, charged at the window from its flank, and swung the blade of his battle-axe between his vast opponent's eyes, right through the thickness of his skull, driving death into his slow-working brain.

And in the next moment, the towering flood that Triton had evoked came thundering and splashing through both windows, a tremendous cataract of seawater in reverse.

———

Through the window of another room, Pelias had caught a glimpse of the second Giant climbing into position to attack. Reversing the direction of his panting, limping flight, the king had just started back to renew his confrontation with the god. Of course it would be deadly dangerous, but Pelias was quite ready to risk what little life he had left, for a chance of added centuries.

Everyone knew that it was impossible to destroy a Face, and Pelias had no idea of trying—he meant to put the Face of Triton on himself. The mind of the god dwelling within it would be severely damaged, and his powers no doubt diminished. But Pelias could still hope that it would bring him virtual immortality.

Several times he had imagined himself ordering his officers, when this moment came: "Butcher him when he falls helpless, and then get me his Face!" But finally he knew he would not dare to say those words. One of his aides, young and agile, might easily be daring enough to seize the Face for himself as soon as it became available. With a god's powers, if not his memory, infused into a young and healthy body, the defector would have little reason to fear a merely human king.

When Triton fell victim to the Giant's invisible weapon, the Trident tumbled from his hand, and Hal watched it go clattering on the floor.

In the next instant, just before the cataract of water struck, the north-man grabbed up the spear. The glassy surface of the dark shaft burned his mortal hand like frozen metal, but still he held it tight, knowing that without the help of Triton, he would need every weapon he could get to fight his way out of this place alive.

And then the crash of water came through both windows, like a blow from the Great Sea itself.

Prince Asterion was watching from a distance, watching as he dreamed, and as he dreamed he felt the shock, and knew in his bones how severe it was. But there was nothing the bull-headed man could do. He was left uncertain how much of Triton had been destroyed this time.

Haraldur, struggling not to drown, clung desperately to the Trident, which had somehow become wedged in an upper corner of the descending stair. There it held fast, keeping him from being washed down with Pelias and Acastus. Father and son had both been swept in that direction, their screams turned to gurgles in the flood, their bodies beaten and broken against the stonework on the next landing down, then flushed away and out of sight in the continuing torrent.

The woman, with her children scrambling to stay with her, had dragged herself across the floor to Triton the moment that he fell. Even as Haraldur came near to drowning, he saw how the rushing, roaring, cascading waters in their furious passage divided neatly around those four clustered living bodies, leaving them undisturbed. Scylla and Charybdis were refusing to do Triton any harm.

———————

He had been thrashing and splashing in salt water—
——and now the flood had stopped, leaving him utterly drenched, shivering with more than cold, lying on stone tiling in a strange, torch-lit room, utter darkness outside its windows. And he could not remember who he was, or where or how or why.

A strange-looking man in a horned helmet, heavily armed and also dripping wet, was standing over him, and had been shouting words at him, words that might have been names, but none of them made any sense.

The man on the floor dragged himself up to his elbows, and then to his knees. Now he noticed a woman in a tattered garment who knelt nearby, wet as everyone else, cradling a pair of small children who were dripping too, and naked but for their bright slave collars.

He said to the woman: "I remember you—I think I do. But not your name."

She did not answer him at once. The whole room and everything in it was littered with bits of seaweed and small crustaceans, and the smell of the sea was very strong.

And now, somehow, the woman struggled to her feet, managing to lift both babies with her, cradling one in each arm. For one of her size and emaciated condition it seemed quite a feat of strength. To the man on the floor she said: "Can you walk? Yes, you can, you must. Downstairs, hurry, we must get out of here."

Getting to his feet was surprisingly easy. He looked down at himself, saw an ordinary loincloth and sandals that told him nothing. He seemed fundamentally uninjured, no blood, no broken bones. His only problem was that he did not know who he was, or where he might belong.

The man in the horned helmet, who was clearly a friend, went ahead of them down the wet and slippery stair. He was armed in one hand with an axe, and in the other with a strange, three-pointed spear. The woman kept on urging the nameless man along. When they had gone down a few steps, he said to her: "I think there was a time when the two of us went swimming together in the sea."

"Yes, there was, I'm glad that you remember that. Now hurry!" And on she went, towing a child with each hand, eager to get out of the half-drowned castle.

Jason, pondering to himself what he ought to do with his remnant of the Fleece, the priceless trophy that nobody now wanted, decided that he would probably go and hang it in the temple of Zeus. Yes, maybe right in front of the gigantic statue of the great god.

In his imagination, he did so. Then he sat there in the temple, waiting for someone to notice his donation. No one did, though many people passed and some glanced at the gift.

On parting from Medea he had said to her: "We found the treasure that everyone had dreamed of, and it turned to dust and ashes in our hands."

Her voice was cool and practical. "I think you might have to recruit an entirely new crew for your next adventure."

"Yes, I have come to understand that. But—I think it will probably not be too hard." Once the word of his successful quest had time to spread, his reputation would be greater than ever. Whether the Fleece was now worth anything or not, he certainly had brought it back just as he said he would. Actually he still had hopes of finding a number of the original Argonauts ready to rejoin him, once they had had their spree in port, and a little time to think about it.

On leaving the castle, Jason walked out alone into the darkness of the surrounding night. As was customary when visitors of no particular importance were departing after dark, one of the servants had given him a cheap oil lamp, no more than a shaped and hardened lump of clay, by which to find his way along the path that led around the harbor, to whatever destination he might choose.

The only destination that interested him right now was much closer at hand. Jason carried the lamp with him as he crawled in under the worn-out hull of *Argo*. He was trying to assess the full extent of the damage, how much of the wood might still be sound, so he could waste no time in getting the ship ready for another voyage.

If he heard in the distance screams of terror, and a certain muffled roaring, the pouring of an enraged and sentient portion of the Great Sea through hollow corridors of stone, he paid such noises little attention. So he was still directly beneath the hull when a great surge of sea-water, the outpouring of Triton's flood, came rushing out of the mouth of the private tunnel-stairway. It bore with it various fragments, some of them human, of the castle's inner life, and these were stopped by the iron grating of the gate covering the mouth. The flood itself was not slowed down at all. The impact of this wall of water tipped the ship sharply from one side to the other, so the man underneath it was caught there and severely crushed.

———

Given the nature of the other events transpiring at the same time, many minutes passed before anyone noted Jason's protruding feet and tried to come to his assistance. Those who lifted the overwhelming weight at last and dragged him out heard his last words upon the earth: "I will call another Tiphys, and launch another Argosy, manned by chosen Heroes . . ."

And he thought he heard a high voice, answering. *Call all you will, unhappy man. But who will answer?*

None of those who came to help the dying man that night reported finding any trace of the Golden Fleece.

———

The man in the horned helmet, and the woman with the two children kept urging him along. He supposed he ought to go with them—but something was very wrong. The days of imprisonment and abuse had left her weakened, and when she handed him one of the children to carry, he accepted the small slippery body automatically.

"But why should they be wearing collars?" he wondered aloud.

"They shouldn't!" the woman told him forcefully, over her shoulder.

That settled that. He took the ring on the girl's small neck between his fingers, and, being careful not to hurt the tender flesh, pinched the metal firmly until it broke. Then he twisted the circlet off and tossed it away.

He descended a few more steps. Then: "Who am I?" he asked again.

"Proteus is your name," the woman said, still going down, not looking back. "I am Rosalind, and you are Proteus. Come along, keep moving."

"Rosalind. You are my woman, then?" Absently he reached out with one hand and started working on the boy's collar. Soon it too parted and was cast away.

She looked back and nodded wordlessly.

Meanwhile, the friendly man in the horned helmet was keeping up with them in their descent, sometimes scouting ahead a bit, sometimes falling behind, now and then nodding encouragement. Proteus had to assume that, for the moment at least, everything was somehow working out for the best.

Proteus was making his way out of the half-drowned castle, coming on shaky legs down one long curving stair after another, with the woman and her two children, and their armed attendant.

Proteus was dizzy, and part of the time he had to lean on other people for support. His body ached as if he had been fighting. There were more stairs to go down, and then yet more. Innumerable stairs, it seemed to him. He thought they must be out of the castle now, and nearly down to the level of the sea; he could hear surf in the background and somehow the sound was welcoming. Where was he, anyway? Was this where he belonged? For all he knew, it might well be, but it was hard to imagine how, and why.

Down and down and down they went, and at every level more people joined them in their flight, until they were inconspicuous and unnoticed among the flow of other refugees, some servants in rags or very nearly, some nobility in finery. It seemed that much of the interior of the castle had known a devastating flood.

Finding himself still leaning on the shoulder of the man in the horned helmet, Proteus asked him, simply: "Who am I?" He wasn't at all sure that he had the right answer yet.

The other hesitated before replying. Then he said: "You are whoever you want to be, my friend."

And now at last they were outdoors. And here the man in the horned helmet left them, to join a small, blond, well-dressed woman who appeared to have been waiting for him. She stared at Proteus and Rosalind, but made no move to approach.

Before going away with the blond woman, the armed man handed Proteus the strange spear, saying: "Keep it. No doubt it'll come in handy, fishing. And if you ever remember, later . . ."

Unable to find the right words, he sheathed his axe, and made a two-handed gesture of casting the whole business from him. "Never mind, just keep it. I wouldn't know what to do with it. And the gods be with you, both of you." He waved a hand and moved away.

Rosalind was staring at the strange spear, as if it mystified her, but she was too exhausted to ask unnecessary questions. And Proteus heard a strange inner voice, that said to him: *The magic of a dying god begins to fail.*

Proteus had no idea what that meant, but it was indeed an impressive spear. His thoughts on the subject were interrupted by an anonymous voice, calling out: "He's dead!"

Turning his head, he saw by the light of torches how a number of people were pulling a man's body from under a large beached boat, or ship, that had two great eyes marked on the prow in faded paint.

"Who is it?" some anonymous bystander asked another.

"Jason," came the answer.

There was a general murmur. "Who is Jason?" Proteus asked his companion.

"Hush." The woman squeezed his arm with her free hand. "Never mind, I'll tell you all about it later."

He couldn't help struggling to gain more information. "What's happened?" Proteus gestured helplessly at the castle behind them. From many windows there came torchlight, and the sounds of lamenting and confusion. "Where are we?" He felt somehow that he should be angry, but had no idea of who or what deserved his anger.

They moved on, heading away from the glow of gathering torches, and into darkness. "I'll tell you all about it later," Rosalind promised him again. It cost her something of an effort, but her tears came to a stop. "Trust me. I think we have a chance now, at least we have a chance."

"That's good," said Proteus. He looked at her—this time he thought he *almost* remembered her. He looked at the clinging children, one girl and one boy. He nodded. The thought crossed his dazed mind that soon he would have to find out his son's name, and his daughter's. Something truly terrible must have happened to him, to all of them, just now, up there in the castle, to wipe his life away. And if he and his family were just fisherfolk, how had they come to be up there anyway? There was something ominous about that.

But it was going to be all right now. He was alive, unhurt, and had his woman and children with him. He asked: "Where are we going?"

"That way." Rosalind pointed away from the uproar, into darkness, and he thought he could hear waves beating on a rugged coast, outside the harbor. His instinct had been right, they were now almost at the level of the sea.

"Home," she said. "Back to the village where my—where our house is. No one will bother us there. No one here in the city will care about us anymore."

"Home," repeated Proteus.

It sounded good to him.

Gods
of Fire
and
Thunder

. . . the moon embrace her shepherd,
And the queen of love her warrior,
While the first doth horn the star of morn,
And the next the heavenly Farrier.

With a host of furious fancies
Whereof I am commander,
With a burning spear and a horse of air
To the wilderness I wander.

—*"Tom O'Bedlam's Song,"* Anonymous

1

NEVER BEFORE HAD Hal seen any fire as strange as this one. Its hungry tongues seemed to feed on nothing at all as they went burning and raging up toward heaven from the flat top of a thick spire of stone that rose steep-sided from the broad river valley. Rarely had Hal felt the glow of any blaze this large. The wall of light and heat went up straight, unnaturally straight, into the air for a good thirty feet. To the right and left the wall of fire swept out in a great, smooth convex curve, making a barrier as high and nearly as solid-looking as a castle's outer curtain. For all Hal could tell by looking at it, that might be just exactly what it was, the magic wall of some great god or monarch's stronghold.

The shape of the flaming barricade strongly suggested that it went all the way round the top of the rocky crag in a smooth curve, which would make it an almost perfect circle, and Hal thought that if it did that, it must enclose a space some twenty-five or thirty yards across. From where he was standing now, on a little saddle of land well outside that enclosed space, there was no telling just what might be contained within it.

Ought such a magic wall to have a gateway in it? From this angle he could see nothing to suggest there might be one.

Hal had been standing in the same place for several minutes, getting back his breath after the steep climb, while he studied the amazing flames. He marveled at how steadily they maintained their position, so frighteningly artificial and regular, neither advancing nor retreating, not letting the chilly evening breeze push them even a little to one side, as any natural fire would have wavered. For several minutes now Hal had been certain that the fiery tongues were born of magic, for they were feeding themselves on nothing, seemingly nothing at all but the rocky earth from which they sprang. But as far as he could see, the ground directly beneath the tongues was not consumed, only blackened by the heat out to a distance of a yard or so.

Overhead, the glare of the fire obliterated whatever stars might have otherwise been coming out now that the sun was down. The strange, unnatural blaze created its own local domain of light and summery warmth. This zone included the spot where Hal was standing, and extended for yards beyond him down the broad grassy slopes and rocky outcroppings surrounding the crag on every side. The sound made by the tremendous fire was not really loud, though it was very steady, a muted roar that blended with the background murmur of rushing water. During Hal's long climb up here from the valley he had noticed several small streams, all plunging down steep hillsides to the river some four hundred feet below.

He was a stocky man, standing with his powerful arms folded under a well-traveled cloak. A few flecks of gray showed in his once-fair hair and beard and mustache. His weatherbeaten face was fixed in a thoughtful expression.

Hal was still puffing slightly from his tedious climb. During the final part of the ascent, climbing the last long slope of grass and rocks, he had felt the heat of the great fire grow steadily more intense on his face and hands. Now he was about as close to it as he could comfortably get, and he could tell that the occasional streaks of flame that rose up green and blue were the hottest, while most of the light was coming from tongues of fire that glowed bright orange.

Part of what made the fire fascinating was that its colors were in constant change, varying rapidly from one part of the bright ring to another. Bands of greater heat and greater light were continually changing places, seeming to chase each other around the circle. What caused the variations was impossible to say.

It had been late afternoon when Hal, making his way north through unfamiliar land along the valley, had first caught sight of the strange burning. At that time it had struck him that for all the flame there seemed to be amazingly little smoke. Now, inspecting the scene at close range, he thought there were certain indications that the peculiar blaze was no more than a few days old—there, for instance, a tree stood just at the outer limit of destructive heat. Trunk and branches were now bare and charred, darker on the side toward the fire, good evidence that no tree could possibly have grown in that location while the fire roared.

It seemed the fire was going to tell him nothing new, however long he stared at it. By now Hal had ceased puffing, and he determined to go completely around the ring, getting a close look at it from every side—if he could manage to do so without frying himself or falling off a cliff. He had what he considered to be good reasons, going beyond his usual curiosity. This process of circumambulation proved somewhat difficult, but Hal persisted, though once or twice the irregularities of the slope brought him so close to the object of his study that he might have roasted himself some meat for dinner—had he any meat to roast. The fire was not merely some kind of magic trick, an illusion that a man might be able to pass through with impunity.

At one point he passed the head of a steep, narrow ravine that went plunging down to end exactly on one curving bank of the broad Einar River. The drop-off was so sharp it made him a little dizzy to look down. The polyphonic murmur of a chain of little waterfalls came drifting up—he had taken note of them during his climb. Their noise now blended with the soft roar of the tall flames.

The surrounding landscape was one of rocks and scattered vegetation, and was mostly unpeopled. For miles, in all the directions he could see, there were only very occasional sparks of other flame to see, the signs of settlements or farmhouses lighting up against the night.

Halfway through Hal's pilgrimage around the fire, he was taken by surprise when a certain small object in his belt pouch suddenly twitched and jumped. It felt like a tiny animal in there, but he knew that it was not alive—unless sheer magic counted as a kind of life. Opening the pouch, he pulled out a small object—which to a casual inspection gave no sign of being anything but a scrap of dirty cloth. But the bit of fabric behaved in an extraordinary way, glowing and brightening (though without fierce heat or flame) in the man's hand even as he held it out and moved it about.

When the strange fabric tugged most strongly at his fingers, Hal reached straight down into a tuft of long wild grass at his feet. The thing that now revealed itself to him was half covered by loose sand and hard to see. Hal spotted it nevertheless and picked it up—a broken fragment of yellow, heavy metal. There was enough of the thing to see that when intact, it must have been part of a crescent shape about the size of Hal's broad hand.

A groove ran halfway round one of the thing's flat sides. Holes had been punched through the groove, and one or two of those holes were still occupied by iron nails. The nails were still wedged in place, though this piece of golden semicircle had been somehow torn loose from whatever object they had once held it to. After a long look he stuffed the object into his belt pouch.

He was frowning by the time he had returned to his starting point without having discovered anything like a gate or entrance to the enclosure of flame. The only thing the circumambulation had really accomplished was to remove any lingering doubts that the fire made a complete and regular circle, almost perfect in its shape.

Obeying a sudden impulse, he bent down once again, snatched up a small stone and flung it uphill. Just before the pebble disappeared into the flames it flared incandescent, as if at that point in its flight the heat had truly been great enough to turn it molten.

Hal gloomily shook his head.

Turning his back on the fire at last, frowning more thoughtfully than ever, Hal retreated to a comfortable distance. He took a morsel of dried meat from his pouch, and stood chewing on the tough fibers while he thought things over. Had he had any fresh meat, he wouldn't have tried to cook it on this particular hearth. These flames were too obviously unnatural. He possessed no real skill in magic, but none was needed to see that. The near-perfect regularity of their ring offered good evidence, as did the fact that they showed no tendency either to grow or to diminish.

On reaching the place where he had decided to spend the night, he made his simple preparations for settling in. Winter was definitely coming on in this part of the world, but this close to the great mysterious burning a man ought to be able to stay comfortably warm. In his preliminary scouting Hal had discovered what he thought would be an ideal spot to sleep, on a small saddle of raised land almost as high as the burning crag, and separated from it by only thirty, yards or so. There the generous Fates, as if feeling some concern for the weary traveler, had caused soft moss to grow upon a handy patch of soil. On this bed Hal now lay down wrapped in his cloak, shadowed by a small outcropping of rock from almost all the direct light of the untiring fire. Still, by moving his head only a little from side to side, he could see a large part of the slope to his right and left, brightly lit by the fire above. He ought to be able to get a good look at anything or anyone that appeared in the area during the night.

The traveler's peaceful rest behind the rock had not lasted much more than an hour when some subtle change in his surroundings awakened him. He came awake with the inner certainty that he was no longer quite alone. Opening his eyes, he lay for a few moments without moving, his battle-hatchet ready in his hand beneath the cloak. Nothing and no one had come very near him yet. Cautiously Hal raised his head and from his niche of wavering shadow studied the slope immediately below the flames, first on one side and then the other.

In a moment, the figure of a young man had walked into his view, no more than a moderate stone's throw away from Hal, but seemingly unaware of his presence.

The fellow was tall and active, dressed in boots, trousers, and a kind of quilted jacket, but wearing no armor except a plain steel helmet that left his almost beardless face exposed. His movements had a kind of nervous recklessness, as well as the jerkiness of deep exhaustion. At the moment he was certainly not on his guard. A short sword was sheathed at his side, and his clothes were so begrimed and tattered that it was hard to guess whether they had originally been of rich material or poor.

This newcomer's attention was entirely centered on the great fire itself, whose gentle roar went on unceasingly. The youth continued a methodical progression, as if he were intent on making his way entirely around the ring of flame, reconnoitering just as Hal had done. He even seemed to be making the same tentative efforts to approach the burning wall as closely as he could, but of course the heat kept him yards away.

Carefully the concealed watcher sat up, peering first around one side of his rock and then the other, to see more of the steep, rough cone of the hillside. He saw enough to satisfy himself that the young man, who presently reappeared, had come here quite alone. Hal rose to his feet, stretched, adjusted his cloak, seated his hatchet once more in its holster at his belt, and remembered to pick up his horned helmet from where he had set it aside when he lay down to sleep. Then, feeling as ready as could be for whatever might develop, he stepped out firmly, striding back across the little saddle of land toward the fire.

The youth's back was turned to Hal, and his attention remained entirely absorbed in the spectacular wall of flame. When Hal had come within thirty feet without being noticed, he judged it wise to halt and call out a few words of greeting.

The tall lad spun around at once, clapping a hand to the hilt of his sword. Hal was waiting open-handed, arms spread in a sign of peace; but even so he realized that his appearance, that of a powerful armed stranger, could hardly have been very reassuring.

"Who are you?" the other demanded, in a hoarse voice that quavered with some recent and excessive strain. Extreme stress and exhaustion were plain also in his young face. "What do you want?"

"No harm, lad, no harm at all." Hal kept his arms spread wide, and made the tones of his own gravelly voice as soothing as he could. "I'm a traveler, just passing through. My home's hundreds of miles to the north. I was heading that way, following the river, when I saw these flames."

After a pause, in which the other did not respond, he went on. "My first thought was that some farmhouse was burning. Then, when I had climbed halfway up these rocks, I thought maybe it was a castle or watchtower—not really farming country just along here. But now I'd be willing to bet there's no building at all inside that fire. It's a strange one, isn't it? Certainly it has to be more than natural."

"They are Loki's flames." The words seemed choked from the youth by some intense emotion. "They feed on nothing but magic. They need no fuel to keep them burning."

"I see." Hal recognized the name, but took the claim in stride. "So, the gods are involved. Can't say I'm surprised. I never saw another blaze like this one." And he shook his head on its thick neck.

The youth had turned slowly round until he had his back almost to Hal and was staring again into the multicolored, undying blaze. His lips moved slightly, as if he might be whispering a word.

The man from the far north cleared his throat. "My name is Haraldur; most call me Hal, to save themselves a little breath and effort. And who are you?"

The tall one turned slowly back. He relaxed slightly, out of sheer weariness, it seemed. His hand still rested on his sword's hilt, but as if he had forgotten it was there. "My name is Baldur," he announced in his strained voice.

"I see," Hal said again. He nodded encouragingly.

Slowly Baldur went on. "I live—I once lived—only ten miles from here." His words had a wondering tone, as if something about that statement struck him as remarkable. Presently he added: "Some of my family—my mother—still lives there."

Hal, exercising patience, grunted and nodded again. Fortune had now blessed him with a chance to talk to a native of these parts, and he didn't want to waste the opportunity. There was information he desired to have.

Baldur now gave the impression of nerving himself, gathering energy, to make some serious effort. At last he went on: "Do you see—anything—strange about me?" He spread out both his hands and turned them this way and that, presenting them for inspection. "Do I look to you like a dead man?"

Hal strolled a few steps closer, and stood with folded arms, looking the young fellow over from head to foot in the fire's clear light. After a moment he raised a couple of stubby fingers to scratch under the rim of his horned helmet.

"I have seen some strange folk here and there," the northman announced at last. "Yes, a fair number who might be described as really odd. And several others who were seriously dead. But I'd say you don't fit in either category." He held up a cautionary hand. "Mind you, I may not be the very keenest judge. I once spent several months as shipmate to a god, and never guessed who he was until he told me."

But the youth had no interest in some stranger's tales of adventure. He had the attitude of one with more than enough of his own. His cracking voice grew no easier as he said: "Three days ago, I was leading a squad of men in battle when I was cut down." Baldur reached up with large and grimy hands to his plain steel helm, and gingerly eased it off his head, revealing the fact that the steel was dented. When he bent slightly forward, his corn-yellow hair fell free, stained and caked with the reddish-brown of old dried blood. "See my wound!"

Hal grunted again, squinting in the bright, just slightly wavering firelight at the head that loomed above his own. He saw what little he could see without getting any closer. There had certainly been a copious flow of blood, but it had stopped some time ago. The wound itself was quite invisible under thick hair and clots.

The northman renewed his efforts to be soothing. "Looks nasty, all right, but maybe not so bad as it looks. Scalps do tend to bleed a lot. Anyway, you survived."

This soothing attitude was not exactly welcome. "I said I fell!" the youth choked out. Baldur's teeth were bared now in a kind of snarl. "I tell you that I died!"

"I see," replied Haraldur in a neutral voice. "If you say so. That's interesting." He resisted the urge to back away a step, compromising by shifting his stance slightly. Head wounds sometimes brought on bizarre ideas and dangerous behavior.

Baldur was still staring at him, not so much threatening now as if pleading silently for some kind of help. After a moment Hal cleared his throat and asked with polite curiosity: "What happened next? After you—as you say—died?"

"What happened?" Now there was outrage, though not directed at Hal. "When I opened my eyes, I saw that the fighting was over. A Valkyrie came flying over the battlefield to choose a hero from among the dead." The voice of the self-proclaimed dead man was turning shrill. "That is what the sworn servants of Wodan can expect, when it comes their turn to fall!"

"Ah, yes, a ride to warriors' paradise." Hal was really a stranger to this land, but some information about its gods and customs had inevitably traveled beyond its borders, enough to rouse his curiosity. Over the past few days he had been doing what he could to find out more. "So, you are a sworn servant of the god Wodan. I see. And if I remember correctly what the stories say, the Valkyries are handsome maidens, who come flying over battlefields on their magic Horses—"

"Have a care how you speak of her!" Baldur had dropped his helmet to the ground, and his right hand had gone back to his sword. His blue eyes glinted wildly in the uncanny wavering of light.

Brain damage, thought Hal again, and now he did retreat a pace. But he persisted in his quest for knowledge.

He kept his raspy voice as soft as possible. "I mean no disrespect, Baldur. Go on, tell me more. So you got knocked down, in some kind of battle, and when you woke up, there you were, lying on the ground with your head a bloody mess. Right? Then this Valkyrie arrived to carry you to Wodan's feasting hall? Isn't that how the story—isn't that what's supposed to happen?"

"Her name is Brunhild." Now the young man's voice seemed on the verge of breaking into sobs. Whatever threat had been in him was melting swiftly. "But she rejected me!" His gaze slid away from Hal's, fell to the ground.

"Ah, but you somehow learned her name. So—"

"She chose another man instead! She would not take me to Valhalla!" In a moment Baldur's legs had folded, leaving him sitting on the ground, face buried in his hands, while his shoulders heaved. It was not an attitude Hal would have expected to see in a man who had pledged himself to a god of war. But people were always doing unexpected things.

The northman cast a swift look around him, to right and left over the curving hillside. It was only a routine precaution. As far as he could tell, he and the agitated youth were still alone.

Approaching Baldur more closely, he squatted down in front of him, taking care to stay out of easy lunging distance—just in case.

"Tell me more," repeated Hal with quiet persistence. "I find this very interesting. The lovely and respected Brunhild came to visit you when you were killed—and just the sight of her made you feel better. But then something went wrong, and you were cheated out of a trip to Wodan's glorious feasting hall."

After a pause, during which Baldur said nothing, Hal added: "Well, at least she told you her name."

Hal had to bend closer to hear the muttered answer: "I knew her name already. In spite of everything, she took another man instead!"

"So you were telling me." The northman scratched his head again, trying to make sense of it all. He wasn't sure that the effort was worthwhile—but there was the gold he had just stuffed into his belt pouch. Beings who used gold for horseshoes might well be able to contribute a little more of it, even if unknowingly, to the retirement fund of a weary but deserving adventurer. Perhaps enough to buy him a small farm. "So, who was this other man? Why did your Valkyrie choose him?"

Baldur shrugged.

"All right, it seems he's not important. How did you come to learn her name?"

No answer.

"So, where is the incomparable Brunhild now?"

A cry of agony burst from Baldur's lips, and he sprawled on the earth face down, one arm extended, pointing uphill, directly toward the wall of fire. Now he was screaming. "She is in there, surrounded by the flames, where no man may approach her!"

That was an unexpected answer. The case was only becoming more complicated. Or maybe it really was all brain damage. "She's in the flames, and not in Valhalla? But why . . . ?"

"Not *in* Loki's fire, but hidden behind it!"

"Ah."

"Wodan has bound her away from me forever, in an enchanted sleep!"

"I see," said Hal, trying to sound as if he really did. He decided to keep trying. "So Brunhild is being punished? For what offense?"

"For daring to look with favor on a mortal!" Baldur was still lying face down, talking into the grass.

"The mortal in question being not the man she actually carried to Valhalla, but—you, the one she left behind. Is that it? All right, I think I do begin to see." Now Hal grunted sympathetically.

He changed position so that his own back was to the fire, meanwhile automatically scanning his surroundings again, then sat down on the ground more comfortably. "That's too damned bad, son, too damned bad." He paused a moment before asking: "But how do you know she's in there?" He hooked a sturdy thumb over his shoulder.

"I know!"

Hal persisted. "Were you listening, watching, when Wodan passed his sentence on this girl?"

"Of course I wasn't there, in Wodan's great hall with the heroes. Brunhild cheated me of that!" The final words came out in a shriek of accusation.

"Aha," said Hal, trying to sound wise. He thought things over, shak-

ing his head. So far there had been no mention in the story of any cache
of gold, and that was where his interest lay.

But he was curious, as usual, about many things. He pulled a stem
of wintry grass, and chewed on the dry fiber. "Still, I keep wondering
how you *know* that she's now behind this wall of fire—did the fight,
the one that you were, uh, killed in—did it take place here on this
hilltop?"

"No, of course not! How could there be room for a battle here?"
Shaking his aching head in exasperation, Baldur gestured at the narrow
space between flames and the steep drop. "We fought in the valley,
miles away."

"All right. Keep calm. Let's go over again what happened. If you
don't mind, I'd like to get it all straight. You were struck down in this
little battle, and then—"

"Only an hour after Brunhild abandoned me, while I still lacked
strength to move from where I had fallen, a messenger from Valhalla
brought me the cursed news. As a courtesy to Wodan, Loki had created
a ring of fire, inside which those who offend the gods can be eternally
imprisoned. Then I raised my eyes to this cliff, and saw the fire, and
knew that it was true."

Having finished that speech, Baldur sat up. Now he seemed to be
making a start at pulling himself together; a tough young man, Hal
judged, who must have been through a few hellish days, whatever the
exact truth might be of what had happened to him.

Hal knew from experience how dangerous it could be to interfere
with the gods' business. But it would not be the first time in his life he
had accepted such a risk. He thought it couldn't hurt to try to learn a
little more.

"What kind of messengers is the old god using these days?" When
the youth did not respond to that, the northman prodded: "Maybe a black
raven? Or a wolf?"

Baldur looked mildly shocked. "No such thing. Great Wodan's messengers are the Valkyries. Girls. Young women, like Brunhild herself."
He paused. "I happen to know that this particular messenger's name
was Alvit."

"Alvit, I see—another worthy name. Another Valkyrie you just happen to know—and how do these girls travel when they go on their
errands? I've heard that they ride magic Horses through the air." Hal
thought that he could feel the heavy little lump of gold in his belt pouch.
"Most people in the world have never seen a horse—even the purely
natural kind is something of a rare animal. But I have. Horses' feet are
not like those of a cameloid or drom. They have hard hooves, and fairly

often their owners fit them with metal shoes. Just nail them on. Then sometimes the shoes come loose."

But it was no use now trying to find out what Baldur might know about horseshoes and gold. The youth seemed to be drifting away again, back into his ongoing nightmare of grief and loss. He had regained his feet and was moving restlessly about.

He was mumbling now, and in his raving he kept returning to what obsessed him as a great horror and mystery: the fact that Brunhild had not counted him properly as a worthy hero among the slain, had refused to carry him away to Wodan's hall. The way in which he spoke of Brunhild strongly suggested to Hal that Baldur and the Valkyrie were or had been lovers. Which added to the mystery, of course. Now Baldur was groaning that he had lost both his beloved and his chance at glorious immortality as a member of Wodan's elite guard, one of those chosen to fight beside the Father of Battles in the final terrific conflict, the twilight of the gods at world's end.

"Tell me no more about glorious heroes, lad, no more," Hal muttered in low tones. "Down south I had my fill of them."

That evoked a twinge of interest. Baldur stopped muttering to himself and turned his head. "What do you mean?"

The older man took thought, and sighed. "Does the Golden Fleece mean anything to you? You've heard of Jason and his voyage?"

A blank look. "No."

Hal shrugged. "I thought the news might have reached these parts by now, but never mind. It's a long story. Tell me more about this fight in which, as you say, you lost your life."

He went on with his gentle but persistent questioning, and gradually Baldur disclosed more information, including the name of the lord whose army—or armed band, rather—he had been fighting in, and something of what the fight had been about.

It sounded to Hal like a simple, more or less routine battle between two local warlords. That was something he could understand, and he took this turn in the conversation as a hopeful sign.

Presently he was nodding. "Then the trouble came down to a matter of gold, didn't it? Barons, minor lords of some kind, squabbling about gold." He added, as casually as he could: "I've heard there are substantial amounts of yellow metal to be found hereabouts."

Now for the first time the youth showed even teeth in a ghost of a smile. "That may be, but those of us who live above ground have never seen much of it. The gnomes have all the gold—or they did."

"Gnomes, hey? I know very little about gnomes," Hal added truthfully. "Practically nothing, in fact. Where do they dwell?"

"Underground." Then Baldur shrugged, as if to ask *where else?* "They have their towns and villages, some of them not very many miles from here."

Hal grunted. "And you say they—the gnomes—*did* have all the precious gold—that means they've lost it somehow? Someone else has taken it away from them?"

The youth did not answer; he was swaying on his feet.

Hal stood up, reminded of his own tiredness. He'd had a long day's hike along the valley, then the ascent of a few hundred feet of steep and rugged trail. Now this. His right knee creaked as he called on it to lift his weight, and for a moment the joint threatened to be painful. Not as young as he once was; in a few more years, provided he lived that long, he would have to worry about getting old. But a poor man could not settle anywhere in comfort; a pauper would have no ease and no respect. "How long since you've slept, lad?"

"Dead men need no sleep." Baldur's voice was slurring now in utter weariness.

"But live ones do. You're no more than half dead. Come this way, I know where there's a bed of moss."

"But Brunhild . . ."

"She's probably waiting her chance to come to you in a dream. If you never sleep, how's she going to do that?"

Five minutes later, Baldur, muffled in his quilted jacket, had sunk, like a drowning man, into the deathlike slumber of exhaustion. And a minute after that, Hal, who had pledged to stay awake and watch, was wrapped in his cloak and snoring almost comfortably with his back against the rock.

———————

It was the middle of the morning before Baldur awakened; Hal, who had been up and about a couple of hours earlier, had patiently let him sleep. Meanwhile the northman quietly chewed another morsel of his dried meat and thought things over.

When the youth did open his eyes at last, he looked and sounded more normal than he had during the night. When questioned directly on the subject of life and death, he was ready to admit that he was still alive.

"That would explain it, then," said Hal. "Why the lovely Brunhild did not choose you."

Baldur sat bolt upright, frowning, shaking his head impatiently. "No! No, you see, the Valkyries have that power, given them by Wodan, to decide the fate of warriors. She could have counted me as fairly slain. She should have done so, and then I would have gone to Valhalla." *What more could a warrior ask than that?* his tone and manner seemed to plead. Then again unutterable woe: "But she rejected me!"

Hal grunted and made vague gestures. "I wouldn't blame her for wanting to keep you alive. I'd have settled for a friend who did that. Most men would, I think."

The youth's lip curled. "True fighting men, heroes, do not fear violent death."

"That's fortunate for them, because they tend to find it early on."

Baldur's smile in response was almost that of a dying man—sweetly tolerant, expressing unbearable sadness, confronting someone who had no understanding, none at all, of his grief's tremendous cause. It was hard to tell which bothered the young man most—the tragic fate of Brunhild, or her equally tragic failure to award him a place in Wodan's glorious company. Obviously they had both been stunning blows.

But Baldur was also very young. He might indeed have tremendous cause for grief, but he soon admitted that he was also ravenously hungry. He could not remember eating anything since before the fight, which, as far as Hal could find out, had been at least two days ago.

A long drink at one of the rushing mountain streams served both men for breakfast; Hal said nothing about his own remaining private store of food. Baldur was in no danger of starving to death, and Hal had the feeling that he himself might well be needing the little that he had. Nor did he mention to his new companion the two very unusual objects that he carried in his pouch. But he did persuade Baldur to wash some of the dried gore from his head and clothing before going home— there was no use frightening his mother or anyone else to death when he appeared.

Now it was possible, in sunlight and with careful probing, to get a good look at the wound. Hal observed cheerfully that it would benefit from a few stitches; but he thought the operation could wait till the lad got home. The dented helmet was easier to fix. Using the blunt end of his hatchet, the northman pounded out the deepest part of the depression, leaving the metal almost smooth.

Turning the conversation around to the subject of Baldur's family, Hal more or less invited himself to pay them a visit. In matters not directly connected with Brunhild and Valhalla, Baldur seemed willing to be told what he ought to do next.

Together the two men set out on what Baldur said would be about a ten-mile walk to the small house where Baldur said his mother lived.

He made no mention of a father. Well, in families where men took up the profession of arms, there tended to be many widows.

When they reached the place where the trail descending to the valley took a sharp turn down, Hal paused to take one more relatively close look back at the enigmatic and unchanging flames, before descending to where they would be hidden by the shoulder of the cliff. They rose as high and fierce as ever, but now in the morning sunlight were pale and relatively inconspicuous.

Baldur had paused with him. "Somehow I will find a way," the youth pledged solemnly. "A way to join her there."

Hal shrugged. "I think you're right to go home first, take it easy for a while, heal that wound. They'll all be glad to see you there. Likely they think you're dead." Then when he saw how Baldur looked at him, he regretted his choice of words.

2

TURNING THEIR BACKS on the central valley of the Einar, the two men trudged along on the road pointed out by Baldur. It led them through a countryside of pastures, orchards, and fields, with modest farmhouses visible from time to time. The trees were barren of leaves, awaiting the coming winter, the fields lifeless under dead stubble. Hal's experienced eye could find no signs of the devastation of recent warfare.

As they walked, Baldur described his home—the modest, simple house owned by his mother, evidently a minor landowner of some kind. Hal got the impression she was widowed, but sufficiently well-off to hire people as necessary to work the land and tend the fruit trees. Baldur spoke in wistful, nostalgic tones, as if he had already been a lifetime away from home and might never be able to go back. It sounded as if he himself had not lived there for many months, or perhaps years.

Baldur was given to long silences, and Hal had plenty of chance to guide the conversation his own way. This included the well-nigh-universal difficulties of farming and the price of land. Presently Hal had brought the talk—cunningly, he thought—to the point at which it was only natural for him to mention certain vague rumors that he had heard—that he had invented, actually. Stories of a great golden treasure hidden somewhere in this vicinity.

He might have saved himself the trouble of trying to be subtle and indirect; Baldur was too wrapped up in his own problems to give a damn for even golden treasure, and only remarked that stories of that kind were always floating around. Which was certainly true enough, in Hal's experience. It was only that he had not been here long enough to hear the local versions. Had it not been for the fragment of golden horseshoe, Hal would have already decided that the stories deserved no more credit here in the valley of the Einar than they did anywhere else.

Around midmorning, the thin road the two men had been following entered a leafless autumnal forest. Shortly afterward they came to a fork in the road. Here Baldur, looking off to their left into a roadside maze of branches, what appeared to be a neglected orchard, observed that some of the trees still held late apples. He announced his intention to make a brief detour and pick some to allay his hunger.

"Fine, lad, you do that. Bring a couple back for me." Hal, looking down the branch road to the right, was less interested right now in wizened apples than he was in information. Some fifty yards in that direction, a small group of people were standing in the middle of the road, to all appearances chatting amiably. He added: "I'll be over that way, having a word with our fellow travelers."

But he had not covered more than half the distance to the little group before he realized that he had come to the wrong place for a peaceful exchange of information. There were two men visible, one of them staying in the background, leaning casually against a fence with his arms folded, as he watched the scene in front of him. Meanwhile, near the middle of the road, a younger and somewhat smaller fellow who wore a sword stood engaged in talk with a youngish woman, who was poorly dressed and had two small children hanging on her skirts.

As Hal came close enough to hear the strained tones of the quiet voices, and to get a good look at faces, he realized that it was less a conversation than a confrontation. This was no family squabble, but an encounter between strangers that gave every sign of threatening to turn violent.

The woman was obviously in a wretched state of fear. Her barefoot children were shivering in the almost wintry cold. A cheap-looking purse lay emptied on the ground at the man's feet, and the current point of dispute seemed to be whether she was going to be completely stripped and searched. Her feeble gesture toward a streak of color on the arm of the man who stood near her suggested that the bandit had already robbed her of a reasonably good scarf.

This fellow now turned at Hal's approach, hands casually on hips, and gave the newcomer a long look of appraisal. His greeting came in a shrill, threatening voice: "Is this any of your bloody business?"

"No." Hal's voice was quiet, and he remained as resolutely mild-mannered as a hopeful salesman. "I just had it in mind to ask some questions. Nothing personal. You can go on with your conversation. There's a strange fire on a hill back that way a few miles. I thought that if any of you people lived in this vicinity, maybe you could tell me—"

The robber was disinclined to be helpful. "Then turn your fat ass around and march back the way you came—hold on, though, not so fast. Let's see what you've got in that belt pouch before you go."

Hal shot a glance toward the fence, where the bigger man, still content to be an onlooker, was leaning as if from sheer laziness against the top course of some farmer's hard-split rails. He, too, was armed with a sword, not drawn. His gaze was penetrating, and somehow his inaction did not give the impression of any reluctance to take part in robbery. Rather his attitude suggested that he thought neither Hal nor the woman worth his trouble. He might have been a master or a teacher, observing an apprentice at his work.

As if to make up for his companion's near-indifference, the younger and slightly smaller brigand gave the impression of being more than enthusiastic enough. Now he was fairly bouncing on his toes. He seemed not in the least put off, as most people would have been, by Hal's formidable aspect. "You heard me. Let's see what you're carrying to-day."

Hal chucked the chin of the long-handled hatchet that rode head-uppermost at his belt, loosening the weapon in its holster. The head was of fine steel, the handle seasoned hickory. His voice was even quieter than before. "Doubtless you can tell just by looking at me that I'm really a prince from the Far East, traveling incognito."

While the other was trying to think of an answer for that, Hal added: "It is my duty, as royalty, to carry fabulous exotic treasures with me all the time. But a look at them will cost you something. Maybe an arm or a hand. Does that strike you as a good bargain?" He still sounded almost apologetic.

It was as if the young bandit had received a long-sought invitation. Something had come alight deep in his eyes. "This is your last warning, fat man. Hand over that belt pouch, or I take it from your corpse."

Hal made a soft meditative sound, and his right hand moved again toward his belt. The pouch stayed where it was, but the slender axe seemed to leap from its holster, as if with some purpose of its own. Hal's thick fingers, as practiced as a fine musician's, caught a solid grip on the low end of its shaft. In the same moment, a long knife had materialized in his left hand.

The nearer brigand had drawn his sword, and in the same moment he launched himself in a rush, yelling loudly. But the intended victim was moving incrementally forward, not back, which tended to spoil the aggressor's timing. At the last moment the attack wavered just slightly, and the clang of the bandit's sword against Hal's parrying knife seemed to vibrate with uncertainty.

For a moment, the two men were standing only a little way apart, just out of grappling range. One of Hal's stubby legs shot out straight from his hip in a hard, thrusting kick. The hard leather sole of his buskined foot struck home, and his attacker went down, bent at the middle, dropping his sword. Through the man's clenched teeth there came a shocking, frightening sound that had not been calculated to shock or frighten. He just lay there in the dusty road, eyes shut, his face now clenched like a fist, his body rocking a little back and forth, uttering the strange noise. He hardly seemed to breathe.

Meanwhile Hal had turned to face the brigand's colleague. The bigger man had advanced two paces from the fence, but then abruptly stopped when faced with the surprising end of the fight. He, too, had drawn his sword, and now he began snarling, breathing heavily, as he waved the blade. He gibbered a few words of nonsense, and his arms and fingers twitched spasmodically, offering more evidence that he was going into a berserker rage.

"I've seen that show before," Hal told him flatly. "Are you ready to dance or not? Yes or no?"

The other only growled and twitched some more. He glared, and a thin string of saliva dribbled from the corner of his contorted mouth.

"I'll take that as a 'no.' " Hal sheathed his knife, after frowning at a deep new nick on its edge. Then he looked at the hatchet in his right hand as if wondering why he had bothered to draw it. A moment later it again hung peacefully on his belt.

The woman had snatched up her emptied purse, and then with daring fingers started to unwind her good scarf from around the fallen bandit's arm—he made no move to resist, his thoughts being still fully occupied elsewhere. Hal was about to try questioning the woman about the fire when behind him sounded running feet.

He turned as Baldur came trotting up, one hand on his own sword-hilt, still clutching a half-eaten apple in the other. He looked ready enough to offer any help that might be needed, but honestly just a little late.

The youth shifted his gaze from Hal to the man still writhing on the ground, and back again. "What happened?"

"Little enough." Hal shrugged.

"I thought the people here were only talking with each other!"

"They were." Hal nodded toward the man lying in the road. "But this one and I quickly got into a little wager about wealth."

"Wealth?"

"Which of us might have the most. Let's see how much he's carrying." And Hal bent to take a look. By now the fellow had almost ceased to moan. Hal judged him in the first stage of recovery—to reach the stage where purposeful movement became possible again was going to take a little while.

The man still standing in the background growled again, but fell silent when Hal looked at him. He was still holding his sword, but now the point was almost on the ground.

Baldur stood gazing uncertainly at this onlooker, while Hal continued rifling the belt pouch and pockets of his fallen foe. The harvest was disappointing, only a small handful of coins.

"I win my bet," said Hal. "He was wealthier than I." But when he straightened up, he looked disappointed, and muttered to himself: "Nowhere near enough to buy a farm."

Suddenly the woman, who had been hovering a few yards away, stepped forward and dared to make a claim.

Her bony finger stabbed at Hal's broad palm. "Those two coppers there are mine."

The children's eyes were staring at the northman. "Important to you, are they?" Hal rasped. "Well, take them, then."

The woman snatched up the small coins, her sharp fingers feeling like a bird pecking at his palm. Then she startled Hal by bursting out with what seemed to be a kind of thanks but sounded like an incantation. The name of the god Thor was mentioned, as were the names of Thunderer and Charioteer, which he thought might refer to the same individual. She swore that she knew him, despite his disguise. A moment later the woman had seized Hal's hand and was kissing it. Her last words were: "The common folk will know you, and you will have our worship, always!"

Then she was gone, almost trotting at an impressive speed, her children scampering on bare feet to keep up with her.

Hal could only stare after her in wonderment. "What in all the hells did she mean by that?" he asked the world at large.

Baldur might have offered an opinion, but his attention had been drawn elsewhere. Now he nudged Hal with an elbow and cautioned in a low voice: "That one by the fence shows signs of being a berserker."

Hal looked that way again, then shook his head. "Not he, not any time soon. Or I'd still be running. The same goes for his comrade here on the deck." He hesitated. "You said you'd pledged yourself to Wodan. But you've never seen the real thing, have you?"

For a moment Baldur seemed poised to dispute the point, but then he shook his head. "A true berserk in action? No, maybe I haven't. But

I *have*"—he hesitated—"have met some of Wodan's true servants. And they have very little in common with this one you flattened." The last words were uttered with contempt. The man who lay on the ground had ceased to moan, and it looked like he might soon be ready to attempt to stand.

"That far I can agree with you, lad. But I think you mean that Wodan's men are somehow on a higher level, and the truth is that they're worse. Now, which way to your mother's house? Think she could spare me a peaceful cup of tea?"

Again Baldur seemed on the point of arguing, but then he caught sight of something that made him nudge Hal again and point away along the road, in the opposite direction to that taken by the fugitives. "Look what's coming now."

About a hundred yards down the road ahead of them, a group of about a dozen men had come into view, approaching at a deliberate pace. All but one were walking, and all seemed heavily armed; a few wore scraps of armor. One man, near the center of the group and clad in furs, was riding on a cameloid. Hal thought he could see that the rider's body was twisted and deformed in some way.

The man by the fence had seen the approaching band, and the sight seemed to meet with his approval.

"Trouble," Hal muttered.

"Probably not." Baldur pitched what was left of his apple away. He sounded more annoyed than worried. "I know those men—more or less. Some of them. They're not likely to do any fighting unless they're paid for it."

"If you say so."

———

As the approaching band drew nearer, it became obvious that he who rode in their midst was the leader, and this despite some evident physical handicaps. The others kept looking to him as if seeking approval or direction. He was missing an arm and an eye, and what remained of his body seemed somehow twisted under the furs. Hal judged he might be around sixty years old.

This fellow came riding slowly up on his cameloid, and with a few harsh words called his crew to heel, when some of them began to take a challenging attitude toward Hal. Others were already jeering at the fallen bandit, whose situation they seemed to find amusing.

But Hal paid little attention to any except the twisted leader. The man wore an array of weapons on bandolier and belt, and his clothes appeared to be mostly furs and leather.

Between Baldur and the crippled man in the saddle there passed a brief look suggesting that they knew each other; but at the moment neither had anything to say.

Hal was the subject of many appraising looks; he was relieved to see that at least some of the others who came walking and riding with their chief were well satisfied, considerably amused, to see the robber who had been more ambitious now stretched out on the ground. They recognized Hal's victim, but gave him no respect.

———

"I am called Hagan the Berserk," the twisted man announced at last. His voice was low and gravelly, much like Hal's. But generally slower, as if every word were being carefully thought out. Seen at close range, he was younger than Hal had first thought, maybe even less than fifty. But whatever the number of his years, they had all been very tough.

At the moment the man who claimed the title of Berserk looked anything but frenzied, but the northman had no intention of expressing any doubts. "My name is Haraldur."

As Hagan dismounted, Hal could see that the cameloid had been fitted with a special saddle to accommodate his rider's disability.

Standing on the ground, the leader was shorter than he had appeared to be when mounted. Now it was more obvious that his spine was far from straight. His one arm was long and powerful, and the forearm below a short fur sleeve, and his hand with which he gripped a crutch, were marked with old wounds, like his face and head.

In fact Hagan's face was hideously scarred, and Hal watching him soon got the impression that he took a kind of perverse joy or pride in shocking and frightening people with his appearance. There was no patch over his empty eye socket.

Even as Hal watched him now, a kind of spasm, evidently painful, rippled through his body. Now Hal could see that one of the man's legs was also twisted, like his torso. The defect made him lurch when he moved, though his movement did not lack speed. The crutch had a hard, almost spearlike point, which looked as if it might punch holes in a wooden floor.

After taking one look at Baldur, who stared back blankly, the bent one turned swiftly to Hal and regarded him in silence.

At last the northman broke the silence. His voice was not quite as easy as before. "My name is Haraldur. Some call me Hal, to save breath."

"Haraldur," said Hagan thoughtfully. "That's a northman's name. You've come a long way from home."

"I was born in the far north. But I have spent some years traveling round the Great Sea."

"Ah." Hagan nodded. He appeared to be listening attentively. Then he shot an unexpected question. "Do you know Theseus?"

Hal blinked. "The famed sea-rover? Only by name, and reputation. Most people think he is a pirate."

The bent man nodded slowly, managing to convey the impression that he approved of piracy in general. "How about Jason?"

"He was my captain on my last voyage."

Hagan's one eye squinted. "Expect me to believe that?"

"Or not, as you choose."

The twisted man was nodding slowly. It seemed that he was choosing to believe, and that Hal's stock had just gone sharply up. Hagan's voice had a new tone, bordering on respectful, when he asked: "Then you were one of the forty Heroes Jason took with him to hunt the Golden Fleece?"

"There were about that number of us rowing the *Argo*, that much is true. As for our being Heroes . . ." Hal let it trail away. "No one else in these parts seems to have heard of us. I'm a little surprised that you have."

Hagan seemed to take pride in his knowledge. "I have my sources." He took another long assessing look at Hal, as if confirming his decision to believe him.

When one or two of Hagan's followers showed signs of wanting to test Hal, Hagan with a look and a growl caused them to restrain their aggression. Then, in a surprisingly mild and reasonable voice, he allowed as how he had been favorably impressed by what he had seen, at a distance, of Hal's behavior.

Baldur spoke to the twisted man at last, asking a question. "A member of your band?" With a nod of his head the youth indicated the man who had now stopped writhing on the ground, and was thinking about trying to sit up.

Hagan's tone changed to one of savage contempt. "To join me was his ambition. His and this other's." The man who had been standing near the fence had not come forward to declare himself a member of the band by blending in with it, as Hal had been more than half expecting. Instead the fellow now seemed to be trying to turn himself invisible. Somehow he had translated his body to the far side of the fence, and was edging away into a barren winter hedgerow.

The twisted man was taking no notice of his departure. "But I would not have them," he went on. "I want no play-actors in my company."

Swinging his weight on his crutch and twisted leg, he brought himself a half step closer to Hal. With a new eagerness in his voice, he asked: "You will have seen the real thing? How men behave when the Father of Battles takes possession of their souls and bodies?"

"I have seen them, true Berserks," Hal replied. He was trying to conceal the fact that it cost him an effort to keep looking into the bottomless blackness of Hagan's single eye.

Now the bent man asked, in his urgent voice: "What of yourself, Haraldur? What is your ambition? Have you ever heard Wodan's call?"

Slowly Hal shook his head. "I have seen how others walk that road, and it is not for me. But let each man choose for himself."

Hagan stared at him a moment longer, then turned his one-eyed stare away. "Well spoken, northman. Great Wodan's way is not for everyone."

Hal felt some of the tension go out of his muscles. Meanwhile the gnarled man glanced with contempt at the figure still sitting in the road. The apprentice bandit's agony had receded to the point where he was now making an effort to get up, glaring about him in his fear and pain and rage. But the only response he got was laughter, from some of Hagan's followers.

In his misery and humiliation the defeated bandit found his voice. "I'll see you again, fat man. I promise you."

———

Hagan continued to ignore the fellow. "Maybe you can see, northman, how matters stand with me. It is my part to serve in this world for a time yet. When the time comes, I will climb the mountains to Valhalla and join my master there." He turned to give his men a narrow-eyed look of appraisal. "As for now, I have some good lads here," he proclaimed modestly.

"I can see that," said Hal, honestly enough. Looking at the crew the bent man had assembled, he thought that if he himself were going in for banditry he could probably not expect to do much better. Somehow Hal got the impression that they were all fiercely dedicated to serving their master. The least formidable among them looked somehow tougher than the robber he had just beaten. Crippled as Hagan was, he seemed to exert an intangible attraction that could make men want to follow.

Hal in his time had known a few others with the same power, and now he himself could feel the tug, though inwardly he recoiled from it as from the taste of some seductive and deadly poison.

"Have you seen Loki's big fire on the hilltop, northman?"

"I have. And it is certainly a wonder."

"You've looked at it closely?"

"Close as I could. Climbed the hill and got within a few yards of it. It warmed me up, but told me nothing. Except that it is more than natural, and I could see that from a distance."

The bent man, who had been listening carefully, now squinted in that direction. "I would like to get a closer look myself. I wonder if a cameloid can climb that hill?"

"The path I found went up a trifle steep for that."

Someone said how long the supernatural fire had been on the hill— it had appeared within an hour or so after the fight in which Baldur had been hurt.

Now Hagan seemed to lose the thread of his discourse. He set aside his crutch and stood rubbing his head, first on one side then the other. At last he said: "Ever since the last time my head was hurt . . . there is a certain god who visits me, now and again . . . did I tell you that?"

"I hope his visits do you some good," Hal told him. "Whoever he may be."

Presently Hagan called his troop together and marched them off, saying he had heard of a local warlord who might want to hire them.

───────

Hal and Baldur watched them go. When the two of them were alone again, Hal remarked: "You and Hagan seemed to know each other."

"We have met before."

"I see."

"He has those spasms . . . in his spine and elsewhere, and sometimes they leave him helpless for minutes at a time."

Hal nodded. "I have seen such things before, the aftermath of head wounds."

"That may be the cause. Or maybe it is a visit from a god. I only know that when it happens, his men seem as afraid of him as ever, perhaps ever more so."

"You seem to know him fairly well."

But Baldur had nothing more to say on that subject. They had walked another hundred yards or so before he began: "Hal, when we reach my mother's house . . ."

"Yes?"

"The people there will naturally want to know what has happened to me."

"Naturally."

"Of course they will see that I have been fighting—this blood on my clothing—and I will tell them about that."

"I suppose they'll be interested."

"But I think it will be better if you say nothing—especially to my mother—about Valkyries."

"I won't if you don't."

They walked on, through a countryside that seemed as peaceful as before.

3

THE HOME OF Baldur's mother proved to be a good match for his description. The house was solidly built of timber, though by no means a fortress, and well kept, pleasantly enough sited on a small rise of ground. As Hal drew near, he thought the building must be roomier than his first look had suggested. It had a sharply peaked roof, suggesting that the local climate could produce heavy snows, and was backed up by a few small outbuildings and a sizable barn. Nearby were open fields, now lying fallow with the onset of winter, with leafless woods at a distance in every direction.

Hal took note of a modest stream meandering at the foot of a slope some yards behind the barn. Looking a couple of hundred yards downstream, he could make out, among scattered trees, a few more buildings at what looked like the edge of an ordinary small village.

Dogs erupted out of the farmyard behind the cottage, at first barking a furious challenge, then changing tone to welcome as soon as they caught Baldur's scent. It had been a long time since Hal had seen so many dogs in one place, and he would have commented on the fact, but it was useless to try to talk with all the racket.

In response to the uproar, people of all ages and both sexes, some twelve or fifteen of them in all, began to emerge from the house and several of the buildings in the rear. Children came running in the lead, and Hal took note of the fact that there seemed to be no men of prime fighting age on hand.

The last to emerge from the house, moving very slowly, was one very old man, leaning on a cane.

There was no doubt which of the women was Baldur's mother, from her attitude and the change in her expression when she saw him standing there alive. She enfolded Baldur in a hug that came near lifting him off his feet. In a harsh voice she cried out: "I thought I had lost you too!"

She was a spare and careworn woman, though well-enough dressed, and in general rather prosperous-looking, wearing a couple of items of silver jewelry.

Baldur looked vaguely embarrassed by this attention. Repeatedly he reassured everyone that despite all the dried blood on his clothes, he was not really hurt. Only a scratch, that was all.

Hal was shaking his head. "And there are those," he murmured to himself, "who scoff at the idea of resurrection!"

Baldur's introduction of his traveling companion was brief and to the point: "This is Hal. We met on the road, and he has been of some help to me. He'll stay with us tonight, and maybe longer."

Moments later food and drink were being pressed into Hal's hands, and he was led into the house and offered a place to sit. The names of a dozen of Baldur's relatives were thrust upon him. He thought he might remember one or two, those of the younger and better-looking women. On entering the house he put aside his helmet, and as a sign of peace, his hickory-handled axe, as soon as he could find a proper place to stand it against the wall, where it was not hidden but out of the way. He was careful to retain his belt pouch, and incidentally his dagger—possibly the latter could be useful when it came time to eat.

Hal was heartily welcomed as Baldur's friend, but Baldur himself remained the center of attention. Now some members of the family were eagerly volunteering that they had heard, from other participants in the recent skirmish, that he, Baldur, was dead. Either some member of the family had already gone looking for his body, or someone had been about to go—Hal couldn't quite determine which. No one here had seen any trace of Baldur, living or dead, for months, but apparently that was not really unusual, so the family had continued to nurse strong hopes for his survival.

The names of several absent men were mentioned, and Hal gathered that they were all close friends or relatives currently engaged in various military operations, though not all in the service of the same lord.

Baldur kept trying to change the subject away from war and casualties, and eventually succeeded, though the change was only slight. "Hal and I met Hagan and some of his people on the road. I said hello to him, but not much else."

That diverted everyone's attention, and brought on a brief silence. All the people in the room seemed to know who Hagan was, but no one wanted to talk about him—not just now, anyway. Very soon the focus of attention shifted back to Hal.

The great joy felt by Baldur's mother at his return, almost from the dead, was shared to a greater or less degree by all the other members of the household.

Several people had brought Hal refreshment of various kinds, but only one remained to sit beside him on the bench. This was Matilda, some kind of cousin to Baldur, perhaps five years younger than Hal, and moderately attractive. A little on the plump side, but brisk and active.

Meanwhile several children were also being introduced as either Baldur's cousins or his orphaned nephews and nieces. Hal lost track of which was which. Two half-grown boys, in particular, Holah and Noden, though shy about actual conversation, were studying the scarred and well-traveled stranger with great interest. They seemed to find Hal's axe even more fascinating than its owner, though so far neither boy had offered to approach closer than ten feet to where the weapon stood resting in a corner.

Half an hour after Baldur's coming home with his new friend, preparations for a feast of celebration were well under way. Hal undertook a visit to the privy, which proved to be about where he expected to find it, buried behind the house in a discreet clump of small evergreens. On the way, he paused in several places to take a better look at Baldur's mother's establishment.

Taking inventory as he strolled along, he observed that the house was considerably bigger than it had looked when he first saw it from the road. Farther back, almost hidden from view, were several shanties that he supposed housed workers on the land and in the house.

One of these in particular, almost behind the small barn, suggested in the shape of its large chimney and general configuration that someone in the family was, or had once been, a blacksmith. The smithy had a disused look about it now.

On his way back to the house, along a path that must be flower-girt in summer, Hal encountered Matilda again. She seemed to be waiting for him, and was making no pretense of doing anything else. He noted that there were now ribbons on her dress and some late-blooming flowers in her hair.

She was obviously not given to blushing and stammering when she had something to say. "You've got the beginnings of a limp there, don't you? My late husband walked that way before he died. That's right, I'm a widow these two years. Childless, too. Some say I'll never marry again, being too sharp-tongued to attract a worthy husband, and too hard to please to accept a lesser one."

Hal framed his answer carefully, considering every word before he spoke. "And what do you say when they say that, Matilda?"

"I say they're wrong. I'm not impossibly hard to please."

"I see. Well, people who know me say I am."

"One more thing I must tell you, Haraldur. Ten days ago I had a sign from the gods, telling me that a stranger would soon arrive at this house, whom I must get to know."

"It's remarkable how those things work, sometimes," Hal acknowledged diplomatically.

By now they were strolling together back toward the house. Matilda had not yet taken Hal's arm, but he was expecting the gesture at any moment. She took the opportunity to point out that she owned some nearby farmland in her own name.

Now they were passing the disused building that had once been a working smithy. Matilda saw where Hal was looking.

"I don't suppose you are a smith, or armorer? Too bad. The man who worked there once made fine weapons. Before he felt the call of Wodan," Matilda added.

Before Hal could craft a good response, she was changing the subject, pointing at something far on the other side of the house. "The land up to that ridge and over it is mine, almost as much of it on the far side as you can see on this; I have clear title by inheritance. Good soil, too. By now the harvest's in, of course, or you could see how fine was this year's crop."

"Then you are a fortunate woman."

"That's as may be. My husband's dying was a grievous stroke, but I have my health, and independence."

Hal murmured vague congratulations.

Having explained herself with apparent candor, Matilda was not shy about offering an appraisal of her listener: "I like a man who's old enough to know his way around in the world. Not so old, of course, that his joints and his wind and maybe other powers are failing him."

Hal looked appropriately grim. "I fear I'm practically at that stage."

She ignored the discouraging admission. "And what do you do? Here I talk on and on, and give you no chance to say a thing about yourself. You're not a blacksmith. Are you a farmer?"

He shook his head. "Never been wealthy enough to own a farm. Why, do I look like one?"

Matilda sighed. "You know well enough what you look like. I was just trying to be polite. As if I couldn't see what . . . but you're close enough to some farmers I've known, who were not exactly gentlemen either. You might be one."

"If you mean I might become a farmer, I suppose that's possible. If you mean I might be a gentleman . . ." He shook his head.

Matilda continued to be selective in what she chose to hear. She eyed his arms and face. "I see a few scars here and there, but you're still strong enough for honest work. No disabilities?"

Hal sighed in turn. "None in particular. Except a lack of opportunity for certain forms of exercise. How about you?"

———

The celebratory dinner was substantial, the long table in the biggest room of the farmhouse crowded with almost twenty people. It was obvious that several neighbors had dropped in. For the first time in many days, Hal truly had his fill of food and drink.

That evening, when some of Baldur's family asked the young man what he meant to do with his life now that he had survived such a close call in battle, he disappointed some and intrigued others by telling them that he meant to find or fight his way to the side of Brunhild.

His mother looked up sharply. "Who?"

"There is a girl, mother. Her name is Brunhild. And she is very important to me. Somehow I will find a way to be with her again, dead or alive."

It was clear from his mother's face that that was not the answer she had been hoping for.

Judging from the silence round the table, and the looks on people's faces, this was the first any of Baldur's family had heard of his affair with a Valkyrie.

It was the very old man with the cane who asked: "Who is Brunhild? What is her family like, and where is she? Is she in some kind of trouble, that Baldur says he will be with her dead or alive?"

As if realizing that he had already said too much, Baldur shut his mouth and refused to utter another word about Brunhild. When it became obvious that Baldur was determined to say no more on the subject, people began to turn to Hal, as if they expected him to come up with some further explanation. He tried to return a look indicating that he had nothing of the kind to offer.

"Not some kind of camp-follower, I hope." That was Matilda's remark, obviously intended as a question.

Hal grunted. Now Baldur's mother, hovering near, wondered aloud if this Brunhild could possibly be from a good respectable family.

Feeling that he had to say something or be taken for an idiot, Hal finally got out: "It's definitely my impression that she is." He could indeed recall Baldur saying something about only the daughters of the nobility being chosen for such exalted roles in Wodan's service.

Matilda pounced. "You know her, then?"

Now the guest regretted opening his mouth on the subject at all. "Never met the girl myself. Baldur's mentioned her name a few times."

———

By evening, a chill drizzle had set in, and Hal congratulated himself on being snug inside, not seeking some crude shelter on the road.

Not that he or Baldur were in the house. What had once been Baldur's sleeping room as a son of the household had long since been reassigned, since he was almost never home. The rain was drumming harder on the roof of the shed, a small and inelegant but comfortable shelter he and Baldur had been assigned to share. The only fundamental really lacking was a fire, but there wasn't going to be a fire in here, not with all this hay.

As if the subject of fire were on his mind, the youth was groaning to Hal that he, Baldur, should have forced himself through Loki's flames when he had the chance, whatever the cost.

"That's a crazy idea." Hal was keeping his voice low. "Your Hildy wouldn't be pleased to have a great lump of fried sausage fall into her lap. And that's what you'd be when you got through that fire. Not that I think you could get through it at all. Anyway, I say it again, you don't really know that she's in there."

"I know." Baldur was calm, resigned.

"You do? How could anyone put anyone in there, without—well—how is it physically possible?"

"You mean to pass through Loki's flames and not be burned?" Baldur shook his head dismissively. "I've seen that done, with my own eyes."

Here was revelation. Hal demanded further details.

Baldur tried to brush his questions aside. "I tell you I have seen it done, by a mere mortal human, never mind how."

"How?" Hal promptly insisted. He waited what seemed to him a decent interval, three or four breaths, then prodded again. "Lad, if she's really stuck up there behind that wall of magic flame, better forget about her. You've seen that fire up close, and so have I. No one's going to get through it." Even as he spoke, he supposed the rain might well be pounding down on Loki's flames, but he doubted it was having the least effect on them.

Baldur's confidence was unshaken. "Someone *can* pass through without harm," he repeated finally. "For the last time, I've seen it done."

"Oh? If you want me to believe that, tell me who and when. And especially how."

After briefly hesitating, Baldur gave in. "I suppose there's no reason I can't tell you. It was another of the Valkyries, on her Horse—I saw them disappear right into the flames, and a minute later emerge again, to tell me the fate of her sister, Brunhild. When she came out, Alvit— her name is Alvit—she told me it was the Horse, and especially the Horse's magic shoes, that made the passage possible. And I saw that she had taken no harm. Not a hair on her head was scorched."

"And when was this?"

"Only a few hours before you and I met, up there on the crag."

Once having got started, the young man was ready to talk on and on. Within a few minutes he was telling Hal that now, seeing no purpose or value in his life apart from the effort to reach Brunhild, he, Baldur, had almost made up his mind to becoming a berserker himself, and prove his devotion to Wodan by achieving a glorious death on the field of battle.

"Why?" Hal asked.

"Why?" Baldur looked at him as if he suspected an attempt at wit. "Because that is the only way a man can ever be truly certain of getting into Wodan's hall."

Hal yawned, reached out a hand to pat and shape the pile of hay behind him. He was looking forward to tonight's soft bed. "Wait a minute. Brunhild's not there, is she? I thought the only object you now had in life was just to reach Brunhild."

"But it's the same thing! You see, Hal, once I am there in Wodan's hall, standing in the presence of the god of warriors, the Father of Battles, I will beseech the All-Highest to set her free."

This seemed to have the makings of an interesting story, anyway. "You think Wodan would do that?"

Baldur stood up from where he had been sitting in the hay. "For a man who stands high in the ranks of Wodan's heroes, anything is pos- sible. Yes, I hope and believe that the god of warriors would grant me that favor. But if he refused, then I would plead to be allowed to join Brunhild. To share her fate, whatever it might be."

The young man remained standing, with one arm raised, as if listening for an answer from above. There was only distant thunder and the sound of the cold rain testing the solid roof.

"I think you mean that," Hal muttered at last, shaking his head. "At this moment you are really convinced that getting yourself cut to bits in some damn fool fight would be a good way to reach your goals in life."

Baldur, sitting down again, gave him his haughty, stubborn look. "Of course I mean it. Were I to die in true berserker fashion, fighting against a dozen men or so . . ." He nodded, as if in private satisfaction.

"Hah!" Hal lay back in comfortable hay, pulling his cloak about him. "Were you to die in true berserker fashion, you'd be mincemeat when you finally fell. The dogs wouldn't want you, let alone your lover. And if Brunhild wouldn't carry you to Wodan the last time you got knocked down, what makes you think another Valkyrie would?"

Baldur didn't want to hear such quibbling. He rolled over in the hay, turning his back. Finally his murmur reached Hal's ears: "I am ready to join Hagan's band."

Hal grunted. "I didn't hear him ask you."

Baldur had the last word, sleepily: "You know, he is my father."

4

ON THE SECOND evening of Hal's visit, he joined the family group round the hearth in the chill evening. The central hall of the house, heated by two fireplaces, was big enough for quite a gathering. The drizzling rain had stopped, but the sky was still a clammy gray, and a chill wind suggested that the first snow of the season could not be far off.

In conversation, he gradually revealed a little more about himself. Baldur's sisters and his aunt had a way of getting a man to talk without seeming to ask probing questions. The small group included the very old grandfather, who smiled encouragingly but had very little to say.

Hal told his listeners that he had spent the last several years in the far south, round the shores of the Great Sea.

Now and then one of the younger members of the family, reassured by Hal's mild and courteous manners, tried tentatively to press him to tell his stories. The two half-grown boys, Holah and Noden, especially were keen in their expectation of tales of adventure from one who had spent years of his life voyaging round the mysterious and legendary Great Sea. Hal had told them a couple of stories, but the more he talked the more they wanted to hear.

The boys by now were growing gradually a little bolder in their questioning. And it was plain they were still fascinated by the battle-hatchet, though neither of them had ventured to lay a hand on it. Probably they had learned in early childhood that men tended to be touchy about their weapons.

Now Noden pointed at the axe, still standing exactly where Hal had put it on his arrival. "I bet this has seen some fighting, Hal!"

Holah chimed in. "Can you throw it, Hal? Stick it in a target?"

"Has it got a name? I've heard that all gods and famous warriors name their weapons!"

Hal only looked at the youngsters morosely, and they fell silent. One of the elders, who had been half-listening, routinely cautioned the boys to mind their manners, not to pry.

Suddenly Hal couldn't remember whether or not the lads were orphans. Some of the children, maybe a majority, in the extended household were, but he had got the various names mixed up in his mind. Battle-orphans generally want to avenge their fathers, bereaved siblings their older brothers; so it has always been, and so it will be. Hal told them that he had to think about it before discussing such serious matters.

When one of the sisters asked him if he had ever met true royalty, he said: "I have seen enough of kings—and of princes and princesses, as well."

"You really have known such people, then?"

He hesitated, then shrugged. "Here and there."

The night was growing late, the fire was beginning to die down, but it was still warm in the snug house. Now Matilda had joined them, but for once she had little to say.

And Hal, responding to another question: "Yes, since you ask me, I was with Jason. But then I decided . . ." Gazing into the distance, he let his words die away.

"Decided what?" Matilda was all in favor of plain talk. Secrets were a sign of something wrong.

That I did not want to be a Hero any longer, caught up in endless games of blood and magic, gold, and power. Games in which I played with some of the high gods themselves and with the human rulers of the earth. Oh, playing for such high stakes can be great sport. Or so it seemed to me. And the very fact of danger has its own fascination. But in the end even the great prizes meant very little.

How could a man hope to find the words to explain things like that? To Matilda, whose mind was in her farmland. And why should he want to try?

"That I wanted to go home," he finally answered.

He wasn't sure if anyone believed him when he said that. Soon someone asked: "Maybe you can tell us, Hal: did Jason really bring home the Golden Fleece? And then it somehow disappeared? That's what we heard a month ago, from travelers passing through."

"I have heard much the same story myself," was his short answer.

"But you were there. You must have seen what happened?"

"There was a great deal of confusion toward the end."

He had not actually told anyone yet that he was even now carrying with him the muddy remnant of the miracle that had once been called the Golden Fleece.

Yes, he had wanted to see his home again. But he had known all along that the home he had left as a boy would not be there when he got back to it, that the people and things that he remembered could no longer exist as he remembered them.

He had been trudging along through the valley of the Einar, on his way home, contemplating how fierce the winter would be just now, up there in the country where he had been born. A great difference from the summery lands in which he had spent the last few years. When he had looked up to catch his first glimpse of Loki's fire on the high crag, it had seemed for a moment like a summons, a beacon of some kind, meant for his eyes in some special way.

"I suppose you'll have people at home, waiting. They'll be glad to see you when you get back." Matilda was at last getting into the discussion.

It took Hal a little while to answer. "If they recognize me at all," he said at last. "They'll look at me and tell me I've been gone a long time. And they'll be right." A few faces came and went in memory. Not, he thought, that anyone up there in the north could really be waiting for him now. Not any longer, not after all the years he'd been away. The young girls he remembered would be raising girls and boys of their own by now, and starting to lose their teeth. By the balls and the beard of Zeus, some of them would probably be grandmothers!

That idea had never occurred to Hal before, and now for some reason it shook him deeply. Had a long time spent in those warm climates made him soft?

He knew he was not handsome, that most people found his appearance more frightening than heroic. Baldur had been telling everyone how neatly Hal had disposed of one bandit and faced down another, and the story had done Hal no harm in the eyes of anyone in this house. He could see in the faces of Baldur's family that in general they were all still a little afraid of him—but he could see also that men who caused fear were by no means a novelty in this household.

———

Other people had retired, rather suddenly, so that before Hal knew it, he and Matilda were sitting alone together by the fading fire.

She had brought some kind of sewing project with her, and her fingers were keeping busy. She said to the fire: "I could see myself marrying a farmer, if he was ready to settle down and work some good land. But never a fighting man again."

Hal had nothing to say to that. Presently he got up and went to find his bed in the soft hay.

———

Part of Hal's long journey toward home had been accomplished without too much effort, riding a succession of riverboats. Part of it he had endured jolting along in a cart behind a drom, and much had been spent on foot. It had been quite a change from the long voyage with Jason, months of steamy sunburned drudgery at the oar, enlivened with occasional hours of extreme peril. And for Hal the aftermath of the great quest had been greatly disappointing, despite the fact (or maybe because of it) that he had been spending time in the company of gods and kings and princesses and Heroes.

Leaving that all behind him, he had abandoned whatever hope he might once have held of achieving a glorious success in the world. Instead he had conceived what had seemed a much more modest plan, that of accumulating enough gold to perhaps buy a sizable farm in his own country. Maybe a farm, or maybe a couple of stout new fishing boats. With that kind of security, a man could settle down and marry.

One trouble with his plan of retiring to a small farm, as he was beginning to discover, was that unless some unusual opportunity came along, the modest success seemed no more attainable than the great one.

And now there was opportunity, in the form of Matilda, her generous body and her farmland. Practically inviting him to plow and plant them both. And what was really wrong with Matilda, if he really wanted to settle down? If she imagined she heard messages from the gods, she was still far less crazy than many another woman that he'd known.

This wasn't home, of course. But then he was far from sure that he any longer had a home, or that he really wanted to find out if he did.

What was the price of northern land this year? he wondered. Maybe eight or ten acres, in one of the good, rich valleys. And what about the price of boats? How many golden horseshoes would it take to establish himself on a substantial farm? More than one, he would be willing to wager. He thought he would begin to feel comfortable if he had four or five such lumps of yellow metal. To be sure, make it half a dozen.

Having survived the long ordeal of Jason's Argosy, and what came after it, Haraldur had started to be tempted by the thought of starting a new life for himself while he was still young enough to raise a family.

Maybe he was being too pessimistic about the costs, and the golden horseshoe fragment already in his pouch might be in itself enough to make him an owner of substantial property when he got home. Maybe. But more likely not.

He had the feeling that more, much more, might be almost within his grasp now, if he were bold enough to take it. Why not try to gather in the wealth of a dozen horseshoes, or a score? After all, there would be nothing *wrong* with owning two or three big farms and a fleet of boats.

The fact that the thing in his pouch was so laden with heavy magic made him mistrust even the permanence of its common value.

———

And again, as he sat talking: "But it all comes down to having some modest measure of wealth, enough to do all these nice peaceful things." As he spoke, his eyes met those of the old man sitting across from him, and it seemed to Hal that a kind of understanding passed between them.

In fact it was Baldur's old grandfather, somewhat hard of hearing, who roused Hal from contemplation by asking him: "It's gold, aye?"

"Beg pardon, grandsire?"

"It's gold, I say, that you're concerned about."

Hal had to agree. "Gold is a thing of constant interest, yes. To a man who must try to plan his future. A subject of which few people ever tire."

The oldster slapped a lean hand familiarly on Hal's knee. "Aye, it's always the yellow heavy metal, isn't it? You can understand that, northman, I can see it in your eyes. Jewels can give wealth too, but gold is more than simply wealth. It's light, and life, and warmth. The softness and the beauty, and the glow. The light in sparkling jewels is much too sharp."

———

And it was practical Matilda, coming in on the end of the conversation, who asked: "Easy enough to say it would be a good idea to have some gold. But how do you propose to get it?"

Hal closed his eyes. He could imagine himself showing his interlocutor what was left of the small scrap of peculiar fabric he had been carrying with him for some months. Pulling it out of his belt pouch, and holding it out.

He could readily imagine what the person he was talking to would say: "Where'd you get that rag? It doesn't look like much."

He saw himself offering it on the palm of his broad hand. "This is gold too, or it once was. Ever hear of the Golden Fleece?"

"It is important magic, then."

"Important, and also exceedingly strange. When I first saw this, it was much larger, and such power as it possessed was of a totally different kind." How could he make a very long story short? Only by throwing most of the story away. "It has—changed, since it came into my hands. First, it is very much diminished. Secondly, it has developed a new power, which astonished me the first time I saw it."

"What power is that? A useful one?"

"A simple one, and tempting. As for useful . . . maybe 'dangerous' would be a better word. Now it shows me whenever gold is near." And it was easy to perform a demonstration on a small golden ornament.

He might of course have told a glorious story, all of it true. Something about how he had picked the little patch of fabric out of the mud of a certain southern beach, on the shore of the Great Sea. The remnant had been lying there ignored, forgotten, after people had died to bring it to that place.

"It was dull and dirty even then. But it was not always so."

"No?"

"No."

And that was all. Hal found that he had suddenly lost his taste for telling stories, even in his imagination.

———————

In real words, Hal questioned Baldur: "Haven't I heard somewhere that the god himself rides on an eight-legged horse?"

"Yes. Or he rides behind one, rather; Sleipnir is the creature's name, and it pulls his chariot."

"You've seen such an animal yourself?"

"No, nor have I ever seen Wodan. But it is true nevertheless." Baldur was firm in his belief, as only those who have not seen can be firm.

After another half-minute had gone by he went on: "I have been thinking, Hal, about the Horses."

"The magic ones, you mean, that the Valkyries ride on? Yes, they seem worth thinking about." *Especially their golden shoes.*

"If one of them can carry a woman in through the flames, to Brunhild's side—why could one not carry me?"

"Oh, we're back on that again?" Hal was about to tell the youth to forget about any crazy plan he might be thinking up for rescuing his girlfriend, or at least paying her a visit. But the golden shoes were still in his mind, and he could not let the subject go.

Yes, Baldur assured him, Alvit had been very clear about the shoes. Even ordinary horses, which were in common use in some parts of the world, wore smooth, curving bands of metal, nailed right on their hooves. "The Horse's hoof, you see, has no more sense of pain than do our hair or fingernails."

"I see." Hal made his expression innocent of knowledge, willing to be instructed.

Baldur was musing. "And in the case of the mounts Valkyries ride, the metal is definitely gold."

Hal had already made sure of that for himself. Delicately, carefully, and in deep secrecy, scratching his secret fragment of a shoe with his dagger's point. He had weighed its heaviness in his hand, assured himself that it was true gold.

Baldur now began quietly and eagerly to explain the plan he had been devising, which involved borrowing at least one Horse from Wodan's stables. Hal's first impression was that it was the kind of scheme hatched by men who had been hit too often on the head.

No one in his right mind would use soft lovely gold to make a mundane horseshoe, and see the precious metal quickly worn away to nothing on hard ground. But gold with a suitable alloy of magic, now—that could be a very different matter.

Hal didn't want to sound too easily convinced. "It strikes me that golden horseshoes would wear out very quickly."

"Not on the feet of a Horse who does most of his running in the air. And of course it isn't just plain ordinary gold, it must be imbued with magic."

Hal had more questions: Exactly why was the Valkyrie riding into the fire, then out of it again, when Baldur saw her at it?

"I thought I had explained that. Because Alvit wanted to—she dared to—visit Wodan's prisoner and see if anything could be done for her. She found Brunhild alive, breathing, seemingly unharmed, but in an enchanted sleep." Baldur's voice almost broke on the last word, and he paused to regain his grim determination. "Hal, I must have the use of one of those Horses."

"Sounds impossible."

"Why? Nothing is impossible, to a true warrior-hero. To a man who refuses to admit impossibility."

"Oh, really? For one thing, you have no idea where the Valkyries' Horses are stabled—or is that another secret you've been keeping?"

"It's true, I don't know where the Horses are, exactly." Baldur admitted. Then he looked up slyly. "Probably they're in Valhalla. But wherever they are, I do know a means of reaching them."

"What way?"

"This must be kept a secret. Have I your word, as—as a warrior and a gentleman?"

"My solemn word as a warrior and gentleman. Oh, of course."

The youth looked all around, then dropped his voice till Hal could barely hear it. "I know who serves as Wodan's farriers. They are gnomes, and I have even visited their village."

Afterward, Hal found it hard to remember whether it was he himself or Baldur who first suggested that they should make a scouting trip to the gnomes' village. Whoever had thought of it first, some such reconnaissance seemed the only way they were going to find out any more about Wodan's Horses—and in particular about their golden shoes, which was the part that interested Hal.

Meanwhile Hal, as usual, kept up his patient search for more information. "Does anyone know what was up on that crag before the fire started? I mean, was there really a castle, watchtower, anything of the kind?"

Even as he asked the question, he was reasonably sure that the answer must be no. If there had been any substantial structure, then there should have been a road going to the top, or at least the traces of an old one. No one could put up a sizable house or fort atop a steep hill without first making a road, or at least wearing a broad path with all the going up and coming down of workers and materials. And of course there had been nothing of the kind.

Baldur had no particular interest in golden shoes, or gold in any form: what he kept coming back to was that the only known way to get through Loki's fire was by riding a Valkyrie's Horse.

Hal just as persistently kept trying to lead the talk from Horses into the related subject of horseshoes.

Hal kept at it. "So, Wodan's cavalry can really fly, then. Not just fly, but carry people through Loki's fire without harm."

"Oh, no doubt about it. I know it's hard to believe, Hal, but—how many times do I have to tell you? If I had a Horse here now, I could be at Brunhild's side within an hour."

Hal picked his teeth and ruminated for a while. They had recently concluded a very satisfactory dinner. Life on a prosperous farm, like this one, could be quite nice, at least for the owners. On the other hand, farming always involved an enormous amount of work.

Some time had passed before he prodded: "You were going to tell me more about the gnomes who handle the farrier work for Wodan's stable. You said you even visited them."

Baldur nodded, then hesitated, as if wondering whether the further revelation he was about to make was wise. Then he added: "I met the Earthdweller who actually does the work."

"You keep coming out with these surprises. How did that come about?"

"Well—it's a long story."

"I'm not going anywhere."

Still Baldur hesitated, as if he feared to allow the escape of dangerous secrets. At last he said: "Brunhild wanted this gnome, Andvari's his name, to look at her Horse's shoes. She thought one of them was beginning to work loose."

"It's none of my business, really, lad—but how long were you and this maiden acquainted?" He had been about to ask *how long and how well* but at the last moment had thought it best to omit a couple of words.

"Well, it was only about six months." Baldur sounded surprised himself when he came to reckon out the time. "No more than that. But it seemed—forever. It seemed that my life only really began on the day that I met her."

Hal nodded wisely. Then he requested: "Tell me more about the gnomes?"

"I don't know much more about them. Why?"

"Well. It seems to me that getting to know them better is the only way you're ever going to find out exactly where to reach the Horses."

And the only way I'm ever going to get any closer to those golden shoes, and the place where they are forged. But Hal did not say that aloud.

5

HAL WAS CARRYING in his pouch good evidence that at least some of Wodan's Horses were truly shod with gold. Possibly they all were. That, he supposed, could easily mean a hundred golden horseshoes nailed firmly on hooves, coming loose, or lying around somewhere as spares. The total ought to buy enough farmland to satisfy a dozen retiring Argonauts. But he was not going to be greedy.

Hal's knowledge of gnomes and gnomeland was practically nil, but Baldur had told him that their towns and villages were generally to be found along river valleys. On the other hand, everyone knew that Wodan's legendary stronghold and headquarters, Valhalla, had to be perched somewhere very high up in some range of mountains. Probably, thought Hal, the gold from which the shoes were made was stored right in Valhalla, or at least nearby. Which suggested that the gnomes who served as farriers for Wodan would have to climb well up into the mountains to do their work.

Of course, any hoard that held a hundred horseshoes worth of gold was certain to be well guarded by one means or another. But in any system of protection there were generally weak points. And Hal had no intention of trying to empty out the divine Wodan's treasury, or even make a noticeable dent in his reserves. No, the northman's ambitions were quite modest, befitting a mere mortal. He would be delighted to just pick up a few more scraps of yellow metal, absentmindedly left lying about by those who seemed to have more gold than they knew what to do with. Just some odds and ends.

For several days now Hal had been incubating an idea in the back of his mind. It was the germ of a scheme which, if successful, should finance the nicest little farm a man could ever want, and maybe the start of a fleet of fishing boats to boot. At first the idea had seemed little more than a daydream, too foolish to be taken seriously; but the longer he thought about it, the closer to the realm of possibility it seemed to drift.

He had to keep reminding himself that he really knew almost nothing about Wodan or magic Horses, and, when you came right down to it, not much about Baldur either. He had no way to test the truth of anything his companion told him regarding Valkyries. So trying to formulate anything like a detailed plan would be a complete waste of time, until he had learned more—a whole lot more. To learn more, he would just have to check out the situation for himself, and the only way he could see of doing that was by beginning with the gnomes.

While Hal kept secretly toying with ideas about gold, Baldur was developing his own scheme for reaching Brunhild and taking Hal into his confidence about it. Now the young man, acting casually and showing a talent for misdirection, so that his family suspected nothing, had begun making clandestine arrangements for his and Hal's planned expedition to the gnomes' village. He was telling everyone that the two of them were going on a fishing trip, just to relax.

Baldur's plan involved finding out from Wodan's gnome-farriers just where the Valkyries' Horses were stabled. Baldur had convinced himself that a Horse could carry him safely through Loki's flames, and once that happened, he would once more be able to clasp his beloved in his arms. Currently he seemed to have no hopes or plans for anything beyond that moment.

Right now, Hal and Baldur were standing on the bank of the stream that ran behind the house, and Hal thought they were out of earshot of anyone else.

As usual, he was playing the role of cautious partner. "We don't have any idea yet where the Horses are kept. At least I don't."

"But certainly the gnomes must know." Suddenly Baldur was ready to offer another revelation; he seemed to dole them out on an average of one a day, like a parent handing sweetmeats to a child. He said: "Brunhild once told me that the farriers' routine work is done four times a year, on the full moon following each solstice and each equinox."

"Is that a fact?" Hal quickly calculated that the next full moon, due in less than two weeks, would be the first after the autumnal equinox. "Then the timing would seem to be in our favor, anyway. How far away is this village of gnomes?"

Baldur, who said he had actually been there once, gave an estimate. Hal thought that with a little effort, they would be able to time their trip so they reached the gnomes' village in a few days. Exactly when the farriers would be starting on their periodic journey to Valhalla was impossible to say, but it would have to be soon, if either departure or arrival coincided with the full moon.

Baldur for once was almost cheerful. "It's a sign, Hal! A very favorable sign, it means that the Fates are with us."

"I'm glad to hear it."

Abruptly the young man turned on Hal. With the air of one who had just reached an important decision and was about to confer a great favor, he announced: "If we can get our hands on two Horses, instead of only one, then you can come with me, when I go to Brunhild." Since Hal was so interested, so ready to join in secret discussions, he must be ready and eager to plunge into the whole bold undertaking up to his neck. What other attitude could a professional adventurer, a former Argonaut, possibly have?

"It will be a glorious adventure!" Baldur added with a grin, inviting his older partner to relax and be enthusiastic.

Hal stared at him. "I'm sure it will."

Baldur had already turned his attention back to planning. "Naturally, our first step must be to think of some good reason to give the gnomes, for visiting their village. We can't just say we were on a fishing trip and decided to drop in."

"Well, we might do worse. But what would you suggest?"

The youth was squinting his eyes, as if his own deep thoughts might be hard to make out. "Tell them you're a merchant, come to trade—no, wait a minute, Hal. That's it. I'll tell them you're a famous warrior, come to commission some kind of special weapon. They fill such orders all the time. They are, as you must realize, the finest metalsmiths in the world."

"I see," said Hal, who hadn't realized anything of the kind. But the world was a big place, and he had to admit that for all he knew, Baldur might be right on this point. "And once we're there, how do we get them to lead us to the Horses?"

Baldur didn't seem to think that that would be a problem. "Either we accompany the farriers when they leave the village—or else we follow them."

"You think we can do either one?"

"Certainly. See, if they don't want company we'll still walk with them openly, part of the way. Then we'll make a show of turning off on a different route. We'll let them get a bit ahead, then follow them secretly until they lead us to Valhalla. Or wherever the Horses might be stabled."

"I see." Hal ruminated for a few strides. "Well, it might work. But why do you assume they're walking? It could be a long journey. Wouldn't they more likely be riding, on cameloids or in a carriage?"

Baldur shook his head decisively. "Gnomes very rarely use such animals."

"You seem to know a lot about them."

And Baldur was suddenly determined to change the subject. Hal wondered silently if the youth might have had a gnomish girlfriend too.

———

Hal could well believe that Wodan might be a little careless with his gold. He had meditated on the subject for some time, and had decided that probably few gods cared much about wealth in itself—after all, they could pretty much help themselves to what they wanted of the world's goods without having to pay. But magic Horses, like the creatures Baldur had described—such an animal would be a treasure indeed, to any god or mortal.

In their secret discussions, Baldur persisted in talking as if it would be the easiest thing in the world to locate a Horse, hop on its back and ride away. *Brain damage*, thought Hal again, reflecting on his colleague's simple faith. Well, maybe his own plan of picking up some odds and ends of Wodan's gold was no more practical. But he could not be sure of that until he knew more, much more, than he did.

Patiently Hal persisted with his questioning. "Suppose we do find out which individual gnomes are going to do the farrier-work. We still—"

"I know that," Baldur calmly interrupted. "A name, and where he lives."

"You do? How?"

The youth was silent.

After a moment Hal pressed on. "So you not only know which village these farriers live in, but—somehow—one of their names."

Baldur said nothing.

Hal pressed on again. "What if they don't want us to travel with them, even partway? And how do you know that gnomes setting out on a journey won't be riding cameloids or driving a coach with droms? It's pretty certain we won't. We don't have any."

"I told you not to worry about the cameloids," Baldur assured him vaguely. "Of course it may be that the gnomes will want to discourage our going with them." He paused thoughtfully. "But I just might be able to find the Horses anyway, even if the gnomes are no help."

"You might? How?"

Again they seemed to have reached an area where Baldur was reluctant to reveal certain matters to his partner. He did explain to Hal that he had come to know one of Wodan's noble steeds by name, the very one that Brunhild had used to ride. That particular Horse had become Baldur's friend, had eaten lumps of sugar, sometimes apples, from his hand. "Its name is Gold Mane. I think that Horse would come to me, if I should call it."

"Call it how?"

"I mean if I were to summon it by magic—assuming you and I could put together some kind of effective spell—the beast might well come to me, across the miles."

"I didn't know that you were any kind of a magician. I'm not."

"Oh, I'm not either, really. Not on a professional level. But when I was a child, I did manage a spell or two."

Hal thought it over. "Better not try anything of the kind unless we have no other option."

"I agree."

In response to careful questioning, Baldur admitted that yes, he had actually even ridden Gold Mane once or twice—which, of course, was a secret that Hal must promise never to divulge to anyone.

"I promise," said Hal, thinking it was no wonder that Brunhild had got herself into deep trouble.

The details of the plan changed as the two men talked it over. But Baldur never wavered in his claim that he had ridden on a Horse, that he could ride a Horse again, given the chance, and that any Horse he got his hands on could carry him safely through the wall of fire.

Again he described how he had once seen Alvit, Hildy's friend and sister Valkyrie, perform that very feat. It did worry Baldur somewhat that Alvit had refused to tell him much in the way of detail about Brunhild's condition on the other side. She would say only that the girl was lying in an enchanted sleep.

———

And so it went. Hal's tentative, private plan, which at the start had seemed little more than a joke, ready to evaporate at the first touch of opposition, was beginning to take on aspects of reality.

Still, there were moments in which it seemed to Hal that he must be brain-damaged himself even to be considering such an undertaking. Even before being hit on the head, Baldur could not have been one of the world's keenest wits. Experience counseled that the only sane thing for a seasoned man of the world to do, in Hal's situation, was to resume his own original northward trek, without pausing to look back. He would say a quick goodbye to the youth with the dented helmet and skull to match, and to all of Baldur's friends and relatives—yes, including Matilda. As far as Hal could tell, none of them had much more sense than Wodan's youthful worshiper.

And yet . . . and yet. There still remained the tantalizing fragment of golden horseshoe, a silent challenge in the form of heavy, real, and lustrous metal. The trouble was that all by itself, that single shard of gold probably wouldn't begin to buy him all he needed for a comfortable retirement. Without any firm idea of current prices, here or in his homeland, Hal could only guess. Maybe his bit of gold would purchase him one plow, along with a pair of droms to pull the plow across the patch of farmland he could not yet afford.

He thought that if he ever saw Matilda again, he might ask her how much she thought her dowry of farmland might be worth in gold. But it didn't take long to come up with several reasons why putting such a question might be unwise.

Alternatively, the piece now in his pouch might pay for no more than one truly glorious celebration—if Hal could think of anything to celebrate.

His real trouble, it crossed his mind to speculate, might be that he still found scheming and struggling to get gold a hell of a lot more fun than farming.

Common sense warned him that there would be only faint chances of success, and probably heavy risks, messing around with the magical property of a god. From Hal's point of view, he might be only picking up a few scraps that their owner would never miss, but Wodan might see the business in an entirely different way. Wodan was not just any god, but one who wanted to be known as the All-Highest, and so far had got away with it.

But on the other hand, when Hal pictured himself returning to his northern home as a poor man in threadbare garments, practically a stranger among folk he had not seen for many years, it was all too easy to imagine the looks of disdain he'd get, the lack of any real welcome . . . the image immediately stiffened his resolve. He could not simply turn his back on what might be a golden opportunity—certainly not just yet. He would have to search and probe a little farther.

For the time being, he would continue to go along with Baldur's plan, just as if he really had some confidence in it. Go along, at least until the two of them had visited the village of the gnomes, and he, Hal, had learned as much as he could there on the subjects of gold and gods.

━━━━━━━━

Baldur, in his desperate craving to rejoin Brunhild, was ready to try anything, and the young man's faith in his own crazy plan now seemed unshakeable. What had seemed a bare possibility only a few days ago was now a certainty in his mind, if only he could come within reach of a Horse.

Hal openly allowed that he had certain reservations about the feasibility of that scheme. But he hastily added that he was ready to go along with it for the time being. Privately he had decided to argue the young man into some more realistic plan as soon as he could think of one; or dissolve their partnership if and when the chance of getting near the gold began to loom as a real possibility.

Of course the idea of just getting on one of Wodan's Horses and riding it away sounded completely crazy. But then, the longer Hal thought about it, the more he realized that as odd and dangerous as the idea sounded, it might not be totally insane. His own experience with gods, admittedly not vast, had taught him a few things. The Face of any deity was bound to confer some great power on its wearer, but it did not necessarily improve intelligence or even guarantee competence in practical matters. The mightiest divinity could, and sometimes had, come to grief through his or her own all-too-human foolishness, forgetfulness and oversight. As it was with ordinary men and women, so it was with gods. A god or goddess, after all, was no more than a human being who had put on one of the ancient and indestructible Faces loaded with odylic magic.

━━━━━━━━

Over the next night or two, as the moon rose later and later, waxing inexorably toward full, Hal and Baldur were careful not even to hint at their true intentions to anyone in the family or village. Meanwhile, they ostentatiously made preparations for a fishing trip—part of the local lore of fishing said late fall was the best time for certain catches.

Baldur told his partner: "We may have to buy a few things—provisions and clothing for the trip. Especially as it seems we will be going up into the mountains."

"I have a little money," Hal admitted cautiously. He had somewhat replenished his otherwise depleted purse at the expense of the would-be robber. "But let's wait, if we can, to buy the mountain gear until we've traveled a way—we still want our departure to look like a simple fishing trip."

"Good idea."

Even if they stayed in the valleys, the strong possibility of cold weather was upon them, this late in the season. There was no telling when the first snow and real hard freeze were going to come along, and acquiring warm clothing and boots gave away no secrets.

Baldur privately remarked that it was fortunate that they would be able to go most of the way to gnome's territory, downstream by water.

Meanwhile, Hal had been casually asking Holah and Noden for information about gnomes, and the boys had been cheerfully telling him some ghastly stories. These tales, of human infants kidnapped and human miners suffocated in subterranean blackness by gnomic treachery, had made Hal wonder if there were not some way to avoid visiting Gnomeland at all. Now he asked his partner: "If we go there, will we be expected to descend into one of their mines?"

Baldur frowned. "No, probably only into their houses. Their dwellings, at least the ones I've seen, are hardly ever dug very deep below the surface. Actually I doubt they'd let us go into a mine, even if we wanted to."

Hal nodded sympathetically. "I can understand why they'd naturally want to keep their gold mines secret."

Baldur looked up at him, as if surprised. "Gold? No, I don't think they really produce much gold. Not any longer. Those diggings were all worked out a long time ago. It's more that they have methods and tools they want to keep secret. When they're in a hurry, they can drive a tunnel through solid rock in no time at all."

"I see." Hal sighed. "So, tell me some more about this place we're going to visit. Don't these holes you say they live in flood out every time it rains?"

Baldur said that in the course of his affair with Brunhild, he had heard her more than once mention the name and location of the gnome settlement where lived the farrier, named Andvari, and his assistant, whose name Baldur did not know.

Hal wondered what else the two lovers might have talked about—apparently they had done a lot of talking.

———————

Then Hal and Baldur began their journey by taking a small boat down the local stream, one of the Einar's tributaries, to the broad Einar itself, which would lead them directly to their secret destination.

Baldur's relatives seemed to accept, largely with indifference, the story he and Hal told them about going fishing. It was hard to imagine weather bad enough to stop a fisherman. So the two men had little trouble in borrowing a cheaply constructed raft from one of Baldur's distant relatives who lived nearby, and who seemed really indifferent as to whether he got it back or not. At one point Hal turned down the offer of the loan of an uncle's trim little sailboat, pleading a lack of knowledge of how to manage one—a totally false plea, but he did not want to borrow any vessel that would be greatly missed if it did not come back. If all did not go precisely well, there would be no use in having an extra set of pursuers on his track.

Baldur had not been entirely truthful with his family, before leaving them this time. His mother and most other members of the family seemed purely relieved that he was undertaking what promised to be an utterly peaceful enterprise.

Holah and Noden, having several times volunteered to go with Hal next time he went to war, swore they knew where the best fishing could be found, and they wanted to come along on that trip if there was no prospect of fighting. But they were vigorously discouraged.

———

As they were poling their raft downstream, Hal said to Baldur heartily: "So, tell me more about these people we're going to see. How well do you know them?"

"I don't know that I would call gnomes people." The young man paused. "Though some of them were very good to Brunhild and me."

Here was more news. "Good in what way?"

Now the young man, continuing his progressive series of revelations, disclosed that over the past few months some of the gnomes had actually connived to provide a secret meeting place for Brunhild and her lover. A place underground, where Wodan and his agents were unlikely to discover them.

"Why do you suppose they were so helpful?" Hal asked.

Baldur lowered his voice, though it seemed unlikely that anyone was within a quarter-mile. "Perhaps I should not be telling you this. But it seems that Brunhild had done the Earthdwellers some good turn previously."

Perhaps you shouldn't. I may someday wish I didn't know it, Hal thought. But, curious as usual, he continued: "What sort of good turn?"

"She never told me that."

Maybe that was the truth and maybe not. Baldur was consistently hesitant about revealing his secrets to Hal, but he kept leaking them out anyway, slowly but surely. In concealing his affair with Hildy, he was also hiding the extent of the knowledge he had incidentally picked up about the gnomes. Certainly no one in Baldur's family suspected that the youth had established any degree of intimacy with certain members of the strange race that he and Hal were about to visit.

Hal's persistent curiosity was a good match for Baldur's need to talk to someone about his troubles. Baldur struggled against the need, but not with much success.

The more Hal learned, the more genuinely interested he became. "So, the gnomes secretly found a way for you and Brunhild to get around old Wodan's rules regarding Valkyrie behavior."

Baldur hesitated. "Yes, that's about it."

"Does the god expect all his flying scouts to remain virgins?"

"Well—something like that, yes."

"Never mind, it doesn't matter. But you and she managed to meet underground, by courtesy of the gnomes."

The young man hesitated. "Yes."

"These Earthdwellers don't much care for the Great All-Highest, is that it? Even though he trusts some of them enough to let them shoe his Horses? And gives them access to his supply of gold?"

Baldur shot his companion a reproachful look. "Wodan is the All-Highest, the Father of Battles. No one speaks openly against him. Not even in jest."

"Was I speaking against him? I didn't mean to give offense, I'm sure." And Hal put on an abashed look, and scanned the sky, as if to make sure no instant retribution threatened.

When rain came, the two men sheltered under oilskins as best they could.

They passed several more or less ordinary villages and any number of isolated houses, and exchanged comments with various fishermen on the quality of the catch. Gradually the land on both banks grew rockier, less and less suitable for farming, and the habitations fewer. In the cold mornings, there were fringes of thin ice along the shore and in the adjoining marshlands.

Stopping at a small settlement of humans of their own variety, called by the gnomes Sundwellers, Hal and Baldur completed their outfitting for winter, including boots and leggings, taking care of such details as had not been done before leaving Baldur's home.

They had come many miles, and the youth said that he could now recognize several landmarks. He added that they were very near their goal.

6

SUDDENLY BALDUR BROKE off their conversation to point at a muddy hole in the riverbank. It was as big around as a man's leg, just at water level, a dark mouth half submerged. "One of the entrances to their village. There'll be a tunnel running from it inland, just above water level."

The black gap looked to Hal intensely uninviting, like the kind of cave that an otter might call home, or maybe some kind of giant snake. He supposed he might go crawling into such a place, if it was big enough, but only if he was fleeing some great peril, desperate to save his life.

Now Baldur was steering their craft closer to the right bank of the river. They went slowly, and more slowly still. Hal kept studying the slope of land slightly above the shore, which carried what looked to him like nothing but virgin forest.

"If that was really one of their tunnels in the bank," he remarked, "then one of their settlements must be near."

"Oh, it is. But you can see how easy it would be to pass it by and never realize that it was there." Baldur went on to explain that almost everything the gnomes created was underground, where they spent nearly all their time. For extensive settlements they favored sites near rivers, for if the tons of excavated earth could be handily dumped into a briskly flowing stream, very little of their presence would be visible.

Having chosen a place to land, the men tied their raft securely to a handy willow stump—even if they were really indifferent to its loss, it might be suspicious to give that impression. Then they ran through a last-minute rehearsal of their supposed reason for dropping in on this particular village. Hal would introduce himself as a warrior of high status, who contemplated commissioning the forging of some kind of weapon or armor.

At that point Baldur suddenly decided there were a few more things Hal should know about the people they were going to visit.

First of all, the gnomes were sometimes called dwarfs, but gave themselves the name of Earthdwellers. Just why the gnomes, or Earthdwellers, insisted on spending their time and strength grubbing in the earth, instead of coming out on the surface like real people, was more than Baldur could explain.

Hal supposed the main reason was probably just that the gnomes had a lot of trouble with sunlight. So few of the occupations normally open to the children of light were open to them.

Baldur informed him that the gnomes were very clever in some ways, and certainly not lazy. Many or most of them were physically deformed, at least by the standards of surface-dwelling humans. They tended to have pale faces and long beards.

"It's only the men who have beards, of course," the young man added after a pause.

"I am relieved."

By now the two of them were walking slowly inland, through a shallow screen of dead reed-stalks. Baldur said: "We humans, of course, can go down into caves and mines, and they can come up into daylight. But neither of our races can ever be really comfortable away from our own element."

"But where do gnomes come from? How long have they been around?"

The young man seemed vaguely surprised by the question, as if he had never thought about it. "Some say they are formed right in the dust of the earth, just as maggots naturally appear in dead meat. But that's not true," Baldur hastened to assure his comrade. "Those are the kind of things said by folk who really know nothing about gnomes. Get down into one of their houses, and you'll see some big-bellied women, and others nursing small children, just as in any human town."

"Well then, they *are* human, are they not?"

The younger man grunted something, and his face showed his disapproval of that idea. He was not ready to go quite that far with what he considered his liberal attitude.

Hal pressed him: "Do they ever intermarry with—what did you say their word is, for people like us? 'Sundwellers'?"

The expression of disapproval became stronger. "I don't know of anyone who's done that. Married a gnome." Baldur sounded vaguely scandalized. "There are stories about people doing that kind of thing in the past."

"What are the children like?"

"You'll have to ask someone else."

───────

They had come inland but a little distance through an almost trackless wintry forest, a domain of barren limbs and fallen leaves, when Baldur paused and indicated a kind of semi-clearing just ahead, an extensive glade whose grassy floor was irregularly raised and pocked by dozens of low mounds. These ranged in size from no bigger than human heads to the bulk of capacious ovens.

Baldur had come to a stop. "Here we are. I'm certain now, I remember the way it looked. This is the place I visited with Brunhild."

"I still don't see any village."

"But it's there, right ahead of us. You can see the holes in the earth, scattered around, if you look for them. The rooms below ground are bigger than the mounds, which are mainly for ventilation."

Hal studied the rugose surface of the partial clearing. Gradually he was able to make out that there were many small openings for ventilation, mostly near the bases of the mounds, or among the roots of the surviving trees, suggesting some kind of elaborate excavation beneath. Hal thought to himself that the drainage system must be ingenious, to keep them all from drowning when it rained.

Cautioning Hal to follow, and to avoid walking on the mounds as much as possible, Baldur advanced to a position close to the center of the complex. There he stamped one foot on the ground, not too hard, in a small flat area, and called out in a loud voice what Hal supposed must be a traditional word of greeting.

Moments later, heads began to peek up out of several nearby holes, some at the base of tree stumps. Shortly afterward, half a dozen gnomes, of both sexes, emerged from one of the larger apertures, blinking in cloudy daylight. They were all unarmed, Hal noted, unless you counted a couple of the men who were holding what must be their miners' tools. The welcome offered the visitors was courteous enough, no more wary than they would have received at many settlements of Sundwellers.

When the visitors announced that they had come on important business, they were warily invited underground, an apparently solid tree stump being easily rotated aside to make a doorway big enough for them. Hal soon found himself in a kind of anteroom, just underground. He realized that this chamber had probably been designed for entertaining the occasional Sundweller. From here, steep, ladderlike stairs led down again, evidence of at least one habitable level lower than this one. It seemed likely that only a small portion of the extensive underground complex would be accessible to people as big as Baldur and himself.

The guests were offered seats on an earthen bench, and then a tray of food. Hal sampled some whitish roots that had a crisp texture and sharp but pleasant taste, along with several varieties of raw mushrooms. Hal found the mushrooms delicious.

Baldur was chewing too. "I've had these little ones before, they're really good. Try one."

Hal tasted and approved. The gnomes who served the food were glum and businesslike. At least Hal felt reasonably confident that he was not going to encounter any gnomish version of Matilda, ready to encourage him with talk of how many miles of underground tunnels, suitable for root farming, she owned, free and clear in her own name.

The natives of this town were small and lean, most of the adults no higher than Hal's armpit. They seemed to Hal not so much deformed as just built on a slightly different body plan. By the time he had exchanged handgrips of greeting with half a dozen or so, he realized that they were surprisingly strong for their small size. The adult males were indeed heavily bearded. All had pale skins, small and rather sunken eyes, large ears and hairy noses. Most were something like fully dressed, in garments of smooth leather and tightly woven cloth.

On his earlier visit, Baldur had briefly met the farrier, Andvari, who had the honor to serve the Valkyries' Horses. Obviously he was a person of some status and importance among his people.

And when the gnome Andvari now appeared, garbed in what looked like leather and stroking his gray beard, he did remember saying hello to Baldur, the Sundweller man who was the lover of the Valkyrie Brunhild. Visiting Sundwellers must be rare creatures here, and no doubt tended to stick in the memory.

———

As Hal could see for himself on entering their town, the presence of gnomish children, warped little creatures to his way of thinking, confirmed Baldur's opinion that they were in the habit of reproducing in the same way as anyone else.

Baldur had told him that the gnomes were abnormally sensitive to sunlight, and generally came hooded and wrapped in extra clothing when they were required to be out in full daylight. They also protected their eyes with special goggles. Hal had seen similar devices in the far north, where they guarded against snow blindness. Each eyepiece was a flat, opaque disk of bone or wood, pierced by a single, narrow horizontal slit for vision.

As far as Hal could tell from listening to Baldur on the subject, there had never been a whole lot of intercourse between Sundwellers and Earthdwellers, and there was always a fair amount of mutual suspicion. The visitors were objects of curiosity, though hardly of awe. Only a few gnomes came to look at them, and those who exchanged bits of conversation with Hal were polite enough, but their manners were reserved, and Hal could well believe that they had misgivings about Sundwellers, at least as great as those Baldur had about them. Doubtless Andvari and his tribe considered those who chose to live on the earth's surface as something of an aberrant offshoot of humanity.

In response to their questions, Hal and Baldur were informed that no one in this village was authorized to contract to produce custom designs of weaponry or discuss the terms of payment. Hal was given directions to another village, many miles away, where skilled armorers could be found.

Privately Hal wondered whether the gnomes had a god of their own—it was the kind of thing that might be awkward to ask about directly, and he wished now that he had found out more from Baldur.

Baldur had been certain that only Sundwelling humans could possibly become gods, but now the gnomes seemed calmly certain that that was nonsense. It seemed that the gnomes felt more akin to the great powers of the Underworld, even though those powers were now their bitter enemies.

In conversation, Hal learned that some of the Earthdwellers firmly believed that the current avatar of Hades was also a gnome, in fact that he could hardly be anything else. That only gnomes could wear that Face, or had ever worn it.

Hal was not going to get involved in any argument, certainly not on matters of religion.

Prolonging their visit just a little, mainly out of curiosity, and also on the theory that it would not be polite to immediately rush away, he studied the walls of the underground anteroom where he and Baldur sat talking.

The walls were of what appeared to be a smooth, light-colored clay, and decorated with an extensive series of pictures, or rather carvings in low relief.

Someone pointed out that here on the wall was Jormungand, the world-serpent, doomed in legend to die fighting against Wodan on the last day of the world's existence. And over on the adjoining wall were other creatures of the nether world—great nasty serpents, shown being trodden underfoot, torn apart with picks, flattened with huge hammers, by some obviously gnomic heroes.

When Hal asked about the pictures, he was told: "This commemorates some of our famous victories in the past—and others that are yet to come."

"Hope I never meet this one in a dark alley," Hal muttered, pointing at an image, when he was sure he would not be overheard. He wasn't certain if the creature he was looking at was fighting for the gnomes in the panel or against them.

———

Suddenly he began to pay close attention to the talk around him. Baldur had somehow worked the subject back to Wodan, and naturally the villagers brought up a matter of which they were obviously proud. Yes, it was confirmed: four times a year, or more often when necessary, two or three of the gnomes made the journey up to Valhalla, to see to the Horses' shoeing, and perform certain odds and ends of metalwork for which Wodan wanted to enlist their special skills.

On hearing that, Hal allowed himself to show some mild interest, thinking it would be strange if he did not.

"I have never seen a god," he lied to his hosts with perfect ease. "What is Valhalla like? There must be wonderful sights."

"Wonderful," Andvari admitted tersely. Contemplating the marvels of Valhalla did not seem to cheer him up at all. "But we tend to our business when we are there, and do not see any more than we have to see, to do our work."

Baldur cleared his throat, and asked tentatively: "I don't suppose human visitors are generally welcome there?"

"No," said Andvari shortly. "They are not."

At that Hal decisively changed the subject, turning the conversation back to the designs of imaginary weapons.

Again he was reminded that he would have to go to the other village if he wanted to contract for such work. The gnomes made no offer of prolonged hospitality, and the visitors soon announced that they must be on their way.

A few minutes later, he and Baldur were out in broad daylight on the surface of the earth, and quite alone. Briskly they tramped away, their footfalls solid on the ground, in the direction where they had left their raft. When they reached their humble vessel, Hal untied it and let it drift away.

Baldur observed: "It wouldn't have been wise to hint that we might want to go along with them partway."

"I quite agree."

"What do we do next?"

"Wait for sunset. And we'd better make sure our water bottles are full. I doubt we'll find much water between here and the mountains."

Presently the two adventurers doubled back toward the village to take up an observation post only about fifty yards from its edge, at a spot from which they could see anyone departing in the direction of the mountains.

Before the sun dropped under the horizon, Hal and Baldur had concealed themselves behind some fallen trunks and underbrush, in a spot from which they could keep close watch over the western end of the village. The full moon would soon be rising in a clear sky, giving plenty of light for such a purpose.

A small road nearby, little used and largely overgrown with weeds, curved sharply near the Earthdwellers' settlement, then headed out, running almost arrow-straight as far as Hal could see, toward the sawtooth horizon of the high country.

There came a brief spattering of chilly rain. As they began their wait, Baldur murmured, peering over a fallen log: "I hope tonight is the night when they set out. But you're right, we can't count on that."

"At least we know they're not already gone. I wonder why the time of the full moon was chosen?"

"Probably because full moonlight makes it easier for night walkers to find their way."

The sun fell lower and the air turned cold. Soon Baldur broke a silence to remark: "It is noble of you to help me in this way."

"I've taken a liking to you, lad. You're a little crazy, but you may amount to something yet."

Baldur smiled faintly, knowingly. "And maybe to Matilda, as well?"

Hal cleared his throat uncomfortably. The smile on his face felt false. "Maybe. Besides, I have a yen to see just what's really inside that circle of Loki's fire." And as he said those words he realized that they were true enough.

As they talked things over while waiting for Andvari and his unnamed helper to appear, the chosen subject was still gnomes. "They don't do any farming, of course, or herding, or anything that would keep them working outdoors all day." Baldur seemed to consider this a troublesome flaw in their collective character.

"But what do they all eat?" Hal continued to be curious. "This village has a lot of mouths to feed. And you say there are many other gnomish settlements, just as big."

"They eat a lot of roots, I'd say. Mushrooms and other fungi, like the ones they fed us. Fish. And of course there are animals and insects that burrow, spend a lot of time underground. And I suppose the Mud-diggers must pick up some food, somehow, on the surface."

And underground there are also worms, Hal suddenly thought to himself. And all those grubs and burrowing insects to consider. It was undoubtedly just as well they had not been invited to stay to dinner.

Despite all Baldur's theories and claims of expertise, Hal could not see the Earthdwellers as anything but an offshoot of humanity, some-what warped by magic.

"Unless we are the ones warped by magic, and they are purely natural?"

Baldur only gave Hal a strange look when he voiced that thought.

"And, by the way, I still wonder how we can be so sure that they make the journey on their own feet? It would put a fine knot in our plans if someone suddenly brought them a pair of cameloids."

"They are walking." Baldur was calmly certain about that. "I never heard of gnomes traveling in any other way. Long journeys are difficult, of course, for at dawn each day they must find a suitable shelter against the sunlight."

Hal thought that probably the cold winds of winter were more un-comfortable for gnomes than for Sundwellers—under the surface of the earth, seasonal temperature variations tended to be small. "So you think you know a lot about them?"

"Not much. I don't care that much."

"I wonder," Hal mused, "How did these particular gnomes come to be chosen to care for the Valkyries' Horses?"

"I think Andvari might have been chosen because he was the best smith among their people. Probably most of them know little or nothing about Horses, or human maidens either. But as they are in general in-comparable metalsmiths, they make great farriers when they set their minds to it."

"What about his companion? The best at working the bellows for the forge?"

Baldur shrugged, as if to say he really didn't know and didn't care. But then he said: "I doubt that. Maybe because he's the best of the gnomish magicians."

"Oh." Hal did not find that reassuring.

"Hal, it must be good to have traveled as far as you have, and seen so much."

"It has advantages. I have even seen something of horses, though never before of the kind Valkyries ride—how did you first happen to meet your Brunhild, if you don't mind my asking?" They were making low-voiced conversation as they kept their eyes open for the gnome-farriers' appearance.

Baldur, whenever he began to talk on the subject of Brunhild, seemed likely to keep on indefinitely. No, of course she had not been born a Valkyrie—no one was. They were not a special race, or anything like that—not in the sense that gnomes were. No one was going to suggest to him that Hildy was not entirely human.

"Of course not. Forgive my ignorance."

"That's all right, you are a foreigner and I suppose you cannot help it. No, being a Valkyrie is just something that girls are chosen for when they are very young."

"A very great honor."

"Certainly."

Eventually Hal managed to extract some details. According to Baldur, his first meeting with Brunhild had come about by sheer accident. He had made a long climb to a remote meadow in the hills, where he had been gathering flowers, actually meaning to take them to some other girl.

The image of a would-be berserker gathering flowers gave Hal pause. But he said nothing, only nodding encouragingly.

Baldur went on: "But those flowers never reached the one for whom they were originally meant. From the moment I saw Brunhild . . . all others were forgotten."

"That's romantic."

She had been on some kind of outing with other Valkyries. On a summer day, swimming in an upland pool, while their magic horses grazed nearby—not that Baldur had had eyes for Horses on that day.

Now the voice of the youth was beginning to tremble. "You cannot imagine . . . such beauty . . ."

"I'll try my best." Hal wondered what the chances were of this kid's living long enough to grow up. Well, Hal meant him no harm. He would try to keep him from getting killed, if that were possible. Merely following a couple of undersized metalworkers did not seem particularly dangerous.

Baldur was still lost in his romantic dream. "It was a holy thing," he breathed.

"I'm sure it was."

As the light began to fade and redden into sunset the woods were quiet. They were also uncomfortably cold for fireless Sundwellers who were trying to be as silent and motionless as possible. As soon as the sun was actually gone, a work party of gnomes, not bothering with special protection, climbed out above ground and began to carry out what was apparently routine maintenance on the shallow mounds that collectively formed the roof of their buried village. Hal could hear them moving about in the middle distance, and as soon as the moon peered over the eastern horizon he was able to see them better. He began to wish that he and Baldur had taken up their observation post at a somewhat greater distance from the village.

Despite his uneasiness and the need to remain alert, Hal had just started to doze off, when suddenly Baldur was poking his arm. "There they are, two of them, on foot. Let's go."

They made two miles along the road by moonlight, then stopped. After waiting to make sure the gnomes were far ahead, they built a fire for warmth, ate sparingly of the cheese and hard biscuits provided for their fishing trip by Baldur's mother, and turned in for some sleep. Sundwellers traveled best by day.

7

AT FIRST LIGHT Hal and Baldur were on their feet again, shouldering their modest packs and hiking westward on the road toward the mountains. They breakfasted as they moved, munching the remnants of last night's dinner.

The master farrier and his assistant had a long start on their pursuers, and the two men kept up a brisk pace for several hours, thinking there was small chance of their overtaking the pair of Earthdwellers any time soon. By moonlight it had been difficult to be sure, but Hal thought that Andvari and his colleague had been carrying only a couple of modest backpacks, which could have held little more than the necessities of the journey. The tools and equipment required for their work must be waiting up there near the god's stable, somewhere on the higher slopes of the mysterious mountains.

All that was very logical. Still, Hal could not keep from wondering whether the pair of artisans might possibly, even now, be carrying with them the gold they were going to use. How much they needed would of course depend on how many shoes needed replacement this time round. That was something an outsider couldn't even begin to guess; Hal supposed old shoes of gold could probably be melted down, reformed, and used again, just like those forged of common blacksmith's iron. How hot did a fire need to be, to melt gold? Not nearly as hot, he thought, as that required to make the darker, tougher metal flow.

But of course if magic was heavily involved, everything about the metal might be different. Possibly it could even be lighter in weight? But no, the fragment in his own belt pouch was solid and heavy enough.

If only he could contrive to get a look inside the packs of Andvari and his companion, while the gnomes were sleeping at midday!

How many Horses did Wodan own? Baldur had said something about there being only ten Valkyries, which seemed ridiculously few, according to the legends . . . but maybe that meant only ten in her particular group, or squadron . . .

Baldur spoke to his companion sharply, asking if Hal was about to fall asleep as they walked.

"Not yet, lad, not yet."

"What're you thinking about, then? You seemed a thousand miles away."

"I am trying to imagine the glories of Valhalla."

It was around midafternoon, on their first day of tracking, when the men reached the spot where the two gnomes had evidently gone to earth at dawn.

Hal put out an arm to hold back his companion. Hal whispered: "Wait a minute. That looks like a little hut." It was a small, crude construction of stone and wood, its only windows mere chinks between stones and logs. A larger hole at one end looked as if it might serve to let out smoke, and indeed when Hal sniffed he could detect traces of fragrant smoke, blended with fainter odors suggesting cookery.

"They're likely still in there now," he whispered.

"So what do we do?"

"What can we do? Wait till sunset, when they'll set out again."

Withdrawing a short distance down the road, Baldur and Hal made their own cold and uncomfortable camp only some fifty yards away, not daring to start a fire that would give away their presence, though Baldur assured his companion that gnomes had a reputation for being observant only in matters connected with their craft.

Shortly after sunset, they heard a muttering in gnomish voices, and presently the sounds of people breaking camp and getting on the road again.

Hal waited an hour this time before he thought it was safe to build a fire.

When in the morning of their second day on the trail Hal and Baldur resumed their advance, their meager tracking skills were helped enormously by the presence of a light snow fallen overnight. The thin white cover on the ground made it ridiculously easy to track the pair they were following; Andvari and his companion had indeed been in the little hut, they had indeed come out of it and marched uphill, and they seemed to be making no effort at all to conceal their trail.

At one point Baldur caught a glimpse of flying sun-shadows on a low cloud, and pointed them out to Hal, who looked up almost too late to see anything at all.

"Could it have been birds?"

"Far too big." Baldur sounded subdued. "They might have been Valkyries, but I could not be sure."

Hal, who was not sure he had seen anything, was uneasy too. The last large flying creatures he had seen had been the hideous Harpies, which still sometimes disturbed his dreams.

The road wound back and forth almost continuously, tending this way and that, but always came back to point toward the mountains, which were still days away. Soon the river and the forest fell behind them, to be replaced by a more open landscape that gave progressively less evidence of human occupation. Since leaving the gnomes' village they had seen only a few human figures, and those all at a distance, farmers and herdsmen evidently. Now the narrow road was taking them steadily into territory even more sparsely inhabited, lacking all signs of human presence. Close ahead loomed foothills, and beyond those were high mountains, barren and unwelcoming in aspect.

Baldur confessed that he had never been this way before, and there was no way to be absolutely sure that Andvari and his companion were still following this road. But no other range of mountains remotely comparable could be seen in any other direction. If Valhalla was anywhere in this part of the world, Hal thought, it must be there, somewhere straight ahead.

After about noon on the third day, Hal and Baldur kept a more moderate pace and an even sharper lookout. It would not do to inadvertently overtake their quarry. They had no way of being certain how fast the short-legged Earthdwellers might be walking. Around mid-afternoon the men slowed their own steps even more, and began keeping a sharp lookout for the camp the two gnomes would presumably be making, in which to spend the day. Since they seemed to repeat this journey fairly often, there might well be a series of small huts, conveniently spaced.

Hal continued to be vaguely surprised that Andvari and his companion were not riding or driving droms or cameloids. But Baldur continued to assure him that such animals were practically unknown among the Earthdwellers.

"But somehow they have no trouble dealing with Horses."

"So it seems," the youth admitted. "Though I don't think they ride them. Lucky for us that Wodan didn't choose to provide his workers with magic transport or an escort of some kind."

"Yes, lucky." Hal subjected his surroundings in all directions to one of his routine scans. "I also find it a little puzzling."

Another light dusting of early snow allowed another period of easy tracking, and when that snow melted in bright sun, additional help was provided by patches of mud and dust occurring at intervals along the sparsely traveled road. Traffic of any kind seemed so rare that Hal did not worry about footprints being obliterated by the tracks of other travelers.

Once more the two men continued walking until the sun had fallen behind the western mountains, without seeing the least sign of their quarry. While traversing a long stretch where there were no footprints to follow, Hal had to admit it was entirely possible that he and Baldur had accidentally passed the gnomes, if Andvari and his companion had gone off the trail to rest or for any other reason. There were many stretches of the road devoid of any clear footprints, where something of the kind could easily have happened. It was equally possible that the journeying Earthdwellers were making such good time that their pursuers could not have overtaken them if they tried.

Moving uphill again, on the fourth morning, Hal was practically certain that their whole scheme had misfired, and he would have to start again from scratch, or abandon all hope of being able to pick up scraps of divine gold.

Then suddenly Baldur was pointing at the ground. "Look! Look, Hal, I think these must be the tracks we want!"

Every now and then those promising tracks appeared again, a few clear prints of small, booted feet, plain enough to tell their story to anyone with eyes. The pattern of bootmarks was consistently that of two people walking side by side, in the short strides natural to short legs.

As far as Hal could tell, the Earthdwelling farriers continued to move only during the long moonlit nights. Hal and Baldur did almost all their traveling during the short winter days, pushing steadily to keep up, while always keeping a sharp lookout on the trail ahead, to avoid overtaking their quarry.

Four days passed on the road, then five. The way the two Earthdwellers were following had gradually lost its wagon-track duality, diminished through frequent branchings until it was only a trail. And then steadily the trail grew thinner, and less deeply worn into the ground, as if few people indeed had ever dared to follow it this far. Hal would have had no means of knowing whether he and Baldur were still on the right path, indeed it would have been hard to be sure that they were on any path at all, had they not now reached an altitude where early winter had already moved in, and snow consistently covered most of the ground. Here the four small booted feet of the two gnomes had left plain record of their passage.

Late in the fifth day, the pursuers had stopped to refill their water bottles at a place where a frosty trickle of a stream, still unfrozen, crossed the pathway under a rude log bridge. Hal's curiosity was alive and well, as usual.

"I still keep wondering why the farrier and his comrade did not choose to ride. Anyone who deals in golden horseshoes ought to be able to afford a couple of cameloids."

"How should I know?" Baldur, now that his great adventure was actually under way, was growing nervous and irritable, which Hal thought was a bad sign. "Maybe the dirt-eaters don't like to get as far above the ground as a cameloid's back would lift them. But their being afoot will make it much easier for us to follow."

Hal grunted something. Following the trail was certainly easy enough. Now and then the trackers even caught a glimpse of the distant pair whose footprints led them on. Only occasionally, at dusk or dawn, could the two slight, dark-hooded figures be seen against the snow. Once Hal spotted them no more than about two hundred yards ahead, and the trackers waited for long minutes before cautiously advancing farther. On and up they went, following a slight trail back and forth, working their way higher and higher into what, after the first few hours of real climbing, seemed an uninhabited and practically uninhabitable wilderness of rock.

The deeper Hal and Baldur were led into the foothills by the twisting path, the more difficult the going became. Hills melded together and became the flank of an undoubted mountain. All river valleys were well below them now, and they were no longer walking so much as climbing, hands as well as feet being necessary to get over some of the steep rock ledges.

"Well," the puffing northman told his colleague, "if those two damned moles can climb it, so can we."

"I only wish they would go faster," Baldur murmured back.

Ever deeper they went into the mountains, and ever higher. Steadily receding into the wintry distance was Loki's ring of magic fire, which still sprouted untiringly from the top of its rocky hill. Several times Hal caught a glimpse of the tall flames, hanging on the rim of the sky, like a signal of warning to the world. Now, at a range that must have been more than twenty miles, the god's handiwork seemed no more than a distant candle.

Once Baldur stood looking back at the fire, murmuring Brunhild's name.

———

At the end of one of their nightly rest stops, while they were waiting for the sky to lighten enough to let them begin a seventh day of tracking, Baldur suddenly asked: "Hal, I keep wondering about Wodan."

"What about him?"

"He is not merciful, that cannot be part of his nature—so if he releases Brunhild, it will be because he is honorable, and generous to his chosen warriors."

Days ago Hal had given up trying to understand Baldur's theology. "If you say so."

"I do say so, Hal—my friend. How much do you know about the gods?"

The northman studied his young colleague warily. "Just what everyone knows, or ought to know."

"What?"

"Well. That Wodan, and Loki, and all the rest are people just like you and me. Except that at some point in their lives, each man or woman of them picked up and put inside his or her head one of the things that we call Faces. And each Face gives its wearer tremendous powers."

"I believe that Wodan must be more than that." The young man's voice was low, but full of emphasis. "The Father of Battles must be something more than just a man with power."

Hal sighed. "Well, I don't want to argue. What makes you think I have knowledge of gods beyond the ordinary?"

Baldur shook his head, as if in disappointment with Hal's answer. "When we first met you told me that you'd once been shipmate to some god, but failed to recognize him."

"Hah, so you were listening after all! But the fact that I once made a fool of myself doesn't qualify me as an expert on the subject."

"You must know something more than you have said!"

"Not much."

"But I have never even seen a god!" Baldur clenched his fists and turned around. "If Wodan should appear now, up there on the mountain . . ." He seemed almost despairing at the prospect.

"You'd deal with the experience somehow. People do. If he appears, then at last you'd get to see what he looks like. Tell me, besides Wodan and Loki, what other deities are most popular around these parts? To which of them do people pray?"

"Well, there's Loki, of course. But I wouldn't say Loki is popular. Feared, yes. He's the subject of talk, not the object of worship." Baldur sounded wistful, adding: "Naturally, those who hope for leadership in battle universally choose Wodan."

"I suppose. Who else?"

The young man meditated briefly. "Thor may be even more popular with the common soldiers—of course he too is a good fighter."

"Of course." Hal was nodding. The mention of Thor had jogged his memory, brought back in sharp focus the face and voice of the poor woman standing in the road with her ragged children, snatching back her copper coins and mouthing the strange prayer, or blessing, with which she had anointed Hal.

He nodded again. "Thor with his hammer, a mean weapon by all reports. As I understand it, he throws it out to kill anyone or destroy anything he chooses. Then back it flies to his hand again. I've heard some stories about that. But what about the ordinary folk? Who do they worship? Not everyone wants to be a berserk warrior, froth at the mouth and ignore wounds."

"Certainly not." Baldur's tone became cool at this irreverence. "As for the commoners who are not fighters . . ." The young man had to stop and think; it was as if he hardly could remember anyone who fit that category. "I suppose Freya is most popular. She's undoubtedly the greatest goddess—and there are half a dozen lesser deities, male and female."

"No more than that?" Hal snorted. "Down south they have 'em by the hundreds."

Baldur's look seemed a polite expression of doubt. If such a swarm of beings claimed divinity, he seemed to be thinking, most of them must be frauds, or at least inferior, and he had no interest in them. "And do the people down there know of Wodan? Are they true warriors?"

"Warlike enough," Hal assured him. "And you may believe me or not, but few down there have ever heard the name of your All-Highest. Round the Great Sea, where I've been living the past few years, everyone would tell you that Zeus is the greatest god of all, practically the ruler of the universe. Of course Zeus frequently has his troubles with Hades, now and then with Neptune. He's chronically at war with Giants.

And down there, if you ask who is the god of war, people will tell you it's a fellow called Mars, or Ares."

Baldur shrugged and shook his head, as if there could be no accounting for some people's crazy ideas. "Our gods, with Wodan leading, know that they will face monsters and Giants in the final battle of the world, when fire and flood destroy everything." He sighed. "Giants are another kind of being that I've never seen."

"I don't know about the end of the world. But no one around here has ever raised a temple or an altar to Zeus? Or to Athena?"

Baldur seemed to be trying to remember. "I've heard those names mentioned. But altars and temples? No, I don't think so."

Hal clapped him on the shoulder, an almost staggering blow. "Lad, it is time you got out in the great world, and discovered what most of the people in it are doing!"

The youth was steadfast in his gloom. "Brunhild is the only part of the world I care about. To join her, or to spend my life in the attempt, is the only adventure I am seeking now."

———

When their journey once more resumed, under a sky grown bright enough to let them identify the marks left by gnomes' feet in the white snow, Hal and Baldur got one more look at the glow of the distant firering, now many miles away.

Drifted piles of old, crusted snow began to appear around the trail as they went on up. The trail itself was covered, and the footprints of the two gnomes were plain to see. The snow was naturally deepest in the places remaining shaded all day long. On and on the two men traveled upward, deeper into the mountains. It was good that they had equipped themselves for cold weather before setting out.

And, since they wanted to avoid freezing to death, a fire was beginning to seem like a necessity, not just a good idea. Hal kept thinking it over, and shivering, until he convinced himself that there was no real reason not to have one, if they built it in a sheltered place and kept it small. At night the Earthdwellers would be intent on their own climbing progress, steadily getting farther ahead, not much caring if someone else happened to be on the trail behind them. Quite possibly, as Wodan's artisans, they felt they had reliable magical protection against assault. Anyway, it was worth a few risks to keep from freezing. As night approached again, they moved aside from the trail, into the midst of a small stand of evergreens, and set about gathering sticks and twigs.

Getting out his flint and steel, Hal soon had created a comforting small flame.

There was no game to be had, and even had there been, neither man was carrying a projectile weapon. The little grove offered nothing in the way of nuts or berries.

With the coming of daylight on the eighth day of their hike, they picked up the trail again and climbed on, trying to ignore the growling of their almost empty stomachs. Hal was thinking to himself that if there was a real Valhalla anywhere—and he had no reason to doubt that some truth lay behind the stories—then it would be hard to find a better setting for it than these mountains.

At one spot, a place where the footprints clearly went off the road and came back, Hal and Baldur investigated. At a little distance from the trail they found a kind of campsite, not much more than a small trampled area, where the gnomes must have sheltered during the previous day. Hal supposed they must be carrying a roll or package of lightweight fabric that they raised as a tent to ward off the dangerous sunlight. He searched the area diligently, but unhappily could discover no forgotten food. He and Baldur had been rationing the cheese and biscuits for several days, but now their supplies were almost gone. Right about now, a few roots and mushrooms would taste very good.

While encouraging Baldur to keep thinking about Horses, Hal kept alight the flame of his own secret enthusiasm. It was a good way to keep from thinking of his stomach.

Baldur never mentioned gold but kept speculating about the Horses. He claimed to know the names of several, had various contradictory ideas about exactly where the animals would be kept, how well their stables might be guarded.

Hal was careful not to argue too strenuously against even the most far-fetched details of his companion's scheme. But at the same time he wanted to prepare Baldur, without alarming him, to face the possibility of a sudden change of plan. The young man would have to come to grips with the fact that their chances of even laying eyes on one of Wodan's magic steeds were very low.

Of course Hal's chance of getting his hands on any scraps of gold might not be any better. But he thought that still remained to be determined.

And as for Wodan's Horses—Hal's mind boggled when he tried to visualize himself, or his naive companion, actually getting astride one of those marvelous beasts, let alone using them in a cavalry raid to plunder old Loki's fire-ring of the fair prisoner supposed to have been confined there.

No, if he and Baldur were really on the path to Wodan's stronghold, and he had to admit that now seemed to be the case, then more likely than not they would soon encounter some insuperable obstacle. Probably something—or someone—would appear to turn them back well before they actually got within sight of their goal, and at that point Hal would be ready to give in graciously and sensibly. The trick was in knowing when certain disaster loomed, recognizing the warning signs before it was too late. He had followed a similar plan for most of his life, and so far as he was still alive.

The trouble was, he didn't think that Baldur would calmly accept the postponement, if not the absolute cancellation, of his last hope of reaching Brunhild—not unless the denial came from Wodan himself.

And was there any reason to think Wodan would be even a little tolerant of casual trespassers? But there was no use worrying about that; not now, while the way ahead still lay open. Hal was advancing warily, thoroughly aware that persistent climbing might well bring a couple of mere foolhardy mortals abruptly to the brink of some kind of suicidal confrontation. Of course he fully intended to turn around before they ran headlong into anything of that kind.

And yet, in spite of all the alarms put up by common sense, despite the foreboding of gruesome danger, he was drawn irresistibly forward by the thought that there was still a chance—a slight, magical, insidious, and wonderful chance—that Baldur's scheme was not entirely crazy. The road to full success, to magic gold and magic Horses, to who knew what, might actually lie open—and there was a much better chance, Hal thought, of simply gaining information that could make him at least a moderately wealthy man.

———

Such trees as still grew at this altitude were sparse, stunted, and twisted with their lifelong struggles against the wind. Now squalls of snow, alternating with freezing rain, came swirling to pester the advancing climbers. Hal found he could no longer tell in which direction they were going, except that it was generally still up. As the howling wind increased in strength, it seemed to him in his more imaginative moments that he could hear laughter drifting down from the still unseen ramparts of Valhalla. He was careful to say nothing of this to his companion.

He was ready to accept that what he seemed to hear was only his

imagination. And what he imagined was of course the laughter of Wodan's elite guard, whose ranks had been closed to Baldur by a Valkyrie's
whim. They were the pick of the bloody crop, or were supposed to be,
men who had been slain in earthly battle but whose spirits had been
snatched by Valkyries from the jaws of Hades, saved from the Underworld. By the will of the All-Seeing, they lived on here, above the world.

According to the legends, the courage and ferocity of these warriors
had so pleased the great god that he, through his flying emissaries,
granted them immortality. They were superbly dedicated fighting men,
miraculously restored to life and health after each bout of combat, who
could imagine no greater happiness than to spend the remaining ages of
the world in a splendid cycle of doing everything they loved, moving
perpetually from evening feast and carousal to brief and dreamless sleep,
then sallying forth to morning battlefield and staggering, wounded, back
again to the hall of feasting, or being carried back by the Valkyries if
they were freshly slain.

Trying to picture in his imagination the great game of perpetual
slaughter, so lovingly described in many legends, Hal wondered if the
players went through rituals and chose up sides anew each night. Or
maybe it was just a glorious free-for-all, with no rules to speak of.
Wodan's finest should be always honing their martial skills, keeping
themselves perpetually ready for the final, world-ending battle in which
the forces of good and evil were ultimately doomed to annihilate each
other.

———

Hal could remember hearing, years ago, one version of the Valhalla
story in which the Valkyries, when not riding forth on their recruiting
missions, served the endlessly rehealed heroes nightly as willing con-
cubines. Hal was not sure how well that system was likely to work,
given that there were supposed to be only nine of the young women.
Presumably by this time there ought to be thousands of heroes, or at
the very least several hundred. Delicately he forbore to raise the subject
with his companion.

In any case, Baldur's thoughts must have been running along similar
lines—and once more there rose up in the young man his sheer dread
of the god he worshiped but had never seen. Easy enough to say that
gods were only humans who wore Faces in their heads; but when you
knew that you were standing face to face with one, there was a little
more to it than that. There were moments when it seemed to Hal that
the young man's nerve was going to fail him.

Once, for no apparent reason, Baldur stopped suddenly in the middle of the trail. The youth was staring into the bleakness ahead and shivering seemingly with more than the wintry wind.

Instinct told Hal that a rough challenge would be the most bracing treatment he could administer just now. "What's the matter, young one? Your feet suddenly gone cold?"

The young man sputtered for a moment, then choked out: "What will Wodan do to men who intrude uninvited upon his celebration?"

Hal kept his answer as casual as he could. Demonstrating what he considered heroic restraint, he kept himself from clouting Baldur alongside the head. "You mean, who come to borrow his Horses? Now's hardly the time to start to worry about that. How in the Underworld should I know? If he admires courage as much as the stories say, he might just give us credit for showing a lot of nerve, and invite us in. On the other hand, he might throw us off one of these cliffs—but as they say, a man has to die sometime.

"Anyway, aren't you the same one I heard only a couple of days ago, talking about becoming a berserker?" Trying to come up with some encouragement, Hal added a flat lie: "Even Hagan was looking at you as if he thought you might have the right stuff to join his band. I suppose you ought to take that as a compliment."

But Baldur only shook his head, as if in silent rejection of his crippled berserker father and all his works. Then he cast a long look back, along what was visible of the trail they had just ascended, marked now by four sets of footprints in the ankle-deep snow. Following his gaze, Hal was struck by the thought that if the gnomes started home before that record melted or was covered by a new fall, they would certainly know they had been followed on their way up.

Time enough, Hal told himself, to worry about that later.

Hal had the strong impression that the youth was fighting down an impulse to turn and run. But so far, Baldur was refusing to let himself do that.

At last the young man choked out a few quiet words. "I must see Brunhild again, in this world or the next."

"You know, young one, I really think you ought to make up your mind which it is you really want the most: Brunhild sitting in your lap, or yourself in Wodan's?"

The only response Hal got to that was an angry stare, and for a moment he was afraid that he had gone too far. Probably it was a question Baldur had not yet answered for himself.

Time to move on again. Hal thought that now they must be truly very near their goal.

8

SUDDENLY THERE WAS real evidence that they had almost reached their goal.

Tilting his head back, Hal could now see, through swirling snow and mist, some kind of construction looming above them, see it well enough as to have no remaining doubts of its reality. The fortress, or castle, was so hedged about by sharp, unclimbable peaks and barren crags, and the single path that seemed to offer the only approach lay so intricately wound among these rocks, that the two intruders were almost upon their goal before they got their first good look at it. And at that point the two adventurers were gazing so steeply upward, into such thickly swirling grayness, that they could be certain of very little, beyond the solidity of a smooth, looming mass, the regularity of artificial walls.

Now they had had a glimpse of their destination, but how to reach it still presented something of a question. A light accumulation of new snow, together with drifting of the old, was covering all signs of a path among the jagged rocks, as well as the footprints they had been following.

As it turned out, there still remained almost a mile of winding trail between them and the structure that loomed above. Hal and Baldur had to spend one fireless and almost-frozen night, huddled together for warmth, when it grew too dark for Sundweller eyes to find their way among the clustered boulders. This close to their goal, they did not dare to show a light of any kind. Fortunately, between big rocks they were able to find a niche in which to shelter from the wind.

When the stars in the clear portion of the sky started to fade in morning light, and the mountain landscape began to grow faintly visible beneath the waning moon, the men gave thanks for their survival and started climbing again. Each time they paused to take their eyes from the trail, they strained them looking upward at a dim and distant parapet, still wreathed in what seemed perpetual mist.

Suddenly Baldur came to a halt. He had his right arm raised, aiming uphill with it as if he meant to use it as a spear. The finger that he pointed with was shaking. His voice was practically a shriek when he cried out what he had seen.

"There's a wall up there. By all the gods, an enormous wall. And a sentry on top of it, looking this way! We have been seen!"

Hal jerked his head back, staring upward, catching nothing but a blinding swirl of mist and snow. "Well, if we have . . ."

He let his words die there. If they had been seen by the powers of Valhalla, it was too late now to do anything about it.

His heart had begun to pound, but he was certainly not ready to turn and run. As far as he could tell, they had crossed no marked boundaries, transgressed no warning signs. He and Baldur ought to have as much right as anyone to this deserted mountain path.

Moving steadily, they trudged on. They had climbed through one more switchback, when both stopped in their tracks. Someone, a single figure, was marching down the path from above, coming directly toward them.

Marching was not really the right word. The means of movement looked more like sliding . . .

Baldur cried out: "It is the sentry! Or it looks like the same man."

"It must be . . ." Hal started, but again he let his words die. He could not tell what it was, this thing advancing upon them. He could only be sure it was no ordinary man.

The man, or image, was following a descending trail, but on drawing near the pair of intruders it ignored them as if they were not there. The appearance it presented was that of a lone soldier whose dress and equipment Hal found completely unfamiliar. The figure's clothing was light, utterly inadequate for the cold weather, and it was carrying a javelin in its right hand, and wearing a shorter, broader spear slung over its back, with a sling knotted at his waist and a net bag of rocks for ammunition.

As the figure drew near, Baldur began an impassioned plea, or greeting, but the thing ignored him totally, and he broke his speech off in midsentence.

Still it seemed to be gliding, rather than striding normally on its two legs. The legs were moving, but not fast enough to account for the thing's rapid progress.

"Hal, is that a god?" Baldur's whisper was tortured, barely audible. Hal's answer was just as quiet. "It looks like none I ever saw."

"Is it a ghost?"

Whether ghost, image, or something Hal had never even imagined before, when it came to the blockage in the trail, it passed through the rock, as if either the stone or the warrior's body were insubstantial.

Meanwhile, as the thing approached, Hal uttered the best that he could manage in the way of a calm greeting, but unnervingly he and his words were totally ignored. Meanwhile Baldur had resumed his jabbering at the figure, pouring out a mixture of pleas and boasting—but the man, or wraith, in gray still paid no attention to either of them, and strode or glided on about its own unguessable business, until it vanished round a turn only a few yards downhill.

Hal felt a chill biting deeper than the cold wind, but actually no great surprise, when he noted that their visitant had left no footprints in the snow. Up the trail, there were still only the two sets left by the gnomes' feet, here spared from the drifting snow by some vagary of wind or shelter.

Well, having come this far, he was not going to be turned back by a speechless ghost. If Wodan meant to warn them, he would have to be a little plainer.

Baldur was too shaken to notice the lack of tracks, and Hal said nothing about it. Instead he asked: "Was that the sentry you saw above?"

"I—I don't know." Baldur scowled and stared up into grayness, but the weather had thickened so it was no longer possible to see anything.

The two men climbed a half-hour longer, making slow progress, panting their way up one switchback after another, before they touched those mist-enfolded walls. They had seen no one else and heard no challenge from above. They had come now to a section of the trail where less new snow had fallen, and still there were only the tracks of the same four feet, marking the passage of the same two gnomes. By now, Hal was confident that he could have recognized the prints of their small but well-constructed boots anywhere.

Presently Hal and his companion rounded the last bastion of the outer wall, and then went boldly in, entering Valhalla through a huge gateway, passing a framework of metal bars that might have been a portcullis before it was overtaken by utter ruin.

The doors that must once have guarded this entry had entirely disappeared. It seemed that at some time they might have been ripped or burned from the ravaged gateway, for there still remained the twisted remnants of their massive metal hinges, along with some of the overhead stonework. What was left was only an open passage between the frowning walls of stone, empty except for drifted snow marked with two sets of gnomish footprints.

An hour ago Hal had thought he was too far from the walls of Valhalla to get a good look at them, and now it seemed he was too close. In a few more moments, the towering stone surface was actually within reach, and behind it an enormous and vastly higher structure, the latter visible only in hints and suggestions, brief glimpses through swirls of mist and snow.

So far, the only portions of Wodan's home—if such it was—that was clearly visible to the visitors consisted of tiers of enormous blocks of stone, each slab so huge it was hard to imagine how it had ever been lifted and set in place. Certainly forces vastly stronger than human arms and backs must have been at work. But still those great ashlars had been fitted together with consummate skill, the joints all fine and straight.

Following the base of the gigantic wall for a couple of hundred yards brought the pair of intruders to a gateway constructed on a matching scale. Whatever door or barrier might once have blocked this portal seemed to have been long since removed, just as the outer gates had been. Through this broad aperture the footprints of the gnomes marched on and in with no sign of hesitation, not even a change of stride. Now Hal could see that the outer wall was all of forty feet thick.

There might have been a sentry on the wall above, but there was none now. Nor was there any visible guardian at the gate.

Having passed the gateway, the two intruders found themselves in an outer courtyard of a savagely ruined but once magnificent castle, built on a scale that Hal thought truly worthy of the gods. He thought the remaining portions of the inner citadel, or keep, even more than half ruined as it was, must be fully a hundred feet in height.

From up above them somewhere, among the giants' stonework, there came a sudden whine of wind, startling both men. But it was only wind.

"Hal—this is not what I thought we would discover here." Baldur's voice was awed, and also troubled. He had moved a step closer to his companion. "Not at all what I expected."

For once Hal had no answer. If this was, or once had been, truly the home of Wodan, then it seemed Zeus had a worthy rival for his claim to be the master of the universe. No doubt about it, this structure was very large and still impressive. But a glimpse through some of the narrow upper windows showed slivers of snowy sky, evidence that the great castle too had been unroofed. Now the still-advancing double trail of footprints was bordered, and in one place partially blocked, by regularly shaped ashlars that had tumbled down from above. The snow hid all details that might have offered a clue as to how long ago the tumbling and scattering had taken place.

———

Hal had never visited the legendary home of Zeus and his most exalted colleagues, nor did he know of any human who had done so, despite all the descriptions in hundreds of detailed stories. He wasn't sure that any such place as high Olympus had ever really existed—but he thought that this might once have been its equal in magnificence.

On the other hand, it looked to Hal like no feasts or ceremonies had been held here in Wodan's castle for many a day. To what height these walls might once have ascended, and what roofs might once have covered them, was impossible to say. Nearly all were fallen in, great beams and stones making vast piles of rubbish, the rubble and the remaining structure alike now half-hidden under mounds of white. On level space, untrodden snow lay inches deep in the mountain's morning sunshine, all across the vast and nearly roofless space that might once have been the great hall of a great god's castle. Here and there, half-shapeless mounds of white suggested snow-buried furniture.

Steadily the double tracks, the same ones Hal and Baldur had been following for many miles, went on, through and around all these wonders. The gnomes had come this way before. Their footprints betrayed no uncertainty on their makers' part, no false turns or doubling back, showing that the farrier and his magical colleague knew exactly where they wanted to go, and had not been tempted to delay and gawk at any ungnomish marvels on the way. Doubtless they were regular visitors to this mountain realm, and to them this was all perfectly familiar.

"Wait!" It was an anguished whisper, accompanied by a hard clutch on Hal's arm. "Look over there!"

Baldur was tall enough to see from their present position, but Hal needed to climb up a step. Raising his head cautiously over the top of a huge tumbled block, Hal saw distant movement in a half-enclosed courtyard—what looked like a squad of perhaps a dozen irregular soldiers, armed men in an assortment of shabby clothes that were not uniforms.

The courtyard was perhaps a hundred paces distant from the place where Hal and Baldur watched, and over most of its considerable area the snow had been trampled into slush and mud. Snow had stopped falling now, and the sun kept trying to extricate itself from scudding clouds, with intermittent success.

Keeping themselves concealed behind huge blocks of stone, Hal and Baldur spent a minute or two gaping at a squad of drilling soldiers in the distance. Hal felt mixed emotions at the sight. It would have been unreasonable to hope that the place where the gnomes were going to work would otherwise be entirely deserted. The soldiers were practicing formally with their weapons, while the harsh, penetrating voice of a sergeant, which doubtless sounded much the same forever and in all armies, nagged and berated them. A thin line of men, no more than a dozen or so, lunged with spears at imaginary opponents, and then withdrew raggedly. At a distance they looked more like sick call than dominating heroes.

The sergeant bawled again, and his squad paired off, one on one, obviously intending to engage in some kind of fencing or sparring practice.

Baldur found the spectacle disturbing. "Those can't be . . ." He let it trail away.

Hal kept his voice low. "Can't be your blessed heroes, enjoying their daily brawl?"

"No." The young man shook his head emphatically. "They can't. Not possibly."

"Then what are they?"

The youth was almost dancing in his worry and frustration. "This can't be it. This must be only some outpost, where they stable Horses. But if this *is* Valhalla, I want to—"

Hal took a hard grip on Baldur's upper arm, shook him into momentary silence. "Keep it quiet. If your girlfriend actually had to carry someone to this godforsaken ruin, filling her quota or whatever, it's clear why she didn't want it to be you."

Judging from the look on Baldur's face, the youth might just have received his death blow. "But I . . . no, that must be wrong."

"Just look around you. The gnomes are real enough. And probably their magic is, for it charms golden shoes, giving Horses the power to fly and carry Valkyries, even carry them unharmed through strange fires. And some peculiar power is producing things like that image of a warrior that met us on the path.

"But you can have the rest of Wodan's glorious domain. It doesn't look to me like any place I'd want to live. Anyway, we shouldn't be arguing about this now. Now get a grip on yourself, and let's see if we can find some Horses."

Baldur turned pale under his soldier's tan, at words that must have sounded in his ears as something very close to blasphemy; but it was hard to argue with the evidence of his own eyes. His manner became a kind of frenzied timidity. At last the youth choked out: "I say the real Valhalla must be somewhere else. And this is only some outpost, where Wodan stables Horses."

Hal was eager to accept that theory, or any theory, if it let them get on with business. "I think you've hit on it, lad. All the better for us if Valhalla's somewhere else. Then its master will likely be there, not here—if he's anywhere right now. So pull yourself together. I thought you were ready to risk all for a chance of seeing Brunhild."

Privately Hal was thinking furiously. The many signs of ruin and neglect and poverty around them strongly suggested a lack of management, to say the least. Hal could readily imagine that Wodan was currently dead, his Face lying lost and forgotten somewhere, unworn by any human. If that was true, the implications were tremendous. If anyone, Valkyrie or not, was really imprisoned behind Loki's fiery curtain, it would not have been Wodan who put the prisoner there; he or she had run afoul of some other power.

Again Baldur was peering back in the direction of the drilling men. "It can't be," the youth murmured.

"You mean those scarecrows with sticks are not your chosen Heroes. I'm sure you're right. It could be they're only—well, enlisted men. Auxiliaries of some kind."

"Yes, that could be." Baldur sounded slightly relieved.

"Or Heroes on sick call," Hal added as a private, murmured afterthought. Other possibilities were whirling through his brain. Gods did die, and for all he knew, Wodan might be really dead. Maybe one of the local warlords had secretly taken over the stewardship of Valhalla, gold and Horses and all.

Not having to contend against a god should make their expedition vastly easier. Whoever was master of the marvelous Horses and their blessed shoes, the farriers' smithy would have to be here somewhere . . . that part of the legend couldn't be entirely a lie. It couldn't be. Because he, Hal, was still carrying a fragment of a golden shoe.

"Auxiliaries." Baldur was still chewing on that word. It did not really satisfy him, but it gave him something to bite on. "That must be it." Then a renewed note of awe crept into his voice. "Hal, look at this."

Hal looked. Another squad of men had appeared from somewhere, to practice against . . . but hold on. Were those in the new detachment men at all? Their gliding movements and stiff poses reminded Hal of the "ghost" that passed them on the trail.

The visitors observed in fascination. Hal, watching as closely as he could at the distance, soon realized that the weapons carried by the gliding images only stung and did not wound, when employed against live flesh and blood. When a weapon in the hand of a live man struck a wraith, the effect seemed even less consequential.

But all this spying was essentially a waste of time. Now he and Baldur turned their backs on the distant drill and withdrew from it, under cover of the scattering of huge tumbled blocks. Meanwhile the blanket of old snow surrounding them remained almost untrodden, so the castle could hardly be swarming with people.

The trail of the gnomes remained as plain to see as ever, but now Hal began to move ever more slowly forward. He paused before he crossed each open space, peering cautiously around each corner before advancing.

He was just at the crucial moment of one such step, when Baldur's touch on his arm made him jump. When Hal looked around, the youth was pointing skyward, whispering fiercely: "Look!"

Half expecting to see an armored maiden straddling a flying Horse, or maybe a truly remarkable ghost or two, Hal raised his gaze. From some unseen base no more than fifty yards ahead, a band of greasy smoke had begun to mount into the sky; it appeared that Andvari was getting his forge working. Moments later there came a preliminary clang of heavy metal, as if a smith might be warming up his arm with a swing or two against an anvil. Hal thought any golden horseshoe that caught *that* blow, the way it sounded, would have been mashed flat.

Working iron ought to need a lot more heat and force than working gold—but of course when magic entered the picture, common sense was often driven out.

Hal's imaginative conception of an underground workshop, created for the convenience of the gnomes, had vanished in cold morning daylight. Soon the two intruders had got closer to the forge-fire, which glowed behind the closed shutters of a small building. They were so close that Hal could hear the master farrier tell his assistant to throw in a handful of salt, "to keep the fire clean." It was a heavily accented voice, filled with dark overtones, and he thought it was Andvari's. Certainly it sounded like the speech Hal had heard in the gnomes' village.

A strange, whinnying sound, unfamiliar to both men but not entirely strange to either of them, carried in the clear morning air.

"Listen!" Baldur's breath puffed like steam from a kettle when he whispered again. This time it was obviously not the whinnying horse that he had in mind.

Hal listened, standing in shadow. All the while, despite his warm coat, he kept shifting his weight and swinging his arms, fearing that he would stiffen if he stood still for very long in the fierce cold. Soon he could hear a few more clangs, of a slightly lighter tone, as if the smith who wielded it were now getting down to serious business. Maybe, Hal thought, there was urgent work on iron and steel to be got out of the way, repairs to harness or armor, before the artisans could get to working the rare and valuable stuff.

"What do we do now?" Baldur was gripping his sword-hilt, and his voice held an agony of fear.

Hal kept his own whisper quiet. "We sneak around there, and try to get a look at what they're doing. Well, we've come to see the Horses, haven't we?" He made a savage pointing gesture. "They must be over there somewhere."

And, he thought to himself, if golden shoes were being forged right here, then the raw material could hardly be very far away.

9

CAUTIOUSLY THE TWO men kept working their way, a step at a time, toward the small building that poured out sounds of industrious activity. Hal, moving a step or two ahead of his companion, thought the little shop or smithy could not have been part of the original construction of the citadel, because it was so roughly built, mortared together of much smaller stones than the towering walls surrounding the courtyard. This structure also enjoyed what seemed to be quite a rarity in Valhalla, an intact roof. As Hal crept closer, he took note of the fact that the covering of the smithy was a fairly recent construction of poles and thatch. A few small birds, their winter nesting evidently disturbed, now flew out screaming.

Energetically, the black smoke continued to pour out of the short stone chimney. Each visible side of the small structure boasted one small window, and each opening was protected by a crude wooden shutter, roughly wedged in place. Hal decided that the building probably served as housing for the visiting gnomes as well as their workshop. Naturally, gnomes would require more shade against intruding daylight than any of the surrounding ruins seemed likely to afford them, all well-ventilated as they were.

Once again, as when he had picked up the fragment of horseshoe in front of the wall of flame, Hal became aware of the twitching of the Golden Fleece in his belt pouch. Elated, he sneaked a look into the pouch, and saw that the bit of special fabric that he cherished was glowing as before.

"What are you doing?" Baldur breathed.

"Nothing! Never mind." With a gesture commanding full attention to the job at hand, Hal led on.

Hal saw that the building had at least two doors. The small one, which he could see, was tightly closed. The other was big enough for large animals to pass in and out, and was guarded only by a tattered canvas that was doubtless meant to keep in warmth and block out the dazzling daylight from sensitive gnomish eyes.

Moving with what seemed to him infinite care, Hal got close enough to the gnomes' forge to get a look inside, peering through a chink at one edge of one of the uneven shutters. He could see and recognize Andvari's face, but not that of the gnome who worked beside him.

The gnomes had removed their outer clothing in the heat of the interior, exposing most of their pallid skin. The master artisan was frowning with concentration as he bent over his anvil, hammer raised in a big hand at the end of a lean arm gnarled with muscle. The assistant was a vague shadow, moving briskly in the background.

It was pretty much the scene Hal had expected to see, and the only trouble with it, from his point of view, was that there was no gold to be seen anywhere. He caught a brief glimpse of something on the an-vil—but all he could tell about the workpiece was that it was glowing metal.

The raw material for magic horseshoes had to be somewhere nearby—but where?

He opened his pouch again to sneak one more look at his fragment of Fleece, and discovered it no brighter and no warmer than before. His talisman was going to provide no further help.

Where in the Underworld would the guardians of golden treasure put it, to minimize the risk of theft? A strongbox of some kind seemed likely. Or it could be simply buried in a hole in the ground, almost right under the forge-fire. And where were the guards? Hal thought there would simply have to be guards standing by, and he had noticed none. That of course raised the ominous suggestion that Wodan might be depending on sheer magic, or invisible beings of some kind, to protect his treasure—and that would be bad news indeed.

Baldur was nudging him. Suddenly it was necessary to temporarily abandon all attempts at spying, and try to conceal themselves in the inadequate shelter offered by a corner of the building, because the crunch of feet on snow and gravel signaled someone was approaching. Here came a scrawny youth who looked no more like one of Wodan's Heroes than he did a gnome, leading one of the strange four-hoofed animals through daylight from a nearby stable to the forge. This indi-vidual was ill-clad and shivering, moved at a shuffling pace, and looked almost as blank-eyed as the ghost Hal had encountered on the trail. He guided the willing Horse along with one hand gripping its mane. The farriers' operation had begun very recently, but already a broad trail had been trampled into the snow between the stable and the smithy.

Hal and Baldur both froze into immobility when this attendant appeared. They were only half-hidden, and it seemed inevitable that the fellow was going to see them, yet he did not. His eyes were fixed in a hopeless stare on the ground some little distance ahead of him.

As soon as the youth had once more passed out of sight, Baldur, whispering something Hal could not hear clearly, something about finding the Horses, began a nervous slow retreat. But Hal had not come this far to be easily scared away. He waited until he felt sure the gaunt fellow was out of the way, and then carefully worked his way closer to the window, thinking that in this case the bright sunlight outside would protect him from observation better than midnight darkness. Baldur took courage and with his hand on his sword-hilt crept up close to Hal again.

Between the intervals of hammering, there were other sounds from inside the workshed, as of some large, hard-footed creature moving on a floor of hard-packed earth. And there were smells that might have issued from a cameloids' stable—but it was not exactly the same smell, with which practically everyone in the world must be familiar.

With each passing second, Hal became less and less concerned that the gnomes, with their poor sight and their concentration on their work, were going to catch sight of the intruders. Nor, with the noise of fire and hammer going on inside, were they likely to be heard. And even discovery would not necessarily be disastrous.

At last Hal could peer in round the edge of the crude canvas drapery shading the doorway. He got one good look at Andvari, and then at last he was granted an eye-shocking glimpse of the glow of gold. With one wiry hand the farrier was fitting an aureate shoe onto a broad hoof, while holding the animal's fetlock clamped between his knees. First it was necessary to scrape the bottom of the hoof, using a rasp or sharp iron tool made for the purpose.

Standing slightly in the background, the assistant gnome, who was really a skilled magician, gestured and muttered at each curved piece of metal before it was nailed into place.

The shoe itself went through some slight variations in color until it was securely fastened on. It grew blurred and dim as the nails went in, one after another, and Hal thought it lost all special radiance the instant the last one was clinched tight.

There was another roofed building nearby, evidently a kind of stable, from which the gaunt assistant was leading the animals one by one to be shod. The pair of intruders looked into that next.

Baldur repeatedly kept whispering: "Gold Mane, Gold Mane." Hal recalled that that was the name of the horse that Brunhild had ridden. Meanwhile, Hal kept silently but fiercely scanning every inch of the place for gold.

Naturally enough there were stalls in the stable, besides sources of food and water that Hal thought might very well be magical. And still there was the strange and half-familiar smell, very earthy and mundane. Hanging on the walls were clusters of leather straps, some kind of harness evidently, but none of the metal attachments to the straps were gold.

Of anything resembling a treasure vault, there was no sign at all.

When Hal had completed a stealthy progress through almost the entire complex of stables and barns, he had actually seen no more than about a dozen Horses in all, in space adequate for many more. The animals present were housed in two different buildings, the majority in one barn where they were waiting to be looked at and worked on by the farrier. Only a couple of Horses were in the other group, standing about restively on their new footwear. Hal was no judge of quality in the rare species, but to him, all the animals looked strong and healthy.

Gesturing silently, Hal led his companion around the smithy where the forge-fire burned, and from which issued the occasional sounds of metallic hammering. He had convinced himself by now that there was no need to be exceptionally quiet. One creature snorted as the strangers passed through the stable; and the straw littering the old wooden or earthen floor of its stall stirred and crumpled and jumped, disturbed by heavy hooves.

Half-expecting at every moment to encounter someone, Hal was ready with what he hoped might be a halfway plausible story; and as a last resort, his battle-hatchet. But they found no human presence other than their own.

This stable, like the others, was a dim place, with a broad central aisle, from which a number of finely built, commodious stalls diverged on each side. Baldur began to look into each of these in turn. Hal thought he had seen a lot of human habitations that were not as comfortable.

Hal could see no droppings in the occupied stalls; maybe some magical power was cleaning the stables as fast as they were dirtied.

There was a strange sound from the next stall, and Hal looked over to discover Baldur in a paroxysm of delight, which he was somehow managing to keep almost entirely silent. At the moment he was kissing a large, pale-haired Horse on the muzzle, and it was obvious that the young man had at last identified the animal he had been seeking. Baldur kept stroking Gold Mane's head and shoulders, and murmuring feverish endearments, almost as if to Brunhild herself.

The Horse seemed pleased by this treatment, as far as Hal could tell, and Hal himself was pleased as well—any confirmation of the wild stories that Baldur had been telling him was more than welcome.

Just as Hal was turning away again, his foot inadvertently nudged a battered metal or wooden bucket, which made a weighty rattling sound. He looked down, and his breath caught in his throat. For once, it seemed, the Fates might be truly with him!

Jumbled carelessly in the bottom of the bucket were at least a dozen golden horseshoes, full-sized and unbroken.

For a wild moment Hal was tempted to grab the container by its rope handle and run for the open gate and the descending trail. But any such mad try would of course be hopeless. Even if his dash to get away went unmarked by any of Wodan's creatures, Baldur would certainly yell after him, maybe even jump on his back and tackle him, for committing such a staggering blasphemy as stealing from the great god.

A second look into the pail convinced Hal that these were the worn shoes, pried from the horses' hooves and casually tossed into a bucket, ready to be melted down, then, with some addition of new gold to replace what had been worn away, reworked into new ones. Now he estimated there were more than a dozen, as many as fifteen. Why they should be here, yards away from the forge and out of the farriers' reach, was not immediately obvious. But a lot of things in the world were awkward and illogical.

Blind greed, surprisingly strong now that it had a real chance, urged Hal to snatch up and carry away the whole bucket, heavy as it was. But the instinct for self-preservation insisted that he not try that. Half a dozen shoes would be plenty, or at least he was willing to bet they would, and he thought he had room for that many in his pouch.

As fast as his hands could move, Hal began stuffing twisted little curves of gold into his pouch; they were heavy, but there seemed little danger of his falling into deep water, so he would be all right.

There was a strange little noise, a kind of choking, and he looked up to see Baldur staring at him. The youth was almost stunned. "What are you doing?" he quavered, in evident horror.

"Providing for my future, lad." Hal kept his voice to a hoarse whisper. "For yours, too, if you like. Let's get on with it!"

"But you cannot *steal* from Wodan!" Baldur was almost hissing with outrage. "I should have known, because all along you have talked of gold, gold, nothing but gold! I should have suspected—but still I thought—"

"I'm only taking a few—"

"You *cannot!*"

Hal drew himself up and tried to speak in a paternal voice. "My son, a great god, a glorious deity like your Father of Battles will never miss a few small metallic crumbs." But he had to heed the look on Baldur's face, inflexible already and getting worse, practically ready to commit murder.

Right now they could certainly not afford a serious argument, much less a brawl. Hal pulled most of the gold from his pouch—carefully retaining his original fragmentary find—and dumped the rest quietly on the ground beside the bucket, thinking the clanging metal would make less noise that way. Even as he sacrificed his treasure he was marking the spot mentally, intending to come back later for what he had already begun to think of as his own property.

Horror and rage were fading from Baldur's face, and he quickly regained some of the happiness that had been his only moments earlier, when he was embracing Gold Mane. In the ecstasy of his excitement he seemed to forget and forgive Hal's attempted crime.

The fact of an exotic stable awoke old memories. "Let me tell you a story about Hercules sometime," Hal whispered to his companion, trying to distract him from his outrage, meanwhile chuckling to himself.

But the youth was in no mood for distraction now, and seized him by the arm. "Hal, do we dare, after all, to do this?"

Hal stared at him. Maybe it was finally dawning on Baldur that Wodan might consider the taking of one of his Horses as great a crime as the pilfering of discarded shoes.

Drawing a deep breath, Hal became heartily encouraging. If it was truly possible for men to ride these creatures, they would provide an excellent means of getting away. "Of course we dare. We are going to borrow—not steal, you understand—a couple of these excellent animals. You will help me find one I can ride. Then they will carry us to a safe spot at some convenient distance. When we are there, you and I will discuss what our next step ought to be."

"*Right now?*"

Hal mastered an impulse to club the young fool down. "Yes, right now! What did you think? Before someone comes nosing around and discovers us. When d'you think we'll have a better chance?"

Hal's sporting blood was up. It seemed that Baldur, though now his will was wavering, had not been entirely crazy after all. In situations fraught with danger there were times—and Hal thought he had learned to recognize them—when the least dangerous thing to do was to move fast and straight ahead.

Experience had given Hal a great respect for the powers that god-Faces bestowed on men and women; but it had also completely freed him of the commonly held notion that gods, especially the truly great ones, could see everywhere and find out everything.

The lord of this ruined fortress might still be formidable—but on the other hand there were certain indications suggesting he might not. Certainly the place had been allowed to go to rack and ruin. It would have come as no surprise to Hal to learn that whoever wore the Face of Wodan now had not visited this scene of embarrassing deterioration for a long time. It was easy to believe that he might never come back. It even seemed quite possible that the most recent avatar was dead, and no one else had yet picked up the Face. Hal had never laid eyes on a naked Face, few people had, but he had no trouble imagining the Face of Wodan lying somewhere, lacking all power and purpose in itself, until, as would inevitably happen, another human being should pick it up and put it on.

If Wodan *was* truly dead, and the gnomes knew it, they were successfully keeping the secret. And if the Valkyries knew it too . . . ? The implications were too complicated and far-reaching to be immediately grasped.

———————

But right now the only thing to do was to climb on a pair of Horses, as quickly as they could, and get away before they were discovered by a stablehand—or by some being far more dangerous. If the Horses could really fly, then they would leave no trail of hoofprints in the snow— and it ought to be much easier that way to carry a truly substantial weight of gold.

Baldur was still dithering. Hal shook him by the shoulder and demanded: "How are you going to reach Brunhild, otherwise?"

Spurred on by this reminder of his beloved, the youth joined Hal in the effort to decide which Horse Hal was going to attempt to ride.

"Of course Gold Mane might carry us both."

"Without a saddle, and a hundred feet in the air? I'd rather not take that chance, let's try for two." Hal had not abandoned his determination that when he left Valhalla he would be carrying some gold—far from it. Which meant he would probably find it convenient to separate from Baldur shortly after they reached their next stop. Of course he hoped, he really did, that the lad would somehow succeed in recovering his beautiful Brunhild.

And still, the methodical clanging racket from the forge went on; evidently the gnomes were unaware that anything was happening outside their door.

While the men were in the stable, deciding which Horses they would take, Hal was looking about for actual saddles, such as he would have employed on any ordinary cameloid. One or two devices of that kind were visible, but stored high up, as if for display rather than for practical use. He looked into another room of the big barn. There was a pile of hay, looking quite mundane, and stuck in one side of the pile a pitchfork, of no use to Hal at the moment.

Hal pointed urgently. "Don't we need saddles?"

Baldur shook his head. "Hildy never used one, nor did Alvit. She said that courage and kind words were all she needed to control her mount."

"We don't have any magic," Hal reminded his colleague succinctly, and began to lead his own chosen Horse away, the fingers of his left hand firmly tangled in its mane. It was a large and capable-looking animal, and did not seem to have taken an immediate dislike to him—he wasted no time worrying about other details. There was a name, Cloudfoot, presumably the Horse's, burned into the worn wood of a railing at the stall's entrance.

A collection of leather straps, their iron clasps and buckles finely worked enough to be considered objects of art as well as function, were hanging on a wall, but Hal dreaded the idea of fumbling around to put strange harness on an unfamiliar animal—that might take him half an hour, if he could do it at all.

He took a close look at some of the harness. Hanging on the planks of the adjoining wall were fat leather pouches that had to be saddlebags. The two pouches in each set were connected with a simple network of straps that must be intended to hold it in place on an animal's back, almost like the saddlebags an ordinary cameloid might wear. Each pair also included a strange addition on one side, in the form of a deep leather cup, that it seemed a rider might use to ground the butt end of a lance or spear.

It raced through Hal's mind to wonder why riders should be furnished with saddlebags when they used no saddles. But of course the Valkyries were not gods, and like the rest of common humanity they must sometimes need practical help in routine matters—there would be missions, journeys, on which they had to carry their own food supplies.

Hal climbed and stretched to reach one set of saddlebags, and snatched them down. A faint cloud of dust came with them, almost provoking a sneeze.

"What do we need those for?" Baldur wanted to know.

"You never know what we might have to carry. Food, for instance."

Baldur looked distracted. "Yes, you're right, we desperately need food. I ought to have a set of those too." And he scrambled to help himself from the display on the wall. Having done so, he announced: "Now we must be on our way."

"Yes, I think we'd better. But wait a moment." Etched indelibly into Hal's brain was a memory of the precise spot, just around there in the stable, where stood the bucket of golden shoes; now if he could only distract Baldur, somehow, for a few moments . . .

"Food," Hal reminded him again. "We must have food. For the Horses, if not ourselves!"

"You're right, I'll find some," the dashing young warrior volunteered. Hal's stocky body could move with surprising speed when it was called upon to do so, and Baldur's brief absence gave him the chance he needed to quickly gather up the gold and load it into his new saddlebags. After picking up the shoes he had earlier dumped on the ground, he scooped a few more from the bucket—maybe farmland in the north would prove more expensive than he thought.

That done, he pitched the empty bucket away into a pile of straw, where it landed almost noiselessly. He strapped the saddlebags tightly closed, to minimize any clinking and jangling when they were shaken. A moment later Baldur was back, timing his return perfectly from Hal's point of view, and carrying his own set of saddlebags stuffed with whatever kind of Horse-fodder he had been able to snatch up.

Hal threw the leather baggage on the animal's back, and then at the last moment, when his gold was loaded and the way seemed clear, fear of the unknown held him back. Bravely defying an absent god was one thing, but climbing onto the back of a creature whose like he had never touched before, in hopes that its wingless bulk would somehow magically carry him into the gray sky like a bird—an adventure like that presented dangers all too clear and present. He hesitated just a moment too long, until the animal caught his uneasiness and started to shy away. Another problem was the simple fact that this Horse had no stirrups. He needed something to stand on, to give him a leg up . . .

Baldur just sprang up on his long, young legs, and with a twist of his body had gained a rider's seat.

That was inspiring. Hal's legs were shorter, but they still had a good spring in them. Still, it took him an extra moment or two to pull himself up into proper riding position once he had gained the animal's back.

———

Hal and Baldur had just got themselves aboard their respective Horses, with a set of saddlebags strapped on each, when animals and men alike were spooked by a frightening distraction.

There came a great swooping, half-visible rushing in the sky, a swirl of noise and cloud reminding Hal of whirlwinds and waterspouts he had encountered in the warm waters of the Great Sea.

He was just starting to say something else to Baldur, when the thought was dashed from his mind by someone or something making a loud noise, accompanied by a dazzlingly great flash of light.

Hal spun round. As soon as his vision cleared he could see, supported by some invisible force a dozen feet above his head, a golden-haired young woman in dazzling silver clothes suggesting armor, sitting a magnificent Horse, whose movements she controlled with her left hand in its mane. In her right armpit she held braced the butt end of a very competent-looking spear, strongly resembling a type of cavalryman's lance. Her fierce blue eyes were stabbing at Hal like darts.

The northman froze in his tracks, and something in the pit of his stomach abruptly knotted. Again there came a powerful swirling in the air—this time it was a whole lot more than smoke.

Baldur evidently recognized the Valkyrie at first glance, for he called her by name: "Alvit!"

She in turn recognized Baldur. Her voice was clear, imperious, speaking the common tongue in what sounded to Hal as a strange but elegant accent.

"Are you insane, Baldur? What do you and this one think that you are doing?" With the sharp tip of her spear, the Valkyrie savagely jabbed the air in Hal's direction.

The young man's answer was drowned out by the Horse's snorting breath, and also by a roaring sound of unknown cause that was now swelling swiftly in the background; but the name of Brunhild was a part of that reply.

Then her gaze turned round on Hal, and to him it looked coldly murderous. He grabbed instinctively for his axe, but the tip of the woman's long spear swung round on him with startling speed, so that before he could even try to parry or dodge the mere touch of it shocked his arm and sent his weapon flying, threw him sprawling in the snow, like a child flicked by some great warrior's blow. He came down hard, on bruising rocks waiting close beneath that cover of deceptive softness.

In a moment Hal was up, flexing his right arm, scrambling instinctively to recover his lost steel. His eyes fell on an axe-shaped imprint in the snow where his weapon had buried itself. His right arm, as he used it to reclaim the axe, was unbroken, not even cut, but tingling in bone and muscle as if he had been sleeping on it for a week.

For the moment the Valkyrie was ignoring him. But she was still holding that spear ready.

Baldur had not tried to draw his sword. Instead, he greeted the mounted girl as if he knew her. When she grounded her flying steed, he tried to grab the animal by its mane, but it pulled swiftly away, freeing itself from his clumsy grasp.

Hal, having recovered his axe, was trying to grab with his free hand for his own animal's bridle, forgetting for the moment that it did not wear one. It took a moment for his fumbling fingers to find the long mane again, and fasten themselves in that.

With shouted warnings and cautions Baldur let Hal know that this Valkyrie was one who had proven herself sympathetic to Brunhild and her affair with a simple warrior.

Baldur sounded as if he had crossed over into panic: "Hal, hold back! Put down your weapon!"

Panicked or not, that sounded like good advice. With a broad gesture, wanting to make sure that everybody saw, Hal slipped it back into its holster, glad of the chance to demonstrate his preference for a peaceful resolution of this misunderstanding. The spear in the Valkyrie's hand was still ready, and he was not going to try to compete with it again. Not unless he had to, to save his life.

When Alvit once more turned his way, he warily introduced himself. His arm still seemed to be on fire, though functioning, and he resisted the urge to rub it.

Something in the Valkyrie's attitude as she confronted Hal strongly suggested that she had seen him stuffing two saddlebags with golden horseshoes, and the hard stare of her blue eye made him feel guilty about it.

In a moment Hal's instincts were proven correct, for she contemptuously charged him as a thief. "And this one has come along to steal gold."

Baldur was lagging mentally a step or two behind, as usual. Reassuringly he told the Valkyrie: "No, I made him put that back."

There came an interruption from an unexpected source. From the direction of the smithy, now out of sight behind some other sheds, came the gnomes, the pair of them stumbling and wincing in daylight. They were pulling on additional clothes and shielding their faces as they cried the alarm. Both small men were crying out in their harsh, accented voices, and struggling with the strings that held their bone-disk goggles on, as they forced themselves to brave the outdoor sunlight. Hal needed a moment to understand what they were saying.

"Someone has carried off the bucket of old shoes!"

Fortunately Baldur once more failed to get the point. "We saw it in the stable," he assured them.

The Valkyrie was briefly distracted as she tried to reassure the two gnomes.

They protested some more, but she had at least temporary success, despite the obvious presence of mutual suspicion.

For a moment at least the gnomes were staring straight at Baldur and Hal, but it was possible, Hal supposed, that in the glaring, show-reflected light they failed to recognize the recent visitors to their village. Moments later the Earthdwellers, at Alvit's urging, had turned away to grope their way back to the smithy.

Now the Valkyrie turned back to Hal and Baldur, and in a low voice urged the foolish intruders to flee.

"Get out of here, and quickly. Yes, you had better take the Horses. I'll get them back later, and think up some explanation. How did you reach this place? On foot? Fools!"

Hal needed only a moment to recover from his astonishment. "Thank you, my lady," Hal bowed deeply. She was welcome to call him whatever names she wanted, for he had never heard sweeter words. "We're on our way at once. Let me just give you back what we have taken—"

But Alvit interrupted, cursing at him. "Never mind that. Take what you have, I say, and go!"

When Baldur showed signs of being unable to move until his mind had been relieved regarding the mysterious problem of the gold, Alvit relented and tried again: "If there is not enough gold to make the shoes, that will get the attention of the All-Highest. Then maybe I can get him to confront our greater problems."

"Greater problems than missing gold?" Even now Hal could not restrain his curiosity.

Alvit's answer burst forth as if she had been holding it back for a long time and could no longer do so. "The guard is greatly under strength, there are shortages of equipment, clothing, even of food—" She broke off, looking anxiously back over one shoulder.

Baldur, who now seemed determined to explain his conduct, began to say something, but she silenced him with a fierce gesture. "Wodan is coming! I will try to delay him, but—no, it is too late." Her last words were almost inaudible, her voice sinking in what sounded like despair.

Baldur took a step closer to her, and for a moment he had Alvit's full attention.

Hal seized his chance. Winding his fingers into a mane of coarse dark hair, he clutched it tightly and leaped astride the Horse, fear lending an extra spring to his legs this time. From the corner of his eye, he could see clearly enough that Baldur had mounted too. As soon as Hal felt himself firmly aboard, he kicked hard with both heels into the animal's flanks.

The next few moments were total confusion.

Using stirrups and saddle, Hal had climbed onto the backs of cameloids and droms more times than he could count. But this bareback experience was every bit as different as he had feared it would be. The beast beneath him seemed harder, bonier than any he had ever clamped between his legs before, and was surely as strong as any cameloid that Hal had ever ridden. In two bounds they were out of the stable and into the air. He caught a glimpse of Baldur near him in the sky, legs forked as they clamped hard round the thick body of a running animal. Both Horses had left the ground in giant leaps, and neither showed any sign of coming down.

Someone, in a voice that sounded remarkably like Hal's own, let out an outcry, as if of fright.

The Horse with Hal aboard was moving quickly, but he had not left the Valkyrie and her steed behind. Their flight had covered only a few yards when in the next moment Alvit, with what seemed a single sweep of her flashing Spear, knocked them both out of their saddles, and sent them sprawling on the snowy ground.

Baldur seemed to have been flattened utterly, but Hal came up from the fall with a bloodied knee and elbow. He also had acquired a mouthful of snow, muffling the words of rage that he was ready to spew forth. His anger was chiefly at himself, for making what now appeared as a long chain of stupid decisions, getting himself into this, and it was doubly fierce because of that. "What now, in all the hells—?"

In the moment it took him to regain his feet, the warrior girl had changed her mind as to what she wanted them to do—her attitude, her shouted commands, showed that they had become her prisoners. And in a moment Hal understood why.

It was already too late. Hal saw with a sinking heart that it was far too late now to attempt flight—because now another airborne marvel had come into view, a single figure riding a black chariot that thundered through the sky behind a pair of Horses, somehow harnessed in tandem rather than side by side—no. Hal rubbed his eyes and looked again.

Pulling the chariot was one monstrous animal, that in fact appeared to be an eight-legged Horse.

One moment this fantastic equipage was hurtling through the air directly toward them. But a moment or two before it ran them down, it abruptly descended until the wheels spun in snow. A moment after that, the chariot had pulled to a stop on the ground no more than twenty feet from Hal, sending up a spray of snow and gravel from the vehicle's two wheels and the eight hooves of Sleipnir. That, Hal now seemed to remember from some legend, was the name of Wodan's Horse.

The Valkyrie and the young man seemed both frozen in position like two statues. Baldur had just dragged himself erect, while Alvit sat astride her own Horse, spear held firmly with the point raised, as if to offer a salute to the new arrival.

Looking at the great god leaning toward him from his chariot, Hal saw an imposing man apparently about fifty years of age, his one functioning eye, locked now in a stare at Hal, deepset under a jutting brow under long hair of silvery blond. A black patch covered the other eye. Wodan was clad in rich furs, and there was a definite resemblance to Hagan, so that the two of them might have been brothers. The big difference that Hal could see with his first look was that except for the missing eye, Wodan's massive body was that of a hale and hearty man.

Baldur was whimpering like a lost child, and he had fallen on his knees.

10

WITH A SENSE that the youth's behavior was utterly unseemly in the eyes of humanity and the gods, Hal grabbed Baldur's collar with one hand and yanked him to his feet. Meanwhile a fragment of some old parody of a drinking song, learned in some exotic tavern from some fellow Argonaut, had begun running through Hal's head. It was something about:

. . . marching with the heroes . . .

Some part of his mind, as usual, kept finding jokes even when the situation was far from funny.

He couldn't remember the next line of the song, and at the moment it did not seem to matter. He was feeling even less heroic than usual, but at least it seemed that he and Baldur were not going to be thrown directly over a cliff. Wodan was staring at them both, but Hal had no sense that the god was particularly angry. Beside Hal, Baldur was keeping silent too, both of them standing there panting and disheveled, about like a couple of boys caught stealing apples. The young man seemed not much worse off physically for having been knocked off his Horse, but his helmet was still dented, and Hal was bleeding freshly from a couple of minor scratches. Anyone who gave them a cursory inspection, as Wodan seemed to be doing, might be easily convinced that they had just fallen on some battlefield.

As far as Hal was aware, only the two gnomes and Alvit had as yet noticed that gold was missing, and only the Valkyrie had connected the loss with him. For her own reasons she was keeping silent about it.

Meanwhile the All-Highest was still directing his one-eyed glare at the pair of intruders, his broad, bearded face betraying not much in the way of interest despite the steadiness of his regard. When at last he spoke, he apparently saw no reason to doubt that they were newly harvested heroes.

"And where are these two from?" The voice of the Father of Battles seemed fully appropriate to his reputation. It gave the impression that if he raised it, it ought to be audible to the farthest corner of any field of war.

Alvit bowed her head and uttered what sounded like a place name, one that meant nothing to Hal. But Wodan accepted it without apparent surprise.

"Have you seen the god Loki anywhere?" was the surprising first question Wodan now shot at the newcomers to his realm.

"No sir, I have not," said Hal clearly, and kicked Baldur in the ankle so that the youngster was roused sufficiently to second Hal's denial.

Silence fell again. The god maintained his dour look, but his gaze was wandering, so maybe his mind was elsewhere. At first Hal kept expecting him to make some comment on the shabby appearance of the two new members of the corps of Heroes. But then Hal remembered under what circumstances the Valkyries generally did their recruiting.

Somewhere behind Hal, in the middle distance, a dozen human feet or so came shuffling and tramping through the snow. He didn't turn, but he thought he could identify the source: a small squad of human soldiers, moving at route step, still some distance off.

Again the god seemed to have drifted away into some shadowy realm of rumination, chewing his substantial mustache and staring now right at Hal, now at something over the northman's shoulder. When Hal looked around at the squad marching toward them, perhaps to escort the two new recruits to the barracks, something about them struck him as odd. As far as he could tell not one of the men was really wearing a uniform, proper or not.

Hal kept expecting rough hands to seize him, strip him of battle-axe and dagger, and probably dump out his belt-pouch too. Wait till someone hefted the saddlebags—then the fun would start. But nothing of the kind happened. All that happened was that Wodan commanded that the two new arrivals be conducted to the barracks.

The tramp of feet grew louder, then shuffled to a halt. Now Hal took a closer look at the squad that had just arrived. He was not impressed. There were only six of them, armed with a miscellany of what looked like second-rate weapons, and none of the men looked really formidable. On neutral ground, and with some other companion than befuddled Baldur at his side, he might have seriously considered trying to fight his way free once the god had ceased to stare at him. Here, under the eye of Wodan, there was no point in considering resistance.

Again the god was speaking, in his voice of rolling, muted thunder. "You are the sergeant—?"

"Sergeant Nosam, *sir!*"

Hal thought there was probably no reason why Wodan had to know the name of every noncom in his army. Still, a god ought to be able to do that, if he made the effort. If Hal were a god, he would have done as much.

Wodan was rumbling. "Nosam, yes. You are to take charge of these two recruits . . ." The volume of the thunderous voice declined, the words trailed off.

The sergeant did not seem to be surprised at his commander's vagueness. "The recruits, yes sir. They will be inducted and indoctrinated according to standard operating procedures."

"My army," Wodan was saying now. "My army needs more men."

"Yes, sir. That has been—that has been my opinion for some time, if I may say so."

Wodan apparently did not care if the man said so or not. Eventually the god grated out an order. "Sergeant Nosam, see that the new members of the guard are issued proper uniforms."

"Yes, my great lord, at once." The sergeant, snapping to attention, saluted and acknowledged the order with military precision. None of the men were wearing any insignia of rank, as far as Hal could tell.

Wodan's rambling voice kept running, on and off, like intermittent rain. Hal would have liked to concentrate more fully on what the god was saying, but he could not. All he could think of was the purloined gold still packed into the saddlebags on the back of the Horse he had been trying to borrow. So far, no one had discovered the theft—no one but the gnomes, and they seemed not to count. Hal was beginning to hope against hope that the matter might somehow, incredibly, be overlooked. But he knew he was not out of the woods yet.

The presence of the animals, as if waiting to be ridden, had suddenly caught Wodan's wandering attention.

"Why are these other Horses here?" the god demanded, pointing with a huge forefinger at Gold Mane and Cloudfoot.

Alvit, bless her, was sticking her neck out to try to save the trespassers. "The heavenly farrier is making his regularly scheduled visit, my lord." Hal hadn't really expected any more help from the Valkyrie, not after she had almost killed them with her damned Spear. But he wasn't going to argue. Still, he feared her noble effort would be wasted.

As soon as someone else discovered the stolen gold, he was as good as dead anyway.

"About time," Wodan grumbled.

To Hal's dismay, the gnomes were back. Andvari was even daring to approach the god directly, while his colleague trailed behind. The daring Earthdweller was babbling to the god something to the effect that the supply of gold was almost entirely missing.

If Wodan heard the plea at all, he ignored it totally.

Alvit looked utterly discouraged. She eyed the two small workmen fiercely, and ordered in a low voice: "Look around carefully. Things are forever being misplaced."

"Yes, my lady," the gnome who had spoken to Wodan rasped, in tones of fear. Then he and his more timid associate began to retreat, walking slowly backward and bowing repeatedly, like dancers or magic toys, until they had passed around the corner of a building.

Suddenly Baldur had fallen on his knees again, and was making preliminary noises in his throat, as if about to utter some impassioned plea, or worse, a miserable confession. Once more Hal grabbed him roughly and jerked him back to his feet, this time twisting his collar and choking him into silence in the process. Wodan had no reaction to this incident; the mind of the All-Highest, if he really had one any longer, still seemed to be elsewhere.

Meanwhile Hal was thinking furiously, or at least trying. The two Earthdwellers ought to have been able to get a good look at Hal and Baldur, and ought to have recognized them from their meeting in the gnomes' village. Yet they had given no sign of knowing them. Possibly the gnomes had been unable to identify the men here in the glare of daylight—or possibly they had simply thought it safest not to recognize the intruders, who were obviously in deep trouble of some kind.

Thinking seemed quite useless at the moment. Wodan was mumbling something into his beard, and Alvit was busy being deferential and soothing to her master. "As you say, lord. I will see to it that the Horses are kept under better control."

"See that they are," said Wodan in a voice that was suddenly clear and sharp. A moment later he picked up the reins of his chariot, and with the sharp tug of an expert driver induced the eight-legged horse to turn the vehicle around, the animal demonstrating fancy footwork in the process. He drove off slowly, staying firmly on the ground, in the direction of his stronghold's massive, towering, half-ruined central keep.

While Sergeant Nosam was trying to get the squad's formation into shape, Hal favored Alvit with his best effort at a pleading glance, hoping she would understand his silent request that she somehow arrange to get them free again. If for some obscure reason she *wanted* him to steal the gold, well, that could certainly be managed; if not, he could live with that decision too.

When she only glared at him, he tried to talk to her again, keeping his voice low.

"That is impossible," the young woman snapped, in reply to his first few words. "Now Wodan knows you are here."

"He does? I mean, with all respect, he doesn't seem to—"

"Here you are, and here you must stay."

"For how long?"

That provoked a savage look. "For the rest of your lives. What did you expect? But take courage, northman. Your life may be over much sooner than you think."

Then the Valkyrie must have signaled to the squad of soldiers with a gesture, for the squad gave up on trying to dress itself into a tight square and loosely surrounded Hal and Baldur, as if officially taking them into custody.

"Forward, march! Route step." Sergeant Nosam might not look like much, but he had the knack of issuing crisp commands.

Dazedly they moved away, the escort looking and sounding as awkward as the two recruits, or prisoners. It was an uneven march, and one of the men somewhere behind Hal, seemed to be straggling, almost unable to keep up. There came a sound of hard breathing, with the slight exertion of this simple walk. Again, Hal thought he could almost certainly outfight any of them, maybe even any two, but it would be berserker madness to take on all of them. Whether Baldur would help him or swipe at him with his sword would be about an even bet. And he doubted that he could outrun any but the slowest.

There was no air of pride, or even of menace, about their escort. Their guide had little to say to his new captives, or recruits; it was as if his thoughts had joined his divine master's, brooding in some distant world.

Their destination, reached after a minute or so of circuitous route-stepping through the sprawling ruins, proved to be a kind of armory or barracks, built into a lower level of the great keep.

Baldur became aware of the low doorway just in time to duck his head. The interior was a shabby place, with makeshift barriers of straw and rags propped with boards over holes in the wall, where they fought to keep out the cold. Better help came from a roaring fire in a makeshift hearth, positioned below another hole that served as chimney. Hal noted with a start that the flames in the crude fireplace seemed to be consuming nothing, just like those on the high crag. More of Loki's magic, he supposed, here in Wodan's headquarters as a gift or on loan.

The sergeant took note of what Hal was staring at. "Never seen a fire like that one, have you? Once Loki was welcome in Valhalla. Some of the flames that he gave Wodan, when the two of them were friends, are burning still. Thank Loki, or we'd none of us survive the coming winter."

Hal was curious. "But Wodan and Loki are friends no longer, is that it? How about Thor? What's his attitude now?"

Now that the god was no longer in sight, Baldur had regained his powers of almost normal speech and movement. He murmured to Hal that this might be a kind of training station where new recruits were kept until they could prove themselves.

"See, Hal, it is only a kind of outpost, as I thought. The stables are here, and a few men to guard the stables. The All-Highest must be only visiting. We won't be here long." He seemed to be doggedly trying to convince himself as well as Hal.

Hal only grunted in response. Alvit's parting remarks, whether they were meant as curse or warning, hadn't offered much ground for hope. And with every passing moment Hal expected a great outcry, a shout from whoever had charge of the Horses now—whoever was going to discover the gold in the saddlebags. And soon horrible vengeance would fall upon the thief.

But moment after moment passed and there was no outcry.

Shortly after their arrival at the barracks, Baldur's outpost-with-stables theory suffered a distinct setback when Sergeant Nosam pointed out to the recruits what he said were the god's regular living quarters, high up in the solid remnant of the still-impressive keep.

When Hal ventured to question the mild-mannered sergeant on the subject of Valkyries' housing, he learned that they were quartered in an upper floor of the same building, very near Wodan's private domain.

There was another entrance to the keep, at ground level, through which the young women came and went, as a rule, without their flying Horses. Even as Hal was watching, he saw a couple of them flying in, the Horses landing on and taking flight from a high terrace, up near the highest level of the still-palatial remnant of a building.

Moments after those maidens on Horses landed, a bright light, like a large lamp newly kindled into flame, suddenly came on in those high rooms. Maybe that was coincidence, thought Hal, or maybe evidence that Valkyries' duties did not end when they put down their Spears. He doubted they were held strictly to their pledge of perpetual virginity.

"The old man's turning in for the night," one of his new comrades in arms observed.

Baldur turned his head sharply. "Who?"

"The old man, I said. Who do you think that is? Our lord and eternal master, Wodan." The tone in which the words were spoken was far from reverent, and the hero let out an ugly laugh through broken teeth.

Baldur rose up as if determined to object to such a sacrilegious attitude, but then remained silent, as if he were either afraid to speak, or didn't know what to say.

Suddenly everyone wanted to avoid the subject.

Hal had not been in the barracks for an hour, when he was surprised to be summoned to take a turn at guard duty. The sergeant led him to a deserted courtyard not far from the smithy and the stables. Was this some kind of trick, to see if he would try to grab the gold and flee again?

Nosam had turned his back and started away when Hal called after him. "Can I ask you a question, Sergeant Nosam?"

Turning, the sergeant was agreeable as usual. "Fire away."

"No one's told me what I'm guarding, or who I'm supposed to challenge if they come this way."

Slowly Nosam shook his head. "Maybe I didn't make it clear. I wouldn't challenge anyone, Haraldur. Just stay on your post, and look alert, in case Wodan or a Valkyrie comes by. Maybe a guard is needed here, maybe not. But there's a standing order to post one, going back a long way, that's never been countermanded. Our job is to follow orders."

"I see."

Hal had not been on guard for more than half an hour, when he was surprised by Alvit, who appeared, on foot and unarmed, and stopped to talk with him.

"Well, northman. What do you think of Valhalla now?"

"So far I am surviving. Give me a little time and I might get used to it."

"Is that all?"

"If you want my opinion of it as a prison, well, I've seen worse. As a military outfit, I have to say it stinks." In fact he had already noticed that the latrine behind the guardroom had a particularly evil smell, despite the fact that it was even colder than the barracks. The walls of both facilities were full of holes and crevices, some of which had been stuffed with straw and rags in a futile attempt to shut out the rising winter wind.

Somewhat to Hal's surprise, the Valkyrie only nodded thoughtfully. "I suppose you were brought to this country as a mercenary?"

"Then you suppose wrong. I was very much on my own, just passing through."

"So you can tell me very little about the intentions of any of our local warlords?"

"Never met any of them, so I can tell you nothing. But I'd think you must know them fairly well. You visit their battlefields, don't you?"

Alvit shook her head. "Battlefields are not good places to discover what people are thinking."

"I am curious," Hal said, taking advantage of the young woman's evident willingness to talk. "I know very little about Valkyries. Do you really make an effort to collect the bravest and the best when you go out recruiting?"

Alvit was shaking her head, as if she marveled at his ignorance. "Haraldur, I believe just this much of what you have told me so far— that you really are a stranger in these parts."

"I am."

"Well, just stop and think about the problem of recruiting heroes. The rankest cowards have run from the battlefield before we Valkyries get there. The brave but ineffective have been slaughtered, unless they are very lucky. Others are trapped, just fighting for their lives. So how are we to know who among the survivors is the bravest? Personally I always look for a man not too badly hurt, but no more than about half conscious, so he won't put up a fight when I drag him aboard my Horse."

"Presumably he should not be dead, either; though the legend has it that you bring the dead to Valhalla."

"Of course, not dead!" Alvit gave a harsh laugh that did not indicate amusement. "Wodan needs fighting men, not corpses."

Hal chuckled too. "I think Baldur more than half believes the legend."

‹ "How do you mean? Believes what, exactly?"

"He's idealistic about Wodan and Valhalla, but doesn't have the details worked out very well. He seems to think that if Brunhild had gathered him in, his dead body would have stayed on the field, while only his spirit would have been carried here to glorious—"

The Valkyrie interrupted, snorting. "Baldur is a fool! And so are you, or you would not be here."

"I won't argue that point. But tell me more about your work on the battlefields. What if you need recruits but can't find a good candidate?"

"We always need recruits, as you can see by looking around you. And it's true, acceptable men, let alone ideal ones, are hard to come by." She sighed. "More often than not we ride home empty-handed after these skirmishes. But Wodan insists we do our recruiting in the traditional way. Some of those we bring back here are failures. We are granted no magical insight. But more likely than not, those struck down in battle have some bravery, or they would not be on the field. I always try to avoid the men who are really trying to run away."

For once Hal had no comment. Alvit ruminated briefly, then turned away and started to leave. Then momentarily she turned back. "Maybe, Haraldur, you will live longer than I thought."

———

Baldur and Hal had been assigned a pair of neighboring bunks, poor berths hardly more than pallets on the stone floor, in a dim-lit, cheerless barracks or guardroom, with a row of some ten or a dozen bunks down each side. Despite the welcome presence of Loki's magic fire, the room was cold.

Hal looked, and pulled his cloak around him. "Damn those holes. Is there a better barracks than this somewhere around?"

A man who was sitting two bunks away looked over. "This is it, friend."

Everything that Hal had seen and heard since his arrival was forcing him to the realization that the Heroes of Valhalla comprised a total of something less than twenty men, most of them not very heroic.

He turned to his companion. "Baldur, do you know what I am beginning to suspect? That this handful of misfits in this barracks are all the army Wodan has."

"That can't be." Baldur looked over as if he suspected Hal of cooking up a joke.

"Maybe it can't be," put in the tired-looking fellow from two bunks away. "But it is."

Other men around them wearily confirmed it.

The tired-looking one sat up; the movement seemed to cost him a great effort. "When did you die?" he asked Baldur. Despite the evidence of illness, there was a glint in his eye that told of joke-making.

Baldur only looked at him, but Hal replied. "It was so long ago, I can't remember."

Then he looked back at Baldur, who seemed to be in shock.

Staring at him, Hal asked in a whisper: "What are you worried about now?"

Baldur only looked at him.

"By all the gods!" Hal couldn't keep his voice from getting louder. "You haven't really been thinking that we're dead?"

Slowly the expression on the youth's face altered. "No. Not really. Though for just a moment, when Alvit swiped at us with her Spear . . ."

Hal was shaking his head. "Look, Baldur . . . I'm not sure how to try to tell you this . . . but none of us here are dead."

Baldur was dignified. "If we are not, we ought to be."

The man from two bunks away was listening now, and went through a kind of spasm, gripped by almost silent laughter. "Dead? Dead? You're not yet *dead*, you clodpate! Though you might soon wish you were." He turned his body and let himself fall face downward onto his bunk, where the sounds of his laughter grew louder, until they turned into convulsions of desperate coughing.

Hal studied his companion. "You have the damnedest eagerness to be dead of anyone I've ever met!"

"So I admit that now we are still alive." Baldur took a long, shuddering breath. "But that being so, I don't know where we are. It should be Valhalla, because Alvit and her sisters are here, but . . . what does it all mean?"

"For one thing, it means that all the old stories about Valhalla have got it just a little wrong."

The man on the other bunk had lain down again, and turned his face away. Baldur was silent, contemplating the impossible. At last the youth got out: "But if this is truly not Valhalla—what should we do?"

"Well, let's not be in any desperate hurry to make up our minds. This is . . . not *too* bad. Let's give them the chance to feed us a couple of square meals first. A little food, a little knowledge—that's what we need right now."

And a little gold, Hal added in the privacy of his own thought.

———

At the dim far end of the large room were two closed doors. Hal pointed toward them and asked a veteran: "Where do those go?"

"Private rooms, for our two corporals, Corporal Bran and Corporal Blackie. You'll know Blackie by his white hair. All white though he's not old."

"So where's the sergeant sleep?"

The man gestured vaguely toward the keep. "Just outside the old

man's quarters, where he can be easily summoned at any time. Being
sergeant in this outfit is not a job I'd want to have."

On their next morning in Valhalla the men were wakened at first light,
and Hal and Baldur, as they had expected, were told that they were
going out to drill.

Nosam had their names down on a roster. "Couple of new ones for
you, Blackie."

Blackie, in his slyly indifferent way, gave Hal and Baldur what he
said was the same warning he gave all new recruits, that there was no
use trying to get away. There were only a couple of dozen live heroes
on hand anyway, and the Valkyries ruthlessly pursued and brought back
any who tried to get away—except for those who died in the trackless
mountains, trying to find their way out.

Hal and Baldur exchanged a look. When it came to planning an
escape, they were conscious of having a special advantage shared by
none of the other men in the barracks—they had not been carried here
on Horseback, but had walked into Valhalla on their own two feet, and
therefore they knew the path that could carry them out. It seemed that
no one but Alvit knew of their advantage.

The joking man from two bunks down, whose name was Baedeker, now
seemed to have taken to his bed more or less permanently. The sergeant
had excused him from all duty, and he did not look at all well. In fact
the more Hal studied him, the worse he looked, and Hal soon decided
that the fellow might well be dying. The victim did not appear feverish,
and so Hal thought there was probably little risk of contagion. But to
be on the safe side, he avoided getting too close, anyway.

During their first morning drill session, Hal and Baldur took part in the
scene they had earlier witnessed from a distance: the daily combat drill,
including the charade of dueling, in which breathing Heroes were pitted
against wraiths.

Hal sparred very cautiously at first, guarding and striking as if he
were in a fight against solid metal and solid muscle. He had to begin

by assuming that the wraiths, with their fierce aspect, had some real power to inflict harm. But this proved not to be the case.

Fairly often during drill and marching these disobeyed the sergeant's orders, or rather simply ignored them, as if they were listening to commands from someone else. The result was that he gave them specific orders rarely; there was after all no way to punish them, by whipping, confinement, or deprivation of pay or rations. The noncoms had long ago given up trying to shout them into obedience.

On the positive side, several veterans assured Hal that these seemed to have no power to do serious harm. If you saw them from a distance, or squinted at them with your eyes nearly closed, they did lend a great air of military bustle and purpose to the establishment. When Hal was matched against them in the practice drills, he soon realized that their weapons were as insubstantial as their bodies, and only stung and did not wound, when employed against live flesh and blood.

"Doesn't seem that they would be of much help in a real battle," he remarked while getting back his breath.

"They do a great job of rounding up deserters," Corporal Blackie assured him with a smile.

"How do they manage that?"

"You felt the sting just now. Their swords and spears carry power and pain enough to harry and drive men of solid flesh back up the trail. Though one or two have chosen suicidal leaps instead."

Some other Hero demonstrated the essential harmlessness of their wraith-opponents by allowing one of them to strike him several times. But such playful negligence seemed to be against orders. When Bran and Blackie bellowed at the offender, he went back to treating his opponents seriously.

The only one who never seemed to slack off during the drills was Bran, though sometimes he would fake a withdrawal. Then with a yell he'd spin around and rout his insubstantial assailant with a powerful blow.

Panting with the effort, he smiled at Hal. "Hit a wraith a real good lick and he disappears for good. Just like a real man in that respect. Like most men, that is."

"If you keep exterminating ghosts, don't they all get used up after a while?"

"Wodan has a device that produces more." Apparently the answer was meant to be taken seriously.

Gradually Baldur was forced to the understanding Hal had already reached—that Wodan's fabled honor guard contained less than a score of living men in all, and most of those were in poor physical shape, hardly able to do more than go through the motions of drilling and practicing at arms.

There were a few exceptions, most notably Corporal Bran, a great physical specimen who seemed to genuinely feel a tremendous devotion to the god. Fighting, even against ghosts, seemed to awaken something deep and terrible in the man's nature. When the drill was over, he seemed to be awakening from a trance. This man seemed to take a liking to Hal, and suggested that the two of them spar sometime with dulled blades.

"Don't think I want to dull my axe."

"That would truly be a shame. By the way, I like that helmet that you wear."

Hal thought that there was something lacking in Bran's eyes, as if he were already dead. Outside of that, nothing in the man's appearance or behavior made him seem particularly threatening at all, at least at first glance, though he was physically formidable enough. Several inches taller than Hal, with sandy hair and beard, he owned sloping shoulders and powerful arms. He walked with a kind of eager, energetic shuffle and carried nothing extraordinary in the way of arms or armor. He was usually smiling, in a way that could easily be taken for mockery. But Hal soon decided that the man really had no thought of mocking anyone.

Minute followed minute in this strange new existence, hour followed hour, a full day went by, and then another, and still Hal had heard nothing about stolen gold. He kept making up imaginative scenarios to explain to himself what seemed a remarkable stroke of good fortune. The most optimistic of these said that whoever had found the treasure had simply decided to keep it, and that even if the loot should somehow be recovered, at this stage there would be no clue to show that Hal had ever touched it.

But then he changed his mind and decided the gold was probably still in the saddlebags. Routine care of the Horses must be sadly neglected here, like so much else, but probably the animals' magic, or that of their golden shoes, allowed them to survive anyway, even to flourish. But sooner or later someone would go to lift those containers off the Horse, and be astonished by their weight. And then . . .

But still there came no alarm, no accusations. It was as if the absence of a few pounds of mere gold was likely to pass entirely unnoticed.

Among the breathing men now quartered in Valhalla, the later arrivals, being better nourished, usually had an advantage in drill and practice, if they were not badly hurt when they came in. But there were some recruits who, seemingly in some kind of shock when they arrived, withdrew into themselves, ate and slept little, and had trouble talking or even understanding orders.

"Those kind never last more than a month or two," was one of the veterans' comments.

Others, usually men of lower rank who had been collected by Wodan's flying girls because no higher were available, took a philosophical soldier's attitude that one outfit was not essentially different from another and life was bad in all of them. These tended to last longer than men of any other category.

───────

When the sergeant summoned Baldur to stand guard duty, he was more insistent than Hal had been, about having the formalities spelled out. "Is there not to be a password, then?"

One of the veterans, overhearing, called out an obscene suggestion in jest.

Baldur ignored the jibe, and in his anger criticized Nosam as being a poor noncom. "When I chose men to lead into battle, I chose none who were like you!"

The sergeant's reply was quiet and unthreatening: "Baldur, I just told you to shut up about passwords and such stuff. That's an order, I want to hear no more. Disobey me and I'll put you on report, and you won't like what happens to you then. You're young and hard, you could probably kill me if we fought, but then Bran would kill you. Or if he didn't—" Nosam's lips smiled thinly. "You might be promoted to sergeant."

Baldur slowly lowered his raised fist. "What do you mean?"

"Just what I said. And you wouldn't want my job, young one." The white-haired Corporal Blackie was shaking his head sadly in the background, while Nosam went on. "Twice a day—and sometimes twice a night, if Wodan's sleep is restless—have to report to the god in person."

───────

Time dragged on, in drill and guard duty and boredom, and Hal began to lose track. Had they now been Wodan's guests for four days or five? And did it matter?

And meanwhile the intermittent presence of wraiths made the armory and barracks seem much busier, more fully occupied, than they really were. At least they consumed no food and filled no sleeping space.

Bran, in his normal mild and almost wistful way, frequently expressed a wish that Wodan would snap out of his listlessness and inattention.

Bran thought that the god must be the victim of some enemy's sly magic. "If only a man could find out who it was . . ."

Loki was a prime suspect, in Bran's thought; and even Thor was not above suspicion.

Bran when he hung around the barracks was a mild-mannered sort, with a tentative and almost gentle smile. His nominal rank seemed to mean little or nothing to him, except that he was never detailed to clean the latrine. But Hal noted that the veterans all went out of their way to avoid antagonizing him.

———

As soon as Hal and Baldur were able to talk privately, Hal said: "It seems that we can walk away, the gates are seldom guarded. If we time it right, no one will miss us for a few hours. But walking won't get us far enough or fast enough. I think we really need the Horses."

Baldur agreed. "If we walk, Valkyries could overtake us quickly."

Hal looked around. "And Valkyries might not be our worst problem. They say that sometimes Wodan sends out his best berserker after deserters."

"You mean Bran? There would be two of us."

Hal did not reply. Corporal Blackie had suddenly appeared, from around a corner, and as if he knew what they had been saying, began in his gently taunting way to talk about escapes.

"Maybe you've been wondering why we don't guard the gates."

"It's not for us to question such decisions," Hal said nobly. Baldur looked at him.

So did Blackie. "No one who tries to leave us can get far. A few who attempt to desert are simply lost in the mountains. The others are hunted down and brought back, the very lucky ones by flying Valkyries. Those who are simply fortunate are harried and driven back by wraiths."

Hal was curious. "Why do you call them fortunate?"

"Because sometimes Wodan sends out the berserker instead—you know what a berserker is?"

"I've heard the name."

Blackie appeared to be reminiscing. "I remember well one such group. There were three men, all recent recruits, all desperate, and well-armed." A pause. "And when they were reported as deserters, Bran volunteered to bring them back, and Wodan granted his request, and sent him out alone." Blackie nodded solemnly.

"Well, what happened?"

"Bran returned, wounded but alive. Not so the others."

Baldur asked it: "Bran brought them back?"

"Not altogether."

"What do you mean?"

"Only their heads."

11

AS FAR BACK as Hal could remember, he had understood that two of the most important things about any military organization were the name and nature of the commanding officer. Ever since he and Baldur had been so irregularly drafted, Hal had been looking around and listening, trying to gather information on the individual, whoever it might be, who held that position in Wodan's divine guard. But for all he had been able to discover so far, the job might be wide open. Hal had yet to hear of anyone who outranked Sergeant Nosam—unless it would be Wodan himself, as supreme commander.

When Hal questioned the sergeant, he was told that for the past year the rank of general had in theory been held by one of the mere ghosts. The sergeant could not remember ever hearing the General—as this wraith was generally called—give an order to anyone, or even speak.

The sergeant's mild attitude encouraged Hal to question him further. "If this General says nothing and does nothing—why is he commander?"

"Because the Father of Battles says so."

"Oh."

"Haraldur, it's not your place as a new recruit to criticize our methods of organization. Rather, you should be learning them, and doing your best to fit in. You don't want to be promoted, do you?" The question made it sound like some exotic punishment.

"No, I don't think so. Since you put it that way, Sergeant, I don't believe I do. So I will try to learn your ways, as you recommend. If in the process of learning, any more questions should come up, I suppose I can bring them to you?"

The sergeant gave him a severe look. "First, just try to forget the things that bother you. Let that be the first thing you learn."

"Right."

Sergeant Nosam relaxed a trifle. "This really isn't a bad outfit, Haraldur. I've been in a lot worse in my time."

"You must tell me about them some day, Sergeant."

"I may do that. Here, if you just go along, as a rule nobody will bother you."

"What more could a man ask?"

Hal and Baldur soon learned that none of their living colleagues had been here in Valhalla for more than a few years, and their average length of service was probably less than a full year. There were probably many real deaths among them, but few of these were casualties from actual fighting. Hal supposed it would be easy to get lost when attempting to escape.

On the evening of their first day of duty as members of Wodan's guard—or as Wodan's captives, but it didn't help to view things that way—Hal and Baldur got their first look at Wodan's great hall. Baldur at first refused to dignify the place by that name, but it was the chamber where the Heroes were expected to put in an appearance every night, for a meal that was often a poor excuse for a feast, enlivened by some sad revelry.

This chamber had thick stone walls, like most of the rest of Wodan's stronghold, and like the rest was well on the way to falling into ruin. Hal thought it must have been designed and built many long years ago, and for some lesser purpose. There was a distinct lack of grandeur. This portion of the stronghold did have the great advantage of a nearly intact roof. Two functioning fireplaces, with one of Loki's roaring, fuelless fires in each, kept the worst of the freezing cold at bay. Hal could see that one good reason for coming to the great hall each night was that two fires made it marginally warmer than the barracks, despite the ruinous condition of the walls.

Half a dozen trestle tables, long, worn, stained, and old, were not only carved with many initials, but much hacked and battered around the edges, suggesting that mealtime was not always peaceful. Sixty or seventy men could easily have been accommodated around the tables, but less than a third of that number were on hand. Once in a while the sergeant urged them to spread out, occupying a greater number of benches, as if he wanted to make it look like the whole room was truly occupied. Here and there the figures of wraiths appeared, filling in empty seats.

Veterans informed the latest recruits that Wodan himself was usually, though not always, in attendance at the nightly gatherings they called his feasts, not at any of the wobbly tables, but sitting gloomily on a high, thronelike chair positioned midway between the fires. Old hands said that the quality of the food and drink would vary wildly and unpredictably from one night to the next. At intervals poor music squawked and wailed, provided by serf attendants with stringed instruments and horns. Hal thought he saw a wraith musician or two, but could not tell if their instruments were making real sounds.

"This can't be *all*, can it?" Hal murmured when he had looked the place over. "This is supposed to be Wodan's entire harvest of Heroes, going back to the beginning of time?"

Baldur shook his head decisively. "It cannot be. This is some elaborate device for testing us."

Sometimes the wraith figures responded when spoken to, lips moving and producing hollow, distant voices. Hal never heard more than a word or two from them, not enough to let him decide if what they said made sense; but he had the impression that no real thought or feeling was behind their words. And when he steeled his nerves to touch one, his hand passed right through, his palm and fingers appearing brightly lighted when inside the spectral body.

To Hal the most realistic of them suggested reflections in a fine mirror, rather than flesh and blood.

Sometimes Baldur was greatly bothered by the wraiths, and kept nagging Hal with unanswerable questions. "If these ghosts come from some strange device, what power sustains it?"

Now and then Hal saw in a wraith some resemblance to someone he had known in life, once to a man he knew to be dead. But he told himself firmly that it was not truly the man himself who walked, but only an image, like a reflection in a pond.

Hal realized that this explanation tended to leave uncertain the fate, the nature, of other individuals . . . he told Baldur he had heard wild stories of certain folk down in Tartarus, people once alive who had passed through the gates of death but still retained their solid, breathing bodies. Sufficient life remained in these dwellers in the Underworld to allow them to move and speak. And Hal had even heard one tale to the effect that when some of these were able to regain the surface of the earth, they were not much the worse for their dread experience.

"Who has ever visited the Underworld and returned, to bring such reports?"

"Not I." Hal shuddered. "I told you that these are only wild stories."

On almost every evening (excepting only those occasional times when Wodan for some unexplained reason did not attend) events in the great hall followed pretty much the same routine. Several times during the course of each nightly carousal, Wodan urged his followers to stand on their feet and laugh, to empty their flagons and sing a rousing song. There arose a thin chorus of broken and wavering voices, creating echoes that soon were lost, drifting away through the cracked stonework high above. Even with one or two men roaring loudly, the overall sound of the song was never more than feeble at its best. The serfs, or the wraith musicians, were still making most of the noise.

Something made Hal look up, into the dim, broken vaulting high above; he felt slightly cheered to see that a bird had flown in, but a better look convinced him that it was a bat.

Now and then a chunk of stone, perhaps disturbed by bats or birds or gusts of wind, or simply coming loose, came falling from the heights to strike with a vicious crack on floor or furniture. Hal decided he'd keep his helmet on.

Strong drink, generally mead, was magically provided, though not on any dependable schedule, and never served by wraiths or soldiers, but only by creeping, starveling serfs. The servers staggered and stumbled as if they were helping themselves when out of Wodan's sight, for which Hal could not blame them. On some nights, the casks and flagons on the tables were filled with all the fermented honey that any man could drink.

After his first cup, Hal made a face. "Is there never any wine?"

"No wine," one of his new mates told him. "Wodan does not consider it a proper drink. Mead is for true Heroes."

On other evenings there was nothing in the men's flagons but weak beer or water. When there was enough mead to let them do so, most of the men generally drank themselves into a stupor.

All too often, the new recruits were told, the rations of real food tended to be scanty. Wodan's quartermaster department was nonexistent, except for the occasional magical efforts of the god himself. Wodan simply never made much of an effort to equip or strengthen his captive army. His magic had grown as erratic as his thinking.

Wodan himself always drank mead, as befitted his legendary reputation, according to which he never ate. Hal was vaguely relieved to note that in practice the god speared some of the choice food morsels for himself—it made the All-Highest seem more human and therefore more fallible.

Though the food varied wildly in quality, the dishes and knives and goblets were consistently magnificent. Hal thought some of the plate might be worth as much as the damned disappearing horseshoes; but the dishes would be harder to carry and more readily missed.

None of the Valkyries ever showed up for the nightly feast, and no one seemed to be expecting them. Hal saw no reason to hope that any of them would accept the idea that solacing the Heroes was part of their duties.

Wodan, when addressing his troops, spoke to his poor handful as if they represented a mighty host. He repeatedly announced it as his own sacred duty, and also his solemn fate, that he must do his best to amass an army for some climactic battle against an opponent of shadowy reality. The god of war was convinced that on that day the treacherous god Loki would be one of his opponents.

At least once an evening he broke off to ask: "Have any of you who feast and drink with me tonight learned aught of the whereabouts of Loki the Treacherous?" And with his one eye Wodan searched the thin ranks of his guard.

On each of the several nights that Hal heard this question asked, the large room remained profoundly silent.

Some members of the guard of honor talked of Loki, as of some being with whom they were almost familiar.

He was a god, that much was certain. But he had now become the enemy of his former colleagues.

Each night, when Wodan had finished with his futile questions, and produced from somewhere an ancient-looking scroll, and unrolled it, a silence fell in the great hall.

Presently the god began to read:

". . . in that evil day, Loki's wolf-child Fenris will lead the monsters of disorder to blot out the Sun and Moon.

"Rising from the sea, the great snake Jormungand will try to swallow up the Earth."

Hal raised his head and began to listen. He had heard that name before.

". . . meanwhile his demon officers will sweep out of the Underworld with an army of ghosts and monsters. Then will follow a tremendous battle, in which the great gods and their enemies will destroy each other. The dead bodies will be consumed in a terrible fire that will engulf the universe and drown its ashes in the sea of anarchy."

Obviously Wodan took his legends very seriously, and this one was fascinating in what it suggested; but still Hal's attention kept being drawn away from Wodan's words to Corporal Bran. Bran always sat listening to the reading with rapt attention, eyes shining, his broad shoulders swaying slightly, as if he dreamed of swinging weapons. This was evidently the high point of the corporal's day, every day. Tonight Bran was murmuring something, in a kind of counterpoint to the reading itself; the sound of his voice was so soft it was smothered by Wodan's stage-whisper, but something gave Hal the impression that the corporal was whispering some kind of prayer.

Meanwhile the god's voice rumbled on. "Know that before these things can come to pass, there will be savage wars all across the world, and a time when each man seeks revenge upon another. The ties of kinship will be dissolved, and the crimes of murder and incest will be common . . . the stars will fall from the sky, and the entire earth will quake and quiver . . . all monsters bound beneath the world will be set free. The . . . sea rises to engulf the land, and on the flood the ship Naglfar is launched . . . fashioned from the fingernails of dead men. It carries a crew of Giants, with Loki as their steersman."

Hadn't the gnomes included Giants in their catalog of enemies? Hal thought he could remember something of the kind from his brief visit to their village.

Wodan had concluded the night's reading, and sat staring into space, as if in contemplation of the horror and glory of the events to come. Looking round his own table, Hal was struck by the absence of two men. "Where's Baedeker?" he asked the man next to him in a low voice. "And Baldur?"

The other whispered back: "Baedeker was too sick to make it out of the barracks tonight. Baldur stayed with him. If anyone should ask, they're both on special duty."

Soon the evening had frayed out to nothingness in its usual way. Wodan had departed and all were free to leave the great hall, Hal returned to the barracks.

There he found Baldur, sitting beside the dying man. Sergeant Nosam had also come in and was standing by. As Hal entered, the man

on the bunk murmured a few words, something that made Baldur burst
out with: "Wodan will not let you die!"

Hal and the sergeant looked at each other, but neither of them bothered to contradict Baldur. Baedeker, his breath rasping in his throat, was
gazing off into the distance, through the stone walls, into some country
that he alone could see.

Presently Corporal Bran came in and joined the group. Standing at
the foot of the bunk, Bran in a firm voice but with gentle words tried
to urge the prostrate man to pull himself together and return to duty.

Baedeker gave him a fleeting glance, and got out a few words: "It's
no good, Corporal."

Bran looked nervous. "That is no way for a man to die. You
shouldn't just lie there like that, on a bed of straw." With a sudden
movement he unsheathed a knife, and held it out, hilt first. "Here. Get
up and fight me, I'll give you a proper end."

Baedeker did not try to move. He had resumed his staring into the
distance, as if he and Bran were now a million miles apart.

Sergeant Nosam intervened. "Bran, I want you to go up and take
the high lookout for a while. I mean on top of the keep. Relieve whoever
is on duty now."

Bran only looked at him, as if his mind was far away. Then he
looked back to Baedeker on his bunk.

It was the first time Hal had seen Nosam nervous. "Do you hear
me, Corporal? I have given you an order."

At last Bran nodded. "I hear you, Sergeant. The high lookout."
Obedience to orders was part of the great scheme of things, ordained
by the All-Highest, not to be disputed. Bran slowly turned and took
himself away.

The sick man's breath, already labored, began to rasp and rattle in
his throat.

And then, before Hal had really been expecting it to stop, it stopped.

No one put the event into words, but no one had any doubt of what
had happened. Baldur sat stunned on the edge of the cot. The sergeant
stood by with nothing to say for the moment, only looking a little grim-
mer than usual.

Hal drew a deep breath. "What's the usual procedure now?"

Nosam seemed grateful for this practical attitude. "Simple rites are
usually conducted around midnight." The sergeant looked all around
him, into darkness, as if seeking some sign that would tell him how far
the night had progressed. "Guess there's no use waiting. Just wrap him
up in his blanket and bring him along."

Baldur was shaking his head slowly. "Is there to be no ceremony?"

"If you want some ritual, make one. But I wouldn't want to remind the Old Man—or Bran—that people actually die here. They know it, but they don't want to know it, if you know what I mean. They manage to forget the fact, in between the times it happens."

Baldur did not respond to that. Hal thought: *Who would he pray to, if we did have a ritual? Wodan?*

Hal moved to pick the body up, but Baldur stepped ahead of him, and gathered up the underweight corpse, wrapped in a thin blanket, to carry it in his arms.

"Follow me."

The sergeant led them out of the rear door of the barracks, through cold and darkness, past the malodorous latrine, then through another unheated vault of stone and out of doors again.

As they walked, Hal's guide pointed with a hand out over the parapet.

"The plain of Asgard's out there. Had we proper light now, you could see it."

"The plain of Asgard?"

"You know, it comes up in the Old Man's readings. Or maybe he hasn't gone through that part of the book since you've been here. That's the great stretch of flat land where the last battle will be fought."

The night was well advanced by now, and Hal took note of the stage of the waning moon. It had been just full, he recalled, on the night when he and Baldur began their walk from the gnomes' village to glorious Valhalla. Somehow he had lost track of the days, but there could hardly have been a great many of them.

Presently they came to a dim, chest-high parapet.

"Here's where we usually put them over," the sergeant said. "The deepest drop is just below. So lift him up, and let him find his rest. Then we'd best be getting right back to the barracks. I've got to see the Old Man yet tonight, and we're due for an early drill tomorrow."

Hal asked: "You're going to see Wodan about—?"

"Not this. No, never about anything like this. Unless he heard it from someone else. Then I'd have to answer questions. Somehow come up with answers."

Someone was still holding the body. "Where do I put—?"

The sergeant patted the top of the parapet. "Just set him up there, I say. Then give him a little shove. There's a good thousand feet of air to cool his fever before the trees and rocks will catch him."

Baldur complied. Then just at the last moment he reached forward with one nervous hand, to tuck in a fold of blanket, as if in the name of neatness or of comfort. It was the sergeant who stepped forward to push the bundle off the wall, over the precipice, to vanish in dead silence. Hal found himself listening for some faint sound of impact, but then he turned away before it came.

———

Next morning, immediately after the early drill, Alvit appeared, and after a few words with the sergeant took Hal aside to talk with him.

He was half expecting to be questioned about Baedeker's death, but Alvit did not mention it.

"What do you think of Wodan's army now?" Alvit asked when the two of them were alone, walking through one of the snowy courtyards. The sun was out this morning, and the trampled whiteness underfoot was turning into slush. "Have you perhaps found the place you have been looking for, here in Valhalla?"

Hal gave the Valkyrie a hard stare, trying to figure her out. "I thought you were willing for us to escape."

"I was, but I have changed my mind."

"I don't understand."

"I have been watching you, Haraldur, and I think you are a real soldier, not just a thug or an unlucky drifter, like most of these. You probably have it in you to be a real leader. To command troops in combat."

Hal stopped walking, and shook his head. "My present position does not afford much scope for leadership."

"Having experience as a common soldier in Wodan's ranks should work to your advantage. You must know the organization before you can be placed in command of it."

He had started to walk again, but now he stumbled and almost fell. "What are you talking about?"

"I am thinking, hoping, praying to all the gods I know, that there might be time to turn this feeble remnant into a real army before it must enter battle." Alvit looked back at the remnants of the morning's drill, a small mob slowly breaking up, and shook her head. "I know it will take months, at least, but we might have that long. Perhaps even a year, if we are lucky."

Hal's curiosity was growing. "Tell me more."

"The point is that we need leaders as well as men. Nosam is too thoughtful and cautious, Blackie too sly, and Bran—I think could not be trusted. And they are all too small in mind to be commanders. Baldur may perhaps someday grow big enough."

"And you think I'm big enough now?"

"I think you may be if you try. In good time we will see. For now, be patient."

━━━━━━━

Alvit's hints gave Hal something to think about as he trudged back to the barracks. It came to him that she might be the true commander here, managing things for Wodan in his dotage. Was the Great Game of power Hal thought he had abandoned about to catch him up again? He was still tired of trying to be a hero.

But Alvit, herself, now . . . she was something for a man to really think about. He could well imagine himself trying to talk her out of keeping any foolish vows of virginity she might have made . . . as Baldur must have done with Brunhild.

12

ON THE NIGHT after Baedeker's death, the evening feast was delayed, and when the food and drink at last were served, both Wodan and Sergeant Nosam were absent.

Corporal Blackie had been left in charge. He and Bran were sitting two tables away from Hal and Baldur, facing in Hal's direction.

Hal thought the food was a little worse than average tonight, though plentiful enough. But the mead was of reasonable quality, and fairly plentiful. The music seemed even feebler than usual, though Bran several times ordered the musicians to play louder and faster.

When the faint hum of talk in the big room suddenly ceased, Hal looked up to see that the pair of gnomes were standing, unbidden and unexpected, in the entrance to the great hall. It was the first time he had ever seen them here.

Blackie growled at them. "Well? What is it?"

Moving a step forward, Andvari asked pardon for intruding, then said they had come not so much to complain as to beg for food, because no one was feeding them lately, and they were still forbidden to leave Valhalla. He doubted that Wodan really wanted to starve them to death. They were almost ready to run out, to just leave anyway.

Hal stood up and scraped food from serving dishes on his own table onto two clean, incongruously elegant plates. Then he carried the plates over to the gnomes, who thanked him profusely, sat down at once, and began to eat.

Baldur tonight had consumed more than his usual share of the drink of true Heroes. When Hal came back to his own table, Baldur waved an arm to indicate the scene before them. "I am now certain of it, Hal.

This—all this nonsense we have here—it cannot be the real thing—all this—it must be a test, I tell you, Hal."

"You've said it, youngster." Looking over from two tables away, Bran vehemently agreed. "I don't believe a man can really die here, the straw death, in his bed. Some kind of lousy magic trick was worked on us. And I don't think Wodan's really sick." His voice was challenging, belligerent, and none of the eyewitnesses to death corrected him. No one was going to try to force Bran to face anything.

"We are being tested," Baldur repeated.

It seemed that Bran, too, had been having more than usual to drink. He slammed a big fist on the worn table. "That's it, you're right, I've said it all along, we are being tested. Those who prove loyal will win to the true reward at last. True Heroes should be fighting every day and every night. Not this . . ." His face and his gesture spoke eloquently of his disgust.

Corporal Blackie, seated at yet another table, had a contribution to make. "If we're being tested, though, how long is the trial to go on? I've been here a year, and all who were here when I arrived are dead now. All of those who tried to escape are dead, and so are many who did not. What kind of a test is that?"

Blackie looked round, as if seeking an answer to his question, and his gaze fell on the unusual visitors. "What's this? Who invited in these bloody dwarfs? Why are they eating our food?"

Hal looked over at him. "I gave it to them, Corporal."

There was a sudden tension in the room, to which the gnomes seemed utterly oblivious. Ivaldr, usually silent, raised a plaintive voice to complain that someone had taken away their essential gold. Without it they could not complete their work, and until their work was finished they could not leave.

He concluded: "We tried to explain all this to Wodan, but he just walked past us as if we did not exist."

Andvari chimed in, shaking his head unhappily. "And all the great god said to us was: 'You are always complaining about something of the kind.' "

Ivaldr was nodding. "I don't know about calling him 'the great god.' Wodan did not look healthy."

That got Bran's attention back. "Careful what you say about the All-Highest," he rumbled.

The Earthdwellers must have heard the words, but they seemed deaf to tone, insensitive to tension. They were busy gulping mead and belching.

"But what can you expect," Andvari concluded, speaking to the

room at large, "from a god of crazy berserkers?" The little man threw
the word out very casually, as if he had no idea of what it really meant.

Hal held his breath. From the corner of his eye he had seen Bran's
head turn round. Suddenly Bran had started breathing deeply and
heavily, and when he spoke again his voice had changed. It was as if a
different man now looked out of his scarred face.

"You have blasphemed my god. And for that you must die, small
man."

This time the message was in the simple words, and came through
clearly. Open-mouthed, the two gnomes sat there looking numbly back
at Bran.

On the bench beside Hal, Baldur seemed not to know whether to
laugh or take alarm.

Hal was very far from laughing. His brain was working rapidly,
trying to calculate the chance of summoning a Valkyrie before someone
got killed. He could see no chance of any other kind of help. There
would be no use trying to reach the sergeant, who was almost certainly
busy attending the god.

The music had long since faltered to a halt. Standing up, Hal called
Bran's name, sending the one word clearly into an aching silence. The
big man's head turned.

Hal told him in a flat voice: "The little one you challenge would
not be here bothering you, were it not for me. So bring to me any
complaint that you might have."

When Bran said nothing, but only continued to stare at him, Hal
added: "You said you admired my honored helmet? Take it, and welcome. A gift." That was the best distraction Hal could think of. He
pulled the helmet off and tossed it across the width of the two tables, so it
bounced on the table where Bran was sitting, and then onto the floor.

He might have spared himself the effort. Bran's gaze did not turn
to follow the clanging, bounding thing at all.

Without another word Bran, moving slowly and steadily, got to his
feet. He stood much taller than Hal, though as Hal had already noted,
there was not that much difference in length of arm.

Hal wanted to try more soothing words, but he could find none, and
suddenly there was no time. Bran was standing on the table at which
he had been sitting. From Hal's position he looked about twelve feet
tall; and when Bran pulled the short sword from its scabbard at his side,
that made him look no smaller.

Without a pause he charged across the tabletops at Hal, sword raised
and howling like a winter wind out of the north.

When a man came leaping through the air at you, the traditional effective counter was to get out of his way by stepping sideways. Hal's first concern was getting his feet and legs clear of tables and benches. Bran's weight splintered a bench when he came down on it. By that time, Hal was out of reach, axe in one hand, knife in the other, trying to find some open space.

Bran came bounding after him, quick as a bouncing ball. This time Hal stepped into the rush, blocked sword with axe, feinted one way and thrust another, feeling his dagger go deep into the big man's side, sliding through tough cloth, digging on into meat. The cut would have brought down any normal man, but it had little immediate effect on a berserker's strength or energy.

Hal had to break away. The next rush forced him backward, and in the swift exchange that followed he neatly broke Bran's sword-blade, catching it in the angle between the head and the tough handle of the war-hatchet.

But to berserker Bran a broken sword meant nothing. He still came after Hal, in one hand the stump of his snapped blade, the other armed with a yard-long wooden splinter, snatched up from a broken bench.

Men were yelling, scrambling desperately right and left and backward, falling to get out of the way. The howling Berserk kept on coming, too fast for Hal to make a conscious plan. He parried, and struck, and struck again. It seemed like two swords coming at him, not one broken one. His forehand swing with the axe was blocked with Bran's forearm on the shaft, the impact feeling as if he'd hit a piece of wood. But then, backhanding with the blunt end, Hal got home solidly on flesh and bone.

A broken leg was not going to stop death attacking, but perhaps would slow it down a bit. Now Hal could see a jagged end of white bone, sticking right out through skin and cloth above Bran's knee. Blood from a wounded arm spouted at Hal, and he realized that Bran was spraying him with Bran's own blood, trying to blind his vision.

Fine dishes, goblets, crashed and clattered underfoot, scattering their contents. In the background, Hal saw another fight had broken out, a skirmish anyway. Baldur, his sword drawn, seemed to be holding off Blackie—and another man was down, not moving.

Hal's foot slipped, whether in spilled soup or blood it mattered not, and in a helpless instant he went down hard on his back. Death leaped upon him, still spraying blood but never weakening, grappling with inhuman strength. The face of death was inches from Hal's own. Teeth tore at Hal's collar, trying to reach his throat. With an all-out surge of effort, Hal got his hickory axe-handle wedged into the open mouth.

In his paroxysm, Bran had screwed one of his eyes shut, as if in unconscious imitation of Wodan's one-eyed glare. Bran's wounded arms still clutched and tore. He howled no longer, but his breath sobbed like a great wind.

Somewhere inside Hal, his own berserker fury had come alive. Enough of it, perhaps. Slowly, slowly his arms straightened, gripping the axe-handle near both ends, forcing the frenzied killer up and back, throwing him violently off so Hal could move again.

His own breath sobbing, Hal staggered and scrambled to his feet. Bran came up right after Hal, almost with him, still quick on his broken leg.

Hal could see it, looking into the one open eye: Bran was dead but he would not fall.

Baldur, you stupid sod, now is the time to hit him from behind with all you've got. If Hal had had the breath to speak, he would have roared the words aloud. But what he could see now and then in the corner of his eye assured him bleakly that no help was on the way. Baldur seemed to have his hands full at the moment, holding other men at bay, those who would have come in on the berserker's side.

Bran had lost his remnant of a sword, but had somehow rearmed himself in both hands with more splintered wood. He still came on relentlessly, stumbling and lurching on broken bones. The lungs of the dead man were still laboring, forcing in and out the air the dead man's muscles needed for their work. This would be Bran's last fight, but while an opponent still faced him, it seemed the spirit of Wodan would not let him fall.

Hal gripped his axe in two hands now . . . a weapon so heavy that it seemed to need two hands to lift . . . and Bran, his body still moving, though no man could say how, was coming after him again. Hal wondered if berserkers had to breathe at all . . .

Later, Hal could not even remember what final blow had brought the monster down to stay.

Berserkers were not gods. And in the end mere human flesh and bone must find its limits and fall down.

———

Hal dropped the axe and fell almost on top of him.

He was gasping, gasping, gasping, and thought he could not have made another move to save his life; Baldur's grandmother could have finished him, right there, with a knitting needle.

He dared not wait until his breath came back, he had no choice. As soon as he stirred and tried to move again, the world immediately started to turn gray before him, as in the beginning of a faint. But he could not allow himself the luxury of anything like that.

Slowly, laboriously, Hal picked up his knife, which had fallen nearby. With his good dagger in his hand, he began the process of slicing and chopping off the berserker's head.

Baldur's hand was tugging at his arm. "What are you doing, Hal? He's dead. He's dead!"

Hal was shaking his head *no*. That was easier than trying to talk. The job done, Hal heaved his grisly trophy into Loki's fireplace. Automatically he sheathed his knife. Breathing was still a full-time job, but now he could make words. "It's the only way. To make sure. Doesn't get up again. And come after us."

Baldur had put away his own sword and was retrieving Hal's helmet for him, putting it on Hal's head. No one else was moving to interfere. Now Baldur was handing him the axe. Hal noted dimly that one of Bran's teeth was still embedded in the handle.

"Hal, you're all blood. Can you walk?"

It took Hal two more breaths to be able to spare the air for two more words: "Not mine."

Both arms still functioned, and both legs. By some miracle he wasn't hurt, not really hurt apart from scrapes and bruises caught from floor and furniture, and from the sheer gripping strength of the berserker's hands.

Someone must have run for Sergeant Nosam, because here the sergeant was, staring in cold horror at the ruin, the dead and wounded men. *Let's see you keep all this from Wodan, Sergeant.* But then maybe he could. Maybe he could.

So far Nosam was saying nothing, and Hal stepped over a body he did not recognize, brushed past the sergeant and the surviving corporal, Blackie, white-faced and clutching at a wounded arm.

"Baldur, this way." Now Hal was almost ready to breathe and talk at the same time. "We go to the Horses."

At last the sergeant found his voice. He only asked: "What happened to the gnomes?"

It was Baldur who turned to give the answer: "I saw them running out. They'll be on their way home."

———

In the stable, Baldur went immediately to start checking out the Horses. As soon as he was out of sight, Hal, now able to walk unaided and almost straight, moved with deliberate speed to recover the golden saddlebags. Miracle of miracles, almost as soon as he looked for them, there they were! He could only think that someone—quite likely Alvit— had simply lifted them from the Horse and set them down against a nearby wall, where they were inconspicuous though not exactly hidden. In the madhouse that was Valhalla, nothing like a thorough search had been conducted.

Besides being equipped with a spear holder, each set of saddlebags came with a water bottle made of some treated skin. The bottles were empty now, but once out of Valhalla it ought to be easy enough to get them filled.

Baldur soon returned, leading the almost-familiar Gold Mane and Cloudfoot. While the young man soothed the animals, Hal quickly strapped on two sets of saddlebags, making sure that Cloudfoot got the gold. He was about to announce that they were ready, when a glance through a nearby doorway spotted something that made him risk delay.

Quickly he muttered to Baldur: "Hold it one second, I'll be right back!"

The doorway led, as Hal had instantly surmised, into what had to be the Valkyries' armory, or at least a branch thereof, conveniently situated here near the stable. What he had glimpsed from outside was a high rack, in which half a dozen of the Valkyries' Spears stood waiting, unguarded and available.

Hal needed only a moment to snatch a Spear and stumble on his bruised legs back to the courtyard. But it was a moment ill-spent, or so it seemed. When Hal emerged, almost staggering, Spear in hand, he saw a sight that made him draw in breath for a desperate yell.

Baldur, not hearing Hal's last words or choosing to ignore them, had mounted the wrong Horse, the one that bore the gold, and was already on his way. But Hal choked off his yell before it could get started, for Baldur was too far away to hear, and too far away to turn back if he did. Besides, an all-out bellow might bring discovery and destruction on them both.

Hal had just dragged his battered frame aboard Gold Mane when Alvit suddenly appeared, on foot and out of breath. For a moment Hal was ready to use his borrowed Spear against the Valkyrie, but her first words convinced him that there was no need.

"There is no help for it, Hal, now you must flee. The sergeant will tell Wodan that Bran and the other man who fell are chasing two deserters." When Hal would have turned his mount away, her hand fell on his arm in a hard grip. "Where are you going?"

"To Loki's fire. Baldur won't go anywhere else."

"Then follow him, and I will meet you when I can. I'll try to bring some food."

13

BALDUR WAS URGING his Horse to its best speed, Cloudfoot's long legs working at a hard gallop, reaching out with each stride to take their magical grips upon huge chunks of air and pull them back. Every time the soles of the two hind hooves turned up toward Hal, the gold shoes on them caught dull gleams from the first horizontal rays of the rising sun, seeming to symbolize his vanishing fortune.

Vaguely Hal realized that if the sun was up already, last night's ritual feast must have started some time well after midnight. It seemed that time itself, like many other things, was coming askew in Valhalla, or at least in the minds of its inmates. Meanwhile he was yelling in Gold Mane's ear, kicking the animal in the ribs, in an effort to overtake his colleague. The trouble was that Hal's mount was slower, though not by much. Trusting that a Horse could be controlled in the same way as a mundane beast, he kicked Gold Mane some more, and shouted out a string of oaths. Their speed increased.

For Hal, the strangest thing about the ride, at first, was not the visible emptiness beneath him. He had been expecting that. It was that his ears kept anticipating the beat of hooves and metal shoes on hard ground—and there was no sound but only the whisper of the passing wind, soft as a woman's breath, and now and then the jingle of an iron buckle on a saddlebag.

In cold blood he might not have been able to force himself to dare this ride. But now with the dead berserker and Wodan and slavery behind him, he was ready to dare anything to get away.

By the time Hal had taken a few gasping breaths, Wodan's stronghold had fallen completely behind them, while ahead and below almost nothing was immediately visible in the gray light of dawn but jagged rock and terrifying space.

<hr />

As if to avoid some unseen obstacle, maybe a passing bird, Gold Mane shifted his flight path abruptly, so sharply that Hal's horned helmet, so narrowly saved from the berserker, tilted clean off his head. His instinct was to make a grab for the helmet before it got away, but somehow neither of his hands was willing to let go its grip on coarse Horsehair. Over the next few seconds Hal grew dizzy watching his prized head-piece grow smaller and smaller, becoming a barely visible dot before it disappeared into a distant cloud.

The falling body of a man, just like the helmet, would take a long, long time to reach even that cloud. Hal slumped forward, clasping his arms around the racing Horse's neck.

But he was not going to fall. He was not going to fall.

What was he *doing*, trying to fly like a bird on the strength of unknown magic? Had he gone completely mad, ready to kill himself trying to regain a few handfuls of stolen gold? Helplessly he yearned after the modest treasure so neatly packaged on the back of Baldur's Horse. And Baldur of course was completely ignorant of the fact that Cloudfoot was carrying gold—or was he? No, Hal had to believe he was. By this time he was certain that he knew Baldur pretty well.

Sternly commanding himself not to look down, Hal managed to overcome his vertigo. Now, glancing back over his shoulder as the clouds flew by, he was heartened by being able to detect no signs of immediate pursuit. To his surprise, they had already covered so much distance that he could no longer see Valhalla at all, but only the moun-tain peaks among which it nested. As far as he could tell, Alvit was the only one in the disorganized stronghold who knew that they had gone.

<hr />

Hal's next shout to Baldur died out awkwardly as Hal's throat spasmed—on reaching a break in the fluffy clouds beneath him, he was suddenly able to see only too clearly the immense altitude that he had now reached. Far, far below him sprawled a wilderness of jagged rock, a scene that lurched and jiggled with the onrushing movement of his steed. Thousands of feet, maybe a mile of empty air, loomed below, a distance that made his gut tighten in anticipation of a fall.

Once again he clutched desperately with both hands at the animal's mane. The strangeness, the unfamiliarity of the Horse that he was riding made the experience all the more terrible—he had to close his eyes again to reassure himself, concentrating on the solid feel of the galloping animal between his thighs.

But voluntary blindness was not going to ease his terror for more than a moment; his imagination was all too ready to furnish the space in front of him with objects of dread. Hal opened his eyes again and saw nothing but rushing clouds ahead, and the galloping figure of Baldur's Horse. This time he did not look down.

———

The world spread out before the flying riders in the dawn of a clear winter morning was an amazing sight, and Hal was awed by this borrowed, secondhand power of the god—for a moment he was utterly terrified by his own audacity.

But his situation as a captive in Valhalla had been bad, horrible to the point where he would have tried anything to escape. Even fighting a berserker, though that had not been his conscious plan when the fight started.

He thought there was no telling how Wodan was going to react on learning of the violence and death erupting in the mess, costing him at least his favorite berserker. Probably the Father of Battles had already been informed. Or even now someone might be bringing him the news. Of course, in the legendary version of Valhalla, beating a true Hero to death and cutting off his head should cause him no more than a little pain and inconvenience—nothing to lay him up for long. Combat in Wodan's realm, as it was so widely celebrated in song and story, was never more than playacting.

There was one more considerable difference between romance and reality. In the legends, no one ever thought of trying to escape from Valhalla. Well, at least this time Wodan would not be able to send out his favorite berserker to track down and dispose of the fugitives.

Which might mean that this time, the god would be conducting the chase in person. But maybe not. To Hal it seemed quite possible that Wodan would prefer the comfort of remaining in his private dreamworld, would refuse to consider the fact that his best berserker was gone for good. Instead the All-Highest would probably be looking forward to tonight's feast, anticipating a good discussion between the winner and loser of last night's rousing fight. And even the absence of both principals in that contest might not matter much; if neither man appeared tonight, the All-Seeing would be perfectly capable of imagining they were there.

Wodan's general ineffectiveness, his wandering attention whenever there were decisions to be made, gave Hal strong reason to hope. Unless someone forcibly brought the fact to his attention, it might be a long time before the befuddled Lord of Valhalla realized that two of his magic steeds were missing from their stalls and faced the fact that two of his exalted band of Heroes had forsaken their eternal reward for the fun of stealing a couple of Horses and a few pounds of gold.

And even if Wodan was ready to confront the truth, he might not be capable of doing anything about it—if only Hal and Baldur could get far enough away.

———

Looking back over his shoulder again, Hal's heart sank when he beheld what looked like a swarm of giant insects on his trail, great wings churning the air in flight. So much for his hope that there would be no pursuit. The insects looked like nothing he had ever seen before. But at least it was not a chariot that now came speeding after him, gaining ground—or air—seemingly with every vibration of what looked like a hundred blurring wings, propelling scores of bodies in a cloud. He could hope that it was only wraiths that followed, and he rejoiced that he had managed to borrow one of the Valkyries' Spears.

Rapidly the vague cloud of semitransparent entities drew nearer, traveling at truly frightening speed. When a whirling vortex of spectral wingbeats swirled around Hal, he resisted the impulse to draw his axe, and put his borrowed weapon to good use—at each touch of its point, an image exploded into nothingness. Though the Spear was unfamiliar in his hands, it proved formidably efficient, and what had been a whole formation of the speeding wraiths soon dwindled to a scattered few that gave up the chase and turned aside.

Before he could relax, he realized he was being pursued by yet more apparitions, traveling every bit as quickly as the first.

As this second wave of pursuit drew nearer, he was soon able to identify a pair of huge unnatural Ravens, with ten-foot wingspans. These came hurtling at him from both sides at once, pecking and slashing with huge beaks, evidently intent on forcing him to land or knocking him off his Horse.

Again he thanked all helpful gods for the mighty Spear. A mere touch from that glittering point produced an almost soundless explosion, obliterating one bird and then the other in a cloud of raven feathers, fragile debris dispersed at once by the rushing winds of the high air.

━━━━━━

Still, only a brief time had passed since the Horse first carried him aloft. The sun seemed to have advanced only a few of its own diameters above the eastern horizon, but Valhalla had fallen completely out of sight, and many miles of air had passed beneath their Horses' flying hooves. The mountains were distant, the valley of the Einar spread out beneath, and Baldur and Hal were drawing near their goal.

Despite Hal's efforts to catch up with his young companion, he had actually lost a little distance, and his shouts for Baldur to slow down a little had either gone unheard or were being ignored.

Studying the object of his pursuit, Hal noticed to his consternation that Baldur was now even slightly farther ahead of him, the young man's Horse still galloping through the air in the direction of the flaming clifftop, which was already noticeably nearer. After only an instant's hesitation, Hal urged his own mount in the same direction.

Of course Hal was looking forward to getting his hands once more on Cloudfoot's saddlebags, stuffed with gold; he thought he deserved that much compensation for long days of unjust imprisonment. But he had other goals in mind as well. Soon Loki's flames would be visible ahead.

Hal was also gripped by a vague, instinctive fear that Baldur, if left to his own devices, would be sure to make some horrible blunder that would result in their both being overtaken and punished by a vengeful god.

━━━━━━

Every time Hal looked over his shoulder he was faintly encouraged, because he could see only a rolling, low, uneven sea of clouds and distant mountains. Let more wraiths come if they would, and he would fight them off with his beautiful Spear; there was still no sign of the one pursuer he truly dreaded, the airborne chariot, pulled by an eight-legged Horse and occupied by Wodan himself.

Then a time came when his head turned again to look and his heart sank, when his eye was caught by distant movement in the sky. There came in view some flying object much too big to be a bird, and looking too solid to be another wraith. Something, just faintly visible between himself and the site of vanished Valhalla, was cruising along briskly on an angled course. What gave Hal hope was that fortunately it was not following directly on his and Baldur's airy trail. The distance was so great that Hal could barely make the object out. But he could tell that it was moving very fast.

Unhappily, Hal soon felt completely certain that it was a solid object, not a wraith, and also that it was indeed a chariot. But he could still hope that the speeding conveyance was not Wodan's. For one thing, this vehicle was of a lighter color than the black Hal remembered.

Every time he looked back, the chariot was somewhat closer, though it was still, thank all the Fates, not in direct pursuit. Hal thought he could see now that there was only a single occupant. It was being pulled by something—what appeared to be a pair of somethings . . . not cameloids or droms . . . certainly not an eight-legged Horse.

Whatever the vehicle was, and however it was being propelled, its course kept diverging more and more from Hal's and Baldur's. But still it was a worrisome sight.

———

Baldur must have caught sight of the same disturbing presence, and only moments after Hal did. For now the young man suddenly changed course, urged the speeding Cloudfoot in a different direction, heading away from the circle of flames.

Then Hal noticed another possible reason for Baldur's change of course: a small squadron of Valkyries were flying on their Horses near Loki's flames, actually circling them like half a dozen or more huge and glorious silver moths. One or two others were sitting their magic mounts on the ground of the clifftop, very near Loki's great ongoing demonstration.

Possibly these young women would share Alvit's cooperative attitude, but Hal was not ready to bet on it. Unless mortal men were armed with something much better than their own mundane weapons, they could expect no success at all in fighting against Valkyries. Hal did have a Spear, but still the odds would be prohibitively heavy against him.

———

When Baldur's mount went diving lower, Hal kept close behind him. Uncertain of how to order his Horse into a descent, he tried pushing gently forward on the animal's long neck. To his great relief he found that that technique worked beautifully.

Down they went, racing through deep vaults of vapor, to burst out at last through the lower surface of a broken layer of clouds. Presently they were quickly skimming low in the valley, about a mile from the cliff of fire.

Baldur, with Hal now very close behind him, guided his mount to a landing on the near shore of the broad Einar, on a bank thickly forested enough to offer some hope of concealment.

A few moments later, Hal guided his own mount to a soft landing at the same spot. At the moment of his own landing, Hal shut his eyes again and gripped his Horse's mane, but Gold Mane managed the business as complete routine. The long-missing sound of hoofbeats came almost as a shock to the ear. He resisted an impulse to immediately leap from his Horse's back and kiss the ground.

Here it seemed to Hal that they ought to be pretty effectively screened by the canopy of some tall evergreens with overhanging branches, long and thick enough to offer effective shelter against aerial observation.

Both Horses were as unexcited by the adventure of flight as if it had been a mere canter through a mountain meadow. Nor did they seem at all exhausted by the terrific speed they had achieved while airborne. They were ready to take a good drink from the shallow eddies of the Einar, and to enjoy some of the long soft grass that grew on the adjoining shore.

Hal, watching Baldur keenly as he approached him, could detect no evidence that the youth suspected anything about the treasure in his saddlebags, or that he had been seriously trying to leave Hal behind. Instead, Baldur looked up almost calmly as the northman appeared at his side and began a congratulatory greeting. The young man's eyes widened only when he caught sight of the stolen Spear that Hal had grounded in the handy holder strapped on with his saddlebags.

"What are you doing with that?" The joyous expression faded from Baldur's face, and his voice was grave.

"Oh, this little thing?" Hal seized the shaft of the Spear and shook it. "Don't let it upset you. I just thought I might need something of the kind. It really seemed of considerable importance that we should get clean away, even if someone tried to stop us. And it came in handy when I met those ghosts and the Ravens."

"What are you talking about?" It soon turned out that Baldur, intent as he was upon his goal, was not even aware that they had been pursued. When Hal had explained about the wraiths and Ravens, Baldur still frowned at the long weapon Hal was carrying.

"Yes, but . . ." he objected. "Alvit won't like it, that you took a Spear."

"You think someone will mistake me for a Valkyrie? Don't know what the Heroes on the battlefield would do if they saw me coming to carry them away."

"I should think they might be inspired to go on fighting."

"Huh. Well, this sticker saved our lives, my lad. But still I'll give it back, next time I see her. I'll gladly give her more than that, we owe the girl a lot."

Half-expecting Alvit to come in sight at any moment—she had said she'd meet them—Hal looked up at the rude canopy of pine branches, through which the sky was visible only in spots and fragments. "I'd say you picked a reasonably good place to land."

"Yes, I thought we had better wait until those Valkyries got out of our way—I'm not sure if they saw us or not." Baldur made no mention of seeing a chariot in the air. Hal hesitated over whether to tell his partner about it or not, then quickly decided to abide by his general rule: in case of uncertainty, keep quiet.

But there was one point he had to raise. "By the way—I thought you were going to take this Horse. The one I'm riding."

Baldur was gracious. "Why, I thought to leave Gold Mane to you. Being more or less used to real humans, he would be less likely to throw off a total stranger. Is there anything wrong with that?"

"No. Oh no, nothing. I see. Thank you. I appreciate it."

In any case they had got away, were free, and no harm done. Now Hal felt free to turn his thoughts to getting at the gold. Looking at Baldur, Hal was sure that the youth had no idea what was hidden in his saddlebags. He could think of no convincing reason to suggest that they switch Horses, and tried to come up with some more subtle method of regaining his lost loot. Meanwhile, both men had dismounted and were crouching by the river to fill their water bottles. Then, sprawling belly down on a flat rock, they drank directly from the stream.

Whether Hal was ever really going to be a rich man or not, the water of freedom had a good taste; he sat up, wiping mouth and beard with the back of his hand. It was, in a way, tiring to have to think of gold again. But he was spared the effort. Before he could decide on the best way to raise the subject with his companion, a lone rider in a flying Chariot burst out of a low cloud, descending rapidly toward them.

14

THE HORSES HAD been quiet, but now they froze, heads turned in the same direction. Hal and Baldur, both on their feet again, stood beside their respective mounts, staring at the one who had just arrived.

The chariot in itself was almost ordinary in appearance, little more than a big cart—but it was pulled through the air by two animals that Hal could only have described as giant goats, the size of cameloids. It was the same strange object that Hal had earlier seen flying at a distance. No more ordinary was the single figure occupying the vehicle. Thank all the Fates, it was not Wodan. But it was certainly not the shape of a mere mortal human either.

"It is Thor." Baldur's whisper was almost as awe-stricken as if this were the first god he had ever seen.

And Hal had to admit the young man must be right. The Thunderer in his goat cart came casually coasting down, steering easily in under the canopy of trees, the wheels of his vehicle spinning just as if they worked against a solid road, instead of air.

The figure in the chariot was male and powerful-looking, to say the least. Red of hair and beard, and with ruddy cheeks that gave him a vaguely jovial look. His head was covered by a broad-brimmed hat, and he was otherwise dressed in sumptuous furs, similar to those that Wodan generally wore, but better cared for. Thor's arms, almost inhumanly thick with bone and muscle, were each encircled by metal bracelets, one gold, the other silver. The god was also wearing dark gloves that seemed to be made of iron, all joints and scales like the finest armor, for when he pulled one off and threw it down, it landed with a metallic thud.

Having brought his vehicle to a stop, Thor looked at Hal and Baldur without surprise, as if he had been more or less expecting to find this pair of mortal humans here. But his interest in them seemed to be only incidental.

Thor's voice was incongruously light and high. "I noticed you fellows galloping across the sky on Horses, but somehow you don't have the look of Valkyries. Is there serious trouble in Valhalla, or what? I'd go see for myself, but I might not be exactly welcome."

The two mortals looked at each other. Baldur's chin was trembling, as if he were trying to speak but found himself unable.

That was all right with Hal, who readily assumed the role of spokesman. "Wodan still occupies his throne, my lord," he grated out. "So I suppose it depends what you mean by serious."

Thor made a little dismissive gesture with one huge hand, as if to say the business was not worth worrying about. "Really none of my affair what goes on in Valhalla," he assured Hal. Then his voice took on a keener edge. "I don't suppose either of you've seen anything of that bastard Loki?"

"Not that we know of, sir," said Hal. And Baldur silently shook his head.

Thor sighed. Just like any ordinary man who had been riding too long in a cramped position, the god descended from his chariot, letting the reins fall carelessly to the ground, and demonstrated to the onlookers that he was not overly tall, at least not for a deity. As the god enjoyed a good stretch, Hal took note of the heavy Hammer, bigger than a blacksmith's sledge, that hung at his belt just as the hatchet rode on Hal's.

Myelnir. Hal stared at it, seeing no signs of awesome power. The handle seemed incongruously short, and he wasn't even sure that it was made of wood. Could the whole Hammer possibly be one piece of forged metal?

Oblivious to the scrutiny of two pairs of human eyes, Thor chose an ordinary riverside rock and sat down on it like an ordinary man. Hal did not really see him draw the heavy Hammer from his belt, but suddenly Thor had the weapon in his hand, and was idly spinning it, head down like a top, on the stone surface.

In his impressive voice he said: "Loki in his capacity as fire-god can whip up a really toasty blaze. I don't suppose anybody here would know exactly why he set fire to that tall hill? Or where he's got to now? At this moment he's of more interest to me than Wodan is. Considerably more."

"No sir," said Hal. Almost in unison with him, Baldur pronounced the same two words. Then Hal added: "That fire's surely interesting, though."

Thor grunted a kind of agreement, and looked very thoughtful. "I've been over there a couple of times, and taken a look around."

Suddenly Hal realized the god was looking steadily at him. "I think you better put that down," said Thor quietly.

"What?" Hal asked, then felt his ears burn with the sound of his own stupidity. There was the borrowed Spear, its butt grounded in his Horse's harness, but the shaft actually still clutched in his right hand.

Thor hefted his short-handled Hammer ominously.

Hal with a flick of his wrist plucked the Spear from its rest, and hastily cast it down at his side. Distantly his mind registered the fact that he did not hear the weapon hit the ground. A moment later he noticed that it had somehow come to be part of the equipment aboard Thor's chariot.

Meanwhile Myelnir had gone back to rest at Thor's belt. The god continued to regard the two men steadily. "Well? Either of you got anything else to say?"

Baldur seemed to be gradually giving way under the strain of the divine presence. Now he was hanging on to his Horse's mane as he stood beside the animal, as if without support he might faint and tumble over.

Hal was hardly at ease, but neither was he about to collapse. He cleared his throat. "Tell me, Lord Thor," he invited, "what the general subject of conversation is to be?"

Whatever Thor's chief concern might be, it did not seem to be the conduct of the two frightened men before him. The god looked grim, but, thank all the Fates, the cause of his grimness seemed to have nothing to do with the puny mortal men before him. "We were talking about Loki," he reminded his interlocutors, gently enough. "I suppose you fellows do know who Loki is?"

"Yes sir," said Hal. "In a vague, general way, that is."

"Well then, let me be more specific. It's important. Either of you see him anywhere, within the last few days? Now remember; he's a great shape-changer. Did either of you see anyone—or anything—that struck you as especially remarkable?"

"I can't remember anything like that, my lord," said Hal. "I mean, considering we've been in Valhalla until very recently. There were some strange things there—but I think not of the kind you mean." He looked at Baldur, who silently shook his head.

Hal was beginning to feel some of the strain that was paralyzing Baldur. In a way, Thor, in his matter-of-fact sanity, was more frightening than Wodan. People had described similar sensations on confronting Apollo. Whatever this god might decide to do, it would not be out of forgetfulness, or befuddlement. But there was a reassuring aspect too. Thor did not seem much interested in who Hal and Baldur were, or what sins they might have committed against Wodan—he only hoped that they might answer some questions for him.

Silently Hal was cursing himself again for getting into this at all. For being so greedy for gold, so big a fool, that he would stick his nose into gods' business for the sake of some farmland and fishing boats. How could he, with his experience, have fallen so completely for the ancient lure of greed?

━━━━━━

Meanwhile, Hal's and Baldur's Horses, in the presence of Thor and his two huge, incongruous goats, had almost ceased entirely to move. The beasts were still standing as if frozen into sleep.

Thor seemed to have decided not to press his questioning any further. "Looks like a hard battle coming soon," he observed, to no one in particular. After studying the horizon in several directions and listening carefully—he briefly held up one huge hand for silence—as if to sounds that mere human ears could not expect to hear, Thor waved an abrupt farewell, climbed back into his chariot, and clucked to his outsized Goats, who scrambled into action. In a moment the god and his strange equipage were airborne and out of sight.

━━━━━━

Hal mourned the loss of his borrowed Spear, but there was nothing he could do about it. "Let's see if the Valkyries are still in sight," he suggested. Baldur agreed, and volunteered to climb a tree—his joints and limbs were, after all, younger than Hal's.

"I won't argue with you there." Hal's body was starting to stiffen, in the aftermath of the battering he'd taken in the fight with Bran. He ached when he tried to move and ached when he did not. If he was still alive tomorrow, he thought, he would be lucky if he could stand on his feet without help. It was as if some enchantment had suddenly advanced him to about eighty years of age.

Baldur had done some fighting in Valhalla too, but had fortunately escaped without wounds, and he seemed to feel no aftereffects. Vaguely Hal could remember what it felt like to be that young. Now the young man nimbly shinnied up a trunk, and presently was peering outward from the upper branches.

"What word?" Hal called up to him.

"Looks like the Valkyries are all gone," Baldur reported. "I don't see them near the flames or anywhere else. We can go on at once," he concluded.

Moving with the agility of youth, Baldur had dropped from the tree again before Hal made any move toward the saddlebags on the young man's Horse. A moment later, the young man was once more astride

Cloudfoot's back. His knees were practically touching the packaged gold, though plainly he had no suspicion it was there. ·

"Maybe," Hal offered, "we should wait a little longer to make sure that Wodan's not coming after us." If only he could think of some reason to get Baldur away from his Horse for one nice, full minute . . .

At this point the young man, thoroughly disillusioned by his experiences in Valhalla, seemed not even to care whether or not an angry Wodan might be pursuing them. Baldur was not going to be distracted now. He did care enough about one subject to say something before becoming airborne again. "I have been thinking, Hal, and now I understand the problem."

"Oh. You do?" By now Hal had hauled himself aboard Gold Mane again. He was going to make very sure that Baldur did not get away from him.

"Yes." Baldur had the air of announcing a great discovery. "It is not really Wodan who has turned senile."

Hal stared at him. "I got a very strong impression that he was about as crazy as two monkeys with—"

"No, what I mean is, the problem lies only with the avatar, not with the essence of the god. A Face cannot become senile, can it?"

"Well. I don't know. I never heard of anything like that."

"Of course it can't." Now Baldur was as certain as if he had been dealing with gods' Faces all his life, turning them out like cheap helmets in the smithy behind his mother's house. "Which means that the problem can be solved. It is just that the time has come for another man to put on Wodan's Face."

The northman stopped to consider. "I hadn't thought of that." True enough, he hadn't, because such a possibility hadn't seemed worth thinking about. Unless, of course, something were to happen to Wodan, which so far had seemed about as likely as the Einar drying up. "But you may well be right."

———

Their argument, or discussion, was interrupted by the arrival of Alvit, who as she rode up announced that she had been watching from a distance.

"I rejoice to see that Thor has not taken your Horses or your lives," was the Valkyrie's next remark, as she slid off her barebacked mount to stretch, in unconscious imitation of Thor. Then she looked at Hal. "What happened to your helmet?"

He shrugged. "I'm lucky I've still got my head."

Alvit had not paused to listen to the answer. "I have warned all the Valkyries to keep clear of the Thunderer," she told them. "I feared he might be grown contemptuous of Wodan, and would confiscate the first Horse he saw, and ride it into the flames, to see for himself just what Loki's fire is hiding. But what did he want of you? Was he curious to know what was happening in Valhalla?"

Hal shook his head. "Not very," said Baldur. "He was asking about Loki."

"In the tone and manner of one who tries to locate an enemy," Hal amplified. "But of course we could tell him nothing. Then he said that some kind of battle was about to start. Any idea what he meant by that?"

"The reasons for it I do not know, except that the creatures of the Underworld hate gods, especially Wodan. But the evidence that we will soon be fighting is very strong."

Hal said: "But you and the other Valkyries remain loyal to him."

Alvit was obviously troubled. "Most of my sisters are loyal—when they are loyal—only because they are afraid. The All-Highest devises terrible punishments for those he thinks have betrayed him. That is why you did well to flee."

"But you wanted us to go for other reasons. Why are you helping us?"

"I had thought there might be time to strengthen our forces before we had to fight, but it is too late for that. Wodan must fight for his life, and he will have no time for distractions. And you would be a great distraction now, so it is better that you simply go."

In the presence of the Valkyrie, Hal dared not say or do anything about the gold hidden in the saddlebags. He couldn't even suggest breaking out the food Baldur had packed, for fear that someone would open the wrong containers.

Baldur was obviously growing restless, impatient with all this talk. Now the young man insisted that he could delay no longer, and was going to ride immediately to Loki's Fire, and clasp his Brunhild in his arms. "You cannot stop me, Alvit, before I have done that, unless you kill me. When I have done it, I will give back this Horse."

"I have no intention of killing you, young man, and you may both keep the Horses yet a little longer. I have no need of them at the moment, nor does the All-Highest. What we need now is not more Horses." On the last words her voice came near breaking, in something like desperation.

Then she pulled herself together, thinking matters over in her serious way. "Yes, go to Brunhild—or get as close to her as you can. Stay there with her, and in a little while I will come in through the Fire and tell you whether Wodan has abandoned his pursuit."

"Could you bring us some food?" Hal asked. "That last feast was a little thin."

"Yes, I will try to do that," she agreed, and noted with approval that they had their water bottles.

"We thank you, Alvit," said Hal. "I still don't understand why you are doing this for us."

She hesitated before adding: "Long I have loved Wodan, too. But now there are things . . . it is strange, almost as if he has determined that his life will end. For his own good, some of us must disobey him." For a moment the Valkyrie seemed on the brink of weeping.

Hal wished that he could do something for her. He also wished that he could think of some excuse, any excuse, for swapping mounts, or saddlebags, with Baldur. But before he could come up with a good idea, Baldur was again on Cloudfoot's back, urging his mount toward the flames. This time Hal had to watch in silence as his farm and his fishing boats seemed about to vanish into the distance. All he could do was jump on Gold Mane and try to keep up with them.

In less than a minute the men were riding very close to where the flames still burned, and quickly they brought their Horses down to land, side by side, on the high hillside not far from the spot where they had first met.

Looking cautiously about, Hal made sure the Valkyrie was out of sight. Now he ought to be able to get his gold back in one way or another—without doing Baldur any damage, if that was possible.

The young man, his face working with some deep emotion, said to Hal: "You have been a true comrade, and I owe you more than I can ever repay."

"Never mind about that—wait! Hold up!" Hal had to force his own mount right next to Baldur's, and jostle him aside, to keep the headstrong youth from plunging right into the fire.

"Let me go!"

"Not yet! By all the gods and devils, man, hold off a moment! Can't you see we must think of what we're doing, before we attempt this? I might have some interest, too, in what's inside the flames." *If you must plunge in there, give me my gold first. Then maybe I'll follow.* But he could not quite bring himself to say that in so many words.

"What more is there to think of? Brunhild is in there, she may be dying, and I am going to—"

"You're still absolutely convinced she's there. Then—"

"Of course she is there. You heard Alvit."

"Yes, yes, but she's already been there for several days—how many is it now?—and she can wait another minute or two. Will you listen to me a minute? I propose we first try riding near the flames, and make sure the heat won't scorch us, that these magic mounts offer us protection." And Hal reached out and caught his companion by the jacket.

"Hal. Let me go."

"Look, I know you saw a Valkyrie do this trick, but it also might be a good idea to drench ourselves in water before plunging into that kind of—wait! Hold up, damn you!"

But Baldur had wrenched free, knocking Hal's arm away with a swinging elbow. The young man kicked his mount in the ribs again, and he was off, headed straight into the wall of fire. The Horse, as if accustomed to such a practice, did not balk or shy away.

Hal's cry went unheeded, and Baldur's mount bore its rider straight into the wall of flame. At the last moment the young man bowed his head so that his face was hidden between his arms, his shoulders in the tattered jacket tensing in the instant before the fiery tongues closed around them.

Raising his head along with his clenched fists, to hurl an oath of anger at the sky, Hal caught sight of something in the distance that stilled his outcry in his throat.

His vision was ordinarily quite good at long range, uncomfortably good in this case, and he had little doubt that the approaching object was a two-wheeled chariot. For some reason he felt vaguely relieved to see that the animals pulling it through the air did not look at all like goats. Then relief faded. At first he had thought there were two Horses, but now he could see that there was only one, and it had eight legs. There was a single rider, who seemed to be carrying a long Spear, a weapon even longer than the Valkyries', and ominously stouter.

Hal hesitated only briefly, taking one last look around. Baldur and his steed had disappeared right into the fire, and they were not coming out. Not immediately, anyway.

Hal's imagination presented him with an unwelcome sensation, the smell of cooking meat.

But Wodan was coming after him, and Wodan was angry. No doubt about it now. The man could feel the radiation of that wrath, even at a distance, and it felt even hotter than the fire. Like the approach of a piece of red-hot iron, or the imminence of a thunderbolt from a black cloud. Choking out a strangled oath, Hal closed his eyes, kicked his Horse savagely in the ribs, and went plunging straight into the flames after his companion.

15

FOR JUST A moment Hal's ears were buffeted by a huge noise. In his imagination it was equal to the roaring of all the flames that Loki in all his avatars had ever kindled. In the same moment, a fierce light came glaring at him, forcing its way in through his closed lids in the colors of blood and gold, far brighter than any natural fire.

But he felt nothing of the blasting heat that he had expected and instinctively tried to brace himself against. The motion of his bounding, airborne Horse kept on unchanged. Then the great light was gone as quickly as it had appeared, and the noise of the divine fire had faded to its usual muted roar. The plunging motion of Hal's mount stopped abruptly, and he thought he felt the Horse's four legs all come down on solid ground.

Opening his eyes, Hal nearly fell from the beast's back in astonishment. He had come through one fire only to confront another. He and Gold Mane had come to a standing stop in the middle of a corridor of clear space, some ten yards wide that ran curving away in two directions, between two concentric walls of fire, so that the strip of free space between them was shaped like a wheel's broad rim. The flames on each side were equally tall and bright, and for just a moment he feared that he would be roasted between them. But this fire was the work of a god, not ordinary nature, and the god had designed this curving space to be habitable by mortal humans. The air immediately surrounding Hal and his mount was clear, free of smoke, and cooler than many a summer's day he could remember.

The ground on which Hal's Horse had braced its legs was mostly rocks and scattered tufts of grass, much like that he had observed outside the outer ring of fire. The chief difference was that in here the surface was almost flat.

The breath Hal had been holding broke from his lungs explosively. His mount had landed quietly and easily, and as if it found this environment familiar, was already tasting some of the grass that struggled to grow here just as it did outside the outer burning ring.

Within this narrow sanctuary, bounded inside and out by Loki's glowing barricades, the air was so quiet that Hal could hear the slight ripping sound made by his Horse's teeth as they worked calmly on the scanty grass.

A pebble's toss ahead of him stood Baldur's mount with Baldur still aboard, facing toward Hal. Cloudfoot was also calmly cropping winter grass. Both animals were behaving as if this little space of rocky soil were some ordinary pasture—somehow, Hal thought, the beasts must be able to distinguish Loki's handiwork from ordinary fire, and they felt no dread of it at all. Or perhaps—and this idea raised new questions—it was as if they had visited this place so often that Loki's handiwork was quite familiar to them.

From where Hal perched on Gold Mane's back, he could see no sign at all of Brunhild. Baldur, also failing to discover his beloved anywhere, shot one haggard, desperate look at Hal, then tugged at his mount's golden mane and kicked the animal into action, so that it bore him quickly away. In only a moment, beast and rider had vanished around the sharp curve of fire-bounded space. And in the next breath the youth and his Horse were returning, coming around the bend of narrow corridor from the opposite direction.

Raising both arms in a despairing gesture, Baldur gave a cry: "She is not here!"

Hal had already reached that conclusion and only nodded abstractedly. At the moment he was less concerned about Brunhild than he was about the fact of Wodan's furious pursuit. Hal found himself holding his breath, expecting at any moment the noise and fury of an angry god to come bursting in through Loki's outer fire-ring. Listening carefully now, the northman could even hear (or imagined that he could) the All-Highest out there somewhere, bellowing in a kind of rage that matched berserker Bran's.

Hal could only pray to the Fates that eight-legged Sleipnir could not breach Loki's barrier as easily as the Valkyries' Horses had. Of course Gold Mane and Cloudfoot had not been harnessed to a chariot. Now if it should occur to Wodan to borrow a Valkyrie's Horse . . .

If Hal was ready to forget Brunhild, Baldur seemed to have already forgotten Wodan. The young man's fears were of another kind entirely.

Again he shouted: "She is not here!" And he waved both arms at Hal, as if he expected his mentor to tell him where she was.

Hal shook his head. "I kept trying to tell you it would be better not to get your hopes up—what're you doing now? Wait!"

Baldur wasn't listening. Instead, he had flung himself from his mount and was dancing and scurrying back and forth, getting as close as he could to the inner barrier of flame and trying frantically to see through it. If Hildy was not to be found in this wheel-rim space between the fires, then maybe she was in there, somewhere deeper inside Loki's sanctuary. There was a kind of logic to the idea. Bending and crawling, her lover brought himself as close to the ground as possible, evidently seeking a favorable angle of sight.

Muttering blasphemies against a whole pantheon of gods, Hal scrambled after the young man, trying with practically no success to get his attention.

In this fashion the two men had made their way almost halfway around the inner barrier when suddenly Baldur froze in position and let out a hoarse scream.

"Here she is! I see her! Hal, look at this!"

Baldur was crouched down, his head only three feet from the inner barrier—about as close as he could get without burning himself—trying with both hands to shade his eyes from the yellow glare, even as he stared intently at something near ground level and just in front of him, on the other side of that incandescent wall.

Hal squatted beside the youth, cupped his hands round his own eyes to shade them from the omnipresent flames as best he could, and studied the indicated region. Then he rubbed his eyes and stared again.

The object Baldur was focusing on was hard for Hal to make out at first, behind the glare and slowly swirling color, but when he had concentrated on the place for the space of a few breaths the thing seemed to come a little clearer—enough to allow him to perceive the outline of what might well have been a supine human shape.

Given the obscuring glare, colors and other details were almost impossible to determine. But there could be no doubt about the general configuration. It did indeed appear to be either a young woman or the statue of one, lying on her back on some kind of bed or slab. She seemed partially clothed in some tight-fitting, reflective stuff that might have been metal armor.

Squinting even more intently, Hal thought he could make out a pale mass of gold, just where the recumbent figure's head ought to be resting, as on a pillow. But as the fire bathed everything in its own bright yellow, it was impossible to be sure.

Abruptly Baldur broke off his contemplation of the image beyond the sheet of fire. Next moment, with a bound and a wild cry, the youth had regained his seat astride his mount. Ignoring Hal's urging to stop and think, he urged Cloudfoot straight at the inner burning wall. But to the surprise of both men, the Horse refused the barrier at once, as simply and conclusively as it had accepted that of the outer ring.

It occurred to Hal that if Wodan himself had carried Brunhild into this nest of fire, then the god must have had some means of getting in and out unharmed. On the way in, he must have protected his prisoner also, unless the terms of punishment had been broadened to include incineration. Of course Hal could not be sure of the exact sequence of events. The girl might have been brought here before Loki called the flames' fierce circles into existence.

Or, and this seemed more likely as he thought about it, the Firegod himself could have carried the disgraced Valkyrie here as a favor for his colleague, the All-Highest, just as Loki had furnished Valhalla with some hearth-fires. That would mean that the two gods had been on good terms until only a few days ago.

It would be something to ask Alvit about, Hal thought, when he saw her again. If he ever did.

"Do you remember, Baldur?"

"Remember what?"

"Back in Valhalla, Wodan asked us several times what we knew about Loki, any contact we might have had with him."

"Yes, of course I remember that. And Thor asked the same thing. What of it?"

"I'm not sure. I was just trying to figure things out."

Hal let it drop. There was no use trying to talk to Baldur, who was growing more frantic with every minute. Again and again he tried desperately to urge his Horse to join the motionless figure half-hidden behind the flames.

Repeated efforts accomplished nothing. The animal showed no reluctance to approach the inner wall of fire, or even to stand near it— only within a few inches of the glowing wall did the heat become unbearable. But Cloudfoot could not be induced to try to pass through it, no matter what Baldur did. The burning inner curtain might as well have been a wall of stone. When Baldur persisted in trying to force the great Horse forward, it reared and finally threw him off.

On his feet again a moment later, he borrowed the mount Hal had been riding and tried again, with exactly the same result.

After being thrown the second time, Baldur lay for a long moment without trying to move. At last he croaked: "Maybe it is my fault—maybe I am unworthy. Hal, you must try!"

Hal argued with him uselessly for a few moments. Then, more to pacify his colleague than in any hope of success, he made the same attempt, and managed to keep from being thrown. But his half-hearted effort achieved no more than Baldur's all-out try.

Now, after stumbling about uncertainly for a few moments, the young man crossed his arms over his face and, before Hal realized what he intended, went lurching blindly forward, trying to reach Brunhild on his own two legs. Heat met him like a solid wall, and his effort accomplished nothing but slightly burning his arms and hands, and scorching some of his long hair until it smoked.

Beaten back once by the intense heat, which when you got close enough was as fierce as that of any fire, he was still ready to try again.

Seeing the expression on Baldur's face, Hal felt compelled to grab him and hold him back to keep him from a suicidal plunge.

"Let me go! Let me go!" The young man struggled frantically, but Hal was stronger.

When the youth attempted a desperate kick, Hal tripped him and slammed him expertly to the ground, knocking out his wind. Then he straddled him to keep him there.

"Let me go!"

"As soon as you get back your wits, I'll let you go. Can't you see, you're going to fry yourself like an egg if you keep on? What good'll you be to her then?"

The youth broke down in helpless weeping.

———

Releasing his prostrate partner and slowly regaining his feet, Hal looked about him. The brief struggle had not been very intense, but it had worsened every ache in his body. It would be too bad to leave Baldur here in this state, but he might have to do so. Still, Hal was in no immediate hurry to stick his nose outside the outer fire-ring, where an angry Wodan might well be waiting to pounce. Alvit had said that she would come to them here, and maybe she really would, bringing food and information.

Meanwhile, *something* must be preventing Wodan from simply bulling his way in. Loki's defensive magic must be powerful. Sleipnir perhaps lacked golden shoes, and Wodan probably could not think straight enough to borrow a properly equipped Horse.

And Hal thought he had better take advantage of Baldur's collapse before the youth revived. Hal himself was nearly exhausted, but he retained the strength and energy to switch the saddlebags from one Horse to the other, strapping the heavily laden pair firmly onto Gold Mane, the animal he had himself been riding, and the light pair on the other. He was assuming that Baldur, when he had pulled himself together, would continue to ride Cloudfoot. But right now Hal's companion did not question what Hal was doing or even notice it.

It eased the aches and pains of battle wonderfully, to think that he had now secured his fortune as best he could. Now, Hal thought, the only thing really preventing his immediate departure was the strong possibility that Wodan was waiting for him just outside the flames. His stay could not be prolonged indefinitely, but he could afford to wait a little longer.

Loki's refuge might be proof against certain angry gods, but it was notably short on such amenities as water and food. Now Hal opened the lighter set of saddlebags, in search of whatever Baldur had managed to snatch up before leaving Valhalla. Hal sighed at what he found. A few handfuls of nothing better than fodder for the Horses, some of it stale-smelling stuff probably left over from some previous Valkyrie ride. Hal decided to postpone trying to eat any of it now—Alvit had definitely said something about trying to bring them food.

Shaking first one water bottle and then the other, to ascertain just how much might be left, he stood over Baldur and spoke to him sharply.

"Look here, young one. Give up this whining and bawling and pull yourself together. Sit up like a man and share a little Horse-fodder with me. Thinking and eating will be better than banging your head against a wall of fire."

Baldur sat up. If his assortment of minor burns, cuts, and bruises were paining him, he gave no sign. Ah, youth! Hal thought again. Sitting down to rest his legs, he groaned with the pain in his chronically sore knee. He wished there was a solid wall that he might lean his back against.

Baldur stirred. He rubbed his head with both hands for a while, then asked: "Where is Alvit? Didn't she say she was going to meet us here?"

"She did say something like that, yes." Hal could feel his eyelids trying to sag shut. It was a long time, years, since he had felt as tired as he did right now. He was going to have to rest before he tried to flee, or made an effort to do anything, for that matter. Not that he wasn't proud as well as tired. Few men—very few—could boast of killing a berserker in single combat.

Still thinking about Alvit, he added: "But she's done a lot for us already, and now she may be caught up in whatever damn fool battle this is that the gods are getting into. We oughtn't to expect much more from her." Privately he was thinking that Alvit would be lucky if Wodan did not discover everything she had been doing for his prisoners and deal her out some terrible punishment.

"I suppose." Baldur had run out of tears and groans for the moment. Now he sat slumped beside Hal, just staring at nothing.

"Let us think," Hal repeated. "How we are going to reach behind the inner flames. There never was a barrier without some kind of a way to get through it." As soon as those words passed his lips, he had serious doubts that they were true. But he let them stand. Baldur needed all the encouragement he could get. And for that matter, so did Hal himself.

At last Baldur said, in a weakened voice: "We need some rest; I don't think I can think straight."

"Truer words were never spoken. Who wants to stand the first watch?"

Later Hal was never sure which of them had volunteered for the first turn of sentry duty, if either did. As things turned out, it did not matter. The two men were exhausted after putting in a day of duty in Valhalla, getting through the nightly feast, then fighting a deadly brawl in the early hours of the morning, and after that a desperate flight. In less than a minute they were both asleep, sprawled on the hard ground.

Hal woke up with a shock, half-strangling on a snore. But he knew it was something more than snoring that had awakened him. There had been a sharp burst of sound, a briefly stuttering, ripping, slamming kind of noise like nothing he had ever heard before. It could have issued from no human throat—but could it possibly have been a dream? The sound had repeated itself once, he thought, and then had come no more.

Now fully awake and sitting up, he listened, as carefully as he could. But everything was quiet, save for the endless murmuring of Loki's surrounding fire, which burned on undisturbed.

"Now what in all the hells was that?" Hal muttered to himself, not really believing the jolt of sound had proceeded from a dream. No one answered him. Baldur was still sprawled out and snoring faintly. A whole team of eight-legged horses could have galloped in through the firewall and trampled over him, and he would not have cared.

Groaning, Hal stood up and forced himself to move about a little. He had a distinct feeling that hours had passed since they had fallen asleep. He was both thirsty and hungry, and his muscles and joints were stiffer than ever from sleeping on the hard ground. But the two confining walls of fire showed no change, and he realized that he had no idea how long he had been asleep. In here, he thought, it would always be impossible to distinguish day from night. This time they had arrived at the crag in the early morning. For all he could tell, the day had passed, and night had fallen; day or night, things would probably look exactly the same in here.

The two Horses were only a few yards away along the curving corridor, still browsing the scanty grass that endured in spite of magic fire. Hal opened a water bottle and took a swig. The Horses were going to have to wait for theirs. He opened the heavy set of saddlebags and checked the gold again, to make sure that something strange and evil had not happened to it while he slept. Then he told himself his nerves were making him inordinately suspicious.

Well, if he had really been sleeping for many hours, that would seem to make it much more likely that by now Wodan had got tired of waiting in ambush outside the fire. Or the Father of Battles might have forgotten about his victims, and gone off to fight an important battle somewhere. Hal was in no hurry to find out. Speaking gently to Gold Mane and Cloudfoot, petting them as he passed, as he had seen Alvit and Baldur do, he took a complete slow turn around the little circle of their flame-protected sanctuary, stretching his arms and legs.

When he had reached a point diametrically opposite to Baldur and the Horses, Hal opened his belt pouch and got out his scrap of Golden Fleece. The little swatch of cloth grew brighter, very definitely brighter, when he held it near the inner circle of flame.

Don't be greedy, he told himself sharply. *All you need is the several pounds of yellow stuff you already have put away. If you can get clean away with that, you'll have had all the good luck that any man could dare to hope for in a lifetime.*

And yet, and yet . . . now the Fleece was indicating a much vaster hoard nearby. For Hal the real lure of great treasure was not so much to possess it, but simply to know about it. To fathom all the secrets of the rings of fire . . .

By the time Hal had put away his talisman and returned to his starting point, his companion was also awake, drinking from a water bottle.

"What we need," said Baldur, when the two began to plan again, "is a skilled magician for an ally."

"Of course. I should have thought of that. Better still, why don't we just enlist one of the great gods as our partner—Loki himself, wherever he is, would be about right."

Irony was lost on Baldur. "Why do you suppose both Thor and Wodan are angry with him?"

"Who knows? If Loki's unavailable, we might instead employ some powerful tool of magical power, something so simple that it can be used effectively even by clumsy clods like us." Hal paused. "Any idea how we can do that?"

Baldur was the picture of gloom. "No. My only clear idea is that I must reach Brunhild, and hold her once more in my arms."

"Then we'd better come up with a different kind of plan. Maybe something totally practical, for a change. How about a scheme that requires us to do nothing outside the realm of possibility?"

What felt like a lengthy period of silence dragged past. At last Baldur offered: "Magic *would* seem to be our only chance. Some kind of magic."

"I hope that's not true," Hal meditated. "Because, as I keep pointing out, neither of us is able to do magic worth a fart. I learned a long time ago that I have no skill along those lines."

There passed another lengthy interval during which no one spoke.

"Clues to magical difficulties are often concealed in riddles," Baldur suddenly announced.

"Are they indeed?" Hal snapped awake; he had been on the point of dozing off again, a vision of a bushel of golden horseshoes drifting in his mind. What was the young fool babbling about? Riddles? Magic riddles? Hal couldn't remember ever hearing anything of the kind.

"Of course!" Baldur was emphatic. "I've heard any number of stories. And I did hear a certain riddle in Valhalla—from one of the kitchen workers—"

Hal made a disgusted noise.

"Wait a moment." Suddenly Baldur stood up straight, rejecting one theory to push another. "Riddles, no, that's nonsense." He raised an arm to point dramatically at nothing. "Gold rings!"

"Brain damage," Hal sighed.

"What?"

"Never mind. All right, gold rings. What in the Underworld have gold rings got to do with anything?"

Baldur had recovered himself sufficiently to begin pacing in the confined space. Once more he looked and sounded full of energy and hope. "Rings are famous for being used in the most powerful magic. I could tell you a dozen stories—"

"Yes, and I could tell a score. But how about a few facts instead?" Hal paused. "You mean a ring like one that Alvit has been wearing?" Come to think of it, he had seen something of the kind on her hand.

Hal did what he could in the way of encouraging suggestions, but soon Baldur's enthusiasm faded. They could not even agree on whether Valkyries generally wore rings or not, or whether Alvit had been wearing one or several.

Hal thought privately that if Baldur were suddenly to insist on some plan that involved their returning to Valhalla in pursuit of some strange magic, that would be the moment when he, Hal, decided he had waited long enough. He would encourage his young partner with some inspiring words, jump on the gold-loaded Horse—yes, that would now be Gold Mane—checking just once more, at any cost, to make sure his treasure was still in the right place—and strike out alone for freedom and security.

Baldur was struggling, as he said, to recall the exact words of some spell that a certain enchantress had tried to teach him as a child, when without warning something large came bursting in upon them through the outer firewall, no more than fifteen feet away. Both Horses started, but only momentarily.

For the space of half a breath, Hal was certain that his doom had come upon him. But he was not lost yet. The intruder was only Alvit, mounted on her own Horse, whose gold-shod hooves came clattering now on the hard rock.

The Valkyrie looked tired, but seemed genuinely pleased to see the two men, and glad to dismount.

"I bring you one item of good news," she began without preliminary. "Wodan has not laid siege to your sanctuary. He is nowhere in sight."

Hal had jumped to his feet, momentarily uncertain whether Alvit had come to skewer them on her Spear or bring them help. Now he relaxed. "That is good news indeed! Then we can leave."

"*Leave?*" Baldur was dumbfounded. "But Brunhild—"

Alvit said: "I suppose you may. But I should tell you, before you go. There is a strange—phenomenon outside."

Hal's surge of relief was abruptly tempered. "What kind of a phenomenon?"

The Valkyrie made awkward gestures that seemed to suggest an object spinning in the air. "There is a glowing circle round the crag, at a distance of about a hundred yards."

"A glowing what?"

Again she moved one hand around. "As if some burning coal, some particle of fire, were speeding steadily in a circular path, revolving around this blazing hilltop, keeping always at about the same distance. I was careful to avoid the thing, whatever it is, as I arrived."

Hal and Baldur looked at each other fearfully. At last Baldur said: "It must be some magical device of Wodan's. As soon as we emerge it will slay us—or at least it will follow us and lead more of Wodan's berserkers to us."

The Valkyrie was shaking her head and frowning. "I do not think that this—thing—belongs to Wodan—I have never seen anything like it in Valhalla. Or anywhere else."

Then she brightened and reached into one of her saddlebags, producing a package that looked and smelled unmistakably like a loaf of fresh bread. Moments later she brought forth a flask of mead and some meat.

Baldur and Hal both expressed their profound thanks.

"How long have we been in here now?" Hal asked, sitting down again, mumbling his words past a mouthful of bread and sausage. Food and drink always made a man feel much more human. Now it seemed the world was going to go on for a while yet, and he would still be in it.

She reassured the men as to how much time had passed—outside the sun was setting, on the same day of their flight. And she reported incidentally that, to the best of her knowledge, Andvari and his comrade had not been seen in Valhalla since Hal and Baldur had fled. She assumed the gnomes had started for home, and she knew of no pursuit.

"And what about the battle?" Baldur asked. "Is Thor taking part?"

"I have not seen Thor since I saw him with you. As to the battle, it's hard to say. I have not been near the actual fighting, but I think so far there have been only scattered clashes. Not all the forces have yet been mobilized on either side. Wodan is grim and determined as usual."

"Has he forgotten about us?" Hal asked hopefully.

"For the moment. He has much greater matters on his mind—and as long as he concentrates on them, his mind is keener than it has been for a long time."

"In a way, I am glad," she added slowly. "It will be better for him to fight, even if he must die, than to go on . . . as he has been, these last few years."

"Then do you think he'll lose this battle?"

Alvit catalogued what she knew of the forces arrayed against Wodan and his few allies. Aside from some local human warlords, it was a roll call of giants and monsters, including certain names Hal could remember from Wodan's reading in the great hall.

She said that Wodan had gathered his handful of living troops around him, including whatever Valkryies were in range of his summons, and made them a speech, while an army of wraiths hung in the background and appeared to listen also. He had delivered to his assembled forces a version of his usual sermon, about the Twilight of the Gods, and of monsters of unspeakable horror being called up from the Underworld by his demonic enemies to overthrow his rule.

"But make no mistake, though his mind is confused, it is still powerful." She stared at Baldur's look of disbelief, and added: "You have not seen his powers in use, and I have."

After a little silence, Hal asked: "What will you do now, Alvit?"

The Valkyrie shook her head slowly. "If I can think of any way to save him, his honor and his life, then I will try. If he is at least partly right about this battle, despite all his delusions, and the monsters of the Underworld are really going to overwhelm him, then I wish to die with him." She paused. "I loved him once."

After a little silence, Hal said: "I think you love him still. But whether gods or monsters win this round, I do not think the world will end."

Alvit only gave him a sad smile.

Now Baldur was saying: "Can you be sure this final conflict isn't all in Wodan's imagination? Possibly there is no real attack at all? He doesn't have a lot of real force to mobilize, as I recall."

"Thor, too, spoke of a great battle brewing," Hal reminded him.

Alvit was shaking her head. "The attack is real enough, I have seen evidence of that. And Wodan's power is greater than you think, when all the wraiths are called to duty. You never saw anything like their entire number."

"But what can they do?"

"They are more effective against certain of the Underworld creatures than they are against humans. At least that is what we are all hoping." After a pause, she asked: "What are you two doing now?"

Baldur had an instant answer ready. "We are of course going to reach Brunhild, somehow, or die trying." Then, looking at Hal, he amended. "*I* am going to die trying. I do not require such sacrifice from my friends."

Hal winced. "Baldur, I hope you find a way to get your girlfriend back. I really do. If I could think of any way . . ."

But Baldur had turned back to the Valkyrie, and was saying: "We had been talking riddles, and were about to go around in rings." When

Alvit looked puzzled, Baldur amplified: "The gnomes are supposed to have forged gold rings of great power in the past. The Earthdwellers have powers that are truly legendary."

Hal put in: " 'Legendary' isn't going to do us much good right now. What we need are powers truly practical. And what the gnomes may have . . ." He suddenly fell silent.

"What is it?" Both of his companions asked at once.

But the northman was not listening. He had risen to his feet, and was staring at the mysterious base of the blazing inner circle. Especially he was concentrating on the way its tongues of fire kept rising, like those of its outer counterpart, seemingly from nothing. He scuffed his booted feet on the solid rock where he was standing. Then he stamped both his feet hard, first left then right, one after the other. He let out what sounded like a battle cry, a kind of screech of triumph.

"What—?" Baldur recoiled from him, but Alvit remained standing just where she was, leaning on her Horse, as if she were too tired to be excited by anything short of a physical attack.

Hal gripped his companion by the front of his worn quilted jacket. He said: "Yes, the gnomes. The Earthdwellers do have great powers, and they just might be able to do us some good. But sometimes the simple method is the best."

"What do you mean?"

Hal waved his arms. "How might we attack the problem if this fire were a solid wall, too hard to break?"

"Well, how?"

"If we are going to take the risks of making a foray back to Valhalla, I have a better goal in mind than ransacking the tyrant's rooms for rings that probably would be of no use to us anyway. I want a juicier bait than a few gold rings before I put my head in the mousetrap."

Baldur and Alvit looked at him in bewilderment.

Once more Hal stamped his right foot hard on the hard ground. "We're going to liberate ourselves a pair of gnomes, along with whatever tools they think they need to do a little job."

"What job?"

"I think they'll do it, out of sheer gratitude. I think they'd better, if they know what's good for them."

"What job?"

"What do you think? Andvari and his friend are going to dig a little tunnel for us!"

——— 16 ———

"WE MUST WASTE no more time," Baldur said after another silence. His voice was alive with renewed hope. "If we are going to find the gnomes, and make them dig a tunnel for us—" He suddenly turned his head and shouted, as if he expected her to hear him: "I'm coming to you, my Brunhild!"

Alvit remounted her Horse, and promptly disappeared through the outer wall of fire. Half a minute later she was back again, reporting that the way seemed clear—there was still no sign of Wodan, or of any entity that she thought might be an agent of the god. She added that the strange phenomenon she had observed earlier still persisted: a faint, sharply curving streak, traced out by something like a spark of flame. Still the spark maintained its course, circling the crag at a distance of about a hundred yards.

The Valkyrie also assured the men that the All-Highest would very likely be distracted now, and for some time to come, by the needs of combat, so he would not be likely to interfere with their endeavor to recruit gnomes, even if their search carried them near Valhalla. "But if you see Thor, or even Loki, remember that my lord needs help desperately. Even when gods have quarreled, they should stand together against the Underworld."

"I'll remember," Hal said.

Impulsively Baldur grasped her by the hand. "We owe you our lives," he said. Hal, standing beside him, solemnly agreed.

"You were never Wodan's enemies," she sadly observed, looking at them in turn. "Nor was Brunhild."

"Then help us save her!" the young man pleaded.

Alvit shook her head. "It may be that you will be able to reach her, with the help of gnomes. I can be of no more help—but I do wish you success. Now I must hurry away."

As soon as Alvit was on her way again, Hal and Baldur hastily conferred, sketching out a plan for the mission they were about to undertake. Then they mounted their Horses and rode out separately through the outermost ring of fire.

It was Hal's idea, at the last moment, for the two of them to take their departure simultaneously but not together, emerging from opposite sides of the outer circle of fire. Then if, in spite of everything, Wodan or one of his creatures was waiting to pounce on them, either Hal or Baldur might have a chance of getting away.

Keeping a sharp eye out as he urged his mount back out through the flames, Hal emerged into the glow of late sunset. He and Baldur were immediately confronted by the strange phenomenon that Alvit had mentioned. Hal could think of no better way to describe it: a small, fiery object of unknown nature, whirling around the crag at about the speed of a thrown stone, while keeping a steady distance from the center of the curve.

The flying spark did not react to the appearance of the two men on their Horses. It made no move to approach or attack, as Hal and Baldur had been at least half expecting, but only maintained its smooth and rapid revolution.

More ominous were certain loud rumblings in the far distance, accompanied by a trembling that must have come through the very bones of the earth, for it made the wall of Loki's flames shiver slightly. There was also a strange glow along the edge of the visible world, in the wrong place to be either sunrise or sunset. Along the far horizon, in the direction of Valhalla, Hal observed strange flashes of light that could hardly have been lightning, flickering as they did where the sky was clear.

Even Baldur was distracted from his great purpose for a moment. "Then it is true," he muttered. "The gods must be already engaged in serious battle. But who are they fighting? Each other, or their common enemies?"

"Either way it ought to keep them out of our hair," said Hal. "Come,

I want to get some digging done, so we can reach Brunhild—and also I want a better look into Loki's secret sanctuary."

Sometimes Hal had trouble understanding his own behavior. Here he was, mounted on a steed that few or none could overtake, and with the package of undefended gold in easy reach. Why not simply take his treasure and ride away?

Well, for one thing, Baldur had probably saved his life when he was fighting the berserker, and deserting Baldur now would not be honorable. Honor did mean something to most northmen. Sometimes to this one it meant a lot. Hal thought stealing gold from strangers was about as respectable as most forms of business, but letting down a shipmate who depended on you was another matter altogether.

Besides . . . having entered the outer room of Loki's sanctuary, had a sampling of its wonders, Hal knew he would regret it for the rest of his life if he retreated now, without even trying to probe its inner secrets.

Tugging his Horse's mane, he made the animal rear and turn around. This riding through the air at terrific speed could get to be fun, as addictive as certain drugs, if a man were granted the chance to practice it a little.

———————

To Baldur, whose mount was galloping beside Hal's—it was still amazing, how quiet hoofbeats were when they fell on air!—Hal said: "It will be safer, I think, if we keep to the interior of clouds as much as possible."

Baldur nodded. "As long as we don't get lost. Now, we must decide which end of the trail to start at—near the village, or near Valhalla."

"Starting halfway between should do the job. If the gnomes ran away from Valhalla at the same time we did, they've only been on the trail for one night—maybe a little more. They can't have made many miles just yet."

———————

Finding the proper road at night was not too easy, even with their Horses trotting through the air only a few yards above the ground. The broad curves of the Einar tended to be confusing in the darkness, but the light of the waning moon led them at last to Andvari and Ivaldr's village. From there it was easy to pick out the right road. Soon Baldur and Hal were cantering briskly along the way to Valhalla, covering in mere hours distances that had taken them days on foot. Yet they dared not go too fast, for fear of missing the men they were trying to find.

"If Wodan sent Valkyries after them . . ." Baldur left the thought unfinished.

"All the pursuit he could scrape together probably came after us. But if we don't find our gnomes on the trail, we'll go to Valhalla. I'd bet the place is undermanned, if Wodan's got his army out in the field. But I'm afraid that in this gloom we'll miss our quarry. They'll see us riding the air, and think we're Valkyries, and hide."

Baldur agreed. Moments later, the two men landed near the trail, tethered their Horses, and allowed themselves the luxury of sleep.

At first light they were up again and in the air. No more than half an hour passed before Baldur stretched out an arm and cried: "There they are!"

Two weary, goggled gnomes looked up from where they had just turned off the trail, evidently in search of shelter against the rising sun. For a moment Andvari and Ivaldr were poised to run, but then they harkened to Hal's bellowing and waited for the riders to arrive.

The two Earthdwellers were also hungry, and made short work of the food Hal brought out from his saddlebags. Of conditions in Valhalla they knew no more than Hal and Baldur, having fled at the same time. And they were much relieved to learn that little of the blood that stained Hal's clothing was his own.

━━━━━━━━━

When Baldur offered them a ride, they were more than willing to be rescued. "Our hearts hunger to see our village again!"

Hal promised them: "And we will take you there, my friend, in good time. But there is something vitally important you can do for us first."

"Of course, anything—anything within reason. Twice now you have saved our lives." But still Andvari seemed a little wary. "What are we to do?"

"It is only a little job of digging. I will explain while we travel," Hal rasped in his best soothing tone.

Despite all their experience in handling Horses, neither gnome had ever flown before. Both admitted they were terrified of riding through the air, but they now feared Wodan even more. In a matter of moments, each was astride a Horse, clinging on behind a massive Sundweller. On becoming airborne, they both groaned and cried out in amazement and alarm.

Hal thought he was able to appreciate the courage this flight must have required of them. If the Earthdwellers found the act of simply venturing out into the open air from underground something of an adventure, how terrible must it be to risk their bodies at such a distance from Mother Earth?

The gnomes said that if digging was required, it would be necessary to stop first at one of several mining towns inhabited by Earthdwellers, where the essential tools would be available. Hal had to agree; even gnomes could not do much with their fingernails. The equipment the miners wanted to obtain included short-handled hammers, chisels, scoops, and shovels. Filter masks were also on Andvari's list of essentials. These were woven of some fine cloth and served to protect the miners' lungs against dust and dirt. Some minerals were notably more poisonous than others.

"Is the digging in a mine?" Andvari wanted to know.

"Well—no," Hal admitted.

"It's right out in the open, then? And I suppose if the need is so urgent, you'll want us to start in daylight? Maybe even with a lot of snow lying about, reflecting sun?"

Baldur was about to answer, but let himself be hushed by Hal, who framed his answer carefully. "The site is pretty thoroughly illuminated."

Andvari sighed. "Well, we have our goggles, and can wrap ourselves against the sun."

When Ivaldr asked him what kind of rock they would be expected to tunnel through, Hal had to admit that he didn't know, being no expert in such matters. Baldur was no help either. About all they could do was warn the Earthdwellers that it wasn't sandstone, or anywhere near that soft and crumbly.

The gnomes received this confession of ignorance in silence, leaving Hal with the feeling that they were too well-mannered to comment on their clients' appalling lack of knowledge.

But as long as they were available he thought he might take advantage of their presence to ask them a couple of very casual questions about matters involving gold. Of course it seemed that his stash of horseshoes would provide all the gold he really needed . . . but he was curious.

"This animal's the first I've ever ridden on that wore shoes made of gold," he began, with what he considered ingenious subtlety. The first with shoes of any kind, he might have added.

"And probably the last." Andvari, clinging on behind Hal, did not sound inclined to enter into any lengthy conversation.

On the other hand Ivaldr seemed ready to discourse on the subject—

though Hal had trouble hearing him across the gap of air between the Horses. Gold, said Ivaldr, was the Earthdwellers' sunlight, the only brightness that many of their race ever saw. No punishment was too severe, he proclaimed, for thieves who stole the yellow metal. All gold, and, to tell the truth, all metal, by rights belonged to gnomes, and it was only by courtesy that they let anyone else use it.

Getting to the mining settlement required a journey of many miles, but at the speed of Valkyries it did not take long, and was happily uneventful.

They landed at a little distance from the miners' village, amid a raw, scarred landscape, marked by many mounds of excavated dirt and rock, some fresh, some very old. There were reddish piles of crumbled material that Hal could recognize as iron ore. Sentries had been posted at the village entrance, and Hal got the impression that regular work had been suspended, as the people mobilized for self-defense as best they could.

———

The sight of the Horses landing immediately drew a modest crowd, all goggled against exposure to the morning sun.

Hal and Baldur remained on the surface, trusting to Andvari and Ivaldr to return from a quick trip underground to gather tools and arrange for an urgent message to be sent to their home village, informing their relatives and friends that they were safe.

By midday they were all four on their two mounts again, the gnomes hooded and goggled against the sun. They were carrying stout canvas bags of stubby-handled mining tools, as well as a new supply of gnomish food.

———

Hal thought he was definitely beginning to develop a certain skill in riding a flying Horse, and he realized he was going to regret the loss when the day came for him to give the animal back. Trying to hang on to it would be tempting, but he understood that it would be hopeless for an ordinary man—certainly if he wanted to retire to anything like an ordinary life.

"What're you thinking about, Hal?"

"Not much. Just trying to imagine Cloudfoot and Gold Mane pulling a plow . . ."

"What strange ideas you have." Baldur looked at him with the sympathy one might reserve for the brain damaged.

———

Hal had planned to wait until the last possible moment, when they were inescapably airborne, to let his new helpers know that they must be carried through a barrier of magic flames to reach the site where they were required to dig. Then, as the last possible moment came and went, he decided it would be best not to tell them at all.

"What is that?" Andvari suddenly demanded, clutching hard at Hal with one hand, and pointing a wiry arm ahead.

"That's where we're going." Now ahead of the cantering Horses appeared the crag where Loki's flames still went soaring and roaring up to heaven, the whole still encircled by the path of the mysterious flying spark.

17

TO HAL, THE smoothly rounded fire on the crag looked no different than it had when he first laid eyes on it. And the only change he could detect in its surroundings seemed minor, having to do with an alteration in the appearance of the object, whatever it was, that gave the crag a halo. The revolving spark still maintained a good, hurtling pace, but Hal thought its glow had been slightly dimmed since he last saw it. He had been privately evolving a theory about the peculiar thing, a theory he now wanted to put to the test.

Andvari, with a bag of short but heavy tools tied to his belt, was still clinging on tightly behind Hal. The gnome now turned his head, averting his goggled eyes from the towering flames as they flew near, and muttered a stream of what sounded like prayers and imprecations.

Without giving any warning of what he meant to do, Hal tugged on his Horse's mane to change direction slightly, then halted Gold Mane in midair. He had chosen a spot where, if he had calculated correctly, the hurtling object in its regular course must pass almost near enough for him to touch it.

Meanwhile, Baldur (who also still had a mumbling gnome, complete with tool bag, clinging on behind him) had seen Hal pause, and had tugged Gold Mane into a short circling pattern, some fifty yards away.

Now Baldur called across the gap of empty air: "What is it, Hal, what are you delaying for?"

"You know my curiosity," Hal called back. He eyed the mysterious object carefully as it shot past him in its orbit. It came so close that his Horse recoiled slightly, but not before Hal had been granted the look he wanted. At close range Hal could recognize the thing easily enough; now he was sure that he had seen it before.

"Damn your curiosity!" Baldur was yelling at him. "We must press on to reach Brunhild! Are you with me or not?"

"I'm with you, and I'm ready." Hal wasn't going to try to explain his discovery now. He tugged Gold Mane around to face the flames. Then, over his shoulder in a low and cheerful voice: "Ready, Andvari? Got your goggles on?"

"I do." The voice of the gnome was somewhat muffled against Hal's shoulder. "We're coming down somewhere near that huge fire, then?"

"Quite near it, but it's perfectly safe. Baldur and I have been there before. Just hang on to me and hide your face. We'll be through in a moment, with no harm."

"*Through?*" Andvari squeaked. "Through what?!"

When they were no more than a hundred yards from the fire, galloping straight toward it, Andvari screamed aloud: "By all the fiends of the Underworld, we're going to be roasted alive!"

Hal was calm and firm. "No we're not. Believe me, Baldur and I have done this before. And forget about the powers of the Underworld, we're too high above the earth for them. The only god who might be involved in this business is Loki, not Hades, and Loki's not objecting."

But by the time Hal had finished saying that, Andvari was no longer listening.

The dreaded experience was over in a moment, and when it proved harmless, the two Earthdwellers recovered rapidly from their fright. Despite the steady glow of the burning walls, the fact that space around them was now tightly enclosed must have been deeply reassuring. Soon the two gnomes had their feet planted firmly on solid ground, and presently, still keeping their goggles firmly in place, they were able to concentrate on work.

At that point, Hal and Baldur had little to do except stand back and keep out of the way.

As soon as they had reentered the curving corridor, so stoutly guarded by two towering rings of fire, Baldur jumped from his Horse and hastened to peer through the inner fires once more at the figure he assumed was that of his beloved. He cried out at once, rejoicing that her blurred image was still visible, and spent a few moments in eager contemplation.

Hal and the two Earthdwellers followed him, somewhat more slowly. Yes, the gnomes agreed. Squinting through their goggles, with eyes barely open, they could see the figure too.

Hal immediately began to issue instructions for what he wanted, the excavation of a small tunnel through the solid rock.

Andvari tugged at his straggly beard. "For what distance?"

"For no great span at all. Just down a couple of feet where we are standing, then straight in that direction." Hal accompanied his words with expressive gestures, pointing toward the hidden center of the flames. "You needn't go far, just make sure you get under this second ring of fire—the flames must be of only modest thickness, since we can see right through them. Then up to ground level again on the other side. We're sure there's a clear, safe space over there." Of course Hal was not really sure of anything of the kind, but he thought there was no use introducing unnecessary complications. "Naturally you must dig the tunnel wide enough for me to get through it."

Andvari, professionally cautious, looked at Hal and seemed to be measuring his breadth and girth. "And nothing will happen to us if we dig under the fire? The god who made the flames has not—defended the ground beneath them?"

"Nothing at all will happen, you have my solemn pledge." Hal did not look at Baldur as he made that promise.

"How quickly must this be done?"

"Quick as you can. Will you be able to manage it in any reasonable time?"

Andvari squinted at his companion, who spat, and nodded. He reviewed the plan. "Straight down here—you say we don't have to go very deep?"

"No reason that I can see."

"Good. Down a couple of feet, then bore horizontally, ten feet or so in that direction"—he pointed inward, then slanted his long gray fingers to the vertical—"and then straight up again? That's it?" His shrug was almost contemptuous. "That shouldn't take long at all. Maybe not even an hour."

"Then do it! Please!"

The next step was for Andvari and his companion, standing alternately close together and far apart, to undertake a round of preliminary testing and probing, tapping and listening, scraping and peering, obviously in search of essential information about the quality of the rock. From time to time this was interrupted by a rapid discussion in some gnomish dialect, promptly followed by another burst of activity in which the two skilled miners took soundings of the ground beneath their feet, one of them tapping on the surface, now with his heaviest hammer, now again with a light one. Meanwhile his colleague, moving to various places, sometimes halfway around the corridor, listened with an ear to the ground.

Progressing in this way, the gnomes finished a complete circuit of the corridor before they agreed on the best place to dig. The spot Andvari finally selected was some four or five feet from the inner wall of flame, and only a few strides from where Hal, on first penetrating the outer ring, had landed on his Horse.

Having determined the exact site of operations, the gnomes wasted no time. They adjusted their goggles, spat ritually on their hands, and then snatched up their tools to begin alternately scraping and pounding on the rock with incredible rapidity.

Watching the speed with which his new allies tore into the earth, Baldur's excitement grew, and Hal could feel his own spirits rise. The Earthdwellers' thin arms flowed in ceaseless motion, and the bones of the world beneath them rang solidly from the impact of their tools. They fractured rock with a hammer and split it with an iron wedge. Hal first squinted and then turned away, protecting his eyes from flying fragments.

"Things seem to be going well," Hal cautiously commented.

Baldur looked strained, as usual. "I will agree that they are going well when we have reached Brunhild."

Hal turned his head from side to side in a futile effort to hear whatever might be happening outside the outer wall of flames. Out there, somewhere, by all accounts, the gods were fighting a great battle, an event that must ultimately be of great importance. Just what the fight was all about was still a mystery to him—well, most wars were like that. But in any case it was no great surprise—it was common knowledge that gods and Giants often clashed.

Though Baldur hated Wodan, he was unable to bring himself to hope that the vile creatures of the Underworld would win. Even though the death of Wodan's present avatar would make it possible for another human, hopefully of clearer mind, to put on the Face of the All-Highest.

———

Hal would have willingly passed on what he had discovered regarding the mysterious aerial token, the whirling dot of fire that seemed to guard the flames. But Baldur obviously was not interested.

When Hal tried to force the subject on him anyway, the young man brushed it away. "As long as it does not interfere with my reaching Brunhild, I care not what it is."

Hal sighed. "All right. Probably won't make a whole lot of difference to you." To himself he added: "But it gives me something to think about."

Meanwhile the diggers were scooping away the fractured rock and loose earth in an almost continuous stream, first with their strong, outsized hands and then with the blades of short-handled scoops or shovels. Hal thought they were making amazingly rapid progress.

When they had dug down the distance of a full handsbreadth, they begin singing or chanting as they worked, spouting words in some rhythmic rhyming tongue that neither Hal nor Baldur could understand, words blurring against the eternal muted roaring of Loki's flames.

───────

This had not gone on long when, without warning, there came another bursting intrusion through the outer wall. Again, all Hal's muscles tensed—again he relaxed gratefully when he recognized the Valkyrie's familiar face.

The gnomes might not even have been aware of Alvit's arrival. They kept working without a pause as she dismounted from her Horse.

Quickly Alvit brought Hal and Baldur up to date on the latest news from Valhalla.

She also remarked that she could not understand the Earthdwellers' chanting either. "But I have heard it before. Someone has told me that it has something to do with gold."

"A subject that seems never to be far from their thoughts," Baldur commented.

"Or from the thoughts of certain other people." She was looking at Hal. "Have you discovered Loki's whereabouts?"

He shook his head. "No. Why?"

"Because Wodan, at a time when his mind was clear, has assured us—myself and the other Valkyries—that he is ready to be reconciled with the Firegod. I can tell you that he hopes to recruit Loki for his side in the battle, or at least to keep him from joining the other side."

"We will certainly let you know if we encounter any god. What of Thor? Has Wodan found him yet?"

Alvit shook her head. "There is a new rumor that Thor is dead— but as far as I know, that is no more than a rumor."

"No big surprise if it proved true," Hal commented.

"Alive or dead, no one can locate him. It is a strange and terrible

THE BOOKS OF THE GODS, PART TWO

time for all our gods." Then Alvit added, unexpectedly, "You look very tired, Hal."

He had been listening with his eyes closed, but now he opened them and nodded. He thought that her voice had a new tone in it, almost tender. "And so do you," he observed.

———

With the gnomes out of sight, he could easily imagine from the rapidity of the dull thudding and scraping noises that four or five men were hard at work.

Baldur and Hal in turn had both made some effort to help the gnomes during the first few minutes of the digging, but each time Andvari shrilly ordered the Sundwellers to keep out of the way. In any event, both men were soon busy trying to soothe the Horses, who were growing nervous in the unaccustomed atmosphere of noise and dust and flying gravel. At last Baldur, saying he was worried that the animals might bolt, led them gently around the curve of cleared space until they were as far as possible from where the digging was in progress.

Hal was on the verge of thinking up some objection to this move, but he held his peace. It just made him vaguely uneasy, seeing his bagged gold being once more conveyed out of his sight. But he told himself that his prize remained very near. Only he knew where it was, and he had no reason to worry.

Under the impact of the gnomes' forged steel and driving energy, what only minutes ago had been a mere marking on the scraped rock had now become a hole. The hole grew deeper with amazing speed, so rapidly that within a few more minutes the foremost of the two diggers was working entirely below the surface of the ground, almost out of sight, his slitted bone goggles left aboveground.

While one pale, wiry figure, turned even whiter with rock dust, battered away at the face of the lengthening tunnel, usually with a hammer driving a chisel of the hardest, finest steel, the other skillfully cleared debris while keeping out of the digger's way. Every few minutes Andvari and his companion swapped places, keeping a fresh man at the hardest job, while the scattered piles of excavated rock and earth rapidly grew higher.

———

There soon followed an interval in which both gnomes were completely immersed in what had now become a tunnel, though it was hard to see how even their small bodies would find room to work in such a confined space. Hal wondered if they might be employing serious magic of their own, if they were worried that Loki had, after all, set up some different and invisible barrier.

Presently he and Baldur were tersely summoned, and commanded to help in the task of scooping away the pieces of fractured rock that were rapidly accumulating, being passed back through the tunnel from the swiftly eroding face.

Then, almost before the Sundwellers had begun to hope that the job might be soon completed, the gnomes shouted at them to stand clear of the tunnel's entrance, and Andvari soon came scrambling out of it, closely followed by his colleague, covered in rock dust. Both of them had taken their goggles off for the moment, and were rubbing their eyes, circles of sallow skin not powdered with rock dust.

"We have broken through," the senior Earthdweller informed his clients tersely.

"What did you find?" Baldur demanded frantically. "Is she there?"

"See for yourself." The gnome's gnarled features were unreadable as he stood aside. Hal took that as a bad sign.

———

Groaning and rushing ahead of Hal, Baldur threw himself headfirst into the narrow tunnel, barely allowing the protesting diggers time to get entirely out of his way.

Moments later, Hal followed, thrusting himself ahead of Alvit, who seemed in no great hurry to finally learn her beloved sister's fate. He found the excavation an exceedingly tight fit in several places; the struggle to get through cost him a couple of small patches of skin, but he persevered.

After some ten or twelve feet of scraping and squeezing his way forward, he came to where the passage turned up, and gradually was able to force his way, sweeping some debris with him like a broom, up through the rising curve to the newest tunnel mouth.

When his head reemerged into direct firelight, he was not entirely surprised to find himself again between two concentric rings of fire. He was in yet another wheel-rim of clear space, somewhat narrower and more tightly curved than the first had been. What had been the inner wall of the first rounded corridor was now of course the outer wall of this one.

Now Hal was able to confirm the existence of something he had more or less suspected: a third wall of flame. Very likely, he thought, this latest discovery was the innermost and final one, for there didn't seem room for another wheel-rim corridor inside it. The third wall looked no different than the other two, except for being more tightly curved, surrounding as it did a smaller area.

Nor was Hal really surprised to observe that there was no more metallic gold to be seen here in the second corridor than there had been in the first.

Consideration of any further details would have to wait. Only a few feet from where Hal was half-emerged from the tunnel, Baldur crouched at the side of a simple bed that seemed to have been formed from a spread-out cloak, occupying a central position between the inner and outer walls of flame.

Pulling the last sections of his aching body out of the hole in the floor, Hal crawled closer to the couple. The impression he had gained by trying to look through the flames had been essentially correct. Lying on her back, upon this rude catafalque, was a slender young woman wearing partial metal armor, loosely fitted over simple cloth undergarments. This outfit left her lower legs, forearms and part of her midriff exposed.

The top of the girl's head was covered only by her golden hair, so long and thick that it spread out in a great fan—this was obviously what Hal had seen from outside the barrier, what had suggested in his eyes a pile or pillow of yellow metal.

Hal's fragment of the Golden Fleece remained quiescent in his belt pouch, not leaping or twitching as he came near the girl. Whatever magic inhabited the Fleece was not going to be deceived by golden hair.

Baldur raised a face transformed and wet with tears of joy. His voice rang out: "She lives, Hal! She lives!"

"I rejoice to hear that," Hal said wearily, painfully getting to his feet. And truly he was relieved to see that the lovely face of the unconscious Valkyrie had the peaceful look of one who only slept, and that a faint blush of life showed in her cheeks. He hoped that that meant something more than skilled magical embalming. But he could not be sure the girl was breathing at all—if she was, the rise and fall of her breast beneath its light steel armor was too slight for Hal to see.

Baldur was clutching one of the young woman's inert arms and pressing his face to her motionless hand. Now his body was again racked by sobs.

Weary of all these demonstrations, Hal got slowly to his feet. "She's not dead," he reiterated in a dull voice, now feeling reasonably confident of the fact. Good news, he supposed—at least now Baldur ought not to absolutely break down—but another complication. Hal had the feeling that he was being battered by events, new things to worry about, first on one side then the other, the impacts coming too fast for a man to cope with them. Was he, after all, getting to be too old for this sort of thing? Shouldn't he already be standing behind a plow, staring at the rear ends of a couple of droms who were content to plod a field and never thought of flying?

Well, maybe he should. Right now the prospect did not seem all that inviting.

Baldur meanwhile had dropped his beloved's hand—her arm just fell limply to the ground—and was trying all sorts of things to wake her up, calling her by name, kissing her one moment and then in the next slapping her—though never very hard. But whatever he did, the young woman's eyes stayed shut, and she showed no sign of regaining consciousness.

Something small, very small indeed and very white, in darting motion, caught Hal's eye and he looked up. Once again light snow was falling, and somehow the soft flakes were managing to escape melting in the air high above the guardian flames; they came drifting down unscathed, to melt only when they touched the enchanted earth within the circle, or more swiftly on the maid's armor.

Alvit had come crawling through the tunnel to join the men. She remarked on the fact they were all standing between fires so large and so close to them that they should be roasted in a short time, yet none even felt uncomfortably warm. The others nodded agreement.

Cautiously experimenting with one hand, Hal decided that the heat within the flames themselves had to be at least as great as that of any normal fire. He could move his own toughened skin to within a few inches of it without being actually burned, but no closer.

"What use are all these speculations?" Alvit asked.

Hal did not answer directly. "I have been watching the snowflakes. If they can fall this far, come down here in the midst of the flames, without melting . . ."

"Ah, I see. Then it might be possible for a flying Horse to do the same? No, Hal, I tried that days ago. It was one of the first things I thought of, when I wanted to see Brunhild. But it will not work. Seen from above, Loki's magic makes this whole clifftop look like one solid mass of fire."

After a pause, she admitted: "Clever of you to come up with the plan of going underneath, right through solid rock. I suppose it never occurred to Loki that anyone would try that."

"Thank you. Maybe he just thought it would take them a very long time if they did."

Hal watched several large flakes settle in the blond hair of the unconscious girl, and several more come down in Alvit's hair, almost exactly the same color as Brunhild's, where they persisted briefly before sparkling into droplets. Another met an even swifter doom, landing on the soft red fullness of Brunhild's upper lip.

Baldur was not interested in snowflakes. He was groaning over his Valkyrie, alternately kissing her passionately, and pleading with her to awake. Again and again he had sworn that all he wanted was to hold her in his arms, but now that he could do that, he wanted more. Well, that was only to be expected. Hal still felt confident she was not dead, but she might as well have been, for all the sign she gave of waking up.

As far as Hal was concerned, Brunhild could wait a little longer. He still believed that Loki must have had some greater purpose here, and was still fascinated by trying to discover what it was.

Suppose that Loki—traditionally the master of fire, and of treachery as well—feared both Wodan and Thor. And suppose, with his knack for making enemies, he had come to be at odds with the powers of the Underworld as well—well, that would be a dangerous situation for even the greatest deity. Loki would have to depend entirely on his own powers, his own skill, for his survival. At least temporarily, until he was able to fashion new alliances. If Loki had wanted to create a defensive stronghold for himself, what better place than here, triply protected by his own wonderful fire?

The gnomes had now followed their Sundwelling clients in through the tunnel, thin wiry bodies accommodating easily to its narrow curves. On emerging from the dark passage, Andvari and Ivaldr put on the goggles they had removed while actually in it, and with their eyes hidden behind opaque disks it was impossible for Hal to even guess what they might be thinking.

Joining the Sundwellers, the gnomes sat down, establishing themselves solidly on the rocky ground as if determined to claim a well-earned rest. One of them helpfully suggested looking for a poisoned thorn, or something similar, embedded in the girl's flesh.

Baldur seemed to be sliding into helplessness. "What should we do if there is one?"

"Why, pull it out!"

Alvit and Baldur began carefully removing more sections of the girl's armor, while Hal sat back, watching and thinking. Baldur's hands were shaking as he set aside, one after another, pieces of metal and cloth.

Alvit seemed ready to take over the operation. "You might turn her over and examine her back."

But there was no need to do that. In the end it was Alvit's keen vision that saw it first: a black dot, coarse but tiny, so small against Brunhild's fair skin, so like a tiny mole, that it might easily have passed unnoticed.

She murmured: "This looks like it. It could be just the end of a thorn that's causing the trouble."

Brushing Alvit's hand aside, Baldur took it upon himself to try to remove the thorn, if thorn it was, stuck so cruelly and outrageously into her tender flesh, near the side of her right breast. With shaking fingers he fumbled for a grip and finally found one.

The thorn was amazingly thin, and horribly long, a couple of inches at least. Baldur cast it away with a shudder.

———

The pinpoint wound where the thorn had been was marked now by a single drop of crimson blood. Almost at once, the recumbent girl drew a deep, shuddering breath and began to stir. Baldur kept pleading with her, clutching her in his arms.

Brunhild's eyes when they opened were dazzlingly blue. She was at first completely bewildered and naturally frightened to find herself enclosed by walls of flame, which she did not remember seeing before. But her recovery proceeded with almost magical speed, and she greeted Alvit joyfully.

Only then did she realize who held her in his arms. "What is this— Baldur? What are you doing here, where are we?" Her voice was thin and weak at first, but soon gained strength.

Her lover was beside himself with joy at her recovery, and did his best to reassure her.

A moment later Brunhild became aware that there were strangers present too. She modestly tried to recover her clothing and her armor. Dressing herself for action, she naturally wanted to know how much time had passed while she remained in her enchanted sleep.

Baldur was horrified when she muttered something about having to prepare herself for combat. It occurred to Hal to discourage her by pointing out that she had no weapons available—and no use trying to borrow any, because probably the only weapon with which Hildy had any familiarity would be the magic Spear.

She was naturally relieved to learn that only a matter of days had gone by since Wodan had sentenced and punished her.

And Brunhild confirmed that she had earlier refused to take Baldur to Valhalla because she wished to save him from an unpleasant fate.

When she learned that he had been there, she was frightened and relieved at the same time. "Thank all the gods you have survived! I wanted to save you from Valhalla—I ought to have told you what it is really like—but I was afraid. And I knew you would never believe me."

At last her gaze focused on Hal.

"Who's this? One of your father's men?"

Hal made a little gesture of salute. "I'm just a type of wandering savage, miss. No more Hagan's man than you are."

At that Brunhild gave him a strange look; but Baldur hastened to vouch for his comrade.

———

The gnomes had been resting, listening to Sundwellers' talk, for only a little while when they surprised Hal by getting to their feet again, showing signs of renewed energy.

"I hope none of you will mind if we dig another tunnel?" Andvari asked the four Sundwellers, indicating with a gesture that he contemplated burrowing under the second ring of fire just as they had the first.

Brunhild only shook her head, not understanding. Alvit seemed surprised, but too tired to take any real interest. Baldur, as if he thought he might have misunderstood the gnome, told him: "You have our eternal gratitude."

Hal also shook his head, not particularly surprised. "No, no, go right ahead and dig. In fact I will be delighted, provided that you make a passage big enough for me to get through. Just a little wider than the last one, if you please. I'd like to see what's in there."

The gnomes nodded silently, their eyes hidden behind goggles. In a minute they had chosen their starting place and work was under way, with fragments and rock dust flying as before.

———

Baldur and his Valkyrie were clinging together as if they both feared to let go. She murmured dreamily: "Whatever happens now, we two will always be together."

Obviously the young couple had no interest in further exploration, and were eagerly, deeply absorbed in planning their own futures. What were they going to do now, where were they going to go? There was evidence of serious disagreement, though so far nothing like a quarrel.

Hal and Alvit both began to urge them to make up their minds quickly.

Hal said: "If I were you, I'd argue about my destination after I was on the road. Head anywhere you like, as long as it's not toward the war."

Baldur seemed too happy to bother to listen closely. "Some day maybe I will go to war again. Right now I do not see the need."

Suddenly Alvit recalled the Horses. "We must make sure they are still safe. We'll need them to get out through the outer ring of fire, it wouldn't do to find ourselves trapped." And one after the other the four Sundwellers slid and scrambled back through the tunnel.

When they had all rejoined the Horses in the outer corridor, Alvit again exhorted the couple to get going. Now, while the battle still raged, was the time to flee the wrath of Wodan. If the Father of Battles was strong enough and lucky enough to survive his current fight—and if he then remembered Brunhild at all—he would certainly try to inflict some extra punishment on her for her escape.

Hal too urged the lovers to move on while they could, while the All-Highest was still distracted with battle.

At last Baldur and Brunhild mounted, on a single Horse, their two bodies molded together and whispering in each other's ears. It was as if, now that they had found each other again, they feared to be out of sight or out of touch for even a moment. Baldur murmured that it would not be the first time the animal had carried them both swiftly.

This time it was Baldur who, automatically assuming the role of leader, sat in front where he could grip the Horse's mane and exert control. And his beloved, Spearless now, no longer a Valkyrie, yielded the place of leadership to him without a murmur. So closely did she cling on behind her lover that it looked like he was sitting in her lap.

At the last moment, Baldur turned his head and swore eternal loyalty to Hal, pledging his honor and his help if Hal should ever need them.

"Thank you, I may need that pledge some day. Meanwhile, get the hell out of here." Hal urged the lovers on their way with a violent motion of his arm, ending with a hard swat on the Horse's rump. The couple and their mount vanished through flames, carrying Alvit's shouted blessing.

Hal's blessing went with them too, silent but just as sincere, since he had first made sure that his gold remained behind.

When Hal looked around again, Alvit was already astride her own mount. But she lingered long enough to tell Hal that she meant to accompany the young lovers on the first stage of their flight.

"And there, your Horse is waiting for your departure." She pointed at the remaining beast.

"I'm looking forward to my next ride," he assured her.

Still Alvit delayed. "Where will you go?"

"I'm not sure yet. What about you?"

The Valkyrie pulled at her golden hair, which was dull and tangled now, evidently from want of care over the last few days. Her cheeks looked hollower than before. "I have already told you, Hal. I mean to return to Wodan, and fight beside him when the enemy draws near— so far I have been unable to do any real fighting."

She reached out a hand to grasp her grounded Spear. "Until now the great powers on each side have only bombarded each other with their terrible weapons at long range. There has been little that ordinary humans like you and me could do. But that will change." The Valkyrie's voice sounded suddenly uncertain. And after a moment she added: "Whether the mode of fighting changes or does not change, whether my god lives or dies, I want to be with him at the end."

Hal said: "I don't know about your sisters, as you call them. But I think you've already done all that the All-Highest could ask of you, and more. Loyalty should work both ways."

Her face and voice were grim. "I have not been truly loyal. I broke my oath to Wodan, in setting you and Baldur free."

Hal had to think that over. At last he said: "I would want all my friends, if I have any, to be as faithful to me as you are to your god. Friends mean more than oaths."

The Valkyrie was shaking her head. "I was all ready to let you steal Wodan's gold—and now I think that was a mistake."

"You only did that for his own good, you were trying to wake him up and save his life. If he was in his right mind, he'd thank you . . . of course he'd probably kill me."

"I hope you are right, I mean that he would thank me. In any case, Hal, I am going to say goodbye to you again." There was something tender and regretful in her manner.

He bowed slightly.

Alvit started to move away, then turned back and said: "We are much alike, northman, you and I. Somewhere under all the differences."

He thought it over, and nodded slowly. "For one thing, it seems that we are neither of us farmers."

She frowned at that. "Farmers? Why should we be farmers?"

He shrugged.

"If I had time, I would ask you to explain."

"I will explain, if you come back to me as soon as you have the chance. I think I'll be here for a while."

Again Alvit was on the brink of leaving, when he added: "And there's another reason I'd like you to come back."

"What?"

"Just so I can see that you are still alive. And, now that I think of it, there's yet another reason after that: I like the way you say goodbye."

"What?"

Hal felt relaxed and confident, the heavy bulk of gold right under his hands in the saddlebags. He could feel it through the leather. Maybe it would never turn into farms and fishing boats, but it meant that he had won. He said: "I'd like to hear you say goodbye to me, oh, another hundred times at least."

He thought that the request pleased her. "If I can, I can, I will." And with that, she was gone.

Now he was all alone, as far as he knew, except for three rings of fire and two gnomes. He could hear the muffled sounds of their tireless digging, only a few yards away.

And a single Horse, of course. But given the fear the gnomes had so far shown of heights and Horses, he wasn't worried about their making off with this one.

18

WITH ALVIT GONE, Hal went back to the inner corridor and put his head down into the new tunnel to talk to the gnomes.

"Have you finished digging?" he asked.

"No, but we must rest again." From what Hal could see in the dimness, indeed the pair of Earthdwellers looked just about worn out. Andvari also seemed worried about something. "Hal, you will not leave us here, will you?"

"No, why would I do that?"

"I don't know. Of course you wouldn't. It's just that we would never be able to manage the Horse by ourselves. We would certainly perish in the attempt."

"And the heights," his companion chimed in, from somewhere deeper in the tunnel's darkness. "I keep remembering how high we are above the valley. If the flames were gone, it would be a terrifying view."

Hal generously agreed. If things here now went as well as he hoped they might, he would owe the little men more than he was ever likely to repay them. So he readily pledged that he would not leave without them, and that he would carry them gently to safety. He didn't expect the Horse would have any trouble carrying him and the two gnomes for a modest distance. It would be awkward but quite possible.

The little men seemed reassured. Soon, after resting for only a couple of minutes, they went back to hammering and scooping away relentlessly at their new tunnel. Still they had offered no explanation of why they were doing it. Hal thought he knew the reason, and he was waiting to find out if he was right.

Sitting down again in the inner corridor, he enjoyed a brief rest, looking around him at the curving walls of fire. The flames were always going up and up, and at the same time they were unchanging, like a magical reversed waterfall. With the gnomes on the job he thought he might actually succeed in probing the mysteries of Loki's stronghold and sanctuary.

Now that the Earthdwellers were out of sight, working away like fanatics in their new tunnel, Hal seized the opportunity to test his fragment of the Golden Fleece in the inner corridor. What he saw confirmed his previous observations: the closer to the center of the concentric rings he brought the Fleece, the more dramatically it glowed and twitched. The talisman was even more active here than it had been in the outer corridor.

He paused to listen to the sounds of a steady hammering, accompanied by a clattering of broken rock, that came drifting out of the near mouth of the tunnel. Despite the eagerness with which the Earthdwellers had undertaken the new task, they now, in spite of all their industry, seemed to be taking a comparatively long time about it.

When Hal called down into the tunnel to ask what was going on, he received answering cries in tense voices, telling him that they had run into especially hard rock.

There was both strain and weariness in Andvari's voice. "The edges of our tools are blunted, from the work we have already done. There is granite just beneath the surface."

"Are you encountering magical interference?" Hal demanded.

He heard a mumble as Andvari and his comrade conferred between themselves in their strange dialect. Then one called back: "We do not think so. Just some very hard rock." The sounds of hammering resumed; Hal thought they seemed to be coming now from a greater distance.

Hal chafed and grumbled to himself, but there was nothing he could do to speed up the digging. Then an idea struck him, and he sat for a time in silence, thinking.

He was still sitting there when at last Andvari and his companion appeared to announce the job was finished. Having emerged from underground, the little men stood aside, and silently gestured that the way through the tunnel was open for Hal. He noticed in passing that the hands of both gnomes were sore and bleeding. But he made no comment.

Seeing light at the other end of the tunnel, Hal started through at once, headfirst. For all the time that the miners had spent in digging it, this passageway was no longer than the first one, and he thought it might be even slightly narrower, as if perhaps the diggers had hoped to discourage the passage of anyone stouter than themselves, without quite daring to make it impossible, against his direct request. He had a real struggle, and once he heard his clothing tear.

When Hal's head came poking up out of the exit, he was at once able to confirm what he had suspected: that the third circle of fire was indeed the innermost. He was emerging from underground very nearly at the center of the final ring. From here it was possible, as it had not been from anywhere else inside the fires, to see a circle of sky directly overhead. This took the form of a disk of orange-washed blackness. He thought he was beginning to lose track of time. Either night had fallen, or this was some strange effect of Loki's light, that the sun's illumination should be kept out even though snowflakes could drift in.

The light in this round chamber was peculiar, somehow not nearly as bright as it should have been, considering the luminous nature of the encircling wall. In fact the whole surface underfoot for some reason lay under a kind of blight of shadow, making it hard for Hal to tell just what he was stepping on, or looking at. There was a small litter of digging tools.

The circular space enclosed by the third ring of fire was no more than about five yards in diameter, and basically level. But further details were hard to see, for the darkened ground was thickly scattered, all across its width, with the loose material of the gnomes' digging—for some reason, in carving out this most recent tunnel, they must have carried much of the excavated material through with them, along with their tools. Hal found that puzzling, but just now he had no attention to spare for such puzzles.

At one side of the enclosed circle, the rocky floor of the space rose up slightly, just enough to accommodate a low mound of something that despite its earthy hue was neither rock nor soil. Whatever hopes Hal might have had for an immediately visible heap of gold went glimmering. But he had not really expected to see spectacular treasure at once. The gnomes would have seen it first, immediately on breaking through.

Suppose they had. What would they have done then?

The answer was simple and obvious. The Earthdwellers would have tried their best to hide the treasure so that no one else, on entering this inner sanctuary, would be able to see it. The only way to conceal a mass of metal would have been to bury it, which meant Andvari and his comrade must have dug yet another hole in solid rock. The surplus material dug from the new treasure pit must have been scattered round evenly with the rest. No wonder the diggers were in a state of near-collapse, with bleeding hands, and no wonder this round of work had taken them so comparatively long.

Hal had dragged his thick body only halfway out of the tunnel when his attention was sharply distracted from the mound by a sharp movement in his belt pouch. The jumping vibration was so intense that it startled him. His fragment of the Golden Fleece was twitching and jumping more violently in his pouch than he had ever felt or seen it do before. It grew relatively active every time he brought it into Loki's stronghold. Overall it had been giving him stronger and stronger indications the closer he brought it to the center of the rings of fire.

But at the moment it was not signaling him to move toward the mound, but in the opposite direction.

Slowly Hal tugged and scraped himself completely free of the tunnel. Getting to his feet, he studied his surroundings in puzzlement; the Fleece was hopping in its pouch like a live thing, but there was not the smallest spark of bright yellow to be seen anywhere. Squinting, he scanned the basically level floor of the enclosed space, which was everywhere heavily littered with loose dirt and chips of stone.

Hal's fragment of the Fleece seemed to be trying to tug him, direct him, to the side of the inner chamber farthest from the mound.

Pulling the talisman from his pouch, he held it in his hand, gripping it firmly so it could not jump clear of his fingers. Then he moved it from side to side, letting the strength of its activity guide him. Quickly he was led to one particular spot of rubble-covered ground, exactly opposite the shadowy mound. Here the scrap of fabric was glowing so that it seemed it must burn his hand, but in truth there was no heat. Hal tucked the fragment back in his pouch, the better to do the necessary digging with both hands.

He had to displace only a few inches of loose rock fragments before the unmistakable glint of gold came into view. Now his hands began to work with great excitement.

The treasure had been hastily but effectively buried, and Hal realized he would never have imagined it was there had it not been for the feverish activity of his fragment of the Golden Fleece.

The uncovering of the treasure went very swiftly now.

In the quarter of an hour or so they'd had available, Andvari and his comrade had carved into the solid rock a repository about two feet in diameter and of unknown depth, just big enough to hold the gold that must have been lying on the surface when they entered this inner chamber.

Hal knew he was looking at what amounted to a king's ransom—

no, make that an emperor's ransom, or a god's. He had little doubt that before him lay the legendary treasure of the race of Earthdwellers.

Tugging at the upper layers of heavy treasure, lifting a few of the larger items completely out of their latest hiding place, he was able to see that the cavity was as deep as his arm was long, and fairly solidly packed with gold.

The treasure was in several forms. There were huge raw nuggets, as well as refined bars, and pieces of jewelry (though he could not see a single gemstone or any metal that was not yellow). Here and there, mostly sifted toward the bottom of the pit, were handfuls of minted coins, bearing faces and script Hal could not recognize, filling up the interstices. How such a great hoard had originally been gathered, and by whom, was more than Hal could guess.

Altogether there was so much gold that he could hardly have encircled it with his two arms, far more than he could possibly have lifted. The sheer bulk of the find made it seem somehow less real than his own secret hoard of thin little horseshoes.

But it was real enough.

Hal's first elation swiftly turned to gloom. He had probed Loki's stronghold almost to its final secret, and his success seemed to present him with only another problem.

Who but a god was likely to succeed in accumulating such a mass of treasure? It would seem to represent the hopes and efforts of a whole tribe or race. Actually Hal thought most gods would not bother to go in for hoarding precious metals. What need had deities for gold, when all the things that humans needed gold to buy were effectively theirs for the taking?

With a grunt, Hal lowered himself to sit on the littered and stony ground, close beside his find. Aching as much as ever, feeling more tired than elated, he sat there staring morosely at it. This was what came of being cursed with insatiable curiosity—whatever fine things you might discover, you were sure to be saddled with new problems. Somewhat to his own surprise, he found himself seriously considering the idea of simply covering up the hoard again.

But even before he made his decision on the hoard, there was, he was almost certain, one more treasure to be discovered here. A thing that might, he feared, have a greater impact on its discoverer than even a ton of gold.

The sight of the immense trove had momentarily knocked everything else out of his mind. But only momentarily, because now the thought of the even more important object trumped everything else.

Turning back to confront the dimly, strangely shadowed mound,

Hal suddenly wished he had had more chance to talk with Alvit, discuss the situation with her. On the other hand, he was now somewhat easier in his mind knowing that Baldur was already far away.

Before he could even approach the mound, he became aware that the gnomes were calling something to him through the tunnel. He called back to them to wait, and then went to take a closer look at what else lay on the other side of this inner, triply-defended room.

Looking closely, Hal could see that the dim little mound was something more than earth. Those were bones, he could see now, as he had suspected, and bones of a special kind, part of a body that had once walked on two legs.

Standing right beside the corpse, Hal confirmed that it was little more than a ruined skeleton, so disjointed that it was hard to say whether it lay curled on its side or stretched on its back. There were a few remaining tatters, burned and shredded, of what had once been clothing. The front of the skull grinned fleshlessly at Hal. Those particular bones were still more or less intact, as if something had halfway protected them from the impact that had shattered most of the rest of the body. The remainder of the head was entirely gone, not even enough of it left to tell what the hair had been like.

There was nothing special about any of the bones—not in their present condition, anyway—to tell him if he was looking at the body of a man or a woman. The ruin of a human body, yes, but also of one that had been more than human. Had it not been for the nearby hoard of gold and certain other indications, Hal would have assumed that the remains must be those of another of Wodan's prisoners.

If you assumed that this unfortunate was only another prisoner, then he or she had evidently been triply confined, inside three rings of fire instead of only two; and so perhaps she or he had been judged guilty of some offense even more serious than Brunhild's.

But it would not be "she." Hal felt certain of that now, and certain the individual's confinement had been voluntary.

Loki had been trying to hide. Hal had no real doubt of which god would have sought safety within a triple ring of fire.

———

The appearance of the body testified eloquently to the force of the blast or blow that had driven the life out of it—Hal didn't see how any merely natural blow, struck by any mortal human hand and weapon, could possibly have mashed a human body, let alone a god, the way this one had been mashed. Not even if the masher had been Hercules. Somehow all the fires and all the magic that this Firegod and Trickster could put up had not been enough to save him.

Hal needed just a moment longer, in the strange, dim light of magic fire, to locate the confirming evidence, but it was there all right. Holding his breath, he bent lower to examine the Face of Loki.

Looking at the first god's Face that he had ever seen, Hal realized that there was nothing intrinsically impressive about it, compared with a pile of gold. All the essentials of Loki's divinity resided in an object no bigger than Hal's hand, and no more conspicuous than a piece of dull glass. It lay close beside the body, near what little was left of the head. There it had come to rest after the skull of Loki's most recent avatar was shattered by some god-blasting impact, an overwhelming force that had come smashing right through the triple rings of fire, penetrating what must have been very impressive magical defenses.

In his wanderings over the past few years, Hal had learned a little about the strength of gods and their magic, and now he shivered slightly when he sought to visualize just what had happened here, tried to imagine the forces involved.

Probably the gnomes had not even noticed the small, dull, ordinary-looking thing lying on the ground—they had been dazzled into ecstasy by finding what they did find, just what they were looking for, and consumed by their anxiety to hide the glorious treasure. Possibly they had looked right at the Face in passing, and simply had not realized what this inconspicuous object was. The Face of Loki, god of fire, and . . .

A Trickster-god as well.

———

Very few people had ever seen the Face of any god. Probably not many people in the whole history of the world, he reflected, for no Face was likely to be lying about, naked and unworn, free for the taking, for very long before someone picked it up. History seemed to confirm what legend taught: powerful forces of magic tended to prevent the Faces from going long unused. When the death of an avatar stripped away the human flesh from some god's divinity, supernatural powers came into play, bringing a suitable human replacement to the exposed Face, or somehow conveying the Face to a man or woman who would put it on.

After looking at the Face for a long moment, Hal shot out suddenly unsteady fingers and picked it up. He was holding what appeared to be a fragment of a carved or molded image of a human countenance, broken or cut from a mask or statue. It weighed almost nothing.

Hal drew a deep breath, and said a prayer to several gods—for years now he had been convinced such prayers were useless, but the habits of youth were hard to break.

Suddenly he knew that he had to make sure the find was genuine, and not some Loki-trickery. Setting the Face back on the ground, he tried to cut it with his battle-hatchet, tapping the object warily at first, then winding up with a full swing. The only result was a recoil that bounced the weapon back, so that it almost hit him in the forehead.

The Face itself jumped only a little on the hard surface where he'd set it down, and when he picked it up for close inspection the cloudy, translucent surface showed not the smallest sign of any damage.

So, it was genuine, the handiwork of whatever unimaginable power had made the gods. Talk about treasure. Compared to this, a pile of gold was worth little more than a pile of lead.

Enormous as the value of the hoard of gold must be, Hal suspected that the market price of this small object, so easily held in one hand, could be greater. There were surely men and women in the world who would pay staggering sums, give value on the scale of treasuries and kingdoms, for the small object Hal now held in his hand. He observed with a kind of awe that he could feel a tingling in his hand, almost a burning in his fingers where they touched the smooth surface.

The eerie impression of life that the thing gave was quite accurate. For certainly something inside it was engaged in rapid movement, reminding Hal of the dance of sunlight on rippling water. Inside the semi-transparent object, which was no thicker than his finger, he beheld a ceaseless, rapid, internal flow, of—of *something*—that might have been ice-clear water, or even light itself, if there could be light that illuminated nothing . . . but when he looked a moment longer, his impression shifted, until it was more one of dancing flames, as if it mirrored the encircling barrier of heat . . .

Again and again Hal kept coming back to the fact that Loki was one of the Trickster-gods, and you would expect his Face to have something uncertain, something deceptive, about it.

It was practically impossible to determine the direction or the speed of flow. The apparent internal waves seemed to be unendingly reflected from the edges, and they went on and on without any sign that they were ever going to weaken.

The thickness of the strange object varied from about a quarter of an inch to half an inch. It was approximately four inches from top to bottom, and six or seven along the curve from right to left. The ceaseless flow inside it, of whatever it was that looked like dancing flame, went on as tirelessly as before.

Whether the modeled face was intended to be masculine or feminine
was hard to tell, except that there was no representation of beard or
mustache . . . the most prominent feature of the fragment was the single
eye that it contained—the left—which had been carved or molded from
the same piece of strange, warm, flexible, transparent stuff as all the
rest. The eyeball showed an appropriately subtle bulge of pupil, and the
details of the open lid were clear. No attempt had been made to represent
eyelashes. An inch above the upper lid, another smooth small bulge
suggested an eyebrow. A larger one below outlined cheekbones. No
telling what the nose looked like, because the fragment broke off cleanly
just past the inner corner of the eye. Along the top of the fragment, in
the region of the temple, was a modeled suggestion of hair curled close
against the skull.

Around the whole irregular perimeter of the translucent shard, the
edges were somewhat jagged . . . now when Hal pushed at the small
projections with a finger, he found that they bent easily, springing back
into their original shape as soon as the pressure was released. Everything
about the piece he was holding suggested strongly that it was only a
remnant, torn or broken from a larger image, that of a whole face or
even an entire body.

The god who had fallen and perished here had once been on such
friendly terms with Wodan that he invited the All-Highest to use one
compartment of his stronghold as a prison for recalcitrant Valkyries.
The same god who had somehow, somewhere, taken possession of the
golden treasure the gnomes were now trying to reclaim. The same god
who had brought the vast hoard here, in an attempt to hide it, keep it
for himself.

The northman knew roughly what powers the Face of Loki would
bring the human being who wore it. But he was not in the least inclined
to put it on.

Instead, he tucked it into his belt pouch, where he imagined he could
feel it burning against his belly. Faintly smiling, he took an inventory
of the digging tools the gnomes had left scattered about in here—he
thought the whole of their equipment was pretty well accounted for.

Then Hal put his head down into the tunnel and called sharply for
Andvari and Ivaldr to come through to him. He was reluctant to go out
to them, lest they assume he had found the gold, and be tempted to
murder him while he was in the vulnerable position of emerging from
the narrow passage.

After a pause, Andvari's voice came back, politely asking Hal to
first pass their digging tools out to them.

He made his own voice neutral, sending it back through the ten-foot tube. "I think you had better come in here and get them. We have some matters to talk over. And as soon as you have tools available, I wish you'd make this tunnel a little wider."

———

When Andvari and his comrade reentered the innermost chamber of Loki's stronghold, they found Hal sitting casually right beside the pile of gold.

For a long moment no one spoke. Then Ivaldr said in a weary voice: "So you have found it."

Hal was letting one big hand rest almost carelessly on the glowing pile. "I suppose this was just lying on the surface in here, and you somehow caught a glimpse of it when you looked in through the second ring of fire? No wonder you just had to dig the second tunnel." He grabbed up a few coins, and let them trickle through his fingers.

Ivaldr started to react angrily to Hal's fingering of the hoard, but then subsided into gloomy silence.

"Well?" Hal prompted.

The two little men exchanged an exhausted look, then nodded in agreement. Andvari said: "Yes, looking through the flames with our goggles we could see it from out in the second corridor. And when we came up through the floor here, it was spread out on the ground at the feet of the skeleton—this second prisoner."

"As if," the other gnome put in, "the prisoner had been gloating over it before she—or he—died. Much good did it do him, or her."

Hal was curious. "Did it ever occur to you to wonder who this second prisoner was?"

Clearly it had not. The pile of gold was what Ivaldr and Andvari cared about. And now that they had handled it, and buried it with great expense of energy and effort, they were probably ready to kill to keep it.

Standing, Andvari drew himself up to his full height, a little over four feet. "The treasure is ours, you see. And now that we have found it, we are not going to let it go." His voice quavered slightly as he confronted the giant warrior before him with this declaration.

"I do not dispute that it is yours," said Hal, mildly. He still sat relaxed. "Others may, but that will be your problem."

They only blinked at him distrustfully. Here in the strange dimness they had taken their goggles off again.

Now in a rush of candor Andvari confessed that he and his comrade had thought of fighting Hal for the gold, but decided against that course. It would be much better if they could trust each other.

"You have been our friend, and saved our lives. And we are miners and metalworkers, not hardened fighting men."

Ivaldr gloomily chimed in: "Also, if we fought, you would probably kill us both in no time."

Hal nodded judiciously. "There is that."

"Besides that, we will need your help. We must all remember," Andvari pointed out, "that we Earthdwellers are unable to manage Horses by ourselves, and without your help we would certainly kill ourselves in a fall from this high place, even if we managed to get out through the outer ring of fire . . . you don't even ask for a share?"

"Would it make you feel better to give me one? You'd be getting no gold at all if I hadn't brought you here."

The two little men looked at each other. "We will have to talk about that," Andvari said.

Ivaldr nodded. "Discuss it with our elders."

Hal had about decided that he didn't really want a share, but still their attitude annoyed him.

———

The two gnomes, saying they wanted to talk the matter of sharing over between themselves, gathered up their tools, left Hal in the central chamber and went out again through the newest tunnel.

If he hadn't been dead certain of their inability to ride the Horse without him, he would have followed closely. As matters actually stood, of course—

Now in through the tunnel—through two tunnels, actually—there came the abrupt sound of hoofbeats, golden shoes on hard rock, followed by terse scrambled dialogue in gnomish voices—followed by sudden and utter silence. Hal jumped to his feet. As clearly as if he could see them, he heard the gnomes somehow scrambling together aboard the one remaining Horse, and riding outward through the fiery curtain.

They were already gone, successfully making their escape. And, whether they knew it or not, they had his pitiful small trove of golden horseshoes with them. He had been utterly wrong about the Earthdwellers and their supposed dread of Horses. The little bastards had tricked him, and now the disaster he had feared had struck.

The strangest thing was that he hardly felt the impact of the loss.

Somehow having the Face in his possession had driven all real worries about mere gold out of his mind.

He said aloud: "Well, if they have my treasure now, I still have theirs. Until they get back with their army to collect it. And that will take a while." Hal looked from the huge pile of gold back to the skeleton, and it grinned back at him. "Didn't do you much good, did it?"

The skeleton made no reply.

"Yes, I have theirs. Along with something even better."

Hal listened, for a sound coming from outside the flames, he wasn't sure exactly what. He thought he could hear several kinds of noise. Whatever he heard, he made no move, but only waited.

19

SEVERAL MINUTES HAD passed, but Hal was still standing there in almost the same position, except that he had taken the Face of Loki from his pouch, and was once more holding it in his hands, when Alvit came writhing through the second tunnel to confront him.

Her blond head popped into view, and she regarded him without surprise. "There you are, Hal. Did you know the gnomes had gone? As I approached I saw them in flight, both of them with their sun-goggles on, clinging desperately to the back of one Horse. The same Horse I left here for you."

Hal let out a great sigh, as if he had been unconsciously holding in his breath. "I realized that they were gone," he said.

"I suppose," Alvit replied after a pause, "that somehow gold is once more at the root of the trouble?" Pulling herself up out of the hole, she stood with hands on hips and glared at him. She was just a little taller.

Hal nodded.

"Where is the gold this time, northman?"

Forcing his hands to move slowly and casually, Hal opened his belt pouch and put away the essence of the great god, so that Loki nestled right beside the Golden Fleece. At the same time he watched the young woman carefully, trying to judge by her reaction whether she recognized the object he had just concealed, or whether she had even bothered to look at it at all.

Alvit was staring at him, but her thoughts were obviously not on Faces at the moment. "So, do you wish to discuss the situation? The gnomes have ridden away on your Horse, and left you trapped in here. And I once thought you might be leadership material. Or were you counting on using their tools to dig your own way out, under the outer ring?"

"No—I mean, I didn't know they were going to take the Horse, but I'm not absolutely trapped."

"You're not? Just how would you propose to get out through the outer ring of fire, lacking a Horse?"

"I'm all right, Alvit. Don't worry about me—not just now. What about you? By the way, I'm very glad you accepted my invitation and came back."

She sighed. "I seem to do a lot of riding to and fro."

"What's going on with Wodan?"

"I think he is happy that his great battle has begun, but he is not well." She went on to report that, since leaving Hal only a little while ago, she had been with Wodan on his not-so-distant battlefield. Her chief reason for returning to the high crag now was that Wodan had dispatched her and all the other available Valkyries to search everywhere they could for Thor.

"And you thought Thor might be here?"

"He was not far from here when last I saw him. You remember when that was."

"What happens when you've found him?"

"We are to appeal to the Thunderer's honor, and to his better nature, for aid against the monsters of the Underworld."

"So Wodan is actually appealing for help? I didn't know he could."

"Of course the All-Highest would not put the matter in those words, he is far too proud—but yes, he needs help and is asking for it. Unlike some men, who can be effectively trapped and need a Horse, but refuse even to admit the fact."

Hal grinned. "I admit that a Horse is likely to be of substantial help to me in getting away from here, when the time comes."

"In that case you may use mine—if I am here when the time comes." Then she dug something from a belt pouch. "Here—I wouldn't want to see you waste away." She handed over another small package of food.

Hal murmured thanks and opened the package. Looking at the food, he remembered his last meal, a nibble of gnomes' roots, and realized that he was hungry.

Alvit's gaze had now moved past him to probe curiously at the modest mound. From the way her face altered, he could tell the precise moment when she recognized that it was largely made of bones.

Her voice took on an edge. "Who's this? Another prisoner? A couple of other Valkyries are unaccounted for."

Brushing crumbs from his fingers, Hal moved that way a step or two, so he was once more standing close beside the remains. "The gnomes, too, thought this was another of Wodan's prisoners. But he wasn't."

"He? It is a man, then? Who?"

When Hal didn't answer immediately, Alvit turned, looking all round the inner chamber. Her gaze fell on the golden hoard, and the question of the bones was momentarily driven from her mind. For the space of two or three breaths she remained frozen in silent astonishment. Then in a hushed voice she said: "I see now why you could be so casual about losing a few horseshoes."

"There seems to be a curse of some kind on me. I'm never going to be rich."

She moved a little closer to the yellow pile. "Surely you will try to take a part of this, at least?"

"It seems the gnomes are determined to have it all. Actually, I've been thinking about another problem."

From the corner of his eye he saw Alvit's pale face turn to look at him. But when he turned to see her expression, her handsome face was unreadable.

Now Alvit was looking from bones to gold and back again, as if an idea had struck, and maybe the truth was beginning to dawn on her. At last she asked again, in a more demanding voice: "Who is this, then?"

Hal gave the skeleton a brief glance. "Not much of anyone right now. But I'd be willing to bet that whole pile of gold that this was the last avatar of Loki."

"This?" And for a moment she drew away, as if in awe, or perhaps fear of some contamination.

"Sure. Gods die, or at least their avatars do."

It took only a second for Alvit to come up with the next thought. Then she was suddenly down on her knees beside the body of a man who had been a god, digging and scraping with eager fingers at the rocky soil around the broken skull. She looked up to see Hal shaking his head.

He told her: "I've looked for the Face too. That was the first thing I did when I discovered him." Now Hal had clasped his hands behind his back, keeping them well away from his belt pouch. If Alvit even suspected where the Face was now, he knew she would try anything, including physical attack, to get it from him, without stopping to heed warnings or explanations. She was desperate to help Wodan, and she would want to stuff the damned thing into her own head at once, turn herself into Loki and go dashing off to save the life of the god she loved.

The Valkyrie was on her feet again. "Hal, if one of us could become a god, we could immediately tip the battle in Wodan's favor. Hal, I beg you, if you have any idea where—" Then abruptly her shoulders slumped. "But no, if you knew where the Face was you'd already be going after it. And if you'd picked it up you'd have become Loki by now."

Hal gave her a wry smile, a slight shake of his head. "You know me pretty well," he said. Then he changed the subject, nodding toward the body. "I have a good idea what killed him. Beyond that it becomes harder and harder to be certain about anything."

Alvit looked at him sharply. "What killed him, then?"

"Understand, there are not many weapons, in this world or the Underworld, that can destroy a god so thoroughly. Not a god as great as Loki. I believe Thor threw his Hammer at him."

It might well have happened, Hal supposed, even without Thor knowing for certain where his rival had concealed himself. Probably the Thunderer needed only to murmur his victim's name to Myelnir, and let it fly; overpowering magic would do the rest. Thor might have believed that Loki was here, but assumptions regarding the behavior of a Trickster could only be tentative.

Again Alvit considered the ruined skeleton. "That may well be. But Loki's Face is not here, which means someone must have picked it up. Who? Did Thor actually come here, inside the flames? Or did he just throw Myelnir from outside?"

"I believe Thor cast his weapon from outside, and I don't think he came in to pick up Loki's Face. Maybe someone took it who—who was in no hurry to be a god."

Alvit was puzzled. "I don't understand. Do you know anyone who would *not* want to be a god?"

Hal drew a deep breath. "I have met the enchantress Circe, who is one example; remind me to tell you more about her sometime. And I myself, like Circe, have seen divinity at first hand, more than once. And never in the countenance of any god have I seen great happiness."

"Are you turning into a philosopher in your old age, northman?"

Hal grimaced. "I hope not. Leaving matters of philosophy aside, I can think of a very practical reason not to be Loki at the moment."

Alvit was not going to be distracted. She shook her head. "I am forgetting my duty. Whatever happened here, Loki is not available. Where is Thor now? I tell you, Wodan is in desperate need of strong allies."

Hal was looking at her intently, trying to find the right way to explain certain things that had to be explained. He said: "I am practically certain that Thor is dead, too."

She stared at him. "Why are you certain?"

"Because I have seen his Hammer." Just at this crucial moment, he was distracted by noticing how—how *pretty*, that was the only word for it—Alvit looked, when her mouth came open in astonishment. He went on: "In fact I've seen it twice. The first time was when Thor's last avatar was still alive and it was hanging on his belt. You've seen Myelnir too, not long ago, though I believe I've had the closer look."

Alvit was now regarding Hal with something like awe. She murmured: "I've never seen the Hammer of Thor, save at a distance, when it was in his hand. That was days ago."

"You are wrong. We've both of us seen it within the past few hours." Hal put out a stubby finger to draw a circle in the air. "It's whirling in a kind of orbit round this crag. You're the one who pointed out the mysterious flying spark."

"That—is Myelnir!" Alvit breathed.

He nodded. "First I suspected, then I made sure. I rode my Horse close to the glowing circle, close enough to get a good look as it flew by. It was Myelnir, all right, but Thor was nowhere near."

Privately, Hal was wondering how effective Thor's Hammer would be in the hands of a mere mortal, supposing he could get his hands on it. He might try to ride his Horse near it again, as it whirled in midair, and try to grab it as it went spinning by.

He might attempt that kind of stunt if he were forced to it, but he was afraid of what the result might be. He didn't want to suggest it to Alvit.

Myelnir's physical dimensions were quite modest, but some of the stories suggested that just lifting it might be more than an ordinary man could do. In the hands of a mortal, assuming he could wield it at all, Hal thought it would still crush other weapons, and kill adversaries. But he doubted that any mortal—Hercules was always an exception in these matters—could throw it effectively; and if he did, once thrown it would not come flying back in perfect obedience to his hand.

Alvit was silent, trying to digest his revelation.

Hal went on: "Some time back, when Baldur and I were lying exhausted in one of these corridors, a strange noise woke me up. I think now that what I heard was the sound of Myelnir coming in through all the firewalls, killing Loki in his hiding place, then flying out again.

"Myelnir did its work on Loki. But then for once it failed to dart right back to its master's hand. I can imagine only one reason for that—

because Thor himself had been slain, in whatever little time there was between his hurling the Hammer and its striking home. Loki and Thor must have died at almost the same instant."

Alvit interrupted. "But then, who killed Thor?" In a moment she had answered her own question. "Of course, it must have been one of those mighty Giants or demons of the Underworld. They have their own means of long-range killing, just as the gods do."

"I expect you're right."

Now Hal, though he could not have said what he was looking for, studied the corpse more closely than before.

"What puzzles me is why would Loki, why would any god, want to hoard gold?" Why would a god, with practically all the riches of the earth lying open and vulnerable to his plundering, fight and struggle to maintain possession of a mere yellow mass of metal? One reason Hal could think of was that Loki might have done it just for fun—for the same reason he, Hal, had been so intent on penetrating all the rings of fire. Otherwise, he could only think that the god was Loki, and Loki's knack for troublemaking was as great as his skill in making fire—that must have had something to do with it.

In some ways, gods were no better or more able than any human. And Hal had known mortal men to die, risking their lives to steal something they did not truly need.

The two other gods he had encountered over the last few days had both been looking for Loki. They had each mentioned him more than once, and not in any friendly way.

The dead skull grinned its grin, as if proud of how very good it was at keeping secrets. The blasted ruin surrounding the bones was good at keeping secrets too. And now an unmelted snowflake came drifting down, to give it the same blessing as another flake had given Brunhild's ruby lips.

"Well, you may contemplate your dead bones, northman. As for me, I must report this find to Wodan."

"Of course."

Alvit had already plunged into the near tunnel, making her way back to the outer corridor. Hal kept right behind her, and Alvit called back: "I don't understand. Are Loki and the Trickster the same god, the same being, or are they not?"

"There's more than one Trickster among the gods, and I think it will be very hard to get a simple answer to any simple question about any of them. Stop and think who you are dealing with."

That answer gave Alvit pause. By this time she was standing beside her faithful Horse.

"For the last time, are you coming with me, northman? We can ride double out through the fire, and then I will set you down anywhere you like, before I go on to Wodan. He would not be pleased to see you."

"I would like to go with you, Alvit. Actually I would like very much to spend a considerable amount of time with you, somewhere where there are no battles to be fought . . . but before I can go anywhere with anyone, there is another matter I must think out for myself. So let me stay where I am, for now."

"Has this other matter anything to do with Loki's Face? Or with the gold?"

"With one of those at least."

"But you are determined to remain trapped inside these flames?"

"If you want to look at it that way."

She shook her head slowly, as if chiding him. "There is too much gold in that pile, Hal, for any one man to carry." Then she suddenly raised her head, to all appearances listening intently. "My god is calling for me," she informed Hal in a tense voice.

In a moment she was astride her Horse, and in another moment after that she and her Horse were gone.

Now Hal was completely alone, standing in the smooth, narrow curve of the outer corridor, surrounded by the enduring magic of a dead god. Not even a gnome remained for him to argue with. Not even a Horse on which to get away.

Turning, he gazed at the outer entrance to the first tunnel, as if pondering whether it could be worthwhile to drag himself through it again. But he had not decided anything before another Horse came bursting in through the outer flame-ring.

For a moment, Hal believed that Alvit had turned round and come back to him, and his heart leapt up.

Then his hopes fell, and his hand moved to the bloodstained hatchet at his belt. This time the mounted intruder was Hagan, with another man, who could only be one of his band of robbers, clinging to the Horse's back behind him.

20

STRANGELY ENOUGH, HAGAN on first entering the fire-sanctuary showed no particular surprise at discovering Hal was there before him.

The Berserk's first words offered a kind of explanation. "Hail, northman! I had word from our mutual acquaintance that I would probably find you here." Then he looked curiously at the second wall of fire. "What is this? Rings within rings?"

Hal nodded slowly. He had been looking forward to getting some sleep, as an aid to thinking out his problems, but clearly rest and sleep would have to wait. "Our mutual acquaintance being your son Baldur?"

"So, the brat told you that he's mine?" Expertly Hagan slid off his mount, keeping his one-handed grip on the Horse's mane. The man who had been riding behind him got off more awkwardly. Hagan went on: "He'll never make a real warrior, and I have serious doubts about his parentage, though his mother was my wife when he was born." He gave Hal a look of frank admiration. "He'll never be a fighter good enough to soak himself in a berserker's blood."

"Baldur acquitted himself well. He saved my life." Hal glanced down with revulsion at the dried stains on his own garments. "But I think your son is done with praying to Wodan, if that's what you mean."

So far Hagan had been balancing, on one good leg and one bad, without his crutch. But now he accepted the aid when his silent attendant handed it over. "Speak no more to me of sons, Haraldur—I'll never get another one on any woman. Wodan, in his tender care for his servants, has seen to that as well." And with the upper end of his crutch tucked into his armpit, Hagan pointed with a jerk of his thumb at his own crotch.

Then Hagan had a question. "You've seen that flying thing out

there, northman? Looping in a circle around this rock, like some de-
mented bird?"

"I've seen it."

"I made sure to keep well clear of it as I approached. What do you
know about the thing?"

Hal shook his head as if the question were beyond him. "It's every
bit as strange as you say." Then, as if just struck by a thought, he added:
"I wonder if it has something to do with the Valkyries."

Hagan seemed intrigued. "Why should it?"

"Some of them have gone to fight at Wodan's side. Are you going
to join them?"

The twisted man looked over his shoulder, making sure his acolyte
was temporarily out of sight. The man had gone off along the circular
corridor, evidently exploring. Then Hagan snarled, in a low voice: "I
am going to tear out Wodan's bloody guts, if I can ever find the means
to do it." When Hal only stared at him, he grabbed Hal by the arm.
"Haven't I been dropping enough hints for you to understand? It's he,
the grand All-Lowest, the Father of Shit, I have to thank for what I am
today. The great Wodan, who has robbed me of all human life!"

Hal was staring, fascinated. But he shook his head. "No, not robbed.
You laid your life on his altar, willingly, when first you went to worship
him."

"I was only a boy then."

"Of course. It is the kind of thing that children do." Hal started to
say something else, but then his eye fell on the Horse. Jarred out of his
own thoughts, he demanded of Hagan: "That's the mount that Baldur
rode. Where is he now?"

The man gave a twisted shrug. "Who knows? I did the brat and his
woman no harm."

"You have the Horse that they were riding."

"Is that what worries you?" Hagan laughed. "I got this beast in a
fair trade. I gave Baldur two nice cameloids for it, and he and his girl
were happy."

"The two of them just rode away?" Hal was not quite convinced.

"I told him he'd do well to ride clear of war, and he gave me no
argument."

Hagan's attendant had returned, having completed his circle of exploration. Now the man put into operation what seemed a prearranged
plan, backing the Horse into the outer circle of flame, in which its
magically protected body seemed to suffer no discomfort. At once, more
of Hagan's men began to appear inside the corridor. They were using
the beast as a kind of bridge or conduit to bring them safely through

the flames. One after another came stumbling through, eyes closed, sliding close along the animal's side and arriving safely, to open their eyes and blink in wonder at the strangeness.

Hal supposed the one Horse could hardly have carried them all here, so most of these new arrivals must have climbed the crag on their own springy legs. Each man of them was young, disgustingly young in Hal's estimation, and he could easily picture them all bounding swiftly up the rocky path, probably not even needing to stop for breath. Their youth and vigor made them all the easier to hate. And now, how proud they all were of having dared the flames.

When about half a dozen had come through, and there seemed to be no more, Hagan interrupted his confrontation with Hal to count heads. He seemed satisfied that everyone he had been expecting had now arrived.

Then he turned back to Hal. "Do you enjoy taking revenge, northman? You look like a man who knows something about that subject."

Hal shrugged. "It's like some other things in life—I find I enjoy it less as I grow older."

Hagan did not seem to be listening. "But how can a mere man ever manage to revenge himself upon a god? Did you ever ponder that question, northman?"

Slowly Hal shook his head. "That's one problem that I've never tried to solve."

"Oh, but I have! I have tried indeed. I've thought and thought about it, northman. And when I had thought enough, and sacrificed enough of my own blood, eventually understanding came. The only practical chance a man can have to be revenged upon a god—*is by becoming a god himself.*"

Hal murmured something and tried to keep himself from backing away a step. He didn't like what he thought he was beginning to see in Hagan's single eye.

"That's why I have come here." Hagan stood closer to Hal and lowered his voice so only Hal could hear him. "I want to get my hands on the Face of Loki, for I have reason to believe that Loki has died here somewhere, inside these rings of fire."

Hal nodded. "Others have had the same idea. Loki is suddenly a very well-liked fellow. Nothing like death to make a god more popular."

Hagan's one-eyed stare was boring into each of Hal's own eyes in turn. "I don't suppose you've seen the little trinket that I'm seeking, northman—? No, of course you haven't, or it'd already be inside your head. And I can see in your eyes that hasn't happened."

Hal had to struggle to keep his own voice steady. "Are you quite sure you'd know the Face of Loki if you saw it? He's one of the Trickster-gods, you know."

That set Hagan back for only a moment. "Oh, I'd know it. Don't try to fool me, northman. You do not wear the Face of any god."

"You're right, I don't."

"But you're right too, there may be trickery." Hagan looked taken aback, as if he had not thought of that before. "Loki's a Trickster, among other things. His Face may change its look from time to time, for all we know. Maybe it can even move itself about, without the help of any human hand."

Hal nodded silently. In fact he remembered how, just as he was stuffing it in his pouch, the Face had twitched like a small animal in his hand, startling him so that he almost dropped it.

Hagan seemed about to say more on the subject, but he was distracted by a call from one of his men.

"Chief, come look at this! Someone's really been digging! Digging like gnomes, through solid rock."

Naturally Hagan went to look. After inspecting the outer entrance of the first tunnel, and snarling at those who had failed to inform him of the excavation sooner, he said: "This work is very new, the dust still drifting in the air." Then he turned on Hal a glare that burned with new suspicion. "Who dug that hole, and when? Where does it lead?"

"Your man there is right, gnomes did the work. Look into it, and you can easily see where it leads." Hal gestured. "No farther than just inside this second ring of fire. Crawl through, and you'll discover a third ring that looks just the same, and a second tunnel going under it. Inside the third ring of fire, at the core of Loki's little stronghold, you'll find an open space, maybe three or four strides across."

Hagan was studying him intently. "And what have you discovered there?"

Hal gestured minimally toward the hole. "Might as well go see for yourself."

━━━━━━━

Commanding his men to stay where they were, and guard the Horse, Hagan plunged in headfirst. He had less trouble than Hal would have expected, dragging his twisted body one-handed through one narrow passage after another and even managing to bring his crutch along.

Presently the two men were standing side by side inside the inner sanctuary, with Hagan eagerly taking in its contents. At first disregarding the exposed surface of the pile of gold, he spotted the skeleton, and went immediately to search near it for the Face that was no longer there. When Hagan raised his head, he was bitterly disappointed. "So, I will have to find some other way . . . who took it?"

Hal was standing back with folded arms. "I am curious, Hagan. Which would you rather have, the Face of Loki, or this pile of gold?"

Hagan's eyes turned in the direction of Hal's gesture. Slowly the expression on his scarred face altered, as he began to appreciate the full magnitude of the hoard.

At last he said: "So, it's real gold? And what a heap! Yes, very interesting indeed. With that much—with half that much—a man could hire and pay an army."

"And even hire wizards, to help him fight a god. If a man had time."

When the bent man had probed the surface of the treasure, he straightened up, as well as he was able. "This gold is now mine, northman. I am here, with my men, and in possession. Unless you want to dispute the rights of ownership with me?"

"Oh no." Hal shook his head. "I wouldn't if I could." He had trouble understanding why everyone besides himself seemed ready to fight and die for the tremendous treasure. What bothered Hal more than missing out on gold was trying hard to win something, coming close to success, and then being denied the victory after all. It was a discouraging thought, but he was beginning to wonder if all of life might not be like that.

To himself he thought: *Maybe I'll still go for one handful of those yellow coins, if I can get the chance.*

Aloud he mused: "That great pile might buy a man his dearest dream. But for some dreams, it still would not be enough."

The ravaged face before him showed puzzlement, followed by a flash of understanding—no, misunderstanding, as it turned out. "Are you trying to tell me there's some way to trade this gold for Loki's Face? I'd do that in an instant!"

Hal was taken aback. "No, I didn't mean that at all."

"Then what?"

"Nothing. Listen to me, Hagan, I—"

"Tell me, damn you to the Underworld! Tell me!"

Hal tried to turn away, but with impressive one-armed strength the bandit grabbed and spun Hal's massive body back.

Hagan's face was evilly transformed. "A god is speaking to me right now, northman. He tells me that you're acting strangely, you must have weighty matters on your mind." The twisted man took a step closer.

"You know where the Face is, don't you? *Tell me!* The gold is yours, all yours, if you can somehow put the powers of Loki into my hands!"

Before Hal could answer, they were interrupted. The first of Hagan's men had found his way through the second tunnel into the central area. Others were right behind him. One after another they came pouring up out of the ground, weapons ready in their hands, in response to the sound of Hagan's raised voice.

"Having any trouble, chief?"

Something in that voice caught at Hal's memory, and when he took a second look at the speaker, the face was unpleasantly familiar too.

Their master seemed about to order them back, but then he stuttered and stumbled. Hagan raised his hand to his head and tangled his gnarled fingers in his hair. Suddenly his voice held hollow desperation. "Ever since the last time my head was hurt . . . there is a certain god who visits me, now and again."

"That's interesting," said Hal in a small voice.

"Ever since the last time my head was hurt . . ." Hagan repeated. A moment later, he sank to the ground in a kind of trembling fit.

"Remember me, fat man? We met once before."

Again Hal heard the voice that he had almost forgotten, and turned to see a countenance to match. When last he saw that face, its owner had been sitting in a dusty road, and it had been contorted with great pain. But now it wore an evil grin of triumph.

Hal said: "I remember."

"I told you, fat man, that this day would come. Now take that hatchet off your belt and set it down—and your knife, too."

Hal took a long look behind him, then in front of him, evaluating the grim and eager faces, the ready weapons. Then he shrugged and followed orders. Greedy, grasping hands picked up axe and dagger as soon as he cast them down. Eager eyes examined the beautifully made if somewhat battered weapons with the proprietary interest of new owners.

By this time Hagan had regained consciousness. In another moment he had pulled himself to his feet, and stood leaning on his crutch, looking thoughtfully from one of his men to another. It was as if he wanted to make sure he knew what had happened while the fit was on him, and what was happening now, before reassuming control. Evidently his men were used to these interruptions of command, for at the moment none of them were paying their leader much attention.

Meanwhile the short bandit was taking his time; obviously he meant to enjoy his moments of power to the full.

Now he said: "In a minute I'm going to pay you something that I owe you, fat man. Give it back with interest. But first, let's see what's in your pouch. This time I think you'll let me have it."

Again Hal hesitated only briefly before he unfastened the pouch from his belt and tossed it over. "That's twice in a row you're right. You're having a good day."

Three men who had been standing behind Hal pushed forward, around him, to join the others. One of the bandits snatched up the oilskin package and dumped out the contents on the ground. A circle of grimy faces stared uncomprehendingly at something they had never seen before. The Face of Loki had fallen among some trivial oddments, including a few crumbs of food—so had the scrap of fabric that once had been the Golden Fleece, but no one even noticed that.

As Hal would have been willing to bet, the bent man still had the wit and spirit, the unthinking berserker readiness, to move faster than any of his followers. Uttering a hoarse cry, Hagan lunged forward with a terrible surge of strength, thrusting with his crutch to knock aside a couple of his followers who were just an instant too slow. His strong hand snatched up Loki's Face, and without a moment's hesitation he pressed it over his own eyes and nose.

Hal had thrown himself down in the same instant that Hagan moved, but in the opposite direction, stretching his body away from the Face as far as he could go. He hugged the hard rock, and wanted to close his eyes, but somehow his private demon of curiosity would not allow him to do that—he had to see what was going to happen next.

Then it came. Again Hal heard the sound that had once wakened him from an exhausted sleep.

His diving body had hardly struck the ground before the air around him seemed to ring like a great gong. Hagan had put on the Face and was just in the act of reaching with both hands—Hal saw dazedly that the Face of Loki had already restored the new avatar's missing arm— eager to embrace the gold.

But before the new god touched the yellow metal, there was a blinding flash, a sense of surging power, ending in a stunning detonation. A small drop of something struck Hal on the forehead, with force that made a spattering of blood feel hard as stone.

Hagan had achieved his apotheosis, and now the body of Loki's latest avatar lay still while a halo of small flames went dancing harmlessly around it. Hagan in his bright momentary life as Firegod might have willed to cut off the magic feeding the three burning curtains, for now they abruptly sputtered and guttered out. The calm daylight of late afternoon ruled the hilltop, and the world surrounding it had abruptly sprung into view. Not even Wodan could have blown those fires out so quickly, like so many candles. But Hagan/Loki had time to do nothing more than that.

No, one thing more. Blooming momentarily back into existence, Loki's giant billows of fire reached out, dying powers only half-alive at best, doing their best to defend the newest avatar. Incidentally they incinerated a pair of bandits unlucky enough to be standing in the wrong place. But the flames of Loki were too late, and too relatively weak, to save their master.

Hal, raising one arm to shield his eyes and squinting into a radiance of yellow light, caught one memorable glimpse of the Face of Loki spinning briefly in midair, after being blasted out of yet another human head. Now the small translucent oval was falling free again. Right into the pile of gold Hal saw it go tumbling, even as that pile melted under the last spasmodic output of the avatar's dying will.

For a moment the glaring glow, the blasting heat, was such that Hal was forced to close his eyes. As he did so, it crossed his mind that Hagan/Loki had just been granted the most glorious cremation that any warrior or Trickster could ever want.

When Hal was able to turn back, and dared to open his eyes again, he watched as the molten pile, seeming to boil with something more than mere natural heat, poured itself fuming down the slopes and crevices of the clifftop, to collide at last with the river at the bottom in a glorious explosion of steam that rose from a deep pool.

The entire bandit crew had been scrambling for the Face. The two or three who had survived the blast, who had not been burned to death or hurled right off the crag, now went tottering and stumbling away in terror and shock. Scorched and blinded, one after another lurched scrambling across the clifftop and over the edge. Their screaming had a thin and hollow sound in the shocked stillness of the air.

Hal was truly alone, and Loki's stronghold was no more. All of the tongues of fire were gone, save for a thin glowing channel in the rock, burned out by molten gold on its way to go trickling over the cliff's edge.

Once again the Hammer of Thor had done its work. Now from atop the crag the view of the sky was completely open. Hal looked up—the fiery dot circling the crag had disappeared at last.

As far as Hal could see, every last ounce of gold was completely gone. Not a drop of it, not a fragment, was left on the hilltop.

Inching his way forward, avoiding the spots where naked, blackened rock still smoked with heat, Hal got his chin over the cliff's edge. He was staring down, hundreds of feet, to where a cloud of steam still hissed. The yellow metal would be undergoing a prolonged quenching and tempering in a deep pool of the river. The heat in several hundred-weight of molten gold must have been awesome, but the Einar was bringing endless, irresistible resources to put it out.

Even as Hal watched, the steam-clouds soon dispersed, and the river flowed on as before, the surface troubled only by occasional huge bubbles, showing something was still stirring in the depths. And presently even that disturbance ceased.

One detail remained etched, brighter than all others, in Hal's memory—the Face of Loki going over, caught up in the flood of useless wealth. If Hal could rely on what his eyes had told him, the end result was going to be a god's Face embedded in the middle of a huge, crude nugget.

Still looking down, he saw with fascination that the flying spark that was Thor's Hammer now circled over the deep pool—in which, even as he watched, the last bubbling and steaming ceased.

Then Hal blinked. Abruptly the Hammer had gone out of sight again—where was it now?

Pulling his head back from the edge of the cliff, he rolled over on his back and sat up, hearing the quick trampling of another Horse's hooves upon the flat, scorched rock nearby, followed by a familiar voice.

"Hal, you are alive!" The gladness in Alvit's words was marvelous to hear.

"So far. Just barely." He rubbed his head, which still felt as if a river of molten gold might be running through it. His eyes were dazzled, but he could make out Alvit's face and form as she bent over him.

She was saying: "As I rode up, I saw something go—pouring—over the cliff. Something tremendously hot it seemed, burning, steaming all the way down—what was it?"

Hal turned slowly to look down at the river again. "A farm and two fishing boats. All gone for good."

"Will you talk sense?" Now the woman sounded unreasonably angry. "Stop gibbering about farms! Or have you been hit in the head too many times, like Baldur and Hagan?"

And like Wodan too. But he did not say that aloud. "Hagan's dead," Hal began to explain. Then, straining his ears, he raised a hand. "Hush! Did you hear something?"

Both of them froze, listening. Hal found himself intently focusing on a sound that might be the rumbling approach of the Chariot of Thor, carrying no passenger—or no living one at least—pulled by its two magic Goats. For a moment his imagination pictured the vehicle arriving at or near the crag, so he would be able to scramble near it somehow and look inside.

But that was not happening. He could imagine any presence that he liked, but there was no sign of any Chariot.

Quite near at hand, though, another noise startled Hal. He grabbed at his belt for an axe that was no longer there, then looked around him for a weapon, any weapon. A rapid, bouncing, scraping noise, like something hard on rock. Then he saw what it was. No, not Chariot wheels.

The Hammer of Thor was no longer circling the crag or skimming the deep pool either. Having now entirely lost its glow of burning heat, it was bounding and skipping around the newly opened and exposed surface of the crag, from which Loki's fires had only moments ago been banished. The rocks were still marked with neat concentric rings where magic fires had blackened them. The four open holes of the two tunnels looked utterly pointless now.

Again Hal was struck by the fact that Myelnir's handle seemed incongruously short, and he wasn't even sure that it was made of wood. Could the whole Hammer possibly be one piece of forged metal?

Hal heard no voice, and yet had the distinct impression that he was being sent a message: *You wanted a weapon. So here I am.*

His fighter's instinct, which he trusted more than any conscious plan, took over. Wodan, or the gods knew what, might be coming at him even now. Spurred by fear of what could happen if he did not act, Hal lunged for the Hammer and managed to seize its incongruously short handle in his right hand.

A moment later he was hanging on for dear life as Myelnir yanked him to his feet, then right off his feet, as if he were a child trying to hold onto a god's hand. But the stubbornness that won in combat had sprung to life in Hal, and he would not let go. Before he had time to draw another breath, he was being swirled away, dragged up into the clouds in a flight at screaming speed. This time there was no Horse beneath him, and his whole weight hung on one hand.

Alvit was crying out in fear. She had been standing right beside him only a moment ago, but now her cries came faintly to Hal's ears, from a great and growing distance.

A plunge into the deep river from the height of the crag's top would have been terrible, but that he might possibly have survived. But before he could wonder whether it was wise to hang on an instant longer, he was at such an altitude that it would have been sure death to let the Hammer go. Besides, now he was no longer over water.

The wind of his passage was roaring in his ears. His weapons that he depended on had all been left behind, just like his gold. Just like his imaginary farm, that now he would never see. He could do nothing but hang on for dear life.

21

NOW ALVIT HAD completely disappeared from Hal's sight, her screams swallowed by the rushing wind of his passage as the Hammer dragged him upward. The Hammer was the one thing in the world Hal could claim as a possession now, outside of a few rags of bloodstained clothing, cloak and leggings torn by the savage wind with every moment of his soaring, roaring flight.

No prospects of a peaceful farm for Hal the Northman now—he could not even reach a handful of dirt. No fishing boats, not even a few splinters from a waterlogged hull. And not an ounce of gold. There was only the rush of air that caught and tore his breath away.

His insane hurtling flight seemed to prolong itself for hours. Had he not earlier begun to accustom himself to flight on Horseback, sheer panic might have broken his stubborn, lifesaving grip upon the Hammer. But as it was, his fingers stayed clamped tight. Presently he thought that if he tried, really made a great effort, he might be able to swing himself up one-handed, against the screaming pull of speeding air, to lock his left hand also on the Hammer's handle. Short as that shaft was, there certainly ought to be room for a man's two hands.

With a gasping exertion he managed, on the third try, to accomplish that. Now his right arm had some ease from the killing strain of his full weight, and his dread of being torn loose at every moment was eased a little.

In his current situation, he had gone far beyond being upset by looking down. Numbly he watched as a layer of broken clouds streamed by beneath him. What little he could see of the earth below, streaked with long slanting shadows as the time neared sunset, strongly suggested that he was being carried into regions that he had never been before.

There were no mountains below him, or immediately nearby. At least he could be sure that he was not being borne back to Valhalla.

How long the journey really lasted was impossible to say. After a flight wilder than any Horse had given him, Hal felt the terrible speed begin to lessen, and he could see that he was coming down. During the descent, the flying Hammer shifted its orientation so the handle was still pointing toward the earth.

Land spread below him, dark and flat and unfamiliar. Trying to see where he was going to alight, Hal saw a flat dull expanse, and in the middle of it an object, dead ahead, that was soon close enough to be recognizable as Thor's chariot, the two Goats still in harness.

Around the motionless vehicle, rapidly growing larger as he flew toward it, there spread what he now perceived as a vast, roadless and unnavigable marsh, clinging to the rim of some great river. Was it the Einar? He couldn't tell. This might well be some other river altogether. Just how many miles had he flown?

At almost the last moment, he realized that his present trajectory would land him not just near the chariot, but right on top of it, and at a dangerous speed. He had no way to steer, no means of control of the force that bore him on. At the last moment, when a crashing impact seemed almost inevitable, Hal forced his cramped fingers to let go of Myelnir's stubby handle. His body went plunging down a few yards away from the hard wood, with a large but anti-climactic splash, headlong into a waist-deep chilly swamp.

The Hammer, released, went bumping and thumping right down into the open vehicle, its landing loud and hard enough that you might think it would have gone right through the floorboards. But no, it simply banged and rattled to a stop—evidently those boards were made of sturdy stuff.

The pair of huge Goats looked round with curiosity, then went on patiently cropping whatever their immortal jaws were managing to dredge up out of the swamp.

Half-wading and half-swimming, spitting and snorting foul-tasting muck, Hal soon got his feet more or less under him. Around the chariot there stretched, for at least half a mile, a seeming forest, practically an ocean, of tall reeds. No one was going to walk to this spot or ride here on a cameloid. Forcing a passage through the masses of vegetation by boat would be a weary job. So no ordinary humans, unless they came somehow flying over it, would find Thor's Chariot here.

Hal took note of the quiet, the loneliness, and the reddening light of approaching sunset. At least there were no sounds or sights of fighting anywhere nearby—it was hard to imagine how anyone could ever organize a battle here. It looked like a place where a man might easily drown, or starve, but he would not be attacked, at least not by his fellow humans.

He hoped that the watery muck engulfing him was too cold to nurture snakes. Wading and swearing, scraping malodorous mud from his eyes and beard, Hal dragged himself right next to the Chariot—it was floating delicately, magically, with only a few inches of each wheel submerged, showing not a spot of mud—and looked inside.

There on the floorboards lay not only the Hammer, now inert, but the body of Thor's previous avatar. The late embodiment of the god was still wrapped in exotic, spotless furs and still displayed enormous metal armbands and iron gloves. The countenance had changed, but it was the same man who had once spoken to Hal and Baldur, and spun his Hammer for them.

At least Hal was reasonably certain it was the same. The body that Hal remembered as so mighty now lay sprawled on its back, shrunken, shriveled, almost mummified, though it was neither mangled nor decayed. There was no sign of spilled blood. The arms no longer came near filling the broad decorative bands. Doubtless the strange appearance of the corpse was some result of whatever Underworld magic had struck Thor down, at a moment when his most potent weapon was miles away. Automatically Hal looked for the Spear that Thor had taken from him, but could not find it. Perhaps Thor had turned it over to some Valkyrie.

Anyway, the northman had little attention to spare for such details. Right beside the body's desiccated forehead, just where you would expect to find it, lay the great god's Face. To Hal's mortal eyes, the small translucent slab looked practically indistinguishable from Loki's.

For a long moment Hal did not move to pick up this new treasure. This time it was not fear of any immediate catastrophe that held him back, but something deeper and more subtle.

"Why me?" he muttered aloud, and one of the Goats turned an inhuman face to look at him.

In all his years of wandering the world, he had never seriously thought that this choice would ever be his to make, but now it had come leaping out at him like a wolf from ambush. And not once, but twice in one day.

What surprised him was that this time the wolf should be so toothless. Because, in truth, Hal had already made his decision, long minutes ago when he moved to pick up the Hammer. And Myelnir in some way had also chosen him.

It was a sobering moment, not entirely one of joy. Before him lay a forcible reminder that becoming Thor's avatar did not guarantee survival. As in the case of Loki, whatever power had demolished the last avatar of Thor might be ready and waiting to destroy the next one too.

Both Goats looked round this time, as if made curious by this strange mortal's actions. Still they seemed to be waiting patiently for something meaningful to happen—something that would call them back to duty. Maybe, Hal thought, they were wondering why this particular human seemed so reluctant to become their god.

Not that it should make much difference to the Goats. Because if he didn't become Thor, someone else soon would. The same magic that preserved Faces from destruction also saw to it that they did not long remain unused. One variation of that magic had brought him here, and if he refused the offer, the challenge, the invitation, the same eldritch power would bring someone else. Or, perhaps, the Goats would somehow be inspired to move the Chariot to a place frequented by people. Either way the result would be the same. The very nature of Faces prevented them from remaining for very long out of the reach of human hands. He thought the Face of Loki, locked in gold at the bottom of a river, would probably be out of reach for some time to come—but it was hard to make any safe predictions about a Trickster.

Hal could remember very plainly how, in his last moment high on the crag, when he had reached to grab the Hammer for himself, he had known an inner conviction that Myelnir had chosen him as well.

He wondered how many humans, down through the centuries, had covered their own human faces with these strange god-things, just out of fear of what would happen if they did not.

Holding the strange, masklike shape in his hands, Hal studied it, even though he already knew all that he had to know about it, and all that he was likely to find out—until he put it on. He had roamed the wide world for some twenty years without seeing the naked Face of any god—and now, in the course of a single hour, he had held two of them in his hands. Well, it came as no news to him that life was strange.

Hal was afraid, knowing that from the moment he pressed Thor's Face over his eyes and nose and let it sink magically into his brain, Haraldur the northman would permanently cease to exist. Oh, not that he expected to die. Not exactly. Hal's memories, his hopes and fears, the things that made him who he was, would all go on. But never again would he be alone in his own head. With him inside his very skull would be all the powers and cravings of the great god, along with all the memories mighty Thor had amassed over many centuries. Those things would henceforward be as much a part of Hal as his own nature, and he thought he could almost feel the pressure of them already, more than enough to fill his old head up to bursting. Over the hours and days to come, they'd stretch him into a new and different shape.

—if the Underworld powers that had killed Thor should allow his new avatar to live that long.

As simple and direct as putting a sharp dagger to your own throat— someone had said that, about the decision to put on a Face.

But what else could he do? And besides . . .

Hal was curious.

Raising the object toward his own face, Hal let out a startled little grunt. Despite all his foreknowledge, at the last moment he had the feeling that the Face attacked him like a striking snake, leaping at him across the last few inches. At the same moment he'd felt it melting in his fingers, dissolved like a piece of ice in flame.

A moment later, the Face had totally disappeared, and Hal knew a burning sensation that told him it had run into his head. He'd felt it go there, penetrating his left eye and ear, flowing right into his skull like water into dry sand. The first shock had been an ice-cold trickle, followed quickly by a sensation of burning heat, fading slowly to a heavy warmth . . .

there was a long moment when his vision and his hearing blurred . . .

Then he knew that it had happened, and he was still Hal, after all.

Still Hal, yes, but . . . now he was different. At the moment, the most profound change was that he was no longer on the verge of physical exhaustion. Hagan had grown a new arm within an instant of putting on a Face, and now Hal thought he could feel himself twenty years younger.

Now his enhanced senses could pick up the distant sounds of battle, a groaning and roaring, and now and then a real clash of arms. His eyes were now keen enough to pick out subtle variations in the strange glow near one side of the horizon.

He also saw, in the far distance, a Spearless Valkyrie, who seemed to be urging her airborne Horse rapidly toward him.

There was the Hammer, now docile and available, and he picked it up at once, knowing it would never dare to play tricks upon him now. Hal hung Myelnir on his belt, where once an axe had hung. Legend, current among gods and mortal humans alike, said that Myelnir had been made for Thor by gnomes, some of whom were as skilled with magic as they were with metal. Was the legend true? Even now, with centuries of divine memories to call on, Hal could not be sure, so ancient were the god and his great weapon.

Even gods, Hal supposed, must have had a birth or a beginning somewhere, sometime. But Thor's origins were lost in the mists of his most distant memories.

In other ways, the memories of a god's lifetime were more helpful. Hal could now at least dimly begin to understand the reasons for the current battle—although those reasons were still far from perfectly clear to either man or god.

———

Hal's stomach, which the god now shared, was ravenously hungry, and Thor remembered several things that he could do about that. In the air there moved a certain power, whose mere existence Hal alone would never have discovered, and on the railing of the Chariot there suddenly rested a pair of delicious-smelling oatcakes, steaming slightly as if fresh from the oven.

Hal tried one and found it very tasty.

The galloping Horse bearing a Valkyrie was somewhat closer now, only a few miles away.

His new memory did offer him one definite assurance: that what he ought to do before anything else was dispose reverently of the body of his predecessor.

Thor's voluminous memories also assured Hal that cremation was the preferred method, in line with some ancient tradition whose origin was probably older than Thor himself.

It took only a minute to straighten out the almost mummified corpse, decently close the eyes and clasp the hands upon the breast. There was no memory suggesting that the god's favorite weapon ought to be burned with him. The Hammer in its present form had outlasted many avatars and would probably outlast many more.

The new god thought, and his old memory confirmed, that Wodan would be pleased to know that this was being done by and for his eminent colleague.

In the swamp it might not be easy to arrange the proper fuel and heat for a funeral pyre. But if he did not take care of this matter now, the body of his predecessor would have to ride with Hal in the Chariot when he set out on his next task, which could not be long postponed; and that was an intolerable thought.

The same servant powers that had brought the cakes now set about the job of arranging a suitable funeral pyre, stripping the dead body of the god's accouterments, and when all was in readiness, igniting flame. Nowhere near the spectacular display that Loki could easily have managed, but it would do.

The pyre had been burning fiercely for half a minute, when the rider Hal had observed in the far distance at last arrived.

The rider was Alvit, of course: her Horse came cantering at low altitude, skimming over the swamp. She had done her best to catch up with Hal in his mad flight, but the flying Hammer had outsped even the best that her mount could do.

He was still just standing in the chariot, when she drew near and tugged her Horse to a standing stop in midair. She gazed at Hal for a long moment.

"So, northman, I see you have survived again. I saw the smoke from a distance, and when I saw the Chariot, too, I thought that Thor was here. What are you doing in . . . ?"

The truth was slow to force itself upon her, but presently it did. Then, while her Horse stood quivering in the air, she gave a long gasp and nearly fell off its back. She let out a little shriek, for once a very girlish sound. "My Lord Thor! You are . . ."

As Alvit fell silent in confusion, Hal reached out and gestured. He was glad he had not yet put on the iron gloves. In a moment the Horse had brought Alvit near enough for him to touch her hand, and a moment later she was with him in the Chariot.

"Never a lord to you, Alvit. I am still Hal." Still Hal, and always would be.

But—not the same Hal that he had been. New differences were coming into view in rapid succession. It was like watching his reflection in a mirror and observing alterations. Thor's new body was not going to stay mud-covered for long, not if the god did not want himself to look that way. Rapidly the stuff of the marsh was drying on his body and falling away like loose dust, along with remnants of dried berserkers' and bandits' blood. He would be able to readily change his clothing, too, just by thinking about it, into something more appropriate for divinity. As soon as he got around to such details.

"Be at ease." He thought his voice still sounded pretty much like his own, like Hal's. "It's all right, I am still Hal, I tell you. Talk to me, Alvit, tell me what's happening."

She was standing close beside him in the Chariot, with her fists clenched nervously at her sides. "I am to tell you, my lord—I am to tell you, Thor—Hal—"

"Yes, call me Hal. Take it easy. Calm yourself."

Presently Alvit was able to inform him that Wodan strongly suspected that Loki was dead. Naturally the Father of Battles was ready to go to any lengths to get control of Loki's Face, so he could have that weapon delivered into the hands of one of his, Wodan's, worshipers.

Alternatively, if there was already a new avatar of Loki, and if the reborn god should still be Wodan's foe, Wodan (or Alvit, serving by default as his strategist) was thinking that it would be best to fight the Firegod early, while he was still relatively ineffective in using the tools of his divinity.

On the other hand, if there was a new Loki and he was inclined to be a friend to Wodan, then Loki might need immediate help in their shared fight against Giants and monsters.

But whatever the true situation was regarding Loki, Wodan was still hoping to recruit Thor.

Now Alvit could carry good news back to her god: that Haraldur the northman has picked up Thor's Face and put it on.

Alvit's countenance showed the hint of a smile. "The face of my lord—Hal—in his present avatar has a . . . a certain majesty about it."

"You can tell him also that my Hammer is now safely resting at my side."

He thought the young woman shuddered slightly, glancing at the weapon. "You knew what it was going to do to Hagan."

"I had a pretty good idea that Myelnir would mangle whoever put on Loki's Face, as long as the order to kill was still in effect. And I thought the world could probably spare Hagan."

Alvit was contemplating him, shaking her head in private wonder. Then she gave a start. "But I am forgetting my duty! When any of us finds Thor, we are to offer him a courteous greeting from our master—there was flowery language, which I have forgotten, but it amounts to a greeting between equals."

"Really? From Wodan?"

Alvit blushed slightly. "As between near-equals, then."

"Then carry my response to Wodan, in such language as you think will not displease him. But maybe I should ride to see him face-to-face, as soon as this ritual burning is completed."

"Yes Hal, you should—but I am forgetting, there is one more thing.

Along with his greeting, Wodan sends an urgent warning that he and Thor had better waste no more time, but get on with the job of slaughtering monsters and demons, the traditional enemies of all gods."

When Hal/Thor thought for a moment, he readily remembered Wodan, and the details and ramifications of Thor's relationship with Wodan, from a completely different perspective than that of Hal the downtrodden recruit. The Wodan of many avatars ago, of ages past, had often been a very different individual from the confused dreamer of today. Thor's memory in this case was encyclopedic, extending through a gulf of time that must have covered many centuries. The exact number of years was something Thor had never bothered to count.

Hal, a neophyte in his god-powers, realized that he might quickly be killed by the same power that had slain Thor's previous avatar. His vast new memory contained several possibilities regarding the precise nature of that weapon, and several suggestions as to which power of the Underworld might have wielded it. Unfortunately, there were some that even Thor knew little of.

The natural-looking flames of the funeral pyre were waning, having accomplished the necessary destruction, and there was no further reason for delay.

"Then let us go find Wodan!" Thor/Hal decided.

He took up the reins with Alvit at his side, and at his touch the Goats sprang into action, dragging the Chariot into smooth and speedy flight. The Valkyrie's Horse kept up, air-galloping obediently just behind the speeding car, as if this were another accustomed exercise, until the speed became too great, and the riderless animal fell behind. The Goats, as Thor expected, seemed ready to provide all the speed that any god could want.

22

"THE PLAIN OF Asgard," Hal/Thor mused aloud. With a gentle, practiced tug on the reins, he brought his Goats to a standstill in midair, so that a moment later the Chariot drifted down to rest on solid ground. Alvit, who had been riding beside him with her Horse following, relaxed a little.

The god's vehicle had come to rest on the top of a bleak hill from which Thor/Hal could survey the scene of intermittent battle spread out before him. The forces of Wodan and his allies were no more than half a mile away, those of the Underworld somewhat farther off, a shadowy no-man's-land of varying width between. Beyond the enemy, some five miles distant, a line of purple hills marked the limits of Asgard.

Alvit, of course, was not going to linger at Hal's side. Taking her leave with a few brief words, she remounted her Horse, and in a moment was riding to report to Wodan, whose own Chariot was visible near the center of his army's line.

Meanwhile Hal paused to survey the scene. He was looking over the same broad sweep of land that Sergeant Nosam had once tried to point out to him when the two of them were standing on the battlements of Valhalla. At the moment, the distant walls of that stronghold were barely visible through a notch in a wall of mountains some miles behind Thor's Chariot.

When the sergeant had been trying to tell him about the plain, the whole scene had been sunk in midnight darkness, and Hal's vision had been no more than human. So he could not recognize the landscape now—nor could Thor, who apparently had never paid much heed to Wodan's longstanding prophecies regarding a Last Battle.

The square miles of Asgard plain might once have been good for grazing, but the land looked practically worthless now, being badly scorched, either by natural fire or magic, across most of its extent. Anyone who might have been living on it when the battle started must have fled days ago. The only remaining signs of human occupancy were a couple of small and distant buildings, already knocked to ruins.

Thor/Hal spun his Hammer in his hand, his god's strength scarcely noticing the weight. It seemed to Hal that his new composite memory could show him very clearly the details regarding use of this superb weapon, the preferred techniques.

But what to use it on? Across a great span of the vague distance, wreathed and muffled in smoke and dust, were the enemy armies. Such human forces as the enemy had managed to enlist in its dark cause— some kind of army scraped together, the Fates alone knew how—were hard to make out behind a haze of smoke and dust, even to the eyesight of a god.

So far, no target worthy of Myelnir had come to Thor's attention. The enemy might well have seen his Chariot arriving on the battlefield, and the important leaders might have prudently retreated.

——————

Another object of Hal's concern was nearer. Shifting to a closer range, Thor's divine eyesight soon discovered the All-Highest. Wodan, as anyone who knew him would expect, was of course leading his troops, taking his place at their head as they entered battle or prepared to do so. And Hal/Thor thought that even the demons of the Underworld might well be affrighted at the sight. The Father of Battles presented a terrible figure, fully armed with his helmet and spear, riding his Chariot behind his eight-legged Horse, the terrible Sleipnir, who at the moment was snorting fire.

Wodan had had much more success at mustering an army than some of his enemies had expected: his corps of fighting humans was relatively weak, but his wraiths and apparitions could frighten fleshly opponents who did not know how ineffectual they really were. This included most of the human mercenaries who now found themselves arrayed against him.

Unless you were gifted with divine eyesight or knew where and how to look for them, the solid physical presence of human beings would be all but lost in the landscape of smoke and mist and magic, among Wodan's shadowy host of several thousand wraiths, their battalions spreading out for a mile to the right and to the left. But using Thor's vision, Hal needed only a moment longer to recognize one group of the real men as his former barrack-mates. On each side of Wodan's Chariot marched, or rather shambled, a crew of a few dozen men, the Heroes from Valhalla. Beside them, extending their ranks for some distance to right and left, was a small corps of human mercenary allies, no more than a couple of hundred, somehow recruited from nearby warlords.

Wodan enjoyed the advantages and suffered the disadvantages of being really, thoroughly crazy.

His behavior became impossible for the enemy to predict, and he thought his army was much grander and more effective than it really was.

If Thor and Wodan had been able to seriously coordinate their power, victory might well have been theirs, and quickly, even against all the monsters. But that was not to be.

———

Above the opposing armies and between them, half a dozen Valkyries, no more, were riding proudly in the air, circling the field with Spears in hand. Alvit had told Hal that Wodan had called the glorious sisterhood together, before sending them to search for Thor, and had addressed them for what he said would probably be the last time.

The god had told his squadron of proud maidens that in this battle they must abandon their traditional role of recruiters. The last days had come, and this shabby force that he now led was all the army he would ever have. Instead, the Valkyries were to fight beside their master and, when called on, serve as Wodan's couriers.

Having surveyed the field from a distance to his satisfaction, Thor took up his Chariot's reins and drove the vehicle directly to Wodan. As he came near the place where the All-Highest waited, Hal looked around for Alvit, but she was not in sight. Either she was with her sisters over the battlefield, or Wodan had dispatched her on some urgent mission.

For the moment, the Chariots of the two great gods stood parked beside each other, Sleipnir's majestic presence in sharp contrast to the grotesquerie of the Goats.

Fixing Hal/Thor with his one-eyed stare, the senior god proclaimed in his rumbling voice: "Thunderer, I know it is a long time since we have seen each other—and yet you look strangely familiar. Have I met this avatar before?"

Thor/Hal only shook his head, and reached out for a handshake, as between equals. "I too have the feeling that it is not long since we parted."

Wodan, after a brief hesitation, accepted his hand. Immediately Hal/ Thor tried to get down to business and open a discussion on matters of strategy and tactics. It seemed to Hal that there was no good reason, except for Wodan's craziness, for Thor and Wodan to fail to stand together against the threat from below the surface of the earth. Both gods were longtime enemies of the creatures from deep hell. The chief point of uneasiness between them seemed to derive from the fact that Thor was a patron god of the more numerous peasants and lower classes, while Wodan's devotees were chiefly of the elite. In the past, certain avatars of each had found this difference grounds for jealousy.

Calling on Thor's vast memory, enlisting his deep intelligence, Hal did his best to come up with some coherent plan of battle. But the effort was practically useless. At the moment Wodan was unwilling to talk about much of anything except how he was going to mow down the enemy with his Spear, when shortly he rode against them.

Suddenly the Father of Battles broke off, as if he had just remembered something of importance.

"Tell me, Thunderer, where is Loki? Have you seen him? Is it possible he's allied with the enemy?"

"In this case," Hal/Thor assured him, "he cannot be, for I have seen him dead."

Wodan was unmistakably pleased. But a moment later he asked the inevitable question: had any other mortal yet picked up Loki's Face?

It did not seem to Hal that now was the time to attempt any lengthy explanation. Sooner or later, some god or coalition of mortals would locate the Face of Loki and find some way of extracting it from its great lump of gold. But there was no point in hurrying the inevitable. The fewer who knew what had happened to the treasure, the better.

At the same time, the mention of Loki had irresistibly evoked some of Thor's more interesting ancient memories. Hal was presented with fascinating scenes involving certain antique avatars of Wodan. There had been one such who, outraged that Loki should be fighting in some ancient battle on the side of the Underworld, had caught firebomb after firebomb on the point of his magic Spear and hurled them back. Of course such missiles had failed to do Loki any harm, but they had certainly scorched his quondam allies, before the Firegod was able to take any effective countermeasures . . .

. . . but here and now, on the plain of Asgard, Wodan was waiting for an answer.

Hal cleared his throat. "My respected colleague, we can expect no help from Loki in this fight. But neither will he appear against us. Listen to me, All-Highest, it is very important that we work out some plan to follow in the battle—"

But Wodan was not looking at him or listening, and Hal had no chance to try to force him to pay attention, because here Alvit came galloping up on her airborne Horse, to report to the gods that enemy action was disrupting the ranks of Valhalla. Many wraiths had already been lost in battle, disappearing like dew in the morning sun, and the flow of replacements had suddenly been cut off. Some force was evidently damaging or interfering with the device that generated and maintained their images.

The news reached the All-Highest at one of his more lucid moments. Announcing that it would be unthinkable for he himself to leave the front line, he said he would much appreciate it if Thor could find out what was killing off his wraiths and stop the slaughter.

Before Thor/Hal could even voice agreement, Wodan had seized his great Spear and brandished it, turned his back unceremoniously on his fellow deity, cracked a kind of whip over Sleipnir's back, and went careening straight ahead, bellowing war cries, toward the center of the enemy line.

———

Alvit, riding her Horse beside his Chariot, directed the newest avatar to a steep-sided canyon, just below the battlements on the north side of the stronghold, opposite the plain. There, she said, the wraith-generating device was located. Only a few, even in Valhalla, knew the place.

Rounding the flank of a mountain, Hal/Thor's Chariot bore him in sight of the narrow entry to a deep cave.

Alvit might have ridden right into the cavity, but Hal/Thor sharply called her back. His divine perception warned him that some demonic or monstrous presence was in the cavern. Myelnir was already in the god's hand, and in the blinking of an eye it sped toward its target. The narrow cave-mouth erupted in a flash of manycolored light, telling Thor's experienced eye that his weapon had wrought annihilation.

He wanted to ride his Chariot straight into the cave, feeling that way he would be better equipped to deal with whatever awaited him inside. But for the Chariot to pass the entrance, it was necessary to enlarge the opening. Myelnir proved a handy tool. Thor tossed his weapon gently, underhand, without dismounting from his Chariot. There was a cloud of dust, a hail of stones. Alvit gave a little cry and dodged as small bits of rock went shooting past her head, and when the dust cleared there was a new look to the cave's mouth. Already Myelnir's handle was snugly back in Thor's right hand. A moment later, the Chariot was inside the cave, where he who rode it could smell the faint, unpleasant residue of the creature he had just destroyed.

Entering an enclosed space many times larger than his Chariot, Hal looked carefully around, with a god's vision keen even in semidarkness. When Alvit pointed out to him the machine that generated the wraiths, he could think of nothing to compare it to, except possibly a tangle of dead or dying tree stumps, projecting from the cave floor, shorn of all branches and leaves. Even Thor had never seen anything just like this before; but his long memory retained garbled stories of a spot deep in the Underworld, where some kind of engine described as similar to this one was said to produce strange images of the dead, in pursuit of some vast project whose purpose all living minds had long since forgotten.

Alvit rode bravely right beside the strange device, whose jagged outline testified, even to one ignorant of proper shape and purpose, that it was broken.

"Hal, is there anything you can do to fix it?"

Hal made a helpless gesture with his powerful arms, limbs grown even thicker with his apotheosis. "Nothing that either Thor or I can think of." The Thunderer's divine talent for constructive building or repair was almost nonexistent, beyond some odds and ends of plain metalworking. Certainly neither god nor man were up to dealing with devices on this level of sophistication.

"Then what are we to do?" Alvit sounded desperate.

Hal didn't know, and Thor's memory was of no help. Being deprived of wraiths would cost the gods' forces one of their chief advantages over the demonic army, for wraiths could duel more effectively against demons than they could against human flesh and blood.

Again Hal was struck by how strongly the mysterious machine resembled an underground complex of tree stumps. Neither Hal nor Thor could make any sense of it—though Thor did have some memory, tantalizingly faint and remote, of having seen something like it somewhere before.

When more creatures of the Underworld suddenly appeared at the cave's entrance, Thor with a swift cast of his Hammer killed two of the latest attackers. The strange, quasi-material shapes exploded at Myelnir's touch, and others turned and fled before entering the cave.

But Thor's defense of the cave had come too late. The engine had been effectively destroyed.

"We can do no more here," he told Alvit, "let's get back to the battle."

She could only agree, and followed on her Horse as Hal drove Thor's Chariot high into the air above Valhalla to get another view of Wodan's deployment and see how the fight was going.

No more wraiths could be generated, and those already in the field continued to vanish under enemy attack, sometimes whole squadrons of them together. Thor looked about him, reveling in senses enormously keener and farther-ranging than Hal the northman had ever dreamt of having. He felt a warrior's joy on seeing that the enemy had come out of hiding and was once more on the attack.

Hal/Thor picked out a target—

And hurled Myelnir!

———

There had been a lull in the fighting. Again the enemy had pulled back out of contact, but no one on the gods' side could be certain if this meant a general retreat, or that the enemy was reorganizing and nerving itself for a final supreme effort.

With his strength augmented by the power of a god, Hal no longer felt the exhaustion that had drained him when he was only mortal man. But even gods could tire, as he was discovering. He had landed his Chariot again, near the spot where he had talked with Wodan, and he was waiting for the All-Highest to come back from his latest foray against the enemy.

Surprisingly, his right knee twinged as he turned round. It was a different kind of twinge than he had been trying to get used to in the last months before his chance came to be Thor. As one who had the experience of many wounds, he recognized this as a therapeutic sort of twang, part of a healing process, almost like a small dislocation popping back in place. He had no doubt at all that the knee, Thor's knee, was going to be just fine from now on.

———

Hal was about to look around for Wodan, when a voice right at his own Chariot-wheel distracted him.

"Hal, remember us?" There stood the youthful figure of Holah—or was this one Noden?—one of Baldur's cousins or nephews, clinging to the vehicle in a familiar way. It was obvious that in the boy's ignorance he did not immediately grasp the fact that the man he recognized had become the great god Thor.

Meanwhile the speaker's slightly older brother was approaching. Being a little more perceptive, he must have realized the truth, for he was trying to drag his younger sibling back.

Hal gave them both a weary look. "So, you couldn't wait to get into a real fight, hey? Well, no more could I when I was your age."

Questioning the boys, Hal learned that they had experienced only a taste of fighting so far. One of them seemed eager for more, the other not nearly so enthusiastic, yet reluctant to admit the fact.

Now the elder asked: "What should we do now, sir—Hal? The men we came to this fight with seem to have disappeared."

"My advice to you both is—keep your weapons handy and don't volunteer for anything." Part of Hal wanted to tell them to go home, and had been on the verge of doing so, but another part admired their youthful daring and enterprise. Meanwhile, his Thor component hardly took notice of the lads at all.

Hal was saved from further discussion by the sudden appearance of Wodan's Chariot, the Father of Battles for once with his back to the enemy, and driving Sleipnir hard. The unaccustomed sight caught Hal's attention—Wodan was beckoning Thor to a conference.

———

Scouting Valkyries had brought the news that the largest and most destructive monsters of the Underworld were once more on the march just below and upon the surface of the earth.

One of the flying sisters reported the presence of the treacherous Giant Skrymir, who could surround himself with illusions as protection against the gods he feared to face directly. Thor himself had no clear memory of what Skrymir actually looked like—and when a fight was over, whether or not he had actually been present was hard to know.

Another Valkyrie claimed to have seen in the ranks of the Underworld the Giant Surt, one who continually brandished a flaming sword. There ought to be no mistaking him, at least.

Hal tried again, but with no more success than before, to work out some coherent plan of battle. But Wodan would have none of it.

The All-Highest was saying to him: ". . . and so, it is too bad, but I cannot offer most of your worshipers Valhalla. Unless of course some of them turn out better than expected, and perform as true heroes should."

Now was hardly the time to haggle over points of honor. Hal simply nodded. "My followers and I will just have to accept that as best we can."

After warning Thor to beware of treachery in their own ranks, Wodan turned, and with an elated war cry, he once more charged against the foe. Soon the Father of Battles in his Chariot was cutting a swath of destruction across the field, right through the thickest of his enemies' ranks. Humans and others fell before him, by the scores, by the hundreds, as he smote right and left with his terrible Spear, much more powerful than the similar weapons used by Valkyries.

Withdrawing slightly from the front line, Thor stayed with the tactics that had earlier been successful, getting the most out of Myelnir's long-range power. He avoided direct engagement, for the most part, killing major monsters at a distance. When one of them died, in contrast to the gods, it was dead, with no chance of a resurrection.

There was a stir in the front line now, the beginning of a retreat on the gods' side, and anxious human yells . . .

A huge shape, or shape-changer more like it, hard to see, was half-materialized behind the enemy's front rank. Skrymir, maybe?

No, no such luck. In the mosaic of legends as so often quoted by Wodan, Thor's prime enemy on the day of the last battle was beyond all doubt Jormungand, the world-serpent. And indeed Thor's memory now assured Hal that god and monster were no strangers to each other.

Hal took aim at the dim shape looming large behind the enemy front, and launched another throw. The Hammer struck home squarely, but for once the victim did not vanish in a blast, or even fall. It was Jormungand, all right.

The dull, gigantic shape, only partially visible through clouds of smoke and dust, recoiled briefly, then resumed its advance. Hal had seen this enemy only in pictures and carvings, but Thor had ancient memories of this horror in plenty. Now man and god were facing Jormungand, the greatest of serpents, who came writhing and winding his way to the attack. Red eyes the size of bushel baskets glowed in an incongruously hairy head, rising easily fifty feet above the battlefield when the long body stretched into the air. Sometimes Jormungand came rolling like some Titan's hoop, biting his own tail. Thor could recall one notable scuffle in which this creature had taken on the form of a cat; but whatever form the huge shape-changer put on, his chief weapon was spitting poison.

For a moment, Wodan seemed confused, and his Chariot was in retreat. Alvit came galloping seemingly from nowhere, to join Thor/Hal in his struggle against the poison-spewing serpent.

Hal shouted and waved a warning to her to keep clear, but on her snorting Horse she came darting in, trying to Spear the demon's eyes. Jormungand was immense, dwarfing the two human-sized bodies that dared to close with him. Hal's own purely human impulse was to turn and run, but Thor's iron confidence and long experience assured his new avatar that the odds were nowhere near as unfavorable as they appeared.

He had thrown his Hammer again, but not yet got it back, when a great fanged mouth came looming overhead, then closing like some castle's portcullis upon the man-sized god. Thor had to grab its upper and lower jaws at the same time, one in each of his two hands, and strain with all his strength to rend them violently apart. Bellowing in pain, the serpent wrenched itself free, almost dragging him from his Chariot in the process. The poisonous exhalation from the mouth would have felled a mortal human in his tracks.

Through dust and smoke and flame the battle swirled. It seemed that Jormungand had terrified the Goats, and Thor had to struggle to regain full control of his own Chariot.

On achieving this, and seeing that the monster still reeled back, Hal looked around for Alvit. He felt a surge of relief as he saw her riding through the air unharmed, Spear still ready to do battle. He told himself that if he had the welfare of the Valkyrie in mind, the best thing he could do for her would be to win this battle. And he told himself that the next time he saw her, he would tell her she was now assigned permanently as Thor's aide. He thought the chances were that if Wodan never saw her again, the old god would never know the difference.

The fact that Thor and Jormungand had come face-to-face in mortal combat made Hal wonder uneasily if crazy Wodan might be right, and the world was really going to end when this battle did.

Alvit had seen him, and came riding near. "Hal, I think that we are winning! If only Loki could be here, and fighting for us, we could destroy these dregs of hell!"

Evidently she had not arrived at the crag in time to see just what had happened to the Firegod. Briefly Hal/Thor considered telling her— because it would be impossible for her or anyone else (except maybe Wodan) to retrieve Loki's Face. But as he had with Wodan, Hal said nothing. He wanted to be sure that Alvit never got the Trickster's Face, because if she had it she would put it on to help Wodan, and it would change her much more than Hal wanted to see her changed. The world could probably get along just fine for a time, with no one wearing Loki's Face—or Wodan's, come to think of it.

———

The fight went on.

As a god, Hal had to admit that Myelnir's handle felt much more comfortable in his grip than any plow handle ever would.

The new avatar of Thor, slamming down row after row of his enemies with his irresistible Hammer—the enemy knew that they would have to kill Thor again or abandon the field.

Finally, the surviving great monsters and the creatures who supported them were slowly retreating, back into the Underworld. By now all of Jormungand's human auxiliaries, those who could still run or walk, had fled the field.

The powers of the Underworld had been defeated for the time being.

But the great serpent and his supporters did not withdraw entirely until there was one more flurry of combat, in which something, perhaps a last parting shot of Jormungand's poison, struck at Wodan and did him serious damage. Hal first realized the fact when Alvit came silently beckoning him, her face showing a look of gloom and doom he had never seen there before.

Thor was one of the first to know that the All-Highest had fallen, and he was first after Alvit to reach Wodan's side. The great god's body lay spilled out of his tipped and broken Chariot and clouds of steam or smoke were coming up. Some force more blunt than poison seemed to have been at work, though it had left no obvious wounds.

Hastily Hal sent his own servant powers to work. They in turn called upon surviving wraiths to form a screen around the tumbled Chariot and those who were near it.

To Alvit he said sharply: "We must keep this a secret, if we can."

As Hal/Thor turned over the old man's body, he could see that Wodan was still alive. The old man's single eye was open, showing the vacant blue of summer skies. The first words that issued from his bearded lips were threats against those the Father of Battles believed had betrayed him.

At first the murmuring was so low that even divine hearing could barely make it out. ". . . must root out . . . treachery."

Thor tried to shift the massive body into an easier position. "Can you sit up?"

Suddenly the voice was louder. "Who're you? All, all have turned against me."

"My respected colleague, that is wrong."

"One of the damned Valkyries was here. They've all failed me. Should never have trusted women. Who're you? Another shape-changer?"

"I am Thor, as much a god as you are, Wodan. We are fighting on the same side." In the circumstances it seemed only prudent to make that clear.

As usual, the All-Highest did not seem to be listening. "All mortals betray me when I trust them, especially the women. But I'll have the last laugh on the traitors."

When Hal/Thor told him that the battle was effectively won, the enemy in full retreat, Wodan reacted with alarm and refused to believe him.

"This is the day of the final battle, and they all must die. I'll see to it!"

There was a long pause. Then: "The end of the world has come!" If the fighting was really ending, then the world must too. The All-Highest could tolerate no other outcome.

Hal left the enclosure momentarily to tell Alvit that Wodan was not yet dead. When he returned, the great god was struggling to get back on his feet. With a surge of effort Wodan had grasped his Chariot and set it once more upright upon its wheels. Sleipnir looked back with the dull fear of a real horse.

Thor tried to be placating. "We have won, great Wodan. You will need your Chariot no more today."

"No, the battle cannot be over! The fighting must go on. The world is going to end. The world must end!" Then he stumbled and would have fallen, but for Thor's supporting arm.

Wodan would have it that the world must end; therefore the battle could not be over yet. Therefore he must order all his remaining forces, human and otherwise, into a suicidal charge.

"If the enemy has retreated, we must pursue!"

Hal tried arguing. "But the enemy has retreated to the lower regions."

"Then we must follow them! We'll invade the Underworld! Drive our own humans forward, Thor! Help me. Help me to my Chariot . . ."

"Maybe when our troops are rested—"

"Damned traitors! I'll give them no rest." Wodan was going to insist on rooting out and punishing the traitors in his own ranks, those who were trying to subvert the Fate of the world for their own mere cowardly survival. Faithless Valkyries! Worthless human trash! Were it not for them, the whole world could have been brought to its proper climax in destruction!

Gradually Hal was coming to the realization that once more Thanatos, god of Death, had failed to claim the god of battles. Hal/Thor knew a sinking feeling. Wodan was not really dying. If he went forward with his mad plan to invade the Underworld, death would probably claim him soon—but maybe not soon enough.

It seemed to Hal that he and Thor now thought as one, with no hint of conflict in their joint awareness.

His god-voice went out smoothly. "Of course, All-Highest. Depend on me to give you the help you really need. See, there, for instance." And he pointed. When the other's head turned, Hal with his right hand slid Myelnir from his belt. The force of the blow was precisely calibrated, getting the job done without causing inconvenient noise or mess. Myelnir was quite capable of fine precision work when such was called for. Nothing to disturb the tranquility of the mindless screen of wraiths surrounding the two gods; all of them were still staring, with great apparent interest, into some distant nothingness.

———

A moment later, Hal was holding the Face of Wodan in his hand, and a moment after that, he had stuffed it into the new belt pouch that Thor had already requisitioned from his powers.

With any luck at all, some considerable time would pass before the retreating enemy discovered that the Father of Battles was dead.

Now, for the third time in only a few hours, Hal had the disposal of divinity.

He shuddered inwardly to think what might happen if the powers of the Underworld should get control of the trinket he had just tucked into concealment. What would they do with it? No demon could wear a god's Face, at least Hal did not think so. No doubt they would hand it to some mortal human maniac, or truly malignant warlord. Or one of Hagan's surviving bandits. However they might dispose of the great power, it was a frightening prospect.

No. To allow that would seem to be against a northman's honor. Once again Hal could feel himself being forced to a particular choice.

———

Parting with a gesture the close ranks of the encircling wraiths, Hal thrust his head and shoulders out between them. A multitude of eyes were turned his way.

"Wodan and I are in conference," he announced. He had already decided that a general proclamation of the All-Highest's death had better wait, until with his next breath he could name the new avatar.

Hal's gaze went skimming along the ranks of waiting humans, pausing briefly on Sergeant Nosam. The sergeant had lived with a god so long that he might be expected to know what a good god would be like. But Alvit had been right about him—he was too small.

Moving on, Hal's speculative eye fell next on Alvit herself—but a different future awaited her, if Hal had anything to say about it. Now he called her to him with a slight gesture, and sent her to find the boys from Baldur's household.

A minute later, Holah and Noden stood before him, two boys not knowing whether to be terrified or overcome with honor.

"Lads, I am about to charge you with an extremely important mission."

Eyes wide, and rendered almost speechless by such words from Thor himself, the boys waited to hear what commission they were about to receive.

Hal/Thor said: "I am loaning you my Chariot, and you are to ride it in search of your uncle Baldur. Then you—"

"He is really our cousin," one lad murmured, as if afraid degree of kinship might make some fatally important difference.

"Whatever he is, wherever he is, you are to find him and bring him back here to me." Hal paused for thought, then added: "If there should be a lady with him who wishes to come along—well, let her."

Seeing the beginnings of great fear in the young eyes before him, fear of their own inadequacy, he hastened to add: "Boys, I am sending help with you, in the form of invisible powers. Magic enough to make sure that you find the man I want."

"Are we to—to give him any reason, sir?"

"Yes. Tell him that Haraldur the northman appeals to his honor, and needs his help. The god Thor has a task for him, a vitally important mission, that none but Baldur can accomplish."

While Hal was speaking, Alvit had approached and looked anxiously into his face, then moved to slide past him into the enclosure of wraiths. He had let her pass.

Now she emerged again, and Hal could see that she was fighting back tears. In a low voice she asked: "And what will Baldur's mission be?"

"Wodan is asking for him," Hal told her. He could see in the woman's face that she had discovered Wodan's death, but did not realize how it had come about. Perhaps sometime he would tell her. Now he only drew her a little aside, so no one else could hear, and added: "I want him to rebuild Valhalla, and to rule there."

"Baldur?" There was grief in Alvit's voice for what she had just seen, but relief as well. "Is it wise to make a god of Hagan's son?"

"Maybe not. But can you name me a wiser choice?"

Hal could see that the Valkyrie was thinking, and he waited but she said nothing. Now it looked like Hagan's son would become the very god that Hagan had so desperately hated. Hal thought that ironic; Thor found it quite amusing.

Alvit plainly stood in need of some kind of help. Hal reached out an arm and pulled the tall young woman gently to him, so that when she slumped a little, her head rested on his shoulder. She seemed content to be there.

After a little while Hal said: "Maybe neither I nor the god in me has any true wisdom. If I did, I'd probably be a farmer. But I want to see how Baldur handles his new job."

Hal was curious.

And so was Thor.